F   Lindsey, Johanna,
Lindsey   author.

Stormy persuasion.

DATE			

Stormy
Persuasion

JOHANNA LINDSEY

Stormy
Persuasion

Gallery Books

New York   London   Toronto   Sydney   New Delhi

G

Gallery Books
A Division of Simon & Schuster, Inc.
1230 Avenue of the Americas
New York, NY 10020

First Gallery Books hardcover edition June 2014

GALLERY BOOKS and colophon are registered trademarks of Simon & Schuster, Inc.

For information about special discounts for bulk purchases, please contact Simon & Schuster Special Sales at 1-866-506-1949 or business@simonandschuster.com.

The Simon & Schuster Speakers Bureau can bring authors to your live event. For more information or to book an event contact the Simon & Schuster Speakers Bureau at 1-866-248-3049 or visit our website at www.simonspeakers.com.

Manufactured in the United States of America

10 9 8 7 6 5 4 3 2 1

Library of Congress Cataloging-in-Publication Data is available.

ISBN 978-1-4767-1427-1
ISBN 978-1-4767-1431-8 (ebook)

Chapter One

JUDITH MALORY KNELT IN front of the window in the bedroom she shared with her cousin Jacqueline, both staring at the ruined house behind the Duke of Wrighton's mansion and formal gardens. Although Judith was the older of the two young women by a few months, Jack, as her father had named her just to annoy his American brothers-in-law, had always been the leader—actually, instigator was more like it. Jack said that she was going to be a rake, just like her father, James Malory. Jack said she was going to be a pirate, just like her father. Jack said she was going to be a superlative pugilist. . . . The list went on. Judith had once asked her why she didn't have any goals to be like her mother, and Jack had promptly replied, "But *that* wouldn't be exciting."

Judith disagreed. She wanted to be a wife and a mother, in that order. And it was no longer a faraway goal. She and Jacqueline were both turning eighteen this year. She'd had her birthday last week, and Jacqueline would have hers in a couple months. So they were both going to have their first Season come summer, but Jacqueline's debut was going to take place in America instead of London, and Judith didn't think she could bear not being able to share this occasion with her best friend. But Judith still had a couple of weeks to figure out how she could change this disagreeable arrangement.

The daughters of the two younger Malory brothers, James and Anthony, the girls had been inseparable for as long as they could remember. And every time their mothers brought them to visit their cousins Brandon and Cheryl at the duke's ancestral estate in Hampshire, they'd spend hours at this window hoping to see a light glowing eerily in the ruins again. The night they'd first seen it had been so exciting, they couldn't help themselves.

They'd only seen the light on two other occasions since then. But by the time they'd grabbed lanterns and run across the extensive lawn to reach the old, abandoned house on the neighboring property, the light had been gone.

They'd had to tell their cousin Brandon Malory about it, of course. He was a year younger than they were, but it was his home they were visiting, after all. The Duke of Wrighton's title and estate had passed to him through his mother, Kelsey, who had married the girls' cousin Derek. His parents had elected to move into it when Brandon was born, so he would grow up aware of his stature and consequence. Luckily, being a duke hadn't spoiled him rotten.

But Brandon had never actually seen the light himself, so he wasn't the least bit interested in the vigil tonight or any other night. He was currently on the other side of the room engrossed in teaching Judith's younger sister, Jaime, to play whist. Besides, having just turned seventeen, Brandon looked more like a man than a boy, and not surprisingly, he was now much more interested in girls than ghosts.

"Am I old enough *now* to be told the Secret?" Brandon's younger sister, Cheryl, asked from the open doorway to her cousins' room.

Jaime Malory leapt up from the little card table and ran over to Cheryl, grabbing her hand and pulling her forward before turning to her older sister, Judith. "She is. I was her age when you told me."

But it was Jacqueline who answered, scoffing at her younger cousin, "That was just last year, puss. And unlike you, Cheryl actually lives here. Tell her, Brand. She's your sister. She'd have to promise never to go investigating on her own and you'd have to make sure she keeps the promise."

"Investigate?" Cheryl looked at her two older cousins, who'd been refusing for years to tell her their secret. "How can I make a promise if I don't know what I'm promising?"

"This is no time for logic, puss," Judith said, concurring with Jacqueline. "Promise first. Jaime had to, and she doesn't even live here. But you do, and without the promise, we'd end up worrying about you. You don't want that, d'you?"

Cheryl gave that a moment's thought before she shook her head. "I promise."

Judith nudged Jacqueline to do the honors, and Jack didn't disappoint, saying baldly, "You've got a ghost for a neighbor. He lives next door."

Cheryl burst into giggles but stopped when she noticed Judy and Jack weren't laughing. Wide-eyed, she asked, "Really? You've seen it?"

"About five years ago, we did," Judith said.

"Judy even spoke to it," Jacqueline added.

"But Jack saw the light first, from this very window. So we just had to go have a look. We'd always thought that old house must be haunted. And we were right!"

Cheryl walked forward slowly and joined them at the window to take a quick peek at the old eyesore her parents had complained about more'n once. She let out a relieved breath when she didn't see any light. She wasn't nearly as brave as her cousins were. But in the moonlight she could see a clear outline of the large, old manor house that had fallen to ruin long before any of them were born, a big, dark, scary outline. With a shudder, she turned and hurried over to her brother for protection.

"You didn't actually go inside that house, did you?" Cheryl asked.

"Of course we did," Jack said.

"But we've all been warned not to!"

"Only because it's dangerous with so many broken floorboards, crumbling walls, and a lot of the roof caved in. And cobwebs. There's cobwebs everywhere. It took Judy and me forever to get them out of our hair that night."

Eyes flaring a little wider, Cheryl said, "I can't believe you actually went inside, and at night."

"Well, how else were we to find out who was trespassing? We didn't know it was a ghost yet."

"You should have just told my father you saw the light," Cheryl said.

"But that's no fun," Jack pointed out.

"Fun? You don't need to pretend to be so courageous just because your fathers are." When the two older girls started laughing, Cheryl said, "So you're just pulling my leg? I should have known!"

Jacqueline grinned at her. "D'you really think we'd keep the Secret from you all these years just to pull your leg? You wanted to know and now we're finally telling you. It was incredibly exciting."

"And only a little frightening," Judith added.

"And foolhardy," Cheryl insisted.

Jack snorted. "If we let things like that stop us, we'd have no fun a'tall. And we had weapons. I grabbed a shovel from the garden."

"And I took my scissors along," Judith added.

Cheryl had always wished she was as brave as these two. Now she was glad she wasn't. They'd thought they'd find a vagrant, but they'd found a ghost instead. It was a wonder their hair hadn't turned white that night, but Judy's gold hair was still streaked with copper, not gray, and Jack was still as blond as her father was.

"We couldn't tell where the light was coming from when we stepped inside the house that night," Jack was saying. "So we split up."

"I found him first," Judy said, continuing the story. "I'm not even sure which room he was in. I didn't notice the light until I opened a door. And there he was, floating in the middle of the room. And none too pleased to see me. I promptly told him he was trespassing. He told me I was the trespasser, that the house was his. I told him ghosts can't own houses. He just stretched his arm out, pointing behind me, and told me to get out. He was a bit harsh. He seemed to growl at me so I did turn about to leave."

"And that's when I arrived," Jack said. "Only to see his back as he floated away. I asked him to wait, but he didn't. He just bellowed, 'Get out, both of you!'—so loud it shook the rafters, or what's left of them. We did, ran right out of there. But we were only halfway back to the mansion when we realized he couldn't really hurt us. And we were missing the opportunity to help him move on. So we went back and searched every room, but he'd already faded away."

"You wanted to help him?" Cheryl asked incredulously.

"Well, Judy did."

Cheryl stared at the slightly older of the two cousins. "Why?"

Judith shrugged evasively, saying, "He was a handsome young man. Must've been only twenty or so when he died. And he seemed so sad when I first spotted him, before he noticed me and got belligerent and protective of his crumbling ruin of a house."

"And because she fell in love with a ghost that night," Jack added with a snicker.

Judith gasped. "I did not!"

"You did!" Jack teased.

"I'd just like to know what caused him to become a ghost. It must have been something quite tragic and frightening, if his hair turned white before he died."

"White hair?" Cheryl said with owlish eyes. "Then he must be old."

"Don't be silly, puss," Jacqueline admonished. "My sister-in-law Danny has white hair, doesn't she? And she was as young as we are now when she met Jeremy."

"True," Cheryl allowed, then asked Judith, "Was he really handsome then?"

"Very, and tall, and with lovely dark green eyes that glowed like emeralds—and don't you dare go looking for him without us," Judy added, sounding almost jealous.

Cheryl huffed, "I'm not daring or curious like you two. I have no desire to meet a ghost, thank you very much."

"Good, because he seems to have magical powers, too, or haven't you noticed that the roof's been repaired?"

Cheryl gasped. "By a ghost?"

"Who else?"

"No, I didn't notice. My room's on the other side of the house."

"I noticed," Brandon spoke up. "And I've never seen workers there to account for it, but the roof has definitely been repaired recently."

"I hope you didn't point that out to your father?" Jacqueline said.

"No, if I did, I'd have to tell him the Secret, and I'm not breaking the promise."

Jacqueline beamed at him. "I knew we could count on you, Brand."

"Besides, Father grumbles anytime someone mentions that old place. He's annoyed that he can't get rid of it. He's tried to buy it so he could tear it down, but the last owner of record was a woman named Mildred Winstock, and she merely inherited it, she never lived in it. And no wonder, with a ghost in residence. It's actually been empty since my great-great-grandfather's day, which would explain its crumbling condition. But then I told you why he built it and who he gave it to."

"Who?" Cheryl asked.

"That's not for your young ears," Brandon replied.

"His mistress?" Cheryl guessed.

Judith rolled her eyes at her precocious cousin and changed the subject. "It's amazing this place didn't fall to ruin, too, being empty for five generations as well."

"Not quite empty," Brandon replied. "The ducal estate has paid to maintain a minimal staff here to keep that from happening. But Father could find no record of who Miss Winstock left the ruin to when she died, so we're stuck with it mucking up our backyard."

Derek had planted trees and thick shrubbery along the property line, though, to block the crumbling, old house from view so people could enjoy the ducal gardens without having to look at that eyesore. But the trees didn't block the view of the old house from the upper floors of the ducal mansion.

Judith sighed as she moved away from the window. "All right, Cousins, time for Judy and me to get to bed, so you probably should, too. We return to London in the morning."

As soon as their cousins left the room, Jacqueline said, "What did you expect? They haven't seen the ghost like we have."

Judith sighed. "Oh, Cheryl's lack of an adventurous nature doesn't surprise me. Derek and Kelsey keep her too sheltered here, while you and I've grown up in London."

"Ah, so that sigh was because we didn't see the light on this visit? We can go search through the ruin tonight if you'd like."

"No, the ghost only revealed himself to us once. I'm quite sure he hides now when we invade his domain. More's the pity," Judith said with another sigh.

Jacqueline threw a pillow at her. "Stop mooning over a ghost. You *do* realize he's not the marrying sort?"

Judith burst out laughing. "Yes, I've had no trouble figuring that out."

"Good, because it'd be quite difficult to get a kiss out of him, much less a nice tumble."

Judith raised a brow. "Tumble? I thought you scratched being a rake off your list last year?"

"Bite your tongue. I'm just going to take a leaf from our cousin Amy's book and not take no for an answer—when I find the chap for me. And when I do, heaven help him. The man won't know what hit him," Jacqueline added with a roguish grin.

"Just don't find him too soon. And do *not* find him in America."

There it was again, Jacqueline's voyage looming in front of them. The first time Jacqueline had sailed off to America with her parents, Judith had been distraught and inconsolable the entire two months of Jack's absence. The girls had sworn then never to be more'n a carriage ride away from each other ever again, so Judy got to go along the second time Jack visited America. But the girls hadn't known at the time about the promise James Malory had made to the Anderson brothers when Jack was born. Her American uncles had agreed that Jacqueline could be raised exclusively in England as long as she had her come-out in America, because *they* hoped she'd marry an American. At least be given the chance to.

When asked why he would agree to something so out of character for him, James had said, "It kept me from having to kill them, which would have made George quite annoyed with me."

True, they were George's brothers, after all, and James hadn't actually been joking, either, about killing them. George was Jacqueline's mother, Georgina to be exact, but James insisted on calling his wife George because he knew her brothers would hate it, but truth be known, even her five older brothers called her that now on occasion. But that promise James had made had kept an unspoken truce in effect all these years with his five American brothers-in-law. Which had been needed, considering they'd once tried to hang James Malory.

"I'm not going to marry until you do," Jacqueline assured her cousin, "so don't *you* be in a hurry to either. We don't need to be following the pack and getting married our first Season, even if our mothers are expecting us to. This year is for fun, next year can be for marriage."

"That's not going to stop you from sailing off without me," Judith said forlornly.

"No, but we still have a couple of weeks to come up with a solution. We'll talk to our parents as soon as we get back to London. It's *your* parents that have to be convinced. My father would be glad to have you along, but when Uncle Tony said no, Father had to side with him. Brothers, you know, and those two in particular, always stick together. But if I tell them that I won't go to America if you can't come with me, they'll see reason. And why *did* your father say no? It's not as if he's looking forward to your come-out. He's been a veritable ogre with it approaching."

Judith giggled. "My father is never an ogre. A bit terse and snappish lately, yes, but—you're right, he'd be quite happy if I never marry."

"Exactly, so he should have jumped at the chance to send you off with me, prolonging the inevitable."

"But is marriage inevitable, with fathers like ours?"

Jacqueline laughed. "You're thinking of Cousin Regina's being raised by the four Malory elders after their sister Melissa died, and how none of them could agree on a man good enough for their niece, and she had to go through numerous Seasons because of it. Poor Reggie. But, remember, back then, the Malory brothers didn't have wives who could put their feet down as they do now. D'you really think *our* mothers won't do exactly that when love shows up for us? Wait a minute, that's it, isn't it? It was Aunt Roslynn who said you couldn't go and Uncle Tony just agreed with her to keep the peace?"

Judith winced as she nodded. "She's *so* been looking forward to my come-out here, much more'n I am. She's even got her hopes set on one man in particular she thinks will be perfect for me."

"Who?"

"Lord Cullen, the son of one of her Scottish friends," Judith replied.

"Have you met him?"

"I haven't seen him since we were children, but she has. She's assured me he's rich, handsome, a great catch by all accounts."

"I suppose he lives in Scotland?"

"Yes, of course."

"Then *he* won't do! What's your mother thinking, to pair you with a man who'll take you away from us?"

Judith laughed. "Probably that she'll buy us a house in London to live in."

Jack snorted. "We don't take chances like that, especially with Scots, who can be stubborn. Wait a minute, is *he* why she won't bend?"

"She *is* worried he'll get snatched up by someone else if I'm not here at the start of the Season. So, yes, I wouldn't be surprised if that's the real reason she's refusing to let me delay my debut for a trip to America."

Jacqueline rolled her eyes. "You silly. We just haven't tackled this together yet. We're much stronger when we do. Mark my words, you'll be sailing with me. I never had the slightest doubt."

Chapter Two

JUDITH LAY IN BED with her eyes wide-open. Jacqueline had promptly fallen asleep, but Judith remained awake because she'd realized she might be married the next time she visited her cousins in Hampshire. Not to Ian Cullen, but to a man she simply couldn't resist. Although she and Jacqueline didn't want to fall in love right away, certainly not this year, Judith had seen what had happened to her older Malory cousins. Love had a way of interfering with the best-laid plans. And as soon as she married, she'd probably forget about her ghost.

That was a sad thought. Whimsically, she didn't want to forget such an exciting encounter or never see her ghost again. Which was when she got it in her mind that the ghost might reveal himself to her if she entered his house alone, and *that* thought wouldn't let her sleep.

She finally gave in to temptation, donned a hooded cloak and slippers, headed downstairs to find a lantern, then ran across the back lawn. But when she reached the dark, old house and tried to get in the front door as she'd done before, she found it locked. Not stuck, actually locked. Had Derek done that? But why, when many of the windows were missing their glass and were easy enough to slip through?

She set her lantern on the floor inside one window and climbed through. She'd seen no light from outside, but still headed straight for the room where she'd found the ghost before. Boards creaked under her feet. If he was in there, he'd hear her coming—and disappear again.

She thought to call out, "Don't hide from me. I know you're here. Reveal yourself."

Of course he didn't. She chided herself for thinking a ghost would do her bidding. She'd surprised him last time. And she'd foolishly lost the element of surprise this time. Nonetheless, she was determined to check that room again before she gave up and went back to bed.

She opened the door. It didn't squeak this time. Had it been oiled? She held her lantern high to light the room. It looked different. A lot different. The cobwebs were gone. The old sofa was no longer dusty. And a cot was in the corner of the room with a pillow and a crumpled blanket. Was someone other than the ghost staying here? A real trespasser now? Even the windows in this room were covered with blankets, so the light of her lantern wouldn't be seen from outside—and was why they hadn't seen the ghost's light in so long. He was probably furious that some vagrant had moved into his house and he'd been unable to scare him away.

But the vagrant wasn't here now. Maybe the ghost still was. She was about to tell her invisible friend that she could help with his vagrant problem when a hand slipped over her mouth and an arm around her waist. She was surprised enough to drop her lantern. It didn't break, but it did roll across the floor—and extinguish itself. No! Utter blackness and a very real man with his hands on her.

She was about to faint when he whispered by her ear, "You picked a lousy place to do your trysting, wench. Is your lover in the house, too? Is that who you were talking to? Just shake or nod your head."

She did both.

He made a sound of frustration. "If I let go of your mouth so you can answer, I don't want to hear any screaming. Scream and I'll gag you and tie you up and leave you to rot in the cellar. Do we have an understanding?"

Being bound and gagged didn't frighten her so much and was even preferable to anything else he might do to her. Jack would find her in the morning because she would guess exactly where she'd disappeared to. So she nodded. He removed his hand from her mouth, but his arm still held her tightly to him so she couldn't run. Screaming was still an option. . . .

"So how soon before the other half of this tryst shows up?"

"I wasn't meeting anyone," she assured him without thinking. Why hadn't she said "Any minute now" instead?! Then he'd leave—or would he?

"Then why are you here and how did you get in? I locked the bleedin' door."

"*You* did? But what was the point of that when some of the windows are open?"

"Because a locked door makes a statement. It clearly says you aren't welcome."

She humphed. "Neither are you. Don't you know this place is haunted?"

"Is it? I'm just passing by. If there are any ghosts here, they haven't made an appearance yet."

"Passing by when you keep a cot here?" she snorted. "You're lying. And you weren't here a moment ago. Did you come out of the wall? Is there a hidden room connected to this one?"

He laughed, but it sounded forced. She had a feeling she'd guessed accurately. And why hadn't she and Jack thought of that before? Even the ducal mansion had hidden rooms and passageways.

But he placed his chin on her shoulder. "Quite the imagination you have, darlin'. How about you answer the questions instead? What are you doing here in the middle of the night if you're not meeting a lover?"

"I came to visit the resident ghost."

"That nonsense again?" he scoffed. "There are no such things."

It would be *so* nice if her ghost would show up to prove him wrong right then. The vagrant would be distracted long enough for her to escape and bring Derek back to get rid of him. But then she realized the room was too dark for her to see the ghost even if he did show up. Frustrated that this trespasser was ruining her last chance to see the ghost again, she just wanted to go back to bed. She tried to pull away from him but he tightened his hold on her.

"Stop wiggling, or I'm going to think you want some attention of a different sort. Do you, darlin'? I'll be happy to oblige." She sucked in her breath and stood perfectly still. "Now that's disappointing." He actually did sound it. "You smell good. You feel good. I was hoping to find out if you taste good, too."

She stiffened. "I'm ugly as sin, with boils and warts."

He chuckled. "Now why don't I believe that?"

"Relight the lantern and you'll see."

"No, the dark suits us. I'll call your warts and boils and raise you a lusty appetite. I think I'm going to win this hand."

Despite the warning, and warning it was, she still wasn't expecting to be flipped around so fast and kissed before she could stop it from happening. She didn't gag. His breath actually smelled of brandy. And for a first kiss it might not have been so bad if she'd wanted to explore it. But she didn't. Her hand swung wildly in the dark but she got lucky with her aim. It cracked against his cheek and got her released.

He merely laughed. "What? It was just one quick kiss I stole. Nothing for you to get violent over."

"I'm leaving now, and you will, too, if you know what's good for you."

A sigh. "Yes, I've already figured that out. But let me get you out of here safely. I don't want it on my conscience if you fall through the floor and break your neck."

"No! Wait!" she cried as he picked her up in his arms. "I know this house better than you do!"

"I doubt that," he muttered, and carried her out of the room and across the main room to the nearest window, which he shoved her through. "Say nothing about seeing me here and I'll be gone before morning."

"I didn't *see* you. You made sure of that."

And she still couldn't. A little moonlight was on the porch, but he stepped away from the window as soon as he released her, disappearing into the blackness inside the house. She didn't wait for a response if he'd even heard her, just ran all the way back to the ducal mansion and up to her room.

She almost woke Jacqueline to tell her about her little misadventure but decided it could wait until morning. It still nagged at her, how a poor vagrant could afford French brandy. The tariff on it was so high, only the rich could afford it. That was why it was the prime cargo of smugglers. . . .

Chapter Three

"WHY DO *you* LOOK like *I'm* in trouble?" Boyd Anderson wondered aloud as he entered the dining room to join his sister, Georgina, for lunch.

His voice was teasing, his grin engaging, but he was quite serious given the frown he saw on her face. Brother and sister both had identical dark brown eyes, but his brown hair was shades lighter than hers. She was dressed today to receive company in a pretty coral gown, but she wore her hair down, as she often did when she only expected to entertain family.

Boyd was the youngest of Georgina's five brothers, and the only one who lived permanently in London. It had been his decision, and a good one since he was the third Anderson to marry into the Malory clan. His wife, Katey, was Anthony Malory's illegitimate daughter, a daughter that Anthony hadn't even known he had until Boyd began to pursue her. Newly discovered as Katey was, the Malorys, and there were many of them, would have been quite up in arms if Boyd had tried to sail off to America with her despite her having been raised there.

Georgina tried to give Boyd a reassuring smile, but didn't quite manage it. "Sit." She pointed at the chair across from her. "I've asked the cook to prepare your favorite dish. It wasn't easy to find white clams."

"Bribery? Never mind, don't answer that. It's Jacqueline's trip, isn't it? What's wrong? Did something happen with the boys?"

"No, they're happy to stay at school. They're not interested in their sister's come-out."

"I thought you were in agreement that she could go?"

"I am. I know you and our brothers only want the best for Jack. And this momentous trip has kept the peace in my family—even if it was forced down our throats."

Boyd winced. "Must you put it like that?"

"Yes, I must, since it's true."

He sighed. "I know we were rather emphatic when we insisted she have her come-out in America—"

"Very."

"—and, yes, I know we're all more often in England these days than in Connecticut as we were back then. But there's another more important reason for her to go to America for her come-out." He paused to glance at the door before he added in a near whisper, "Your husband is absent from the house, I hope? I wouldn't want him walking in on this conversation."

"Yes, James has gone to the dock to make sure all the provisions have been delivered for the trip. But I wouldn't be surprised if he drags Tony to Knighton's first."

"Damn, I wish they'd let me know when they do that. I do so enjoy watching fights of that caliber."

"You wouldn't today. James is rather annoyed, so it's bound to be brutal."

"All the better! No, wait. Why is *he* annoyed? Because you're upset—with someone?"

"I'm not upset with anyone, just worried. It's Jack who's having the bloody fit."

"About the trip?"

"In a roundabout manner."

"But I thought she wanted to go."

"Oh, she did, but she thought that Judy would get to go with her. But that's not happening. And now Jack refuses to go without her."

Boyd laughed. "Now, why doesn't that surprise me? They've always been inseparable, those two. Everyone knows it. So why can't Judy go?"

"Her mother won't allow it. Roslynn has been preparing for the Season here for months, has been looking forward to it even more than our daughters are. She already knows who will be hosting what parties and balls, has promises of invitations for them all. She already knows who the most eligibles are, including a Scotsman she favors for Judy because he is the son of a close friend of hers. She's leaving nothing to chance and thinks that Judy might miss a significant event if she sails with us."

Boyd cast his eyes toward the ceiling. "But they will be back in time for the Season here, might only miss a week or two of it. They'll still have the rest of the summer here. That *is* why we're leaving now, in the spring."

"But missing the beginning is what's turned Judith's mother stubborn, and she can be very stubborn. And I even understand her reasoning, since the very beginning of a Season *is* when attractions first spark, pairings get made, courting starts. To arrive even a week late can make a world of difference, with all the best catches already taken. Of course she's most concerned about that Scotsman. She doesn't want another girl to snare Lord Cullen. So she's making sure Judy will be here when he is, right at the start of the Season."

"Do you really think that will matter for the two prettiest debutantes this year?"

"It won't matter for Jack. She'll go after who she wants as soon as she claps eyes on him, consequences be damned, this side of the ocean or the other."

"For God's sake, Georgie, you're talking about your daughter, not one of the Malory rakes."

She raised a brow at him, a habit she'd gotten into soon after marrying James Malory. "You're surprised she'd take after her father?"

"Too much after him, obviously," Boyd mumbled, adding the complaint "And that should've been nipped in the bud."

She chuckled at him. "There's no nipping an influence that strong. But that's beside the point. Unlike Jack, who occasionally acts before she thinks, Judith is too kindhearted and considerate of others to even come close to stepping on toes. And Roslynn knows that about her daughter. Which is why she won't budge on Judy's not missing the first ball of the Season here. I'm afraid if we can't change Roslynn's mind, we won't be sailing. Jack has simply *and* furiously declined to have a Season without her best friend beside her."

"Damnit, Georgie, we're three days away from sailing. It's too late to cancel. Katey has been looking forward to the trip."

"D'you think I like this situation? We're already packed. *The Maiden George* has been brought up from her dock in the south and a full crew hired. She's anchored in the Thames as we speak. We've been browbeating and cajoling Roslynn for months, and now we're down to the last few days and she's still saying no."

"But our brothers are all on their way to Bridgeport. And Amy will be there soon to oversee the preparations. She sailed with Warren last week. They will all think something horrible has happened if we don't show up as expected!"

"James would sail anyway to let them know what's happened, if it comes to that. They won't be left to worry. I'm sorry, Boyd. I know you and our brothers have been looking forward to this. I just don't want all of you to be angry if James doesn't keep his promise. It's *not* his fault."

Boyd gave Georgina a pointed look. "Since when does Jack rule the roost? I'll get her on the ship myself if you and James are reluctant to insist."

"You're missing the point, Boyd. There *is* no point to this trip if my daughter spends the entire time miserable. None of us expected Roslynn's opposition. We've all tried to change her mind. But she won't budge. She's a Scot, you know, and she's lost her temper more'n once, with all of us trying to change her mind."

"Then don't count on Jack's ever marrying," Boyd said flatly.

Georgina shot to her feet. "Excuse me? You take that back, Boyd Anderson!"

He rose as well, his brow as furrowed as hers. "I will not. I told you there is another even more important reason for Jack to have her come-out in America. You know she's going to have a much better chance of finding love with a man who isn't familiar with your husband's reputation. The young men here are going to be scared to death to approach her because of him."

Georgina dropped back into her chair but was still bristling on her husband's behalf. "Jack isn't worried about that happening and neither are we."

"Then you're deluding yourselves, because it's human nature. There isn't a man who knows him, or who has even merely heard the rumors about him, that would risk having James Malory for a father-in-law—that's *if* James doesn't kill him before they get to the altar."

Georgina gasped, even sputtered before she said furiously, "I now agree with Jack. In fact, I'm not going either. I wouldn't be able to bear weeks at sea with someone as pigheaded as you!"

Boyd lost his own temper, snarling on the way out of the room, "I won't let my niece throw away a golden opportunity just because *you* don't know when to put your foot down!"

"How dare you!" Georgina yelled, and threw a plate at him.

The plate missed and shattered in the hall. The front door opened before Boyd reached it, and Jacqueline remarked wide-eyed, "Is she breaking dishes on you again?"

Boyd snorted and took Jack's arm to lead her back out of the house. "She never did have good aim." And then sternly: "Do you know how much trouble you're causing?"

Jack grinned cheekily, not the least bit repentant. "It's all part of my plan."

"To drive us crazy?"

"To get Judy on the ship with us."

"I've a better idea. Come on, we're going to find a certain Scotsman and arrange a little accident for him."

"Really?!"

"I'm definitely in the mood to, but I suppose we can try to reason with him first."

"Reason with a Scotsman?" Jack started laughing.

Boyd tsked. "Just tell me he's in town. I don't want to kill a horse riding to Scotland and back in three days."

"He is here on business, actually. Arrived a few days ago and has been calling on Judy each day. I've had a devil of a time making sure she's not home to receive him, hoping he'll get the hint and just go away. But Aunt Ros guessed what I've been up to after Judy found the nerve to tell her that she'll have no Season a'tall if she can't have one on each side of the ocean."

"Did that work?"

"No, not yet, but it has to eventually. For now, Aunt Ros is sure Judy will come around once our ship sails without her. She is calling me a bad influence, though," Jack ended with a grin, rather proud to be called that.

"So Judy hasn't even met Lord Cullen to know whether she would like him or not?"

"Not since he was a boy. He, on the other hand, has seen her in recent years and is quite besotted. But she's in no hurry to find out what the man is like. She's supposed to be meeting him right now in the park. Roslynn was taking her. But Judy's going to pretend to be sick."

"Then let's meet him instead. We can use his infatuation to good purpose, tell him he'll be doing Judy a favor if he cooperates and claims he's had an accident that will prevent him from joining the Season for a few weeks. As long as he agrees to assure Roslynn of it, so she'll no longer have a reason to object to Judy's coming with us, I won't actually have to break any bones."

Jacqueline grinned. "You realize you sound like my father?"

"Bite your tongue, Jack."

Chapter Four

"**H**AVE YOU THOUGHT OF something yet? We're down to two days before we sail, and now neither Jack nor George intends to join us thanks to your wife's intransigence," James said as he landed a hard jab to Anthony's chin that moved his brother back a step.

Word had spread fast in the neighborhood when the Malory brothers were seen going into Knighton's Hall together. The seats around the ring were already filled as if this fight had been scheduled. A crowd was at the door fighting to get in. Knighton had thrown up his hands and stopped trying to prevent access. Anthony, the youngest Malory brother, had been coming to Knighton's for most of his life for exercise in the ring, but his fights weren't very exciting since he never lost—unless his brother James stepped into the ring with him. No one ever knew which brother would win, and thus bets were flying about the hall today.

Anthony's black brows narrowed on his brother. "No, and you can stop taking your frustration out on me."

"But who better?" James said drily, and another hard right landed. "What about now?"

"Blister it, James, it ain't my bloody fault."

"Of course it is, dear boy. You are the only one capable of talking your wife around. Lost your touch? Good God, you have, haven't you?"

Anthony got in a solid punch to James's midsection for that slur, followed by an uppercut. Neither one moved James Malory, who had been likened to a brick wall more'n once by men who had tried to defeat him, his brothers included. But Anthony was knocked off his feet with James's next blow, deciding the matter of his giving up this round. Bloody hell. James won too easily when *he* was annoyed. But Anthony was saved from having to concede when his driver climbed up on the side of the ring and waved for his attention. Seeing the man as well, James stepped back.

Anthony got up to fetch the note his man was waving at him, reading it as he returned to James in the middle of the ring. He snorted before he told James, "Judy suggests I save my face a bruising today and come home to pack. Apparently, Ros has given in."

James started to laugh at the good news, which was how Anthony caught him off guard with a punch that landed his older brother on his arse. But James's own annoyance was completely gone now with the unexpected news, so he merely raised a golden brow from his position on the floor to inquire, "Then what was that for?"

"Because now I'm no doubt in the doghouse," Anthony grumbled, though he offered James a hand up. "I don't know who changed her mind or how they did it, but I know I'll end up catching her anger for it."

"Then it's just as well you'll be sailing with us and your wife will be staying home. She will have more'n enough time to calm down before we return."

Both men knew that Roslynn wouldn't sail with them because of her seasickness. She and Anthony's younger daughter, Jaime, suffered from the same malady, so even if Roslynn was willing to endure the discomfort for Judy's sake, she wouldn't subject Jaime to it again. Nor would she leave Jaime at home alone for the two months they expected to be gone.

But James noted that his remark didn't seem to ease his brother's concern. "Come on, old man, don't tell me London's most notorious rake can't redirect a lady's anger into passion of another sort," James said as he leaned forward to take his brother's proffered hand.

Anthony abruptly withdrew it. "It's against my code of honor to hit a man when he's down, but I *could* make an exception just for you."

James chuckled as he rose to his feet. "I'll pass on that favor. Don't want Judy to think her message didn't get to you in good time."

In the middle of the Atlantic, *The Nereus* was making good headway toward Bridgeport, Connecticut. While the Andersons' family business, Skylark Shipping, had many ships in its fleet, each sibling also had one of his or her own, and *The Nereus* was owned and captained by Warren, the second-oldest Anderson brother and Amy Malory's adoring husband. The couple spent half of the year at sea, along with their children, Eric, and the twins, Glorianna and Stuart, and of course the children's tutors. The other half of the year they spent in their house in London so their children could get to know their large family.

"No pain."

"Then . . . ?"

"Something—bad—is going to happen."

Warren immediately looked up at the sky for an approaching storm that might cripple them, but not a dark cloud was in sight. "When?"

"I don't know."

"What?"

"I don't know!"

He sighed. "If you're going to have these feelings, I really wish you could interpret them more specifically."

"You always say that. And it never helps because I can't. We have to go back, Warren."

He tsked, helped her straighten, and turned her around so he could hold her in his arms. "You're not thinking clearly. We'd miss half the family that are already heading this way. Even James and Georgie will have departed with Jack long before we could get back."

"I wish there was a faster way to travel," she growled in frustration against his wide chest.

He chuckled. "That's never going to happen, but we don't sail with cannons anymore—"

"You still acquired a full cargo that's weighing us down."

"Of course I did, that's my job. And despite the cargo, we're making damn good time. Another week, give or take a day or so, and we'll be in Bridgeport."

"If the wind holds," she mumbled.

"Naturally. But you know, no matter what your feeling portends, you can lessen the blow and make sure it isn't devastating. Do it now. Say something to relieve your mind, sweetheart. Make a bet. You know you always win."

Amy was basking in the spring sun on deck, despite the wind's being nippy. As the only woman in the Anderson family who had experienced a successful social Season in London, she'd been asked by the Anderson brothers to plan the social events for Jacqueline's two-week visit to Bridgeport. Of course, Drew Anderson's wife, Gabby, had had a London social debut, but it had been cut short and turned into a scandalous disaster by Drew, so she couldn't offer much advice about come-out parties. Amy wasn't simply relying on her own experience. She had conferred with her cousin Regina, the Malory family's expert in social events.

Amy had to get the Anderson family home ready for these events. She had to plan the menus and send out the invitations. Warren would help her with the invitations since he knew whom to include. Although Amy had been to Bridgeport with him dozens of times over the years and had met many of the Andersons' friends and acquaintances, she couldn't be expected to remember them all. Yet everything had to be perfect before Jacqueline and her parents arrived.

Her own children were more excited about this trip than she was, since they were going to get to attend each event. In England they'd have to wait until they were eighteen to be included among the adults, but in America rules like that didn't apply. Amy was too frazzled to be excited. So many things to do, so many lists to make.

With so much on her mind, she almost didn't notice the feeling that started to intrude, and then she did, doubling over from it, as if she'd received a blow to her stomach. Warren, approaching her from behind, noticed and was instantly alarmed.

He put his hands gently on her back. "What sort of pain is it, sweetheart?"

She glanced up at him and gave him a loving smile for the reminder. "I bet nothing is going to happen that my family can't handle."

"Are you sure you want to be that vague?"

"I wasn't vague. That covers everyone in my family, everyone in your family, all wives, husbands, and children."

Chapter Five

THE HOLDING CELL, ONE of many, was the only one currently in use. The cell wasn't in a jail or a prison, although it certainly felt as if it were to the men detained there. Underground, no windows, the prisoners would have no light at all if a single lantern weren't kept burning day and night. That light was for the guard, not the prisoners.

The revenue base had been built toward the end of the last century when the Crown got more aggressive in patrolling her southern waters, mainly along the Cornish coast. The base had started out as no more than a dock and a barracks halfway between Dorset and Devon. As it had expanded over the years, a community had grown up around it. Shops, a stable, taverns, but the main business was still the apprehension of smugglers, and they were dealt with severely. Sent to the colonies in Australia or hanged. One or the other with trials that were a mockery.

Nathan Tremayne had wished more than once that he'd been born in the last century, before the revenue men got organized. Then, smuggled cargoes could be unloaded right on the docks of a village with everyone helping. Even the local nabobs would turn a blind eye on the illegal activities as long as they got their case of brandy or tea. It had been a simple way to get around exorbitant taxes, and the long expanse of rocky Cornish coastline made that section of England ideal for bringing in rum, brandy, tea, and even tobacco to otherwise law-abiding citizens at reasonable prices. With so few revenue men patrolling back then, the smugglers faced little risk. Not so anymore.

These days the few smugglers still operating were running out of places to hide their cargoes. Even the tunnels built into the cliffs were slowly being discovered and watched by the revenuers. Smugglers had resorted to storing their cargoes farther inland, away from the revenuers, before their cargoes could be distributed. But the goods still had to be unloaded onto shore for transport—or loaded back onto a ship if a smuggler suspected his hiding place had been discovered by a meddlesome wench who would likely inform the authorities. That's how Nathan had been caught last week. His crew had gotten away, scattering like rats in a sewer. He and his ship hadn't.

It had been a setup. The revenuers had been lying in wait. He just couldn't prove it unless he could escape. But that wasn't happening from a cellblock such as this. Chained hand and foot with the chains spiked to the wall behind him, he could barely stand or reach the man chained next to him. Four in the cell were in a similar position. He didn't know them, didn't bother to talk to them. An old man had been left unbound. His task was to pass out the tin bowls of gruel to the rest of them. If he was awake. If waking him didn't get him angry. Nathan had already missed a few meals because of that old man's temper.

Nathan was asleep when they came for him, unchaining him from the wall, dragging him out of there. The last man to be removed from the cell had gone out screaming about his innocence and hadn't returned. Nathan didn't say a word, but a slow-burning anger was inside him. He'd had other choices, other kinds of work, other goals, too. He might have stuck to that path if his father, Jory, hadn't died. But one thing had led to another, a long chain of events, and now here he was about to be hung or sent off to prison for life.

The two guards dragging him didn't even give him an opportunity to walk. That would have been too slow for them, with the chains still on his ankles, and they weren't removing those. He couldn't even shield his eyes from the daylight that blinded him when they got aboveground.

He was taken into a large office and shoved directly into a hardback chair in front of a desk. The fancy room had more the look of a parlor with expensive furnishings, indicating that the man behind the desk was important. The man who, Nathan guessed, was maybe five years older than he was, which would put him around thirty, wore a spotless uniform with gleaming buttons, and had curious blue eyes. He had the look of an aristocrat. A common practice was for second sons to work for the government in some capacity.

The guards were dismissed before the man said, "I'm Arnold Burdis, Commander Burdis to be exact."

Nathan was surprised he'd been left completely alone with the officer. Did they think a week of nothing but gruel in a bricked and barred hole had made him weak? The office might be in the middle of a base crawling with revenuers, but still, it wouldn't take too much effort for Nathan to overpower this man.

He'd immediately spotted the old dueling pistol on the desk, which was there for obvious reasons. Nathan eyed it for a few moments, debating his chances of getting to it before the commander did. The likelihood that it had only one bullet in it decided the matter because he would need at least two, one for the commander and one for the chain between his feet in order to escape. Unless he wanted to take the commander hostage . . .

"Would you like a brandy?"

The man was pouring one for himself, and two glasses were actually on the desk in front of him. "One of my own bottles?" Nathan asked.

Burdis's mouth quirked up slightly. "A sense of humor despite your dire straits, how novel."

The commander poured the brandy for him anyway and slid the glass across the desk. The rattle of his chains as he raised it to his lips screamed of those dire straits, but sarcasm wasn't humor. And he only took a sip to wet his dry mouth. If the man intended to get him drunk to loosen his tongue, he would be disappointed.

"You are quite the catch, Tremayne. But it was just a matter of time. You were getting sloppy, or was it too bold for your own good?"

"Try desperate?"

"Were you really? Dare I take credit?"

"For dogged persistence, if you like. I prefer to blame a wench."

Burdis actually chuckled. "Don't we all from time to time. But my informant wasn't wearing skirts."

"Care to share his name?" Nathan tossed out the question, then held his breath.

But the man wasn't simply conversing with him or distracted enough to reflexively reply to a quick question. He was cordial for a reason; Nathan just couldn't imagine what it was. But he was beginning to think he was being toyed with. A nabob's perverse pleasure, for whatever reason, and he wanted no more of it.

"Do I even get a trial?" he demanded.

The commander swirled his brandy and sniffed it before he looked up curiously and asked, "Do you have a defense?"

"I'll think of something."

A tsk. "You're far too glib for your situation. Admirable, I suppose, but unnecessary. Has it not occurred to you that I hold your life in my hands? I would think you would want to rein in that sarcasm, at least until you find out why I've summoned you."

A carrot? It almost sounded as if he wasn't going to be hanged today. But it raised his suspicion again. If this wasn't his trial, the commander his judge and jury, then what the hell was it? And he'd been caught red-handed. He had no defense and they both knew it.

He sat back. "By all means, continue."

"I am successful in this job because I make a point of finding out all there is to know about my quarries, and you are something of an anomaly."

"There's nothing peculiar about me, Commander."

"On the contrary. I know you've been involved in other lines of work. Lawful ones. Quite a few actually, and you mastered each one, which is an amazing feat for someone your age. Couldn't make up your mind what to do with your life?"

Nathan shrugged. "My father died and left me his ship and crew. That made up my mind for me."

Burdis smiled. "So you think smuggling is in your blood? I beg to differ. I already know about you, Tremayne, more than I expected to learn. Privilege of rank, access to old records."

"Then you probably know more'n I do."

"Possibly, but I doubt it. Moved quite far down the proverbial social ladder, haven't you? Did all the women in your family marry badly, or just your mother?"

Every chain rattled as Nathan stood up and leaned across the desk to snarl, "Do you have a death wish?"

The commander immediately reached for his pistol, cocked it, and pointed it at Nathan's chest. "Sit down, before I call the guards."

"Do you really think one bullet would stop me before I break your neck?"

Burdis let out a nervous chuckle. "Yes, you're a strapping behemoth, I get the point. But you have an earl in your bloodline, so it was a logical question."

"But none of your bleedin' business."

"Quite right. And I meant no offense. I just found it a fascinating tidbit, who your ancestors are, a bit far back in the tree, but still . . . D'you even realize that you could be sitting in a chair like mine, instead of the one you're in? It boggled my mind when I realized it. Why did you never take advantage of who you are?"

"Because that isn't who I am. And you ask too many questions of a man you've already caught."

"Curiosity is my bane, I readily admit it. Now *do* sit down, before I change my mind about you and send you back to your cell."

There was that carrot again, alluding to a different outcome to his capture than the obvious one. Nathan drained the brandy in front of him before he dropped back in his chair. He could handle at least one glass without losing his wits. Bleedin' nabob. Nathan still suspected he was being toyed with, and now he guessed why. His lordly ancestor probably ranked higher than the commander's did. Why else would the man want to sit there and gloat?

"Are you going to tell me who your informant was?" Nathan asked once more.

"He was just a lackey, but can't you guess who he works for? I have it on good authority that you've been searching for the man yourself. He must have thought you were getting too close to finding him."

Nathan stiffened. "Hammett Grigg?"

"Yes, I thought that might be clue enough for you. The same man suspected of killing your father."

"Not just suspected. There was a witness."

"An old grudge finally settled between the two men, was the way I heard it."

"My father was unarmed. It was murder."

"And is that what you had in mind for Grigg?"

"I want to kill him, yes, but in a fair fight—with my bare hands."

Burdis actually laughed. "Look at yourself, man. D'you really think that would be a fair fight? I've nothing against revenge. I feel the need for it m'self occasionally. But I'll have Mr. Grigg caught and hung long before you can get your hands on him. He is my next quarry, after all."

"And I'll be dead before you catch him."

Burdis refilled Nathan's glass before he replied, "You misunderstand why I've brought you before me. I'm going to give you the opportunity to thank me one day."

"For what?"

The commander opened a drawer to retrieve a clean, unfolded piece of paper that he set in front of him. He tapped it. "This is a full pardon already signed, an opportunity for you to start over with a clean slate. But it's conditional, of course."

Nathan's eyes narrowed. "Is this some joke?"

"Not a'tall. This document will remain with me until you fulfill the terms, but it's a legitimate offer."

"You want me to catch Grigg for you without killing him? You really think I could resist the temptation if I get my hands on him?"

"Forget about Grigg! I told you, *assure* you, I'll see him hanged for you."

For the first time, Arnold Burdis didn't look or sound so cordial. Nathan was done with second-guessing him, other than to say, "You sound angry."

"I am. My man guarding your ship was killed, left floating in the water where your *Pearl* should have been."

"You've lost my ship!?"

"I didn't *lose* it," Burdis growled. "It was stolen, and, no, not by Hammett Grigg. We caught one of the thieves. Nicked as they were sailing away, he fell into the water and was recovered. We gave chase, of course, probably would have caught them, too, if we'd known their direction. We searched up and down the coast, while they did the unthinkable, sailing straight out to sea and beyond."

"Who were they?"

"They're not Englishmen, but they've been stealing English

ships for some ten years now, just so sporadically, and never from the same harbors, that no one linked the thefts. At first they were just taking the vessels offshore and sinking them, but then they decided to have their revenge and make a profit at it."

"Revenge?"

"It's a couple of Americans who bear a grudge against us for the last war we had with their country, which orphaned them. They were just children at the time, which is why they only got around to getting some payback a decade ago." A folded note was tossed at Nathan. "Those are the particulars I got out of their man. My superiors don't give a rat's ass about this crime ring targeting our harbors. They only want you and your ilk. But I don't like having my toes stepped on, and these thieves did that when they killed one of my men and stole *my* prize right off my docks."

Nathan raised a brow. *His* prize? "Tell me you're not asking me to bring my ship back to you."

"No, if you can recover *The Pearl*, she's yours again, but good luck with that. They refit them with new paint, new names, then auction them off to their unsuspecting country-men, who actually think they are legitimate shipbuilders. And they've gotten away with this for years. But you're going to end it. It won't be easy getting the Yanks to do you any favors, but you'll need to figure out a way to get the authorities over there to work with you in closing down that operation. That's my condition. I want a letter from an American official stating that the thieves have been arrested and put out of business."

"That's all?" Nathan rejoined drily.

The commander's eyes narrowed with the warning. "Don't even think of running away once I give you your freedom for this task. As I mentioned, I found out more'n I expected to about you, including that you have guardianship of your two remaining relatives. I would hate to see your nieces end up paying for their uncle's crimes. So do you agree to my terms?"

"For my freedom, did you even need to ask?"

Chapter Six

IN GROSVENOR SQUARE, AT the home of Edward and Charlotte Malory, most of the extensive Malory family in England and a few close friends were gathered for a send-off party for Jack and Judy, who would be sailing in the morning for America. The crew was already aboard *The Maiden George*, the trunks had already been delivered. It only remained for the seven members of the family bound for America to row out to the ship at dawn, too early to expect good-byes at the dock, thus the party tonight.

Glancing about the room, Judith was looking for Brandon so she could ask him what had happened with the vagrant. She'd told him that she suspected the vagrant was a smuggler, and Brandon had assured her he and his father would send the man packing. But it appeared her cousins from Hampshire weren't going to make it tonight. She wasn't surprised, when she and Jacqueline had visited them so recently and they had already given Jack their good wishes for the trip.

Derek had even told Judith, "I bet your mum will change her mind, so I'm going to wish you a wonderful voyage, too."

"I wish *Amy* were saying that," Judith had replied, and she hadn't been joking.

Derek had laughed. "Yes, that would guarantee your sailing to America, wouldn't it?"

It would indeed. Amy never lost a wager. Judith realized she should have asked Amy to bet on it before she'd sailed with Warren. Maybe Amy had and *that's* why Judith was going now.

Jacqueline came up beside her and said in an annoyed tone, "*He* shouldn't be here when he's not a close friend of the family and only your mother knows him."

Judith followed her cousin's gaze and saw Roslynn fussing over Lord Cullen. "But now we all know him, and besides, my mother is right. It was quite thoughtful and gallant of him to come here tonight to wish me well on my voyage when he must be in pain from his injury."

"He's here because he's got his heart set on you and your mother's got her heart set on him *for* you. Tell me your heart's not getting set here, too, when you and I swore not to marry this year."

Judith grinned and teased, "Now that I've met him again after all these years, I have to admit he turned out rather handsome, don't you think?"

"If you like dark red hair and pretty blue eyes. Flirt all you want, just no falling in love yet."

"Stop fretting. I'm not eager to get back here because of him when we haven't even left yet."

In a corner of the room, Boyd joined James and Anthony, who were looking at the Scotsman, too. Anthony was saying, "Ros should've confessed what she was up to, trying to match him with Judy. But I'm not complaining when he managed to bring peace to the family by getting himself laid up. But if it weren't so obvious that my baby ain't interested in him, I bloody well would."

"Noticed that," James agreed.

"He's head over heels for her, though," Boyd put in.

"And how would you know anything about it, Yank?" Anthony asked.

"Because as a last resort, Jack and I tracked him down and asked him to feign an injury to help Judy convince her mother to let her go to America."

"That splint on his leg is wrapped up rather tight for a fake," James remarked.

"It's not a fake," Boyd said with a grin. "The man is as clumsy as an ox. He got so excited by the scheme he really did fall off his horse and break his leg."

James rolled his eyes.

Anthony said, "I see I'm going to have to have a word or two with Roslynn, after all. What the deuce could she be thinking, matchmaking our daughter with such a bungler?"

"It was a brilliant plan, though, you have to admit," James said. "The broken-limb part. You should have thought of it, Tony."

"I didn't even know about *him*, so how could I?"

"Just remember you owe me one, both of you, the next time you lay into me," Boyd said before quickly walking off.

"Did he just goad you?" Anthony said with an incredulous laugh. "And with a smirk, too!"

James shrugged. "He should know by now that I have a faulty memory when I find it convenient. And my memory will definitely be faulty when it comes to being beholden to an Anderson—wife excluded, of course."

Lord Cullen didn't stay long, shouldn't have come at all when his doctor had ordered him to stay off his feet for three months. After Judith thanked him again for coming and wished him a swift recovery, Jacqueline steered her toward their mothers.

"D'you feel the excitement?" Jack asked. "We're going to have a grand time, you know. I feel it, I'm bubbling with it."

"You're bubbling with triumph, not excitement. Note the difference."

"Pooh, whatever it is, let's go share some of it with your mother. She might have given in when she learned the Scot won't be here for the start of the Season either, but she's still not happy about it or what she termed our 'collective tantrum.' And if she's not happy, then Uncle Tony won't be getting a nice good-bye from her tonight, and he'll be in a rotten mood the whole trip."

Judith blushed at that statement as Jacqueline dragged her across the room to their mothers. Despite how brazen Jack could be at times and how used to it Judith was, she believed some things just shouldn't be mentioned or even alluded to, and what their parents did behind closed doors was definitely one of those things.

Both girls walked up to Roslynn and put an arm around her waist. Judith was now as tall as her mother at five feet four inches and had the same sun-gold hair streaked with copper, but her father's exotic cobalt-blue eyes, a stunning combination, or so her family liked to remind her. But Judith's features also resembled her mother's. She had a heart-shaped face and finely molded cheekbones, a small, tapered nose, even the same generous full lips. Jacqueline, on the other hand, looked nothing like her mother. She didn't inherit Georgina's diminutive height. She was taller at five feet six inches and had James Malory's blond hair and green eyes, but her features were uniquely her own: a pert nose, high cheekbones, a stubborn chin, and a mouth far too sensual for a woman.

Her lips were turned up now in a smile meant to melt hearts. Few people were immune to it, and Roslynn wasn't one of them, but she still admonished her niece, "None of that now. You won't be cajoling me out of this snit."

"Are you sure?" Jacqueline asked. "I haven't heard your Scot's brogue yet to prove you're in a snit. But Judy won't take my word for it, so a little reassurance from you before we sail is in order." Then, in one of her more serious tones: "Don't make her suffer because there's been a little dent—"

Georgina cut in with a gasp. "Jacqueline Malory! Not another word!"

Jacqueline merely met her mother's eyes with a steady look that offered no apology. She was protective of family, always had been, and most particularly of Judith. It wasn't the first time she had stepped up to be Judy's champion, and Roslynn loved her all the more for it.

"It's all right, George," Roslynn said, and then to Jack, "You've made your point, sweetheart. And I wasn't going to let my darling leave without my best wishes." Roslynn leaned her head toward Judith's. "You can have fun. In fact, I want you to enjoy every minute of your trip." But her tone turned stern when she added, "But don't you dare come back in love. You will wait and fall in love here. And that's the last I'm going to say about it." But Roslynn ended that with a smile.

Jack still leaned forward around Roslynn and said to Judith, "You didn't tell her?"

"Tell me what?" Roslynn asked.

Jacqueline chuckled. "We're not getting married this year. Next year maybe, or even the year after that. We're in no hurry to. Really we aren't."

"It's true, Mother," Judith confirmed. "The fun is going to be in the trying, not the doing."

As the girls moved off to circulate about the room, Roslynn remarked to Georgina, "That was no doubt word for word from *your* daughter."

"I quite agree," Georgina said.

"But they can't be that naive. When it happens, it's going to happen, and there's not a bloody thing they can do to stop it."

"I know, but still, I wish Jack had let her father know that was her intention. James has been masking it very well, but he's been a powder keg since the beginning of this year, with the thought of Jack getting married by the end of it. He's not going to deal gracefully with her falling in love, you know."

"You think Tony is? He used to only visit Knighton's Hall a few times a week, but it's been daily for several months now. He wants to stop time from advancing but he can't, and he's extremely frustrated because of it. Truth be told, that's why I didn't want to delay Judith's Season here and hoped she would favor young Cullen before it even began. The sooner Judy gets married, the sooner my family can get back to normal—until Jaime comes of age."

Georgina laughed. "You *really* should have owned up to that sooner, m'dear."

"Prob'ly." Roslynn sighed. "I swear, our husbands were never meant to have daughters. Sons and more sons would've been fine, but daughters! It was just asking for trouble. I fear for their suitors, I really do. Our men don't have the temperament to just stand back and let nature take its course."

Chapter Seven

JUDITH TRIED TO MASK her smile when she and Jack moved away from their mothers. She was starting to feel some of the excitement that had infected Jacqueline. And her cousin was so proud of having been right, she might as well have been crowing with it. To keep her from bragging with an "I told you so," which would have annoyed Judith because she'd heard it so often, she put a finger to Jacqueline's mouth when she started to open it.

"Don't say it. Let me. You were right—as usual. My mother is not angry at me for the way this turned out, so the burden is gone and now I can fully enjoy the trip."

"I wasn't going to mention *that*," Jacqueline replied, and turned Judith around to face the parlor's double doors. "Who's that and why does he look familiar?"

Judith saw the man then, a stranger, elegantly clad if not quite in an English style. He wasn't wearing a greatcoat, but a cloak edged with black ermine. The frock coat underneath it was a bit too full skirted to be fashionable. And was that a sword poking out from under the cloak? He appeared to be a foreigner, but Jacqueline was right, he did look familiar. And they weren't the only ones who thought so.

Their uncle Edward put his finger on it, taking a step forward to say in his typically jovial tone, "Another long-lost relative? Come in!"

Everyone more or less turned in unison to see whom Edward was talking about. The young man at the door seemed embarrassed now that he was the center of attention, and perhaps a little overwhelmed, with so many people in the room. Even though Judith doubted that the tall, handsome young man was related to them, she didn't think her uncle had been joking. But then, when did her uncle ever joke about family?

And the stranger didn't dispute her uncle's conclusion. In fact he appeared rather amazed when he replied, "How did you know?"

Judith's cousin Regina stepped forward, grinning. Jack's brother, Jeremy, stepped forward, grinning. Anthony just stepped forward. They all resembled the stranger with their exotically slanted, cobalt-blue eyes and raven-black hair.

"Another Malory," James stated the obvious in his drollest tone.

The young man looked directly at James and, not seeming the least bit intimidated by him as most men were, said, "No, sir, I am not a Malory. I am Count Andrássy Benedek, of Hungary."

"Are you now? A blood relation nonetheless. Tell us, which Stephanoff you are descended from?"

"Maria—apparently."

"Our grandmother Anastasia's grandmother?" Anthony remarked. "You don't sound too sure."

"I obtained the information from my great-grandfather's journal, which is only a memory now."

Anthony began to laugh. "Another journal?" At Andrássy's curious look, he added, "We found one, too, some ten years back, written by my grandmother Anastasia Stephanoff. Prior to that, it was only rumored that Gypsy blood ran in our family."

Andrássy nodded. "I had never heard of this Stephanoff ancestor. I don't believe my late father was aware of her either. Gypsy bands pass through Hungary, never staying long. I have never met one myself. So for me, there was no rumor or other clue until I found the journal. Ironically, I might never have known of it, or had a chance to read it, if my stepsister hadn't found it in our attic while she was hiding there during one of her tantrums, but that is some unpleasantness I don't need to burden you with."

"Another time, perhaps," Edward said as he stepped forward to lead Andrássy into the room. "What happened to your ancestor's journal? Why don't you have it anymore?"

"It perished in the fire that destroyed my home and all my family heirlooms."

"How awful," more than one person said.

"You're destitute?" Edward asked.

"No, not at all. My father might have distrusted banks, but I never shared that sentiment. I had an inheritance from my mother. May we speak in private?"

"No need, m'boy," Edward said. "Everyone in this room is a member of our family."

That rendered the young man speechless, but then all four of the eldest set of Malory brothers were present: Jason, the third Marquis of Haverston and the oldest, Edward, the second oldest, and James and Anthony. Their wives were present, too, and most of their children, including their children's spouses and a few of their older grandchildren. More than twenty Malorys had shown up for Jack and Judy's send-off, and the young count was obviously overwhelmed.

"I had no idea," Andrássy said, his blue eyes moving slowly about the room, a little glazed with emotion. "I had hoped I would be able to track down one or two of Maria's descendants, but . . . never this many. And you don't even seem surprised by me."

Edward chuckled. "You aren't the first member of this family to show up full grown, my boy, albeit one more distant than we might have expected. And I am sure we are all interested in hearing what you read in the journal about our great-great-grandmother Maria Stephanoff."

Anthony handed Andrássy a drink, which he merely held as he spoke. "The journal belonged to my great-grandfather Karl Benedek, Maria's son. Karl's father, understandably, didn't want to speak of his indiscretion with a Gypsy woman, and he didn't until the night he thought he was dying. Maria's caravan was merely passing through and he allowed them to spend one night on his land. She came to him and offered herself in payment. She was young and pretty, but he still refused her, until she said a son would come of it. He had no children, even after going through four wives trying to obtain one. He was desperate enough to believe her that night, but come morning he was angry over what he guessed was a deception."

"But it wasn't a lie?"

"No, it wasn't. Somehow Maria knew and swore she would bring him the boy when he was born. He still didn't believe she was carrying his child, but just in case, he refused to let her leave. He kept her a prisoner until exactly nine months later when she gave birth to a son. He let her go, but he kept his son, whom he named Karl. Maria said the boy would be able to find her if he ever needed her, no matter where in the world she was. Such an odd thing to say. My great-great-grandfather never saw her again and did not tell his son, his only heir, about her until the night he thought he was dying."

"Did he die that night?" James asked curiously.

"No, not for another ten years, and he and Karl never spoke of his strange tale again. But when my great-great-grandfather did die, Karl went in search of his mother, Maria. He found her in England, still traveling with her band of wandering Gypsies. Her granddaughter, Anastasia, had just married an English marquis."

"Wait," Jason spoke up with a frown. "That can't be all that Karl wrote about Anastasia's husband. Merely that he was a marquis from this country?"

"No, Christopher, Marquis of Haverston, was the name written in the journal. I went to Haverston first, only to be told the current marquis was in London. I was given this address, but I almost didn't come here tonight since I am only passing through England on my way to America to search for my stepsister Catherine's real father. I had planned to get her settled and out of my life before I tried to find any descendants of Maria's here. I simply couldn't resist the chance to meet at least one of you before I left England."

James guessed, "I'm beginning to suspect we don't want to meet your stepsister?"

Andrássy sighed. "No, you don't."

"Not to worry, dear boy," Edward said. "My brother James deals remarkably well with difficulties that arise in the family, so we've learned to leave such things to him, trivial or otherwise."

By the young count's expression he had obviously taken offense. "I didn't come here for help. I am capable of dealing with my responsibilities and she—"

"Yes, yes, she's your albatross, we get that," Anthony said, putting an arm around Andrássy's shoulder. "But you haven't heard my brother complaining about being your champion, have you?"

James raised a golden brow. "Give me a moment," he said, but was ignored.

Anthony continued, "As luck would have it—ours, yours, who knows—we happen to be sailing for America in the morning. You're welcome to join us. No need to say another word about your sister if you'd rather not. Think of it as giving us a chance to get to know you a little better, and vice versa. You might want to consider it fate that led you here tonight."

Andrássy didn't agree, but he didn't decline, either. And before he decided either way, the rest of the family wanted a chance to speak with him. James and Anthony stood aside, watching how readily the family took to him. Jack and Judy had him cornered now.

"They're going to talk his ear off," Anthony remarked.

"Jack will," James agreed. "She's rather good at that. And if she thinks he ought to come with us, the matter is as good as settled."

"You don't doubt he's one of us, d'you?" Anthony inquired thoughtfully. "You weren't exactly throwing open those beefy arms in welcome."

"There's no harm in checking into his background," James

replied. "I'll ask Jeremy to see what he can find out about him while we're away. But considering we're heading into Anderson territory, it might not hurt to have another Malory relative, however remote, on our side." James paused a moment. "On the other hand, I'm not so sure it's a good idea to stick him on a ship with us. Once he gets to know us, he might want to run in the opposite direction."

"Speak for yourself, old man."

"Regardless, it's been known to happen. And on a ship, there's nowhere to run."

Anthony chuckled. "Do we need to wake up Knighton tonight? Get rid of all our aggression before we sail? Might work for a week or so."

"No need. I had a ring installed in *The Maiden George*'s hold for us. I do like to plan ahead."

Chapter Eight

"You sure you want to do this, Cap'n?" Corky Menadue asked hesitantly as he stood with Nathan on the London dock.

Nathan smiled. "Get my ship back? Damned right I do."

"I meant work your way over to the colonies."

"I believe they call them states now."

"But it ain't like you couldn't pay for passage instead," Corky said, and not for the first time.

Nathan looked down at his first mate. He had inherited Corky when he'd inherited *The Pearl*, but he'd known the older man most of his life. Corky had been Jory Tremayne's first mate, and Nathan had pretty much grown up on his father's ship—until Jory had kicked him off it. Such impotent rage he'd felt back then, but nothing he'd said or done would change Jory's mind. It was for his own protection, Jory insisted, as if Nathan couldn't protect himself. And he was haunted by the thought that his father might still be alive if he *had* been there the night his father was shot.

"Forget about Grigg! I told you, assure you, I'll see him hanged

for you." Not if Nathan could find him before Commander Burdis did. But he had a ship to find first.

Nathan reminded his old friend, "The other vessels aren't leaving for another week and they're not bound for Connecticut, which is where I need to go. This one is actually going about fifty miles west of my destination. Damned lucky, and about time some luck came my way. Besides, time isn't on our side even if I wanted to waste the coin on passage, which I don't. *The Pearl* will be sold if we don't get there soon."

"I'm just worried about your temper. Last captain you took orders from was your father and that was five years ago. D'you even remember how?"

Nathan barked a laugh, but Corky added, "And this captain is some kind of nabob, if you can go by the high wage he's paying us. And I know how you feel about nabobs."

"You don't have to come along, you know," Nathan told his curly-haired friend.

"And what else would I be doing until you come back with *The Pearl*?"

After Burdis had released Nathan, he'd found Corky and most of his crew in the haunt they frequented in Southampton, where Nathan had settled after leaving Cornwall. At first they'd been shocked to see him and then quite rowdy in expressing their relief that Nathan was a free man. After he'd been captured by the revenuers, they hadn't expected to ever see him again. He didn't begrudge them their escape the night his ship and cargo had been confiscated. In fact, he was fiercely glad they had escaped because they wouldn't have been handed the boon he'd been given. He still couldn't quite believe he was walking free again.

Burdis turned out to be not such a bad sort—for a nabob.

He'd arranged for Nathan to have a bath, a good meal, and his personal belongings returned to him, even his pistol. Then they'd transported him to his home port of Southampton.

After telling his men what had happened and what he had to do now, they'd wanted to snatch a ship for him that very night. He'd been tempted, but with the commander's terms still fresh in his mind, he'd had to tell them no, that he needed legitimate passage.

"If you steal a ship other than your own, our deal is off," Burdis had said. "No more breaking laws of any sort for you, Captain Tremayne."

Too many bleedin' conditions, but he was going to abide by them since it meant a shot at getting his ship back.

When he'd elected to follow in his father's footsteps, he'd known it wouldn't be easy. Still, he'd enjoyed the challenge of smuggling, enjoyed thumbing his nose at the revenuers when they gave chase. They never came close to catching him when he was in the Channel. But constantly having to find new places to store his cargoes had taxed his patience and caused him no end of frustration.

He'd thought he'd finally solved that problem a few months ago when he'd figured out the perfect hiding place: the abandoned house a little ways inland in Hampshire. The house had an extra advantage as its closest neighbor was the Duke of Wrighton. No revenuers would dare snoop around there. But he hadn't counted on the duke's having nosy servants. If that wench hadn't come ghost hunting or meeting up with her lover, which is what he suspected she'd really been doing, he wouldn't have been forced to move the cargo so soon and wouldn't have gotten caught because of it.

After he'd sent word to his crew in Southampton to bring

the ship to their usual unloading cove, so it could be reloaded, one of his crew must have mentioned the plan to someone in Grigg's crew. Or maybe someone in Grigg's crew had heard his men talking about it. It wouldn't be the first time the two crews had ended up in the same tavern. He preferred to think that than that he had a traitor in his crew. But the ghost-hunting wench was still ultimately to blame.

He hadn't been joking when he'd told Burdis he blamed a woman for his capture. He should have put more effort into securing her silence. A kiss usually softened them up, but not her. He'd gambled that he'd be able to get her feeling friendly and agreeable toward him, so she'd keep his presence a secret. Maybe he should have lit her lantern so she could see whom she was dealing with. One of his smiles tended to work wonders on wenches, too. But kissing her hadn't yielded the result he'd hoped for, and he had ended up insulting her instead. He hadn't needed to see her to tell she was bristling from it.

"We've time for a pint and a quick tumble, Cap'n. You game?"

"Thought I asked you to stop calling me that? I'm not your captain for this trip."

Nathan *was* bored, though, just standing around waiting for wagons to show up. He glanced around the London dock, but the last wagon had left ten minutes ago and no others could be seen heading their way. There would probably be more, though, and he didn't want to risk a delay in sailing to America by getting fired because he wasn't there to unload wagons. Every day mattered with *The Pearl* on her way to being altered and sold. It was annoying enough that the ship he'd signed on to in Southampton was making this short detour to London to pick up passengers.

"Come on," Corky cajoled. "We were told to wait, but no one said we couldn't do that waiting in yonder tavern. Watch from the door for the next wagon if you've a mind to, but the rowboat ain't even back from the ship yet to carry another load. And it's going to be a long voyage. One more wench to see me off is all I'm interested in tonight."

Nathan snorted. "You just enjoyed the company of a wench three nights ago in Southampton. Were you too drunk to remember?"

"Oh, yeah." Corky grinned. "But that was then and this is our last night on land. Three weeks at sea is a bleedin' long time."

"The voyage could be as quick as two weeks and besides, *you* don't need to be here. You can still head back to Southampton to wait for my return."

"And leave you without a first mate for the return trip? It's a shame we heard about this ship too late to get the rest of our boys on her."

"I wouldn't have known that her captain was hiring a crew at all if I didn't stop by to tell Alf and Peggy I'd be gone for a few months."

Old Alf was the caretaker of a cottage a few miles up the coast from Southampton. Nathan had been steered to the couple when he'd been looking for someone to care for his nieces while he was away on *The Pearl.* It had proven to be a nicer arrangement than he'd first thought, since the cottage had its own private dock, and Alf let him use it as a berth for *The Pearl.*

Alf had been generous in that after his wife, Peggy, had agreed to watch the girls for Nathan. He hadn't even charged Nathan a fee, merely laid down the rule that no cargo was ever to be unloaded there, since he knew what business Nathan had got into. Alf refused to say much about the bigger vessel at his dock, or why she sat empty, and Nathan was in no position to pry when the elderly couple was doing him such a big favor.

"At least you got me on her with you," Corky said.

"Only because they still needed a carpenter and I bargained to have you included. Alf even hesitated to mention the job, since he knows I no longer practice carpentry. It was his wife, Peggy, who brought it up. Every time I visit the girls, she nags me to go back to work that won't land me in prison. The old gal worries about me."

"She's fond of your nieces and worries they will be left without a guardian again. And she's right, you know. Look how close you came to fulfilling her fears this time. Are you sure you even want your ship back?"

"Are you going to nag now, too?"

"Is that pint of ale suddenly sounding like a good idea?" Corky countered.

Chapter Nine

NATHAN CHUCKLED AND GAVE in, steering his friend across the docks. The tavern Corky had his eye on stood between a warehouse and a ticket office. Nathan didn't know London at all, had never been there before, and had never heard anything good about it either. But taverns were taverns, and this one looked no different from the ones he'd find at home in Southampton. While Nathan had no interest himself in a woman his last night on land because he had too much on his mind to spare any thoughts on a wench, a pint of ale would indeed be welcome.

He'd never asked for them, but now he had responsibilities that he didn't have last year when he would have been the one to suggest a quick tumble. Not anymore. Not since his sister died and he was the only one left in their family who could care for her two children. Not that he hadn't had an agenda before that happened. He just hadn't been in a hurry to achieve his goals.

His nieces, Clarissa and Abbie, were darling girls. He never expected to get so attached to them so quickly, but each time he visited, it was getting harder to say good-bye. At seven years of age Clarissa was the younger and the more exuberant of the two. She never failed to throw herself into his arms with a happy squeal when he arrived. Abbie was more reserved at nine years of age. Poor thing was still trying to emulate her father's snobby family, thinking that's how she ought to behave. But she was starting to come around. She expressed delight now when she saw him and he'd even felt dampness on her cheek when she'd hugged him good-bye a few days ago. My God, that had been difficult, walking away from them this time.

They didn't deserve to live in poverty just because their parents had passed on. He had to do right by them, give them a home, a stable one. One way or another, he was going to provide them with the comfortable life they used to have.

The girls had been raised so differently from him, but then his sister, Angie, had married well. She'd had a fine house in Surrey and her daughters had had a governess, tutors, and fancy dresses. It was too bad it had all come with such disagreeable people for in-laws, the lot of them thinking they were grander than they were just because they held a minor title. Nathan hadn't liked Angie's husband because it had become apparent soon after the wedding that he had only married her because she was descended from an earl. Nathan hadn't even been able to visit her or her children without sneaking in to do it because his brother-in-law had found out Jory was a smuggler and assumed Nathan was one, too.

But everything his nieces had had was gone now, taken back by their father's family when he'd died, killing Angie with him, because he'd been foxed and driving his carriage too fast. Nathan hadn't thought it possible, but he'd come to hate the nobility even more than he already did when those heartless snobs turned their backs on their own granddaughters just because they'd never approved of Angie. All the girls had left were the fancy dresses that didn't even fit them anymore, and an uncle who only hoped to accomplish goals that a sane man would realize were impossible.

He ordered that pint, then another. He was starting to feel the anger that tended to show up when he thought about his situation too long. Maybe what he should be looking for this last night on land was a good fight.

Ale in hand, Nathan turned to glance about the room, looking for someone who might accommodate him, but the tavern was so crowded, he didn't doubt one punch would lead to a full-scale brawl. While it wouldn't be the first time he'd spent a night in jail for starting one, he couldn't afford for that to happen tonight if he wanted to get *The Pearl* back.

He started for the door, but turned about when five new customers stepped through it and he recognized one of them. What the hell? Hammett Grigg's men in London, of all places? The last time he'd seen Mr. Olivey, Hammett's first mate, who was the one he recognized, had been in Southampton five years ago. Grigg and a handful of his crew had tracked Nathan down to find out where Jory was holed up. Still furious with his father, he'd told them he didn't know and didn't care. They'd actually had him watched for a while, thinking he could lead them to Jory. But he never saw his father again, and Hammett and his men finally found Jory on their own. . . .

Was the Cornish smuggler actually crazy enough to deliver a load of untaxed goods to the biggest city in the country? Not using London docks, he couldn't. He had to be in London for some other reason, maybe to line up new buyers. But if his men were here on the docks, Grigg might be nearby, too. Could Nathan really get this lucky and find the man before Commander Burdis did?

Well, he'd wanted a fight. Trying to find out Grigg's whereabouts would definitely get him one, but he preferred that it take place outside if possible. Or he could just wait and follow them when they left. Would he have time for that?

He glanced behind him without turning. The five men were still by the door, looking about the room. There were no empty tables they could use. If they didn't leave, they'd be coming to the bar where Nathan was standing and that brawl would then be inevitable. . . .

Decision made, Nathan walked to the door and shouldered his way past them. Easy enough to do when he was taller and brawnier than them. And as expected, they followed him outside. Five of them against one of him would make them cocky. They just didn't know him well, and he'd like to keep it that way for a few minutes. Cocky men tended to have loose lips.

"Leaving without paying your respects, boyo?" Mr. Olivey said, grabbing Nathan's arm to stop him. "Thought we wouldn't recognize you?"

"Wot are ye doing 'ere, eh?" another asked. "Why ain't ye—? Heard ye got locked up."

"I heard you helped with that," Nathan replied. "Where's your boss? I'd like to thank him."

" 'Ere now, don't be blaming us 'cause you got careless, boyo."

"I bet 'e's plannin' to wield 'is 'ammer in London. Now the revs got 'is ship, wot else is there left for 'im?"

The men's chuckles were cut short when Nathan gripped the man's throat with one hand and pinned him to the tavern wall. "My business here is none of yours, but yours is certainly mine. I repeat, where's your boss?"

"You're in no position to ask," Olivey said behind him. "Or did you really think you could take us all on?"

"Let's find out." Nathan leapt to the side to position himself so that all five men were in front of him again.

Five against one might be lousy odds, but he had passion and purpose in his corner, while he guessed they just wanted to have some fun at his expense. He didn't have to wait long for the first swing to come his way. He blocked that one and threw one of his own. Two quick jabs at another had a second staggering back.

Blood pumping, Nathan had no doubt that he could do this, despite the odds, and get the answer he wanted before he was done. He just needed to leave one of them standing and able to talk.

The next sailor to come at him he knocked to the ground, but the man got back up too quickly, wiping blood from his mouth. "Should take to the ring, boyo, instead of wasting time with a hammer. You'd make a fortune."

Olivey's comment distracted Nathan a moment too long. Bleedin' hell. Both his arms were suddenly pulled forcefully behind him and Mr. Olivey stood in front of him laughing.

"Should have run while you had the chance. Should have left well enough alone, too. Hammett was done with your family—until he heard you were looking for him. Look where that got you, eh."

"Go to hell," Nathan spat out.

But suddenly his arms were freed and he heard the distinctive hollow sound of two heads cracking together. He didn't need to look behind him to guess that two of Grigg's men had just been hurt if not put out of commission. Then he was yanked aside, out of the way, and a strong arm fell over his shoulder. He tried to shrug it off, but the hold tightened enough to stop him. Blood *still* pumping, he was about to swing at whoever was holding him immobile until he got a look at him.

Tall and dark haired with shoulders as wide as Nathan's and wearing a fine greatcoat, the man could pass for a nabob except for one glaring fact. A member of the gentry wouldn't get involved in a street brawl, would he? No, he'd merely yell for the watch. Another man, too, a big, blond brute specimen unlike any Nathan had ever seen was pounding Hammett's sailors with his fists. Were they just a couple of rakehells out looking for trouble? Then they could add him to the count before they were done and he didn't think he'd walk away from that, could even miss his ship because of it. But right now he needed at least one of Hammett's sailors conscious so he could question him.

It was all he could do to sound reasonable when he said to the black-haired man, "Let go so I can help him." Stop him was more like it.

"Bite your tongue, youngun. That's not a snarl my brother is wearing, it's a grin." Then the man sighed because all five sailors were now sprawled on the ground. To his brother he complained, "Really, old boy, you could have dragged it out just a *little*."

The blond bruiser merely gave the black-haired man a bored look before he turned his piercing green eyes on Nathan. "Need a job? I could use a sparring partner."

Nathan choked back an impotent snarl. He'd just lost his chance to get answers. He should have stopped the bruiser from knocking them all out, but the demolishing had happened so fast. And they actually thought they were being *helpful*.

He got out, "No thanks, I have a job."

The black-haired one who'd held him back let go of him now, saying, "No pearls of gratitude? Do we need to teach you some manners, youngun?" But then he added, "Behind you, James."

What happened next left no room for thought. It did flash though Nathan's mind that he had been left for last and was about to get the beating of his life. But he saw one of the sailors staggering to his feet. Nathan yelled, "Wait!"—but the man named James turned to the sailor, while the black-haired taller one put his steely arm around Nathan's shoulder again.

It was too much. Nathan swung, catching the black-haired man completely off guard and connecting with his chin, taking him down. He doubted he could do the same with the bruiser who was now staring at Nathan with a raised brow.

Nathan stiffened. He could probably bolt as the sailor was now doing, but he didn't want *this* one following him.

He broadened the distance between himself and the bruiser and, pointing to the fleeing sailor, quickly said, "I need answers that you and your friend are keeping me from getting."

"Then run along and get them. My brother's going to be in the mood for a fight now, but not to worry—"

Nathan didn't wait to hear the rest. With a nod, he ducked around the strange twosome's carriage, which had stopped in front of the tavern, and took off down the dock, chasing down the sailor. He thought he heard someone laughing behind him, but it was probably just someone in the tavern, and he didn't look back.

The sailor had ducked around a corner onto a wide street. It was dark, but not deserted. A good number of sailors were making their way back to their ships, some drunkenly. Nathan ran down the street, glancing at each man he passed. It took him a few minutes to spot Hammett's sailor just as the man turned another corner.

Swearing, Nathan reached the spot only to find a narrow alley filled with broken crates and other garbage. A dog barked to the left. He headed that way. He found the dog but the sailor was nowhere in sight. He could have entered any number of buildings through their rear doors. A light suddenly appeared in an upstairs window of one of them. He tried the door to that building and found it locked. He moved on to the next building. The door was unlocked and he slipped inside. The corridor he found himself in was dark—but not so dark he couldn't see the shadow crouched in it.

Nathan leapt forward and dragged the sailor outside before whoever had lit the lantern could come down to investigate why the dog was barking. He didn't stop until they rounded another corner and he shoved the sailor up against the side of a building.

"I distracted that bruiser so you could get away, but I'll be finishing you off m'self if you don't—"

"Wait!" the man pleaded. "I'll tell you what I know, just no more punches."

"Where is Grigg?"

"He ain't in town yet, but he'll be here tomorrow for the delivery."

"To who?"

"Man on the west side, runs a fancy tavern. The cap'n's been supplying him with brandy off and on for a year now."

"Who's the man? What's the name of the tavern?" Nathan tightened his grip on the man's shirt.

"Don't know. All I know is this is a big delivery, so the captain is coming to town himself for it. He's got quite a few establishments here eager for the finer stuff that he supplies now, those that cater to the gentry. Cuts them a deal they can't refuse."

"I need names."

"I don't know, I swear! Mr. Olivey does. You should be asking him—"

"He's not going to be answering anything tonight, but you aren't telling me anything useful either. That better change, and quickly."

"It *was* the captain who set you up. He had a man watching your crew in Southampton. You shouldn't be so predictable, boyo, always coming back to the same port."

Nathan ignored the gloating tone for the moment. "Is that how Grigg has managed to avoid me?"

"Aye, he never docks in the same place twice. But since you do, it was easy to set a spy on your crew when they were in Southampton. He was there when you sent your men that message that you needed to reload your cargo to move it to a safer spot. He even overheard where they were to meet you with your ship and when."

"How was that ambush arranged so quickly?"

"Because Captain Grigg was in town that night. He was told about your change in plans. He sent his spy to a revenue ship in the harbor, and the rest you know."

"What I need to know is where I can find him, *boyo*. So if he doesn't have a base, why don't you tell me where he stores his cargo."

"I can't because he doesn't. D'you really not know how many men work for him? Half of them just drive the wagons and simply wait for him to beach, unload, and they cart the goods straight to the buyers. No hiding it like we used to. No giving the revenuers that patrol the waters a chance to find us. He arranges everything in advance and has been operating that way for years. There's nothing more I can tell you."

"Yes, there is," Nathan said in a quieter tone. "You can tell me why he killed my father."

"Well, your sis—you don't know?"

Nathan lifted the man a little off his feet to get his point across. "Tell me."

"I know nothing. Nothing!" The sailor's jaw was clenched, but he was shaking like a leaf. "I wasn't working for him back then."

Nathan pulled the man away from the wall and raised his fist warningly. "The tavern?" he growled. "Last chance to say something useful."

The sailor's eyes widened. "There's an alley behind it, that's all I ever see of it. The cap'n's of a mind that the less we know the better. Only Mr. Olivey gets told when, where, and who. But I heard him call the bloke we deliver to Bobby."

"The owner?"

"Don't know, never asked."

Nathan smashed his fist into the man's face. "Too little, too late," he muttered, but the man couldn't hear him.

Nathan hurried back to the tavern to rouse Mr. Olivey for more information, but he slowed as he approached. The watch had found Grigg's defeated crewmen. All four of them were still unconscious, didn't even stir as they were lifted and placed in a wagon to be taken to jail. Nathan wasn't even surprised. The man who had laid waste to them really was a bruiser.

Nathan was disappointed, but if the sailor he'd questioned could be believed, and he probably could be, Nathan knew much more now than he had before. And if his new turn of luck held, Grigg wouldn't be caught by Burdis before Nathan returned to England.

Corky was in the small crowd gathered in front of the tavern, but he was nervously looking around for Nathan rather than watching what was going on. Nathan waved to draw his attention.

Corky ran over to him immediately. "We better get back to our post and quickly. The owners of the ship came by to see how the loading was going and got caught in a fistfight. Someone actually knocked out one of them and he's furious."

"That's—unfortunate," Nathan said with a sinking feeling. "Did they board?"

"No, not tonight. Where did you take off to?"

He gave Corky the short of it, saying, "Grigg's men are in town. I had words with one of them."

"He's operating out of London? I know he's cagey, but I didn't take him for a loony."

"He only delivers here to a number of buyers, but I got a lead on one of them. It's the first clue I've had about Grigg's whereabouts since he killed Jory. And now I know where to look for him when we get back to England."

"Or you could send word about him to your commander friend."

"Hell no, and he's not my friend. He's just a revenuer

using me to get himself a promotion. Our goals merely line up—temporarily."

Corky tsked. "Connections have their uses, particularly if they come with titles. It doesn't serve your best interests to hate all nabobs just because of your sister's in-laws."

"I don't hate them all. Only the ones I meet. Now it's late and we sail in the morning. We need some sleep. They can wake us if any more wagons show up."

"I'd agree, 'cept this one might be for us."

Corky was talking about an approaching coach, not a wagon. Yet it did stop and the driver called down, "Are you with *The Maiden George*? If so, I have passengers who want to board now."

Chapter Ten

Last night, nathan had thought the couple were an odd pair, as he and Corky rowed them and an inordinate amount of heavy luggage out to *The Maiden George*. The man had introduced himself as Count Andrássy Benedek, a relative of the ship's captain. The woman's name hadn't been mentioned. They spoke English but the man had a foreign accent. And they didn't seem to like each other. Although the pair had been whispering to each other, Nathan had gotten the impression that they were bickering and didn't want to be overheard. The woman's pretty face had looked angry.

Nathan had felt sorry for the bloke, though. A henpecked man if he'd ever seen one, and he looked no older than twenty-five, his own age. Far too young to be stuck with a shrew for a wife, pretty or not, if that's who she was to him.

But this morning as the dawn sky brightened, Nathan was surprised to see Benedek joining him at the rail. Escaping the shrew? Nathan might have remarked on it, one man commiserating with another, if he didn't want to avoid drawing attention to himself on this trip. Besides, the man was titled.

Class distinctions didn't used to mean anything to Nathan. Having an earl for an ancestor probably accounted for his attitude, not that he'd ever mentioned that to anyone or ever would. It was galling that Burdis had found out. In fact, if someone called him gentry these days, he'd probably punch him in the face. He preferred to simply treat all men as equals whether they wanted to be or not, but most nabobs felt differently.

His reticence turned out to be a good decision because the count wasn't alone for long. His companion from the night before arrived a few moments later, saying, "You can't ignore me, Andrássy!"

"Can't I?" Benedek shot back. "Not another word about it, Catherine. I am *not* going to ask them for any more favors when I only just met them."

"But one of them could have the insight, could tell me if my father really is alive, or even where he is. You could at least ask."

"And have them think I'm crazy? The supposed magical abilities of Gypsies is just superstitious nonsense and trickery. That's what Gypsies do. They prey on the hopes and dreams of the gullible. They tell you what you want to hear and get paid for it. None of it is true and I'm not going to insult this branch of my family by mentioning these notions of yours. My God, do you listen to yourself, spouting such nonsense?"

"Of course I believe it, when I've seen you display the Gypsy gift occasionally. Deny it all you want, but you know it's true."

"All I have is the instinct of a tracker and luck. There's nothing mystical about that, Catherine. And I'll use those instincts to find your father, if just to be rid of you for good!"

"How dare you! You wouldn't even know about these relatives of yours if not for me! I found that journal that mentioned them. You owe me!"

"I owe you nothing, although I will honor the obligation my father saddled me with when he married your mother!"

"Perfect, luv. You really are a master of improvis—"

Nathan couldn't hear any more as the pair moved farther down the deck, but the woman's voice had changed to a purring tone there at the end, as if she really was offering praise.

But glad to be alone again at the rail, Nathan raised the spyglass he'd borrowed from Artie, the crusty, old first mate, for a closer view of the wharf. A longboat had been dispatched for the passengers because there were so many of them. Quite a crowd of well-dressed people were on the dock, waiting for it. But he wasn't interested in them.

He trained the eyepiece up and down the wharf as far as he could see. He was meticulous, stopping to peruse faces, making sure he didn't recognize any. He didn't expect to see any of Grigg's men this soon, but Grigg might show up himself looking for them. And if he spotted the man, he couldn't say if he would risk losing *The Pearl* to get his hands on him now.

Jory had decided to send Nathan away five years ago to protect him. Despite how angry Nathan had been because of it, he'd still loved the man. He felt angry to this day, but for a different reason: because he and his father had never made amends and it was too late to now. But that had been Jory's decision, too. No communication at all was to pass between them that could lead Grigg to Nathan, who could then be used against Jory. But settling that score for his father was *his* decision. And even with the ship soon to sail, he still had that on his mind.

As Nathan continued to scan the wharf with the spyglass, he found it a bit disconcerting to come across a fellow with a spyglass of his own trained right on Nathan. No one he recognized, well dressed in a greatcoat, a gentleman by all accounts. The man gestured to his head, as if tipping a hat to Nathan for having discovered him spying on *The Maiden George*. The man was even smiling before he put his spyglass away and got into a rowboat that took him out to one of the other ships.

Many ships were anchored in the river, unable to dock yet. Southampton's port was crowded, too, but nothing like London's. Weeks could go by before a ship could get a berth in this town, or so he'd been told.

"See anything interesting, Mr. Tremayne?"

Nathan glanced at the sailor who'd come up next to him. He'd said his name was Walter. Nathan knew him in passing from Southampton, but then the whole crew had been hired out of Southampton.

"No, just someone a little too interested in this ship. He actually had a spyglass trained on us."

Walter shrugged. "So? Just looking for someone."

"I suppose." Nathan glanced down at the stretch of water between the ship and the dock.

The longboat was halfway back to the ship, and it wasn't full of passengers after all, just four men and five ladies, not counting the sailors rowing them. He figured a few of those people could be ladies' maids and valets. Most of the people he'd seen on the dock must only have been there to see their family or friends off, because they were now getting back into carriages.

"There don't appear to be many passengers," he said.

"Well, it's a privately owned ship designed to accommodate family comfortably. The captain had her built to his specifications. All of the main cabins are like rooms in a fancy hotel."

Nathan knew how lavishly appointed the cabins were. He hadn't mentioned it to anyone, but he hadn't been able to resist inspecting *The Maiden George* when he'd been docking *The Pearl* next to it for the last year.

"You've sailed on her before?" Nathan asked Walter.

"A few times over the last decade, and I'm glad of it. I actually gave up the sea, but I'm always up for a voyage on *The Maiden George*. It pays too well to turn it down, and it's never boring. Did you not wonder why the purse was so high for this crossing?"

Nathan hedged. "Well, this is my first time across the Atlantic, so I had nothing to compare it to."

Walter chuckled. "It's triple the standard, mate. A pity she leaves her berth so rarely, or I'd be rich by now."

"If she doesn't get much use, why does the owner even keep her?"

"Because he can."

"Merely for convenience?" Nathan said. "That isn't normal, is it?"

"Not even close to normal. But then, neither is the captain. That's him there, Viscount Ryding, just one of many titles in his family."

Nathan followed Walter's gaze back to the approaching longboat. Now that the sky had brightened and the boat was closer, he could make out the occupants more clearly, but he looked no farther than the large man in the front of the boat. Blond, with broad shoulders under a greatcoat, he was the bruiser who'd rescued Nathan on a whim. And his dark-haired brother was in the boat, too.

Nathan's sinking feeling returned. He'd actually hoped when they hadn't boarded last night that the owners weren't going to sail with their ship. Many didn't, merely hired captains for them. But it looked as if his luck had just taken a swing for the worse, and now he was going to have to make himself scarce, at least until they got out to sea where it would be less likely that they'd toss him overboard. Up in the rigging would suffice before they boarded, and he might even stay up there for the duration of the trip down the river.

It didn't matter which of the two was the captain. They were both nabobs and he'd struck one of them. And even if he could somehow make it right with them, he was still going to hate working for a lord no matter how long the trip took. The nobility had a whole different way of thinking compared to ordinary men. As different as night and day. They could take offense at the simplest thing that wouldn't normally raise a brow. You wouldn't even *know* you were insulting them until it was too late.

Then the sun rose over a couple of buildings in the east to cast a beam along the water. Copper hair lit up like a flame in the sunlight and instantly drew his eyes. The young woman ought to have been wearing a bonnet to hide magnificent hair like that, but she wasn't. She was old enough—eighteen, nineteen?—to have her hair done up fancy, but it was simply tied back at her nape. Because it was so long, the wind still tossed it over her shoulders. Her clothing, though, was clearly that of a young lady, a blue velvet coat tied at the waist, a white fur cape that merely capped her shoulders, ending only halfway down her arms. But it was her beautiful heart-shaped face that tugged at a memory that wouldn't quite surface in his mind.

"The red-haired wench, she looks familiar."

He didn't realize he'd said it aloud until Walter admonished him, "I wouldn't be calling that one a wench if you don't want to end up in the ship's brig or worse. The cap'n's a fair man, but he can be a might touchy when it comes to family, and she's probably a member of his. Never seen him take on passengers who weren't related to him in one way or another."

A whole ship full of nabobs? Corky had been right. Bleedin' hell. But he assured the sailor, "I meant no disrespect."

"Was just a friendly warning, mate. You know how that family is. Very, *very* protective of their own."

"I wouldn't know. Never heard of the Malorys until I signed on and was told the captain's name."

"Really? Thought everyone knew who they are."

"So they're famous? Or notorious?"

"A little of both." Walter laughed as he walked away.

Nathan hightailed it over to the rigging and started climbing, determined to postpone his next meeting with the Malorys for as long as possible.

Chapter Eleven

"I HOPE *YOU* ARE NO' going tae prove as stubborn as your cousin," Nettie MacDonald said as she entered Judith's cabin to help her prepare for dinner.

Roslynn had insisted on sending her own maid on the trip to see to both girls' needs. Nettie was more a member of the family than a servant, so Judith was delighted that she was accompanying them. Nettie was the only maid aboard. Since *The Maiden George* didn't have an abundance of cabins Georgina and Katey, Judith's older sister, had elected to just hire maids when they reached Bridgeport, but then they both had husbands who could help them dress on the ship if they needed assistance.

"Jack is always stubborn," Judith replied with a grin. "But what's she being stubborn about tonight?"

"Wouldna let me touch her hair. Wasna going tae concede on wearing a dress either till I put m'foot down. Told her I wouldna be washing those breeches she loves sae much if she didna at least dress proper for your dinners."

Jacqueline had also had ship togs made for Judith, not that Judith planned to wear them if she didn't need to. She'd rather deal with her skirts whipping about in the wind than feel self-conscious in sailor's garb. But Judith had already braided her hair for tonight, quite in agreement with Jacqueline that putting her hair up in her usual coiffure on a ship was just asking for it to be blown apart by the wind. However, she moved straight to her little vanity and sat down, just to make Nettie happy, and the old girl did smile as she unbraided Judith's hair and started arranging it more fashionably.

Although Judith's cabin was a decent size, it was still rather cramped with a full-size bed, a wardrobe, and a comfortable reading chair, a little vanity, even a small, round table for two, and her trunks, which had been pushed up against one wall. But she didn't plan to spend that much time in her cabin. Today had been an exception. With most of the family unpacking and recovering from the party last night as well as the early-morning departure, she'd spent most of the day reading and resting. And getting her sea legs, as Jack called the adjustment to the constant motion of the ship.

Judith didn't mind that at all. In fact, she was exhilarated to be on a ship again. Possibly because she liked sailing even more than Jacqueline did. It was too bad Judith's mother and sister didn't, or she might have had more opportunities to sail with her uncle over the years.

She was looking forward to joining her family for dinner tonight in her uncle's much larger cabin and seeing their new cousin again—well, she assumed Andrássy and his stepsister would be invited to dinner. And Nettie made sure Judith looked as if she were going to a formal dinner at home. Her gown, sheer white over blue silk and embroidered with lilacs, wasn't new, but her new wardrobe for the Season hadn't yet been finished because her mother hadn't expected her to need it for another month. She'd still brought all of it along, which was why she had twice as many trunks as Jack did, clothes to wear on the ship and for the first few days in Bridgeport, and a full wardrobe that still needed a seamstress to put the finishing touches on it.

"There, you look lovely as always, lassie," Nettie said when she had finished putting up Judith's hair. "I'll get a sailor in here tomorrow to dig out your jewelry box. I'm no' sure why it's packed wi' the unfinished gowns."

"Because I didn't think I would need it until we get to America and I don't, not just for family dinners, so there's no need to unpack it." Judith hurried out of her cabin before Nettie disagreed with her.

Closing her door, she jumped in surprise when a woman behind her said much too sharply, "Move out of my way!"

Judith immediately stiffened and turned to see stormy gray eyes pinned on her. The woman's brown hair was bound up tightly, and the angry expression on her face prevented Judith from determining whether she was pretty or plain. The woman was angry because her way was blocked for mere moments? Judith couldn't imagine who she was, and then she did. Andrássy's stepsister, Catherine?

She opened her mouth to introduce herself, but Catherine was too impatient to let her get a word out. "Nearly knocked me over and now you just stand there gawking? I asked you to move!"

She was about to shove Judith aside when Jacqueline yanked her own door open behind them and snarled into the narrow corridor, "No screeching on the ship! Learn the bloody rules before you embark or get tossed overboard." And Jacqueline promptly slammed her door shut again.

Trust Jack to say something outlandish when she was annoyed. The woman's face turned red. Judith had to get out of there before she burst out laughing, which would only make the situation worse. But poor Andrássy! He hadn't been joking last night when he said they didn't want to meet his stepsister, and now she knew why.

She squeezed past Catherine and ran upstairs to the deck before she did in fact giggle. She waited there a few minutes for Jacqueline to join her.

"I suppose that was the stepsister?" Jack said as she came up the stairs.

"That red velvet she was wearing doesn't bespeak a servant from the galley."

Jack huffed, "If she was heading to her cabin, let's hope she stays in it permanently. I heard every word. Rudeness like that—"

"Usually has a reason." Judith put her arm through her cousin's as they headed up to the quarterdeck. "Her face was pinched. It could have been from pain, rather than a horrible disposition."

Jacqueline tsked. "You always see the good in people."

Judith laughed and teased, "And you always try not to!"

"I do not! Besides, more often than not, first impressions are accurate. However, I'll reserve judgment this once, but only because I know you want me to."

A few minutes later they entered the captain's cabin. Accessed from the quarterdeck with only a few steps in front of the door that led down to it, they didn't knock. James and Georgina were on the sofa, his arm around her shoulders. Anthony and Katey were already present and sitting at the long dining table.

The large room resembled a parlor. A long sofa and stuffed chairs with two card tables were on one side, and a desk long enough to hold the charts was on the other side by the dining area. An intricately carved partition in one of the back corners closed off the bed from the rest of the room. The long bank of windows in the back had the drapes open, revealing the ocean behind the ship and the moon shining down on it.

That was Judith's favorite place on the ship. She loved to stand and gaze out of those windows. During the day the windows offered a wonderful windless view of the ocean, and at night, if the moon wasn't hidden behind clouds, the view was almost breathtaking.

After giving her father and sister quick kisses in greeting, she moved to the windows. She couldn't actually see the moon with the wind currently taking them on a southwesterly path, but its light was reflected on the waves.

Jacqueline had joined her parents on the sofa, and Georgina, glancing at the pale green gown Jack was wearing, teased her daughter, "I'm surprised you're not in breeches yet."

"The Scot wouldn't let me," Jack grumbled. "I've a mind to bar my door."

"Nettie means well, so why don't you try a reasonable approach instead."

"Reason with a Scot?" Jack said, looking directly at Anthony as she did.

Anthony burst out laughing. "Ros would box your ears for that slander if she were here."

"Only if she could catch me." Jacqueline grinned.

"I really wish Roslynn and Jaime were better sailors so

they could have joined us." Anthony sighed, but his spirits were too high to dwell on it. "But with the Yank indisposed for a few days, I intend to make the most of this rare situation. After all, how often do I have my two eldest daughters to myself?" He raised his glass of brandy high. "Here's to seasickness!"

"That's not funny, Father," Katey said, quick to come to her husband Boyd's defense.

"I thought it was," James remarked.

Andrássy arrived a few minutes later. He knocked. James merely called out for him to come in. Their new cousin was formally dressed in black with a short cape with a pearl clasp and snowy cravat under it, and he was still wearing his sword. Even his greeting to everyone sounded a little too formal, or perhaps he was merely nervous.

With a smile, Georgina got up to lead him to one of the chairs, inquiring, "Is your sister coming?"

"No, she feels uncomfortable joining the family for dinner because she is not one of 'us' and doesn't want to interfere or be a burden. In fact, she insists on repaying you for your generosity in allowing her to travel with you by working for her passage. Perhaps in the galley or—"

"That's highly irregular and certainly not necessary," Georgina said.

"Actually, it is. Catherine can be quite mercurial"—Judith and Jacqueline looked at each other and rolled their eyes—"and she will be calmer if she keeps busy."

Was that really Catherine's idea, Judith wondered, or was it Andrássy's? If it was his, that might be why his stepsister was so angry tonight. Put her to work like a scullery maid?

Georgina must have had the same thought because she

sounded a little annoyed when she replied, "She's not a servant and won't be treated as one."

"I tried to tell her exactly that," Andrássy said. "I just worry if she is too idle—I wish we had thought to bring material she could work with on the ship. She's highly skilled with a needle, even makes all her own clothes, she loves sewing so much. So if any of you ladies need any clothes repaired, Catherine would be delighted to help in that regard at least."

"I could rip a few seams, I suppose," Georgina replied with a grin.

A few people laughed. Judith held her tongue and shook her head at Jack to keep her from mentioning that Judith could use a seamstress. She wasn't about to saddle herself with Catherine's company before she had a chance to form a better opinion of the young woman—if a better one could be had.

But the subject changed with the arrival of Artie and Henry announcing dinner. They got stuck in the doorway, both trying to enter at the same time. Which didn't surprise anyone other than Andrássy. Those two old sea dogs might be the best of friends, but a stranger wouldn't figure that out with all their bickering. Part of James's old crew from his ten years on the high seas, they had retired when James did to become his butlers, sharing that job and this one, too, both acting as his first mates for the voyage.

They all moved to the dining table as the many platters were brought in. Andrássy was quick to pull a chair out for Jack and then sit in the one next to her. A little too quick? Judith wondered if she was going to have something to tease Jack about later.

Judith wasn't hungry because she'd already had samples of tonight's fare when she'd visited the galley late that afternoon.

She noticed that Katey, seated beside her, was also picking at her food, but for a different reason.

"Worried about Boyd?" Judith guessed.

Katey nodded. "I hate seeing him so miserable. You'd think after so many years at sea he would have conquered his seasickness by now."

"I don't think it can be conquered."

"I know." Katey sighed. "I just wish—you know he used to have his ship's surgeon make him sleeping drafts so he could just sleep through it. I offered to do the same for him, but he refuses because he wants to stay awake and talk to me. Yet he's usually too sick to say a word! So I end up sleeping too much, like I did today. I'm not going to be able to sleep tonight now, while that is the only time he *does* manage to sleep."

"At least his seasickness only lasts three to four days. But didn't you bring any books to read while you keep him company?"

"I didn't think to, no."

"I did and I just finished a very good one. I'll go fetch it for you in case you do have a sleepless night."

"Eat first," Katey insisted.

Judith grinned. "I did this afternoon."

Telling her father she'd be right back, Judith slipped out of the captain's cabin. A few lanterns were lit, but they weren't needed with the deck currently bathed in moonlight. She caught sight of the moon in the eastern sky and paused. She wished it were a full moon, but it was still lovely. After she got the book, she decided to go to the rail for an unobstructed view of the moon before returning to her family. But as she hurried back upstairs, she dropped her book when she slammed smack into a ghost. And not just any ghost, but the Ghost.

Chapter Twelve

ALL SHE COULD DO was stare at him as light from a lantern on deck illuminated him. Hair as white as she remembered and floating about his shoulders. His eyes a deeper green than she remembered. And tall. No, taller than she remembered she realized now that she was standing next to him, six feet at least. He was too close. She realized he'd grabbed her shoulders to keep her from tumbling backward down the stairs. But he should have let go of her now that she had steadied herself. Someone might come along and see them. Someone such as her father.

With that alarming thought, she stepped to the side, away from the stairs, and he let go of her. All she could think to say was "You're dead."

"No, I ain't, why would you say so?"

"You don't remember?"

"I think I'd remember dying."

"We met a few years ago in that old ruin in Hampshire, next to the Duke of Wrighton's estate. I thought you were a ghost when I found you there. What are you doing here?"

It took him a moment to connect the when and the where, but when he did, he laughed. "So that's why you seem familiar to me. The trespassing child with sunset hair." A slow grin appeared as his emerald eyes roamed over her, up, down, and back up. "Not a child anymore, are you?"

The blush came quickly. No, she wasn't a child anymore, but did he have to look for the obvious evidence of it? She shouldn't have left her evening wrap in the cabin. Her ghost was a common sailor. She shouldn't be talking to a member of the crew for so long, either. Devil that, he was fascinating! She'd wanted to know everything there was to know about him when she'd thought him a ghost. She still wanted to.

To that end, she held out her hand to him but quickly pulled it back when he merely stared at it. A bit nervous now that he didn't know how to respond to her formal greeting, she stated, "I'm Judith Malory. My friends and family call me Judy. It would be all right if you do."

"We aren't friends."

"Not yet, but we could be. You can start by telling me your name?"

"And if I don't?"

"Surly for an ex-ghost, aren't you? Too unfriendly to be anyone's friend? Very well." She nodded. "Pardon me." She walked over to the railing. She gazed at the wavering reflection of the moon's light on the pitch-dark ocean. It was so dramatic and beautiful, but now she couldn't fully appreciate it because she was disappointed, much more than she should have been. She almost felt like crying, which was absurd—unless Jack had been right. Had she really fancied herself in love with a ghost? No, that was absurd, too. She'd merely been curious, amazed, and fascinated, thinking he was a ghost, that there really were such things. Even after Jack and she were older and admitted he couldn't *really* be a ghost, it had still been more fun and exciting to think of him that way. Yet here was the proof that he was a real man—flesh and blood and so nicely put together. Not as pale as she remembered. No, now his skin was deeply tanned. From working on ships? Who was he? A sailor, obviously. But what had he been doing in that old ruined house in the middle of the night all those years ago? The ghost had told her the house was his. But how could a sailor afford to own a house?

She was more curious about him than ever. Unanswered questions were going to drive her batty. She shouldn't have given up so easily on getting some answers. Jack wouldn't have. Maybe she could ask Uncle James . . .

"Nathan Tremayne," said a deep voice.

She grinned to herself and glanced at him for a moment. He was so tall and handsome with his long, white hair blowing in the sea breeze. He was standing several feet from her and staring at the moonlight on the ocean, too, so it didn't actually appear that he had spoken to her. But he had. Was he as intrigued with her as she was with him?

"How do you do, Nathan. Or do you prefer Nate?"

"Doesn't matter. D'you always talk to strange men like this?"

"You're strange?"

"A stranger to you," he clarified.

"Not a'tall. We are actually old acquaintances, you and I."

He chuckled. "Telling each other to get out of a house five years ago doesn't make us acquainted. And why were you trespassing that night?"

"My cousin Jack and I were investigating the light we saw in the house. That house has been abandoned for as long as anyone living can remember. No one should have been inside it. But we could see the light from our room in the ducal mansion."

"And so you thought you'd found a ghost?"

She blushed again, but they weren't looking at each other, so she doubted that he noticed. "When we saw you there, it was a reasonable assumption."

"Not a'tall, just the opposite." Was that amusement she heard in his tone? She took a quick peek. It was hard not to. And, yes, he was grinning as he added, "You drew a conclusion that no adult would have come to."

"Well, I wasn't grown yet. That *was* quite a few years ago. And you were holding your lantern so that its light only reached your upper body. It looked as if you were floating in the air."

He laughed again, such a pleasant sound, like a bass rumble. It shook a lock of hair loose over his wide brow. His hair wasn't pure white as she'd thought. She could see blond streaks in it.

"Very well. I can see how your imagination could've played tricks on you."

"So why were you there that night and looking so sad?"

"Sad?"

"Weren't you?"

"No, not sad, darlin'." But instead of explaining, he said, "Do you really believe in ghosts?"

She looked up and saw his mouth set in a half grin and the arched eyebrow. Was he teasing her? He was! She also noticed his green eyes were gazing at her intently. Quite bold for a common seaman if that's what he was. Quite bold for any man, actually, when they'd only just met—that first time didn't count.

In response to his teasing she said, "Jack and I admitted to ourselves a few years ago that we'd been mistaken that night. But we continued to refer to you as the Ghost because it amuses us. It was our special secret that we only shared with our younger cousins. It was much more fun to say we'd found a ghost than the new owner of the house. But you can't be the owner of the house. What were you doing there?"

"Maybe I like secrets as much as you do."

On the brink of discovery and of clearing up a mystery that had intrigued her for years, she was more than a little annoyed by his reply. "You really won't say?"

"You haven't tried convincing me yet, darlin'. A pretty smile might work. . . ."

Judith went very still. So still she thought she could hear her heart pounding. She couldn't believe what had just become crystal clear to her. She *knew* who he was. It was that second instance of his calling her *darlin'*. She'd been too flustered to pay much attention to it the first time he'd said it, but this time she remembered where she'd heard it before. A mere two weeks ago from a man who she suspected was far more dangerous than a vagrant.

The moment it had struck her that night of how odd it was for a vagrant to be drinking French brandy, she had known he wasn't what he'd first seemed to be. But that wasn't all. He claimed to know the abandoned house better than she did, so he'd either been staying there a long time or had visited it more than once. His putting a lock on a door that didn't belong to him. His coming out of a hidden room where he could have been storing smuggled or stolen goods. And his warning her to tell no one that she'd seen him there. All of it pointed to his being a criminal of one sort or another.

Of course she'd told Jacqueline about him in the morning, and of course Jack had agreed with her conclusion and suggested she tell Brandon, who could prevaricate a bit and warn his father without revealing that Judith had had a run-in with a criminal in the old ruin. Before they'd left for London, Brandon had told her he'd spoken to his father and assured her they'd catch the smuggler red-handed that very day. So what was he doing here, on *The Maiden George*?

He appeared to be waiting for her to answer him. She did that now, hissing, "You deserve to be in jail! Why aren't you?"

Chapter Thirteen

NATHAN WAS TAKEN ABACK by the girl's angry question. He almost laughed at how close to the mark it was, yet it didn't make sense. Nonetheless, the instinct for self-preservation kicked in, and quickly.

"You've mistaken me for someone else. But I'm not surprised. First you thought I was a ghost, then you took me for a landowner. Isn't it more obvious that I'm just a hardworking seaman trying to earn a living?"

"I don't believe you."

"Why not?"

"Because I'd never forget a face that's haunted me for five years, and now I recognize your voice, too."

"From five years ago? I doubt that's possible."

"From two weeks ago when you accosted me in that ruined house," she said hotly. "You're a criminal and I won't have you on board endangering my family."

So it was her, he thought, and not one of the duke's servants as he'd assumed that night. And maybe she was not quite a lady either, except in title. That was an intriguing thought and even likely, considering how he'd met her, both times, out and about alone at night. And now tonight.

"It seems to me you're the one guilty of criminal behavior, breaking into houses that don't belong to you. And more'n once? Tell me, darlin', does your family know about your late-night rendezvousing?"

She sucked in her breath. "Don't *even* go there. You know I spoke the truth about why I was there that night."

"If I wasn't there, how would I know? Or wait, were you there to see me again?" He grinned, suddenly beginning to enjoy himself. "Well, me in ghost form, but me nonetheless. And you already admitted you did that at least once."

She scoffed, "You're not turning the tables on me here, but nice try. There's simply no comparison to a smuggler, or is it a thief? Which one are you?"

"And why would I be either of those?"

"Because the facts add up precisely, and there's a long list of them. You even proved yourself to be a liar that night. You weren't just passing by, not with your own cot set up in that room."

"A criminal who carries a cot around with him? Do you realize how unlikely that is?"

"You put a lock on the door."

"If whoever you are talking about did that, I'd think he did it to keep pesky ghost hunters from waking him in the middle of the night. Didn't work, did it?"

"You think this is amusing?"

He smiled. "Did I say that?"

"You didn't have to when it's written all over your face," she snapped.

"Well, you have me there, darlin'. But it's not every day I get accused of criminal activities. I have to admit, I do find a certain humor in that."

"You were hiding illegal goods there and that put *my* family at risk! My cousins could have been implicated. No one would believe they couldn't have known what was going on in their own backyard. The scandal would have touched my entire family!"

Enraged in defense of her family? Well, that at least he could understand. It just didn't alter that he needed to convince her she'd made a mistake.

So he chuckled. "Will you listen to yourself now? No one in their right mind would blame a duke for anything, much less something illegal."

"So you admit it? You came out of the hidden room, and I tasted brandy when you kissed me. You were *not* just a vagrant passing by as you claimed! I don't doubt you've even been using that ruined house to hide smuggled goods for five years, haven't you?

He was hard-pressed not to laugh. She'd figured everything out and with amazing accuracy. Smart girl. Beauty *and* intelligence. When was the last time he had come across that combination? But she was merely making charges she hoped to hear him confirm. That wasn't going to happen. He did need to get her off the scent though. . . .

His voice dropped to a husky timbre, his smile broadened. "You know, darlin', if you and I had actually shared a kiss, that would be a pleasant memory I'd not soon forget. And now you make me wish it had happened. . . ."

She was staring at his mouth. As he'd hoped, he was distracting her. He just hadn't counted on his getting distracted, too. The pull was incredibly strong to kiss her again, right there on the deck in the moonlight. Utter madness.

But he was saved from finding out what might have happened next when he heard two of the crew talking, their voices getting louder as they approached. She heard them, too, glancing nervously beyond him.

"Good night, darlin'. I better fade away like a ghost. I'd hate for your family to learn of your predilection for late-night trysts."

Nathan walked away. The subtle threat plus the doubts he'd tried to put in her mind would hopefully be enough to keep her mouth shut for the time being. He was going to climb the mainmast again, but unable to resist the urge to look back, he merely moved into the mainmast's shadow. She was halfway to the quarterdeck before she turned to look back as well. Had she thought of more aspersions to cast on him? But he relaxed when he saw she wasn't looking for him, but for the book she'd dropped. She came back to retrieve it.

A few moments later he lost sight of her when she entered the captain's cabin, but her image was still in his mind. The woman was too beautiful—but she was trouble. He was going to have to come up with a better way to keep her from voicing her suspicions to other people. But that could wait for tomorrow.

Chapter Fourteen

IN THE MORNING, NATHAN found Corky to discuss his newest problem—Judith Malory. But his friend had been tasked with swabbing the main deck, a chore so menial Corky couldn't stop grumbling about it long enough to offer any suggestions. Nathan still kept him company while he checked the railings for loose nails. It wasn't something he would have thought to do so early on the voyage if he hadn't seen Judith leaning against a rail last night.

"Watch out, Cap'n," Corky suddenly said behind him. "I think that trouble you were telling me about is coming your way."

Nathan turned to see Judith marching toward him and Corky quickly getting out of the way. She looked even more beautiful in daylight with the sun on her glorious red-gold hair, wearing a long velvet coat left open over an ice-blue dress trimmed with yellow-dyed lace—and the light of battle in her cobalt-blue eyes.

She'd lost a few hairpins last night, which he'd found on the deck after she'd gone, so he wasn't surprised to see she'd braided her hair today. Diamond-tipped pins. He'd thought about keeping them as a memento, but dug them out of his pocket now and handed them to her, hoping it would forestall another tirade. It didn't.

"I do *not* care for the way you threatened me last night!" she began.

He shrugged. "If you're going to make outlandish accusations about me, I can make a more realistic one about you—that you seem to have a habit of conducting nighttime trysts with strange men."

"When you put my family at risk, there is no comparison!" she said furiously. "I demand an explanation."

Nathan gnashed his teeth in frustration. He wasn't about to spill his guts to her and tell her about his unusual situation when he didn't know her and had no reason to trust her with the truth. Beautiful in the extreme, she was still a nabob. And he wasn't so sure she was going to spread her suspicions around either. If she was, why would she have come looking for him this morning to discuss them again? He just had to come up with a way to ensure her silence, or at least some explanation that she would believe so she could laugh off her damned conclusions. Or maybe another bit of truth would suffice. . . .

"Tremayne!" was suddenly bellowed from the quarterdeck.

Nathan hissed under his breath, "Bleedin' hell. I knew better than to talk to you when you've got relatives crawling all over this ship—including my captain."

"Why are you even aboard? Escaping a hangman's noose in England?"

In exasperation he said, "No, chasing down my ship, which was stolen."

"Yet another lie? Good God, do you ever say anything that's true?" Then she smirked, "But that was just my uncle's 'come here' voice, not his 'come here and die' voice. You'll hear the latter after I tell him who you really are, Nathan Tremayne."

He was out of time to talk her around, so he said, "Give me a chance to explain before you do anything we'll both regret. It's not what you think."

He left her with that, and hopefully enough doubt to keep her pretty mouth shut for the time being.

Nathan approached Captain Malory with a good deal of annoyance. The man's summons couldn't have come at a worse time, when he still had an ax hanging over his head from the man's niece. But he didn't think a few more minutes with Judith would remove that ax. She'd had two weeks to convince herself that her suspicions about him were accurate. He might need just as long to change her mind—if he could. And if he couldn't? If she spread her tale anyway?

He supposed he could jump the gun on her and make a full confession right now to her uncle—captain to captain. Like hell he would. That would only be a logical path if the man weren't a lord, too. Damned nabobs were too unpredictable. And he knew nothing about Judith Malory's uncle other than he was a rich lord with sledgehammers for fists—and he liked to fight. Nathan had definitely gotten that impression the other night.

At least he didn't think this Malory was the one he needed to avoid. He doubted the captain was going to want retribution for what had happened on the docks, not when he'd let him go after Hammett's sailor. However, as captain he was king of this ship for the duration, his word law, his dictates followed whether they were fair or not, and if Nathan had just gotten on his bad side because of a woman, Nathan was going to be furious—with himself.

He'd been so stupid last night, letting that pretty face dazzle him. Talking to her as if there could be no consequences for it, and then to forget that entirely after she made her accusations, which could bring even worse consequences. He should have walked away when he had the chance to, before she realized who he was.

It was laughable. This was supposed to be the easy part of this trip. The hard part wasn't supposed to start until they arrived in Connecticut and he had to convince the law-enforcing Yanks over there to help him, an Englishman, take down their own criminals. At the most he'd be giving them a good laugh over that. At the worst, they could toss him in jail instead for his audacity or run him out of town. But he still had a few weeks before he found out how strongly animosity still ran between the two countries that had gone to war with each other more'n once.

He didn't look behind him to see if the reason for his latest predicament had scurried off. He could still see her in his mind's eye, though, softly rounded, exquisite in every detail, lush, sensual lips, far too beautiful for any one woman to be. If he couldn't talk her around, maybe he could seduce her into keeping silent instead.

The moment the thought occurred to him, he made his decision. That's how he would handle Judith Malory. He hadn't felt so good about a decision in ages. So what if she was surrounded by family on this ship and the lot of them were aristocrats. He was used to living dangerously.

When Nathan approached James Malory, he saw him conversing with his first mate. Artie looked contrite, as if he'd just received a tongue-lashing.

"I didn't know you wanted it set up before we sailed . . . ," Artie was saying.

The captain's back was turned toward Nathan, so he didn't intrude. Malory in a billowing white shirt open at the neck, tight, buff breeches, black, knee-high boots, and hair to his shoulders didn't look any more like a nabob now than he had the other night. Glancing around, Nathan realized he was the only member of the crew who was properly dressed. Like the captain, the other sailors had all stowed their jackets and were working more comfortably in their shirtsleeves. After all, it wasn't a military ship where the crew had to button up in uniforms.

Nathan was about to shrug out of his own coat when Malory turned and noticed him. "My brother has a bone to pick with you," he stated baldly.

Nathan winced. "I was hoping you wouldn't remember me from the other night."

"Forget hair like yours? Not bloody likely."

But the captain was grinning as if from a fond memory, prompting Nathan to ask cautiously, "You aren't angry that I punched your brother?"

"Not a'tall. Found it highly amusing, actually. Ain't often Tony gets taken by surprise like that. But he'll want a rematch, so you might want to avoid him for a few days. As it happens, the project I have for you will see to that nicely. I'm told you're my carpenter, but how experienced are you?"

Relieved he wasn't going to be questioned about the fight on the dock or be reprimanded for talking to the captain's niece, Nathan answered honestly, "Three years, sir. Two to master building and repairing, and then I spent a year branching out to furnishings. Before that I built chimneys. Before that, I tried my hand at painting and roofing."

"A jack-of-all-trades—for landlubbers? Then what are you doing on *The Maiden George?*"

"I inherited my father's ship a few years ago, but she was stolen last week. This group of thieves has been plaguing England for a good decade, but not so often that the authorities could piece together who they were or what they were doing with the ships."

"That doesn't answer my question, dear boy, but it does pose another. A captain reduced to ship's carpenter? Do you like the sea so much that you'll sail in any capacity?"

"Your destination is exactly where I need to go to get my ship back."

James chuckled. "Ah, there we have it, an ulterior motive. So your thieves are Yanks, are they? I find that particularly priceless, 'deed I do. Can't wait to mention it to my brother-in-law. But fess up, how did you figure that out?"

"I didn't. A Commander Burdis captured one of the thieves and he has an ax to grind with them because they killed one of his men. He agreed to tell me where to find the thieves and my ship if I agreed to put them out of business for him."

"So you're actually working for the government?"

"Unofficially."

"Of course, can't step on Yank toes without stirring up another war, can we," James said drily.

"Something like that was mentioned."

"Well, a captain you may be, but not on this voyage."

"I'll earn my way."

"You will indeed, and that begins now. My first mate remembered to load the materials for it, but now he tells me he forgot to inform *you* that I want an exercise ring built in my ship's hold. Fetch your tools and meet him below. He'll show you where to build it."

"An exercise ring?"

James had started to turn away but stopped and a frown formed. "Do *not* tell me you don't know what an exercise ring is."

Nathan stiffened, ready for battle. The man looked downright menacing when he frowned. But Nathan had to know what he was building in order to build it. The only rings he knew about were for pugilists. Surely that's not what the captain was talking about. Or was he?

"For fisticuffs?"

The frown vanished. "Splendid, so you do know."

"How large do you want it?"

"The size of the tarpaulin will determine the dimensions for the platform. A foot off the floor will suffice. I've been assured everything you will need for it is down there. And, Tremayne, don't take too long building it. I'm already feeling a need to make use of it."

"It shouldn't take more'n a day, Captain Malory."

"Excellent. Do a good job and you can test it out with me—yes, yes, I know I already offered you that job and you turned it down, but it sounds now like you might have some frustration to work off, lost ship and all, so you might want to reconsider. By the by, did you get your answers from that sailor the other night?"

"Yes."

"I suppose I should apologize for interfering in that little contretemps you were in. You didn't really look like you needed help. I just deplore passing up a spot of exercise when it presents itself so handily. But run along now. You've my ring to build."

Malory didn't seem to be a bad sort—for a captain. Nathan had told him nothing he didn't mind sharing. And the man was right, he could use an outlet for his frustration, just not for the reason he'd stated. But to spar with his captain, at sea, probably wouldn't be in his best interests. The man obviously didn't expect to lose, but what if he did? And ended up angry because of it?

No, the better course would be to avoid any further discourse with the captain altogether, which shouldn't be too hard. The first mate and the boatswain would be getting their orders from him. Those two had to deal with James Malory on this trip, Nathan didn't. Thank God.

Chapter Fifteen

As soon as Nathan had stepped up on the quarterdeck, Judith had moved to stand just below it, where she could hear what was being said without being seen. But what she heard just fueled her anger all the more. More and more lies. Did the man *ever* tell the truth? But he was going to have to. His "Give me a chance to explain before you do anything we'll both regret. It's not what you think" was the only reason she hadn't gone over to her uncle with him. Well, there was also the fact that James was the only member of her family who would just shrug at the news that a smuggler was on his ship.

It was her father she needed to inform, not his brother. Yet she didn't go in search of Anthony either. The smidgen of doubt that Nathan had planted in her mind held her back.

She went to Jacqueline's cabin instead to see if she was awake yet. Her cousin would never forgive her if she wasn't the first to know that their ex-ghost had been found and who he *really* was, but Judith hadn't had a chance to tell her yet. Last night after retrieving the book for Katey, her father had engaged her in a game of backgammon, which they had still been playing when Jack went off to bed.

But Jacqueline was still sound asleep now, and it only took Judith a moment to realize where she wanted to be. With Nathan Tremayne still firmly in her mind, she headed for where she knew she'd find him. But when she got there, she could hear him talking to Artie, so she went back on deck. She knew it was inappropriate for a lady to be alone with a member of the crew, and she didn't want Artie to mention to anyone that she'd sought Nathan out.

The moment Artie appeared back on deck, she headed down to the hold again. She peeked into the cargo deck before she took the last few steps down the stairway. Nathan was alone now. He was unpacking one of the crates so he didn't notice her approach. He'd removed his jacket and had even unfastened the top buttons of his shirt, which wasn't surprising because it was warmer in the hold than it was on deck. She couldn't take her eyes off him. He looked rather dashing like this. If Jack could see him, she would say he looked like a pirate—no, Judith reminded herself, like a smuggler.

The reminder got her eyes off him for a moment. She looked around the large cargo hold, which appeared almost empty because the ship wasn't carrying any cargo for sale. Provisions were stored along the sides in crates and barrels of various sizes. Toward the stern, pens contained farm animals that would be brought to the galley as needed. She could hear the clucking of a few chickens in the distance. Nathan was standing next to a pile of building materials, but otherwise, most of the space was empty, so there was plenty of room for the exercise ring he'd been tasked to build.

"Not exactly what you expected a ship's carpenter to have to do, is it?"

He stiffened at the sound of her voice, but he didn't glance up. "Go away, trouble," he said in a grouchy tone. "We can continue our *debate* after I'm done working."

She ignored the unflattering name and the suggestion. "We need to clarify a few matters. And the sooner you accomplish your task, the sooner we can do that. I can help."

"The devil you can."

"You need to measure the tarpaulin before you begin building the ring, don't you? I can help you spread it out."

He turned to her. "So you were eavesdropping?"

She saw no reason to deny it. "I was just making sure that my uncle didn't kill you."

His eyes narrowed. "Spit it out. Are you joking about him or not?"

She shrugged. "That's a matter of perspective. To me he's the sweetest man, my best friend's loving father, my father's closest brother. Really, he's just a big, cuddly bear."

"But what about to people who aren't members of his family?"

"Some people do fear him, I suppose, but I can't imagine why."

Nathan grunted. "I can. I saw him make mince of four blokes in a matter of minutes the night before last. He's bleedin' well lethal with his fists."

"Well, everyone knows that. He and my father are both superlative pugilists. They have been for years. It's a skill they honed when they were London's most notorious rakes."

"D'you even know what you're talking about? Fighting and seducing women have nothing to do with each other."

"Course they do, when you consider how often they were challenged to duels by angry husbands. But they had no desire to kill a man just because the poor chap had an unfaithful wife, so they took a lot of those challenges to the ring instead. They still won either way."

Nathan took a step toward her. "I would think such worldly matters would be kept from tender ears like yours."

She backed up. Was it the subject matter that had turned his green eyes sensual? Her pulse began to race. She took a deep, steadying breath, but it sounded like a sigh even to her ears. So she blurted out, "It was common knowledge, not a family secret."

He kept moving toward her. "Does your family have secrets?"

She continued to step back, away from him. "There's a skeleton or two in most closets, but not as many as I suspect are in yours."

She thought only briefly about standing her ground. Was he trying to make her nervous about being alone with him down here? It might not have been the smartest move on her part when the man had his own secrets to hide and she was the only one who knew them.

She continued to back away from him, but something got in the way. Caught behind her knees, she abruptly sat down on a crate. He took a step back as if he'd just gotten the results he wanted and said with some amusement, "Stay out of the way if you're staying."

He'd done that deliberately!? Her hackles rose immediately as she watched him walk away. She was about to lambaste him for trying to frighten her when he stopped to add, "Unless you want that kiss I was thinking about." He glanced around. "Do you?"

He'd only been going to kiss her? Well, he could have made that clear! "Certainly not," she humphed.

He faced her again to say, "Don't get indignant, darlin'. I was just going to show you the difference."

"What difference?"

"Between your smuggler's kiss and mine. Thought it might be a more pleasant way to clear up the confusion for you."

"I doubt that would indicate anything a'tall."

He laughed. "He was that good?"

She raised a brow. "That implies you think you'd be better at it?"

He shrugged. "I don't get complaints, just the opposite. So you might want to think about the offer—instead of worrying that a smuggler might break your pretty neck to keep his secret. That *did* occur to you, didn't it?"

"Is that a not-so-subtle threat?"

"No, I would never threaten you. In fact, I think I'd protect you to my dying breath."

He'd managed to startle her. "Why?"

"Because only a few things are worth dying for, family, country—and the love of a beautiful woman."

Why would he even say that!? Merely to plant the seed that something romantic could develop between them if she kept his secret? But he didn't wait for her to reply. Instead he went about his work, ignoring her, taking the tarpaulin out of its crate and dropping it in the middle of the hold before he began unfolding it.

As she watched him, she saw how efficiently he worked. There wasn't a single pause to suggest he didn't know what he was doing, forcing her to conclude that he had really learned carpentry at some point. But had he worked at it for three years as he'd told James? When would he have had time to do that if he was smuggling five years ago? Very well, she conceded, maybe he hadn't been smuggling all that time, but definitely more recently. He'd admitted he owned his own ship—if what he'd told her uncle was true.

She couldn't take her eyes off him, fascinated by the way his muscles flexed as he staked out the four corners. He was far too muscular for a common seaman. She could see him captaining his own ship, though. Had he built the ship himself? Is that why he'd learned carpentry? Then who had taught him to sail it?

Good God, she had so many questions. One just led to another. Yet she still didn't ask him any, was even having trouble breathing when he removed his shirt and tossed it aside as he began hammering together the first side of the platform. His chest was already gleaming with sweat. She was feeling warm, too, so she shrugged out of her coat and draped it over the crate she was sitting on.

"Besides, I can think of much nicer things to do with your neck," he suddenly said, as if there had been no break in their conversation. And then: "No blush?"

She took her eyes off his chest and saw that he was looking at her again, had caught her staring at him. That brought on a blush. But had he actually been thinking about her neck all this time?

"There were more'n two rakes in my family, so there isn't much that can embarrass me."

"I seem to be having an easy time of it," he said with a chuckle.

"You're deliberately trying to embarrass me, so stop it."

"Not deliberately, or do you think I'm in the habit of talking to fine ladies like yourself? Believe me, the women of my acquaintance don't blush." He gave her a grin, then turned more serious. "What made you think you'd heard my voice before last night—aside from five years ago, which even you know is too long ago to remember something like that?"

"It wasn't your voice. It's what you keep calling me. 'Darling.' The smuggler called me that, too."

"You think sweet words aren't commonly used? That I'm really the only man to use that one?"

"If you're not a smuggler, what are you?"

"As has already been established, a shipowner and a carpenter. You should let it go at that."

"When you also said you were just here to earn a living?" she reminded him. "You realize one lie means everything you say is suspect."

He chuckled. "You're very suspicious for someone so young. A fine lady like you, how do you even know about smugglers and the like?"

"You'd be amazed what some of the members of my family have been involved in."

"Like?"

"I'm not sharing secrets, you are."

"Not while I'm working, I'm not."

She ignored that to ask, "Can you really finish this ring in a day as you told my uncle?"

"Yes, even if I had to cut the lumber, which I don't. Artie said he got all the materials from a man who builds rings for a living, so it's already cut to specifications and just needs to be put together. Are you worried I'll get on your uncle's bad side if I disappoint him?"

"No, when that happens, I doubt it will have anything to do with your carpentry job."

"It will if you keep distracting me," he retorted.

She suppressed a grin. "I *was* being quiet. You brought up necks."

He snorted but continued to hammer, even when he asked a few minutes later, "How often did your father and your uncle lose those challenges you mentioned?"

"They never did."

"Never? Even when they get taken by surprise?"

"Who would dare do that?"

He didn't appear to like her answer, but since he could apparently work and converse at the same time, she continued, taking a different tack. "I have to say, that was a very good excuse you came up with, instead of admitting that you're running from the law."

"What excuse?"

"That you're chasing a stolen ship. Did you build it yourself?"

"No, I inherited her from my father two years ago."

"So you've been smuggling for only two years?"

She slipped that in hoping to get him to tell the truth while he was distracted by his work, but it didn't happen.

He glanced her way. "I've told you how wrong you are, yet you do seem to be very curious about me, so why don't we make a deal. I'll answer your questions over the course of the voyage if you'll answer some of mine, and we'll agree to keep each other's secrets."

"I don't have any secrets that would land me in jail," she said pertly.

He shrugged. "Neither do I, but if you don't want to strike a bargain, so be it."

"Not so fast, I didn't say that. Let me be clear, you're offering to tell me your life story, the truthful version, if I agree to keep what you say to myself?"

"You'll have to do more'n that. You can tell no one that we've met before. That will have to be *our* secret."

"But my cousin Jack—"

"No one."

She snapped her mouth shut. She wasn't sure she could keep secrets from Jack and certainly didn't want to when they always shared everything. Annoyed, she said, "I seem to be getting the short end of the stick. I'll have to think of something else you can do for me to more evenly balance this agreement."

"Then we have one?"

"We do." She got up to shake hands on it, but heard her name being called. "I have to go. Jack's calling for me."

"That's a woman's voice."

"Yes, it is, but there's no time to explain."

"There's time for this."

She was already hurrying to the stairway and wasn't going to stop to find out what he meant. So she didn't see him put down his hammer and reach for her. But suddenly he was holding her quite intimately with one of his arms around her waist and the other halfway around her shoulders with his hand behind her neck. She was bent slightly back as his lips moved softly against hers.

Such a classic pose he had her in, romantic really, yet it did run through her mind that he was stealing kisses from her again. But this time she knew who was doing it, not some faceless rogue, but an incredibly handsome one. So when she did what she knew she was supposed to do and tried to push away from him, the merely halfhearted effort brought her hands sliding up his bare chest to his shoulders. And before she could try again, the pleasant way his lips were moving over hers caused such scintillating feelings to flutter inside her that she didn't want to pull away from him.

The foray was simply too sensual, the way he parted her lips with his, sucking on her lower lip, nibbling at her upper lip, then running his tongue over both before flicking it teasingly at hers. His hold tightened and he deepened the kiss, sending her pulse thrumming erratically and a wave of heat over her whole body.

Utterly immersed in what he was doing to her, she was surprised when he let her go and she found herself standing there without his help. Her eyes flew open to find him giving her a curious look she couldn't fathom.

"Was there a difference?" he asked.

That's why he'd kissed her? "You already know there was a difference because you know how brief that other kiss was and that it ended like this."

She didn't slap him as hard as she'd done that night at the old house. Which was probably why he laughed. "I guess the bargain is off?"

"No, but I *will* think of something unpleasant for you to do to keep up your end of the bargain—besides giving me the truth."

"I doubt anything to do with you could be unpleasant, darlin'."

"Even if I keep you at my beck and call, subject to my whims?"

He grinned. "Sounds like the pot just got sweetened for me."

"I wouldn't be so sure," she huffed.

"Oh, I am. As long as it doesn't get me in trouble with the

captain, I'm yours to command. Would you like to seal our bargain with another kiss?"

She didn't answer as she marched up the stairs. She'd amused him more than enough for one day. When they met again, she'd have the upper hand and she planned to keep it that way.

Chapter Sixteen

"S HE LOOKS LONELY AND sad," Judith said to Jacqueline as she gazed at Catherine Benedek, who had just appeared on deck, her brown hair so tightly wound up the wind hadn't disturbed it yet.

"And why is that our business?" Jacqueline asked.

They were sitting on one of the steps between decks nibbling on pastries, far to the side so the sailors could navigate to and fro without having to ask them to move out of the way. Judith hadn't yet quite recovered from lying to Jack when she'd asked where Judith had been. And her cheeks had gone up in flames because of it. But Jacqueline had already grabbed her hand to lead her to the steps, so she hadn't noticed.

Oh, God, lying to Jack already. Before she'd gone topside, Judith had run to the galley for a couple of pastries. She'd needed an excuse for why Jack hadn't found her on deck. She'd handed Jack a pastry and said, "I went to the galley for these." Yet she was still agonizing. *How* was she going to be able to keep a secret from her dearest friend, when no one knew her better than Jack did?

But the mysterious Catherine Benedek was a useful distraction to get her mind off secrets and kisses and ex-ghosts, at least briefly. "Aren't you curious about her?"

"After the way she spoke to you last night outside our cabins, no."

"I am. Who yells like that for no reason?"

"Her."

Judith rolled her eyes. "Let's introduce ourselves."

"Fine. But if she screeches again, I'm going to toss her over the rail."

Jacqueline threw the rest of her pastry over the railing and dusted off her hands on her breeches as she stood up. She'd already donned her ship garb: baggy pants, a loose shirt, and a pink scarf over her head, which kept her long, blond hair securely bound up. And she didn't bother with shoes or boots, preferring to go barefoot. She'd had three sets of work clothes tailored for the voyage and three sets made for Judith, too, even though Judith had told her she wouldn't wear them. They both loved sailing, but Judith had no desire to help with the actual work of sailing, as Jack did.

"You barely touched that pastry," Judith said as she dusted crumbs from her hands, too. "Are you feeling all right?"

"I probably should have resisted the fresh milk Nettie brought me last night. I got too much sleep because of it and now I feel a bit sluggish, is all."

"Nettie brought me a glass as well, but it didn't cause me to oversleep, so I doubt it was the milk. Are you sure you haven't caught something? Are you feverish?"

Jacqueline swatted Judith's hand away when she tried to feel her brow. "Stop fussing, Mother. I'm fine."

Judith tsked. "Aunt George would send you back to bed. I only wanted to see if you have a fever."

"I don't. Now can we get our meeting with the harridan over with?"

They had nearly reached the elegantly clad woman, so Judith whispered, "Be nice," before she made the introductions.

A warm smile revealed the woman was quite pretty, after all. "I'm Catherine Benedek. It's a pleasure to meet you under better circumstances."

"So you aren't always so disagreeable?" Jacqueline asked baldly.

Taken aback, Catherine assured them, "No, only when I'm in pain, as I was yesterday. I had an excruciating headache. Caused by lack of sleep, I suppose. I was rushing to my cabin for some laudanum to help with it. I do apologize for being terse."

"You still have an American accent," Jacqueline noted. "You weren't in Europe very long?"

"I was." That sadness was back in Catherine's light gray eyes. "But my mother was American, so—"

"Was?" Jacqueline cut in.

"Yes, she died in the recent fire that took Andrássy's father, too."

That would certainly account for Catherine's sadness, Judith thought. "How awful. I'm sorry for your loss."

"You are kind. But I suppose I have my mother's accent. I'm surprised you would recognize it."

"Jacqueline's mother is American, and five of her uncles are, too," Judith explained. "That's why we're sailing to America.

We're having a come-out in Connecticut to please the American side of her family. Then we'll have another one in England to please the other side. I was only able to get permission to go with her at the last minute. I'm actually quite unprepared. My entire new wardrobe still needs some finishing work, mostly just the hems."

Catherine's expression lit up. "So Andrássy told you that I love to sew? I would be delighted to assist you."

"It seems like an imposition."

"On the contrary, you would be doing *me* a favor by relieving my boredom. Say you will at least consider it."

Judith grinned. "Of course."

The smile remained on Catherine's lips, a little wider now. "How very accommodating of you to travel for such a reason. I, too, have family in America, though Andrássy doesn't think my father can still be alive after all these years."

"But you do?"

"Indeed. He was only assumed dead after his ship went down off the coast of Florida. But there were survivors of the shipwreck who returned to Savannah, which was where we lived. My father could have survived, too. Maybe he was injured and was recovering somewhere. That could have accounted for his not returning home. He might have come home much later and found us gone and had no idea where to look for us."

"Then you don't think your mother's marriage to Andrássy's father was even legal?" Jacqueline asked.

"No, I don't. God rest her soul, it was stupid and shameful of her to remarry so quickly. I hated her for many years for doing that."

"Really? Your own mother?"

Judith intervened before Jack turned the woman unpleasant again. "Anger can sometimes be mistaken for hate. It's understandable, though, that you would be angry at your mother for giving up on your father when you thought he could still be alive."

"Thank you for that." Catherine smiled at Judith. "Barely a month had passed before my mother packed our bags and took us to Europe. She told me that we were only going to visit an old friend of her mother's in Austria. But within three months of arriving there, she met the count, who was in the city on business, and married him. Three months! And then I was forced to live in that archaic country of his where English is barely spoken."

"I'm sorry—*we're* sorry," Judith said.

But Jack ruined it by adding, "Sounds exciting to me. A new life in a country that is so different from your own. Have you no sense of adventure a'tall?"

"Adventure? Are you joking?"

"I guess so," Jacqueline said drily.

Catherine didn't seem to notice Jacqueline's tone and changed the subject. "You two look nothing like Gypsies, as Andrássy does."

"You expected us to as far back in our ancestry as Anna Stephanoff was?" Jacqueline asked.

"You do have his eyes though, even the exotic shape."

"Only a few of us have the black hair and eyes you're referring to," Judith said.

"What about the gifts?"

Judith frowned. "What exactly are you—"

Jack interrupted with a laugh. "I think she means fortune-telling and other things Gypsies are renowned for."

Catherine suddenly looked quite excited. "Yes, indeed. Do you have any special abilities? Or does anyone in your family? I begged Andrássy to ask, but he doesn't believe in such things."

"Neither do we," Jacqueline said firmly.

The woman looked so disappointed, Judith took pity on her. "Our family does have more than its fair share of luck, but no one would call it a Gypsy gift."

"Yet perhaps it is," Catherine said quickly. "Can you explain?"

Jack was glaring at her, but Judith continued, "Well, for instance, our uncle Edward is incredibly good with investments, but only some people call him lucky. Others view him as being very knowledgeable about financial matters. Our cousin Regina is rather good at matchmaking. The men and women she pairs up usually end up quite happy together. My father and Jack's brother, Jeremy, who take after the Gypsy side in looks, were always lucky with women, and now they're lucky with their wives, but again, that's hardly considered a gift. And—"

"—that's the extent of it," Jacqueline cut in to finish for Judith. "Now, it's your turn to tell us what you expected to hear and why?"

"Is it not obvious? I hoped for some help in finding my father. I plan to start my search in Savannah, but as I and my mother were his only ties to that city, it is unlikely he is still there. His trade routes were between there and the Caribbean, where he lived before he met my mother. It's daunting to think we might have to visit every port in the Caribbean to find him! I at least hoped for assurance that he's alive *somewhere*."

Jacqueline raised a brow.

Judith saw that Catherine was becoming distraught and quickly said, "I'd trust your instincts and start your search in

Savannah. It really does seem the most logical place to start. No doubt you will find some new information about your father there. If you'll excuse us, we have some unpacking to do."

Jack dragged Judy away, mumbling under her breath, "Did we have to listen to her life's story?"

"We were being polite, and why did you interrupt me back there?"

"Because you were about to tell her about Amy, which is none of her bloody business."

Judith tsked. "We were just discussing luck, and Amy's *is* phenomenal, you'll have to admit."

"Yes, but that's all it is. Don't think for a minute that Catherine can be trusted, Judy. I don't fully trust Andrássy either, for that matter."

"Really?"

"You don't think it was a bit too convenient, him showing up the night before we leave and ending up on this ship with us? Just because he's got eyes like yours doesn't mean he is a relative."

Judith laughed. "You're forgetting he knows all about the Stephanoffs."

"From a journal that he could simply have found somewhere and decided to use the information in it for some nefarious end."

Judith laughed again. "You don't really believe that."

"All right, maybe not nefarious. And maybe he *is* related by blood. But that doesn't mean he isn't up to no good. So just watch what you say, to both of them. We don't need to spill family secrets just because he *seems* genuine."

Did Jacqueline *have* to mention secrets when Judith had such a big one of her own now?

nd Henry brought in the food, so they all took their
e table.

ássy had, unfortunately, been placed across from the
nack between James and Anthony, which didn't bode
r him. In fact, after what Jacqueline had confided to her
luncheon, Judith suspected Andrássy was in for quite a
ng. Jack had gloated that she wasn't the only one with res-
ations about Andrássy. She'd overheard their fathers discuss-
g the same thing. Of course, it was *Jack's* father who shared
er suspicions that Andrássy might not be who he claimed to
be. But then when did James Malory ever take anything at face
value? It was a throwback to his wild youth and ten years of
raising hell on the high seas to be suspicious first and agreeable
later—maybe.

Georgina inadvertently initiated the interrogation of Andrássy with the query "Your sister didn't want to join us for
dinner again?"

"I didn't mention it to her."

Georgina glanced at the empty seat at the table. "Why not?"

Another innocent question. But then Georgina was completely trusting, unlike her husband. So James obviously hadn't
shared his reservations with his wife yet, only with his brother.

"As I mentioned last night, Catherine has moods and isn't
always pleasant company," Andrássy explained.

And he didn't want to subject his new family to that? Judith
felt compelled to say, "I've seen her at her worst, but anyone
with a severe headache can get snippy, myself included. Jack
and I also had a nice conversation with her when she was feeling better."

"I wouldn't call it nice," Jack put in.

"It wasn't unpleasant," Judith insisted.

Chapter Se

❦

"WHERE IS JACQUELINE?" ANDRÁSSY asked Judit[
she arrived alone for dinner that night in the captain's cab[

"She's coming. She's just a little off-kilter today. She ov[
slept this morning, then overslept again from the nap she took
this afternoon."

Georgina frowned. "She's not getting sick, is she?"

"She doesn't have a fever. I checked."

"Probably just too much excitement over the last few days,"
James guessed, and added for his wife, "I wouldn't worry,
m'dear."

"Whatever you do, don't suggest she go back to bed," Judith
said with a grin. "She's quite annoyed with herself for spending
too much time in it today."

After that remark, only Andrássy still looked concerned. Judith wondered again if their new cousin might be a bit smitten
by her best friend. But Jacqueline did arrive a few minutes later,
eyes bright and wide-awake now, the picture of good health.
Vivacious in her greetings, she arrived only a few minutes be-

"Matter of opinion," Jack mumbled for just her ears.

James gave his daughter a quelling look before he said to Andrássy, "So you would describe your stepsister as hot-tempered? Many women are, including my Jack."

Jacqueline laughed, no doubt taking her father's comment as a compliment. But Andrássy said, "I never thought of it that way, merely that she can be moody. A new home, a new father when she wasn't reconciled to giving up finding her real father—it was a difficult time when she and her mother came to live with us."

"What happened to her father?" Katey asked.

Judith stopped listening as the conversation turned to what Catherine had already told her and Jack. She hoped Jacqueline was noting, though, that the pair did pretty much have the same story, which made it even more believable. Who could make up something like that? But Nathan Tremayne came quickly to mind. *He* could. He seemed to be quite adept at tall tales, making himself sound like a hero instead of the criminal he actually was.

She wondered if he had finished his job down in the hold. Likely no, since he probably wasn't *really* a carpenter. Any man could wield a hammer, but did he actually have the skills to build a proper ring? Oh, God, she hoped her uncle and her father didn't get hurt when they used the exercise ring and it fell apart beneath them.

Why didn't she just tell her father about the smuggler so Nathan would be spending the voyage in the brig where he belonged? She should never have agreed to a bargain with him, when it just gave him more time to get creative with his lies. Yet, if she didn't have to keep him a secret from Jack, would she be quite this uneasy about it? And why the deuce did she want to come up with an excuse to leave the table so she could go down to the hold to check on him?

She glanced across the table at Andrássy, who was saying, "It's why she ran away so often when she was a child. She was trying to get back to America where she grew up, so she could look for her father."

"Instead of traveling all over the world looking for someone who could be long dead, why don't you just marry her off?" Anthony suggested.

"I would if I thought it would make her happy. But until this matter of her missing father is settled, I doubt she will ever be happy in a marriage."

"So you're actually concerned about her happiness?" James asked.

"Of course." Andrássy seemed a little insulted to have been asked that. "The tantrums she had as a child were understandable. I don't even mind her temper. As you say, it's not something unique. Many women have one. It's merely embarrassing when it erupts in public. That is all I wanted to warn you about, so you wouldn't take offense if you witness any unpleasantness of that sort. Because of the fire, she has nothing and no one but me to depend on. But she is my burden, not yours."

"Are you going to rebuild?" Georgina asked.

"Perhaps someday, but my wish is to return to Austria where I was schooled and continue my studies there. I paint."

"An artist?"

"I dabble. I hope to do better one day. But I can do nothing with my life until I settle my stepsister's."

"A burden like the one you're shouldering can kill inspiration," James said thoughtfully. "What I don't understand is why you would go so far above and beyond when there isn't even a blood tie between you. Don't take offense, dear boy, but that smacks of coercion on her part. So I must ask, does she have some hold over you that you haven't mentioned?"

"James!" Georgina protested.

But Andrássy actually chuckled. "I am glad you feel you can speak so plainly with me. But consider, I am the last of the Benedek line, but not the last of Maria's line, and yet I would never have known that if Catherine hadn't found my great-grandfather's journal. So when she beseeched me to help her find her missing parent, I couldn't in good conscience deny her when I was about to embark on a similar search myself. For family." Andrássy looked around the table, a warm smile on his face. "You Malorys are so much more than I ever could have imagined. You've welcomed me without reservation." Only Jacqueline looked a little guilty over that comment. "But my father made Catherine a member of my immediate family. Despite the turmoil, he never regretted doing that because her mother made him happy."

"Is it as simple as that? Obligation, responsibility, and a debt you feel you owe?"

"Sounds like something that would rope you in, James," Georgina said with a pointed look. "Oh, wait, it already did, or aren't those the same reasons you agreed to help Gabrielle Brooks?"

He chuckled. "Guilty."

"Not to mention, ending up in a pirate's prison because of it."

"Point *taken*, George."

No one jumped in to explain that byplay to Andrássy, but then it was a touchy subject that the Andersons, wealthy shipbuilders and owners of a large merchant fleet, now had ex-pirates in the family on more than one shore. One long since retired (Georgina's husband, James) and the other turned treasure hunter (Drew's father-in-law, Nathan Brooks), but still, both guilty of wreaking havoc in their day.

Judith steered the conversation back to Andrássy's efforts to help his stepsister, telling him, "I think what you are doing is admirable. You've given Catherine hope, haven't you?"

"Yes, I believe so, but I fear she has yet to learn patience."

Jacqueline opened her mouth, but Judy pinched her under the table, knowing that her cousin was about to say that they'd already experienced the woman's impatience, and that she'd got it into her head that a Malory with Gypsy gifts could help her more than Andrássy could—which wasn't going to happen and didn't need to be discussed.

Judith said to Andrássy, "It may not be a quick undertaking, but you may find that it changes her for the better. You might consider pausing your journey in Bridgeport to allow your sister to have a little fun before you continue on." She stood up then. It was as good an opportunity as she was going to get to slip away before everyone else finished eating. "Now if you will all excuse me, I didn't get as much rest today as Jack did. I'm rather tired."

"Of course, poppet," Anthony said.

But before Judith left, she leaned down and whispered in Jacqueline's ear, "I got your foot out of your mouth. Don't put it back in as soon as I leave."

Jack merely snorted.

Chapter Eighteen

ONLY TWO LANTERNS WERE left burning in the hold, both by the exercise ring, but Judith didn't find Nathan there. The ring wasn't finished but the platform was. The tarpaulin had even been tacked to it, and two of the four posts were secured to the corners. It only needed the other two posts and the ropes strung between them, so Judith figured he thought he could finish that quickly in the morning before James came down to inspect it.

Judith was disappointed that Nathan had quit working for the day as this might well be her last chance to speak with him alone. She supposed she could ask him for instruction on some nautical matter during the voyage, maybe even get him up in the rigging where they *could* speak without being overheard. But then she'd have to wear those unflattering clothes Jack had had made for her, and besides, Jack would say that *she* could teach her anything she wanted to learn about sailing—unless Judith confessed her interest in Nathan. That wouldn't be giving away the secret, would it? Course it wouldn't. Once Jack got a look at the man, it would be blatantly obvious why Judy was interested in him.

She might as well turn in for the night, but she moved over to the ring to examine it first. She thought about climbing up on the platform to make sure its floor was as sturdy as it should be, but it was a bit too high off the floor for her, so she just pressed down on it with her palms.

"Couldn't stay away?"

She swung around with a gasp. Nathan was sitting on the floor between two crates, one of which still had her coat draped over it. He was leaning back against the bulkhead, holding a plate in one hand and a fork in the other.

She slowly walked over to him, noting that at least he had his shirt back on, and yet her heartbeat still accelerated. "I thought you'd gone."

"Only long enough to fetch some dinner. Damn fancy grub for a ship, too. Definitely not what we were served on the short trip from Hampshire to London."

"There probably wasn't an actual cook aboard yet. The one we have now isn't a seaman. My aunt and uncle sail with their own servants, most of whom boarded in London."

"All the luxuries of home, eh? But now I'm never going to be happy with my own cook again."

She smiled at his grumbling tone. "You actually have one? I thought smugglers only make short jaunts across the Channel and back, hardly long enough at sea to warrant needing a cook aboard."

"I wouldn't know. But I'll take your word for it, since you seem to know more about smuggling than I do. But have a seat. You can watch me eat while you tell me about my life."

Sarcasm, and quite blatant, too. Yet his tone was friendly,

his lips even turned up in a grin. So he was merely teasing her again?

"I came for my coat," she said, though she sat down on top of it again anyway.

"I was going to return it to you."

She raised a brow. "How, without giving away that I was down here?"

"You don't think I could have found you alone?"

"Not when I'm with Jack most of the day and we're with our family in the evenings, so, no, I don't think so."

He chuckled. "I have a bed in the carpenter's storeroom. Well, at the risk of stirring up a hornet's nest, I'll mention it's just a cot." He waited, but she wasn't going to address the cot issue again and merely snorted at his assumption that she would. So he continued, "But I've claimed it as my own for a little privacy. You're welcome to visit any night you feel like—"

"Stop it. You might find this all very amusing, but you should recall, you still have a noose hanging over your head."

"Breaking a bargain? Really? Thought you nobles had more honor than that."

"It was a silly bargain—"

"But it was struck—even sealed. Ah, there's that blush I remember so well."

"You are insufferable."

"No, I just have a lot on my plate, including you. And if your word is as wishy-washy as a mood, then it's not reliable, is it?"

"I'm keeping it, but only for the duration of the voyage as we agreed."

"That wasn't the stipulation."

"*That* was a foregone conclusion," she stressed, not giving in on that point. "But don't worry, you'll have time to disappear after we dock."

"Think you'll want me to by then?"

The question implied they were going to get much more intimately acquainted. His tone had even dropped to a husky timbre! It jarred her and brought all sorts of questions to mind that she should be asking herself, not him. She was *too* attracted to this man and out of her depth to deal with it. It had held her back from doing what she should have done the moment she realized who he was. It had impelled her to strike the Bargain. But she couldn't let that last question stand.

"You and I won't—"

His short laugh cut her off. "I merely meant, by the time we dock you'll be convinced that I'm innocent and not the black-guard you wrongly think I am."

Was she using her suspicion as an excuse to keep herself from giving in to this attraction? No, he was just good at stirring up doubt.

She reminded him pertly, "Our bargain was for the truth. Do you even know how to tell it?"

"Course I do, darlin'. But d'you know how to recognize it when you hear it?" Yet he didn't wait for an answer, not that there was one when his tactics were so evasive. Instead, he got back to the subject he didn't get to finish that morning. "So tell me how a woman gets a nickname like Jack?"

"Because it's not a nickname. It's the name her father gave her at birth."

"Really?

"Of course the fact that her maternal uncles, who James doesn't like the least little bit, were all present at the birthing might have influenced his decision a tad, but he couldn't be swayed to change it."

"He's that stubborn?"

Judith smiled. "Depends on who you ask, but in this case, he was absolutely inflexible. However, Jack's mother, George, made sure—"

"Good God, another woman with a man's name?"

"No, Georgina is her real name. James just calls her George. Always has, always will. But she made sure Jacqueline appeared on her daughter's birth record. Nonetheless, among the family the name Jack had already stuck."

"I'm guessing that explains the odd name of this ship, *The Maiden George*?"

"Yes, James's original ship was named *The Maiden Anne*, but he sold her when he retired from the sea. This one he had built when Jack's mother wanted to take Jack to Connecticut to see where she was born. An unnecessary expense, really, when George and her brothers own Skylark Shipping, which is a very large fleet of American merchant ships, and at least one of them is docked in England at any given time. But as I mentioned, my uncle doesn't exactly like his five Anderson brothers-in-law. He refuses to sail on their vessels short of a dire emergency. And now it's my turn to ask a question."

He stood up abruptly at the noise suddenly coming from the animals down at the end of the hold. She looked in that direction, too. Probably just a rat scurrying past them, or a cat on the prowl for one. But Nathan set his plate down on the other crate and went to investigate anyway.

Not exactly adhering to the Bargain of tit for tat with questions, she noted with some annoyance, which she would point out when he came back. But he didn't come back. . . .

Chapter Nineteen

NATHAN DIDN'T EXPECT TO find anything in the back of the hold. He just didn't want to lose his advantage in this bout of verbal sparring with Judith, which would have happened if she started interrogating him again so soon. He preferred to keep her distracted from the facts as long as possible, or at least until he could better ascertain her reaction to them.

He hadn't decided if he should appeal to her sympathy—if she had any—with some truths he could share? Or admit everything, including that he owned the house in Hampshire and had a pardon waiting for him? Unfortunately, he didn't think she was likely to believe either. But if he told her too much and did convince her that he was innocent, their bargain would come to an end and he'd lose her company. And he liked her company. Liked teasing her, too. Liked the way her mouth pursed in annoyance. Liked the way her eyes could spark with anger or humor. Definitely liked the way she'd felt in his arms. Bleeding hell, there was nothing about her that he didn't like—

other than her stubborn insistence that he was a smuggler. *Why was she so certain? What was he missing?*

He was jumped the moment he passed the crate where the man had been crouched in hiding, and it was his own damn fault for having his mind filled with Judith instead of the matter at hand. And it was no scrawny runt either that tackled him to the floor. He was nearly as big as Nathan. In the brief glimpse he'd caught of him, he'd seen a young man with queued-back blond hair and dark eyes, who was barefoot but not poorly clad in a shirt made of fine linen and a fancy gold-link chain at his neck. Nathan didn't recognize him as a member of the crew, and he doubted one of the servants Judith had mentioned would attack him.

The noise of their hard landing startled the chickens into squawking and set one of the pigs squealing. Nathan was only startled for a moment before instinct kicked in. He rolled, taking the man with him, and got in one solid punch before he was thrust back and the man scrambled to his feet. But he didn't run. He pulled a dagger from the back of his britches and took a swipe at Nathan just as Nathan got to his feet. He felt the sting of the blade on his chest, but didn't look down to check the damage. His anger kicked in full force because of it.

He'd never been in a knife fight before and had no weapon on him to counter it. He could have improvised with a hammer or a file, but his toolbox was too far away and he would likely get that dagger in his back if he ran for it. He positioned his arms instead to block the next swipe, but doubting that would be effective, he just tried to stay out of reach instead. But that wasn't going to be possible for much longer.

Weighing his options, he saw they were sorely lacking.

Knock the dagger out of the man's hand so he could have a fair fight with him, which he knew he could win, or send Judith for help if she hadn't already run out of there. The second option didn't appeal to him in the least, and he would be dead before assistance arrived. Then a third option slid across the floor and stopped near his feet. His hammer.

The man spotted it, too, and quickly stepped forward with his dagger extended to move Nathan back from it. There was no time to think, but there was no way he was giving up the opportunity Judith had just given him. He turned his back on the man, dropped to the floor, and, bracing his hands on the floor, kicked backward. He didn't connect with his attacker, but it startled the man sufficiently to give Nathan the time he needed to grasp the hammer and rise to his feet, swinging it. He connected with the man's shoulder and the man stepped back. Nathan had the upper hand now and they both knew it.

He took the offensive with some steady swings. Sparks flew when the hammerhead struck the blade, but the blond man held fast to his dagger, although Nathan had him moving backward. He'd soon be out of room to maneuver with the animal pen behind him, but he might not know that yet.

With the advantage his now and not wanting to actually kill the man, Nathan said, "Give it up, man. Better than getting your head bashed in."

"Bugger off!" the man snarled, but desperation was in his expression, which warned Nathan the man was about to try something, and he did, flipping the dagger in his hand so he was holding it by the tip and raising his arm to throw it. Nathan only had a second to react, and the quickest way to get out of the path of that dagger or to stop it was to dive at the man.

He did, plowing them both into the fence of the animal

pen, which broke with their combined weight. They hit the ground, animals scattering and raising a cacophony of panicked noises. But Nathan pressed his broad chest against his attacker's dagger arm so the man couldn't move his weapon, if indeed he still held it. Letting go of the hammer, Nathan smashed his fist into the man's face, once, twice, three times. Twice had been enough to knock him out.

Nathan took a deep breath and sat up. The dagger was still within his assailant's reach so Nathan shoved it out of the pen before he glanced down at his chest to see if he was wounded. The blade had sliced open his shirt and his skin stung. He'd been scratched, but not seriously enough to draw more than a few drops of blood.

"Are you all right?"

She was still there? He glanced up and saw how upset she looked and assured her, "I'm fine."

"But he attacked you. Why?!"

"Damned if I know." He got to his feet and dragged the man out of the pen before he added, "He's not a member of the crew, obviously."

She was frowning down at the man. "He's not a member of my uncle's kitchen staff either. I know them all."

"Must be a stowaway then."

"But stowaways don't try to kill people once they've been discovered."

She had a point. It was a minor crime that usually only got the culprit some time in the brig or forced labor until the ship reached land. Then most captains would simply let the stowaway go. The man's aggression didn't make much sense. He couldn't have been in the hold since they'd left London. Nathan was sure of that. The animals would have given him away sooner, and sailors who came down here several times a day for provisions would have noticed him. The man had to have been hiding somewhere else and snuck down here when Nathan went to fetch his dinner.

He grabbed a crate and used it to block the broken part of the fence so all the animals didn't get out before he could repair it.

Judith, watching him, suddenly gasped. "You're hurt!"

"No, it's nothing."

"Let me see."

She rushed over to him. He rolled his eyes at her, but she was too intent on opening the tear in his shirt wider so she could check his wound. But it gave him time to realize she was a little more concerned than she ought to be about someone she wanted to see in prison. Was she so compassionate that she'd help anyone in need?

She finally brought her eyes back to his. "It's just a scratch."

He smiled. "I know. You should have run the other way when the fight started, but I'm glad you didn't. The hammer tipped the scales in my favor. Clever of you to think of it."

She blushed. "I got angry that he wasn't fighting fairly. I *did* think about hitting him with a plank of lumber first, but I had no confidence that my swing would be effective."

He laughed at the image that brought up. He seemed to be doing a lot of that around her—yet another reason why he liked her company. "Never thought I would end up grateful for that temper of yours or have to thank you for it, but you definitely have my thanks, darlin'."

"You're welcome."

He bent down and hefted the unconscious man over his shoulder.

"Where are you taking him?"

"Your uncle needs to be informed about this, so take your coat and go before the commotion starts. He could order the entire ship searched tonight for more stowaways, and I doubt you want to be found down here."

"Quite right. I'm leaving now. No need to wait on me."

He still paused at the stairway to make sure Judith was safely out of there before he went up. The possibility that there was more than one stowaway would explain why the unconscious man had jumped Nathan instead of just giving himself up. Had he been distracting Nathan from finding his partner? When Nathan reached the main deck, he dropped his heavy load.

The man didn't stir even a little, but Nathan couldn't leave him there alone, so he simply yelled for the first mate. Only a few sailors were on deck at that time of night, but they came forward to investigate, one of them bringing a lantern.

"Cor, you decked one of the cap'n's London servants?" a sailor guessed. "Cap' won't be pleased."

"Fetch him and we'll find out," Nathan replied.

Artie arrived and peered down at the man. "He don't belong here. Where'd you find him, Mr. Tremayne?"

Nathan explained to Artie what had happened, then had to repeat it all when the captain joined them. If Malory was annoyed that someone would dare board his ship without permission, he hid it well. In fact, the man's face was without expression of any sort.

"He's not one of the crew, Cap'n, and from what Mr. Tremayne is telling us, he doesn't appear to be a typical stowaway, either," Artie pointed out.

"No, he doesn't." James stared down at the man and

nudged him with the toe of his boot to see if he was close to coming round yet, but the man didn't move. "Did you have to hit him quite so hard, Mr. Tremayne?"

"I dropped my hammer first" was all Nathan said in his defense.

The slight quirk to the captain's lips was too brief to tell if it was amusement. "Our conclusion that he's not on board for the ride begs the question, what is he doing on my ship?" James said. "And why hasn't someone fetched water yet so we can bring him to and ascertain that?"

But the moment a sailor ran off for a bucket, Andrássy appeared with sword in hand, yelling, "How dare he endanger my family? I'll kill him!"

The count looked enraged enough to do just that as he ran down from the quarterdeck. Nathan leapt toward him to stop him.

Looking annoyed, James did, too, shoving Andrássy back. "What the devil d'you think you're doing?" James demanded ominously. "I need answers, not blood."

"But—are the women not in danger?" Andrássy asked, lowering his sword.

"Bloody hell," James snarled. "Just stay out of—"

"Cap'n!"

Nathan turned back and saw that the stowaway must have leapt to his feet, knocked down the only sailor still next to him, the one who'd just yelled, while they'd been distracted, and dived over the side of the ship. Nathan only saw the man's legs before he disappeared.

Incredulous, Nathan ran to the rail. "What the devil? Does he think he can swim back to England?"

The others had come to the rail, too. One sailor shouted, "Should we fish him out?"

"How?" the one with the lantern said in frustration as he held it over the rail. "Do you even see him down there? I don't."

Nathan couldn't spot the man either. Unlike last night when the sky had been clear, tonight a long bank of clouds covered the moon. More men arrived with more lanterns, but the light still didn't extend far enough for them to spot the stowaway. Nathan could hear the sounds of splashing, which indicated the stowaway was swimming away from the ship. And then he heard something else. . . .

"Oars," he said to James. "There's at least one rowboat nearby, so there must be a ship, too."

"Artie!" James started barking orders. "Get every man on deck armed in case this is a sneak attack. You two"—he pointed at the sailors—"get one of our smaller boats in the water and go after them. If it's not an attack, I want that bloody stowaway back. Henry, get the man in the crew with the best night vision and send him up in the rigging. I want to know what's happening down there."

Nathan ran to the other side of the ship, but he *still* couldn't see anything in the water. Moving around the ship, he did ascertain that the sound of the oars could only be heard on the side of the ship where the man had jumped. The sound was growing fainter, and finally it could only be heard from the stern.

He was on his way to inform James of that when Walter, the sailor with the best night vision, who hadn't needed to climb far to use it, called out, "Behind us, Captain!"

James moved to the stern immediately with the crew following him. Artie handed him his spyglass, but James didn't bother to use it. He glanced up at the thick clouds overhead instead and swore foully.

But Walter yelled down again: "Just one rowboat, moving swiftly back to the big ship. Our boat isn't close yet, Captain. Doesn't look like we can overtake it."

Then the clouds thinned, just enough for the moon to cast a dim light on the water. James quickly brought up the spyglass and said a moment later, "She's three masted and fully rigged— and pulling about to show off her cannon."

"To fire on us?" someone asked.

"No, she's not close enough. I'm guessing it's merely a ma- neuver to deter us from attempting to bring their man back for questioning. Artie, call our boat back. I'm not going to risk their lives if they don't have a chance of overtaking the other boat." Then James swore again as the light faded. "Bloody mys- teries, I deplore them."

The comment hadn't been directed at any one of them in particular, but members of the crew tried to figure out what had just happened.

"Not piracy or they would have fired on us."

"Only one rowboat, so it wasn't a sneak raid," someone else said.

"For that rowboat to be halfway to *The Maiden George* when the man jumped means that a rendezvous had to be ar- ranged for sometime tonight," Nathan speculated.

"Since I am doubtful of coincidences, I agree," James said. "But we have been at sea only two days. What could he have expected to accomplish in so little time?"

"Sabotage," Artie offered.

"To sink us?" James shook his head. "Too drastic and forfeits innocent lives."

"Perhaps they don't care," Artie said, "But I'll have the ship searched from top to bottom."

"If he was here for revenge, he might have been prepared to do the killing tonight and then jump ship."

"But you caught him first? I suppose that is possible, but my enemies tend to be impatient. The man would have tried to kill me by now if he wanted me dead. I suppose the crew can be questioned to find out if anyone else has a relentless enemy."

Nathan did, but Grigg wouldn't send a man on a suicide mission to kill him even if he had discovered Nathan was on this ship, so he didn't mention it. He suggested something not quite as nefarious instead.

"It could be that the stowaway was retrieving something that ended up on the ship by accident. He might have thought he could find it in a couple of days and maybe he did. He could have been waiting for me to leave the hold where he was hiding, but I found him instead."

"That possibility isn't wholly implausible, but it doesn't explain his immediately attacking you instead of trying to talk his way out of the hold. He could have claimed to be a crewman or a servant. No one but the first mates knows everyone aboard my ship."

Which was how the man could have gotten around on the ship without much notice, to eat and do whatever else he was there to do, Nathan thought. But he was done guessing when that's all they could do. It accomplished nothing.

"Do we turn about then, Cap'n?" one of the men asked.

"No, we're not giving chase, not with my family aboard,"

James said. "But I want constant surveillance of that ship that's trailing us. If it approaches, I want to know about it. And set up shifts of armed crewmen to patrol the *The Maiden George* tonight."

"I'm beginning to hate mysteries m'self," Nathan mumbled.

James nodded and turned to his first mate. "I suspect this will go unsolved for the time being, but gather the rest of the crew and search the supplies for anything out of the ordinary. And every nook and cranny, for that matter, to make sure this wasn't a joint undertaking. Give me the results as soon as you're finished. I'm going back to my cabin." Then James paused to turn to Nathan again. "Did you finish my ring, Mr. Tremayne?"

"I'll have it done within the hour, Captain."

"It can wait until morning. You've done enough for one day."

Nathan nodded. "You said 'unsolved for the time being.' Do you think they'll continue to follow us if they didn't get what they were after?"

"Oh, I'm quite depending on it."

Chapter Twenty

JUDITH COULDN'T BELIEVE SHE was going to do this. Again. It was so against her nature to sneak about like this. There had to be another way to talk to Nathan without stirring up any curiosity about it. But she couldn't think of anything.

She hurried down to the lower level, aware that she had so little time she might as well not even bother. It was midmorning already. She hadn't meant to sleep this late and Jack would be looking for her soon if she didn't oversleep again, too. She might, though, after coming to Judith's cabin last night before she retired. Jack had had to share with her everything that she'd learned from her father about the stowaway, and Judith couldn't even admit she already knew half of it. Darned secrets . . .

She found Nathan putting his tools away. The exercise ring was finished. And he'd already repaired the animal pen. A few more minutes and she would have missed him.

He confirmed that, saying, "I was just leaving. Didn't think you were going to pay me a visit—and what the devil are you wearing?"

"Clothes that are easy to put on. My maid let me oversleep and I was too impatient to wait for her to come back. As it is, I don't have much time to spare."

The way he was staring at her britches brought on a blush. She'd tucked them into midcalf-high riding boots, but the britches weren't thick. Jack liked her clothes comfortable, which usually meant soft. So Judith didn't tuck in the long, white shirt, allowing it to fully cover her derriere instead, but she did belt it. She had no doubt she looked ridiculous, but that's not what his green eyes were saying.

"You're actually allowed to dress like that?"

"On board ship, yes. I wore breeches the last time I sailed years ago. My mother agreed. Better than a skirt flapping in the wind."

"For a child, maybe, but you're a woman now with curves that—"

"Stop looking!" she snapped.

He laughed. "There are some things a man just can't do, darlin'."

Her eyes narrowed. "Are you deliberately wasting what little time I have before Jack starts wondering where I am?"

His eyes came back to hers. "Doesn't work out well, you having me at your beck and call, does it? Not if you have to arrange it around your cousin."

She'd already figured that out but did he have to sound so amused about it? "If you have somewhere else to be, by all means—"

She didn't get to finish. He actually put his hands on her waist and set her on the crate next to him. It was a bit high for her to have chosen as a seat, leaving her feet dangling a few inches off the floor. But then he sat down on it next to her! It wasn't wide enough for two. Well, it was, but not without their thighs touching.

She might not even have noticed it if she were wearing a skirt and petticoats, but in the thin, black britches, she could feel every bit of his leg against hers and the warmth coming from it. She could feel the warmth of his upper arm, too, as it pressed against hers, since he wasn't wearing a jacket. The position was far too intimate, reminding her of how it had felt being pressed to his half-naked body yesterday when he'd kissed her. . . .

That pleasant fluttering she'd experienced yesterday showed up to fluster her further. She started to get down until she realized that sitting side by side, she wouldn't have to look at him and get snared by his handsome face and sensual eyes. If she could just ignore that they were touching. If she could not wonder if he had put them in proximity because he wanted to kiss her again. She groaned to herself. She was *never* going to get any answers from him if this attraction kept getting in the way.

"Where did you grow up?" she blurted out. There, one simple question he couldn't possibly evade.

He did. "Does it matter?"

Staring intently at the exercise ring in front of them, which was well lit with two lanterns hanging on its posts, she demanded, "Is this really how you're going to adhere to the Bargain?"

"Well, if I say where I was raised, you're just going to take it wrong."

"Oh, good grief, you grew up in Cornwall?" she guessed. "Yes, of course. The one place in England well-known for smugglers. Why did I bother to ask?"

"I warned you'd take it wrong. But Cornwall has everything every other shire has, including nabobs, so don't paint everyone who resides there with your suspicions."

"Point taken."

"Really?" he said in surprise. "You can actually be reasonable about something?"

"I favor logic, and that was a logical statement about a region."

He snorted. "I've given you lots of logic—"

"No, you haven't, not on matters that pertain to you personally. So did you learn carpentry before or after you took to the seas?"

"It's my turn."

"What? Oh, very well, ask away. I have no secrets to hide other than *you*."

"I rather like being your secret."

Why did that bring on a blush? Just because his tone dropped to a sensual level didn't mean he intended it to. Or it could mean he did. The man *could* be trying to deliberately discompose her. Or was he getting as caught up in this attraction as she was? The thought made her feel almost giddy. If he wasn't a criminal—but he was, and she had to keep that firmly in mind.

"Was that a question?" she asked.

He chuckled. "How big is your family?"

"Immediate? Both parents are hale and hearty. My sister, Jaime, is two years younger than I and doesn't take well to sailing, so she stayed home with my mother. My half sister, Katey, is much older and is aboard with her husband, Boyd."

"I meant the lot of you."

She suspected he didn't, but she answered anyway. "Don't

think I've ever counted the number. My father is the youngest of four brothers. They've all got wives and children, even a few grandchildren, so if I had to guess offhand, there's more'n thirty of us."

It sounded as if he choked back a laugh. She was *not* going to glance his way to be sure. Keeping her eyes off him was working—somewhat. At least she'd stopped wondering if he was going to kiss her—oh, God, now she couldn't think of anything else. It had been thrilling, if a little overwhelming, but the feelings it had stirred in her had been too nice not to want to experience them again.

"—most of my life," he was saying.

"What?"

"Your previous question."

"But what did you just say?"

"Where *did* your mind wander off to?"

The humor in his tone made her wonder if he already knew, which made her blush even more. "Would you just start over, please?"

"When you ask so nicely, of course. I said that I was a sailor first, that I sailed with my father most of my life."

"Except for the three years you worked as a carpenter. You mentioned that to my uncle. Where and why did you learn that trade if you already had a job with your father?"

"No cheating, darlin'. That's three questions in a row you're asking."

She huffed, "I wouldn't have to if you would elaborate, instead of giving me terse answers that only lead to a dozen more questions."

He chuckled. "So you adhere to logic and exaggeration, oh, and let's not forget stubbornness. I'm starting a list."

"And you adhere to evasion. D'you really think that isn't obvious?"

"You know, I'm having a hard time keeping my hands off you."

She sucked in her breath, her eyes flying to his. His expression said that he wasn't just trying to distract her. Blatant desire, poignant and sensual. It struck a chord, lit a flame. . . .

"Just thought you should know," he added, then looking away, asked, "Where did you grow up?"

Judith needed a moment to come back to earth. Actually, longer. As if he *had* touched her, her nipples still tingled from hardening, her pulse was still racing. She would like to think she would have stopped him from kissing her just then, but she knew she wouldn't have. Why didn't he!?

Oh, God, the man was more dangerous than she'd thought—to her senses. She jumped off the crate to put some distance between them. She was going to have to be more cautious of his tactics.

"London," she said, and said no more. Still watching him, she noticed when his mouth tightened just a little, but enough to guess he didn't like short answers either. "Annoying, isn't it, lack of elaboration?"

"I'll survive."

She snorted at his glib answer. "Well, since I'm usually more thorough, I'll add, I was born and raised in London, as well as tutored there. In fact, I rarely left the city except to visit family in other parts of England, such as Hampshire, where I first met you."

"And at least twice to America."

She smiled. "Before I comment on that, I require another

answer from you. Why did you learn carpentry if you already were working with your father?"

He glanced at her again and laughed heartily. She liked the way humor disarmed him so thoroughly, his face, his mouth, his eyes, all revealed it. It said that he was getting used to her and wasn't the least bit afraid that she might land him in jail. Confidence that he could change her mind about him, or actual innocence? There was the rub. If she had that answer by now, then she wouldn't be here—or she would, just for a different reason.

He addressed her last question. "I had a row with my father that led to my leaving Cornwall for good when I was twenty. I ended up settling in Southampton, which is where I took up carpentry."

She repaid him in kind. "My first trip to America was with Jack, too, to visit her mother's hometown of Bridgeport. This trip is for her come-out there before we have another in London. It's unusual to have two, of course, but her American uncles insisted. If you don't know what a come-out entails—"

"I do. It's what you nabobs do to get yourselves a husband. So you're going on the marriage mart, are you? Somehow, I didn't expect you'd need to."

Had he just given her a compliment, but in a derogatory tone? "I don't *need* to. I've lost count of how many men have already petitioned my father for permission to court me this summer."

"So you've got a host of eager suitors waiting for you to return to England?"

"No, as it happens, my father threw all those hopeful gentlemen out of the house. He didn't appreciate the reminder that I was approaching a marriageable age."

"Good for him."

She raised a brow. "Really? Why would you side with him about that?"

"Because women don't need to get married as soon as they can."

"You're talking about someone you know personally, aren't you?" she guessed.

He nodded. "My sister. She should have waited for a better man who could have made her happy instead of accepting the first offer to come her way. It didn't turn out well."

Judith waited a moment for him to continue, but she heard the sound of approaching voices. She gasped. "That's my father and uncle."

"Bleedin' hell, hide."

Chapter Twenty-One

THE TIMING WAS HORRIBLE on all accounts. Nathan had just opened up, answering questions without asking any of his own. That could have gone much further if they weren't interrupted. But Judith didn't need to be told to hide. She was hurrying toward the crates when Nathan's arm hooked around her waist and she was pretty much deposited on the floor behind one. At least she had room to hide there because none of the supplies were placed close to the hull since it needed to be checked regularly for leaks. It was one of Nathan's jobs as the ship's carpenter— when he wasn't being interrogated by the captain's niece.

She crouched down behind the crate with a few moments to spare before she could distinguish her father, just entering the hold, saying, ". . . answered too readily, without a single pause. Didn't have to think about it even once."

"And your point?" James replied.

"Thought that would convince you the lad is telling the truth."

"I never called him a liar, Tony. He can be exactly who he

says he is and still have an agenda other than the simple one he claims. Telling us nothing but the truth doesn't mean he hasn't left out some pertinent details."

It almost sounded as if they were talking about Nathan, but Judith knew better. They were discussing Andrássy, although Nathan might not guess that. And why hadn't he left yet? She could still see him standing between the two crates by his tools, his back to the entrance, and less than two feet from her. He was providing her with more concealment, but she could tell from the aggressive set of his wide shoulders that he was tense. Did he expect a confrontation? Or just expect he might have to protect her from one? Decent of him, but she wouldn't let it come to that.

As if she weren't anxious enough, she felt dread when it occurred to her why her father and her uncle had come down here. To use the new ring. They wouldn't be leaving soon, which meant she couldn't leave either. It also meant they'd hear Jack calling for her when she didn't see her on deck, and that would be anytime now. She could even imagine her father initiating a search of the ship by everyone on board.

James's voice had sounded farther away, as if he'd already gotten into the ring. Judith didn't peek around the crate to find out for sure. But once they started sparring, they might be distracted enough for her to slip out of there. She'd have to crawl most of the way behind the supplies, but that would be easy enough to do in her britches.

"My nephew's wife has hair like yours," Anthony said in a deceptively affable tone.

Judith's eyes flared wide. It sounded as if her father was standing right in front of the crate she was hiding behind! But she knew he was talking to Nathan.

"Be a good chap and tell me you *aren't* related to the Hilary family."

"Never heard of them," Nathan replied cautiously.

"Good."

Judith didn't have to see it to know her father had just punched Nathan in the gut. The sound was unmistakable. But *why*? And not just once. She winced with each blow that followed. She knew how brutal her father could be when it came to landing punches. Was Nathan even trying to defend himself? She was afraid to look. She couldn't *not* look.

Nathan ducked the next blow. He'd maneuvered the fight so Anthony's back was to her. James was facing her from his position in the ring, but his eyes were on the two men below him and his tone was quite dry when he said, "You're allowed to fight back, Mr. Tremayne. My brother won't be satisfied unless you do."

Nathan blocked a blow to his face and followed it with a right jab that caught Anthony in the chin and snapped his head back slightly. She winced for her father now, yet she wondered if he wasn't secretly pleased that he wasn't going to win easily. He loved a good fight. There's wasn't a Malory who didn't know it. But if he appreciated that Nathan *wasn't* flat on his back yet, he gave no indication of it. He continued to deliver blow after blow, concentrating on Nathan's midsection, while Nathan got in two more punches to Anthony's chin and cheek.

James finally said, "Enough, Tony. I don't want him damaging his hands on you. He needs them to do his job."

"Someone else can do his bloody job," Anthony replied in a snarl.

"Actually, they can't," James rejoined. "We only have one carpenter aboard."

"*He's* the one found your hidden miscreant last night?"

"Yes."

One more punch. "Very well, I'm done. I shall consider us even—Tremayne, is it? Unless you do something to tip the scales again."

"Your idea of *even* stinks—my lord."

Judith groaned to herself at that less than conciliatory answer, but Anthony merely seemed to be amused by it and quipped, "On the contrary, dear boy. You're still standing, aren't you?"

James offered magnanimously, "If you need to rest up after your exertions, Tony, I can wait another day to test out this ring."

"Bite your tongue, old man. That was just a warm-up." Anthony proved it by joining James in the ring.

Nathan should have left, but instead he sat on the crate that Judith was still hiding behind. She was sitting cross-legged now, facing the hull, her back against the crate. She assumed Nathan was just catching his breath, watching the action in the ring.

So she was surprised a few minutes later to hear him say in a low, if incredulous tone, "How does he do that at his age and after what I just meted out to him?"

He was talking about the punches her father and her uncle were doling out to each other in the ring. She whispered back, "Don't equate age with skill. My father has had years of conditioning, not to mention frequent matches with his brother like the one you're watching now."

Nathan snorted quietly. "I gave you the opportunity to leave—why didn't you?"

She didn't answer that and instead asked, "Did he hurt you?"

"What d'you think?"

"How badly?"

"I might survive."

She started to frown until she recognized the teasing note in his voice. There was something else she wanted to know. "What did you do to provoke his anger?"

"I have to be at fault?"

"I know my father. I can tell when he holds a grudge against someone. Why?"

"I might have knocked him out on the London docks before we sailed."

She gasped. "How? The only one he *ever* loses to is my uncle James."

"Caught him by surprise, you could say. But you heard him. We're even now."

She almost said, "Don't count on it," but she didn't want him to turn leery of talking to her because of her father. That might happen anyway now, but she wasn't going to help it along.

Then he added, "Go now while they're distracted. Stay low."

"You should leave as well."

"Not a chance. People have to pay to watch fights of this caliber. Besides, don't take it wrong, darlin', but I want to see your old man lose."

That infuriated her, enough to make her hiss, "You won't see it today. Mark my words, my uncle is going to *let* him win that bout."

"Why would he do a fool thing like that?" Nathan sounded surprised.

"Because those two are very close. It might not always seem

like it, but they are. And because it will soothe ruffled feathers, even put my father in a good mood—which might help him to forget about you for the duration of the voyage. Just don't expect my uncle to do you that favor after we dock and you're no longer working for him."

Chapter Twenty-Two

"I PROB'LY SHOULD HAVE MENTIONED this sooner, but someone's caught my eye," Judith told her cousin.

They were sitting in the middle of the double bed in Jacqueline's cabin, both cross-legged, cards in hand, more cards on the blanket between them. Jack was barefoot and wearing her ship togs, which she would probably wear every day until they docked. Judith still preferred not to wear them and even more so after seeing Nathan's reaction to them. She was outfitted in a simple, blue day dress with short-capped sleeves.

They often played whist by themselves, despite its being a four-person game. They merely skirted the rules with each of them playing an extra hand. It was not as exciting with only one player to worry about instead of three, but it passed the time for them, and Judith found it more fun than a game of chess, which Jack *always* won.

But Jacqueline didn't even glance up at Judith after her statement, which Judith found rather disappointing because it had taken her several days to get up the nerve to make it. But she was still tense. Normally she'd be bubbling with excitement when she shared something like this, but she was too worried that she'd inadvertently reveal too much.

"In London?" Jack asked as she picked up her extra hand to play a card from it.

"No, on board."

That got Jack's immediate attention and a laugh. "Good God, not Andrássy! I know he's quite handsome, but he's our cousin."

Judith found the mistake amusing enough to point out, "Too distant to count, actually. What would you add to it, that he's our fifth cousin, sixth, tenth, when they usually stop adding numbers after second? But no, it's not Andrássy."

"Who then? There's no one else aboard except common sailors—oh, no, you don't!" Jack made a sound that was half gasp, half snort. "It's a good thing you mentioned it so we can nip this in the bud *right* now. Your parents will never let you go to a man who doesn't have at least *some* prospects!"

Judith rolled her eyes. "Are you forgetting what happened when I turned eighteen? Half my inheritance from my mother was turned over to me, more money than any one family could ever need. Prospects, I believe, won't be an issue."

"That's beside the bloody point and you know it," Jack was quick to stress.

"You're being a snob."

"I am not! Just realistic. Of course if you intend to elope instead of getting permission, then I won't say another word."

Judith started laughing, couldn't help it. This was not how she'd expected this conversation to go. But at least her tension was gone for the moment, thanks to Jacqueline's overprotective nature.

"You are getting *so* far ahead of yourself, Jack. I didn't say I've found my future husband. I'm just highly intrigued by this man and want to get to know him better, perhaps find a few moments alone with him when we could speak freely. And he's not just a common sailor, he's a carpenter." *And my ghost,* she wanted to add, but instead mentioned what Nathan had told James about his stolen ship.

Jack grinned, which brought forth her dimples. "Alone with him, eh? Are you sure you won't be too nervous to say a word, let alone have a conversation? You've never been alone with a man who isn't a relative."

"I think I can manage. And we're on a ship. It's not as if he can hie off with me or one of your father's sailors or servants wouldn't be within shouting distance."

Jack chuckled. "Point taken. And he does sound quite interesting. His name?"

"Nathan Tremayne."

Jack raised a golden brow so like her father's habit. "I even like the sound of it." But then she speculated aloud, "Judith Tremayne. Judy Tre—"

"I *told* you I'm not—"

"Yes, yes. And *we're* not getting married for at least a year. Doesn't mean you can't take that long to get to know this chap. Besides, options are good things to have, and you'll want lots before the time comes to choose a husband." Then Jack scooted off the bed, scattering their cards and pulling Judith with her.

"Where are we going?"

Jack tossed her some shoes, but didn't bother getting a pair for herself. "I have to meet this young man of yours for myself. Let's go find him."

Judith wasn't about to protest when she hadn't actually seen

Nathan for two days. And she'd looked for him each time she came on deck. But short of sneaking around and looking for him, which she had decided she was never going to do again, she hadn't been able to find him and had concluded that his job was keeping him busy elsewhere.

They found him in the first place Jacqueline looked, in the carpenter's storeroom. Jack knew exactly where it was, but then she'd explored every inch of this ship the last time they'd sailed on it. And learned every aspect of running it, too. Of course, she hadn't given up yet on her goal of being a pirate back then. She'd even tried to teach Judith everything she was learning, but Judith, not sharing the same interest, had only listened with half an ear.

The room was smaller than their cabins, but big enough for one man to work in. Materials weren't stored here, but in the hold. Only a long workbench and a wide assortment of tools were kept in the room. And the narrow cot Nathan had mentioned, replete with rumpled bedding to show he'd been using it.

He was standing at his bench twisting apart old ropes to make oakum from the fibers, which was typically applied between planks in the hull to keep them from leaking. Judith vaguely recalled Jack's mentioning the process. His white shirt was tucked in, half-unbuttoned and sweat stained, the sleeves rolled up. The door had been open, but the room was still hot. His hair wasn't quite long enough to club back, but he'd tied a bandanna across his brow to keep the sweat from his eyes. Some of his shorter locks had escaped it. It made him look roguish, and far too masculine.

Jacqueline, having pulled Judith into the room with her, was definitely caught by surprise, enough to whisper, "You forgot to mention he's a bloody Corinthian and so handsome it hurts the eyes."

Judith's cheeks lit up instantly, but Nathan didn't appear to have heard the whisper. As he turned toward them, he merely stated, "You must be Jack."

"Judy mentioned me? Yes, of course she did. And did she tell you that neither she nor I am getting married this year? Shopping, just not buying yet. Keep that in mind, Nate."

He laughed, that deep rumble Judith had missed hearing. "Has anyone ever told you that you're a little too outspoken for your age?"

"Wouldn't matter if they did," Jack retorted. "Malorys don't adhere to golden rules, we create our own."

He glanced at Judith. "Is that so?"

She rolled her eyes. "For some of us."

Jacqueline nodded toward the rope still in his hand. "That's something you could do on deck where it's cooler. Why aren't you?"

"Maybe I was avoiding meeting up with the two of you," Nathan replied with a slight grin.

"Why? I don't bite—without reason."

"He's just teasing, Jack. I'm beginning to recognize the signs."

Jacqueline glanced between them. "Just when did you two get so well acquainted?"

"We're not," Judith replied with only a slight blush. "We've only spoken a few times."

Jack nodded and told Judith, "I'm going to find Andrássy and see if he actually knows how to use that sword he carries. Don't be too long in joining us on deck." Then Jack actually smiled at Nathan. "It was a pleasure meeting you, Nate." But

she ruined the cordial remark by adding, "Nothing inappropriate happens in this room or I'll have to gut you—if her father
doesn't beat me to it."

Jack left as quickly as they'd arrived. Judith peeked around
the door to make sure her cousin really was going up to the
main deck.

"That was a little too direct," Nathan said.

Judith turned back to him. "That's just Jack being Jack.
She's very protective of me, well, of everyone in the family, actually. It's a Malory trait we all share. But I think she's annoyed
with me now that I didn't mention you sooner."

"You weren't supposed to mention me at all."

"No, your condition was to refrain from saying we'd met
before and I've adhered to that. I told her nothing other than
what you said to her father. But all that sneaking I was doing
behind Jack's back was far too nerve-racking to continue. As
you can see, it's no longer necessary."

"Yes, but how did you manage that?"

"By convincing her that I was interested in you."

He grinned. "That must have been hard to do."

"Yes, it was," she gritted out.

He abruptly tossed the rope in his hand on the workbench
and reached for her. She gasped, but he was just setting her on
the bench. Deliberately disconcerting her again? He must have
remembered how easy that was for him to do. It did put her
closer to him, right in front of him actually, and he didn't move
away to correct that.

Flustered, she demanded, "*Why* do you keep setting me
down on things?"

"It's up, actually, and because you're a half-pint." But he

leaned a little closer to add, "And maybe because I like touching you."

She blushed and jumped down to put some distance between them, only to feel his hands on her waist again. He put her right back on the bench, he just didn't let go as quickly this time. His hands lingered on her waist. And those pleasant sensations were showing up again that had nothing to do with anything except him. She couldn't breathe, couldn't think, waited . . .

"So you like my touch, do you?"

"No—I—"

"Then maybe you'll stay put this time?"

She snapped her mouth shut. How bloody high-handed of him! And he did let go of her now, but too late. She was of a mind to leave but didn't doubt he was persuading her to do just that with his manhandling tactics. Had he hoped her interrogation was done when she didn't seek him out these last two days? Wanted to assure that it stayed that way? Too bad. She was too stubborn to let him manipulate her like that or to give up on getting at the truth.

She was angry now. Not because he didn't kiss her just then as she'd thought he was going to do, but because it appeared he was trying to renege on their agreement.

Not having seen him the last two days, she'd had plenty time to dwell on him and had realized that none of her questions to him had been about smuggling. She'd merely questioned him to satisfy her curiosity about his personal life. So she'd accomplished nothing so far other than to nearly get caught hiding in the hold. By her father no less.

"I've missed you."

She blinked. The anger simply drained away and too quickly, making her realize he could be doing it again. Saying things designed to distract her.

And he wasn't done. "I thought I caught your scent a few times." Then he laughed at himself. "Kept glancing behind me, expecting to see you. I even opened a few doors I was so sure I could smell you nearby. Just wistfulness on my part, I guess."

Her brows narrowed suspiciously. "You know I don't believe a word of that."

He grinned. "I know."

He moved farther away, over to the cot to sit down. She was surprised he hadn't sat next to her again, but guessed the workbench wouldn't support their combined weight. She caught the wince, though, as he sat, making her wonder if he was still in pain from that fight with her father.

"Everything I say is going to be suspect," he continued. "Because you don't know me well enough to know when I'm telling you the truth. If you come over here and sit on my lap, maybe we can change that."

She snorted to herself. *That* didn't sound as if he were in pain. Or he simply knew she wouldn't be doing anything like that. It didn't even warrant a reply, it was such an outrageous suggestion.

Instead, she asked, "How bad was the bruising?"

"Black."

"Still?"

"I think he ruptured my stomach. I can't keep anything down."

Her eyes flared, but she quickly realized he had to be teasing. "Nonsense, you'd be dead by now if that was so." Then she smirked. "Maybe you're seasick. Now *that* would be hilarious, wouldn't it?"

He snorted. "No, just absurd."

"But you've never been at sea this long to know, have you?"

"I was just exaggerating, my way of letting you know what I think of your father."

"Oh."

A compliment to Anthony's prowess in the ring, or a slur? It was unusual to see someone at odds with her father. Her instinct was to defend her parent, but she held her tongue, recalling how rough that fight had been. She supposed Nathan was due a little grouching about it, at least until he was fully recovered, even though by the sound of it he'd started the animosity in the first place. Of course, she didn't know what that had been about. Yet.

"Now I'm craning my neck in the opposite direction," Nathan complained. "At least come sit over here." He patted the spot next to him on the cot.

"On a bed? With you? That's far beyond the pale of inappropriate and isn't happening."

"Close the door first. Who will know?"

Her eyes narrowed. "Stop trying to seduce me."

He shot off the bed and didn't stop until he was leaning into her. "But it's working, isn't it? If you're going to admit to anything, darlin', admit you want me as much as I want you."

Oh, God, did she? Is that what these feelings were? No wonder she was so confused and excited by him by turns. She'd never experienced desire before.

He'd pushed between her legs even though her skirt wasn't wide enough to allow him to get that close. She didn't know

how he'd done it until she felt his hand on her outer thigh—
against her skin. Steadily moving upward and bringing her skirt
up with it.

Simple instinct moved her hand to his to stop its ascent.
And it worked, he just didn't take his hand away, and she
would remember later that she didn't either. She was too deep
in the throes of anticipation. Yet the fear of discovery was present, too, with the door wide-open, when anyone could pass by
and see them. But it didn't occur to her yet to simply push him
away.

His cheek rasped across hers before he bent his head to
breathe deeply by her neck. "There it is again." His lips brushed
against her skin as he said the words, causing gooseflesh to
spread, leaving a trail of tingling sensations across her shoulders
and back. "The smell of ambrosia."

"Jasmine," she corrected breathlessly. "And vanilla . . . with
a touch of cardamom . . ."

"Then it's just you, that's ambrosia."

He leaned up, was suddenly staring deeply into her eyes.
He did that for the longest moment. Such intensity! As if he
were trying to see into her soul. Then he kissed her with such
passion it took her breath away.

"I'm going to hate m'self for this moment of gallantry."
His words brushed against her lips. "But if you don't leave this
second, I'm going to carry you to that bed. That's a promise,
darlin', not just a warning."

Sanity returned with a vengeance, crimson embarrassment
with it. But he didn't move back so she could get down from
the bench without sliding against him. She heard the groan as
she did, just before she ran out of there.

She stopped at the end of the corridor near the stairs, and

the trembling set in. She put her back against the wall and closed her eyes for a moment. Her cheeks were still scalding hot. What just happened?! But she knew, because once again she hadn't got a chance to ask a single pertinent question. He'd found the perfect way to avoid that. He was chasing her away with sex. And what would have happened if she didn't leave? Would he really have made love to her?

Oh, God, she wasn't even near him now and yet that single thought made her knees go weak.

Chapter Twenty-Three

NATHAN LEFT THE STOREROOM before he demolished it. What the bleedin' hell was wrong with him to let her go like that? She'd been his for the taking. He'd seen it in her eyes. And a woman always got soft and friendly—and trusting— afterward. Which is exactly what he needed. But getting angry at himself for letting her go pointed out just how much of a fool she was turning him into.

The saner thought was that he needed to stay far away from her. He'd been managing to do just that, knew very well she was trouble in more ways than one even before her father convinced him of it. Yet he still couldn't get her out of his mind, had found himself thinking of her at all times of the day. He did want her. There was no denying that. He just couldn't have her, and he needed to keep that fact uppermost in his mind.

They could *not* be left alone again. Today proved he couldn't keep his hands off her when they were. The only way to make sure she stopped tempting him like that was to give her the truths she wanted so she'd stop seeking him out. So he went up on deck where he expected to find her. She was there, looking calm and composed. He wasn't, so he decided not to approach her yet and moved to the stern of the ship and took out the extra spyglass Artie had found for him. The first mate was there, too, doing the same thing.

Yesterday Nathan had seen the captain surveying the ocean with a spyglass as well. But James hadn't mentioned the ship that had been trailing them the night the stowaway had escaped, and it hadn't been sighted since then. He'd surprised Nathan by volunteering information of a different sort, saying, "There's a Yank aboard named Boyd Anderson who you might want to have a chat with. Spends a few days seasick every voyage, which is why you might not have noticed him yet. But he can steer you to the people you need to discuss your plan with after we arrive. Might save you some time."

"Appreciate it, Captain."

"Don't mention it. Some Yanks do come in handy occasionally—good God, I need to bite my own tongue."

And he'd left with that odd statement.

Now, Artie lowered his own spyglass and, noticing Nathan, asked, "You've been watching for them, too, mate?"

"Curiosity compels me to."

Artie nodded. "No further sightings. They either got what they were after, gave up—or they know where *The Maiden George* is heading, so they don't need to keep us in view." Then he grumbled, "The day was when we would've circled behind and boarded them—or blasted them out of the water."

"Really?"

The first mate snapped his mouth shut and marched off, obviously unwilling to elaborate—or realizing he shouldn't have said that. Nathan turned to pursue the subject, but spotted Judith instead. She wasn't looking his way but was watching the fencing match between her cousins on the main deck. Leaning against the rail, her back to it, her arms crossed, her red-gold locks were whisked about her shoulders and back by the wind. She was so engrossed in the match that she might not even know he'd come on deck. He could keep it that way—if his feet didn't have a will of their own.

He stopped two feet away from her and watched the fencers for a few minutes. It immediately became apparent that Jacqueline Malory wasn't just amusing herself; she actually knew how to use that thin rapier in her hand. The lunges and feints, the quick responses, she wasn't giving Andrássy much of a chance to do anything other than defend himself.

Incredulous, Nathan asked, "Just what sort of tutors did you girls have?"

"Normal ones."

"Normal for whom? Pirates?"

Judith burst out laughing.

He glanced at her. "What was funny about that?"

"You'd have to know the particulars," she replied, still grinning. "So tell me, when you were a child, what did you want to be when you grew up?"

"Is that a trick question I shouldn't be falling for?"

"No, but when Jack played that wishing game, she decided she wanted to be a pirate. Of course, she's outgrown that notion. Thankfully."

"Are you sure?"

"Yes, quite."

"Yet it appears she mastered one of the skills of the job."

Judith giggled. "I know."

"Did you as well?"

"Goodness, no. We shared the same tutors since we live close enough to. We merely altered the weeks and subjects, one week at my house for literature, geography, and several languages, then the next week at her house for history, mathematics, even a smattering of political science, then my house again, et cetera. We just differed in our personal curriculum. She was interested in fencing, pugilism, and becoming a crack shot, all of which her father was happy to teach her. I was interested in needlepoint and learning to play an assortment of musical instruments. And you?"

"The rudiments of a general education taught at a local church. But I don't believe that she took up pugilism. There'd be no point, since it's not something she could ever make use of."

He caught the smile on Judith's face, which she wasn't directing at him since she'd yet to glance his way even once. Then she confided, "I would agree with you if I hadn't seen her in the ring with her older brother. Jeremy can easily hold his own in a fight. He is like a younger version of my father, but she was still able to beat him. Speed and a few tricks can counter size and brawn." Then Judith laughed. "Of course that only works once. Onto her tricks, Jeremy didn't let her get away with it twice."

Jack might be a few inches taller than Judy, but Nathan still couldn't picture what she had just described. But it did make him wonder if Judith might be good at lying, too, or just good at exaggerating. She still wouldn't look at him. Didn't trust herself? He started to smirk but ended up groaning to himself. He *had* to stop thinking she was as attracted to him as he was to her. It might even just be a ruse on her part to get him to confirm her suspicions. And why didn't he think of that sooner?

A pretty older woman appeared on the quarterdeck, elegantly clad in a hooded, green velvet cloak that she no doubt wore to protect her coiffure from the wind.

"Your aunt George?"

"Yes," Judith replied.

Noting the woman's serene expression as she watched the fencing, he said, "She doesn't mind her daughter's antics?"

"D'you really think she could be unaware of the lessons Jack had from her father? Of course she doesn't mind. She's proud of all of Jack's accomplishments, from never missing what she aims at with a pistol to her grace in a waltz—speaking of which, do you know how to waltz?"

Startled by the question, he quickly turned to look at her and saw she *still* wasn't looking at him. It was starting to annoy him. "Why would I? If you're going to dance, it should be fun."

"You think waltzing isn't fun?"

"Course it isn't, it's just what you nabobs do to make sure you don't work up a sweat. I've seen it. There's nothing fun about it."

"You won't think so after I teach you how. We'll have the lesson here on the deck."

He snorted. "Not bleedin' likely. You can't single me out like that."

"I won't. I'll get Jack involved and a few other sailors, so it will merely appear as if we're just amusing ourselves to counter the boredom of the voyage."

"Do whatever you like, but you can count me out of nonsense like that."

"On the contrary, I'm going to call in my beck-and-call card and insist you learn some manners—at least how to treat a lady. We're merely going to start with the waltz."

"Why? Once I'm off this ship, I'll never be around ladies

again, so your lessons will be pointless. And besides, d'you think I'm not aware that a lady is never left alone with a man? That she has a chaperone at all times? Maybe it's you who needs some lessons, darlin'."

"Our circumstances are—unusual. Or would you rather I ask my questions in front of an audience?"

"You're doing a good job of pretending I'm invisible right now, aren't you? We're talking and we're not alone. Keep it that way and I won't think you're seeking me out for more—"

"Stop it!" she cut in with a hiss. "The things you say, you *know* they are inappropriate."

He chuckled. "But it doesn't appear that we need to be alone for me to say them. Or would you like me to leave until you have someone else standing here with us? An actual chaperone? Like you're supposed to have?"

He probably shouldn't put her on the spot like this. She might be blushing now, but she was unpredictable, too, and adept at turning the tables on him.

"I wasn't suggesting the lessons on proper etiquette begin immediately," she said stiffly. "In fact, right now you're going to tell me why you looked so sad the night I thought you were a ghost."

"We're back to that?"

"Yes, we are, and no evasion this time."

Chapter Twenty-Four

"Answer me," Judith demanded when Nathan stood there without saying a word.

He said instead, "I wonder what Artie and Henry are arguing about."

"You're changing the subject?" she said incredulously. "Really?"

"Yes, really."

Exasperated, she followed his gaze. "You've been on the ship long enough to know those two are always arguing about something. It means nothing. They actually enjoy it. What you may not know is they are not only *The Maiden George*'s first mates, but Uncle James's butlers at his house in London. Yes, they share that job, too. They're also best friends, though at times, like now, it appears otherwise. They used to sail with my uncle. When he retired from the sea—"

"He used to sail regularly?"

"When he was young, yes, for about ten years. But as I was

saying, Artie and Henry retired from the sea with him and became his butlers."

"Two butlers? Is that normal?"

"Not at all normal. But my uncle James isn't a conformist. Artie and Henry were going to draw straws to see who'd be first mate this trip, then decided to just share this job, too. Now—"

Nathan interrupted with the guess "The captain used to be a pirate, didn't he?"

She gasped. "How—did you arrive at such a ridiculous notion?"

"Something I heard Artie say about blasting things out of the water in their day. And you just admitted your cousin aspired to be like her father."

"I said nothing of the sort! Do *not* put words in my mouth."

She couldn't believe he'd guessed so accurately, but that was one thing about her family that was kept strictly in the family and was going to remain that way. James's days of being Captain Hawke, gentleman pirate, as cousin Regina liked to refer to his former profession, were long since over. He'd even faked Hawke's death when he finally returned to England to make peace with his brothers, though that run-in with the pirate Lacross a while back had let a few of his old cronies know he was still quite alive and well. But Nathan wasn't going to be told any of that.

She demanded, "So you think of pirates instead of the military? Yes, of course, a smuggler would."

"Keep your voice down."

"Then don't make statements designed to enrage me. If you want to know about my uncle, ask him yourself—if you dare be that bold. But first, you're going to answer me. Why were you sad the night we first met?"

He sighed. "I wasn't. Disappointed, yes, and if I'm admitting things, a little angry, too. My maternal grandmother had just passed on. I didn't know her well, hadn't even seen her since I was a tyke. She lived alone in London, I lived with my parents in Cornwall. My father and she didn't get along, and she wanted nothing more to do with us after my mother died. So I was surprised when her solicitor tracked me down to hand me a deed to that property."

"Are you saying you actually *do* own the manor?"

"I told you that when you were a child. If I *had* been there this other night when you intruded yet again, I would have done the same thing—simply told you to get out, that you were trespassing."

"I'm to believe this *now*? You had your chance to make the claim of ownership when I asked before. You didn't because it's obviously not true."

"It's a bleedin' wreck of a house."

"One that comes with a lot of land. My cousin Derek would even pay you a fortune for it, so you'd never have to work again."

"Maybe I don't want to sell it."

"Maybe because you don't really own it!"

He suddenly raised a brow at her. "Why so angry, darlin'? Because you found another trespasser in that house, or because you didn't find me when you hoped you would? Are you angry that I'm not your ghost?"

She almost sputtered, but took a quick, deep breath instead. She wasn't even sure why she'd just gotten so angry. Merely because he hadn't confirmed sooner that he was related to Mildred Winstock, who was an aristocrat by birth?

But he wasn't waiting for her to answer him. He continued with a shrug, "It's nothing to be proud of or boast about that I own a house that's falling apart."

"You didn't know it was a ruin until that night, did you?" she guessed.

He barked a short, bitter laugh before he said, "No, I actually went there to take up residence. It was just after the fight I had with my father, which I've already mentioned to you."

"Which led to your leaving Cornwall, yes, but you never said what that fight was about."

"I'd rather not talk about that. It's painful enough that I never saw my father again before he died."

Was that true, or was he just being evasive again? She glanced at him to check the expression on his face and got distracted by how handsome he was. He wasn't wearing a bandanna now, and with the sun shining brightly, his hair looked pure white again as the wind blew it every which way, including across his face, which he didn't seem to even notice.

Something in his expression was angry, but mixed with melancholy, too, which compelled her to finally say, "I'm sorry."

"So am I. At the time, I was angry enough to break ties with him and live on my own, but only because I thought my grandmother had left me the means to do so. What a joke that turned out to be."

"Surely not intentional."

"No, I doubt she ever stepped foot in that house herself and didn't realize she was leaving me nothing but a shambles. It had belonged to my grandmother's grandmother, but according to my mum, my grandmother had been born in London, raised in London, and never left London. It was probably just a nice

excuse for why my grandmother never came to visit us in Cornwall, instead of telling me the truth, that the old bird hated my
father."

Judith was inclined to believe him, which warned her she
probably shouldn't. He might be making all this up to elicit her
sympathy. He hadn't admitted to owning the house the first time
they'd spoken on the ship. And he hadn't mentioned it in any of
their earlier conversations. Then she realized she could confirm
whether what he'd just told her about the house was true.

"What was your grandmother's name?"

"Doesn't matter."

"Actually, it does. I know who the last owner of record was.
If you don't, then—"

He glanced at her sharply and demanded, "Are you this suspicious with everyone?"

"Just smugglers," she said without inflection. "And I notice
you're not offering up a name."

He snorted. "Mildred Winstock. And now you can tell me
how you know my grandmother."

She was surprised how relieved she was to have proof that
he was telling her the truth. Now their earlier encounters in
Hampshire were beginning to make sense to her. His owning the house explained the lock on the door and his claiming
to know the house better than she did, even the cot that he'd
added. Only his telling her not to say she'd seen him there was
odd. And his accosting her. That wasn't how a property owner
behaved. Or that he didn't want the lantern lit again so she
could see who he was. So try as she might to exonerate him in
her mind, she still couldn't, not when so many clues pointed to
illegal activities.

"I didn't know your grandmother," she explained. "My

cousin Derek tracked down the identity of the last owner of record so he could buy the house."

"Why?"

She was hesitant to tell Nathan the truth, but he had to realize what an eyesore his property was, sitting next to a grand ducal mansion. So she said in a roundabout way, "He wants to give it a proper burial."

"It's still standing."

"Barely."

"I know better'n anyone the condition it's in, but I'm not selling it just so your lordly cousin can tear it down. It's the only thing I have left from my mother's side."

She tried to sound cheerful for him as she suggested, "Then repair it."

"I intend to."

"Really?"

"Why do you sound surprised? It's the only reason I mastered carpentry."

Her eyes widened. Derek would probably donate whatever Nathan needed, anything that would improve the view from the back of his home. "You've had five years to get started. If it's a matter of materials—"

"It was, but not anymore. I've been stockpiling what's needed, stashing materials in that hidden room so no one would run off with them when I'm not there. I just wasn't in a hurry to get started with the repairs until recently. I did some work on the roof, I just haven't tiled it yet. I could redo it all in cheap slate, but slate doesn't belong on a house like that."

"You want to match the clay tiles that are currently on it?"

He nodded. "What's left of them. Just didn't realize how expensive clay is. And didn't expect this trip to add to the delay."

"What changed recently to prompt you to start repairing the house?"

"I'm not alone anymore."

Her eyes flared. "You have a *wife*!?"

He burst out laughing. It drew a few eyes their way, Georgina's and Jack's in particular. Jack even slipped up because of it, giving Andrássy his first chance to take the offensive. Jack's sound of exasperation could be heard across the deck.

Nathan noticed, too, and said uncomfortably, "I should leave."

"What you *should* have done was tell me you're married *prior* to kissing me," Judith said furiously. "I *despise* unfaithful husbands!"

He raised a surprised brow at her, but only briefly. He was still glancing about the deck to gauge the damage done from the attention she'd drawn to them. But he said, "That's a bit heated for an assumption, darlin'. Jealous?"

"Not in the least!"

"Then stop yelling at me and look away," he warned, but then suddenly hissed, "Bleedin' hell. Meet me up in the crow's nest tonight and I'll explain why you're mistaken. But I'm not staying for this."

This was James and Anthony. They had just appeared on the quarterdeck and were standing with Georgina now, one on each side of her. But neither was watching the fencing match. They were looking directly at Judith and Nathan instead.

Chapter Twenty-Five

NATHAN DID ABANDON SHIP, as it were, returning belowdecks again. Judith couldn't do the same, not if she wanted to put out the fire before it started. If anyone was going to tear Nathan apart for being *married*, it would be her, not her father. So she pulled up a bright smile, waved at her father, and joined him on the quarterdeck. And did a good job of hiding her fury.

Her father didn't. He was scowling even as he put an arm around her shoulders. "What were you doing with that chap?"

"Debating whether to toss him overboard."

"I'll kill him if he insulted you."

She rolled her eyes. "You say that about every man I talk to. But I was joking, so there's no need for you to kill anyone this trip. He was just shocked by Jack's display of fencing skill. I was merely explaining why and how she came by it."

"None of his bloody business."

"I thought we agreed you weren't going to hate every man I meet. Mother even assured me you wouldn't."

That was pulling out the trump card, and it seemed to

work. Anthony relaxed a little, even chuckled. But Georgina, having heard them, remarked, "Quite a handsome fellow, this one, isn't he?"

"And you noticed this why, George?" James asked.

Georgina laughed. "Am I to pretend to be blind?"

Judith jumped in, "Handsome, but sorely lacking in manners. Still, he's rather interesting."

Anthony looked over Georgina's head to say to his brother, "Blister it, James, did you tell *everyone* about his unusual mission?"

"Only you, old boy," James said, then proceeded to tell his wife about it.

Anthony peered down at Judith and demanded, "Just how did you find out?"

She didn't deny it. "You think his commission to track down ship-stealing thieves is the only thing interesting about him? Yes, I've spoken to him before today, which was when I found out he owns that big old house behind the Wrighton estate. You know the story of it, don't you?"

"Don't believe so."

"I do," Georgina put in. "It was built for the old duke's mistress, wasn't it, and given to her to lure—er, that is, it was a bribe?"

"Incentive, yes," Judith concurred. "She was gentry and a widow, but the duke wanted her closer to him than London, where he'd met and fallen in love with her. Derek found all that out when he tried to buy the property. Mr. Tremayne is the woman's great-great-grandson."

"So he's gentry?"

"Doesn't matter," Anthony insisted in a mumble.

"Course it does," Georgina said, giving Judith a wink. "A

dashing captain *and* a landowner of note, perhaps you should let this one run its course, Tony."

To which Anthony snarled, "James, kindly ask George to *butt out.*"

James merely laughed. Judith took a moment to glance up at the crow's nest, so high in the rigging. Several rope ladders were attached to it, but still, she was *not* going to climb up there tonight. In fact, she didn't care if she ever saw Nathan Tremayne again. But she wanted that to be her decision, not her father's.

So before he warned her off, she told him, "I'm just bored and he's interesting, it's no more'n that. I'm not like Jack, who manages to find dozens of ways to have fun on a ship—steering it, climbing rigging, even fencing."

"Have I been ignoring you, poppet?" Anthony asked in concern.

She smiled. "No, of course not, and you don't need to entertain me. You don't often have Katey to yourself like you do now while Boyd is indisposed. I do understand."

"Doesn't mean you can't join us when Jack isn't by your side."

She giggled, reminding him, "And how often do you think that is?"

Anthony rolled his eyes.

That's when Jacqueline bounded up to them. Out of breath, she hooked her arm through Judith's to drag her away, yelling back, "Time to change for dinner!"

It wasn't, not quite, but no one protested since Jack obviously needed a bath after her exertions. But as soon as they were out of hearing, Jack asked, "Did I rescue you? Do say I did!"

"Possibly. At least, father didn't get around yet to forbidding me to speak to Nathan again."

"As much as he'll try to, you can't let him whittle down your options, Judy. I'm sure to be in the same boat someday, so we have to stick together on this."

"I know."

But Judith did suddenly realize, much too late, that in trying to explain to Anthony why she might be interested in Nathan other than romantically, she'd broken the Bargain with him. Well, not exactly, not if Jack didn't hear that he owned the ruin and put two and two together to conclude that Nathan was their ex-ghost. But she should probably warn Nathan—the devil she would. The way he'd warned her he was married?

Still incensed over that, it wasn't a good time to hear Jack say, "I'm so thrilled for you. He's incredible looking, isn't he?"

"Yes."

"And daring. Chasing after a stolen ship is going to be dangerous."

"Yes."

"Feel free to volunteer more'n yeses."

"He's going to inform the authorities, so he'll have help. It might not be dangerous a'tall."

"Or he might not come back alive."

"Jack!"

"Worried about him already? That smacks of a little more'n smitten," Jack teased.

"No, and, no, in fact, he's got some explaining to do," Judith retorted. "My conversation with him was cut short when our fathers arrived on deck, so I'm going to meet Nathan after dinner to finish it."

"Explaining about what?"

"I'll tell you afterwards. Don't want you going after him with your rapier in hand."

Jacqueline raised a brow. "Sounds like you've already thought of doing that yourself. You're actually angry with him, aren't you?"

"A little. Very well, a lot. But don't try to drag it out of me when it could just be a complete misunderstanding. I don't want you getting the wrong impression based on an assumption."

"Like you have?" Jack guessed. "Goodness, if you're touchy about the slightest things, you *are* smitten. Confess that at least."

Judith didn't, but not answering at all convinced Jack she was right, so at least she didn't get in a huff about not being told everything immediately.

And at least Nathan wasn't mentioned that night at dinner, either. But Boyd was responsible for that. Finally making an appearance, the Yank was back in good health and therefore fair game for James and Anthony. Boyd wasn't just James's brother-in-law, he was also Anthony's son-in-law, so of all the Andersons, he was doubly entrenched in the family. Which didn't stop them one little bit from ribbing him mercilessly throughout the dinner about his seasickness.

"If you need another week in bed, Yank, be assured we'll get along without you," James said. "Won't even notice your absence."

Boyd's malady used to cause him acute embarrassment, shipowner that he was. But he was so used to being the butt of the Malorys' jokes that he took them in stride these days, following the example of his brother Warren, who also came under the gun from these two and either laughed along with them or ignored them. It tended to work.

But James gave ground tonight for another reason. Andrássy was flirting with Jacqueline a little too openly, complimenting her on everything from her hair, her dress—Nettie had won the battle tonight—to her fencing skill. Jack was amused by it. James wasn't. While the ladies might have thought Andrássy had been quite brave to want to defend the family during the stowaway incident, even if he had misjudged the situation, James wasn't going to overlook that Andrássy's interference had given the stowaway the opportunity to escape.

Judith knew that her uncle had had doubts about Andrássy before, but after Andrássy had cost him the answers he wanted, even if unintentionally, any chance of James's warming to their newest cousin had probably been lost.

But Judith didn't spend much time thinking about it, not with her rendezvous with Nathan fast approaching. She didn't even yet wonder why his being married was a worse crime in her mind than his smuggling was. But a while later, she would climb up to the crow's nest to find out what he had to say about it.

Chapter Twenty-Six

JUDITH DRESSED FOR THIS excursion in her ship's togs, even braided her hair to make sure it didn't get in her way during the climb. She'd also left her shoes in her cabin, thinking bare feet would allow for better purchase on the rope rungs. But when she stood by the rope ladder and put her hand on it, she couldn't take that first step. She didn't have to look up to find out how high that crow's nest was. Were the answers she wanted really worth such a daunting climb? The ladder wasn't even steady! It was swaying so much it moved right out of her loose grip.

She stepped back, changing her mind, only to see Nathan drop down to the deck next to her, which explained why the ladder had been swaying.

"Didn't actually think you'd take me up on my suggestion of a tryst in the crow's nest, darlin'."

She was relieved he was on deck instead. "Now that you're here we—"

"Come on." He took her hands and placed them on the

ladder and moved in so close behind her that she had nowhere to go but up. "I have the watch tonight and I can't do my job from down here."

She glanced back. "Then why did you come down?"

"Did you really think I'd let you make this climb alone?"

Actually, she'd expected to have to climb up herself and had assumed he wouldn't even know she was there until she arrived up top. But he must have been watching for her.

He added, "And miss a chance to be your hero and catch you if you should fall—into my arms?"

He'd just added a teasing note to his gallantry. She wondered if he was embarrassed to show her he had this chivalrous side. But she started climbing. She wasn't the least bit nervous now, not with him behind her. And he didn't touch her again, probably afraid it might startle her into slipping—until they reached the nest and she felt his hand on her derriere, giving her a push to get her over the edge.

The crow's nest was shaped like a big tub. Some nests were just flat platforms, some were mere rounded frames, and others were rounded and made of solid wood with planked sides such as this one.

"I'd already volunteered for the watch tonight, or I wouldn't have put you through the ordeal of climbing that ladder," he said as he followed her over the rim.

She stood up and gasped softly at the view. "Oh, my."

The full moon tonight looked so much bigger from up here and was incredibly beautiful. Not long over the horizon, it was still quite huge. Seen from this unobstructed vantage point, with its wavy reflection off the water, it was breathtaking, even highly romantic. She got her mind off that thought rather quickly and turned to Nathan.

But he was still gazing at the moon. "This is why I took the watch when it's not one of my duties."

"What if there had been too many clouds tonight instead?"

He looked at her before he said, "That's the chance you take to see something this beautiful."

She felt warmth in her cheeks, and inside her, too. She couldn't let him distract her with flattery, if that's what his comment was. "I believe you have something to tell me?"

"That I'm not married? I'm not and I've no plans to be. I'm not sure how you came to that conclusion from what I said earlier."

"Because *not alone anymore* doesn't imply family, it implies recent acquisition of family, which tends to mean getting oneself a spouse."

"Not always and not in my case. My sister and her husband died last year in a carriage accident. They had two young daughters that his family didn't want, so I have the care of them now."

For once he wasn't evading answers, but she certainly hadn't expected this one, or to be so relieved that he wasn't married that she was almost giddy from it. "How old are your nieces?"

"Clarissa is seven, Abbie is nine. They're all I have left now in the way of family, and I intend to give them a proper home as soon as I can. But in the meantime, I found a nice couple to look after them. You might even know them." He explained where the girls were, ending with "Ironic, isn't it, that they're currently living in a house your uncle owns?"

"Uncle James only bought that property so he would have a place to store his ship away from the crowded docks of London. But, no, I don't know his caretakers. And why didn't you mention your nieces earlier?"

"My responsibilities are not your concern. Besides, you were painting me only one color—black."

Reminded of that, she retorted, "I haven't seen any shades of gray yet. In fact, I find it irresponsible that you didn't give up smuggling when you became your nieces' guardian."

She was prompting him to deny it, but he didn't. He looked away toward the moon. And she immediately regretted sounding so condemning when she didn't know *all* the particulars.

He might have good reasons for not abandoning what he'd been doing prior to becoming the girls' guardian. Other obligations or debts, or perhaps he simply couldn't afford to quit yet if he'd been putting all of his money into materials for that ruined house. Or he could simply be addicted to the excitement and danger of smuggling, knowing it would mean prison or worse if he was caught. And she shouldn't be angry any longer now that he'd told her he wasn't married. If it was true. Good God, was she ever going to just believe him without wondering if he was lying to her?

"I'm not going to apologize—" she started.

"Course not. Nabobs never do."

"You think *that* excuses you?"

He glanced her way in confusion. "What?"

"It's been established that *you're* gentry. If you think that puts you above the law—"

His laugh was genuine. "Third son of a third son and so far back, no one remembers the lord who used to be in our family. No, I'm not gentry, darlin', and don't wish to be. Call me a blackguard all you want, but don't call me a nabob."

"Actually, you don't have a choice when it comes to family."

He snorted. "If you don't know who your ancestors are, if you can't name them, then it don't matter."

"It's a matter of record—somewhere. You just haven't looked."

"Maybe because it's not something I need or want to know."

Frustrated by his attitude, she remarked on the obvious. "You seem to have a distinct animosity toward the nobility. Why is that?"

"That, darlin', is none of your business."

"This is how you hold up your end of our Bargain?"

"My opinions and sentiments aren't part of our Bargain."

"Well, if you're going to skirt the rules, you might as well know I let it slip to my family that you own the manor house. Not that we met there. And Jack doesn't know yet, so she hasn't made the connection between you and our ghost . . . and the smuggler who accosted me."

"But if it's mentioned to her, she will?"

Judith winced. "Probably."

"You don't keep secrets very well, do you?"

He didn't sound angry, merely disappointed, making her feel awful now. And chilled. She'd cooled off enough from the climb to feel the chill, so she sat down in the crow's nest to get out of the wind. Over the rim of the nest she could still see most of the moon. And Nathan's silhouette in front of it.

"I didn't do it deliberately. Why does it matter if my father, aunt, and uncle know you own the ruined house?"

With the moon behind him now and so bright, she couldn't see his face when he turned to her. He sat down next to her before he said, "I don't want your family seeing me as an equal whether I am or not. I don't make friends with aristocrats."

"It must be extremely difficult, your having to deal with me, then, isn't it?"

"Oh, no. *You*, darlin', are about as big an exception as there can be."

Mollified—well, much more than that actually, after what he'd just said—she felt a sense of anticipation rise within her. They were sitting so close, not actually touching, but she could feel heat radiating from him. It made her a little breathless, a little nervous, too, to be up here alone with him. He was so unpredictable.

To distract herself *and* him, she said, "Tell me more about your nieces. What are they like?"

She saw a shadow of a smile as he said, "Clarissa is exuberant and affectionate. She took after my sister and me with light blond hair. Abbie's hair is a darker blond and she's more the proper little lady. But both girls love ribbons and are always asking me to bring them some. Turn around for a moment."

She wasn't sure why she did as he asked, possibly because she was enjoying hearing him talk about his nieces. But it was her own ribbon he was after. She could tell it was gone as her braid started to unravel.

"Sometimes the girls like to wear a ribbon on this side of their head." He leaned forward and kissed the right side of Judith's head. "Other times they prefer this side." He kissed the other side of her head. "But sometimes they wear the ribbon around their neck, pretending it's a necklace."

She gasped softly when she felt his fingers, so lightly, brush across her throat just before his lips pressed against the side of her neck and not briefly this time. The sensation was so delightfully tingly, she closed her eyes and bent her head to the side to give him better access.

"I figured this would be the least likely place that I'd be tempted to kiss you," he suddenly said, then added with a sigh, "I was wrong."

Her eyes flared wide, but he was already drawing her across his lap to capture her lips with his. Cradled there, her head resting against his arm, he worked the magic she'd twice succumbed to—and sparked the desire she now recognized, too. Her own. She'd spent so much time with him, too often staring at his long, magnificent body. That first day in the hold when he'd been half-naked had stirred up primitive urges in her more strongly than she'd realized. The far too many inappropriate remarks he'd made that had shocked her came back to her now, playing havoc with her innocence. She slipped an arm around his neck and wrapped her other arm around his back as she moved her legs so that she was straddling him. She did all this without thinking while his tongue parted her lips for a deeper kiss.

He groaned. She barely heard it over the pounding of her heart. His hand was caressing her along her thigh, around her derriere, provoking a rush of warm, delicious sensations that she felt too keenly. The material of her britches was so thin, it was as if it weren't there! It was why she'd felt chilled, which wasn't the case now, far from it. But when he cupped her breast, she moaned with pleasure as a wave of almost unbearable heat surged through her. He'd popped a button to get inside her shirt and under her chemise. But she didn't care. All she could think about was arching into his strong hand, gripping his shoulders even more tightly.

She kissed him with abandon, letting her tongue duel with his as both of his hands now claimed her breasts, kneading them gently. She almost screamed when he used a finger of each hand to circle her nipples, teasing her with the softest of touches and making her wild for more. All of her reactions were out of her control. If she had any thought at all, it was a hope that this night wouldn't end.

"You are the sweetest kind of trouble I've ever met, darlin'."

His hands moved to her derriere as he started kissing her again, deeper and then more deeply, and she realized he'd pulled down her britches. The feel of his callused fingers on the softest of her skin had her writhing in his lap, moaning with pleasure as he hardened beneath her.

But some things could still shock her innocent sensibilities, and feeling his fingers move between her legs did just that. She broke the kiss with a startled gasp and pulled back to gaze into his burning emerald eyes. They couldn't look away from each other, and Judith felt she finally knew what it meant to be inti-mate with a man. He leaned forward and kissed her lightly on the lips as he pulled up her britches.

"I won't apologize for wanting you, but this isn't the place for it. Too cold and not soft enough for you. Give me a mo-ment and I'll help you down the ladder."

She said nothing, but she had to disagree. With a moon like the one shining down on them, it was a romantic place for kissing—and everything else they'd done. And irrationally, she felt some regret now for having stopped him.

Chapter Twenty-Seven

NETTIE WAS LEAVING JUDITH'S cabin, having just finished helping Judith dress that morning. Catherine arrived before the door closed, Judith's yellow ball gown draped over her arm and, by the looks of it, nicely hemmed now. Nettie had tried to put the finishing touches on Judith's wardrobe, but Nettie MacDonald didn't see well enough these days to do such intricate work, so Judith had stopped her and had decided to take Catherine up on her offer to do some sewing for her. Catherine had already finished three dresses. She spent a few hours every day in Judith's cabin, working on Judith's come-out wardrobe. And Andrássy hadn't been exaggerating about her skill with a needle. Her work was so fine that Jack was even considering asking Catherine to re-hem her own ball gowns.

Catherine had joined the family at the last few dinners in James's cabin and would probably continue to dine with them for the duration of the voyage. Her behavior had been polite and so pleasant that Judith wasn't the only one who wondered if Andrássy hadn't only exaggerated his stepsister's shortcomings, but had deliberately given them the wrong impression of her. While they believed that she might have rebelled in her earlier years against being thrust into a family she didn't want, which was understandable, her behavior indicated that she'd outgrown that resentment.

Judith turned to Catherine now and suggested, "Why don't you join us on deck right now? We're going to conduct some dancing lessons. It will be fun."

"Surely you already know how to dance?"

Judith giggled. "Of course. Jack and I are going to teach the crew."

Catherine smiled. "Thank you for the offer, but I confess I'm not very fond of dancing. Truly, I am happiest with a needle in hand, so you go ahead without me."

Judith shrugged. "Make yourself comfortable then, either here or with Georgina. She did invite you to spend your days with her."

"Yes, I sat with her yesterday . . . well, until your uncle came in. He makes me nervous, I'm not sure why."

"He has that effect on a lot of people. You just have to get used to him. But Jack's waiting on deck for me, so I must run now."

She didn't run, but she certainly had the urge to. Two days had passed since she'd seen Nathan. She'd done the avoiding this time, staying close to one member of her family or another so if she did see him, she wouldn't be able to talk to him. But enough time had passed for her embarrassment over what had happened in the crow's nest to have ebbed. He'd carried her down from the nest that night on his back. Insisted, mentioning that he didn't want her abraded palms on his conscience.

She hadn't complained about the soreness, but figured he'd guessed that her palms stung because sailors were familiar with rope burn.

He'd only made one inappropriate comment on the way down, telling her in a cheeky tone, "I've dreamed of having your legs wrapped tightly around me, but I enjoyed it more when we were sitting in the crow's nest."

She might have slapped him if she hadn't had her arms around his neck in a choke hold. The man wasn't accustomed to being around gently bred ladies. But two days without seeing him had left her feeling a little bereft, so she'd had a note delivered to him last night, telling him what time to present himself on deck this morning. She didn't mention why, not when he'd made it clear he didn't want dancing lessons.

Jacqueline was already there teaching two sailors to hum a tune. She'd called in three others as well, and even Artie had come over to find out what she was doing. Judith's intention wasn't to single Nathan out, and Jack knew that. The size of the group would assure him of that—if he showed up.

Judith laughed as she joined them, asking Jack, "Is that going to work?"

"Course it will. Besides, there isn't a single musical instrument aboard, so we've no other choice. You do recognize the song, yes?"

Judith answered by humming along while she carefully surveyed the decks without seeming to and even glanced up in the rigging. But there was no sign of Nathan. Jack was ready for a demonstration and grabbed Judith to waltz with her. Jack had even worn her pants so there would be no confusion over who was assuming the role of the man for the lesson.

"Pay attention to the position of the hands," Jacqueline told her audience, "and the distance you must maintain from your partner."

They danced a bit before Judith was forced to whisper, "You were supposed to lead, not make us a bungling pair with neither of us leading. Let's try it this way instead."

Judith let go of Jack and, with her arms still up in the appropriate positions, began twirling about by herself. She even closed her eyes for a moment, imagining that she was dancing with Nathan. But that just brought forth some annoyance because she had expected to dance with him, and he wasn't cooperating by showing up.

Behind her, Jack said, "Artie, you've seen enough waltzing to know how it's done. Come show your men."

"Don't even—" Artie started to balk.

But Jacqueline cut in, "Don't force me to get my father for this demonstration."

"He wouldn't," Artie snickered.

"He would for me. Of course, he'd still be annoyed about having to participate, and he'd take that out on everyone else afterwards."

Artie grabbed Jack's waist and began twirling her, if a little rambunctiously. But Jack started laughing. She was having fun. So was Artie after a few moments. And then Judith spotted Nathan watching from a distance, arms crossed as he leaned against the railing. She waved him over. He didn't budge. If she had to go get him, that *would* single him out. But Jack noticed him, too, and bounded over to him and dragged him forward, starting a lesson with him.

Judith was satisfied to watch them, avidly actually, so she

was startled when Andrássy was suddenly dancing her around the deck. His engaging grin kept her from being annoyed with his presumption that she wouldn't mind.

"You should have let me know you needed a partner," he said, showing her there wasn't much difference between the English waltz and the European version.

"We're not dancing just to dance, we're teaching the crew. But since you're here, we can demonstrate how refined and elegant this dance can be. My father and aunt have been keeping you company?"

"I have enjoyed learning the card games favored in your country. Your father is brutal at chess, though."

"I know." She grinned. "He taught me."

"I could use some lessons on how to beat him, if you are willing."

"Perhaps later today. But I've been meaning to ask you about Catherine. She's been most helpful, even sweet, a far cry from what you led us to expect."

"I apologize. Sibling squabbles perhaps made me sound harsher than I intended. She can indeed be charming when she tries, and I'm delighted she's presenting her best qualities on this trip."

Judith held her tongue, trying not to read too much into that about-face. She had to remind herself that she'd been on Andrássy's side to begin with when Jack and James hadn't been, so she didn't want to start doubting him now. And it was easy enough to believe that Andrássy had only given them the wrong impression due to a recent squabble with his stepsister.

But then he added, "I confess I was more worried that she would become testy simply due to boredom than anything else, but you have come to our rescue in that regard, and for that we both thank you. She is never more content and calm than when she is sewing."

Jack had released Nathan and grabbed another sailor. Nathan didn't stay to watch, though, was walking away. Judith stopped dancing with Andrássy to go after him, telling her cousin, "Thank you for the dance, but I need to get back to our task before these men are called back to work."

She thought she could stop Nathan by skirting around in front of him, but he started to put up his hands to move her aside. Without a word, too. And he looked annoyed, even impatient. Or was he jealous? Jealous? Over Andrássy?

She quickly took his hand instead and thrust it out to her right with hers, then draped her other wrist over his upper arm. "Show me what Jack just taught you."

"No."

She grit her teeth. "This was all for *your* benefit. Don't disappoint me."

He just stared down at her for a long moment. But she could see in his green eyes that he was relenting, before he said, "You looked silly when you were dancing by yourself."

She tried not to grin. "I'm not out to impress, I'm here to teach. And now that we have your hands in the right places—"

"Not the right places for me. Just my opinion, darlin', but I'd much rather be touching—"

"Lesson number one." She leaned a speck closer and hissed, "Keep your risqué thoughts in your head, *not* on your lips."

She started them off. He quickly took the lead, making her wonder if he had done this before, until he said, "If I step on your toes, are you going to cry?"

"It wouldn't be the first time, but a gentleman doesn't usually wear such heavy boots, so do try not to."

But he got back to her previous remark, saying, "I thought you favored honesty."

"I do, just not the sort that might only be shared by married couples."

"So what you're saying is I'd have to marry you before I could speak my mind?"

He was teasing, but she still missed a step. "I see you *do* understand."

He shook his head. "Too extreme. I'll suffer the blushes instead, and yours are too pretty not to see them often."

"So you're choosing to be incorrigible? Never mind, no need to answer what's obvious. But one thing a waltz allows is *polite* conversation while dancing. Let's see if you can keep track of your feet and talk at the same time, shall we?"

He chuckled. "Isn't that what we were doing?"

"The operative word is *polite*."

"Very well, what did you want to discuss politely?"

"What will you do with the manor after it's repaired?"

He raised a brow. "You're allowed to scratch nerves but I'm not?"

"This isn't a touchy subject."

"It is for me."

She sighed, deciding now wasn't the time to persist in her questioning of him, so she was surprised when he added, "I'm going to live in it with my nieces."

"While you work as a carpenter again in Southampton?"

"No, the house comes with land. I was thinking I might try my hand at farming."

She winced for her cousin Derek, knowing he wouldn't like

a farm in his backyard any more than a ruin. But she didn't quite believe Nathan, either. A farmer? She just couldn't picture it. Of course, a man in his position wouldn't need to plow fields himself. Gentlemen farmers hired workers. But she was sure he'd meant tilling the land himself.

So she said, "You're right, the house comes with a lot of land, the tract stretching to the east. Have you considered building houses on it that you could rent out? The income would support you very well."

He appeared surprised by her suggestion. "That's something I would never have thought to do."

She grinned. "Broadening your horizons, am I? Then it's a good thing you met me."

He snorted. "When you're nothing but trouble? And you've spent too much time teaching me something I already know."

She blinked. "The waltz? But you said—"

He laughed as he let go of her. "I'm a quick learner, darlin'. It only took a few minutes for me to figure it out."

"Selective learning," she humphed as he sauntered away.

Chapter Twenty-Eight

T HE TWO TO FOUR weeks Nathan had mentioned to Corky that the trip could take hadn't seemed like such a long voyage to him before they'd set sail, but it did now. Of course, like Corky, he'd never sailed so far from land before. Crossing the Channel between France and England on his runs was nothing compared to an Atlantic crossing. So he hadn't known what this sort of isolation was going to be like. Now he did, and it was hell with such a desirable woman as Judith aboard—a woman who wouldn't leave him alone.

She was dangerous to him in so many ways. She'd gotten him to open up. He couldn't remember ever saying so much about himself to anyone else before. She made him want more for himself. She made him wish their circumstances weren't so different. But the worst thing was that knowing he couldn't have her didn't stop him from wanting her.

He picked his times on deck carefully now, first making sure she wasn't there. But he had been trying to find Boyd Anderson alone for several days now, without having to disturb the man in his cabin. Today he finally saw him, not alone, but on deck.

"The captain suggested I speak with you, Mr. Anderson, if you have a few minutes?"

The woman Boyd was with said, "It's a little too windy for me up here today. I'm going to return to the family."

"You have a beautiful wife," Nathan said as they both watched her walk away.

Boyd turned back to him with a smile. "I know." But then his eyes were drawn to Nathan's waist. "Ask whatever you like as long as you tell me what you have crawling around in your shirt."

Nathan laughed and pulled out the kitten. "It *was* sleeping."

"You weren't going to toss it over the side, were you? They're valuable aboard."

"Not this size they aren't, but no. I found it strolling down the corridor by itself. I looked for its mother for a while, but she's hidden her litter well."

Boyd was still staring at the kitten, curled up now in the palm of Nathan's hand. "I know Artie brought his tomcat along, but I didn't think he was such a romantic that he'd bring along female companionship for him."

"I'd have to agree with that assessment." Nathan grinned. "It's more likely a female jumped aboard on the southern coast, long before we sailed, to have kits this size."

"Well, good luck finding the mother. But don't let my wife see that tiny thing before you do, or she'll want to adopt it. Women can get silly when it comes to adorable babies. Now, I'm sure you didn't want to speak to me about lost kittens?"

"No. The captain, as well as the first mate, both steered me to you. Artie said you're as American as one can be, and I'm going to need American assistance after we dock."

"How so?"

"Are you familiar with the town of New London?"

"It's maybe a half day's ride up the coast from Bridgeport. It's a whaling town and one of our competitors."

"For whaling?"

"No, shipbuilding. My family has owned a shipyard for longer than I can remember. We don't just build ships to add to our fleet, we build by commission as well."

"Would you know if any of those competitors only claim to build ships?"

Boyd laughed. "That's an odd question."

"Not odd when you hear the rest of what I have to say." Nathan explained his situation, ending with "I didn't know the thieves are operating out of a whaling town. The thought of them overhauling *The Pearl* into a whaler turns my stomach. I need to find her before she's sold."

Boyd was shaking his head, his expression incredulous. "A decade of stealing ships right under the noses of the English? I wonder . . ."

"What?"

"Skylark had a ship disappear out of Plymouth harbor in England four years ago. We thought it merely departed ahead of schedule, and when the ship and captain were never seen again, we had to conclude they ran into trouble on the seas."

"If your vessel was one of the stolen prizes, they may have killed your captain if he was still aboard when they took it. The thieves killed a man when they stole mine, so they don't care if anyone gets hurt. But the information I have is that they only steal English ships."

"You can't tell the difference with ours. We got out of the habit of keeping our colors up in English ports after we dock.

Damned lot of rubbish gets tossed on our decks in the middle of the night if we flaunt that we are Americans. Old grudges not forgotten on both sides, apparently."

"But your vessel could have been lost at sea as you surmised. You don't know that it's related."

"We don't know that it isn't. Regardless, while it's probably nothing that can ever be verified, the people you've described still need to be stopped. I don't know anyone in the town government of New London personally, but I have an old friend who settled there who would. John Hubbard and I go way back, and he owes me a favor."

"I'll be sure to look him up then."

"*We* will," Boyd corrected. "I'm going with you."

Chapter Twenty-Nine

FINDING BOTH CATHERINE AND Andrássy in her cabin disconcerted Judith a bit when she returned there to change her clothes. A sailor hurrying past her had dropped a bucket of water, which had splashed all over her. The sailor had apologized profusely, but she understood his haste and sudden clumsiness. He'd probably just noticed the storm heading their way and had been startled by the sudden crack of thunder.

Nonetheless, she smiled at her cousin and his stepsister and said, "Time to batten down, as they're saying topside."

"And that means?" Andrássy asked.

Judith laughed. "I'm not really sure. But if you haven't noticed yet, there's a nasty storm bearing down on us. So you should put away everything in your cabins that might fall when the ship starts rolling and make sure your lanterns are secured and extinguished."

"But I can't work in the dark," Catherine said, annoyed.

Judith ignored the urge to roll her eyes. "A storm isn't the best time to be plying a needle, I would think. Besides, we're all meeting in my uncle's cabin for an early meal. They might be putting out the fire in the galley oven if the weather becomes extreme, so it could be our last hot meal until the storm passes. And do hurry. It's going to be upon us soon."

She realized the moment Catherine was gone that she should have asked her to wait a moment to help her into another dress. Getting out of the one she was wearing proved more difficult than she'd expected. At least one fastener tore as she struggled to twist the dress around to reach the others. With Nettie already warned about the storm and helping to secure the galley, and Jack in the captain's cabin already, getting into another dress was impossible.

She had no choice but to don Jack's favorite garb. At least she got into the britches and shirt in half the time it would take to put on a dress. And in only a few moments she had grabbed everything that was lying about the room and dropped it all into one of her trunks. She finally doused the two lanterns Catherine had been using, grabbed a cloak in case it was already raining, and hurried back to the main deck, which she had to traverse to reach James's cabin under the quarterdeck.

The storm was imminent; the only thing that hadn't yet arrived was the rain. Strong gusts were already upon them, the crew working swiftly to rope down anything that wasn't secure and to lower the sails. A laugh from overhead drew her eyes and made her pause. Nathan was hanging on to the mainmast, working in tandem with another sailor to tie down one of the bigger sails. His shirt had been blown loose from his britches and was flapping about as wildly as his hair, but he looked exhilarated, completely unconcerned about the dangerous storm that would soon overtake the ship.

"You like storms, do you?" she shouted up at him.

He looked alarmed when he saw her and immediately dropped down to the deck next to her. "Why aren't you inside?"

"I will be in a moment. Do you?"

He'd already taken her arm to usher her straight to the captain's cabin. "Love them—at least at sea. On land, I wouldn't even notice. Here, it's a fight against the elements, with Mother Nature cracking her whip, and there's never a certainty who will win in the end. Now—"

The wave cut him off, a huge one that suddenly washed over the deck, knocking them both off their feet. But it actually carried Judith with it. She screamed, her arms flailing wildly, trying desperately to find something to grab onto. She heard her uncle shout her name, but he wasn't close enough to reach her before . . . oh, God, not into the water! She wasn't that good a swimmer, would drown before anyone could reach her in the churning water surrounding the ship.

All of that flashed through her mind before she felt a hand on her foot. Spitting out water, she raised her head to see that she was only mere inches from the side of the ship, which was tipped precariously low to the water. She quickly closed her eyes as water rushed over her face, as the wave receded. Her heart was still slamming in her chest when she opened her eyes and saw water draining through the slats of the railing. As high as the railings were, she might not have washed over the side, but she'd almost been smashed against them. That could have killed her or, at the least, seriously hurt her.

She found out who had saved her when Nathan picked her up in his arms. "That was too bleedin' close."

"Are you all right, Judy?" James asked from beside them.

Nathan *still* didn't set her down! He was holding her so tightly to his chest she could hear the pounding of his heart.

With her uncle peering down at her with a concerned look, she quickly said in a trembling voice, "Yes, I'm fine now."

"Get her inside, Tremayne," James said briskly before he started shouting orders to the crew again.

Nathan carried her up to the quarterdeck. "If you leave his cabin—just don't. You've been splashed enough for one day."

Splashed? Then he'd seen the mishap with the bucket? But she hadn't noticed him on deck and she'd looked for him. She always looked. It was becoming quite annoying how easily he managed to avoid her within the relatively small confines of the ship.

But he didn't give her a chance to ask about it; in fact, she barely had enough time to say, "Thank you—for keeping me on board," before he set her down to open the door to James's cabin and closed it again the moment she was inside.

Anthony immediately noticed she was soaked and walked over to her. "Are you all right? What happened? It's not raining yet."

"No, it's not, but I was splashed by a little ocean spray." Judith grinned slightly to alleviate his concern.

Georgina rose from her chair. "Come with me, Judy. I'll find you something dry to wear."

She nodded and followed her aunt to the bedroom section of the cabin. She wasn't going to mention what had happened when Katey, Catherine, and even Andrássy already looked worried, and the worst of the storm hadn't even arrived yet. She changed quickly with Georgina's help, then spent a few minutes drying her hair with a towel before she braided it again and joined her family to wait out the storm.

Jacqueline nodded at her, but was already playing a game

of whist with her mother, Katey, and Boyd at one of the card tables.

Anthony had been waiting for Judith to start up a game at the other table with Andrássy and Catherine and called her over. "Where have you been? What delayed you, poppet?"

"I had trouble changing." It was a pet peeve that she couldn't dress or undress herself without help. "One of these days high fashion will take into account a shortage of maids."

"I wouldn't count on it," Catherine said with a slight smile before her expression turned tense again.

Andrássy didn't seem relaxed either. Neither Benedek had experienced a storm at sea before. Judith hadn't either. Her first voyage had been smooth all the way. Georgina looked anxious, too, but then James was still on deck and she wouldn't relax until he joined them. Jack was her usual exuberant self as if she weren't even aware of the storm. Boyd seemed calm, apparently only concerned about Katey, whose hand he was holding.

Judith wasn't worried about the storm anymore, even though she'd almost been swept away in it. Her outlook didn't change even when the ship started rolling and dipping. Witnessing Nathan's attitude toward the storm had given her an odd sort of calm now that she was safe and dry in the cabin. But at one moment the table tipped so sharply that the cards slid halfway across it before the ship righted itself—and her mind flew to Nathan, hoping he was holding on during pitches like that. But she merely had to remind herself that *he* was having fun out there and, with so many years at sea, would know what precautions to take.

The card games, which were supposed to take people's minds off the weather, succeeded for the most part. Boyd, an old hand at sailing, assured them that the more violent a storm was, the quicker it would blow past them. Judith didn't find that particularly reassuring, but it held true. The storm was strong enough to pass over them in under an hour, leaving behind a gentle spring rain that didn't last long either.

There was cause for celebration afterward. Nothing had got damaged and the strong winds preceding the storm had pushed them ahead of course, even though the sails had been down during the rough weather. But celebration meant extra wine at lunch and again at dinner. So Judith was feeling quite sleepy by the time she retired for the night. Wearing a dress once again and waiting for Nettie to arrive to help her out of it, she lay back on her bed and was almost asleep when she heard the knock at the door.

"You don't need to knock," she called out to Nettie.

"I think I do" came back in a low baritone.

With a gasp, Judith flew off the bed and to the door to yank it open. Nathan stood there, his clothes neat and dry and his hair combed back but still wet, though apparently from a bath. He looked a little abashed, though she couldn't imagine why until she noticed one of his arms was behind his back, as if he was hiding something from her.

But her eyes went to his when he asked, "You weathered the storm all right?"

Had he really come to ask that so many hours after the storm had ended? "Yes, quite, but I think I have you to thank for that, too. After seeing how much you were enjoying yourself out in the midst of it, I didn't find it nearly as frightening as I thought I would."

"So you weren't frightened *for* me?"

She wasn't going to admit that she had briefly been or that

she'd sought out Artie the moment the rain stopped to ask if all hands were accounted for. She raised a brow instead to say, "Are you fishing for a declaration of concern?"

"A bit too obvious, am I?" he said with a grin.

"A little. Now, what have you there that you appear to be hiding?"

"Come closer and you can see," he suggested with a roguish lift of his brows.

"Or you can just show me," she retorted.

"But that's not as fun."

The man was incorrigible. He wasn't trying to conceal the humor in his eyes, either. She was no stranger to teasing, her family being quite prone to it, but this sort of teasing wasn't at all the same and too closely resembled flirting of the more rakish sort. It flustered her. It made her blush. At times it made her feel positively giddy. Tonight she fought the urge to simply laugh, which warned her she might be getting too used to Nathan's risqué form of teasing.

But then she felt his hand lift hers and the sudden warmth he placed in her palm. She glanced down and blinked at the white ball of fur she was now holding, then laughed a moment later when it uncurled and she realized what it was. Looking up at her was the most distinctive little face, with silver streaks fanning across its cheeks and up its brow, large, green eyes rimmed in black as if painted with kohl, and a black button of a nose. More silver streaks were on its bushy tail, but otherwise, it was all white.

She couldn't take her eyes off it, even as she wondered aloud, "And what am I supposed to do with a newborn kitten?"

"Feed it, pet it—love it. You know, what you usually do with adorable things."

That answer sounded a little too personal, as if he weren't

talking about the kitten at all. And she did find his green eyes back on her when she glanced up at him.

She had to clear her throat to say, "Of course I'll keep it, if you'll promise to bring me fresh milk each day from that dairy cow in the hold."

He wasn't expecting to hear that. "You want *me* to milk a cow?"

She grinned. "Did you think you wouldn't have to do that if you took up farming? Farms usually do keep livestock on hand."

He snorted, but he didn't refuse the stipulation. Not that she would give him back the little gift if he did. It was too late for that. And she was sure he'd figure out soon enough that he could get the milk from the galley after someone else had milked the cow.

"And what have ye there, hinney?" Nettie asked as she finally arrived.

"A new addition to my cabin."

That Nettie immediately looked Nathan up and down after that answer had them both laughing. But the old girl took the kitten from Judith and held it up for examination. "Och, what a bonny-looking wee one. I'll fetch some grain from the galley fer a box that it'll be needing."

"Sand works, too," Nathan mentioned. "And we've plenty of that barreled for ballast. I'll bring you a few buckets full tomorrow."

Nettie entered the cabin with the kitten cuddled in her arms. Judith took a moment to tell Nathan, "Thank you for the gift."

He shook his head. "It's not a gift, but a favor you're doing me, taking it off my hands."

"You don't like cats?"

"Never gave them much thought, but I was starting to like that one a little too much, after caring for it for the last few days."

"Ah, and it's not a manly pet, is it?" she guessed.

"You really think that would matter to me? I've just got things to do once we land and can't be taking a kitten along, so better to get rid of it now. And you're the only one I could be sure would give it proper care."

"Sure, are you? Why?"

"Because I've never met anyone as kind as you are, darlin'. So take good care of our kitten."

She gasped after that sank in. "*Our* kitten? I'm not just babysitting it. It's mine now!"

But whether he'd heard her or not was debatable, since he'd already walked away.

Chapter Thirty

J ACQUELINE WAS HAVING ANOTHER match with Andrássy on the main deck this morning. Judith was watching them from the quarterdeck. It was such a warm spring day her aunt and sister had come out to join her, standing on either side of her.

"How's Nettie's cold, any better yet?" Georgina asked Judith.

"Her sniffles are abating, but she had a fever last night, so at least she's agreed to stay abed now. Catherine offered to finish my last gown in Nettie's room to keep her company, and I'll be sitting with her this afternoon."

"Not too close," Katey warned. "Can't have you catching a cold, too, when you'll probably be at your first ball before week's end."

Then Georgina remarked casually, "I haven't seen your young man since he thrust you into the cabin the day of the storm."

Neither had Judith, at least not enough to suit her. And she'd thought she had come up with the perfect plan to make long moment before he said, "You have incredible eyes," then spoiled the compliment by adding, "It's too bad your father has them, too."

She grinned. "Are you going to tell me I remind you of my father?"

"No, he reminds me of you."

"You've had more words with him?"

"Just nasty looks. But I'm not fueling that fire by being seen with you again."

Having said that, he left before she could think of a reason to extend the visit. She went to the door to call after him, "What about Silver for a name?"

"That'll do," he replied without looking back.

So frustrating, and the trip *was* almost over. Three to five more days depending on the winds, she'd been told last night at dinner. She had the feeling once they docked, she'd never see Nathan again. Yet she still wasn't completely certain that he wasn't a criminal. Well, obviously she was leaning toward not, or she would never have formed this tentative bond of friendship with him.

She could trust him to protect her if she needed protecting. That said a lot. She could trust him not to endanger her family anymore—if he'd been doing that. Yes, they had become friends—of a sort. And he probably knew by now that she wouldn't turn him in if he did admit he was a smuggler. But was he really going to go back to that career if he *did* get his ship back? When he had two young nieces depending on him? She should ask him that at least—if she was ever alone with him again.

Georgina, still waiting for a reply to her remark, added, "Would you like me to invite him to dinner?"

sure she did see him every day for the remainder of the trip. The milk she'd asked him to deliver for the kitten. But twice now she'd returned to her cabin to find fresh milk already there, and Nettie wasn't the one bringing it. Once Nettie answered the door and took the bowl from him, then promptly closed it again with a mere "Thank ye, laddie." Just one time was Judith actually alone in the cabin when he showed up, yesterday, their twelfth day at sea.

She'd just changed into her ship's togs, which she was re-signed to wearing for a few days until Nettie recovered, when Nathan had knocked on the door. He'd handed the bowl of milk to Judith and brushed past her to enter the cabin without a by-your-leave. Without even making sure first she was alone! And he went straight to the kitten.

Picking it up and setting it in his palm, which it fit in with room to spare, his hand was so big, he'd asked, "What did you name it?"

"I didn't."

"Why not?"

"Because I couldn't tell what it is. Do you know?"

"Never bothered to check. I was just calling it Puss."

"And I've just been calling it Kitten."

He flipped the kitten over to examine it, then laughed. "I can't tell either. Something neutral then for a name?"

"Such as?"

"Furball? By the looks of it, it's going to have longer hair than normal."

She shook her head. "I'd take exception to that name if I were a female kitten."

He glanced at her, but if he'd been about to say something, he didn't. He seemed to be caught by her eyes instead. It was a

"Good God, no—and he's not my young man."

"Really? I got quite a different impression the day you spoke of him, that you were forming an attachment."

"No, I—no."

"Haven't made up your mind?"

"My father doesn't like him. Putting them in the same room isn't a good idea."

"Who are we talking about?" Katey wanted to know.

"Nathan Tremayne," Georgina answered. "Have you met him yet?"

"Briefly. Boyd is quite looking forward to assisting him. In fact, he intends to desert me as soon as we land and hie off to New London with the chap. What about James?"

Georgina laughed. "Oh, I've no doubt he'd love to get involved in that. He'd much prefer to jump into a fight of any sort than attend parties—if the parties weren't for Jack and Judy. Boyd shouldn't miss them either."

"I don't think he expects to be gone long," Katey said. "A few days at the most."

Listening to them, Judith realized that what Nathan had told her about chasing down his ship had to be true. Why make up a tale like that and enlist others' aid if it wasn't? In fact, most everything he'd said about himself was probably true. But had he ever clearly stated that he wasn't a smuggler? No, she didn't recall his being clear about it one way or the other, just evasive.

Later that night, she checked on Nettie once more before she retired, but the old girl was fast asleep so she didn't disturb her. Entering her own cabin a few minutes later, already pulling off the ribbon that held back her hair, she was halfway across the room before she noticed she wasn't alone and came to an abrupt halt. Nathan was there, slouched down in the reading chair, his head slightly tilted, a lock of hair over one eye, his hands folded across his belly, fingers entwined. He was sleeping! And the kitten was smack in the middle of his chest, stretched in a classic upright pose, legs bent, head up, eyes closed. She could hear it purring from across the room.

Incredulous, she sat on the edge of her bed and just stared at them, so much feeling suddenly welling up in her that tears nearly came to her eyes. The two of them made such a heart-warming picture, sharing contentment, love, and trust. The kitten had obviously made its choice about which human it wanted. She was going to have to give it back to Nathan, per-haps when he was done with his business in America. She knew where in England she could find him to do so. So perhaps this trip wouldn't be the last she ever saw of him. She found that thought more than comforting.

She was loath to disturb them and didn't do so immedi-ately. The light next to Nathan wasn't bright. It merely gave the cabin a soft glow, but it allowed for a thorough scrutiny. It was breathtaking how handsome he was. She'd been entranced by his appearance even when she'd thought him a ghost. But as a flesh-and-blood man he could stir her in uncounted ways. Sleeping, he looked endearingly boyish. Awake, he was fascinat-ing in just how masculine he was in size and strength. He was roguish, for sure. Outrageous, too. Yet, if he did ever behave in a gentlemanly manner, she'd probably tell him to stop it. Had she really gotten so accustomed to him with all his rough edges?

With a sigh, she finally approached and carefully picked up the kitten and set it down by the milk Nathan had brought tonight. Then she gently nudged his shoulder and moved back, in case he lashed out when he was awakened, as some men did.

But his eyes opened gradually, looked at his chest first, where the kitten had been, then landed on her and opened wider.

He sat forward and stretched before he said somewhat abashed, "Sorry. I thought I'd be out of here long before you finished your dinner."

"The purring probably lulled you to sleep. It is such a pleasant sound. So you're still avoiding me?"

"When I have to fight myself tooth and nail to keep my hands off you, I thought it best."

Trust him to say something designed to make her blush. True or not, he grinned when the blush arrived, causing her to point out, "That's hardly adhering to our Bargain."

He raised a brow. "I'd think you'd be out of questions by now."

"Not quite. For instance, having told me you're responsible for two little girls who have only you to depend on, are you going to give up smuggling for them?"

"You *still* haven't let go of that notion?" he said, clearly exasperated. "If I ever was a criminal, I'm not one now. I'm going to retrieve my ship or die trying. What I do with her afterwards I haven't decided. But I promise you there's no noose waiting for me in England or anywhere else."

"I believe you."

He was suddenly looking at her in a completely different way. He stood up, cupped her cheeks in his large hands. "Do you really?"

"Yes."

He took her by surprise, hugging her. In relief? Possibly. But when she looked up at him, something else entered his expression. What happened next seemed a natural explosion of the senses. He didn't just kiss her, he brought her up to his mouth, lifting her off the floor, wrapping her legs around his waist to keep her there, pulling her so tightly to him she felt engulfed by his masculinity. And thrilled beyond measure. She'd been wanting this more than she realized, wanting to feel him like this, to embrace his passion and revel in it.

She wrapped one arm around his neck and slid her other hand up through his hair, gripping a handful as she returned his kiss with a fervency she scarcely recognized in herself. She didn't even realize he'd walked them to the bed until he laid her down on it. But she held on tight, dragging him down with her, unwilling to let him go for even a moment. Feeling him hard between her legs was so unexpected that a groan of desire escaped her. He moved off her so quickly, she might as well have burned him.

He was halfway off the bed when she realized he was leaving her and said, "Don't go."

She didn't want the kissing to end. He must have thought she meant something else because he glanced back at her with such yearning, and at that moment she realized she did. She smiled slightly. He made a sound as if he were in pain as he gave in.

He came back and straddled her hips so he could easily remove her shirt. It still wasn't easy. The chemise that followed was. Then came the blush and the moment of indecision. He was watching her, his eyes locked to hers as his hands began to explore what he'd uncovered. She was mesmerized by the desire she saw, then by what she felt, so tender at first, then the kneading, fanning the fire, then the flick of his finger against her nipple that sent shocks clear to her core. She wanted, needed to touch him, too, but all she could reach was his thighs, spread apart, one on each side of her.

She caressed them while he literally tore out of his shirt. She heard the rips and almost laughed. He moved off the bed to step out of his pants, but was back in a moment, at her side now, much better. She could reach his shoulders, his neck, his hair. It felt like silk against her chest when he leaned down to fill his mouth with her breast. She gasped at the heat that rushed through her body. Oh, God, the swirl of his tongue against her nipple before he sucked hard drew gasps from her, evoked another groan. He didn't pull away this time. Now, he seemed to know the sounds she was making were expressions of pleasure, not a plea to desist.

He was taking his time now, caressing her breasts and stomach, her neck and arms, as he kissed her, wanting to know every part of her that he could. Her shoes and britches came off so gradually she barely noticed because far too many other sensations were surprising and delighting her. Riddled with calluses, his hands weren't soft. But his lips were. They felt like molten velvet as they moved over her body. But the two opposite sensations—one excitingly rough and the other seductively soft—had such an amazing effect, arousing her and soothing her by turns, fanning her passion even hotter.

He rolled over to his back, taking her with him and placing her on top of him. She liked the position she was in with her knees resting on either side of him because it gave her better access to his wide chest, where she could feel the muscles ripple beneath her fingertips. She was delighted to discover that his nipples were just as sensitive as hers. But he didn't let her stay there for long. He flipped her onto her back again. He bent one of her legs at the knee and she did the same with the other as he slid his chest up hers for a deep, penetrating kiss that seemed to draw moans from her soul.

His voice was raspy as he said, "You can't imagine how often I've thought of this, nigh every bleedin' minute, but nothing in my wildest dreams could have prepared me for what you make me feel. Do you feel it?"

With his mouth hot on her neck again, sending involuntary tremors throughout her body, she could barely think much less answer. But she gasped out, "What I feel is—akin to joy—"

He leaned up with a grin. "Really?"

"And so much frustration I just want to choke you!"

"You know why you have that urge?"

"Yes, I believe I do."

"Then have at me, darlin'. Or better yet . . ."

His idea of "better" was to entwine his fingers with hers and kiss her hard just before he entered her. This is what she'd been dying for. If she cried out, it was lost in his kiss, but she didn't think she did. Their joining was too smooth, too quickly done, and far too welcome. And with that thick heat filling her, she didn't move, just wanted to savor how deeply satisfying it felt. He accommodated her, holding himself perfectly still except for his mouth moving over hers. All he was doing now was kissing her deeply but tenderly.

So sweet of him to do that, but she'd had her moment to relish him and now every nerve in her body was clamoring for more. Her muscles flexed around him. He began to move, thrusting slowly into her at first, but she gave him every clue that that wasn't enough. Her grip on his shoulders tightened as she moved with him now, wildly as if she were being pushed toward some unknown precipice. But when it arrived, that indescribable burst of ecstasy, washing over her in waves, throbbing in her heart and loins, she merely held on tightly and rode out the storm until it vanquished him as completely as it did her.

His breathing rasped by her ear, his face dropped to the mattress over her shoulder. He was still trembling. Feeling it brought a smile to her lips. But when he finally rose up, he moved up toward the head of the bed, drawing her with him. With all that cavorting across the mattress, they hadn't been anywhere near the pillows until now.

With his arm around her and her cheek resting on the side of his chest, he assured her, "I'll go before dawn. Let me just hold you for a while."

In answer, she put her leg over his. She didn't want to talk. She'd never felt so deeply satisfied and—happy. Yes, happy. That was the glow she was basking in.

So she was almost asleep when she heard him say, "I'm never going to forget you. I want you to at least know that."

Beautifully said, but it sounded like a good-bye. It probably was. She knew these were stolen moments. But he didn't know she now had every intention of seeing him again when this trip was over.

Chapter Thirty-One

"SINCE WHEN DO *you* sleep the day away?" Jacqueline complained as she plopped down on the bed.

Judith curled into a ball, turning away from Jack and pulling the blanket up to her neck. "On those rare occasions when sleep eludes me, of course. Now go away."

"But—"

"A few more hours or I'll be yawning all day."

"Fine, but I'll be back if you're late for luncheon," Jack said, and flounced out of the room.

As soon as the door closed, the kitten jumped up on the bed and tickled Judith's nose with its whiskers. "Shoo. I'm not getting attached to you if I'm giving you back to him."

The kitten didn't obey, just settled down on the pillow next to hers. Judith hadn't been asleep. She had been awake for several hours. She had just been too content with her dreamy thoughts to want to get up yet. She could have spent the entire day in bed just thinking about last night. She should at least have gotten dressed, though, before someone showed up. Explaining to Jack why she was naked wouldn't have been easy when their cabins weren't overly warm.

She should probably have some regrets that she'd stepped so far beyond the pale, but she didn't. Not one. But she did wish Nathan had still been there when she woke. Actually, she wished he could be beside her every morning when she woke. But that required a commitment he wasn't interested in making. She shied away from that thought. Anything was possible and she wasn't done with Nathan Tremayne yet.

She rose and dressed quickly before Catherine made an appearance, too. She couldn't help smiling when she found her clothes from yesterday scattered about the floor. Jack was rather messy in that regard so it wasn't likely that she had noticed. Nettie would have. Judith was so neat she actually folded her dirty clothes before putting them in the pile for washing. And she might have to do the washing herself if Nettie didn't recover soon.

Catherine did indeed arrive before Judith vacated the room and went right to the wardrobe to put away the final gown she had finished. Judith was making her bed, but gave her a cheery smile. She hoped that wasn't going to be a problem today, not being able to stop smiling, even when she was alone.

Catherine paused for a moment to ask, "Are we sure this is the last gown? Your maid said it was, but she was sneezing when she said it, so she might not have checked all your trunks."

"I'll need a sailor to move the top chests so I can check the lower ones," Judith said.

She knew just the one to ask. Another smile, this one quite brilliant. But she had no *reason* to smile over what she'd just said. This bubbly happiness she couldn't seem to tamp down *was* going to be a problem.

Catherine nodded. "Which evening gown are you going to wear for the last dinner? I'm surprised your family wants to dress formally for it."

"The yellow and cream I think." Judith had put that one away yesterday, so it was still fresh in her mind.

"You have jewelry to complement it? If not, I have an amber pendant you can wear."

Judith chuckled. "I have every color gem there is, but I'm not sure if I brought my amber. Since we've had no reason to wear jewelry thus far, I can't remember everything I threw into my jewelry box for the trip."

"I can check if you like. Where do you keep it?"

Judith laughed again. "I'm not sure of that either! It's in one of the trunks. You didn't see it when you were taking the gowns out?"

"Your maid has been putting the ones that still needed work in your wardrobe for me, which is where I have been hanging the gowns I finished so she could put them back in your trunks."

"I'll find it when—"

"You there!" Catherine called to a sailor who was passing by in the corridor. "We could use your help, if you please." Turning to Judith, she said, "You look for your jewel box while I make sure all the gowns are indeed done."

Judith sighed. So much for getting Nathan back in her room with a legitimate excuse. She easily spotted her jewelry box in the third trunk she opened. But when she opened the box, she drew in her breath. "They're gone!"

Catherine, still bent over a trunk, said, "Who is, dear?"

"My jewelry, all of it!"

Actually, not all. She was relieved to see her most valued

possession was wedged in a corner of the box, the tiny grass ring Jack had made her when they were children. Jack had one, too. They'd spent all day making them for each other. They had worn them for months until the rings had started to unravel and Judith had put hers away to preserve it. Even though it was too small to wear anymore, it was still precious to her. And, thankfully, worthless to a thief.

But everything else that had been in the box was worth a fortune because Roslynn had gone quite overboard in ordering extravagant jewelry for Judith's come-out. Her mother's bane was that her husband never allowed her to contribute any part of her large fortune to their living expenses. Anthony insisted on paying for everything. So she spoiled her children with gifts they didn't need, but it made her happy to do so.

Catherine peered over Judith's shoulder at the empty box. "Could the jewelry have spilled out in the trunk? Perhaps during the storm?"

"Actually, one trunk did slide off the pile that day. It got dented, but it was latched so it didn't open."

Judith dug into the trunk to check. It only took a moment. The jewel box had been filled to the brim because of the three large tiaras in it that took up so much room, and two tiered necklaces in hard settings that wouldn't bend. Any one of those would be easy to spot among the clothes. But just to be absolutely sure, she took every single gown out of the trunk and even shook them. No jewelry fell to the floor.

Judith sighed. Catherine put an arm around her shoulder. "Don't assume the worst yet," she said encouragingly. "Ask your maid first. She might have moved your jewelry for some reason. Servants that old sometimes forget to tell you what they've done."

Judith shook her head. "No, Nettie might be old but her mind is as sharp as a tack. I've been robbed. You might want to check your jewelry as well. I doubt I was singled out for this."

Catherine gasped. "But I can't afford to replace my jewelry! Go tell your uncle immediately. The ship will have to be searched to find the culprit and recover everything he took before we land. He can hide it, but it's still on board somewhere."

Judith nodded. At least she didn't have to worry about smiling any more today.

Chapter Thirty-Two

JUDITH RAN TO THE captain's cabin, but James wasn't there, so her father, who was playing chess with Andrássy, sent a sailor to fetch him. Jacqueline, red-faced with anger—that *would* be her first reaction—ran out immediately to check her cabin. Katey followed to check hers. Georgina quickly determined that her jewel box hadn't been touched, but no one expected her jewelry to have been stolen because the captain's cabin was never empty.

"Could this have happened at home before we sailed?" Anthony speculated.

"I don't see how," Judith said. "My trunks were packed and delivered to the ship the night before we sailed, and our servants handled that. And all of my trunks were locked and were still locked when I got to my cabin. I carried the key. And I didn't actually unlock my trunks until later that day, after we were out to sea."

"So you haven't opened your jewel box since we've been aboard? Until today that is?" her father asked.

"No, there was no reason to."

"What baubles did you bring along for the trip?"

"Too many. All the full sets mother just had made for me, diamonds, sapphires, emeralds—"

"Good God, she didn't!"

"Yes, of course she did. And I packed the pearl tiara you gave me, the choker Jaime—"

"I'll get you another tiara, poppet."

"But I remember your giving me that one on my sixteenth birthday, and how pleased I was to have my first grown-up piece—"

Anthony hugged her tightly. "Baubles can be stolen, love, but memories can't be taken away. You'll always have that one."

She gave him a teary smile but it didn't make her feel any better.

Catherine rushed in, going straight to her brother, crying, "They took everything, Andrássy! Everything of value I had left. Do something!"

Andrássy appeared embarrassed by his stepsister's over-wrought state, but he put his arms around her to comfort her. "I'll buy you some other trinkets."

"You can't replace my mother's brooch. You have to find it!"

Jacqueline burst in next, snarling, "I'm going to gullet who-ever did this!"

"So yours are gone, too?" Georgina asked.

"Every last bloody jewel. This is going to *ruin* our come-out. Without proper glitter, a ball gown is just another dress. I am *so* furious!"

"Of course you are, dearest," Georgina said soothingly. "And you'll wear my jewelry if it comes to that."

But Jack wasn't easily appeased, huffing, "No offense, Mama, but your baubles are *old-fashioned*."

Georgina rolled her eyes. "Jewelry is *never* old-fashioned."

Katey came in next with Boyd and, with a sigh, said, "Mine are gone, too."

Anthony exclaimed, "Does *no* one lock their bloody door except me?"

Katey, the only one who had been robbed and did not appear upset about it, said, "Goodness, no, whatever for? It's a private ship filled with family."

"And a thief."

"Well, yes, obviously."

Andrássy, still trying to comfort Catherine, who was crying, asked, "Could it have been that stowaway?"

"No," Katey replied. "My jewelry was all still accounted for after that incident."

Judith dried her eyes with a handkerchief Georgina had given her and went over to Catherine. Judith felt bad for her. The rest of them could easily replace their losses. Judith and Katey had their own wealth, and Jack had eight uncles and two adoring parents who would fill her jewelry box to the brim again. But Catherine was dependent on Andrássy, who supported both of them with his inheritance. He was going to America to rid himself of his stepsister so Judith doubted he would willingly incur the expense of replacing all of Catherine's stolen jewelry.

Judith slipped her arm around Catherine's waist and took her aside, pointing out, "All isn't lost yet. It's an outrage that this happened, but our possessions are still on the ship somewhere, and no one is getting off it yet. And thanks to you, we found out much sooner than we might have, so there's plenty of time to find what was taken before we dock."

"You're right, of course. I shouldn't have let myself get so emotional. It's just that the broach is all I have left from my mother. I'll be devastated if I don't get it back."

"But you will, I promise."

"What happened?" James asked as he walked into the room, but too many of them started to talk at once, so he bellowed, "George!"

Georgina tsked at his tone and asked, "What took you so long?"

"Artie had trouble tracking me down, since I was up in the crow's nest. He said one of my crew has turned into a jewel thief?"

"I would guess the opposite, that our thief pretended to be a sailor. It was too neatly done, and too thorough. Aside from myself, *all* the women in this room were robbed, and none of them realized it until Judith found her jewel box empty a quarter of an hour ago, and they went to check theirs. That doesn't smack of a sailor acting on impulse. That's *four* different cabins snuck into, James."

Judith saw her uncle's gaze drift over to Catherine and then to Andrássy. Catherine must have noticed that James was looking at her because she leaned closer to Judith and whispered, "I didn't do it, I swear! I know Andrássy told your family I was rebellious when I first arrived at his home. He might even have mentioned that I used to take things in anger to get back at my mother, but I was just a child then, for God's sake, and I never took *any*thing of value. I—I can't imagine why he would even mention it, it was so long ago."

Judith couldn't either, for that matter, if Andrássy had actually told a member of her family that—unless he had done it to deliberately plant a seed of suspicion in his mind. For this? Good God, was Andrássy even who he said he was? They knew he was living off an inheritance only because he'd told them that. And James and Jack had both had doubts about him. Judith had staunchly defended him, but it wouldn't be the first time she had misjudged someone's character. Look how wrong she'd been about Nathan.

"It's been determined that at least some of the thefts oc- curred within the last week," Georgina was saying.

"Within the last four days, actually," Katey clarified. "I'm sure that's how long it's been since I took my amethyst earrings out of my jewelry box to wear to dinner. They simply go too well with that lilac dress I wore the other night. You'll have to replace them, Boyd."

"No," Boyd said, but quickly added with a chuckle, "I'd much rather find you the originals and I will."

"Indeed," James agreed. "All of the missing jewelry will be found before we dock. I want all of the baggage searched, and every inch of your cabins scrutinized. And because one tends to overlook things in familiar surroundings, I want a fresh set of eyes in every room, so you take Boyd and Katey's room, Tony. Boyd will take Andrássy's, and, Andrássy, you take Tony's room. Katey, you take Catherine's room. Jack and Judy, you switch with each other. Catherine, you can help my wife, since this is the largest of the cabins. Look into every nook and cranny, dear ones. The thief might be hiding his plunder where we'd least expect to find it."

"Do we at least get to eat first?" Anthony asked, only half joking.

James stared at his brother but didn't relent. "No meals

until I have the culprit in my brig. If any of you missed break-fast, as my dear brother obviously did, stop by the galley before you begin. Once you finish the rooms, join me to help with the rest of the ship. If the first sweep doesn't yield results, then we will do it again. Before day's end, I'm bloody well going to know who dared to commit robbery on my ship."

Chapter Thirty-Three

"I'M BEGINNING TO ENJOY this." Jacqueline grinned as she lifted a small wooden carving of an elephant out of a crewman's locker. "It feels like we're on a treasure hunt, doesn't it?"

Judith, who was next to her, sorting through another locker, said, "Don't you mean scavenger hunt?"

"Considering what was stolen, I don't believe I do. You know, all combined, that jewelry is probably worth a king's ransom. Yours alone would be!"

Judith didn't blush or try to make excuses for her mother's extravagance. Everyone in the family knew how carried away Roslynn could get whenever she found something to spend her money on.

Judith had hoped to find Nathan working with James's group in the crew's quarters when she and Jack joined her uncle there after completing their search of each other's cabin. But although James had divided the crew who weren't actually manning the ship into two groups—one searching the cargo hold with Artie supervising, and the other assigned to the main deck and the battery deck with Henry in charge, James didn't trust any of the sailors to search the crew's quarters because he considered it the most likely hiding place for the jewels.

Working alone there, James hadn't made much progress, so he was glad to have Jack and Judy's help, and later Anthony's, too, when he joined them, although Anthony was mostly distracting James with his suspicions about who had robbed them. Boyd was at the other end of this deck working his way toward them. They didn't need to rip open the mattresses in the large bunkroom because the mattresses were thin enough that any jewelry that might have been sewn inside them could be detected by touch.

Boyd entered the crew's quarters and spoke with James. A few moments later, James called the girls over to him. "Boyd just found this," James said, holding up an amber ring. "He says it's not Katey's. Do either of you recognize it?"

Judith did. The amber ring went with her amber locket and bracelet. So she had brought her amber after all. It wasn't nearly as expensive as her other sets, but still beautifully made, especially the oval locket, which was circled with tiny seed pearls.

Her father had come over to have a look at the ring and answered for her, "That's Judy's ring. Gave her the amber m'self. The other pieces weren't with it?"

"No," James said, and nodded to Boyd, who left immediately. James didn't exactly look relieved by the discovery and told the girls, "I need to let George know she can stop keeping an eye on Catherine. I believe we're done here for the time being, so you might as well come along."

"You suspected her, too?" Jack asked, keeping up with him. "*I* did."

Judith tsked, but James agreed, "Her—or her brother. Why do you think I sent you all to different cabins? It was to keep them out of theirs."

"Well, don't let *her* know you suspected her," Judith said quickly as she followed behind them. "She felt bad enough when you only *looked* at her earlier." Then, a little red-cheeked, she added, "Though I confess I did have a moment's doubt about Andrássy."

"Where this was found doesn't implicate either of them," James said.

"So a sailor got greedy?" Jack guessed.

"Or planned this well in advance," James replied. "But we'll find out soon enough. Boyd is having him brought to my cabin."

Judith was frowning before they reached James's cabin. If the ring hadn't been found in the crew's quarters or a specific locker, how did he know whom to bring in for questioning?

"George, *really*?" James complained the moment he entered his cabin to find her rifling through his desk, the papers on top of it all scattered.

She glanced up to give him a sweet smile. "I was running out of places to look, m'dear."

"You can stop looking."

Catherine, standing in front of the bank of windows, turned to ask him hopefully, "So am I exonerated?"

Judith was surprised that Catherine would actually ask that. So was James. Judith didn't think she'd ever seen her uncle look discomfited, but at that moment he did. He merely said, "Of course."

Anthony sat down on one of the sofas, stretched his arms

over the back, and asked, "So who is our culprit? I've a mind to tear him limb from limb just for sneaking into Judy's room, much less for stealing from her."

James tsked. "He'll need to be in one piece when we turn him over to the authorities when we dock."

"Then just a few minutes with him. Really, James, you can't tell me you aren't just as incensed that the blighter would dare—"

"Course I am."

Anthony rolled his eyes at that calm reply. He should have known getting James to show what he was feeling was next to impossible. He'd tried, and failed, often enough in the past.

Boyd, looking grim now, returned with Katey, and they both joined Anthony on the sofa. Boyd had seemed the least disturbed of all the family members when he'd learned about the robbery. After so many years at sea, he traveled with nothing of real value that couldn't easily be replaced, and he had tried to convince Katey to do the same. So it was odd that he now seemed more disturbed than anyone else. Georgina noticed it, too, and moved over to perch on the arm of the sofa next to her brother to quietly question him.

Jack was standing next to Judy and leaned closer to her to whisper, "Who do you think it is?"

"I'm more curious to know why your father hasn't given us a name yet."

"Because we wouldn't recognize it if he did. Do you know all the names of the crew? I surely don't."

"Of course, I didn't think of that," Judith whispered back, then sighed. "I'm letting my suspicions run amok today. This is all so disturbing."

"Worse than that," Jack growled low. "We've never been

robbed before, neither of us. I bloody well don't like how it feels."

"But the thief has been caught and we will soon have our jewels back. You shouldn't still be so angry."

"Can't help it," Jack mumbled.

Artie arrived, four sailors with him. Nathan was one of them. Judith's pulse picked up at the mere sight of him, but she was overcome with shyness, too, after what they had done last night. She still cast him a smile, but it faltered when she saw how tight-lipped he was. And he hadn't noticed her yet. He was staring at James, as were the other sailors.

James walked over to the sailors and held out the amber ring. "Recognize this?"

He didn't seem to be asking any one of them in particular, yet Nathan answered, "Why would I? I'm not your thief."

"Yet it was found under your bed. Dropped it by accident, did you? Didn't hear it fall and roll out of sight? Rather careless, that."

Judith blanched, every bit of color gone from her face. She was too shocked to remain quiet. "My God, a smuggler *and* a jewel thief! How *could* you?!"

Nathan didn't reply, but his emerald eyes weren't so lovely when they narrowed in anger. They were downright menacing instead. Because he'd been found out obviously. She was going to be furious as soon as she stopped feeling like crying.

"A what?" more than one person asked.

Catherine's timing couldn't have been worse when she added, "That's the man who entered your cabin, Judith, with a bowl of milk for that kitten you adopted. He was quite surprised that the room wasn't empty when he found me there working on your gowns."

Judith was even more horrified to realize Nathan had probably robbed her before last night and had *still* made love to her. Icing for his cake? Or was that so she'd defend him in case this very thing happened? He'd had plenty of opportunity these last four days to rob them. She'd given him that because of the kitten. Had he used the animal as a ploy, in case he got caught alone in her room? It was a perfect excuse, wasn't it? And she'd played right into his hand, insisting he bring her milk. And last night he hadn't said he wasn't a criminal, only that *if* he had been, he wasn't one now. The man played with words, and they'd *all* been burned because she was gullible enough to trust him!

"Why didn't you tell us he was a smuggler?" James asked her.

Judith's cheeks turned bright red as she was forced to confess, "Because it was just a suspicion. I thought I could keep an eye on him and ferret out the truth."

"He tried to buy your silence, didn't he?" Georgina said gently. "By toying with your affections?"

"Seducing me into silence, you mean?"

"Well—yes."

"I'll kill him!" Anthony snarled, and shot off the sofa.

"Wait!" one of the other sailors said.

But James was already grappling with his brother. "Not *now*, Tony. Jewelry first—then you can kill him if you've still a mind to."

The other sailor spoke up again, this time in a tone of disgust. "You nabobs are a bleedin' odd lot. Nate's no thief. I can vouch for that."

James pushed Anthony back before he turned to the man. "How?"

"I'm his first mate," the man said proudly.

"Are you now?" James said, and then to Nathan, "And how many more of my crew were previously yours?"

Nathan looked beyond furious, so it was just as well the other two sailors were holding him now by the arms. "Just Corky, and leave him out of this."

"It makes sense that you'd have an accomplice, a lookout, as it were. Lock them both up," James said to Artie. "The ladies don't need to be present for the questioning."

Chapter Thirty-Four

"JUST LET ME AT him for a bit," Anthony said to his brother as he paced the floor of the captain's cabin. "I'll get the location of his hiding place out of him."

James raised a brow at him. "I thought you were done with that grudge."

"He robbed my daughter. It's back in spades." Anthony looked over his shoulder at Judith, who was sitting on the sofa between Georgina and Jack, being consoled by them.

James's arms were crossed and he was leaning back against the door in a relaxed stance. But he was obviously blocking the exit, his not-so-subtle way of letting Anthony know James wasn't going to let him rip anyone apart just yet.

James said, "Artie is getting the rest of the ship searched, though considering our thief is a carpenter able to create his own hiding places, that's likely a useless endeavor. But I'm still going to give Tremayne a few hours to figure out that the only way he's not going to rot in an American prison is if he cooperates by returning the jewels and appealing to our mercy."

"No mercy, James," Anthony warned. "Jewels back or not, he's still a thief and deserves to rot. *And* he's a smuggler. He'll be lucky if he ever gets out of prison."

James chuckled. "The Yanks aren't going to imprison him for thumbing his nose at English revenuers. They're more apt to pat him on the back for that. Besides, our smugglers aren't a cutthroat lot, they're merely a result of high taxes, protesters as it were. You could even say they are revolutionaries. They've taken up the gauntlet to help others. Jewel thieves are a different breed. They steal just to help themselves—or when they have no other choice."

"What the deuce does that mean?"

"Kindly recall that Danny, *my* daughter-in-law and your niece by marriage, was a thief. So you are aware that extraordinary circumstances can force someone to do something they'd rather not do."

Anthony snorted. "That is *not* the case here. The man's not a pauper. He's got his own bloody ship and a rich property in Hampshire."

"Exactly."

"Eh? Now what are you getting at?"

"Settle on one or the other, Tony, not both. If he's the thief—"

"If?!"

"Then everything else he's said about himself is likely a lie," James continued. "Consider this, a thief who gets easy access to wealthy people's homes because he is a carpenter. He hears about our trip and that four wealthy families will be on board *and* a carpenter is needed. Rich pickings all in one place. Sounds like a thief's dream come true, doesn't it? And free passage to a new continent where he can rob some more before he returns home to England. All plausible. But what isn't plausible is that he's gentry *and* a thief. The man's a damn good liar though. You realize he would never have come under suspicion if that ring hadn't fallen out of his stash without his noticing before he hid the rest. Foiled by a bit of carelessness. Bloody rotten luck, that."

"Makes me sick to my stomach that he lied about *The Pearl*," Boyd put in as he came over to join them. "Well, a ship he even invented a name for. And, no, I'm not seasick again," he added testily before one of his two standard ribbers thought to mention it. "I was looking forward to helping him recover his ship in New London."

"Am I the only one who wasn't gulled by him?" Anthony demanded.

"Give it a rest, Tony," James said. "Tremayne—if that's his real name—is not a stupid man. He wouldn't have done what *you're* thinking."

Anthony didn't deny his other suspicions. "Wouldn't he? He had the gall to rob her, so I can't believe that's not all he stole from her."

"Ask her," James said simply.

"The devil I will," Anthony replied uncomfortably, glancing behind him at Judith on the sofa. "That would be Roslynn's department and she's not—"

"George," James called out. "Ask her!"

"George doesn't know what we are discussing," Anthony hissed.

"Course she does," James replied. "You mean to say Ros can't read your mind as easily as George reads mine?"

Judith had heard them well enough. When her father was angry, he was rarely quiet about it. "The only thing he seduced out of me was my friendship—and trust," she said hollowly. "He convinced me of his innocence when he's not the least bit innocent. I should have followed my instincts. I *never* should have trusted him."

"It's not your fault, sweetheart," Georgina assured her. "He fed you a tale designed to appeal to your kind nature, so of course you'd believe him." Georgina added pointedly to James, "We all did. And he's had enough time to stew. Wrap this up, James, so we can put it behind us."

The ship's brig was more a cooling-off room for members of the crew who got into fights or just needed a mild reprimand. It wasn't set up for an extended stay. It could only be called a brig because its door was made of iron bars. It was actually a tiny room, one of four, in the hallway by the galley, where the cook had been storing sacks of grain.

Corky was using one of the smaller sacks as a pillow for his head, not that either of them was sleeping. Two narrow shelves or benches were built into the walls on either side of the five-foot-square room. But what they couldn't be called were cots. Yet they'd have to serve as such. There was nowhere else they could sleep other than on the floor.

There wasn't even room enough to pace in, though Nathan felt more like smashing his fist through a wall. He'd never been so angry at a woman in his life. The rest of them had behaved no differently from what he'd expect of nabobs, but Judith? After what they'd shared, how could she think he'd steal from her? From her! Being falsely accused didn't even compare to what he felt over that betrayal. But it was his own fault for trusting an aristocrat. Now he might have to spend the rest of his life in prison because of that error in judgment.

"I'd like to know who set you up so we know who to keel-haul afterwards."

Corky wasn't taking their incarceration seriously yet, but then his attitude was based on their innocence and the certainty that they'd be released with profuse apologies as soon as the real thief was caught. But there was evidence, which meant people were not going to look any further when they believed they already had their man.

"I don't think there's going to be an afterwards, at least, not for me," Nathan said, gripping the bars in front of him and giving them a hard shake, but he got no satisfying rattle out of them. "You, they'll have to let go. They don't imprison men for confessing to friendship."

"At least Artie left us a lantern. Surprised he did, after that angry look he gave you. Speaking of which, have you made an enemy you failed to mention?"

"Other than Lord Anthony, you mean? No, not that I know of. And as much as I don't like that lord, he wouldn't set me up by placing a missing ring under my bed. He's more direct, favoring revenge with his fists."

"He prefers Sir Anthony."

Nathan turned around. "Who does?"

"Sir Anthony does. He's the son of a marquis, so of course that *makes* him a lord, but according to the second first mate, he prefers to be called Sir Anthony, since he actually earned that title himself."

"I don't give a bleedin' damn what he prefers." Nathan sat on the bench across from Corky. "I was more likely picked as the culprit because aside from the two first mates, I'm the only other member of the crew who claimed a bed away from did. The real one. Yet here I sit, framed for something I didn't do. A smuggler does *not* a thief make—not that I'm confessing to either charge."

"Let's be clear, Tremayne. It doesn't matter to me what you used to do, only what you've been doing since you boarded my ship. All that remains now is for you to fess up to where you've hidden the rest of the jewelry."

"So you've already searched everyone on board?"

"And the point of that would be? What was taken was from four separate jewelry boxes, and some of it quite bulky— necklaces and tiaras that don't bend, far too much bulk to conceal on a person."

"I've never stolen anything in my life, but if I did, I sure as hell wouldn't be dumb enough to hide it on a ship that hasn't sighted land yet. I would have waited until an escape was within view."

"But you're a carpenter, dear boy."

"So?"

"So who better to fashion a hiding place? You could have built a cubbyhole in any wall, floor, or ceiling and concealed it from view. A simple task for a carpenter of your skill. I'm going to be quite annoyed if I have to rip my ship apart to find your cubbyhole. Exceedingly so."

"I would be, too."

James actually laughed at that reply. "Yes, I suppose you would be—if you were telling the truth. Unfortunately, my family has been robbed, so I'm not inclined to believe the number one suspect just now. Proof, on the other hand, speaks for itself. I'll give you some time to think about your current situation, but not too long. I expect to see land tomorrow north of our destination, so we could be in Bridgeport late the main quarters. Planting that bauble in the communal area wouldn't have fingered anyone in particular as the thief. But planting it in my room points a finger directly at me."

"I've gotten to know the men," Corky said in a thoughtful tone. "Was feeling them out to see if any might want to join us on the trip home. Never would have guessed one of them could be cunning this way, much less be a bleedin' jewel nabber. If I had to make a guess—"

"Don't bother. Nothing short of finding the trinkets *on* someone else is going to get me out of this. Quiet!" Nathan cautioned, standing up and gripping the bars again when he heard footsteps. "Someone's coming."

"Or just passing by on their way to the galley," Corky said with a snort. "You'd think they'd put a brig in the bowels of the bleedin' ship, not close enough to the galley that we can smell food cooking."

Nathan didn't reply when he saw the captain was paying them a visit. Malory glanced around to locate where the key was hung before he continued down the hall. Nathan almost laughed. Where could he go if he could reach the key? But he couldn't. Even with a shoe to give him an extra foot's extension, he couldn't stretch to the front of the little hallway. But the captain's not knowing where the key was hung proved this room wasn't used often. Nathan wouldn't be surprised if Malory had had to get directions to it.

James stopped in front of the cell. His expression wasn't indicative of his mood, but his words were. "I'm disappointed in you."

"The feeling is bleedin' well mutual. Anyone could have put that ring under my bed and you know it. Obviously the thief tomorrow night. Volunteer the location so the jewelry can be recovered and I might be able to calm my family down enough to let you go."

Nathan snorted. "We both know that's not happening *if* I'm guilty, but since I'm not, I can't very well tell you where the stash is, now can I?"

James shrugged. "Who knows what my family's sentiments will be once the jewels are recovered. But right now I know exactly what they are, and it's just your blood they want."

"You mean your brother does."

"Well, yes, that goes without saying. You managed to inveigle his daughter's trust. If you went a step further and bedded her just to get her on your side for this bit of pilfering, I'd kill you m'self. Did you?"

"You think I would say so after that statement?"

"I suppose not."

"Why don't you just ask her?"

"Oh, we did. But the darling chit has a way with words that can boggle the mind. If she gave a definitive answer, I'd have to say it only seemed so."

Corky joined Nathan at the bars. "If you'd stop barking up the wrong tree, Cap'n, you might open your eyes to other motives. Grudges, revenge, even jealousy, or just simple anger. I've seen a man break a priceless heirloom in a rage. Deliberately. And cry like a baby afterwards. And wouldn't take much to toss a sack of baubles over the rail, now would it? They'd be gone in an instant. Too late to regret doing it. You see my point?"

"You're talking about a fortune, a bloody king's ransom. No one in their right mind—"

"Exactly. Who's in their right mind when they're enraged, eh?"

The captain was shaking his head. Corky gave him a look of contempt and sat back down. Nathan hadn't thought of motives yet, but he did now.

"My friend's suggestions are a little far-fetched, but here's one that isn't. There was a stowaway who didn't have time to do any obvious damage, but was picked up by a ship that was on our arse. That was planned, and being so, one or more of the crew could have been in league with them all along. Just because there hasn't been another sighting of that ship doesn't mean it's not still following us."

"To hurt me or my family?"

"No, for what you just admitted is a king's ransom. That stowaway could have put the jewels in a crate that could float and lowered it over the side and then signaled that ship to look for it. The jewelry could very well be on that ship. That's what they were after all along."

"Or you could be the one in league with them and could have done exactly that," James said as he walked away.

"This nonsense is going to cost me my ship, damnit!" Nathan growled after him. "No bleedin' baubles would be worth that to me!"

He waited for a reply but there was none, which had him furiously shaking the bars again. Still not even a little rattle from them. He and Corky weren't getting out of that cell. His ship was going to end up sold. He was going to see the inside of a prison despite his pardon. Even if the Malorys didn't have an enemy out there on the high seas, they had one now aboard their ship.

Chapter Thirty-Five

"You can't fool me," Jacqueline said as she joined Judith at the rail. "Didn't touch your food last night or this morning. Haven't even remarked on the land you're staring at. You're still heartbroken, aren't you?"

Am I? Judith wondered. Is *that* what I'm feeling? She was still somewhat in shock and utterly disillusioned, and she'd cried herself to sleep last night. Her eyes were quite red from it. But then not even a full day had passed since Nathan had been apprehended as a jewel thief.

"I'm not saying I am, but will it ever go away?" Judith replied.

"Course it will."

"How do you know? You've never felt heartbroken."

"Because it stands to reason, don't it? Half the world would be in tears if it doesn't."

"I highly doubt half the world—"

"A quarter then, but if you want specifics, didn't your sister fancy herself in love with young Lord Gilbert last winter? She certainly cried for several hours over him. And not two days later she was happy as a lark singing the praises of Lord Thomas instead."

"Jaime was barely sixteen. She's allowed to float in and out of love until she figures out what it really is—which she hasn't done yet. She's too young—"

"So have you figured it out?"

"I just feel so betrayed. He led me to believe we were friends, then he robbed me, us, all of us." .

"Friends and lovers?"

"Jack!"

But while Judith's cheeks had turned pink with a blush, Jacqueline was rarely embarrassed by any subject and wasn't dropping this one. "You wouldn't make love without telling me about it, would you? I don't think I could forgive you for keeping *that* a secret from me."

"I—wouldn't."

It wasn't a lie, it wasn't! She'd tell Jack eventually. She just couldn't bear to yet when the mere thought of just how close she'd gotten to Nathan made this pain even worse. It was clouding her mind and squeezing at her heart.

So she was completely broadsided when Jack said, "But you didn't tell me he was our ghost."

Judith actually groaned. Jack wasn't going to forgive her, ever, for the secrets she'd kept from her.

"You guessed?"

"Not a'tall," Jack replied in a tone that sounded hurt. "The hair so blond it looks white didn't give it away. Others have hair that color. But after you excused yourself from dinner last night, I heard my mother whisper to my father that at least he's not Derek's neighbor after all, and wasn't that the worst crime, his impersonating gentry? So I asked what she meant by that and she explained. Suddenly your immediate fascination with Nathan Tremayne made sense."

"He asked me to keep that secret and now I know why, because it was just another lie. He doesn't own that house. He was just hiding smuggled goods there. I told you about my suspicions when we were visiting Derek and his family."

"So he's the smuggler you saw the night before we left Hampshire?"

"I didn't actually *see* him that night. But when I saw him on the ship and recognized him as our ex-ghost, something he said made me realize he was the man who had been at the ruined house behaving so suspiciously. I accused him of being a smuggler. He denied it, of course, and promised a full explanation if I'd hold off saying anything about it."

"It's not exactly a high crime," Jack pointed out. "Some people even consider smugglers folk heroes, you know. I mean, how would you feel if you couldn't afford a cup of tea anymore when you've been drinking it all your life?"

"I know. And that's the only reason I held my tongue."

Jack snorted. "I suppose how handsome he is had nothing to do with it. Or that you've fancied yourself in love with his ghost all these years?"

"Only his handsomeness—maybe."

"There's no maybe about that. He was fascinating to you back then and still is. Of course you could lay claim that he compromised you whether he did or not—if you want him for a husband. That might be the only way to keep him out of prison—*if* you want him for a husband."

"You're repeating yourself."

"Some things bear repeating. Prison can ruin a man. The time to save him would be now."

Already suffering from heartache and now overwhelmed by guilt, Judith suddenly burst out, "We *did* make love."

"I know."

Judith gasped. "No, you didn't!"

"I bloody well did," Jack retorted. "Think I didn't notice that silly grin you couldn't keep off your lips yesterday morning? Think I haven't seen that countless times on the women in our family? Even my mother, for Pete's sake, gets that look after she and my father—"

"I get the point."

"I'll wait until you get over your heartbreak to insist that you share every detail, but not a minute longer. I can't believe you kept *any* of this from me. *Me!*"

Judith winced. "I know. He tricked me into keeping silent. I was trying to get at the truth, and agreeing to his terms seemed to be the only way I could. But I realize now all I did was give him time to make up an elaborate tale I would believe."

"One you *wanted* to believe, you mean."

"Well, yes. And time to convince me he could be trusted. That's the worst of it. I can't believe I trusted him!"

"Good God, don't cry again! Forget I said a word. We're not saving that blighter. Prison's too good for him!"

Jacqueline said no more, just put her arm around Judith's waist and squeezed. The wind quickly dried her tears. She continued to gaze at the coastline, which she figured was in one of the states north of Connecticut. She didn't care. She'd lost interest in this trip, lost her appetite, too, as Jack had pointed out. All she could focus on was the abysmal pain that was overwhelming her.

She had thought about confronting Nathan. This morning she'd even gone down to the corridor that led to the improvised brig. She didn't go any farther than that because she had started crying again. It was too soon to talk to him without screaming or crying, and what could he say to her to explain why he'd stolen from her? She wouldn't believe him anyway, could never believe him again, he'd lied to her about so much.

She couldn't stop thinking of him, though. The image of Nathan and the kitten asleep together in her cabin, so adorable, so—innocent—was stuck in her mind. Of course, even murderers could love their pets. His affection for a kitten did *not* make him innocent of anything. But it had been so heartwarming, seeing him like that. It had made her draw conclusions she wished she could now forget.

Her uncle James had said it wasn't plausible that Nathan was gentry *and* a thief. He should also have pointed out that Nathan's being a smuggler and a thief wasn't plausible either. Why would a thief smuggle when smuggling wasn't nearly as profitable as stealing? He couldn't be both. But he certainly wasn't adept at thievery when he'd carelessly left evidence behind. Was this his first attempt at it? Or had he been coerced into it, his nieces threatened . . .

She groaned to herself, aware that she was searching for reasons for him to be innocent because the thought of his going to prison made her sick to her stomach. No matter what he'd done, that single thought filled her with dread, as if she were the one facing such a dire future. Is that why she felt so miserable? Maybe it wasn't heartbreak she was experiencing, just gut-wrenching compassion for a friend. A supposed friend. No, he wasn't a bloody friend, damnit.

"I wonder what town that is," Jack said. "I'm going to read the charts and dig out my uncle Thomas's map to find out. Have you seen the one he gave my father? It's a map of the entire east coast of America and well enough drawn that my father didn't immediately toss it out simply because an Anderson drew it." Jack laughed. "Cartography might only be a hobby for Thomas, but he's quite meticulous at it."

Judith took a closer look at the town that had sparked Jacqueline's curiosity. She could see single-story houses, a church steeple, a few short docks with only fishing boats tied to them. *The Maiden George* was close enough to shore that she could make out some people waving at them, or more likely waving at the children swimming in the water.

Her eyes flared wide. A strong man could easily swim to shore from this distance. She didn't have to marry Nathan to save him from prison. She just had to let him out of his cell.

She hurried after Jack to have a look at that map herself. James had said they'd reach Bridgeport sometime between midnight and dawn. They would still get a good night's sleep since he didn't plan to dock the ship until daylight. So she could do it anytime after they were anchored in the harbor or even before that, if she could figure out where they were along the coast.

At least that sick feeling of dread had gone away, now that she had a positive plan. She did have a few second thoughts, though. The jewelry still hadn't been found. Her family would be furious at her for helping Nathan to escape. Jack was the only one who would understand why she had to do it. But when she snuck down to the brig late that night, she found it empty. Nathan was already gone.

Chapter Thirty-Six

LATE AT NIGHT THE weather was more than brisk in Connecticut—if they were even in that state. Clothes soaking wet, tired from the long swim to shore, Nathan and Corky were shivering as they walked up the beach toward the lights of the one place in town that appeared to still be open that late, a tavern.

Nathan still couldn't believe they were free. The set of circumstances was astounding. A noise had woken him in the middle of the night by mere chance. Even so, he almost went back to sleep before he noticed the door to the brig was open. Then, forgetting how narrow his makeshift bed was, he nearly fell to the floor getting up so fast to make sure he wasn't dreaming it. The door was open, but no one was in the hallway, so he didn't know whom he ought to thank for it. Most likely one of the crew who knew he was getting a raw deal from the Malorys. Or the actual thief, who regretted framing him?

In either case, he and Corky had bid *The Maiden George* farewell in quick order. They didn't even consider gathering their belongings first. They dove straight over the side and swam toward the lights onshore.

"Tell me you had coins in your pocket when we were tossed in the brig," Corky said hopefully. "A strong drink would be more'n welcome right now."

"My pockets are as empty as yours."

Corky groaned. "Wet, cold, no money, no belongings that we could trade, and a powerful local family will soon be trying to recapture us. This ain't looking too good, Cap'n."

No, it wasn't—yet. But if he could just get to *The Pearl* as soon as possible, their immediate problem would be solved because he knew something about the ship that no one else was aware of, not even Corky. At least, he hoped no one else knew it yet. But if they weren't even in the right state . . .

Nathan dredged up an encouraging tone for his friend. "We'll be fine as soon as we get to New London."

"Aye, the Yank's friend will help us."

Nathan shook his head. "We lost that opportunity when we got thrown in Malory's brig. We can't take the chance now that John Hubbard will simply believe us if we arrive without decent clothes and no letter of introduction from Boyd Anderson, which Anderson didn't bother to write since he planned to come with us. Hubbard would likely send a message to the Andersons to confirm our story first."

"As I said, this ain't looking good," Corky mumbled.

"Stop worrying. I have an alternative plan, but we need directions first, and I'm not waiting till morning to get them. Come on."

They entered the tavern. Aside from the skinny barkeep and one barmaid well past her prime, there were maybe a dozen customers, half of them lined up at the bar. While the sudden warmth in the room was welcome, Nathan wasn't there to waste time.

"Evening, mates," he said loud enough to draw every eye in the room to him and Corky.

All conversation and rowdiness stopped abruptly until one muscular young fellow at the bar demanded, "Who the hell are you?"

"Come to wash the floor, did you?" someone else snickered.

That started the laughter. Well, Nathan had to concede they did look ridiculous with their hair and clothes so soaking wet that puddles were forming at their feet, and not even a jacket to ward off the cold night air.

"If you can point us in the direction of New London, we'll be on our way," Nathan said.

But that caused even more laughter and a couple replies. "You're in the middle of it."

This was New London? But that couldn't just be a lucky co-incidence. Someone on the Malory ship must have intention-ally opened the brig door as the ship approached the town he intended to visit.

But before Nathan had a chance to ask about the shady shipyard and its owner, whose name Commander Burdis had given him, the big fellow came over to him and shoved Na-than's shoulder, hard enough that a slighter man would have fallen. Nathan stood his ground, but the man's aggressive stance didn't alter.

Nathan was shoved again as the man said, "We don't wel-come strangers in our town, least of all suspicious Brits who show up all wet in the middle of the night."

Someone else with a grudge against England or just a local troublemaker? Nathan wished he'd thought to tone down his accent, if he even could. But tonight was a perfect opportunity to reach his first goal, so he wasn't about to leave without directions to the shipyard.

He quickly decided to try to nip this man's aggression in the bud and hoped the crowd wouldn't rally to help their friend. "We're not here to cause trouble," Nathan said as he planted a fist in the man's belly, following up with a blow to his chin that knocked him to the floor. "Really we aren't."

Unfortunately, the fellow quickly jumped to his feet. He was big, even had a few inches on Nathan, and he exuded confidence, was even grinning now. But Nathan couldn't afford to lose when this tavern was a prime place to get some help, maybe even the men for the crew he would need for the trip home. That wasn't going to happen if he lost or backed down from this fight.

Nathan hoped for a charge he could easily avoid or take advantage of, but his antagonist wasn't unskilled and tried a few punches just to test Nathan's reflexes. Nathan did the same. For a few minutes neither of them was getting anywhere.

Already tired from the long swim, Nathan knew he wouldn't have the stamina to outlast the man if they continued to cautiously test each other's mettle. So the moment the man broke through his guard with a solid punch to Nathan's chest, Nathan came up with a backhanded left fist to the side of the man's head and leapt up to slam a quick right-handed blow to the man's jaw. With Nathan putting his full weight behind it, the fellow dropped to the floor again.

"*Really* we aren't here to cause trouble," Nathan repeated, and, willing to roll the dice, offered the man he'd decked a hand up this time.

The man stared at Nathan's hand and a moment later

laughed and took it. Nathan introduced himself. His former antagonist told him his name was Charlie and ordered Nathan a whiskey, which Nathan passed on to Corky. He then asked the group at large if anyone there was familiar with Henry Bostwick and his shipyard. He got more responses than he expected.

"I worked for him a few years back, but the work wasn't constant and he shorted my wages to boot, so I didn't hire on again," Charlie said.

Someone else said, "Shorted my wages, too, and no excuse for it neither, when he auctions off ships three to four times a year. Course, buying them old and just bringing them here and prettying 'em up, he's only making half what he could."

"Don't make excuses for him, Paulie. My brother swears Bostwick is up to no good. There's been other ships he sells privately, and who knows the difference when that yard is all closed up like it is."

"Is this how Bostwick explains not actually building ships from scratch?" Nathan asked.

"He builds new ones, too, he just pulls the crew off 'em to work on the old ones when they show up, so it can take years for a new one to get finished. But that's how he's always done it, far as I know," Paulie said with a shrug.

"Always wondered how he manages to find so many ships," Charlie said. "The few I've seen come in over the years weren't actually old, so he would have had to pay a high price for them. How's he make a profit that way?"

"He makes a profit because he's not buying them, he's stealing them out of English ports," Nathan replied.

Someone laughed. "Is he now?"

Nathan stiffened, wondering if that was going to be everyone's sentiment, and asked the man, "You know something about that?"

"I know some of the ships brought in were indeed British. Had a peek at the logbooks before they were burned. But who cares?"

"I understand why you might not find his business practices objectionable, but I do, since I have reason to believe the ship he currently has in his yard belongs to me."

The man just shrugged and turned back to his drink. Charlie asked Nathan, "Is that why you're here?"

"Yes. To retrieve my ship and get the local authorities to put Henry Bostwick and his ring of thieves out of business."

"Good luck with that," someone snickered. "The word of a Brit against a local man of business?"

"There are a few things I know about my ship that Bostwick wouldn't know and hopefully hasn't discovered, but I need to find out if she's here first. Can someone take me there—now?"

"Why would we do that?" Paulie asked. "There's guard dogs let loose at night inside the outer fence, and any ship on the property is closed up in the big shed where they're worked on. There's no way you're getting in there to see anything."

There was a round of agreement with that assessment. But with the likelihood that *The Pearl* was still in New London, Nathan wasn't going to wait until morning to find out. His ship had to still be here. She was over twenty years seasoned. It would take a while to sand her down to give her the look and smell of a new vessel. That had been his only hope, actually. The time it would take to polish her.

"I'll pay handsomely to see my ship tonight," Nathan offered.

"Let's see some coins, Brit."

Nathan ignored that. "And I'm going to need a crew for the return trip to England. I'll wager some of you who aren't in your beds at this hour could use the work."

Some laughed over that remark, confirming it. But the same doubting Thomas called out, "Show us a ship before you go hiring a crew."

Corky warned in an urgent whisper at Nathan's side, "You're promising what we don't have!"

"Trust me" was all Nathan whispered back.

It was actually Charlie who downed the rest of his drink and volunteered, "I'll take you."

Nathan smiled and, grabbing Corky, followed the big man out of the tavern.

A while later, they approached Bostwick's shipyard on the shore. The fenced-in yard to the side of the big shed had plenty of space to build ships in, but it was empty except for a few piles of lumber and the roaming dogs. Was the shed there so that work wouldn't have to stop during the harsh winter months—or to hide whatever was going on inside it? But it wasn't tall enough to accommodate masted ships unless the ground in the work area had been dug out.

"Corky, stay on this side of the fence to distract the dogs if I can't get the front door opened quickly enough," Nathan said.

"No reason for the door to be locked if there are guards inside, and I know there's at least one," Charlie said. "I live near here. I've seen him come out to patrol the place at night."

Nathan nodded and amended for Corky, "Follow if the door's open, distract if it's not. Charlie—"

"Let's do this," the big man said, and hopped the fence before Nathan could finish.

Nathan grinned and followed. Unfortunately, the door was

locked. But it was old. He could break it down easily, but that would immediately alert the guards, and the dogs. And they didn't know how many armed guards they would have to contend with.

"Kick it in?" Charlie asked.

"No, let's try pushing first, quietly," Nathan whispered. "It won't take much for the hinges to give way, but the dogs are going to get our scent soon, so we need to do this fast."

They both put their shoulders to the door and shoved, but it didn't give way quickly enough. A dog started growling—too close. Nathan didn't have to think about it; he raised his foot to kick the door in, but it suddenly opened before he could.

The guard that stood there looked so surprised to find them in front of him that he was slow in raising his rifle. Nathan grabbed it from him and smashed the butt of the rifle against the man's head. Fortunately, he didn't have to do it twice because Charlie was already shoving Nathan out of the way so he could close the door on the dog. It barked now on the other side of the door, but only for a moment. Corky must have figured out some way to distract it.

Around the shed on this upper level was a walkway, ending at an office on the other side. The windowed office looked down on the main area, which was indeed much lower. A light in the office revealed two more guards sitting at a table. A ship was below them in the center of the shed, but the large area was too dark for Nathan to tell anything other than that the ship was the same size as *The Pearl*. If it was in a trench, he could probably sail it out at high tide once the two enormous barn-like doors of the shed had been opened.

"Do we take out the other guards?" Charlie asked.

"That might lead to shots being fired, which I would as

soon avoid. I just need to board the ship to confirm it's mine, and I think we can do that without their noticing. Come on."

Two sets of stairs led down to the work area, one by the office, one by the front door. Nathan led the way down and hurried up the long ramp to the ship.

"Hide here and keep an eye on that office," he told Charlie as they reached the main deck. "Let me know if the guards come out of it."

It took Nathan only a few moments to find what he was looking for: the concealed compartment he'd built in the deck below the wheel. He had to resist the urge to laugh aloud when he found all his money still in it. Bostwick hadn't found it. Nathan's initials carved in the hold probably hadn't been noticed either, but the compartment was all the proof he needed that the ship was his.

Once the two were outside again and back over the fence, Corky came running toward them. "Well?"

"They were nice enough to remove *The Pearl*'s barnacles for us."

Corky gave a hoot of laughter before he held up his bare foot. "I had to give up my boot to get that dog interested in something other than you."

Nathan patted his shirt where he'd stuffed his smuggling profits. "We'll get new clothes in the morning."

Charlie spoke up, "I'd like to sign on for your crew, but I still don't see how you're gonna get your ship back. There's no way the authorities will believe a Brit who's accusing an American of stealing ships."

"Who is Bostwick's biggest competitor?" Nathan asked.

"That would be Cornelius Allan. Why?"

Nathan grinned. "Because he'll believe me."

Chapter Thirty-Seven

Thomas, georgina's third-oldest brother, was waiting on the docks for them, having just received word that *The Maiden George* had been sighted. Jack was waving at him from the deck, but she laughed when she saw how many carriages and wagons were pulling up behind him.

"I wonder if my uncle expects more Malorys than we have on board?"

"Isn't he the most practical of the Andersons?" Judith replied. "Easier to dismiss carriages than to find more if they're needed. And I can't wait to set my feet on land again!"

"Don't pretend you didn't enjoy the trip—most of it, anyway."

Judith didn't reply. She'd asked Jacqueline not to mention Nathan to her again. It was bad enough that everyone else was talking about him this morning, speculating about his escape. She didn't report it, but one of the crew did when the family was sharing a quick breakfast before James maneuvered the ship to the docks. Of course more than a few eyes had turned to her at the news. She had been able to say honestly that she hadn't done it and just kept to herself that she would have let him out of the brig if someone else hadn't had the same idea and beat her to it.

With Silver snug in Judith's arms, she and Jacqueline were the first down the ramp. Georgina's three other brothers arrived at the docks before the rest of the family debarked. Georgina introduced Catherine and Andrássy to them, briefly mentioning Andrássy's connection to the Malorys.

Andrássy was quick to assure the Andersons, "My sister and I will not impose on you. We will be continuing our journey immediately."

Georgina protested, but surprisingly, so did Catherine. "Actually, I would like to accept their invitation to enjoy some of the festivities. Please agree, Andrássy. It's been so long since I've been to a ball."

For a moment, Andrássy glared angrily at his stepsister for putting him on the spot like that, but gentleman that he was, he politely said, "Very well. We can stay for a few days."

A while later, Judith and Jacqueline were seated in a comfortable open carriage, riding with their parents to the Andersons' redbrick mansion not far from town. Four of the Anderson brothers on horseback, two on each side, escorted them so they could continue speaking with Georgina on the way.

James, glancing to either side at the in-laws he least favored, remarked, "Why does it feel like I'm riding to the gallows, George?"

"Location, m'dear," Georgina answered with a grin. "Will you ever forgive them for wanting to hang you here?"

"Course not," James mumbled.

"Thought you'd need reinforcements, James?" Drew said on their left, looking at Anthony.

"My brother wouldn't let his daughter come alone," James replied.

"Well, we're delighted to see *her* again. You, on the other hand . . ." Drew laughed and rode ahead.

"Can I kill just a few of them while we're here, George?" James asked his wife. "I'll be gentle."

Georgina tsked. "That sort of killing is never gentle. And you promised you'd behave."

"No, I promised to suffer in silence."

"Well, no one expects you to do *that*. But you knew they'd get in a few licks, being on the home front, as it were. Don't begrudge them that when you and Tony are unrelenting when they visit us in London."

When they pulled up to the Anderson mansion, Amy ran out to greet them. "Was it a smooth trip? Everyone in good health?"

James raised a brow. "You expected otherwise, puss?"

Amy blushed, confessing, "Well, I did think something might go wrong, but you know what a worrier I am."

"Something did go wrong," Anthony put in. "The ladies were all robbed of their jewelry, every last bauble."

"That's all?" Amy looked relieved, but quickly amended, "Well, it could have been worse."

A few of them rolled their eyes at Amy.

James said, "I do need to return to town, and now's a good time while the ladies get settled. I'd like to hire a few local carpenters to pry open parts of *The Maiden George* to see if the jewels are hidden somewhere on the ship. Several searches produced no results."

"Aren't you forgetting something?" Anthony asked, giving James a pointed look. "We also need to inform the local authorities that we caught the thieves, but they escaped from the ship last night. They'll be easy to find with their British accents and lack of money, as long as the search starts immediately."

Judith felt her heart sink. Nathan was going to be a fugitive now?

"These new boots are damned comfortable," Corky said, not for the first time. "I could get used to togs like this."

"You do look more presentable than usual," Nathan said with a grin.

He'd gotten them rooms at the local hotel last night. Hot baths, some decent food, and a few stops this morning for new clothes had them both looking like local businessmen as they waited in Cornelius Allan's office for the shipbuilder to join them. He was a well-respected citizen, successful businessman, and Henry Bostwick's main competitor, so Nathan was counting on Mr. Allan's *wanting* to believe him when he presented his case against Bostwick.

The middle-aged man looked hopeful when he arrived and said, "My manager just informed me that you claim to have proof that Henry Bostwick is a thief? This better not be a joke, young man, because I haven't heard such delightful slander in ages."

"It's very much the truth," Nathan assured Mr. Allan. "I confirmed last night that the ship he is refurbishing in his shipyard right now is mine. When his men stole it, a man was killed. But one of his men was also captured. The information gleaned was that Bostwick and his ring of thieves have been stealing ships from English ports for the last decade. It might have started as revenge against the British, but it's turned too profitable for that to be his only excuse anymore. Understandably, my government wants his operation closed down—and I want my ship back."

"An interesting story," Cornelius said. "But you understand why your word alone won't be good enough? No offense— Treemay, was it?"

"Nathan Tremayne, and none taken."

"Well, it's no secret that I detest Henry Bostwick. He's been a thorn in my side for years. He doesn't just undercut my prices, he's ridiculously secretive, enclosing his entire yard the way he did. But he claims to buy the ships he refurbishes, and while I would love to see the records of those purchases, I've never found a viable reason to ask him to produce them for inspection."

Nathan smiled at the older man. "Until now. If he has any records, they are bound to be fake. But he's gotten away with this for so long, I doubt he even bothers to cover his tracks with records."

"So why have you come to me with this story?" Allan laughed. "Other than the enemy of my enemy is my friend."

"Because as a respectable member of your community, your support could get this wrapped up quickly, perhaps even today. And I did mention I have the proof you would need to do so. There are two things about my ship that no one knows but me. I carved my initials in the hold when I was a child because my father had just told me his ship would be mine one day and I wanted to put my mark on it. But I didn't want my father to notice, so I carved them on the backside of one of the beams nearest the hull. Even if Bostwick has had the hold painted, the painter wouldn't have noticed those initials to sand them down first. I also built a secret compartment on *The Pearl* that Bostwick hasn't found."

"Nor would he, if he merely bought an old ship. But the initials do sound promising."

"There's more. I've also spoken with some of the local men who've worked for Bostwick in the past. A few of them have actually seen some of the ships that were snuck onto his property in the dead of night. They are willing to testify they were British ships, not American ones, and that he passed them off as being newly built when he sold them. That was from just a handful of men. There are probably others in town who will have more to say about his illegal activities. But since the locals also say that Bostwick actually does build a ship every so often, don't give him a chance to say he bought mine. Simply demand to see the purchase document before he has a chance to say anything. If he doesn't yet have a falsified document to show you, then he might make the claim that he built my ship. If he does that, you'll then have him red-handed, because he can't show you where the ship's secret compartment is, whereas I can."

Cornelius Allan grinned with a good deal of relish. "You got me on board when you mentioned local witnesses. But tell me, after all this obvious thought you've put into bringing Bostwick to justice—not that I'm complaining, mind you—you appear to be in quite a hurry to see it done. Is there another reason you bear him a grudge?"

Nathan chuckled. "Stealing my ship isn't enough? No, I've just been away from home too long. I'm eager to return with my ship, and with an official document attesting that these thieves have been put out of business." Of course he couldn't add, *Before the Malorys show up with the law to arrest me, which could be as soon as today.*

Chapter Thirty-Eight

JUDITH AND JACQUELINE WERE enjoying an exhilarating ride that morning, ending with a race back to the house. Judith won, but their groom hadn't been able to keep up, which was why Jacqueline was laughing as they dismounted in front of the house.

"I'm so looking forward to seeing Quintin again tonight," Jacqueline confided as they handed their reins to the tardy groom.

"First name already?" Judith replied. Jack had met the young man at Amy's soiree last night.

Jack grinned. "Yes. He's delightful, charming and funny—and I hope he'll try to kiss me tonight."

"On your second meeting?!"

"I'll wager he does." Jack grinned widely. "Yanks aren't as concerned with propriety as Englishmen, and besides, he knows I'm not going to be here for long, so an accelerated courtship is quite in order. *You* keep that in mind and start enjoying yourself. This is our third day here and I've barely seen a smile out of you!"

"I've just been distracted."

"Is *that* what you want to call it? You need to forget about that bounder who's going to be in jail soon and get into the spirit of the festivities. Honestly, Judy, you should be excited about meeting Raymond Denison at the ball tonight instead of worrying about a man you'll probably never see again. Amy confided in me that she's sure you'll adore Denison."

"If she bet on it, I might have to ring her neck."

Jack rolled her eyes. "She wouldn't do that."

Catherine suddenly called out to them, and they turned to see her walking toward them on the road from town. "If you wanted some fresh air, you could have joined us for our ride," Jack said as Catherine reached them.

"Thank you, but I'm not very good with horses. And I needed to visit the shops in town for some trimmings to spruce up my dress for tonight. I didn't actually pack a ball gown for this trip, but it doesn't take much to turn a dress into one."

It didn't? Judith thought. Well, maybe not for someone as skilled with a needle as Catherine was. Catherine and Andrássy were still at odds, too. He might have relented on staying a few more days before they continued their journey, but he obviously wasn't pleased about it. They'd even been seen arguing in whispers.

The girls followed Catherine inside. Servants were rushing around, getting the house ready for the ball, with Amy in the hall calling out orders. She looked frazzled, but she wanted everything to be perfect for her first ball.

Catherine excused herself to go upstairs. Amy joined the

girls and with a nod toward Catherine said, "I have a funny feeling about that woman."

Jack laughed. "Many people do. Judy is the only one who really likes her."

"That's not true," Judith said in Catherine's defense. "Your mother does, too."

Jack snorted. "My mother is too gracious to show what she *really* thinks."

"I saw her talking with a young man in town yesterday," Amy mentioned. "A bit too familiarly for a first meeting. Does she have friends in Bridgeport?"

"That isn't likely," Judith replied. "She hasn't been in America since she was a child."

Jack snickered, guessing, "Maybe she found herself a beau our first day here while the rest of us were settling in. You know she could be more worldly and experienced with men than we thought."

Upstairs, Andrássy slipped quietly into Catherine's room. He didn't expect to find her packing. "Going somewhere, Sister, without telling me? I thought you weren't ready to leave Bridgeport yet."

She swung around in surprise. "We're both leaving tomorrow as agreed. There's no reason to wait until the last minute to pack."

His eyes narrowed in anger. "You're lying. You're planning to sneak off without me."

He grabbed her and tried to kiss her, but she shoved him back. "Stop it! I warned you there'd be no more of that when you began the role I hired you for. And you've played that role superbly, but it ends tomorrow when we go our separate ways. Nothing has changed from the original plan, Andy."

"You already changed that plan by sticking around when we were supposed to leave as soon as we docked. So you could sneak off without giving me my cut?"

She tsked and tossed him a small bag. "Satisfied now?"

He opened the bag, saw the jewelry on top, and stuck it in his pocket. But it still made no sense that she was risking everything by delaying their departure.

Then his eyes widened. "You're not going to carry out your friend's lunatic plan, are you? It failed once and you can't risk it again, not here with so much family around. Your father will be happy enough with the fortune in jewels you stole for him. You assured me he would be."

"I know my father. He won't be happy unless he gets *everything*!"

"I won't let you do it!"

"If you say or do anything to stop me, I'll tell the Malorys who you really are and that it was *your* idea to steal the jewels, that you forced me to help you!"

"They'll never believe you. They love me, consider me one of their own. I've played my role well."

"Oh, they'll believe me all right. I got the jewels off the ship by sewing them into the hems of my dresses, but I also sewed a few into your clothes, and I won't tell you which items in your extensive wardrobe are currently serving as jewel cases. But I *will* tell the Malorys if you insist on ruining this evening for me." Then Catherine added more sweetly, "I've so been looking forward to my first American ball."

She tried to further lighten his mood. "Did you remember to get them some ribbons?"

It didn't work. He was suddenly glowering at her, what was on *his* mind finding voice. "How could you believe I stole from you?"

"I was shocked by the robberies, and you never did directly deny that you're a smuggler. You were always so cryptic or evasive whenever I asked. So I didn't know what to think, but when I calmed down, I realized you couldn't have done something that awful. But you must admit how bad it looked. It had even occurred to me briefly, as it did to members of my family, that you'd been paying attention to me because you wanted to keep me quiet about my suspicions that you were a smuggler, and so you could gain access to my cabin and help yourself to my jewels."

"Underestimating your own attractiveness, aren't you? Let me give you a little advice as you begin your come-out season, darlin'. You are one woman who doesn't need to worry about ulterior motives in the men you meet. You're as fickle and pretentious as all those other aristocratic women, but never doubt that you're beautiful."

His tone was so scathing she was completely surprised when he grabbed her by the shoulders and pulled her up against him. His mouth claimed hers in a deep, angry kiss that conveyed even more depth of feeling than his words had expressed. But Judith didn't care why Nathan was kissing her so passionately, only that he was. Her heart soared as everything she felt for him was drawn to the surface. But he gave her no chance to reciprocate, no time to even put her arms around him! He simply let go of her and walked away.

"Happy husband-hunting, darlin'," he tossed over his

shoulder before he climbed onto the ledge of one of the windows and actually leapt toward a nearby tree.

Judith ran to the window to make sure he didn't get injured in that jump. She saw him just before he dropped the last few feet from the tree to the ground and disappeared into the darkness.

Judith moved back into her room and picked up the vanity stool she'd knocked over. She caught her reflection in the mirror and laughed at the silly grin she was wearing. He'd come to find her before he left the country, even climbed a tree for her! He was angry, yes, still hated her family, true, but she didn't care. At least she still had a chance with him, and if he didn't find her in England, she'd find him. Finally she had something to look forward to.

Chapter Forty

THE RECEIVING LINE AT the ball was long with so many Andersons and Malorys present. Clinton stood at the head of the line with Georgina and Jacqueline next to him so he could introduce his niece to old friends of the family's. The Willards, who were renowned for hosting their own balls each winter, came through first.

Reverend Teal was next and paused to say to James, "I'm delighted to see you and Georgina are still married." When James had shown up bruised and battered at the private marriage ceremony that Teal had been asked to perform all those years ago, the reverend had been quite sure that James had been forced to participate, so his remark tonight was genuine.

"We tried to undo that, Reverend," Warren said on James's right. "Really we did. Unfortunately, James couldn't be coerced twice."

James raised a golden brow at Warren. This Anderson used to have the worse temper of the lot, had tried to hang James. But Warren's temperament had changed completely when he married Amy, so much so that James couldn't get a rise out of him no matter how often he'd tried over the years.

"Feeling brave on the home front, are you?" James said drily to his brother-in-law. "If I'd known that's all it took, I would have visited more often."

Warren grinned. "Like hell you would have. It's too bad you didn't figure out a way to avoid this. We hoped—er, *thought* you would!"

"The thought of taking on you and your brothers again at the scene of your brief triumph was too much to resist, dear boy, I assure you. Of course, George will insist it be one-on-one this time—not five on one."

"She won't allow it and you know it," Warren rejoined confidently.

"We can wait until she goes to bed."

But Georgina overheard that and leaned forward to tell her second-oldest brother, "Don't bait him, Warren. James has promised me that he'll be on his best behavior tonight."

"More's the pity," James said, waiting only until Georgina turned away to jab Warren with his elbow, hard. "But do take this up again tomorrow, Yank."

Once the last guest arrived, James and Anthony took to the floor with their daughters to start the ball off. Their dark formalwear was the perfect foil to the girls' sparkling gowns, Jack in pink silk, Judy in pale blue. Drew and Warren joined Georgina on the side of the floor.

"He actually knows how to dance?"

"Shut up, Drew," Georgina said without glancing at him, wiping away a tear as she watched her husband and daughter twirling by.

"But you must admit, this is just *so* not like him," Warren said on her other side.

"Tonight it is. He'll do anything for Jack, including adhering to traditions he would otherwise thumb his nose at—including bringing us here."

"*That* was writ in blood long ago," Drew reminded her.

Georgina rolled her eyes. "Remember who you're talking about, as if something James said on the day of Jack's birth, when he was so overwhelmed with emotion, would make a jot of difference now—particularly considering *who* he said it to."

Drew laughed. "*James* overwhelmed?"

She tried to swat his shoulder, but Drew was adept at staying out of his sister's reach when he saw it coming. "It was Jack who wanted to come," she told them. "She didn't want to disappoint you, so we came."

Warren put an arm around her waist and squeezed. "We know how much he loves her, Georgie."

On the dance floor, Jacqueline was having nearly the same thought as her uncles. "I didn't expect this, you know."

James smiled. "Didn't you?"

"As if I don't know how much you hate dancing? You could have claimed a sprained foot. I would have backed you up and helped you hobble around."

"Hobble? Me?" He rolled his eyes before he stressed, "*And* I don't sprain feet. But I am exactly where I want to be, m'dear. Besides, now these young bucks know who they have to get past to get to you."

She beamed a smile at him, whether he was serious or not. Dancing past them, Judith was smiling at her father, too, which made Anthony comment, "Your mood seems remarkably improved, poppet. I hope it's not because one of these Yanks has caught your eye already."

She laughed at his less than subtle attempt at slyness. "D'you really think I'd mention it if they did?"

"I promise I won't kill him."

He said it with a grin, which she returned. "I know you won't. But, no, no one here has caught my interest yet."

"Not even young Denison? Amy was so sure you'd like him."

Raymond Denison was supposed to be there tonight, but she couldn't recall having met him yet. "He wasn't able to come to the soiree last night. Perhaps he couldn't make it to the ball, either."

"Judy!" Anthony said, looking at her incredulously. "He gave you three compliments in the receiving line. If he had spouted one more, I was going to forcibly move him along. You really don't recall?"

She blushed slightly, but then grinned. "I was probably distracted, remembering Mama's admonishment to enjoy myself here without falling in love with an American. But if you want me to form an interest in Mr. Denison, you can take me to meet him again as soon as we finish this dance."

"Bite your tongue. If he wasn't memorable enough for you, we'll keep it at that."

She did meet Raymond Denison later, though, and danced with him. He appeared to be quite the catch. Jacqueline even pouted that he was more handsome than her Quintin. Judith wasn't sure if she was teasing. But Raymond was the equivalent of an English gentleman, an American man of leisure. His family apparently owned long-established businesses not just in Connecticut but all over New England, and he was the young heir to it all. He was amusing. She laughed quite a bit with him, much more than with the other young men she danced with. But she had a feeling even bad humor would have made her laugh tonight, she was feeling so bubbly inside. And no matter whom she danced with, she wished it were Nathan instead. . . .

Amy was ecstatic. As the evening wound down, she'd received so many compliments it was clear her first gala event was a resounding success. Even her first attempt at matchmaking appeared to have worked. She said to Jacqueline when she joined her at the refreshment table after dancing with Andrássy, "Judy seems quite taken with Raymond Denison. Have you noticed how often she's laughed with him tonight?"

Jack grinned. "Like Jaime, it just took a new man for her to stop lamenting over the wrong one."

"Then she said something to you about Raymond?"

"She hasn't stopped dancing long enough for me to ask!"

"If you mean Judith, I quite agree," Catherine said as she stepped up to them. "I was hoping to get her opinion about this wonderful man I've met."

"Who?" Amy asked, but amended with a laugh, "I'll ask again later! I must find out why the champagne is running low."

"But the night is almost over!" Jacqueline called after her cousin, not wanting to be left alone with Catherine, but Amy didn't pause as she hurried off.

"Will you join me in the garden for a moment to meet him?" Catherine continued. "I just want to see what another young woman thinks of him before I consider delaying my trip even longer—because of him."

"Is this the man you met in town while shopping?" Jack asked.

"Why, yes, it is."

"Then why don't you bring him inside?"

"Because he wasn't invited. But we danced in the garden. That was quite romantic. I'm surprised you haven't tried it with your young man."

Now *that* was a sore subject. Jacqueline had twice tried to get Quintin out to the garden tonight, but both times he got distracted by one of his many friends. Maybe if she disappeared for a while, he'd get the idea. So she agreed to accompany Catherine, but spotting Quintin, she still waved at him so he could see where she was going.

The terrace was well lit with the pretty lanterns Amy had decorated it with for the ball, but that light didn't extend far. The extensive garden did have old lampposts though, interspersed along the many paths. But a few had gone out, leaving long stretches of darkness between them. Catherine kept moving deeper into the garden.

"For a party crasher, he's doing a good job of staying out of sight," Jacqueline remarked impatiently.

"He *must* still be here," Catherine whispered beside her. "I assured him I would return."

The man suddenly stepped out of the shadows and smiled at Jacqueline. She drew in her breath. He was handsome, very handsome. Black-haired, dark-eyed, wearing a double-tiered greatcoat and an oddly shaped hat with feathers drooping off to the side of it. She guessed that Catherine didn't want an opinion about him at all. She just wanted to show off that she'd found the most handsome man in Bridgeport!

But Catherine suddenly whispered, "Hurry!"

That broke through Jacqueline's momentary surprise. With a frown, she turned toward Catherine, only to get a gag shoved in her mouth and a steely arm clamped over her chest. But she also saw Andrássy running toward them, his sword in hand. Thank goodness! Whatever Catherine was up to, her brother wasn't going to let her get away with it.

"Let Jack go, Catherine!" Andrássy ordered furiously. "I warned you—"

Jacqueline's eyes flared as someone else snuck up behind Andrássy and hit him over the head. The sword fell to the ground. So did Andrássy, and he didn't move again. They'd killed him?! But it was the last thing she saw. Without a word from these men, she was bundled up and carried away.

Chapter Forty-One

JUDITH JOINED GEORGINA, AMY, and Gabrielle, who were standing near the entrance. There might be a few more waltzes, but most of the guests had already departed, and Judith had had quite enough dancing for one night.

"Well, how was it, your first official ball?" Georgina asked, putting an arm around her.

"I'll probably have sore feet in the morning." Judith grinned. "And where's Jack gone off to? Surely not to bed yet?"

"Not without telling me, she wouldn't."

"Like you, she was dancing most of the night," Gabrielle said. "But I haven't seen her lately, now that you mention it."

"The last I saw her, she was with Catherine at the refreshment tables, but that was quite some time ago," Amy replied.

Judith glanced about the room again. "I don't see Catherine, either."

"Nor Andrássy, for that matter," Georgina said, beginning to frown.

"Those two wouldn't sneak off tonight without saying their good-byes, would they?" Amy asked,

But Georgina was a little more than concerned now. "Never mind them, start looking for Jack. I'll send the men to search the grounds."

Judith groaned and hurried upstairs with Gabby to check the bedrooms. Jack was probably in the garden getting the kiss she'd wanted from Quintin, and she would be mortified when their fathers found her there. And it would be Judith's fault. She should have looked for Jack there first.

Jack's bedroom was empty, as Judith figured it would be. Gabrielle met her in the corridor to say Catherine's belongings were all still in her room, and Gabby hurried downstairs to report that. Judith started to follow her, but thought she better check on Andrássy first. As fond of Jack as he was, he might know where she was or at least where his stepsister was. Catherine's absence might be a matter of concern after Jack was found.

But Andrássy's room was empty, too, his trunks still there. An envelope propped up on his bureau was odd enough for her to grab it along with the little velvet pouch pushed against it that was holding it upright. James's name was on the envelope. Perhaps Andrássy and his sister did sneak off, after all, and this was their farewell note? But without their belongings?

She hurried downstairs just as her father and uncle were coming in from the garden—without Jack. She felt a pang of fear, seeing how worried they looked. Clinton was informing them, "I've sent for the militia, James. We'll search the entire town and beyond if we have to, but we'll find her."

"You might want to read this first, Uncle James." Judith

handed him the envelope. "I thought it was only a farewell note from Andrássy that he left in his room for us to find tomorrow morning, but it could be more than that."

James opened the letter and started reading it.

Anthony complained, "Blister it, James, don't keep us in suspense. Read the bloody thing out loud."

James ignored Anthony until he finished reading. His rage was apparent, the more so because he said not a word, but he handed the letter to his brother. Anthony was about to simply read it silently, too, but Georgina snatched it out of his hand and read it aloud to everyone:

> *The only reason you are reading this is because I have failed to stop my former lover Catherine's plot to abduct Jacqueline. I never wanted this to happen, but she and her accomplices are determined to commit this foul deed to please her father. You will receive a ransom note tomorrow by post. No, I am not who I said I am. I am a professional actor who foolishly fell under her spell. She hired me to aid her in her plot because I do actually have Gypsy blood and she wanted me to pass myself off as your relative. I helped her steal the jewelry, but I am leaving my portion of it here to prove I am a man of honor. No harm will come to Jacqueline. I will see to that and to making my amends to the Malory family the next time we meet.*

Georgina had started crying before she finished.

Anthony was the first to respond; "Dead men can't make amends."

A round of angry agreement followed that statement.

"This must be what I had a premonition about," Amy said

miserably. "I knew something bad was going to happen, but I thought it was the theft when you told me about it. I should have known it would be something worse than that."

Judith was so shocked by Andrássy's revelations, she almost forgot about the pouch, but she handed it to James now. "This was with the letter."

He opened it and emptied the contents into his hand. No more than a few pieces of cheap costume jewelry rolled out along with a lot of stones added for weight.

Anthony snorted, "Of course he's not a Malory. He's too stupid. She gave him little more than a pile of rocks in payment."

"And he has stunningly bad taste in women," James added, referring to Catherine.

Judith felt hollow inside. She'd befriended Catherine, defended Andrássy! "I believed them without question, but you didn't, Uncle James. You had doubts from the beginning."

"His only proof of being related to us having been destroyed in a fire was too convenient, leaving just his word, and a stranger's word isn't good enough when it comes to my family. It would have been easy enough to learn about the Stephanoff side of the family, particularly in Haverston, where people still remember Anastasia."

"Can we even trust what he's written?" Katey asked. "After all, he's a Gypsy."

"Perhaps not even that is true," Boyd said to his wife.

But just then someone ran in and yelled that the ships in Bridgeport harbor were under attack. James left immediately, everyone else following as quickly as the horses could be saddled or hitched, the ladies in the carriage, the rest on horseback. What they found in the harbor defied description. *The*

Maiden George was tilted on her side, the wharf she'd been tied to demolished under her as she sank into it. The ship on the other side of that wharf was also starting to tilt in the other direction. There didn't appear to be a single ship along the docks that wasn't sinking. It was as if the entire area had been fired upon, yet there were no fires and no ships out in the harbor to account for so much destruction.

James was actually walking on the side of his ship, looking for the hole that had sunk her. One of his crew swam out of the hold to report, "A sawed and pried-loose plank, Cap'n, just as you suspected. Had to be done earlier tonight and underwater, which is why the watch saw nothing amiss until it was too late."

James leapt ashore and told Anthony, "I sent Artie to wake the postmaster. If Catherine and her cronies didn't want us to get their ransom note until tomorrow, it could have a clue in it about where they're taking Jack."

"Out to sea, obviously, or they wouldn't have sunk our means to give quick chase," Boyd said.

"Possibly," Warren replied, "or that's just what they want us to think."

But someone suddenly yelled, "Look there!"

A ship was coming into view, moving out from behind a bend just beyond the outskirts of town. It was heading out to the middle of the Sound—and the ocean beyond. James started swearing. Judith thought she saw a woman on the deck, but it was too dark to be sure.

But Henry was on hand and had his spyglass. He handed it to James. "That's Catherine."

It was infuriating to just watch them sail away with no way to stop them. James wasn't the only one swearing now. Then

Artie returned with the ransom note. James read it aloud this time:

> *Come to St. Kitts if you want to obtain your*
> *daughter's release. You will be contacted there*
> *with further instructions. It will be a simple*
> *exchange, you for your daughter.*

James snarled to no one in particular, "They want me, why the bloody hell didn't they just take me?"

"Speaking from experience," Warren said cautiously, "you're not an easy target to take by any means. Whoever wants you apparently knows that."

"But why make Uncle James travel so far for this?" Judith exclaimed. "Why not do the exchange right here?"

"Because James can gather an army here," Georgina said, quietly crying again. "They obviously want him isolated, which means—"

Georgina couldn't finish that thought, but Judith could fill in the blanks. Money wasn't being demanded as it had been when she'd been kidnapped as a child. They wanted James specifically, which could only mean one thing. They planned to kill him.

"But this makes no sense," Boyd put in. "They want you to follow but take away your means to?"

"They obviously don't want a sea battle, likely aren't prepared for one."

"Neither were you," Boyd replied.

"But that wouldn't stop me from ramming them out of the bloody water."

"Not with Jack on board you won't," Georgina admonished even as she put her arms around James.

James conceded that point, correcting, "Or from boarding them."

Judith couldn't bear it, knowing how frightened Jack must be, remembering her own terror when she'd been abducted right out of Hyde Park. Watching her aunt and uncle, she knew they were just as frightened. James just dealt with it differently from most people. He'd move heaven and earth to get his daughter back—and demolish anything that stood in his way. She *knew* he'd rescue Jack. But at what cost to himself? His only real chance was to get to Jack before her abductors reached their destination.

She moved over to speak with Artie for a few moments before Clinton approached James to assure him, "We might be able to find you a ship before yours is seaworthy again. I'll send men tonight to the other harbors along the Sound. We probably won't find a new one, but I'm sure we can locate a captain willing to sell his. It still won't be soon enough for you to catch up to them."

"I can't count on that," James said. "I bloody well wouldn't sell my ship for a rescue that means nothing to me, so I don't expect anyone else to."

"No, but you'd help," Georgina said. "You've done it before."

"In either case, I'll rouse our shipyard employees to get to work immediately on your ship," Thomas offered. The calmest of all the Anderson brothers, even he looked grim tonight.

James nodded, but Warren added as Thomas left, "It's still

going to take several days or more. It won't be the first time I've assisted in dry-docking a ship, though it's much easier to do at our shipyard. Everything needed will have to be hauled here. We'll just need to dismantle the wharf to make room. As soon as the tools get here, we can get started on that."

Drew remarked, "You instead of money, James? You know who that sounds like, don't you?"

James shook his head. "Lacross is in prison for life. It's not him."

"Are you sure? How do you know he didn't scheme his way out? And don't forget a few of his men escaped that night we rescued Gabby's father. One might be trying to get revenge for Lacross."

James snorted. "That was too many years ago, Drew. Besides, you really think that pirate had any friends? Most of his men were coerced to work for him toward the end, your father-in-law included. This was Catherine's doing, for *her* father, whoever he is."

Drew conceded with some exasperation, "It was just a thought. I don't like not knowing exactly what we're up against."

"Neither do I," James said, then peered at Drew's wife. "I don't suppose your father was planning to attend this reunion and is just late getting here?"

"I'm sorry, James, no," Gabrielle replied. "He got his hands on a new treasure map recently, which means we won't see him for months."

James was reaching an explosive point, being foiled at every turn. He started ripping up the wharf with his bare hands long before the workers got there. It was painful watching him as the hours passed, because he knew—they all did—that tomorrow would be too late for him to catch up with Catherine and her cohorts before they reached St. Kitts. Even if a ship *could* be bought, it wouldn't happen soon enough.

And then *The Pearl* sailed into the harbor.

Chapter Forty-Two

"OF ALL THE BLOODY nerve," Anthony was saying while he held Judith protectively close to him. "Sail in as bold as you please when he expects a noose to be waiting for him here?"

At least half of them had moved down the dock to where *The Pearl* was being directed to an empty slip. James had confirmed Nathan was on the ship after he put his spyglass away, but he said to his brother, "Kindly remember that's no longer the case. Stop grousing about one thing when it's another thing that's got your dander up. And do *not* antagonize him. I need that ship, preferably with his cooperation."

Judith didn't understand why Nathan was even here. She'd sent Artie to find him up the coast, hoping Nathan would be willing to help with Jack's rescue. But Artie had returned just as *The Pearl* was sighted to tell her that he hadn't been in time, that Nathan had already sailed.

She searched for Nathan on the decks, but all she could see were men in unusual uniforms who looked nothing like sailors. "He's brought the military with him?"

"Looks like some of our local militia boys," Clinton confirmed, recognizing one of them.

"Ha!" Anthony crowed. "So he's spent the last few days in chains after all."

"You better hope not—for James's sake."

"Why?"

"Because right now your brother has a ship *and* a captain on hand to negotiate with, which is much more than he had a few minutes ago. But if this captain is under arrest, then his ship will be locked down until after a trial."

"That won't stop my brother, Yank."

"You might want to remember this is Georgina's hometown. He won't want to be outlawed from it."

With a hard stare from James, Anthony held his tongue for the moment. One of the militiamen jumped down to the dock to tie off the ship. James and Boyd went to help him when it appeared he wasn't sure how to do it. A wide ramp was dropped for debarking. But before any of them could board the ship, a few horses were led off, already saddled, then the militia followed.

Anthony stopped one of them. "Is Nathan Tremayne under arrest?"

The man actually laughed. "Arrest? The man's a hero. He helped New London take down a band of thieves who were operating right under their noses for a damned decade."

Well, that explained why Nathan was bold enough to sail into Bridgeport, Judith thought. He didn't just have the local militia on his side, he had them with him!

"Tony, for the *last* time . . ."

That's all James said, but it had Anthony snarling, "I get it. So he told the truth about his ship being stolen. That changes nothing—"

"Then give it a little more thought, because it does."

"A welcoming committee? I'm touched."

They turned. Nathan was standing at the top of the ramp, arms crossed, tone icy. He looked ready for a fight. And Judith couldn't take her eyes off him.

"I'd like a word, Tremayne," James said as he moved halfway up the ramp.

Nathan didn't change his stance or step aside from blocking the way onto *The Pearl*, didn't even acknowledge that he'd heard James. But he was staring at Judith now, who still stood with Anthony's arm tight around her.

James, glancing between them, asked, "What did you come here for?"

Nathan's eyes moved back to James. "New London is full of whalers. Hard to get a full crew there that doesn't want to be off chasing whales instead and I've been trying for two days. These militiamen figured I'd have better luck in their town, getting the last few men I need, even offered to help get us this far by way of thanks."

"So you're just here for a crew?"

"Just that. Disappointed I'm not in chains instead?"

"Not a'tall. We found out who stole the jewelry tonight, but that's not all she's guilty of. I need your ship to take us to the Caribbean. I'll—"

Nathan's harsh laugh cut him off. "I'm not helping you bleedin' Malorys after what you did to me."

"That's—unfortunate—considering you were assisted out of that predicament by someone on my ship."

Nathan gave James a long, hard look. Whether he read anything into that statement was unclear. Judith did. So did Anthony, who was swearing under his breath now.

But Nathan's next question wasn't odd, since they were all still wearing their evening apparel. "You're having a ball on the docks tonight?" A glance down the pier. "Or a war? What happened here?"

"My daughter has been abducted. The bastards went out of their way to make sure I couldn't follow immediately."

"Judy's cousin Jack?"

James again glanced between the Nathan and Judith who were staring at each other, before he made the decision easier for Nathan by saying, "I'll pay you thrice what your ship is even worth."

"Some things don't have a price," Nathan said angrily.

James took another step forward. "You really don't want to know the extent I will go to, to get my daughter back. Take my offer, Tremayne. It's more than fair, and it even leaves you to captain your ship, which isn't actually how I'd prefer it, but I can be reasonable."

"As long as you get what you want?"

"Quite right."

Nathan didn't answer for a moment, which was better than another outright refusal. But Boyd came forward to sweeten the offer, saying, "I'll even throw in a full cargo, once you return us here. Give you a taste of the trader's life—if you haven't tried that yet."

"Us?"

"My brothers and I. Jacqueline is our niece. While we're not incredibly fond of our brother-in-law, we'd rather he not be exchanged for Jack. So we need to recover her before that happens."

"*You're* the ransom?" Nathan said to James.

"Yes."

"Our—your mystery ship?"

"Undetermined, but possible."

Nathan glanced down at the dock at so many expectant faces staring back at him. His eyes lingered the longest on Judith, again, but he stiffened when he stared at Anthony.

Yet he told James, "Come aboard, alone, if you want to hear *my* terms."

Judith let out her breath in relief. Nathan was agreeing, just with stipulations. Which was fine. At least he was going to help! But of course he was. He had his own agenda, might still be furious with all of them, but he had a good heart. And as long as *The Pearl* got under way soon, it still had a chance to catch up with that ship before it even reached the Caribbean, so both Jack *and* James could come out of this unscathed.

On the ship, Nathan led James to the center of the deck, where they couldn't be seen from the dock. James had already guessed: "I suppose you don't want my brother to come along?"

"Correct. He isn't setting foot on my ship—ever."

"If that's all it takes—"

"That's not all. You can bring only three Andersons with you. Counting you, that's the number of men I still need to round out my crew. You can choose, but you might want to check if one of them can cook."

James rolled his eyes. "So we're agreed?"

"If you can supply my new cabin boy—Judith."

James went very still. "And I was so hoping I wouldn't have to kill you."

"That's not negotiable. And don't be a hypocrite. I overheard Artie teasing your wife about the time she acted as *your* cabin boy, when you knew she was a female but she thought you weren't aware of it."

"I ended up *marrying* her," James growled.

"Beside the bleedin' point. Those are my terms, Viscount Ryding."

James didn't answer for a long moment. He finally said, "You have a cabin for her?"

"Yes, one. The rest of you will have to sleep with the crew."

"Then let's be clear. If she agrees to this nonsense, and the decision must be hers, you don't touch her, not even by accident. I'll need your word on that."

"Agreed. But if you're leaving it up to her, you might remind her of the Bargain she struck with me—tit for tat is owed."

James just narrowed his eyes before he left the ship. He pulled Judith aside to explain Nathan's demands and what he'd said about their Bargain. Anthony joined them before she could give her answer.

"Well?" Anthony asked. "Are we going or is he still sulking over a few hours in your brig?"

"His terms are, you don't go—but Judy does."

"Like hell she does!" Anthony snarled. "This isn't a bloody pleasure jaunt. She stays here with the rest of the women."

"I've already accepted his terms."

Judith put her hand on her father's arm. "I was going to insist on it myself," she said, not even sure if that was a lie. "This is Jack we're talking about. I'm going. I'll just gather a few things and be back before the supplies are loaded."

She started to leave, but heard behind her, "Damnit, James, why didn't you just toss him in the water and take his bloody ship?"

"Because his chums are still here, who hail him a hero and have the authority to gather the entire town against us. We aren't getting Jack back if we're tossed in jail instead. Judy will be fine under my protection."

Would she? She'd seen the anger in Nathan's eyes. He might have kissed her earlier tonight, given her such hope because of it, but he was still so furious with her. And she couldn't see that ending, not when he'd just included *her* in his terms to help them. Tit for tat? Or just payback for her and her family's accusing him of something he didn't do?

Chapter Forty-Three

"Y OU MISSED A SPOT."

"This floor isn't even dirty!"

"Because you're keeping it that way."

Nathan couldn't take his eyes off Judith as she angrily stood up with her bucket and came over to the side of his desk where he was pointing. Getting back on her hands and knees, she grabbed the rag out of the water and slapped it hard enough on the floor for the water to splash in his direction.

"If you wanted to polish my boots, you should have said so." He turned in his chair so she could reach his feet.

She glared up at him. "Enjoying yourself, aren't you—a little too much?"

He grinned. "Actually, yes."

He'd been embarrassed when she'd first entered his cabin the morning after they'd sailed from Bridgeport. It had none of the luxuries she was used to and barely any furniture. He couldn't imagine what she'd thought of it. *The Pearl* was three-masted like her uncle's ship, but not as long and not as wide.

His cabin might be located in the same part of the ship as the captain's cabin on *The Maiden George*, but it wasn't even half the size. His father hadn't slept in his cabin, merely used it as a chart room and a place to dine with Corky—and Nathan, when he was aboard. Nathan had turned the cabin into his personal quarters and had added a hammock, which was where he slept. One of Bostwick's men in New London had put a cot in it, an alteration that Nathan didn't mind.

Nathan didn't know the three Andersons, Warren, Thomas, and Drew, whom James had picked to accompany them. He would have preferred for Boyd to join them, but he recalled James saying that Boyd would be useless for half of the voyage because of his seasickness. James and the three Anderson brothers were pulling their weight, though Nathan had caught all of them giving orders to the other sailors, or starting to before they remembered they weren't in command on this voyage. For men who'd been captains for most of their lives, it was a hard habit to break.

The first morning at sea Judith had made his bed, dusted his desk, swept his floor, and fetched his breakfast, all without saying a word. She didn't castigate him for putting her in the position of a servant, she didn't demand to know why he'd done that, and she displayed no resentment either. She had seemed more the martyr, willing to do whatever it took to rescue her cousin. She'd even appeared a little grateful to him for helping them with the rescue mission. But Nathan didn't want her gratitude. Although he was keeping his anger in check, he still felt plenty of it—especially, toward her.

He'd trusted her. That's why the rancor wouldn't go away. He'd never trusted anyone quite like that, when the odds warned that he shouldn't. She'd even made him look at nabobs differently, showing him they weren't all heartless snobs the way Angie's in-laws had been. Only to prove in the end that he'd been right all along.

Corky had given up his cabin for her. *The Pearl* only had three of them, and the Anderson brothers had claimed the other. Nathan didn't know where James was sleeping, but he wouldn't be surprised if it was in the corridor outside Judith's cabin, or even on the floor inside it. Nathan had given his word he wouldn't touch her and he wouldn't, but James was still helping him to keep his word.

The man never knocked when he entered Nathan's cabin and made no bones about deliberately failing to do so, unless he knew Judith wasn't in there. *Then* he knocked. But when she was in the cabin and Nathan was, too, James showed up once or twice. Unexpectedly. Quietly. He didn't even provide an excuse for it! Nathan found it annoying, but he wasn't fool enough to ask him to stop it, when he knew very well he'd crossed the line with his terms. It had been a moment of madness that James would no doubt make him pay for as soon as James had his daughter back.

Ironically, Nathan shouldn't even be here. He could have checked in other towns for more sailors to hire for his crew instead of the town Judith was in. He should have been on his way back to England and his own nieces, instead of embroiling himself in Malory family problems. If only he didn't know Jacqueline, gutsy, brazen, funny—and Judith's dearest friend. He could have said no if he'd never met Jack or hadn't seen that pleading look in Judith's eyes there on the dock. . . .

And Judith hadn't remained the silent martyr for long. Her testiness had showed up the first time he ordered her to do something she wasn't expecting to have to do, such as washing his clothes or scrubbing his floor again today when she'd just done it yesterday.

"This isn't tit for tat a'tall," she pointed out now. "I barely asked anything of you."

"But you could have, darlin'. You can't imagine how many sleepless nights I had, thinking of all the ways you could have taken advantage of me."

She blushed furiously. He relented and put his feet back under his desk before she actually reached for them. But he couldn't keep his eyes off her as she began scrubbing around the corner of his desk. Beautiful as she was in a dress or a gown, she looked quite fetching in her boyish garb, which was all she'd been wearing on his ship. Right now he had a glorious view of her derriere, which was outlined nicely by her britches as she leaned forward to swab the floor. It was getting harder and harder for him not to touch her, particularly when he saw her in such an alluring pose and she got so close he could smell her, as she was now. He had to be a masochist to put himself through this when he still wanted her so much, just so he could squeeze out a few more days with her before they parted and he never saw her again.

Glancing up at him again, she suddenly asked, "Who let you out of the brig?"

Pleased that she was still curious about him, but angry because of the subject she'd just raised, he realized she was doing it again, stirring contradictory emotions in him. But he wasn't surprised. She had no idea of the depth of emotion she'd tapped in him. He'd never given her a clue about his feelings, not even that amazing night when he'd made love to her. But the truth was, he was afraid he'd fallen in love with her. That there was no hope for a future with her and had never been fueled his anger.

"I wasn't awake to see who it was, but it obviously wasn't you," he said bitterly.

She started to reply, but changed her mind, started to again, but again closed her mouth.

His brows snapped together as he watched her. "What?!"

She glanced down at the floor and said so quietly he barely heard it, "I was going to."

"Going to what?"

"Let you out. I waited until everyone was asleep. I waited too long. You were already gone."

He snorted. "How convenient for you to say so now."

Her cobalt eyes rounded in surprise as they met his again. "You don't believe me?"

"Why would I?"

"Perhaps because I've never lied to you? I've lied *for* you, but never to you, well, at least nothing of import that I can recall."

"Import? What does that even mean?"

She shrugged. "I might have lied about members of my family, but family secrets are family secrets, you understand, and they are not to be revealed except by those members involved and at their discretion. Certainly not at my discretion. You, on the other hand, lied to me. Or are you going to maintain at this late point that you were never a smuggler?"

"D'you really think I'd answer that? You, darlin', can't be trusted."

She stiffened, obviously insulted, but he couldn't miss the hurt that briefly flickered in her eyes, too, which twisted his gut. He started to reach for her, but caught himself at the last second. That damned promise . . . And like clockwork, James

opened the door—and frowned when he didn't immediately
see Judith.

But she stood up, guessing who had arrived without knocking, and with her bucket in hand, told Nathan stiffly, "The
floor is finished and it's time for your lunch."

She hurried out of the room without glancing at her uncle,
but James didn't leave with her. He came forward slowly, his
ominous demeanor predicting payback might be coming
sooner rather than later.

"I know this isn't your fight, Tremayne, which is why your
terms were outrageous—"

"No dire predictions, please. I'm not abusing her in the
least. And you are mistaken. I was compelled to come along."

"Oh? I didn't realize I was so persuasive."

Nathan barked a laugh. "You aren't. But my reasons are
my own. As long as nothing happens to this"—he picked up a
document from his desk drawer and dropped it back in—"then
when I return to England isn't an issue."

"And that piece of paper is?"

"Proof that I accomplished my mission."

"I'm all the proof you need, old boy. Or in case I don't survive this, my family is."

"No offense, Lord Malory, but I prefer the document that
was demanded of me."

"I begin to see . . . stipulation for a pardon?"

Nathan laughed again. "You are amazing. Your deductive
reasoning astounds."

"So you don't care to own up to why you need a pardon?
You don't need to. I've led an eventful life, seen more things
than I ever cared to. Even though you will be sailing home with

your ship, the fact that you must still deliver written proof that you accomplished your goal speaks for itself. You're aiming for a promotion or a pardon, and since you aren't a military man . . ." James sauntered back to the door, but paused a moment to glance back. "I liked you from the start. Decking my brother, for whatever reason, took guts. I hope I'm not going to have to end up killing you."

Nathan leaned forward. "Did *you* let me out of the brig on your ship?"

James's expression didn't change, not even a little. It was annoyingly devoid of emotion of any sort. "That would mean you owe me a favor, wouldn't it?"

"You aren't going to answer?"

"Me? Do good deeds?" James laughed as he left the cabin.

Nathan stared at the door for a moment, frustrated. That was a detestable habit Malory had, of leaving things up in the air like that. Of course he hadn't done the deed, when he was the one who'd put Nathan in that brig in the first place. The Malorys now knew that Catherine was their thief, but they hadn't known it when they were all on *The Maiden George*. Nathan was *not* going to look for a reason to be beholden to that man. He much preferred it the other way around.

iled. "Eating with you isn't appropriate—while I'm

your servant."

not releasing you from your job as my cabin boy."

id I ask you to?"

No, you didn't—and why haven't you?"

She was surprised. This was the first time he'd revealed that complete compliance with his demand might have baffled m. But she would never admit how thrilled she'd been to e included in his terms. She'd been a little nervous at first, but that hadn't lasted long when it became clear that he only wanted her to perform the customary chores of a cabin boy. He had no way of knowing that the work she was doing actually made her feel as if she was help... ll way to get Jack back.

In answer, she said, "So you could tell me no? That's quite all right, thank you." Then she quickly mentioned, "We're getting close to St. Kitts. Strategy needs to be discussed with my family. I suggested we have dinner tonight here in your cabin so you could be included."

He raised a brow. "A little presumptuous of you, wasn't it?"

She gave him an innocent look. "You don't want to be included?"

"With *you* serving dinner? I can imagine how well that will go over with your family. How many of them will I have to fight off before they get around to discussing anything?"

"I won't rub their faces in your orneriness. Tonight I'll eat with you."

He laughed. "Is that what I am? Ornery?"

"Better than acknowledging that you're getting revenge against me."

"Never that, darlin'."

Chapter For[ty]

{ornament}

FOUR DAYS OUT AND they still hadn't sighted the ship [they] were trying to catch. James had said it could take upward [of] a week to reach St. Kitts, less only if they were lucky with the currents and the wind. They'd been sure that overtaking Catherine's ship en route would be the only way to rescue Jack without a loss of life—on their side. But obviously the other ship's head start was an advantage they couldn't overcome, so an alternative plan had to be considered.

To that end Judith had a purpose other than delivering Nathan's breakfast when she arrived at his cabin this morning. He was standing at his desk, but he immediately glanced at her, his eyes lingering for a long moment, before he looked down again at the charts that were spread out on his desk. James's charts of the Caribbean. They had been soaking wet when Artie had fetched them from *The Maiden George* before they had sailed. But now that they had dried out, they were still readable.

"Only one plate again?" Nathan said before she could broach her subject. "You don't follow orders very well, do you?"

"Then what would you call it?"

"A simple need for a cabin boy."

She twisted her lips in annoyance that he wasn't any more willing to tell her his real reason for making her his servant than she was willing to say why she didn't mind. She went over to make his bed. She could *feel* his eyes still on her. It was almost as if he were actually touching her. And why didn't he?! Yes, he'd promised her uncle he wouldn't, and James had assured her that he and his brothers-in-law would mutiny if Nathan did, but she'd never expected Nathan to adhere to his word so literally.

Then he suddenly said, "I woke up this morning with a crick in my neck that isn't going away. Come over here and see if you can work it out."

Her eyes flared wide. She straightened and turned slowly to find him sitting at his desk now. She asked carefully, "What about your promise to my uncle?"

"I'm not breaking it. Your uncle said I can't touch you, but he didn't prohibit you from touching me."

Her stomach fluttered at the thought, but she was worried about getting that close to him, worried that she couldn't do what he'd asked without touching him the way she wanted to touch him. Her breathing quickened before she even reached him. When she stood behind him, staring down at his wide shoulders, she felt a rush a warmth and desire for him. She had to pretend it wasn't *him* she was touching. She closed her eyes and tried that, taking care to keep her fingers on his shirt.

"I can barely feel you." He rose from the chair, turned toward her, and starting unbuttoning his shirt.

Judith groaned to herself yet couldn't take her eyes off him, and when he removed his shirt and hung it over the back of the chair, her gaze roamed from his muscular chest down to his belt buckle.

"Now, try it again." When she looked up, she saw a half grin on his face. He was enjoying this!

Judith took a deep breath, deciding to make him as uncomfortable as she was in this intimate situation he'd concocted. She put her fingers on the soft skin of his neck and rhythmically moved them up and down, and then lower to the tops of his shoulders. His hair brushing against the backs of her hands was so sensual she almost gasped at the sensation! While she might have started out stroking him, soon she was kneading his shoulders, deeply massaging them, then lightening her touch to a caress. She heard him groan and then sigh. Soon she was lost in her ministrations, which were clearly giving him pleasure, lost in thoughts of what could happen next. . . . She leaned forward and asked, "Can you feel me now?"

"This wasn't—" Nathan shot out of the chair. "Leave. Now!"

Judith ran out of there, straight to her own cabin, and stayed there until the flush left her cheeks and her hands stopped trembling. Contradictory man! She hoped his sore neck got worse—no, she didn't. Or did he even have a sore neck? He'd sounded a little smug when he'd told her she could touch him. Had it just been a ploy that had backfired on him? That thought had her feeling a little smug now. But she didn't return to his cabin before dinner—with her family.

That could have turned out much worse than it did, but the Andersons were actually neutral where Nathan was concerned, even though Judith was their brother Boyd's sister-in-law and Georgina's niece. Judith had seen to that by assuring them she didn't mind helping with the "cause."

But Nathan's cabin wasn't exactly designed for guests. His table only sat four and was so filled with the food that arrived that no one tried to eat at the table. And the discussion had already begun.

Thomas and his brother Drew were leaning against one wall as they ate. Warren, James, and Judith used three of the chairs, while Nathan remained behind his desk.

"You can't just turn yourself over to them," Thomas was saying to James. "When we get there, we must find out where they're holding Jacqueline *before* they know we're there."

"Dock elsewhere?" Drew suggested.

"That won't be necessary," Warren put in. "Catherine is the only one who will recognize any of us, but she won't know this ship."

"Enter the town disguised then?" Thomas said.

Warren nodded. "Long enough to find one of them that we can question."

"When Jack might not even be there?" James said.

"What are you thinking?" Warren asked.

"They are directing me there just for further instructions. That doesn't mean that's where they are going."

"And what's the point of that?" Thomas asked.

"To get me on a different ship—alone."

"Don't do it, James," Thomas warned. "You can't just give them the only leverage we have. You."

"I still think if you can figure out who Catherine's father is, then we can ascertain how to foil him," Drew insisted. "Think, man. Who wants revenge against you so badly they'd go to this much trouble to get it?"

"We already ruled *him* out, and it's pointless speculating. I stepped on too many toes in my day, yours included. I can't honestly count the number of enemies I have on this side of the world."

"Yet most of them think Hawke is dead," Warren reminded James. "That alone narrows it down."

"Who's Hawke?" Nathan asked.

Silence greeted that question, but a few Andersons glanced at James to see if he would answer—or lay into Warren for mentioning that name. But James stared at Nathan for a long moment before he said, "It was a name I used to go by when I sailed these waters years ago."

"When you were a pirate?" Nathan persisted.

Worse silence. Tense silence. Judith groaned to herself, almost blurting out that *she* didn't tell Nathan that. But James actually laughed. "Like you were a smuggler?"

Nathan snorted. "Touché."

"But I *am* the black sheep of my family," James continued. "And for a time I felt compelled to protect them from my antics by using a false name. Couldn't give them more reasons to disown me, you understand, when they already had so many."

Nathan tipped his head to that vague reply. "Then might I point out that you're overlooking the obvious? If you're going to sneak around St. Kitts, grab Catherine while you're at it. Then you have a more palatable exchange."

There was full agreement with that idea. But James also pointed out, "That's if her ship is even there. They might merely have someone planted there to direct me elsewhere. But we have contingencies now, so we are at least prepared for numerous outcomes."

Chapter Forty-Five

CATHERINE WAS STEWING. IT wasn't the first time she'd felt frustrated on *his* ship. She wanted him. It would have been nice to add the bonus of a passionate interlude to the real reason she'd convinced her father to send her along on this venture. With such a lengthy voyage to England and back, she'd been so sure she could seduce the captain. But she'd found out too late that he despised her father, and because of it, he could barely tolerate her presence on his ship. She *should* have known that, but her father never told her anything!

"I thought these men were yours, but they don't seem to like you," Andrew said as he joined her on the deck.

"Shut up. You shouldn't even be here."

"Then why am I?"

"Do you really need to ask, after you took that silly moral high ground? I couldn't trust you not to spill your guts to the Malorys before we sailed."

He quickly changed the subject from that reminder. "Where are we going?"

"After St. Kitts? To another island, one so small it doesn't even have a name. You won't like it though."

"Why not?"

"Pirates," Catherine said smugly.

"So that's who these men are?"

She snorted. "Do they look like pirates to you?"

"Actually . . . ," he said warily, glancing around the deck.

She chuckled. "That's just the flamboyance of the Caribbean, nothing more. These aren't my father's men."

"So *you* hired them?"

"No, but the captain does my father's bidding. He was tasked with getting Jacqueline. Amassing a fortune in jewels for Father was the only reason he let me go along on this venture. He thinks I'm as incompetent as his other bastards. This was a test for me, one he was sure I'd fail. But I haven't failed. I even helped with the captain's mission, so now Father will know I can be an asset to him. He won't send me away ever again."

"You barely know the man. Didn't it take you most of your life to find him? Why do you even want to impress him?"

"He's my father! The only real family I have left."

"But since you were not tasked with kidnapping Jacqueline, you could let her go."

"Don't be absurd. She—"

"Has the captain's full attention. You think I haven't noticed how you look at him—like you used to look at me."

Her eyes narrowed on him. "They were going to keep you locked up. Don't make me regret letting you out."

"I'm only pointing out the obvious. You want him, but you're not going to get him with a beauty like Jacqueline aboard—kept locked in his cabin. He hasn't let her out once. Do you even know if she's all right?"

"Of course she's all right. She's his *precious* cargo," Catherine said scathingly, turning to glare at the locked door Andrew had mentioned.

"I still don't understand why you snuck their man aboard *The Maiden George* when they were following us to Bridgeport anyway. What was the point of that?"

"You ask too many questions," she mumbled.

"You don't even know why, do you?" he guessed.

"It was the captain's doing. I'd already devised a way— you—to get *me* on that ship that was about to sail with a fortune in jewelry on it. They tried to get to Jacqueline before the Malorys sailed, without success. The captain didn't want to waste time following the Malorys to America if he could get Jacqueline off that ship a few days out of England."

"He even had his man drug her, didn't he? She kept saying how tired she felt the first few days at sea. That smacks of desperation when stealing her off that ship could only have saved a week or two of time."

She shrugged. "*He* thought the timing was important. He didn't say why, so don't ask me! He's so closemouthed I don't even know his damned name."

Andrew was incredulous. "But he works for your father."

"My father doesn't tell anyone anything they don't need to know, about his men or anything else."

The captain suddenly left his cabin, slamming the door, looking furious.

"What's wrong?" Catherine asked.

"She won't eat. Not once has she touched her food, and we're four days out. Her belly cries, but she refuses!"

The food *was* horrible compared to what they'd had aboard *The Maiden George*, dry, flavorless, half the time burnt, but that wouldn't be causing Jacqueline's rebellion. As handsome as this man was, she was amazed he hadn't cajoled the girl into being reasonable. So captor and prisoner weren't getting along at all? That eased her jealousy a little, but not enough.

"Let me talk to her," Catherine suggested. "I'll get her to cooperate if I can see her—alone."

"When you led her out to me in that garden? She thinks you're one of us."

"Did you tell her that?"

"I've told her nothing."

"Then I can convince her to at least eat."

He started to deny the request, but then nodded stiffly and extended his arm with a flourish toward the door. She expected Jacqueline to still be wearing her ball gown, but when she entered the cabin, she found the girl wearing one of *his* long shirts and nothing else! She stared at bare legs from the knees down and saw red. Had they made love?

Jacqueline was standing at the windows that faced behind the ship, not a full bank of them, just two, but with clear, clean glass. Hoping to see her father's ship appear, no doubt. Back stiff, arms crossed, she turned at the sound of the door's opening with eyes blazing. And the anger didn't dissipate at the sight of Catherine.

"What do *you* want?" Jack demanded.

"My lover isn't happy with you, Jacqueline."

"Your *what?*"

"He didn't mention our relationship?"

"Are you mad? How can you consort with that bastard? They're going to kill my father!"

Catherine tsked. "Whatever happens, you won't be able to

help, will you? Not if you're so weak you can barely stand up because of this childish refusal to eat."

Jacqueline marched over to the captain's desk, where a plate of food had been left, untouched. Catherine smiled, anticipating the captain's gratitude for her success in making Jacqueline behave reasonably. But the girl didn't lift the plate to eat from it. Catherine ran out of the cabin, but not before the plate came flying after her to break on the deck and make quite a mess.

She smiled to herself, despite the scowl the captain was now giving her. She could not care less if Jacqueline ate before she was delivered. She didn't need to be in good health when the exchange was made.

Andrew noticed Catherine's smirk as she sauntered away. He took a chance and approached the captain himself. "That was a mistake, you know. Jack has never liked Catherine. She wouldn't listen to anything she had to say, but she'll listen to me. I guarantee if you let me speak to her, she'll start eating her meals."

"You have until more food arrives and not a moment more."

Andrew nodded. Catherine hadn't bothered to close the door. He peeked around it to make sure Jack wasn't ready to throw something else before he rushed inside. But she wasn't happy to see him, either.

"You, too, Andrássy?" Jack snarled.

He gave her a weak smile. "It's actually Andrew, but there's no time to explain. You know I'm not part of *this*," he whispered urgently. "But I might be able to help you escape."

"I've thought of nothing other than escape—when I'm not thinking of ways to kill *him*. But how? He keeps me tied at night, the door locked in the day."

He nodded toward the two windows. "Use a blanket to break those, as quietly as you can. I will knock three times on the door to let you know when we are nearing the harbor at St. Kitts. That's when you must do it and quickly, while the captain is distracted by docking the ship and the noise in the harbor. But you must eat in the meantime, or you won't have the strength to do this."

"Catherine said nearly the same thing, just without mentioning escape, so how can I trust you?"

"I'm only going to give you the signal, Jack. The rest is up to you. But once you escape, I would advise you to hide and stay hidden until these people give up and go away."

"And if they don't leave?"

"Do you really think they will stay and face your father without you in hand?"

She grinned for the first time. "No, that wouldn't be very smart of them."

Two days later, they reached St. Kitts late in the morning. Andrew had given his signal to Jacqueline, but since he was not allowed to debark and the captain's cabin was locked, he had no way of knowing yet if she had successfully escaped. The captain went ashore to arrange for a go-between. The exchange wouldn't happen here. They just wanted to make sure that James Malory wasn't going to arrive with a flotilla of ships before he was directed to the next and final location. But by the time the captain returned and gave the order to sail again, Jacqueline had been gone for several hours. They might even have sailed without knowing that if the captain hadn't gone straight to his cabin when he got back.

Of course he was in a panic when he saw that Jacqueline had escaped. He began to send his men to search the docks nearby. Catherine approached him quickly. "Call them back," she warned. "There's no time to waste here now that your hostage is gone and her father could arrive at any moment."

"He won't. I sank every ship in their harbor."

"You underestimate him if you don't think Malory would have found another ship within hours. We need to report to my father right away. The fortune I am bringing him will lessen the blow of your failure—or I could lie for you."

"Lie?"

She coyly put a hand on his arm. "I can tell him she jumped ship and drowned. That there was nothing you could do. You will of course assure him that you will leave immediately to obtain another Malory to use as a hostage instead. His wife, perhaps, while she's still in America. Or you can return here to try and catch Malory yourself while he's looking for his daughter, though I do assure you that isn't likely to go well—for you. But in either case, I insist you return me to my father now. You can't risk losing the fortune I went to great risk to get for him, by allowing me to be discovered here."

Andrew was close enough to have heard most of that and note how annoyed Catherine was when the captain didn't answer her either way. But they did pull up anchor and depart in haste. Andrew looked longingly at the shore as they left, wondering if he should dare to jump overboard. But Catherine would probably send the ship back for him. He knew too much now. And Jack couldn't come out of hiding until they'd gone. So he didn't jump and just hoped he wasn't making an even bigger mistake than he'd made when he'd succumbed to Catherine's wiles.

Their final destination was only a few hours away. The tiny island was overgrown with plants and tall palms. It didn't look inhabited, yet two other ships were anchored there in the aqua waters. The only building that could be seen from the ship was the top of an ancient, crumbling fort. There was no dock. They rowed ashore and started climbing a steep, sandy hill. At the top, a small village of huts was spread out in a clearing in the jungle. Inside the fort, near the huts, was a new building, a big one, which is where they headed.

Catherine was obviously happy and excited to be home, particularly since she'd succeeded in her own task, and she ran ahead of them to crow to her father about it. The captain, having failed in his task, looked distinctly worried, which infected Andrew to the point that his feet stopped moving.

He called after the captain, "I'll just wait on your ship, if it's all the same to you."

The man turned. "You aren't my guest, you're hers, and she would have left you in St. Kitts if she was done with you. Come along."

"But—is her father actually dangerous?"

The captain took Andrew's arm to get him moving again. "Yes. But if you still have her protection, then you have nothing to worry about. Just try not to draw his attention to yourself, and if you can't, address him respectfully as Captain Lacross."

They entered a big, open room that contained large, long tables and resembled a medieval great hall. The balcony in the back had rooms off it upstairs and below. But this main room was where men were gathered. Catherine was hugging an older man who had stood up at one of the long tables.

But then she turned and pointed an accusing finger at Andrew. "Daddy, he helped Malory's daughter escape!" Then she pointed at the handsome captain. "And your captain took no steps to prevent it!"

Chapter Forty-Six

D REW KNEW ST. KITTS WELL; his father-in-law lived here. But most of Drew's brothers knew it, too, since the well-populated island had long been on Skylark's trade route. The plan was for all the Andersons to debark immediately to begin scouring the town and asking questions. It wasn't necessary. Jack was standing on the dock waiting on them, wearing her soaking-wet ball gown and barefoot.

James didn't wait for the ship to be tied off nor the ramp to be dropped, he simply jumped to the dock and gathered Jack into his arms. And ushered her onto the ship the moment the ramp was dropped. They still didn't know what they had to deal with. He wanted her out of harm's way before they did.

Jack was passed around; everyone needed a hug, and now they were all damp from her gown.

Judith got hers last and didn't want to let Jack go, whispering, "I was *so* frightened for you, Jack!"

"I was fine," Jack replied with a short laugh. "Enraged, but fine."

"Were you simply let go, or did you escape?" James wanted to know.

"I broke a window and jumped into the water just as they were docking."

"But you're still dripping. Did this only just happen? Are they still here looking for you?" The gleam of battle had entered James's green eyes. He was only waiting on her answer before he charged off to find her abductors.

"That was a few hours ago. I swam behind the other ships moored here. I had hoped one would be a Skylark vessel, but it appeared not. And I was hesitant to cross the dock looking like this, which could have gained too much notice, and someone might have led them in whatever direction I took. So I just stayed in the water, hiding behind the last ship down at the end of the pier. I was still floating there when I saw them just sail off without me about an hour ago."

"Uncle James, please," Judith interceded. "If they are gone, can I at least get Jack into some dry clothes before we hear what happened?"

James nodded. "Of course. Bring her to Tremayne's cabin when you are done."

"Tremayne?" Jack asked as Judith led her below to her cabin.

"This is his ship and not really designed for passengers, but he showed up in the nick of time and agreed to assist in your rescue. They'd disabled *The Maiden George*."

"Yes, I know, I heard all about it," Jack said with disgust. Judith tossed a pair of breeches and a shirt on the cot for her. "Oh, thank God, I was afraid you were going to hand me one of your dainty dresses."

Judith laughed as Jack stripped out of the wet gown and

petticoats. It seemed like forever since Judith had been able to laugh. "How on earth did you swim in that? Your legs didn't get tangled?"

"I tied the skirt up first, sort of like swaddling, and just dropped it before I climbed out of the water. It left me tired though . . . well, my limbs are. You can't imagine how exhausting it is to try to stay afloat in one place for over an hour."

Such mundane subjects when Judith had so many questions she was nearly bursting with them. But she didn't want Jack to have to repeat herself, so she held her tongue.

But Jack wanted to know, "So you've forgiven him?"

"It doesn't matter, when he hasn't forgiven me."

Jack winced for her. "Well, don't fret it. He'll come to his senses if you want him to."

"Oh?" Judith managed a grin. "Wishful thinking will do it, will it?"

"Not a'tall! But a nudge or two will, so we'll figure something out—after we get home. I do want to go home, Judy. I don't like this part of the world anymore."

Judith nodded as she hurried Jack to Nathan's cabin. Kidnapping, sunk ships—heartache. Judith would just as soon go home, too.

The only one sitting was Nathan, behind his desk. He glanced at Judith as she arrived, even stared at her for a long moment before he gave Jack a slight smile in greeting. But then he just stared pensively at a long-tipped pen he was winding through his fingers, as if he had no interest in this reunion.

He'd told Judith before they'd arrived that he was releasing her from her duties because he knew she'd want to spend every moment with Jack as soon as they got her back. Magnanimous of him, but she didn't want to be released! She'd hoped they'd have enough time together for her to breach his defenses. She'd been so encouraged every time he laughed or smiled at her. But then that stiffness would sneak back into his demeanor, the obvious anger just under the surface, and she was afraid whatever they'd had between them was truly gone. She couldn't even blame him when she'd accused him of stealing as quickly as her family had. How did you forgive someone for thinking the worst of you?

"Did they hurt you?" James asked carefully as he approached Jack.

"No, just my pride. I was captured too easily."

James smiled as he hugged her to him fiercely. "Do you know what he has against me? Why he did this?"

"The captain who took me? He doesn't even know you, he works for someone else. Never even gave me his name, so I gave him one. Bastard. You can refer to him like that. I certainly did."

Quite a few smiled over Jack's disparagement. James wasn't one of them. "Why were you kept in the captain's cabin?"

Jack blushed. "How did you—?"

"It's the only cabin on a ship that would have a window big enough for you to escape from."

"He pretended I had a choice, there or his brig. When I chose the brig, he just laughed. He didn't want his *prize* to suffer deprivation. But nothing untoward happened—other than me trying to kill him. And then Andrássy—well, it's actually Andrew—he helped me escape. It was his idea to go out the window and he gave me a signal when the time was right for it."

"So it appears he told the truth then," James said.

"About what?"

"He left us a letter of confession. He admitted he's no relation to us, that Catherine hired him to pretend to be one just to get them on *The Maiden George* so they could steal the jewelry."

"*They* did it?" Jack asked in surprise.

A few embarrassed eyes went to Nathan. His expression was no longer pensive or detached. His eyes moved over the room and ended on Judith. His anger was definitely back.

But James and Jack weren't watching this byplay, and Jack said to her father, "I knew this wouldn't surprise you, that they were impostors. You didn't trust them from the start."

"No, but the theft wasn't enough for Catherine. Andrew suspected she was going to abduct you, too. Instead of warning us before it happened, he foolishly thought he could stop it."

"He did try, actually, but he got knocked out. I didn't even know they'd taken him, too, until he was allowed to see me one time on the ship, which was when he assured me he'd help me escape. I really wish Catherine would get blamed for that, but she probably won't be. She and Bastard are quite chummy. *Very* chummy, if you get my drift."

Judith gave Jack an odd look. That had been said quite scathingly. But then Jack hugged her father again and added, "I just want to go home."

Nathan stood up. "I'll begin departure."

But James stopped him. "I need to go ashore first, Captain Tremayne. I won't be long."

Drew followed James out of the cabin. "You think some of them might still be here?"

"If they are, they'd be the proverbial needle and would take too long to ferret out in a town this size. However, first instinct is usually the accurate one, so come along and take me to your Skylark office here. I want to arrange for someone you trust to find out if our mutual nemesis is still in prison and send me word. I would like him crossed off the list, or not, before I return to settle this."

"I hope you will include me in your numbers when you do."

"Itching for a fight, Yank?"

"I don't like how this played out. None of us do. Lacross or not, they stepped over the line when they took our Jack."

Chapter Forty-Seven

"JUDITH MALORY, I INSIST. If you don't tell me what's wrong *this* minute . . ."

They'd just finished breakfast together. Whenever her mother used her full name *and* that tone, Judith knew she was in trouble. But she just didn't want to talk about Nathan, didn't know where he was, didn't know if she'd ever see him again. Of course that didn't stop her from looking for him every place she went.

Roslynn had been given a full account of the trip, so she even knew who Nathan was and had nothing but good things to say about him, how he'd changed his plans and sailed to the Caribbean to find Jack. She had also expressed regret at how shabbily he'd been treated by the Malorys, her husband in particular.

"You should be asking Jack that," Judith replied to her mother. "She's been behaving most odd. She is angry more often than not for no apparent reason."

"No, I *know* you. I've caught those sad looks when you

think no one is watching. Are you just worried about Jack? Did you fancy one of the men you met in Bridgeport? Or are you disappointed Lord Cullen got engaged before the Season even began here? That was so unexpected," Roslynn complained. "But that cast on his foot got him far too much sympathy from the ladies—"

Judith cut in tonelessly, "I assure you I'm not lamenting over the Scotsman."

She was worried about Jack, but she was equally worried about her father. Finding out that Nathan was innocent, that he'd been so wrong about him, didn't sit well with Anthony Malory a'tall. He did apologize when Nathan returned them to Bridgeport. It had been an exceedingly embarrassing moment for him that Judith had watched from afar. Or her father's foul mood could be a result of the tiff her parents were having. She didn't even want to know what that was about. Or it could simply be because she had half a dozen young lords aggressively courting her. Two of them had even whispered to her that they were going to ask for permission to marry her—from her mother.

Ordinarily Judith would have laughed at their admissions of which parent they preferred to approach. She hadn't told them not to, but only because she didn't want to have to explain why. She would tell her mother instead. Actually, she ought to sit both her parents down and have a talk with them. But not today. She had a recital to attend this afternoon, a dinner tonight, a ball tomorrow. A Season in London was a whirlwind of activities.

So Judith was appalled with herself when she suddenly burst out, "I found out what love is like, Mama. It's horrible. I hate it!"

"Only if— Who would dare not return your feelings?" Roslynn demanded hotly, but then she guessed, "Oh, good God, your father was right? You got attached to that young man from the ship, Nathan Tremayne? But Tony didn't say it was serious!"

"Because it's not—not anymore. He couldn't forgive me for doubting him. I can't even blame him for that. But we were mismatched from the start, never meant to be. I'm beginning to accept that. Well, I have to, don't I?"

"Not if you don't want to, sweetheart. Or do I need to point out that you should never *ever* say never. Or perhaps I need to remind you that your father and I didn't marry for love. He merely made the ultimate sacrifice of his bachelorhood to protect me from my cousin Geordie. Tony was the worst rake in London, with the exception of his brother James, of course, so I was sure it would *never* work. Look how wrong I was. So tell me more about Mr. Tremayne. . . ."

Mere blocks away in the West End of town, Nathan was hiding around the corner of a building, waiting. He wasn't alone. Arnold Burdis leaned against the wall next to him, six of his men lined up beyond him. Nathan thought he heard a wagon pulling up to the back entrance of the tavern, but when he peeked, there was nothing there. It was just sounds from the street out front that he'd heard.

This was one of three fancy taverns in this wealthy part of London. Commander Burdis had groups of men posted at the other two, and single men watching four other establishments that weren't quite as fancy, but still in the general area. If normal deliveries weren't made in the mornings, they wouldn't even be there yet. But Nathan had a feeling Grigg would be that bold. Night deliveries, with the tavern filled with nabobs, might draw suspicions. But Nathan and Burdis had been doing this for a week now, ever since Nathan got back to England and reported to the commander—and confided what he'd learned before he'd sailed from Grigg's man.

He was beginning to think Grigg's man had lied about those London deliveries. Yet everything the man had said that night had made sense. Why would smugglers come to London except to do business? Why wouldn't Grigg hit this lucrative market after finding it nearly risk-free? His runs across the Channel would be much quicker, and he'd avoid the heavily patrolled southern coast. And revenuers didn't police the city. They might keep an eye on the docks, but the city was too big. And they weren't expecting smuggled goods to get in by land routes.

"Are you sure this plan will actually bear fruit?" Burdis asked, not for the first time.

"This tavern is almost out of brandy. They are charging exorbitantly high prices for what little they have left. Last night I went in and ordered a glass. When I commented on the price, I was told to stop complaining, that they'd be getting a shipment soon."

"Yes, yes, I know it looks promising, but—"

"You didn't have to come along."

"You mean you hoped I wouldn't. But the man's got to hang, Nathan, publicly, legally. I can't let you just have at him."

"But he'll be hung for smuggling, not for killing my father," Nathan growled.

"Does it really matter why he hangs, as long as he hangs?"

It mattered, but obviously only to Nathan. Grigg had caused the rift between Nathan and Jory, made them part ways with anger, and killed Jory before Nathan could fix that, before he could tell Jory how sorry he was for leaving the way he did.

"You still going to that ball tomorrow night that I arranged for you?"

The commander's attitude toward Nathan had changed quite a bit after Nathan returned to England, almost as if they were friends now. Having "worked together," as it were, and successfully, Nathan wasn't even surprised. But he'd found it useful, having friends with connections, when he'd got it into his head to enter *her* world.

Which had been a crazy notion to begin with, and since he didn't even know if Judith would be at the ball, he said, "I don't know."

"My tailor didn't come through for you in time?"

"He did. I'm just having second thoughts about it."

"I had to call in a huge favor someone owed me to get you that invitation. What the devil d'you mean, you don't know?"

"Just that. I'm not so sure it's a good idea now, to see her again."

Arnold, who hadn't questioned why Nathan had wanted to attend a ball in London, rolled his eyes. "So it's a woman. That's what I had to promise my life away for? I should have known."

"Your life?" Nathan said with a chuckle.

"You can't believe what that hostess is capable of demanding in return. If I wasn't already married, she might even demand that I propose marriage to her. She's a widow."

As exaggerations went, that one had to be a whopper. Nathan should never have asked the favor. He just didn't like the way his relationship with Judith had ended. At least that was the excuse he'd convinced himself of. He'd behaved like an ass.

He knew it better than anyone else. But he wasn't used to these feelings she had stirred up in him. They were driving him crazy. She had given him no clue about how she felt about him. The sadness he'd seen in her eyes was as likely to have been disgust as disappointment. During the entire trip back to Bridgeport, he'd never seen her alone. She'd always been with Jack or her uncle. She wore her family like a shield. That damned, infuriating family . . .

Her father did apologize, but how sincere could an apology be when a threat was laced into it? "You might be innocent on one count, but not all," Anthony had added that day. "I know what you did. Stay away from my daughter. I won't warn you again."

Nathan might have demanded an explanation if his first thought hadn't been that the man knew he'd bedded his daughter. But saner reasoning later suggested Anthony couldn't know that. Nathan was still alive, after all.

But not every member of her family was hostile to him. Her American uncles weren't bad sorts at all. Boyd had been true to his word. He had rounded up a crew and a full cargo for Nathan and had even suggested where he could sell it quickly, in Ipswich or Newport, for the best prices. Nathan hadn't declined it when a free cargo would turn quite a tidy sum. But he was almost feeling rich now since James Malory had also come through with the handsome fee he'd promised him for his help.

It was nearing noon. Burdis would be taking his break soon but would resume surveillance again that evening. He'd been doubtful of a morning delivery from the start, was still sure the smugglers would prefer to operate in the shadows of night. Nathan knew Burdis was just here now to humor him.

"I'm going to have to start bringing a chair for this mission," Arnold said, only half joking.

Nathan started to laugh, but stopped at the sound of another wagon nearby. He glanced around the corner again. A slow, satisfied grin spread across his lips. A wagon was approaching the tavern's back entrance. Three men were on the perch, another three in the back sitting on crates. It didn't take that many men to make deliveries.

"He's here," Nathan warned in low tones. "And with enough men to stave off trouble. He obviously doesn't take risks with a load this big."

"You're sure it's him?"

"I've only seen him once. But Hammett Grigg has a face you can't forget. He's got his top man with him, too, Mr. Olivey."

"I want his ship as well," Arnold reminded Nathan.

"I'm sure you can persuade one of them to take you to it afterward—if any of them are left alive. So we're handling this as we discussed?"

"We discussed *not* killing them, as I recall," Arnold grumbled, and sent half his men around the tavern to come up on the other side of it. He wanted no one escaping. "Go ahead and distract them. If you can manage a confession, I'll add murder to his list of charges. If it looks like he'd rather just shoot you, get out of the bloody way."

"Yes, Mother," Nathan said drily, and stepped around the corner.

The wagon was just coming to a stop with all six men still in it. Nathan walked to the front of the wagon and patted one of the horses as he positioned himself between the two animals.

The reins were within his reach, but he'd have to lean forward to make sure he got both of them. The wagon was the only way Grigg and his men might still escape, simply by charging forward down the alley. But Nathan knew grabbing the reins was too aggressive a step to take just yet.

Olivey noticed him first and nudged Grigg. The older man glared at him. "You again? You Tremaynes are a bleedin' bane," Hammett said, drawing a pistol.

"There's no need for weapons," Nathan replied calmly. "Killing my father wasn't enough for you?"

"Who says I did that?" Hammett smirked.

"One of your men."

"Like hell," Hammett began, but then he laughed. "Jory horned in on a couple of my buyers and wouldn't let me go near your sister, preferring that damned nabob. He had it coming. And now you do, too."

"My sister? You bastard—"

The shot was fired. Nathan dodged, then leapt for the reins, yanking them out of Olivey's hands. Grigg had used an old pistol with only one charge, but now he was reaching for another tucked in his pants.

Arnold's voice rang out clearly as he moved in with his men, "You will cease and desist! In the name of King William, I am placing you under arrest for stealing from the Crown with the crime of smuggling—and for the murder of one Jory Tremayne."

The revenuers behind the wagon had already come forward, their rifles aimed at Grigg's men. The three in the back of the vehicle didn't reach for theirs. The third man on the perch jumped down and ran to the tavern's back door, but it was locked. A shot to his leg made sure he didn't try anything else. Nathan started to calm the horses, worried they still might bolt from the noise, but they'd merely raised their heads, well trained or used to loud noises. He still quickly used the reins to hobble one of them for now. Olivey had immediately raised his hands. Grigg did so slowly now. He still might reach for the pistols tucked in his pants, but with so many rifles pointed at him, that was doubtful.

Nathan headed toward Grigg, but Arnold yanked him back as someone else got Grigg down from the wagon and confiscated his weapons. "We have his confession. The charges now include murder."

That bleedin' well didn't help. "Just give me five minutes alone with him," Nathan asked.

But Arnold knew him by now. "Out of the question. I can't hang a dead man."

"One minute, just one."

It took a moment, but Arnold nodded reluctantly, saying, "But not a second longer."

Grigg put up his fists when he realized what was about to happen. But he wasn't a fighter. His style was to shoot someone in the back, send his men to do it, or fight dirty. He tried dirty, drawing a concealed knife while he was bent over from Nathan's first punch. But whatever had hold of Nathan, it didn't include caution. He lunged for the knife the moment he saw it, grabbed it, and tossed it aside. Grigg's attempts were pathetic after that. Nathan even allowed one of Grigg's wild swings to land, just to make the fight *feel* fair for himself, but it wasn't. He got no satisfaction in beating the man unconscious, not when the first blow to his face knocked him out. It didn't even take a minute.

Chapter Forty-Eight

JUDITH AND JACK GOT to ride alone to the ball in one coach, their parents following in the other. Jack's armed escort—all four of them—was with the girls, though, and had been with Jack ever since they'd returned to London. Although the men dressed in livery, they were too big and brawny to look like servants. James had insisted on the guards, and they were going to remain with his daughter indefinitely. Judith thought that could be why Jack's moods were far from sterling. She wouldn't like being hemmed in.

She glanced at Jack, who was staring out the window. They both sparkled tonight. Jack's gown was dark pink silk, but a layer of white chiffon over it created an appropriate pastel color. Even her jewelry was pink, rose quartz mixed with diamonds.

Judith's gown was new, ordered the day after they got home, even though she already had a half dozen others she hadn't yet worn. But she didn't object when shopping calmed her mother, and Roslynn had needed calming after learning what had happened. The new gown was Judith's favorite color, pale blue.

Half of her wardrobe was that color. But she'd boldly picked a much darker blue for the edges, a mere inch. Roslynn didn't complain when she saw how the color matched Judith's eyes. And of course Roslynn had seen to buying Judith more jewelry immediately, too. So her gown was complemented by sapphires tonight.

"You look magnificent tonight, Jack. I wish I could wear pink like you, but Mother thinks it makes me look wan—are you listening?"

"What?"

Judith sighed. "I wish you'd tell me what's wrong. You're either distracted or snapping at me over something—more *often* snapping. If your eyes were red, too, I'd think you're going through what I went through with Nathan. You aren't, are you?"

Jack snorted. "Believe me, when I fall in love I'll know it. And *you'll* know it. Everyone will, because I'll drag him straight to the altar, kicking and screaming if I have to—well, my father will see to that."

Judith couldn't help chuckling over the image that created. "Very well. I was just worried you might have gotten overly attached to Quintin."

"I might have, if we'd had more time together, but no. Bastard cut that short."

Jack was *still* calling her abductor by that name, and she usually got angry every time he was mentioned. Not just snappish, but really angry. But Jack's tone had been even just then, so Judith wasn't going to press it, when anger was the last thing Jack should be taking to a ball.

Instead Judith said, "And any of these new lords who've been courting you since we got back?"

"Not yet, but we're in no hurry, remember?"

How could she forget that? They weren't supposed to fall in love anytime soon, either, but so much for well-laid plans. So she took another guess, nodding toward the roof of the coach where the escort was riding. "You hate these precautions, don't you?"

"My guards? No, actually, they're nice enough chaps."

Judith was running out of ideas, so she tried her mother's tactic. "Jacqueline Malory, you're going to tell me *right* now what's been bothering you. I insist!"

Jack snorted again. Judith was encouraged. Jack's snorting was normal. "I don't like being so helpless, as I was during—it's made me hate being a woman!"

Judith was taken aback. She would never have guessed *that* could be the problem, and yet she should have. Jack was always so in control, always in the lead, always sure of herself and her capabilities. To have lost that control, even for a little while, would have hit her hard.

But Judith replied pragmatically, "Nonsense. D'you think a man really would have fared better? A man would merely have been knocked out and dragged off, instead of being carried off. And he would have been bound before he woke. Truly, Jack, men can be rendered just as helpless in such a situation. But— is that really all that's been bothering you?"

Jack wrung her hands in indecision, then admitted, "No."

"Then what?"

"I didn't tell my father everything." When Judith's eyes rounded, Jack added, "No, nothing like that. But there was another note, the original one penned by Bastard's boss. When I found it, I accused Bastard of not leaving any note at all, so my father would have no idea what happened to me. I could have killed him that day. Actually, I tried to. But he assured me that Catherine had sent a more polite version of the original one."

Eyes still round, Judith said, "A polite kidnapper? Are you serious?"

Jack actually grinned for a moment. "I had that exact thought at the time, you know." But then she wrung her hands again. "I was afraid that if I told my father about it, it would stir an old memory for him, and he'd know exactly whose idea it was to abduct me and where to go to find him. The original note from Bastard's boss implied he would. And I don't want my father to go after him, at least not when they are expecting him to. I couldn't bear it if *my* words led him into a trap."

"Don't you think you should let your father decide the matter?"

"I'll tell him, after enough time has passed for his anger to wane a bit so that he doesn't hie off and get himself killed."

"But it's been weeks since we got home."

"I know, and maybe Bastard has warned his boss to change the location of his lair and this can all just be forgotten."

"Is that who you're trying to protect?" Judith asked carefully.

"Gads, no, *he* should be drawn and quartered!" Jack spat out.

Judith sighed. "It's your choice, Jack. I just hope this decision doesn't come back to haunt you someday."

"You can't imagine how much I've been agonizing over this. The indecision was making me furious with myself. But I've never been so afraid for my father before. They were going to control him through *me*! Kill him because of *me*! I *am* going to tell him, whether it helps or not, but after the Season is over. Besides, by then he'll probably have more information. Uncle

Clinton assured him that all the Skylark captains who pass down that way will keep an eye out for Catherine, Andrew, and Bastard. Something is sure to come of that."

Judith didn't usually disagree with Jack but she tsked now, "I hesitate to say it, but I think you should simply have more faith in your father. As long as he doesn't have the rescue of loved ones to contend with, he won't be restrained. And you know how that works out."

Jack grinned, then laughed. "Yes, I know. I'm just making sure it does happen that way, by letting enough time pass so whoever did this won't be expecting him. That's all, Judy. I just want my father to have a better fighting chance. And I did consider how torn up he'd be if he missed my Season just to wrap this up."

That was sound reasoning, so Judith said no more on the subject. And Jack obviously felt better for having made a clean breast of it. She was still smiling when they arrived at the ball.

Chapter Forty-Nine

Lady spencer's ball wasn't the first of the Season. They'd missed that one due to their detour to the Caribbean, which had delayed their return to London by a week. It wasn't the second ball, either, but at least they'd managed to attend that one, with a mere one day's notice, which was why Judith had so many suitors already. But she'd hoped she might actually enjoy this third ball. Nasty thing, hope, when it didn't stand a chance in hell . . .

Jack's suitors converged on her immediately, but then Georgina had held James back when they arrived, so the young bucks hadn't yet noticed that Jack's father was in attendance. Georgina had insisted on taking this precaution. Because James was such a social recluse, rumors about him of the dastardly sort had always abounded and were still whispered to this day. He simply never gave the *ton* a chance to get to know him and never would. Georgina had had to hold him back at their first ball, too, so Jack would at least be able to meet a few young men before he was noticed. James was actually amused by his wife's ploy.

Judith didn't face the same challenge on entering the ballroom with her parents. The only rumors that had ever circulated about her father concerned his having been a notorious rake and having had his share of duels because of it, most of which were long forgotten. It was still well-known that he was a master in the ring, but what young buck didn't know that when they had all at one time or another visited Knighton's Hall to witness firsthand his renowned skill.

Judith knew it was simply her father's demeanor that gave young men pause about approaching her—whenever Roslynn didn't have her eye on him, urging him to smile or at least keep a neutral expression on his face. But at the first ball, Roslynn had managed quite well to keep Anthony from scaring away every man who approached Judith, and Roslynn had been overly nice to all of them as well, which was why Judith already had a handful of suitors. They came forward tonight, just more slowly since Anthony was still at her side.

But an elbow was discreetly jabbed in Anthony's ribs as his wife whispered, "Behave. Be cordial. Be their bluidy best friend."

"Now *that's* going too far, sweetheart, 'deed it is," Anthony complained. "But I'll give the first option a try if you'll stop frying me—and put your brogue away."

The byplay was brief but long enough for Addison Tyler to whisk Judith onto the dance floor with a relieved laugh. "Gad, I thought she'd never distract him."

With barely ten minutes passed since she'd entered the ballroom, she knew that was a gross exaggeration. But Addison was still smiling, so it was obviously intended to be. Firstborn of an earl, Addison would eventually inherit that title. With blond hair, dark gray eyes, and a handsome visage, he knew he was quite the catch this Season. The ladies did, too. Quite a few had set their caps for him before Jack and Judith had arrived home. Judith knew a good number of the debutantes, those who lived in London with whom she and Jack had socialized while growing up, and she'd been snubbed by a few of them as if she'd stolen Addison Tyler away from them.

"Does your father hate me for some reason?" Lord Tyler asked as he glided her smoothly in the current waltz.

"No, he hates you all equally."

"So he's that sort of father, eh? Can't bear to let you go?"

"Something like that."

Addison was one of the two young lords who had already decided that they wanted to marry her. Hadley Dunning was the other. They'd both called on her every day this week at the appropriate midmorning hour. They weren't the only two who had done so. But Addison was behaving somewhat aggressively toward her other suitors, too, as if he'd staked his claim and they ought to know it and back off. Some harsh words had even passed between him and Lord Dunning at the recital yesterday. The hostess had expressed concern they were going to come to blows right there in her music room. Judith doubted that they would have done so because they knew each other well. But their hostess had still asked them to leave.

Addison hadn't apologized for that yet, might not think he ought to. Roslynn had been amused that men were fighting over Judith already. Anthony didn't know because he had taken his own aggression to the ring yesterday afternoon.

"But at least your mum is nice enough."

Nice enough? What the deuce did he think, that it was him

and her against her parents? But then she groaned to herself. She was looking for a reason not to like him, wasn't she? Yet she'd favored him from the start, but only because he was the most handsome of the lot. Yet having gotten to know him better, she still found him acceptable. A little carefree, a little too bold, quite the flirt. But he hadn't made her laugh, not once.

She actually liked Lord Dunning more. Hadley wasn't quite as handsome as Addison, but he was definitely more amusing, and she needed some humor in her life right now. And he was much more friendly. He was actually trying to get to know her and wasn't attempting to immediately sweep her off her feet as Addison was doing. But she wasn't going to be rushed into a decision, and she was feeling rushed, by both of them. That had to stop. The Season had barely begun.

So she held her tongue, waited for the apology that didn't come, and managed a smile when Addison escorted her back to her parents. But he blocked Hadley from getting close enough to her to ask for the next dance. Deliberately. There was even a slight shove.

Which prompted Anthony to say, "I'm good at cracking heads together. If I have to behave, you bloody well do, too."

His saying that with a tight smile kept Roslynn's hackles from rising. In fact, as soon as Hadley Dunning led Judith onto the floor, she whispered to her husband, "Lord Tyler's jealousy might be amusing, but not if it gets out of hand."

"Say no more, m'dear. I'll—"

"Oh, no, you won't." Roslynn knew exactly what Anthony was itching to do. "If they want to fight over Judy, let them. We can only hope they will not do it at one of these large events— actually, I suppose it wouldn't hurt for you to discreetly say a few words to him, just to help tone it down—if you can do that without laying a hand on him. If it scares him off, so be it. It's not as if she favors him or anyone else here."

"Music to my ears," Anthony said with a *very* genuine smile.

They were still whispering, but only because two more of Judith's beaux were lingering with them instead of moving off to find a partner for the current waltz. Inconvenient, but these young bucks had made *their* choice and didn't want to miss catching Judith for the next dance.

"You should be asking yourself why your daughter isn't thrilled with any of these young lords," Roslynn warned.

"I already know why. She and Jack made a pact. They're not getting hitched this year. Thank God."

"That's not why and I think you know it. She's in love with someone else. I just haven't met him yet."

"An infatuation, that's all that was, and it was nipped in the bud. She's over it."

"I happen to know otherwise. And it's high time I met Mr. Tremayne."

"I'm happy to say he's gone and good riddance."

"Are you now?" she said sternly. "Happy? That your daughter isn't?"

He snorted. "Look at her, Ros. She's laughing. Does it look like she's pining over that blighter?"

"She hides her feelings well, but she confided in me. So let me ask you this. *Would* you stand in the way of her happiness?" He didn't answer, so she added, "You should track him down for her."

He actually laughed. "No, I will not. We're not interfering

for one simple reason. The man doesn't want her. If he did, he'd be here asking me for her hand before someone else does, but he's not, is he?"

"Because you obviously don't like him and he knows it."

Anthony shook his head, disagreeing, "No, he's actually not afraid of me, Ros, not even a little. That's the one thing I *do* like about him."

"That's some progress." She smiled.

He rolled his eyes. "One sterling quality does not make him acceptable to me as a son-in-law."

"No man is *ever* going to be acceptable to you for our daughter. I'm not even surprised this is turning out to be so difficult. But you have to think of Judy, not yourself. You knew this day would come."

"But it hasn't come yet. I repeat, he doesn't want her, and she'll just have to—"

"Would that be him?" Roslynn suddenly asked, nodding toward the entrance at a handsome man with white-blond hair.

Anthony hissed, "Of all the bloody nerve."

"Well, you *did* say he wasn't afraid of you," Roslynn smirked.

Chapter Fifty

JUDITH SAW NATHAN THE moment he entered the ballroom only because her eyes kept venturing in that direction, hoping he would. But when he did, it took her a moment to believe it. Dressed in black evening attire tailored to perfection, blond hair queued back for the occasion, he fit right in as if he belonged here. Well, didn't he? He had the credentials to be here, but how had he finagled an invitation? He must have one, she supposed, to have gotten through the door.

As if she cared how he'd managed it. He was here! Her heart was already racing with anticipation. He'd come to his senses, finally. He'd come to find her. But to do it this boldly? When he could have just come to her home? He would have been let in. Every day since she'd been back, she'd warned the butler to expect him, then had dealt with the disappointment when he didn't show up.

Their eyes met across the room, but she couldn't hold the look because she was still dancing with Hadley. But the moment the music ended, she hurried back to her mother to make herself available for Nathan to approach her. Her father was conspicuously absent. Thankfully! But then she noted Anthony on the edge of the room. He'd gone to join forces with James. Those two had better *not* chase Nathan off, not tonight. Tonight was going to be magical now, the veritable highlight of her Season, of her life, for that matter. Nathan would make it so.

Roslynn wasn't alone. The two beaux Judith hadn't danced with yet were still waiting for her, and two others had joined them, one she knew, one she didn't. Three of them asked to have the next dance, which she promptly declined. Yet they didn't leave!

Roslynn whispered to her, "I suggested they find other partners while they wait for a turn on the floor with you, but I think their feet have grown roots."

Judith was flattered, but right now it was quite vexing. Would Nathan even come forward with so many lords presently vying for her attention? She couldn't see where he'd gone.

But then Roslynn said in an even lower tone, "Perhaps you are thirsty? Lady Spencer has laid out extensive refreshments to suit everyone's tastes."

Judith guessed, "You saw him?"

"Your father confirmed your Mr. Tremayne is here, yes." Roslynn added with a grin, "I'll hold down the fort and tender your excuses."

Judith beamed a smile at her mother and started toward the other side of the room. But she'd barely gone ten feet before she saw Nathan dancing by with someone else. She stopped as it dawned on her that he might not be here to see her at all. This could merely be his introduction to high society, a means to an end, since he intended to take his guardianship of his nieces more seriously. Just planning ahead for the connections he would need when his nieces came of age? Or was he just making sure that Anthony would leave him alone if he devoted his attention elsewhere for the moment? Or worse, making sure that *she* knew he was done with her. But in any case, she didn't like his tactics, not one little bit.

She returned to her beaux and said to the newcomer, "We haven't met. Shall we rectify that with a dance?"

He didn't decline, even though he hadn't asked her for one when he'd had the chance. "I'm Robert Mactear," he said once he began to waltz with her. "I was just paying my respects tae yer muther. She's vera good friends wi' mine."

She heard no more than the name, which sounded familiar, for her eyes and attention were elsewhere. Nathan passed within a few feet of her. The pretty chit he was dancing with was talking his ear off. He appeared raptly interested in her every word.

"She had a handful o' invitations sent tae me long afore this Season started. I ken she had high hopes for us."

Judith blinked. "You and I?"

Had her mother *really* looked for another Scotsman when Ian Cullen got snatched up by another debutante? But this would have been while Judith was in America—before her mother knew about Nathan.

"Aye," Robert confirmed it. "I had tae return tae London on business, so I thought I should let yer muther know I'm already taken, well, as soon as my lass says yes tae me."

She might have laughed. Roslynn was simply *not* destined to be a matchmaker. But she grouched instead, "So am I, though *my* lad appears to want to ignore me tonight."

"In that case, ye might want tae laugh and pretend yer flirting wi' me? Just tae nudge him a wee bit. I know from experience how bluidy well that works."

She did laugh. "You're a good sport, Robert."

A while later Jack found her and asked, "What the devil is *he* doing here?"

"Causing a stir," Judith said. "The ladies can't take their eyes off him, if you haven't noticed."

Jack peered at her. "You've obviously noticed. Why don't you just tell him how you feel?"

"That's not how it's done."

Jack's brows shot together. "You're joking, right? That's how *we* do it."

No, that might be what Jack would do, but Judith wasn't nearly that bold. She wished she were, though, and visited the refreshment tables a few times to see if that might give her more courage, but it didn't. It did allow her to flirt outrageously with her beaux though, per Robert's suggestion, but that didn't help either. Nathan didn't notice because he was too busy dancing with every debutante but her. Bloody blighter, he was going to take his anger to the grave?

But when she saw him heading for the exit, she actually ran across the room to stop him. "You're leaving? Really? Without a bloody word to me?"

He turned. "Yes. This is your world, darlin'. Not mine."

She didn't know what to say to that, but it was coming back, that pain in her chest, constricting her heart, squeezing. Yet, he seemed to be waiting for her to say *something*, but all she could do was stare at him, at his handsome face that she hadn't seen for nearly a month, the bruise on his cheek that was barely discernible, but *she* noticed it, the tight line of his lips, his stiff jaw, and the intense emotion in his eyes. Hot or cold? She couldn't tell!

But the only words she managed were "What's that bruise from?"

"Unfinished business finally put to rest."

"And is that your only unfin—?"

The question died off. He'd walked away and right out of the ballroom! Oh, God, why did she flirt so hard with the other men? Had he just given up because of it?

She got through the rest of the night. More champagne helped, perhaps too much champagne because she was aware of being a little foxed when she found herself in bed and didn't even remember the ride home.

But she went right to sleep that night. She was sure she was still foxed when she heard *his* voice, felt *his* hand on her cheek, a touch that healed all her wounds. But of course she wasn't sleeping.

Now she was wide-awake. "How did you get in here?"

"Through your window." He was still caressing her cheek. Like their kitten, she felt the need to lean toward his hand and tilted her head slightly so she could. "It's not the first time I've stood below it."

That surprised her. "But how could you know which was mine?"

"Earlier this week I found one of your kitchen maids out back and convinced her that I wanted to throw pebbles at your window to get your attention. She was happy to point it out to me. She thought I was one of your many swains trying to impress you with a private serenade."

The idea of him singing to her made her giggle. "You wouldn't have."

Enough moonlight was in the room that she could see his smile. "No, I wouldn't."

"You could have just come to the front door."

"Knowing your father, I couldn't. But I threw some pebbles tonight, so many of them I was afraid the glass would break. You just didn't hear them."

Damned champagne—no, she was glad the noise didn't wake her, glad that he must have found the ladder leaning against the apple tree in their garden. But why did he? What little he'd said at the ball suggested she'd never see him again, certainly not like *this*.

"What are you doing here?" she asked breathlessly.

"Tell me you didn't expect me."

"No, I didn't."

"Deep down, you did."

She didn't correct him again, yet he'd assumed something that wasn't so, while she'd been crushed by his seeming indifference tonight, sure he was still angry. Had they both fallen prey to false assumptions? When mere actions could speak much louder, as his were doing right now?

But remembering that hurt, she said, "We should have spoken at the ball, at least, more'n we did."

"I thought we would. I even thought we would dance. But when I got there, I was a bit stunned by how beautiful you looked—and how perfectly you fit in that glittering room. And I was afraid I would kiss you, right there in front of everyone, if we—"

She sat up immediately to kiss him, cutting off his words. It's what she'd wanted to do from the moment she'd heard his voice. He'd been at the ball, for her. He'd come here tonight for her. She didn't need to hear another word. But she needed to feel again what only he could make her feel. She'd longed for this, cried for this, for him. She ought to take him to task for that, but not now when he was showing her the depth of his feeling, crushing her to his chest, devouring her lips.

So when he pushed her back to her pillow, she could have cried, until she heard, "Give me a moment, darlin', please. I don't want to hurt you, but you can't imagine how much I want you."

She understood. She could have said the same thing. But she didn't want a moment. "Take a deep, calming breath if you must, just do it quickly," she insisted, *demanded*.

He laughed shakily, saying, "That worked, your silly humor."

It was no time to tell him she wasn't joking. But he stood up and shrugged out of his evening jacket, then took off his cravat and shirt. She kicked her covers away so she could kneel on the side of the bed in front of him. Within close reach of him, she slid her hands over his bare skin. So fascinating to all her senses. He had such a magnificent body, perfectly proportioned, big, lean, rock hard. Just looking at him had always affected her on a primal level she never quite understood. But right now, he was the flame and she was the moth, finding him a lure that was impossible to resist, and her body was on fire for him.

He was undressing quickly, yet not fast enough for her. Her nails scraped over his nipples, not intentionally, yet she heard the groan. Arrested, she wasn't sure what she'd just done to him, caused him pain or pleasure? But she tossed off her loose nightgown to find out and scraped her own nipple to feel what he'd just felt . . . oh, God!

He said it aloud, "Oh, God," as he tumbled her backward on the bed.

They rolled together. She laughed and ending up beneath him, gave him a brilliant smile. He appeared transfixed by it. She was caught by his eyes and the wealth of feeling in them. He loved her! She wished he'd say so, but she was content just seeing it. His lips were gentle on her now, her face, her shoulders, her neck. His love for her was in every touch. Even when he entered her a while later, it was with such tender care. They were like two pieces of a whole that were meant to rejoin, fitting together perfectly.

The ecstasy arrived for her first and rather quickly. She hoped it wouldn't always be so, because reaching that pinnacle was half the pleasure. Perhaps she could persuade him to make love to her again. But the champagne caught up with her as she finished the thought and nodded off.

"I want to marry you—if I can have you without your family." Nathan was only half joking, yet she didn't respond. "Judy?"

He sighed when he realized she was already asleep. Or pretending to be, and that would be his answer, wouldn't it? No, he was done with doubts, had experienced far too many when it came to her. He dressed, kissed her brow, and slipped out the way he'd come in. It was her turn now. If she wanted him in her life, she knew where she could find him to let him know.

Chapter Fifty-One

JUDITH WOKE WITH A smile and a nasty headache. The head-ache went away as the morning progressed; the smile stayed. It had been a magical night, just not at the ball. It would be nice if she could remember it in more detail, but her joy was still overflowing. She ought to caution herself that she'd felt this way before after the first time Nathan and she had made love, but she didn't. This was different. This time she was sure Nathan loved her.

Jacqueline showed up midmorning instead of staying home to receive her own callers, which wasn't unusual. Jack didn't have the patience for *all* the formalities of a Season. But she still couldn't escape all of her beaux. Having been told where she'd gone, some of them followed her to Judith's house, so the parlor on Park Lane was quite crowded today. Which was why it took so long for Jack to find a moment alone with Judith.

When she did, Jack observed, "You seem quite chip-per today, though I have to admit that *was* a splendid ball, wasn't it?"

"No, but it was a splendid night."

"I thought you went home angry?"

Judith didn't reply to that, grinning excitedly instead. "I've made a decision. You were right. I should have told Nathan long ago how I feel about him and I will, just as soon as I see him again."

"He barely said two words to you last night. D'you really think that's going to happen?"

"Yes, for the simple reason that he made quite an impression last night on the *ton*. He's no doubt on everyone's lips this morning."

Jack glanced over her shoulder, then nodded with a snort. "He's definitely on *their* lips."

"So every hostess is going to want to include him now."

"They might want to, but no one will know where to send invitations!"

"But I do." Judith grinned. "And I'll make sure they do."

"You're going to break our pact to wait, aren't you?" Jack said with a sour look.

Judith hugged her tightly. "I have to. You will, too, once you feel this way. It's the most glorious thing, Jack, really it is."

"Just so you know, if he hurts you again, I'll do the same to him."

Judith laughed. "So will I!"

She canceled her engagement for that afternoon so she could go through all of her own invitations and jot brief notes to each hostess. She gave his address in care of Derek, so she sent her cousin a note, too, to deliver them to the ruin. She even added the postscript "It will be repaired soon!"

Of course Nathan might not go straight to Hampshire. He might be staying somewhere in town until he could declare his intentions to her. But in that case he'd finagle his own invitations, just as he'd done last night. So she did expect to see him again, and soon. The only thing she didn't expect was for him to call on her on Park Lane. He'd made it perfectly clear that he didn't want to run into her father. But he could come through the window again. . . .

Her confidence started to wane by the end of the week. She didn't get despondent, though. She got determined instead. She confided in Jack about what she was going to do. Jack merely cautioned her not to go alone. So they found her parents in the dining room that morning, and just in time. Anthony had just stood up to leave. His habit was to escape the house before the callers arrived.

"Sit down, please," Judith requested. "And don't worry, the house is now officially back to normal."

"Did a few months fly by without my noticing?" Anthony said drily as he resumed his seat.

Judith might have laughed at his quip if she weren't putting the cart before the horse, as it were. "No, but I am henceforth declining all callers, well, except—no, he won't, and we know *why* he—" Before she got any more tongue-tied, she declared firmly, "I've canceled all my engagements, too. The Season is over for me."

Roslynn might have had some warning, but she still exclaimed, "Judy! It's barely begun!"

"But there's no point, Mama, when I already know who I'm going to marry."

Judith was looking at her father as she said it. He didn't ask her who, merely said, "I don't suppose he intends to ask my permission first?"

"And risk a resounding no?"

"But has he even asked you yet?"

"No, but he will, just as soon as I get to Hampshire. Will you take me?"

He didn't answer. He looked at Jack and asked, "Are you responsible for the courage in her words?"

Jack grinned cheekily. "No, actually, I just wanted to watch."

Anthony snorted. "Minx."

He didn't look angry, and it was usually quite easy to tell when he was. Judith still held her breath as he stood up and came over to put his hands on her shoulders.

"Is he who you really want, poppet?"

"More than anything."

"That's quite a lot. And since I've already had my brow beaten quite enough lately, I suppose I should summon the coach."

She gave a delighted cry and hugged him, but he wasn't quite done. "Of course, if he should disappoint you, I'll want to know why."

At least her father didn't say he'd kill him. One hurdle down, the bigger one to go. . . .

Chapter Fifty-Two

THE RUIN LOOKED THE same from a distance . . . well, except for the roof, which appeared to be finished, and all in clay tiles, too. But as Judith got closer, she saw that many of the windows had been replaced as well, perhaps all of them. Nathan had obviously been busy this week. Too busy to open the invitations she'd arranged to have forwarded to him? Or had he deliberately ignored those?

The front door was wide-open. So were the new windows. As she stepped inside, she noticed that a nice breeze was circulating. The entrance hall and the parlor hadn't changed much, but at least the cobwebs were gone and the staircase had new boards, all but one, which Nathan was still hammering in place.

His shirtsleeves were rolled up, his tool belt strapped to his hips. And he was wearing knee-high Hessian boots? She almost laughed. Did he not realize he shouldn't be working in such fancy footwear? But he probably found them too comfortable to resist. He'd obviously done some shopping while in London.

Or collected the rest of his wardrobe that he'd left in England when he sailed.

She'd been filled with such determination and resolve. Why the deuce was she suddenly so nervous now that she was here? But she didn't have much time. Her father was allowing her a brief visit alone with Nathan, but warned if she took too long, he'd come to find out why. Did he really think they'd make love in a crumbling old ruin? Well, rake that he used to be, he probably thought exactly that.

She carefully stepped inside because he'd replaced some of the rotted floorboards in the foyer, but not all.

"Are your nieces here with you? I've looked forward to meeting them."

He glanced back, straightened, and came down the stairs without taking his eyes off her. "They'll be remaining with Peggy and Alf, your uncle James's caretakers, until the house is fit for them."

"You mean until it's finished?"

"No, just until it's no longer a danger to curious children. Which won't be much longer. The attic and the first floor sustained the worst of the weather damage. The second floor hasn't needed nearly as much work. The girls' rooms are already done."

She was surprised. "And furnished?"

"Well, no. And I've still got to paint or wallpaper them and figure out what to put on the new floorboards."

"You don't think they'd like to be a part of that? Watch the progress? Make choices for their own rooms? They could stay with my cousins next door in the meantime. They've got an army of servants to watch over them, including my cousin

Cheryl's old nanny. And Derek's cook makes such wonderful desserts. They'd be thrilled."

His brow furrowed with a frown. "Too thrilled. I don't want them getting used to a grand mansion like that because then they might be disappointed with the home I'm giving them."

Judith knew his nieces would be delighted with this manor once she added her touch to it, but she didn't say that. He was annoyed enough with her suggestion to finally take his eyes off her face—and notice the kitten in her arms. She'd brought it as an excuse to visit him—if she ended up needing one.

"I never expected to see it again." He couldn't help smiling at the furball. "Figured you would have found it a home by now."

"Bite your tongue. Silver is quite entrenched. And *it* has been determined to be a he by my mother."

His eyes came back to hers. "Why did you bring him?"

"I know you only gave him up because you had nowhere to keep him while you finished your business in America. I thought we might share Silver, now that you appear to be staying in England for the time being."

"Share?"

"We can—figure something out." She looked away.

Her nervousness had just shot through the roof. This wasn't exactly how she had expected this meeting to go. Why wasn't she in his arms already? Or was he as nervous as she was?

She set Silver down on the floor. He didn't wander off, just started licking his paws. Nathan might have picked him up, but he followed her instead when she walked over to the room she'd first met him in—when she'd thought he was a ghost. And had, more recently, been kissed by him. He never did confirm that he was a smuggler. Still, she was sure he used to be one, but hoped he was done with that part of his life.

The room looked the same with blankets hanging over the windows and a rumpled cot in it. But the blankets looked clean. She guessed he simply preferred this old study for now to a moldering master bedroom upstairs.

"Show me the hidden room."

She wasn't sure he would, yet he moved past her to one of the decorative wooden strips spaced several feet apart on each wall to cover the seams of the old wallpaper. One had a switch on the side of it.

"A bookcase used to hide this," he explained as a panel opened in the wall next to him. "It was empty, the books likely stolen, and wasn't worth keeping, so I used it for firewood long ago. Then I noticed the latch when I was here one day, trying to see how easily I could punch my fist through these walls."

She grinned. That must have been one of his angry-at-the-house days. She went over to peer inside the room. The decent-size space was filled to the brim with stacks of lumber and other supplies—and an open case of brandy up front, a few bottles missing from it.

"Ahha!" she couldn't help saying.

He laughed behind her. "When *The Pearl* became mine, her crew expected me to continue in my father's footsteps. Smuggling I knew how to do. Merchant trading is much more involved, and I didn't know the first thing about finding markets that would turn a profit instead of a loss, or making contacts for cargoes. I do now, thanks to the Andersons."

She swung around. "So you're going to try legitimate sailing?"

He shook his head. "I'm actually thinking of hiring a captain and sending *The Pearl* to join the Skylark fleet, which was

Boyd's suggestion. They already know all the markets and have all the necessary contacts."

"And you'll turn a tidy profit from that while you—farm?"

He laughed again. "No, I think I'm more partial to your idea of building a few rental cottages. After the house is done, of course."

They were talking about such inconsequential things while she . . . "I don't have much time." She hurried back to the main room to make sure her father hadn't yet arrived.

He followed her and put his hands on her shoulders to keep her there. "I was going to give you two weeks."

"Two weeks for what?"

"Before I returned to London for your answer. But I'm not exactly partial to climbing through windows, so I'm glad it only took one week for you to bring it to me. But if you heard my question, I'd like a chance to rephrase it."

"I'm pretty sure I would have answered if I'd heard one," she said breathlessly, her heart starting to soar. "When—did I miss it?"

"Last week, and thank God you don't know what I'm talking about."

She swung around with a gasp. "Excuse me?"

"I mucked it up, darlin'. You would have been too angry to say yes."

He obviously wasn't talking about what she hoped he was, if she would have been disturbed by what he'd said. She'd rather not get angry with him ever again, so she wasn't going to ask him to repeat whatever he'd mucked up.

Instead she said, "About that rephrasing?"

He grinned and put his arms around her. "I'd get on my knees for this, but I don't trust these floorboards to risk—"

"Yes!" she squealed, and threw her arms around his neck.

He leaned back with a chuckle. "You're supposed to wait for the question."

"Go ahead, but my answer is still going to be yes." She smiled.

"So you guessed that I love you?"

She grinned. "It's nice to hear it, but I had my suspicions."

"Did you now? And that I want to marry you?"

"That I wasn't so sure about—until now."

"I do, darlin'," he said tenderly. "It was agony fighting with you, and for that you can't imagine how sorry I am. But it's even more agony being apart from you, and it didn't take long to find that out."

"I don't feel whole without you either. I've loved you for so long." She giggled happily. "Even when I thought you were a ghost."

"I was never—never mind. Just tell me how soon we can marry. Today can't be soon enough for me."

"My mother will want to arrange it. We can't deny her that."

"If you insist."

"And you should probably formally ask—"

His hands cupped her cheeks, his words brushed her lips. "Will you marry me, Judith Malory?"

"I meant ask my father."

He groaned, placing his forehead against hers. "I would do anything for you, but you must know I'd rather be shot than ask his permission—"

"Then it's a good thing I've already given it," Anthony said from the open front door.

Nathan immediately stepped back from Judith to demand, "How long have you been standing there, Sir Anthony?"

Anthony was leaning against the doorframe, relaxed, as he replied drolly, "Long enough." But then he straightened. "Just so you know, Tremayne, the only thing I had against you was that my baby was falling in love with you. I wasn't ready to accept that yet, it was too bloody soon, but I've had it beaten into me that there's no accounting for *when*, merely that it's happened. So you've my blessing, for what it's worth. But if you ever hurt her or make her cry again, I'll bloody well kill you— just so we're clear on that."

Judith was grinning. "Go away, Papa, we were about to kiss."

"No, we weren't," Nathan assured Anthony.

Judith grabbed the front of Nathan's shirt. "Yes, we were."

She started it, but he soon forgot they had an audience, embracing her fully, kissing her deeply. But she couldn't quite lose herself with a *parent* in the room. She didn't let go of him though, just ended the kiss so she could lay her cheek on his chest, a happy smile on her lips.

"Is he gone?" Nathan whispered after a moment.

She bit back a giggle to peer around his shoulder. "Yes. You *will* get used to him, you know. You'll probably even become great friends."

"Somehow I don't see that ever happening. But as long as he doesn't visit us too often."

"He might, at least for a while. He'll want to see for himself that I'm going to be blissfully happy here. He's not going to just take my word for it. But it won't take long for him to believe it."

"But he won't want to reside in this house when he visits, will he?"

"Probably."

"Then I won't repair the guest rooms."

"Wait—"

"No."

"But there's something you don't know about me. I'm rich, and I don't mean my family is. I have my own money and a lot of it."

"And why does that warrant a 'wait'?"

"Because you have to promise me you won't be like my father. He refuses to let my mother spend any of her own money on things that are needed. It quite infuriates her."

"You had me at 'don't be like your father.' I bleedin' well *won't* be like him."

"So I can decorate our house?"

"I love the sound of *our*. Yes, to your heart's content, darlin'. As if I know anything about decorating."

"And furnish it?"

"Don't press your luck."

She laughed. Compromising with him was going to be fun. She brought his lips back to hers to prove it.

STORY THIEVES

THE STOLEN CHAPTERS

JAMES RILEY

ALADDIN

NEW YORK   LONDON   TORONTO   SYDNEY   NEW DELHI

ALADDIN

An imprint of Simon & Schuster Children's Publishing Division

1230 Avenue of the Americas, New York, New York 10020

First Aladdin hardcover edition January 2016

Text copyright © 2016 by James Riley

Interior illustrations by Chris Eliopoulos copyright © 2016 by Simon & Schuster, Inc.

Jacket illustration copyright © 2016 by Vivienne To

ALADDIN is a trademark of Simon & Schuster, Inc.,

and related logo is a registered trademark of Simon & Schuster, Inc.

For information about special discounts for bulk purchases, please contact Simon & Schuster Special Sales at 1-866-506-1949 or business@simonandschuster.com.

The Simon & Schuster Speakers Bureau can bring authors to your live event. For more information or to book an event contact the Simon & Schuster Speakers Bureau at 1-866-248-3049 or visit our website at www.simonspeakers.com.

Book design by Laura Lyn DiSiena

The text of this book was set in Adobe Garamond.

Manufactured in the United States of America 1215 FFG

2 4 6 8 10 9 7 5 3 1

Library of Congress Cataloging-in-Publication Data

Riley, James, 1977–

The stolen chapters / by James Riley. — Aladdin hardcover edition.

p. cm. — (Story thieves ; 2)

Summary: Mysteries abound as memory-erased Owen Conners, boy magician Kiel Gnomenfoot, and their half-fictional friend Bethany confront secrets, stolen memories, hidden clues, surprising twists and endings, and some very familiar faces.

[1. Books and reading—Fiction. 2. Characters in literature—Fiction. 3. Adventure and adventurers—Fiction. 4. Magic—Fiction.] I. Title.

PZ7.1.R55Sp 2016

[Fic]—dc23

2015012733

ISBN 978-1-4814-0922-3 (hc)

ISBN 978-1-4814-0924-7 (eBook)

Dedicated to the fictional. Remember,
you don't have to do what your authors say.

CHAPTER 1

Kiel Gnomenfoot

the Magister

Charm

CHAPTER 2

The library

CHAPTER 3

"WHERE ARE YOU?"

CHAPTER 4

smiling half-robotic girl.

trapped in the nonfictional world

sidekick,

CHAPTER 5

███████████

 ethany!" ████████████████████████
█████████████

████████████████████████████████

████████████████████████████████

████████████████████████████████

████████████ what she'd done █████████

████████████████████████████████

████████████████████████████████

████████████████████████████████

████████████████████████████████ she

couldn't face them.

████████████████████████████████

████████████████████████████████

CHAPTER 6

██████████████ ██

Mr. Holmes ████████████████████████
████████████████████████████████████
████████████████████████████████████
████████████████████████████████████
████████████████████████████████████
████████████████████████████████████
███████
████████████████████████████████████
████████████████████████████████████
████████████████████████████████████
█████ A pistol ██████████████████████
████████████████████████████████████
████████████████████████████████████
████████████████████████████████████

CHAPTER 7

backup plan,

"Moira Gonzalez,"

CHAPTER 8

the key

Baker Street School

found her dad

CHAPTER 9

scared

terrified

CHAPTER 10

Someone was trying to steal Owen's life, and there was nothing Owen could do about it.

"Your life is *mine* now," said the story thief, a brown-haired boy wearing the exact same T-shirt, the exact same jeans, and the exact same face as Owen.

"No!" Owen tried to shout, but he couldn't move or talk. His body just wouldn't respond.

The duplicate leaned in, hands reaching out for Owen . . .

And that's when Owen woke up with a start.

Wait, he'd been asleep! It was just a *dream*! A scary, sweaty, awful dream.

Owen wanted to laugh. "It was all a dream" was the worst possible ending to any story, but right now, it definitely felt comforting. It had felt much too real, though he supposed that

was dreams for you. Owen ran his hands over his sheets, happy to still be in bed.

Except his sheets felt a lot like carpet, and he wasn't lying on a pillow.

Also, his carpet-feeling sheets were orange for some reason.

"Uh?" Owen said. He picked his head up a bit from the carpet, only to wince and drop his head back to the floor, squeezing his eyes shut. A huge ache pounded through his temples, and everything smelled weirdly smoky.

He tried opening his eyes again, but even the little bit of light in the room caused his headache to scream at him. But Owen knew that orange carpet. He knew it like the back of his hand. Which, admittedly, he didn't know all *that* well, but still.

This was the library. He was facedown on the floor of his mother's library.

And he had no idea how he'd gotten here.

Gathering all of his courage, Owen opened his eyes again to look around.

"Owen?" said a voice to his side, followed by a painful groan.

"Kiel?" Owen said, and groaned too as he turned slightly to face the direction the voice had come from.

Kiel Gnomenfoot, former boy magician and hero to millions as star of his own book series, looked like he wanted to burst into tears. "Owen," Kiel repeated, as if the word tasted bad. "Why . . . head . . . hurt?"

Owen tried to bring up a word or two, something along the lines of *I have no idea, but it's obviously for evil, evil reasons,* but all he managed to croak out was, "Unnh." Figuring that wasn't enough, he slapped his hand a few times on the floor, then cringed at the noise.

How had he and Kiel gotten to his mom's library? The last thing Owen remembered was . . . wait, what *was* the last thing he remembered? It was like everything in the recent past was just gone. He remembered Kiel being introduced to their class as Kyle, a new student, but that was the last thing. How long ago had that been? And why couldn't he remember anything else?

Thunder crashed, and Owen grabbed his head as it erupted in pain, which made him face-plant onto the floor. After a moment of pure agony, something more urgent than the ache seeped through his brain.

"Do you smell smoke?" he asked Kiel. Owen pushed himself up and over onto his back, so at least he wouldn't hit his face again if he fell.

"Probably," Kiel moaned from his side. "Is something on fire?"

Dark black smoke began to curl into sight above Owen on the library's ceiling, and in spite of the pain, Owen immediately sat up. "Kiel!" he shouted. "The library's on fire!"

"No yelling!" Kiel shouted back, and they both groaned. Kiel slowly pushed himself up too and looked around. "Oh. Fire. That's not a good thing. Hold on, I'll use . . . whatever it is I do. Magic. To put it out."

"Holding," Owen said, gritting his teeth and waiting. "Hurry. *Hurry.*"

A pause, and then Kiel gasped. "They're not there!"

"What aren't?"

"My wand-knives!" he said, then paused. "Owen, I can't remember any magic, and my spell book's gone too. I can't do magic without it or my wands."

"A brilliant observation," said a too-deep, fake-sounding voice from behind them, as if someone was talking into a voice changer. "Which begs the question, what exactly *can* you do,

13

Mr. Gnomenfoot? What use are you without your magic?"

Owen turned to find himself staring at a short figure wearing a brown overcoat, a Sherlock Holmes hat, and a white mask with a black question mark where the face should have been.

Well. *That* wasn't good.

"Gentlemen," the masked figure said, crossing his arms over his chest. "I would say the game is afoot, but unfortunately, your game is already over."

CHAPTER 11

And you are?" Kiel asked, pushing himself to his feet a bit unsteadily. Owen followed his lead, but the whole room decided to spin at that moment, and he stumbled sideways into one of the library's study tables.

"Doyle Holmes," the masked boy said in the strange voice. "You have, of course, heard of me." He wasn't asking.

Kiel shook his head, wincing at the pain. "No. Should I have?"

Owen shook his head too, but for a different reason. "No," he groaned. "No, no, no, no, *no*. He shouldn't be here. He *can't* be here. Kiel, Doyle Holmes is, like, the great-great-great-something-grandson of Sherlock Holmes. He's a . . . he's like you." Owen winced and lowered his voice so that only Kiel could hear. "Only he's from a book that no one read. I heard it wasn't good."

Kiel straightened up, and his hands automatically flew to his belt, where his wand-knives usually were, before he sighed. "Maybe he's wearing a costume," Kiel said, not sounding hopeful.

"Ah, no," Doyle Holmes said. "I am, in fact, fictional, just like you, Kiel Gnomenfoot. Though that is the only thing I imagine we have in common."

Owen's eyes widened. He knew Kiel was fictional? This was *so* not good!

"Not possible," Kiel said, taking a step toward the boy in the mask. "You couldn't have gotten out. Not without—"

"Your friend Bethany?" Doyle finished. "You're very correct. Which brings up the question: Where might she be now?"

No! "What do you want?" Owen said.

Doyle shrugged, his mask betraying no emotions. "What does *anyone* want? To be the world's greatest detective? To solve the most challenging mysteries of all time? To ensure that no one breaks a law ever again without me catching them?" He paused. "All of those things, of course. But right now I want to see you story thieves pay for your crimes."

"*Magic* thief," Kiel corrected. "Get it right. *Kiel Gnomenfoot, Magic Thief.* It's right there in the title of my first book."

"Don't worry, your stories are now over," Doyle said, and

16

Owen could almost hear the boy smirking behind the mask.

Behind the detective, a flickering orange glow grew brighter, and the smoke along the ceiling began to thicken. And for the first time, Owen noticed that there were gas cans stacked around the library shelves.

And Doyle was holding a long match. He slowly lowered it to his fingers, snapped them, and the match lit.

"No!" Owen shouted, and grabbed his phone to call 911. Was a fictional character actually burning down his library? He punched in the numbers, but somehow, his phone had no service. Not even one bar, even though it always had service in the library.

"Don't worry," Doyle said, holding up a phone of his own. "I've already made the call. The police and fire department should be here momentarily. I've informed them that I saw two kids of your description setting fire to the library, so I imagine they'll have some questions." He nodded at the gas cans. "And once they discover Owen Conners's fingerprints all over these, I'm fairly certain they'll have all the evidence they need to put you away."

What? He was *framing* them? Why was this all happening? And why couldn't Owen remember anything that'd happened before he woke up?

"You know, I haven't had to fight someone without using magic for a while," Kiel said, stepping forward. "I think I've missed it. Owen, want to hold him down?"

"I wouldn't," Doyle said, pointing his match at the gas cans. "Not unless you want these going up prematurely."

"Why would you do this?" Owen said, pulling Kiel back, away from the boy in the question-mark mask. "And where is Bethany?"

Doyle shrugged. "I wouldn't worry about her." He held up his hand and tapped his watch. "Well, at least for the next two hours or so." He glanced at his wrist. "Sorry, two hours and ten minutes. Don't worry, I've put watches on both your wrists as well. Consider that part of the punishment. As soon as the timers reach zero, you'll never see your friend again."

Owen looked down at the rubber band on his wrist. The amount of buttons and markings on it made the band look far more complicated than just a watch, but the only thing on the face was a timer counting down: 2:10:09.

Kiel pulled his arm out of Owen's grasp and stepped forward. *"Where is she?"* he shouted, angrier than Owen had ever seen him.

"That's a good question," Doyle said, stepping back into the

burning section of the library. "But one you won't need to concern yourself with. No, I'd worry far more about the police if I were you."

Outside, the sirens grew louder, and Owen grabbed Kiel again. "What have you done to her?" Kiel shouted, struggling against Owen's hand.

"It's not what *I'll* do, but what she'll do," Doyle said. "Figure out where you are, and you'll have half the mystery solved."

"Why are you doing this?" Owen asked. "And why can't we remember anything?"

"The headaches?" Doyle said. "My apologies. I forced Kiel to use his little forget spell on you both. Couldn't have you using what you knew to find Bethany, now, could I? No, this has all been planned out from the start." He leaned forward, and in spite of the mask not having eye holes, Owen felt like Doyle was staring right at him. "Just remember, I did all of this *by the book*."

Owen grimaced. Amnesia? Seriously? What a horrible cliché.

"The police won't capture us," Kiel said, pointing at Doyle. "We'll rescue Bethany, and I'll find my wands and spell book. And then you and I will have a pleasant talk, where you don't say much, and I smile a lot." He winked then, though it didn't look easy for him.

Doyle shook his head. "Oh, Kiel Gnomenfoot. I'm a *Holmes*. There's nothing you can do that I can't see coming." And with that, he tossed the match into the stack of books right next to the gas cans. "You have about thirty seconds before the fire hits the gas. I'd *run*."

"NO!" Owen shouted, only to have Kiel grab *his* arm and yank him toward the library doors. Owen glanced back as they ran through the automatically opening doors, and he saw Doyle slip out the back way right as the fire reached the gas cans.

Kiel pulled Owen to the side of the building, just as an enormous explosion shattered the library doors and all the windows. The force of the blast sent Kiel and Owen flying, then crashing into the library's bushes.

As sirens filled the air, Kiel groaned, then turned to Owen. "What did he mean, 'a homes'?" he asked.

"That's the great-great-great-great-great-grandson of Sherlock *Holmes*, the greatest detective who ever lived," Owen said, his eyes wide as he turned back to watch his mother's library burn in the night. "And if anything, I think Doyle was written to be even *better*. We're in so, *so* much trouble."

CHAPTER 12

02:04:14 remaining

As the fire grew, Owen pushed his way out of the bushes, staring at the flames in horror. This library was his entire life. He'd spent so many days here, after school, weekends, even vacations, helping out, waiting for his mother, and especially reading all of its books.

The sirens drew closer, and Kiel pulled Owen back into the bushes to hide. Kiel seemed less angry, though he was still breathing hard. "I think this Doyle guy just made things a bit hotter for himself than he realized," he told Owen, then winked. "Don't worry, we'll find Bethany and then make him pay for this."

Owen slowly turned to Kiel in disbelief. "Did you just make a *joke*? The library's burning down! We need to help."

"But we'll be caught if we do," Kiel said, his brow knit in

confusion. "Doyle said the police are coming, and if they're anything like the Science Police, that's a bad thing. This will have to wait, Owen. If we get caught, we might never find Bethany and save her."

"Then we tell the police the whole thing!" Owen said, realizing that tears were streaming down his face as smoke filled the air. "This isn't a *book*, Kiel. This is my real life! We can't just run, not from the police. We need to tell them what happened, and they can help us find Bethany."

Kiel raised an eyebrow. "Think about what you're saying, Owen. You're going to tell the police that a fictional character escaped his story to kidnap your half-fictional friend, then set fire to your mom's library?" He shook his head. "Who would believe you? There's a reason Bethany keeps her powers a secret. This is something *we* need to take care of. By ourselves."

"I don't care if they believe me!" Owen shouted back. "This is my entire life! My *mom's* entire life. She put so much work into this place. I can't have her thinking I did this! I *can't*."

First a fire engine, then two police cars sped into the parking lot of the library, slamming on their brakes to skid neatly to a stop within inches of one another. As firemen poured off the truck and hooked up their hoses to a fire hydrant, four

police officers leaped out of their cars, noticing Kiel and Owen instantly. "Freeze!" one shouted, reaching for his gun.

"Hands in the air!" another shouted.

"We didn't do it!" Owen said, his hands flying straight up.

"Descriptions match the suspects," one of the police officers said into the radio on his chest. "Moving to apprehend."

"We're not suspects!" Owen shouted. "And there's no need to apprehend. We're surrendering!"

"This is a terrible idea, Owen," Kiel said, taking a step backward toward the bushes. "I don't have my magic, so I can't help you if this goes badly. You sure you want to do this?"

"No," Owen whispered. Then louder, "The guy who set fire to the library ran out the back. You can still catch him! He's wearing a brown coat and a creepy mask with a question mark on it."

The four police officers moved closer, their guns drawn. "Don't move!" one said.

"Tell it to the judge!" another said.

Tell it to the *judge?* Even with his headache and the fire and everything falling apart, Owen couldn't believe his ears. Who talked like that? Someone had seen too many cop movies.

"We need to get out of here," Kiel hissed, backing away as

the firemen began hosing down the library, not that it was doing much good: The fire was blazing out of control now. "Bethany's depending on us. We have . . . two hours, exactly, to find her. There's no time to waste with this."

"The police will find her," Owen said, not quite as confidently as before. He glanced at his watch and saw Kiel was right: 02:00:00, right on the dot. "This is how things work in the real world, Kiel. Kids don't solve crimes here, the police do. We have to let *them* handle it."

"Cuff 'em," one of the officers said, and two pulled out handcuffs while the others kept their guns pointed at Kiel and Owen.

"We didn't do it," Owen said, practically pleading with the police. "You have to believe me. The guy who did is getting away!"

"Owen Conners, you have the right to remain silent," the police officer said, then began to mumble something about an attorney and a few other things, getting so quiet that Owen couldn't hear any of his other rights.

Handcuffs snapped around Owen's wrists, and he was jerked roughly away from Kiel, who sighed and held his hands out in front of him. A second officer went to handcuff the boy

magician, but Kiel didn't take his eyes off Owen. "Sorry, my friend," he said, shaking his head. "I want to believe you, but chalk it up to too many years living under the Science Police."

And with that, Kiel knocked his hands up into the police officer's, reversed the handcuffs, and latched them onto the officer's wrists instead. Then he disappeared into the night, his black cape and clothes cloaking him in the fire's shadows.

"Suspect escaping on foot!" one of the cops shouted into his radio. "We need backup!"

"He didn't do it!" Owen shouted as an officer dragged him by his cuffs back to the police cars. "Why won't you listen to me?"

The officer opened his squad car door and tossed Owen into the back, as even more sirens filled the air, and the whirring of a helicopter sounded from a far-off distance. A *helicopter*? The police officer jumped into the front seat and began fiddling with his computer.

"The guy who did this is named Doyle Holmes!" Owen shouted. "He kidnapped a friend of mine, Bethany Sanderson!"

The police officer frowned, then pushed some buttons on the computer screen. "I'd advise you to keep your mouth shut until you get to the station. Anything you say can and will be used against you, as I said." The computer beeped, and he

paused. "Also, there's no record of a Bethany Sanderson in this town, so maybe come up with a better story next time."

"*What?*" Owen said. "Of course there's a record. She's my classmate! Call her mom, she'll tell you!"

"I have a Stephanie Sanderson, thirty-nine," the police officer said. "No dependents, though." He abruptly shifted the car into reverse and, without looking, slammed on the gas, narrowly missing the other squad car and two light poles. "Base, I'm coming in," he said into the radio on his shoulder. "Have one of the arsonists from the library. Throw the book at this one." The officer turned to glare at Owen. "He deserves it."

Owen's eyes widened, and he turned to the door, only to find it had no handle on the inside. Had Kiel been right? Was this a huge mistake?

And why was there no record of Bethany?

"*Please* believe me," Owen said to the police officer. "My friend is in danger. This guy, Doyle Holmes, said that we've got two hours before we never see her again."

"You might never see the friend who doesn't exist again?" the officer said. "I'll be sure to alert the FBI."

"I'm serious!" Owen shouted as the officer slammed on the gas again, sending the car bursting out into traffic. Owen

quickly grabbed the door's arm rest just to hold on as the car weaved in and out of the few vehicles on the road this late at night, driving at least ninety miles per hour down the street. "She's in real danger! This Doyle guy isn't from around here!"

The police officer looked back at Owen, his eyes not even on the road as he continued to swerve. "Boy, you're just really digging yourself in deeper, aren't you?" he said, smirking.

Owen sighed and collapsed back against the seat, then glanced down at the watch on his wrist: 01:55:46.

Kiel had been right. This was a huge mistake.

But maybe that was okay. Kiel was still free, and he was a *hero*. He was probably out there right now, finding Bethany all on his own. Knowing Kiel, in fact, Bethany was probably free already!

CHAPTER 13

01:55:46

I t took Bethany several minutes to realize that she wasn't dreaming the sound of running water. She opened her eyes and immediately gasped.

She was in a room made entirely of cement, it looked like, though it was so dark she almost couldn't see. The only light came from the ceiling, where grates let in streams of water. The room was empty except for large metal shelves against one wall, cameras in each corner, and whatever she was sitting on.

Bethany tried to stand, only to find she couldn't move her arms or legs. Heavy chains were cuffed to her wrists, binding her to an old green chair with the cushions half missing, while her ankles were tied to the chair's legs with rope.

Meanwhile, the water pouring through the grates in multiple waterfalls was starting to collect on the floor.

"Help!" she shouted, everything coming back at once. Owen and Kiel. Kiel's forget spell. *Doyle*. Her heart began beating out of her chest, and she tensed, ready to jump.

"I wouldn't," said a voice from behind her, and a boy in a Sherlock Holmes hat and coat wearing a mask with a question mark, stepped into the light.

"Let me go!" Bethany shouted, pulling at the chains as hard as she could.

Doyle didn't move. "I don't believe I will. But please, feel free to escape."

She bit her lip to keep from screaming at him. "Why are you doing this? I've done nothing to you!"

"Really?" Doyle said quietly. "What about humiliating my family, Bethany Sanderson? You've revealed our secret to the entire world. And maybe worst of all, you've presented me with a mystery I haven't been able to solve. We can't have that, now, can we?"

Bethany just stared at the detective as the water flowed into the room. He was *insane*. "Where are Owen and Kiel?"

"You won't be seeing them again," Doyle said. "I imagine they're both being arrested as we speak. If I were you, I'd be far more concerned with what will be happening to you

in"—he looked at his watch—"just under two hours."

"Two hours?" she said. "What happens—" But she stopped midsentence, realizing she didn't want to know.

"That's when this room fills with water," Doyle said, then glanced up at the ceiling. "Don't worry, I had this room specifically modified so I'd know exactly how long it'd take. Of course, the water will rise above your head far before then if you're still tied to the chair, so let's say you have about a half hour, tops."

Bethany's eyes widened. "You're trying to kill me?" she asked quietly.

"Me?" Doyle said, managing to look indignant despite his mask. "Of course not! I'm just providing motivation. After all, you can't have a mystery without a motive. And you, Ms. Sanderson, are my only lead in solving your mystery."

Jump, her mind said. *Get out of here!* Her whole body tensed, but she couldn't. "This isn't a mystery, Doyle. This is my *life*!"

Doyle waved a hand around. "What's the difference? All of our lives are mysteries, Ms. Sanderson. What will we do at any given moment? How far will we go to get what we want? Who will we sacrifice to save ourselves? All mysteries, and I, for one, am excited to see their solutions."

Bethany glanced up at the water flowing in. "You're insane. This is a death trap! You're acting like some kind of villain—"

Doyle leaped forward, his mask stopping within inches of her face. *"Some kind? I'm the greatest villain,"* he hissed almost too softly to hear. "But this isn't a death trap. It's a mystery!" He slowly stood back up. "A true classic, what we call a locked room mystery. How did the victim die when the murderer couldn't get into the room? In this case, the murder weapon is water, and the victim is you, dying from drowning. The fun comes when you're discovered, and the water has been drained." He gestured around proudly. "You'll have drowned in a dry room! Don't you see how fun that'd be to solve?"

Bethany just stared at him in shock. "Why, Doyle?" she asked. "I paid you what you asked for."

Doyle leaned back in. *"Sometimes a story just needs a good villain,"* he whispered, then stood back up. "But don't think of this as punishment. It is, of course, but don't think of it that way. This is an experiment! I'm here to learn from you. Whether you want me to or not."

With that, Doyle turned and walked over to a small door in the wall, the rising water sloshing on the floor as he went.

Bethany yanked on the chains again in frustration, then stopped. He might be crazy, but he still had his family to think about. "This is crazy, Doyle!" she shouted. "You know that. This isn't worthy of a Holmes! What would your great-great-great-whatever-grandfather think?"

Doyle paused, then slowly turned back to her. "Nice try, Ms. Sanderson. I know what he'd think. My family's known what he thought since that day at the waterfall." He shook his head. "A *flying man* saved his life. That's what he claimed, and for the next three years, he searched the entire world for the man, the secret of flight, anything. *Three years.* There's nothing Sherlock Holmes couldn't find in that time, but this was one mystery that defeated him, and he was never the same afterward. We all thought he'd lost his mind, that Professor Moriarty had beaten him." Doyle pointed at her. "But no. It was *you*, you and Kiel's Magister all along."

Bethany's eyes widened, remembering the Magister chasing her through books, and his flying form accidentally saving Sherlock Holmes from a fall over Reichenbach Falls. "We saved his life!" she shouted. "He might have died!"

"Better to die with one's reputation than live without it," Doyle said, and turned his back on her.

"I can just escape!" Bethany shouted, pulling on her chains. "You and I both know I can!"

"Please do," Doyle said, his hand on the doorknob. "And my cameras will record it. Should be all I need." He turned and faced her. "But we both also know what happens if you do. You'll never see them again, Bethany Sanderson. You'll have lost two more, just like you lost your father."

Bethany screamed again in rage, pushing off the floor as hard as she could, almost toppling the chair she was chained to.

"I'd be careful not to fall over," Doyle said, opening the door. "Wouldn't want to drown in just six inches of water, would you?"

"I'm going to get out of this," Bethany told him. "And I'm going to make you pay. Do you understand me?"

Doyle shrugged. "Just remember, *you* came to *me*. So whose fault is this, really? Like I said, life is a mystery, isn't it? I never would have thought you'd break every one of your rules just to get what you wanted, but here we are. Who could have deduced that?"

Bethany gritted her teeth, holding back another scream.

"Good luck," Doyle said, then closed the door behind him. Bethany heard some sort of spinning noise, and a huge lock clicked into place. And for the first time, she noticed she had

a black band on her wrist that showed a countdown in red: 1:50:19.

Jump, jump, jump, jump, jump, her mind said.

No. Kiel and Owen would find her. Of course they would. Whatever trouble they were in, they'd find a way out of it. Owen was probably a huge fan of mysteries and had read them all. And Kiel was a hero! He'd know *exactly* what to do.

CHAPTER 14

01:50:07

Kiel Gnomenfoot, former hero to millions as the star of his own book series, current boy magician without any magic, had no idea what to do.

Things used to be so easy. There were keys to find, Charm to help him find them, and Dr. Verity to fight. But now there was this Doyle guy, Bethany was missing, and Owen had surrendered to the police at the very first chance he got, which just felt so wrong that it made Kiel's stomach ache. Back on Magisteria, whenever the robotic Science Police had caught someone, that was it. You never saw them again.

Tended to leave a bad taste in one's mouth about the police.

"We've got you surrounded!" shouted a voice from just a few feet away in the darkness. "Come out with your hands up!"

Usually, this would be the point where Kiel would cast some

fun, probably ironic magic spell, then say something amazing, often with a wink and a grin. Charm seemed to appreciate that sort of thing, so Kiel made sure to push it, even when he was scared or uncertain. Even without magic, part of him wanted to take this police officer down, steal his radio, then spout off something snappy and daring, just so the police knew who they were dealing with.

But this wasn't his world, or even a fictional one, so instead, Kiel inched his way back into the shadows. The roaring fire offered up lots of shadowy hiding spots as it consumed the library where Kiel, Bethany, and Owen had all met most nights to have exciting, dangerous, amazing adventures. Just like the last time, where they . . .

They what? Kiel couldn't remember the last adventure they'd been on. For some reason he thought of the Magister, and . . . and a spell book. He rubbed his forehead, trying to bring that memory to the forefront. Why was it so hard to think of it? Clearly he was just too amazing at magic, if he'd erased his own memories this well.

He heard footsteps go by, and Kiel counted to five, then silently stepped out and made his way in the opposite direction. Overhead, a large flying carlike object with what looked

to be a sort of halo above it floated loudly in midair, shining a light down onto the library's grounds. As the light shifted closer, Kiel dove beneath a car, which had just enough room for him to fit easily.

This was all wasting time, and there was only an hour and forty-eight minutes left before something terrible happened to Bethany. The very idea left a hole in his stomach and made him want to punch something, and hiding when he should be looking for her made it even worse.

Still, it'd waste even more time if he got caught, so Kiel took a deep breath and stayed out of sight.

As soon as the flying car's light passed, Kiel rolled out from beneath the car in what he hoped was an impressive way, then leaped to his feet and took off at a noiseless sprint in the direction he'd seen Doyle go right before the explosion. Bethany could be anywhere, but if Kiel got ahold of Doyle, this would all be over in moments, with or without magic.

Maybe more than a few moments. After all, Kiel planned on enjoying interrogating Doyle. Whoever he was.

Unfortunately, more police were flooding the grounds now, and it took longer than he'd have liked to make his way around to the other side of the burning library without being caught.

Firefighters were also running everywhere, and steam rose from the roof as they sprayed the building with water.

If he still had his magic, he could have put out this fire instantly. Doyle would pay for that, too. While the library seemed to belong to Owen's mother somehow, it still had given Kiel some pretty happy memories. Or at least, he *thought* it had. Granted, he couldn't remember them now, but he was confident that they had been good.

As he moved, he reached out with his mind, trying to sense his spell book. Even when it was lost, he could at least pinpoint its general direction. That was part of the magic, after all. He was connected to his spell book, and it to him.

This time, though, he got no sense of the spell book at *all*. That wasn't good.

Kiel reached the back door of the library and slowed to a stop, looking around for signs that anyone had passed by. The hard surface of the road wouldn't show footprints, though, so Kiel moved on to the woods nearby, where the softer dirt would hopefully be more useful. The darkness obscured almost everything, though. Kiel wanted to scream to whoever was listening in either the fictional or nonfictional world how much he hated having to rely on his own eyes

instead of just using magic, like the universe had intended.

The sound of footsteps pushed Kiel back into the trees, and he barely breathed, all his thieving skills coming back to him instinctually. Whoever it was stopped just a few feet from him.

"We got one of them, sir," the voice said, then paused. Kiel waited, but the same voice spoke again. "No, the boy in normal clothes. Owen Conners. The other one, Kiel Gnomenfoot, got away."

Kiel pushed forward an inch at a time until he could just make out the silhouette of a police officer speaking into his shoulder radio as he flashed a science torch through the air. Who was the officer talking to? And how did he know Owen's name? Obviously he'd heard of Kiel, as everyone had. But that raised another question: Didn't nonfictional police officers think that Kiel was just some heroic, amazing wizard from a series of books? This guy didn't even seem the slightest bit surprised to be talking about a fictional person.

"I know you said this Kiel boy wasn't dangerous and that the Conners kid was the one to worry about, but are you sure?" the police officer said, then stopped. "No, of course I didn't mean to doubt you! I apologize, sir."

What? Kiel Gnomenfoot not dangerous? And Owen Conners

was the one to worry about? What sort of upside-down world *was* the nonfictional world?

Kiel loved Owen like a brother, of course, but dangerous wasn't the first word that came to mind. And Kiel had taken down dragons, giants, and fire-breathing unicorns! Not dangerous?! Whoever was on the other end of the line was clearly not dealing with a full spell book.

"We're taking the Conners kid to the station," the police officer continued. "We'll interrogate him there, and . . . no, you're right. Whatever you say. This is your case, after all. Yes sir, I'll keep you updated. Yes, sir, thank *you*, Mr. Holmes."

Kiel's eyes widened. Holmes? *Doyle* Holmes? Were the police working with the boy who kidnapped Bethany? Or was there another Holmes? Owen had mentioned a grandfather, so maybe there were more family members involved.

Of course, the Holmes family was also supposed to be fictional. Or was just Doyle fictional? Kiel shook his head. If Owen hadn't surrendered, he'd be around to answer these questions, instead of letting them give Kiel *more* of a headache.

This would have been the perfect time for any number of spells, but instead, Kiel just waited until the police officer moved out of sight, then went back to searching the ground.

Just as he was about to give up, the fire's light lit up footprints in the dirt, leading away from the library.

Ah. Let's see who was dangerous now, *Doyle.*

Kiel followed the trail through the woods and down through some backyards. The path struck Kiel as a bit familiar, but that wasn't too surprising. He, Owen, and Bethany had gotten used to walking back and forth to the library at night for their adventures. Hadn't they?

And then the footprints ended at a house, and Kiel skidded to a stop, sighing heavily.

Owen's house. The footprints led to the back door of Owen's house. He'd been following Owen's footprints the whole time, probably from the last time they'd all jumped into a book, which was . . . recently? Maybe?

Kiel started back toward the library, then stopped. Doyle would be long gone by now, and the only thing back there were police. But without another clue, how exactly was he supposed to find Bethany or Doyle? Especially after wasting so much time following the wrong tracks?

Wait. He *did* have another clue. The police were working with a Holmes, maybe Doyle. And that meant there was definitely a place he could go to find out more.

And he really should rescue Owen. It wouldn't do to leave his friend locked up, even if Owen had unwisely given himself up. And who else knew the boring, unmagical, nonfictional world like Owen?

With new purpose, Kiel set out for the police station, shaking his head at the idea of having to jog the whole way. Magic was just so much easier for getting around!

Kiel had been without magic before, of course. Both before he'd met the Magister, and then when the Magister had made him forget all of his magic after they'd met Bethany, and his master had gone off the deep end.

But he'd gotten the magic back . . . somehow. Somewhere in the fog, there was a memory of what he'd done.

Kiel slowly breathed in and tried to think of something, anything that'd help him remember.

Bethany's face came to mind, and he smiled in spite of himself.

Then Bethany's face morphed into Charm's, and he gasped out loud as the memory slammed into his head like a hammer.

MISSING CHAPTER 1

Two months ago . . .

"So I'm not real," Kiel Gnomenfoot said quietly, staring at his hands.

"What makes you think that?" the Magister asked, the hints of a smile playing over his face.

"I'm made of science, Magi," Kiel said, shaking his head. "Dr. Verity formed me from that unnatural—"

"Science is about as natural as you could possibly *get*," Charm said, her robotic eye narrowing in irritation. Kiel glared at her, and she turned away guiltily. "But, um, I understand your point," she finished.

"He *made* me!" Kiel said, shouting now. "I was never meant to exist. All I am is a clown—"

"Clone," Charm pointed out.

"Of the man who's currently trying to destroy Magisteria." Kiel sighed. "And Magisteria isn't even *my* world, is it? If I'm a clown—"

"Clone."

"Then I'm actually *Quanterian*." Kiel grabbed his apprentice spell book, his face contorted in anger, and threw it across the room.

The spell book froze as soon as it left his hand, then turned in midair to glare at its owner. Kiel ignored it, dropping to the floor to sit cross-legged with his head in his hands.

"I'm not even *real*," he said again.

The Magister circled around Kiel, then kneeled in front of the boy and pulled Kiel's chin up to look his apprentice in the eye. "You assume that real is something anyone would want to be."

Kiel gave his master a sad look. "Magi, now isn't the greatest time for a lesson."

"What is magic if not forcing unreality to *become* real?" the Magister asked. "So Dr. Verity recreated

44

himself, giving us you. Do *you* want to destroy Magisteria?"

Kiel shrugged. "Only sometimes. When people annoy me."

"And what could be more real than that!" the Magister said, clapping Kiel on the shoulder.

Kiel snorted, then shook his head. "I can't be him, Magi. I *can't*! What if I turn out just like he did? What if I'm destined for evil? And look at him! *That's* what I'm going to look like when I'm older?"

"Ugh," Charm groaned, and Kiel could almost feel her rolling her eyes.

"You will be whatever you *decide* to be," the Magister told Kiel gently. "The idea of destiny is something we made up to justify whatever we wanted to do. You are no more destined to become Dr. Verity than I am to turn Alphonse into a dog."

Alphonse, Kiel's cat, stopped licking his wings for a moment to look at the Magister, then shrugged and returned to his important bathing.

"I'm not sure any of this is helping," Kiel pointed

out as he pushed to his feet. "But I suppose I don't have time to feel sorry for myself. Charm can't get the last three keys by herself—"

"*Actually—*"

"Even if she's far too proud to admit how much help she needs," Kiel continued. "I'll just have to soldier on and hope that my natural talent and intelligence is enough to keep me from turning into Dr. Verity."

The Magister smiled. "I have the utmost faith in your . . . talent and intelligence."

"Of course you do," Kiel said, shrugging. "We all do."

Charm clenched her fists and slowly took several deep breaths. "If we don't leave *now*, I swear I will ray gun you."

"She has trouble admitting her feelings for me," Kiel whispered to the Magister, who nodded, still smiling. Kiel walked over to stand next to Charm and made an impatient gesture. "Uh, let's *go* already."

Charm's eyes widened, and she opened her mouth to scream at him just as they both disappeared in a flash of light.

The Magister smiled, dropping into his chair. So

Kiel Gnomenfoot had finally learned he was a clone of Dr. Verity. The day the Magister had dreaded for so long had now come, and the boy was taking it about as well as anyone could, finding out that he was the creation of a madman.

But would the boy take the truth about the Source of Magic quite so well?

To be continued in Kiel Gnomenfoot and the School for Wizardry, *book five of the Kiel Gnomenfoot saga.*

"Magi?" said a soft voice from behind him, and the Magister turned around in his chair to find Kiel looking at him strangely, Charm standing just behind him. Oddly, Charm was giving the Magister a look of almost palpable hatred. Usually those looks were directed more at Kiel than himself.

"Back so soon, my boy?" the Magister asked.

"I, uh, forgot my spell book," Kiel said, and held out a hand toward the still-floating, still-angry apprentice spell book. The book floated over to him in a sulking sort of way, then shrank down to the size of a coin, and Kiel slipped it into a pouch on his belt.

"I thought you had moved beyond the need for it?" the

Magister asked. "You didn't need it to find the Fourth Key, after all."

"Can't hurt to have a backup," Kiel said, then slowly took a step back.

"Kiel," the Magister said slowly, "I know why you're here."

Kiel froze. "You do?"

"Because it occurred to you that if you're a clone, then I have misled you about your parents," the Magister said.

Kiel paused. "That's it. You're right. But just hearing you admit it, that's really enough. I should get back to things—"

"I couldn't tell you the truth, my boy," the Magister said, his voice dropping low. "I cannot apologize enough, but you had to find out on your own, when you were ready."

"I'm not sure I was *ever* ready for some truths," Kiel said.

The Magister nodded. "I understand, believe me. Truth is a sword with no hilt. We grab for it at our own peril, at times."

"The truth, like how you're secretly planning on destroying Quanterium?" Charm mumbled, and the Magister blinked. He must have misheard her.

"I'm sorry, what did you say?" he asked the glaring girl.

"Nothing," Kiel said, throwing Charm an annoyed look.

"We really should get going. Keys to find, crazy madmen to fight, that sort of thing . . ."

"Kiel," the Magister said, and opened his arms. "Please tell me you forgive me."

Kiel's eyes widened slightly, and oddly, he looked up at the ceiling. "Seriously?" he whispered to no one in particular.

"Of course I am serious," the Magister responded, a bit confused. He gestured for Kiel to hug him. "Please, my boy. I can't tell you how sorry I am to have deceived you."

Kiel gritted his teeth, then stepped forward and hugged the Magister, who smiled and let out a sigh of relief. Kiel quickly pushed back, then stepped away. "Well, gotta go!" he said, and raised a hand into the air.

"You don't have your teleport button," the Magister pointed out.

"Charm's got it," Kiel said as she took his hand.

"Good luck, my boy," the Magister said.

"Magi," Kiel said, avoiding his teacher's eyes, "if *you* ever find out something that turns your whole life upside down, like I just did, try not to turn crazy and evil. As a favor to me."

The Magister smiled. "You have my word."

Kiel sighed, then disappeared with Charm from the Magister's tower, reappearing in the middle of a dark library.

"I *really* wanted to hit him," Charm said. Kiel mumbled some words and the disguise spell faded, revealing Bethany in Charm's place.

"Did you see him *hug* me?!" Kiel shouted at her, his face contorted with disgust. "UGH. I need to bathe."

"But he's the Magister!" Owen said from where he sat on a nearby table. "You *love* him."

"It's amazing what happens to your relationship when your adopted father tries to kill you," Kiel said with a shrug. "Plus, if he hadn't forget-spelled the magic out of my head, I'd never have had to steal my own spell book in the first place." He reached into his pocket and pulled out the tiny still-sulky book, which quickly expanded into a normal-size still-sulky spell book.

"So you're sure this book has the spell?" Bethany asked, shifting her weight from foot to foot nervously.

"Trust me," Kiel said, winking at her. He tried to open the cover, and the book snapped at him. *"Hey!"* he shouted. "Bad book! Don't do that again." He pointed a finger in warning at the book, and it pouted, then flipped open to the right page.

Kiel held the book up for Owen and Bethany to see.

Illumination of Location, the page said.

"So who wants to find Bethany's father, then?" Kiel asked, grinning widely.

The memory hit Kiel hard, and it almost staggered him.

Just like it did to Owen, who looked around almost in disbelief, his head throbbing. Where had *that* come from?

CHAPTER 15

01:42:56

Memories weren't supposed to almost knock you over. Since when did that happen? And why had it hit him so suddenly, out of nowhere? For a second Owen almost lost track of where he was, but the sight of a police officer filling out paperwork at the counter of the police station reminded him quickly enough.

Someone bumped into him, and Owen looked up to find a burly man who smelled like burned hair staring down at him. Owen quickly backed up into the police officer, who pushed him back toward the man.

One meaty hand hit Owen's shoulder. "Excuse me," the man said politely. "Sorry about that. Didn't mean to bump into you." And with that, he pulled off a beard and tossed it onto the counter, followed by his stinky overcoat.

As the man peeled off his disguise, he revealed a tailored suit, hair that wasn't even mussed by a wig, and a face with no smile lines. He patted Owen's shoulder once, then dropped the rest of the disguise onto the counter and turned to walk away.

"How'd it go, Inspector?" the officer at the counter shouted.

The man in the suit jabbed his thumb over his shoulder, and Owen turned to find police officers dragging in what looked to be an entire criminal gang, all dressed in black. "Book 'em," the man in the suit said. "These boys are going away for a long time."

Just then one of the officers yelled, and before Owen knew it, the largest of the criminals broke free and grabbed a gun from an officer's holster, aiming it right at Owen. "Let me go or the kid gets it!" the man shouted.

The man in the suit sighed and, almost faster than Owen could see, kicked the criminal in the back of the knees, grabbed the gun from midair, and punched the man in the face. The criminal collapsed to the floor, and the man in the suit handed the gun back to the officer. "Try holding on to this a bit more tightly next time," he said, then turned and walked away.

Wow. Apparently, police stations were exactly like every cop

53

movie or TV show Owen had ever seen. Who knew those were so realistic? Right down to the innocent kid getting threatened when a criminal breaks away. It was almost a cliché, it happened so often.

Like a fictional cliché.

Owen frowned, something small and annoying tickling his brain. There was something off here. Not by much, just—

And then a shove in the back derailed his train of thought.

"Move," said the police officer who'd arrested Owen, pushing him farther into the police station. In spite of everything that was happening, a familiar feeling of excitement came over Owen. It was like when he and Charm had been under fire on the *Scientific Method*, Charm's spaceship. Sure, he was being arrested, but at least it was happening in an awesome way.

The officer led Owen down one of the quieter hallways and into an empty room with two metal chairs, a table, and one lone light—exactly what Owen expected. He was going to be interrogated! Classic.

The man shoved Owen into one of the chairs, which faced a long mirror on the wall, then slammed the door as he left, leaving Owen to stare at himself in the mirror. It was probably one-way glass, with people on the other side watching him,

right? That was how it worked in movies. The boss watched as the police interrogated the criminal.

That thought killed the excitement instantly. *He* was the criminal here, and *he* was being framed for his mother's library burning down. The image of the building going up in flames hit him almost as hard as the memory of Kiel returning with his spell book did, and he felt like throwing up. He had to convince the police that he was innocent and get them to find Doyle. If not, Owen would be going to jail, probably for the rest of his life. But, even worse, he'd have to explain this to his mother!

Not to mention that Bethany was missing, and they only had . . . an hour and forty minutes left to find her before, well, *something* bad happened.

Why did this all have to be such a stupid mystery? Owen *hated* mysteries. Why spend an entire book just waiting to find out what had actually happened? It was like the world's longest magic trick, only usually really lame when you found out how it was done.

Okay, so *exactly* like the world's longest magic trick.

He'd read a bunch of mysteries, of course. Sherlock Holmes, Encyclopedia Brown, all the ones his mom recommended, but he just couldn't get into them. Magic was just so much cooler, and involved a lot fewer details and clues and convenient plot

devices that revealed exactly what the detective needed to know exactly when they needed to know it.

But since he was clearly living out a mystery now, he might as well embrace it. Doyle had said he'd planned this mystery by the book, so maybe that was a hint. Owen would just have to treat this like a mystery in a book, and maybe he'd be able to figure out what was going on. So first, he needed to list the questions that needed answering.

Where is Bethany? No idea. Could be anywhere.

How did Doyle get out of his book? Bethany had to have done it. Who else could have?

But why would Bethany take Doyle out of his book? Maybe by accident? But how did you accidentally take a freakishly masked guy out of a book with you? Maybe he grabbed her at the last minute. But how would he have known to grab ahold, anyway?

And that led to the next question:

How does Doyle know who we all are? It's not like Kiel's books existed in the fictional world. Did they? Did books also exist in the fictional "real" world, the realistic place where all non–fantasy or science-fiction stories took place? Was there a library in the fictional real world with Kiel's books?

The idea of a fictional real world just gave Owen an enormous headache, so he moved on. Even if Doyle had Kiel's books, how did he know *Owen's* name? He couldn't have gotten that from any book. Maybe he'd learned it when Doyle had escaped, somehow? He just couldn't remember, and that was the most frustrating part.

Speaking of not remembering:

Why did Doyle make Kiel remove their memories? What was so important for them to not remember? Maybe where Bethany was? Even so, Doyle had gotten them arrested, so it's not like he thought they'd be able to run around looking for her. So what was the whole point? Or to put it differently:

Why is Doyle doing this? Yeah, seriously. Why?!

Okay, so those were the questions, none of which had any answers. He did have a guess here or there, but none that helped him. Perfect. This whole detectiving by the book was going *so* well.

And this was exactly why Owen hated mysteries.

Minutes passed, and Owen kept checking the watch Doyle had put on his wrist: 01:38:47. 01:37:19. 01:36:12. Where were the police? Couldn't they just throw him in jail already and get this over with?

At least Kiel was out there, a real hero. If anyone could rescue Bethany, even without any magic, it was Kiel Gnomenfoot. After all, he'd been written to do just that kind of thing, hadn't he? When Owen had tried living Kiel's life, he'd almost died. But this was what Kiel was made to do, beat the bad guys and rescue the good guys. He'd have Bethany back in no time.

Or hopefully in 01:35:34. 01:33:29. UGH.

A knock came at the door, and after a pause it opened, revealing the man in the suit from earlier. The man nodded at Owen, then turned his gaze to the file in his hands. He slowly closed the door, his attention on the file, then sat down in the chair across from Owen.

"I didn't do it!" Owen said as soon as the man's behind hit the seat.

The suited man's eyes briefly rose above the file, gave Owen a look, then went back to reading.

"Listen to me, my friend's in danger!" Owen said, his voice rising. "There's this crazy person who kidnapped her, and said that after an hour and a half I'll never see her again. She might die!"

Again the man's eyes flicked up from his file, but this time

they stayed locked on Owen's. "Your friend is this Bethany Sanderson?" the man said.

"Yes!" Owen shouted, just thankful that someone had been listening. "She's *completely* not fake. She goes to my school. She has a library card. How could someone not exist but still have a library card?"

The man just looked at Owen, then glanced back down into the file. He closed it now and laid it on the table, then folded his hands on top of it, giving Owen an unreadable look. "I'm Inspector Brown," he said finally. "From the city."

The city? Which city was that? But that could wait.

"I'm Owen Conners," Owen said, sticking out his hand.

The inspector glanced down at Owen's hand, then shook his head. "I hate to say it, but you're in a lot of trouble here, Owen Conners. We've got a witness claiming you set fire to the library where your mother works. I'm told the lab boys are pulling prints now, but preliminary work suggests they're yours."

"But I didn't do it!" Owen shouted, standing up. "I saw the guy who did it! He admitted that he was framing us! *And* he kidnapped my friend!"

"Can you describe this person?" the detective said, his hands still folded.

"Yes! He's wearing some kind of weird white mask with a question mark on it." Owen paused, realizing how this sounded. "I know it's hard to believe, but it's true. And a Sherlock Holmes hat and coat."

"A deerstalker hat," the inspector said.

"What?"

"It's called a deerstalker hat, the hat that Sherlock Holmes was rumored to have worn. Not that he ever appeared in photos that way." His hands still hadn't moved, not even to jot down a note. This didn't seem to be going that great.

"You don't believe me," Owen said, falling back into his chair hard.

"Oh, I know who you're referring to," the inspector said. "But considering his history with the force and me in particular, I'd find it pretty hard to believe that he's been setting any fires."

What? History with the force? How would a fictional character have—

"Yo, Wikipedia," said a police officer, opening the door. "No sign of the other suspect. We think he got away."

The inspector flinched. "I've asked you all not to call me that," he said, and the police officer just smirked, then shrugged and shut the door. The inspector shook his head, turning back

to Owen. "Sorry. They think it's funny because of my child-hood nickname. Owen, do you know where your friend, this Gnomenfoot boy, might have gone? Things might go easier for you if you cooperate."

"He didn't do it either!" Owen shouted. "Don't you get it? We're being framed! I don't even know why, because none of it makes sense, but I saw this masked guy with my own eyes. He set the fire, not us. Kiel and I almost blew up! Why would we do that to ourselves?"

The detective stared at Owen for a moment, then sighed. "I've spoken to your mother, Owen. Would you like to know what she told me?"

Owen flinched. "Probably not?"

"She claims you're home in bed right now, at this moment. Said she was looking right at you." The inspector raised an eye-brow. "Now, I don't know what to make of that. Do you?"

She'd said *what*? Why would his mother lie like that? Or was there some way Kiel had cast a magic spell to make it look like Owen was still in his bed? What was *happening*?

Owen concentrated as hard as he could, trying to remember anything from earlier that night. Fighting through the fog in his brain to get to an actual memory was like trying to punch

actual fog, though: it wasn't accomplishing anything, and probably made him look really stupid.

"Tell me about this Kiel Gnomenfoot boy," the inspector said. "We don't have any record of him, either. Did he put you up to this in some way?"

"No, he's a *good* guy," Owen said, his mind racing. Why couldn't he remember leaving that night? Kiel's magic was so annoying sometimes! "He'd never do anything like this either. We both just want to find our friend."

"Bethany Sanderson," the detective said. "You're right that there's no record of her, either. No one in your school by that name. No one in this city, even." He raised an eyebrow. "Not even a library card."

How was that possible? Owen's mind raced, launching through all kinds of different explanations. Was he going insane? Had he dreamed Bethany this entire time? Was this all a dream now?!

He pinched himself hard and jumped at the pain. Well, at least he was awake. But how could there be no record of Bethany? "That can't be true," Owen said, almost pleading with the inspector. "She's my friend! I've known her for . . . well, for just a couple of months. I think. But I've seen her for longer, in class, in school. She *exists*!"

The inspector sighed. "I don't know why you're lying, kid, but this is getting us nowhere," he said. "Tell me what's going on. Tell me how this all started. From the beginning."

"I don't know!" Owen said, dropping his head into his hands. "I don't—"

But just like that, a memory hit him like a hammer, and he *did* know.

One month ago . . .

The library was silent, with just one light left on in the back by the study tables, which were all covered in books. As if by itself, one of the books opened, and a cartoon hand pushed its way out, followed by two lines for an arm and a doodle of a head.

"So weird!" Bethany said as she emerged, her mouth in the shape of a large O, while her ponytail lines bounced behind her. She used her cartoon hands to pull herself all the way out of the book, then reached in to pull out two more life-size doodles.

"But *so fun!*" Owen said, a smile line stretching from one side of his round head to the other. "Look at this!" He yanked on the lines that made his body, then released them, letting them twang back into place. "It's like they're rubber bands!"

"I know I agreed to this," said Kiel, "but when you said 'diary,' I can't say I was expecting *that.*" He held one cartoon hand up to his circle mouth as if he might vomit.

"Turn us back already, will you?" Bethany told Kiel, gesturing with her four pudgy fingers for him to hurry. "The last thing I want to do is figure out how to go to the bathroom like this."

"Wait!" Owen said as Kiel raised his cartoon hands into the air, holding two straight lines that were his wands. "Just give me, like, five more minutes. I want to see how far I can pull my arms out before they snap back."

Bethany sighed and shook her head. "That is the last time we go into an Owen book," she whispered to Kiel. *"The last time."*

Kiel waved his wands, and he and Bethany both immediately turned back into their normal selves, Bethany in jeans and a T-shirt, her red hair in a ponytail, Kiel wearing all black, with his cape and wand-knife holsters.

Owen, still a cartoon, grinned widely as he began tying one arm to the table leg.

"So?" Kiel said to Bethany as he took deep breaths, thankfully not looking quite so sick anymore. "Are you ready now? You said we should all pick one adventure to have before we do this, and we've done that. Some were . . . *odder* than others, but . . ."

Bethany couldn't help smiling at Owen slowly pulling his body away from the table, grunting as the arm tied to the table began stretching. "Everyone has their own idea of fun."

"At least mine didn't almost get us eaten," Owen said, then returned to his pulling.

"By fake dragons, no less," Kiel pointed out.

"They're called *dinosaurs*," Bethany said with a sigh. "And unlike dragons, they actually were real here. But now they only exist in stories, so I wanted to see them. I still feel like you two missed the entire point of that."

"My arm's taller than I am!" Owen said, and turned to show them, only to have his arm snap back, yanking him with it right into the table. Owen hit hard enough for little stars to pop out above his head as his pupils turned around and around in his eye circles. "Owwww," he moaned as Bethany and Kiel just lost it.

It took a few minutes before Bethany could even speak, and even then she had to wipe tears from her eyes. "Please do that again?" she said, her voice still high-pitched from all her laughing. "I vote you stay in cartoon form for the rest of the night, and just do that over and over."

"Mean," Owen said, his frown filling up his face. "*Fine*, turn me back."

"You don't want to try using your body as a bow and arrow first?" Bethany asked.

"I mean, *yes*, but not if you're going to make fun of me for it," Owen said, and nodded at Kiel. The magician, still laughing, mumbled the spell and Owen instantly turned back to his normal self. He pushed himself to his feet, then held out both arms in front of him, frowning. "Does the right one still look longer?"

"Definitely," Bethany said, wiping the smile from her face. "Like, by at least a few inches."

"Are you serious?" Owen said, frantically trying to measure them. "Kiel, turn me back, *quick*. I need to fix this!"

"So are you ready?" Kiel asked Bethany, ignoring Owen. "You promised we'd do the spell tonight. We can't keep putting it off forever."

Bethany's joy faded, and a chill went through her body. "Are you sure you don't want to jump in another story? We could each pick another one. . . ."

Kiel grabbed Bethany's shoulders and turned her around, giving her a comforting smile. "Don't worry," he told her quietly. "Your father is fine, wherever he is. I'll use the location spell, we'll jump into whichever book he's in, and that'll be that. You'll have your dad back home by morning."

"It might even be *more* than a few inches," Owen said, squinting at his arms.

Bethany winced. "*If* my father's okay. And if he even *wants* to come back."

"Of course he will," Kiel told her, giving her a confused look. "How could he ever not want to see his daughter?"

Bethany swallowed hard, not wanting to think of all the reasons. She'd come up with a long list over the last few days, ever since she'd jumped Kiel back into his series to retrieve his old practice spell book. Owen and Kiel had wanted to use the location spell that same night to find her father, but she'd convinced them that they should all pick one last story, since bringing her father back would definitely put an end to their adventures. It was hard enough to hide what she'd been doing

from her mother. Her father showing up would pretty much get her grounded for a few hundred years.

But that wasn't the real reason. There were too many bad ways this could go, and now that it was finally here, she half expected the worst. Maybe even three-fourths.

"We can still wait if you're truly not ready," Kiel said, but Bethany could see him practically dancing from foot to foot, anxious to finally get on with it.

"No, let's just do it. I'm ready enough." Kiel seemed to believe her lie, so she turned to Owen, who was trying to shove his arm toward his shoulder. "Can you be serious for a second? We're doing this."

Owen flashed a look at her, then straightened up immediately and nodded. "Totally serious. Not that my arm being longer isn't serious too, but that can wait. Though really, not for much longer." Still holding one arm, he led the other two to the center of the library, where Bethany turned to look at Owen and Kiel.

"I've used this spell before," Bethany told them. "When I cast it in the Magister's tower to find Jonathan Porterhouse, the spell created a little ball of light that floated off to the right book. So just be ready to follow it, okay?"

Kiel looked hurt. "I *have* used my magic before, you know."

Bethany glared at him, and he shrugged. "But sure, we'll do what you say." He then winked at Owen, who giggled, which managed to make her more irritated.

Kiel pulled a wand from its sheath and began to speak the words for the location spell, as Bethany's hands and feet both turned to ice. What if her father wasn't alive? Or what if he was, but he'd moved on and had a new family? Or what if he'd been trapped this entire time, tortured by some evil villain, all because of her? Her heart beat so quickly she almost couldn't think straight.

But then a small ball of light appeared right in front of Kiel's wand, and Bethany stopped breathing completely.

All three of them leaned forward, waiting to see where it'd go. The ball hung in place for just a moment, then jumped toward the mysteries section.

Bethany's heart leaped into her throat, and she took a step to follow it, only to stop as the light paused in midair. It seemed to shake just a bit, then move toward the romance books.

Then it paused again and just quivered in midair, like it wasn't sure where to go.

"What's it doing?" Owen whispered.

"I don't know, I've never seen this before," Kiel whispered back.

The ball trembled harder and harder and began to glow brighter as it did, the light soon becoming hard to look at. As it shook, smaller balls of light exploded out of the original, flying off in every direction. First dozens, then hundreds, maybe even thousands of balls filled the air, so bright that Bethany could barely see anything, as if the sun had just appeared in the middle of the room.

"Turn it off!" Owen shouted. "Someone's going to see!"

Kiel shouted some magic words, but the balls of light kept popping out of the first one, then flying off into every corner of the library. Finally, the original ball flew off as well, and the three kids covered their eyes as best they could to see where the light balls had gone.

They didn't have to look far.

Each and every book in the library had a ball of light directly in front of it.

Every single book.

Bethany's mouth opened and closed, but no sound came out. Somewhere in the distance a siren began blaring, and Owen grabbed her hand, pulling her toward the door of the library. She stumbled after him as Kiel followed, behind them the location spells fading away into nothing.

None of them said another word as they quietly made their way into the bushes beside the library while a police car slowly pulled up. The police officer shined his light into the now-dark building, then shrugged and got back into his car. A moment later he pulled away, and Kiel and Owen both turned to Bethany, their eyes filled with questions.

"I knew it," she whispered, her voice trembling. "*I knew it.* It never works. Nothing does. This is my fault, and he's never coming back."

"Bethany," Kiel started to say, but she shoved him away.

"NO!" she shouted. "I'm done, do you hear me? I give up! I can't do this anymore! I just . . . I can't take this. He's gone and he's never coming back. And I'm done! Leave me alone!"

And with that, she turned and ran, the cold wind whipping her face so hard she found it covered in tears by the time she got home. Once there, she snuck up to her room, locked the door, and screamed as loudly as she could right into her pillow, until her throat hurt and she saw spots in front of her eyes.

Finally, she reached under her bed, grabbed a specific book, and dove right in, not wanting to spend another minute in the real world.

CHAPTER 16

01:29:56

With water reaching almost to her knees, Bethany rocked the chair left and right as hard as she could. Finally, momentum sent her over the edge, crashing the chair onto its side and spraying water in every direction.

"AH!" she shouted as the cold water splashed over her from head to toe. Why did it have to be cold? Couldn't this stupid death trap at least have had warm water?

She bent forward in the chair, trying to see where the ropes were attached from her ankles to the chair. As far as she could tell, it looked like the ropes had been tied to the chair's feet. She managed to slip the knots down off the chair legs, then pulled her legs up to her and untied the ropes, freeing her ankles.

Unfortunately, the chains around her wrists were a different story. They looked to be bolted to the chair legs somehow.

She groaned, then took a deep breath, trying to stay calm. There had to be a way out of this. She pulled on the chains, but the chain links bit into her wrists painfully the harder she pulled, and when she tried grabbing the chain itself, she found it was far too slippery to hold on to. Wrapping the chain around her hand was even more painful than just pulling with her wrists.

After a few minutes of experimenting, she pushed her head into the arm of the chair and screamed as loud as she could.

"You seem to be having some difficulty," said a strange voice from somewhere behind her. Bethany instantly looked up, but saw no one.

"Who's there?" she said, not liking how vulnerable she felt, chained up and about to drown.

"Nobody important," the voice said. "I do think it's time we had a little chat, if you don't mind."

Bethany wanted to laugh. A little chat? Who *was* this? "Did Doyle send you?"

"No," the voice said. "He has no idea that I'm here."

"He does now," Bethany said. "He's got cameras all over this place."

"He won't see *me*," the voice said. "I'm here to speak to you. Alone."

That sounded promising. Either that, or he was going to kill her. "Could you help me, then? Get these chains off of me?"

"You can get out yourself. We both know you can."

Bethany eyes widened in surprise, and again, she tried to turn to look at whoever was speaking to her. She caught the briefest glimpse of what looked like the top of a bald head before whoever it was pulled back out of sight. "Who *are* you?" she said, not entirely sure she wanted to know.

"I already told you. Nobody of consequence. But I'm not here to talk about me. We need to discuss your trips into the fictional world, Bethany."

Even with the freezing water, somehow that statement made Bethany feel even colder. "I don't know what you're talking about," she lied, trying not to show how terrified she was.

"Yes, you do," the voice said. "And the trips need to stop. You're never going to find what you're looking for."

"And what's that?" she asked slowly, her heart racing. "What am I looking for?"

"Your father," the voice said, and Bethany almost stopped breathing. "What you're doing is dangerous, girl. Far more dangerous than you realize. There are people in the fictional world who'd do anything to find you, if they learned of your

existence. For now, they're unaware, but every time you enter a story, every time something like *this* happens, you create ripples." She heard the person dip what she imagined was a hand into the water, then watched as small waves passed by the chair. "Too many ripples, and people start to notice."

"Who?" Bethany said quietly. "Who are these people?"

"The less you know, the better," the voice said. "For now, just believe me when I tell you that you need to stop."

"*No!*" she shouted, jerking around in the chair and trying to get a better look, even though the chains bit painfully into her skin. "Tell me who they are. Tell me who *you* are! How do you know me? Do you know where my father is? *I need to know!* Please!"

"Stop trying to find him," the voice said, almost sounding sympathetic. "Looking will only lead to darkness and pain for both worlds. Let him go, and take solace in what you still have: a mother who loves you."

Bethany growled in frustration. "I'm not going to stop!" she screamed. "I *will* find him, I don't care what it takes!"

"And that attitude is what got you here."

Her eyes widened. "How do you know any of this?"

"Oh, I know far more than you think," the voice said. "I

77

know about you and your friends . . . even your father. So believe me when I tell you that you must *never* find him. That is all I can say."

"No, please!" Bethany shouted. "Help me get out of these chains. Let me see who you are!"

"You know how to free yourself," the voice said, getting farther away.

"No, I *can't*," she said, not sure if there was water on her face or if she was crying. "I can't do it again. Not to *them*, too. I can't!"

"It's the only way," the voice said, even farther now. "You must leave and save yourself."

"Please, help me!" she shouted. *"Please!"*

"I saw what you did on Argon VI," the voice said, and this time she could barely hear it. "I know how you feel, and what this means to you. That is why I *cannot* release you. Escape, Bethany. Leave all of this behind, and forget about it. The worlds will both be safer if you do."

Argon VI?! How could this person have seen her there? "What do you mean?" she shouted. "How would they be safer?"

But this time there was no response.

Bethany shouted again, and flailed around in the chair so

hard that she splashed water all over herself. Crying in frustration, she yanked on the chains over and over, but all she did was make her hands bleed from the hard metal.

Argon VI. How could anyone have seen her there? She hadn't told Owen or Kiel. Doyle didn't know. *No one* knew, other than EarthGirl.

The memory of her time on the other planet filled her mind, and somehow, it actually managed to calm her down. She stared at the chains, then at her red, scratched hands, and finally at the chair she was laying on.

She'd been going about this the wrong way. Too much doing, not enough thinking.

She dropped the chains, and instead reached behind her for the soaking wet cushion on the chair, which she pulled out as best she could. Once she'd managed to get it off the chair, she unzipped the cover and yanked out the cushion. That she tossed aside, then took the cushion cover and wrapped it around her hands for protection.

Then she grabbed the chains again.

The cover protected her skin enough for her to pull as hard as she could. First one chair leg, then the other pulled free, and instantly she jumped to her feet, pulling against the heavy

weight of the unattached chains on her wrists, searching for whoever had been talking to her.

Except nobody was there, and there was no way out of the room, other than the door Doyle had used. And that had been in her sight the entire time.

Who was her visitor? And how had he managed to see her on a completely different planet?!

MISSING CHAPTER 3

One month ago, the same night . . .

The green sun of Argon VI beat down on Bethany as she punched a hole straight through a mountain, screaming at the top of her lungs until her throat hurt. She leaped into the air, flying hundreds of feet into the yellow sky, then turned her laser vision on the desert floor beneath her, burning the sand into glass. She then dove back down to the surface, splintering the glass into dust so fine it felt like snow.

"WHERE ARE YOU?" she screamed into the empty sky as she sank to her knees, her voice like thunder. She punched the ground a few more times, tears falling and mixing with the dirt on her face. "WHY CAN'T I FIND YOU?"

She leaped back into the air and rocketed off toward the ocean, a sonic boom exploding behind her. She hit the water

with a sound like a bomb going off, tunneling through it so quickly that she left only steam behind her, then aimed straight down. She hit the sea floor hard enough to send tremors in all directions, then spun around in a circle as fast as she could, twisting the water into a funnel all the way to the surface, an enormous whirlpool a mile deep.

She stopped, and as the ocean water began to collapse in on her, she clenched her fists and exploded up through it, leaving behind another cloud of steam as she flew off—

Only to be hit in the face by something that felt hard as a rock. Everything went dark as Bethany spun around, crashing back to the ground in the middle of a field, sending corn flying. She looked up in surprise and found someone floating in the air in front of her: a girl in jeans and a white T-shirt with a blue ball on it and a black hoodie that covered her face. Beneath the hood two red eyes glowed like lasers, and Bethany could feel the heat from where she stood.

No. *No, no, no!* What had she done?!

"Good morning!" EarthGirl said, her burning eyes staring straight into Bethany's. "Now, I'm not sure who you are or why you're being all crazy. But please stop destroying things, if you don't mind. Wouldn't you rather just discuss your problem, so I

can help you fix it?" The glow in her eyes began to fade, and she gave Bethany an embarrassed look. "I'm really sorry I punched you, by the way. I *hate* punching. It always feels so ridiculous."

"I . . . I can't talk to you," Bethany said, frantically trying to figure out what page in EarthGirl: *Doomsday on Argon VI* she'd jumped into. Was she interrupting the plot? Had she just pulled EarthGirl away from something important? "I'm sorry, for . . . for all of this. I need to go." And with that, Bethany took off into the air, another sonic boom exploding behind her.

"Thank you!" EarthGirl said from right beside her, her voice somehow reaching Bethany despite them both flying faster than the speed of sound. "Apologies are a good place to start. But I've never met anyone who could do what *I* do before. What's your name?"

"It's not important," Bethany said, abruptly skidding to a halt in midair. The green sun gave anyone from Earth super-powers here, which meant that anywhere Bethany could go, EarthGirl could easily follow.

"I'm Gwen," EarthGirl said, pulling her hoodie off to reveal a dark-skinned girl about Bethany's age with long brown hair. She stuck out her hand, then wrinkled her nose at it. "I hope

I'm not offending you. I've read that people from my home planet used to greet each other this way, with their hands. I'm from a place named Ay-arth."

"Earth," Bethany corrected, then winced.

"So you *do* know it," Gwen said, a small smile playing over her face.

Bethany turned bright red. "You tricked me?" How many rules could she break here at once? Talking to a main character was bad enough, but EarthGirl knew that there were other people who knew about Earth now too!

Gwen shrugged. "Not tricking so much as just skipping some steps. What's your name?"

Ugh. "Bethany," she said, taking Gwen's hand. "I really, really hope you weren't busy just now. Because if I'm interrupting anything—"

"Nah," Gwen said, waving a hand. "I just finished disassembling this robot thing that was trying to destroy the world. A girl at school built it. We're actually good friends." She sighed. "Well, she's friends with Gwen. She kind of hates EarthGirl." She pointed at the T-shirt she wore. "It's a whole thing, and I keep wanting to fix it, but, honestly, I have no idea how."

"Sounds complicated," Bethany said, inwardly sighing with

relief. If Gwen had completed the book's story, at least Bethany might not be changing much, assuming she got away without making things worse. "Listen, I really shouldn't take up more of your time. I was just in the, uh, solar system, and—"

"So you're from Earth too?" Gwen said, pulling Bethany gently by the hand back to the ground. "How did you survive it blowing up? How did you get here? *I have so many questions!*"

"I know you do," Bethany told her, inwardly screaming. "And I promise, someday you're going to find out everything you want to know." Like, two books from now, even. "But I'm not the one to tell you, okay? Trust me. I'm . . . I'm just like you, I have no idea how I survived, or where I am."

Gwen's face fell, and Bethany felt even worse. "Listen, I'm sorry," Gwen said. "I didn't mean to be so pushy. Of course you don't have to tell me anything you don't want to."

"It's not that, really!" Bethany said quickly.

"I hope I'm not weirding you out," Gwen said. "It's so hard to know anything about Earth culture. All I have are some old books my parents put in my rocket, but most of those were about these people called detectives, who are always solving crimes." She sighed. "I'm trying to be a good detective *here*, on Argon VI, but I never know if I'm doing a good job, or if I'd

85

just be embarrassing my real parents, you know?" She paused, her eyes lighting up again. "Wait. Do *you* know anything about detectives?"

She had to get away. This conversation could only lead to bad, bad things. But how? Could she burrow into the ground fast enough to hide before Gwen caught up, so she could jump out of the book? "Sure," Bethany answered, glancing around for a likely spot. "You're doing a great job. Detectives solve crimes, help the police, that kind of thing. Just like what you're doing."

"The police, yeah!" Gwen said, getting excited. "They show up a lot! Only they're usually not very smart, and the detectives have to figure things out for them."

Bethany half smiled in spite of herself. "Don't believe everything you read."

"Bethany, please, talk to me," Gwen said, sitting down on the ground and locking her arms around her knees. "Who are you? Where do you come from? I'll take whatever I can get. I just . . . I just really want to know about my parents and my world."

Bethany gritted her teeth. Maybe she could run fast enough to disappear into the distance before Gwen was back on her feet? She started to turn, then looked down at her hand, which Gwen had grabbed. *"Please,"* Gwen said, her expression one

Bethany had seen far too often on her own face. "Please, I just need to *know*."

And suddenly, the rules just didn't seem that important. "I'm . . . from the future," Bethany said, thinking of the plot of an upcoming EarthGirl book. "I've come back to your time to . . . to look for *my* father. He's lost here somewhere, but I have no idea how to find him."

"The future?" Gwen said, her eyes widening. "There are Earth people in the future? How?"

"I can't tell you that," Bethany said, hating herself for lying to this poor girl. "It'd mess up the entire time line. You know how it is."

Gwen nodded, but her face fell. "Oh. Sure, I guess. Well, at least I can help you find your father. Let's get started. Where have you looked?"

Bethany just stared at her. "You can't . . . I mean, I appreciate the help, but—"

"Detectives help *find* people, Bethany," Gwen said, leaping to her feet. "If I'm going to be one, then this is the least I can do. Besides, you seem nice, when you're not breaking up my mountains." She grinned, and for a moment Bethany almost considered letting her help.

Then something she had said sank in.

"Detectives help find people," Bethany whispered, and all the frustration and horribleness of the night faded away, just like that. "Gwen," she said quietly, "you have no idea how amazing you are. Spectacular. Incredible. All the adjectives."

Gwen blushed, then shoved Bethany's shoulder, a hit that would have sent Bethany flying if she hadn't dug her feet into the ground. "*Stop* it," Gwen said, smiling shyly. "I'm sure all Earth people are like this."

Bethany started to laugh, then stopped and nodded instead. "Yes. They are. All Earth people are incredibly nice and helpful." She hugged Gwen, then stepped back. "*Thank you*, seriously. So much." And then she said something she never, ever thought she'd say. Part of her screamed at the idea, but the rest of her didn't care. "Maybe I can come back and hang out a little more, when I'm done?"

"That'd be great!" Gwen said, giving her a grin as she pulled her hoodie over her head. "By the way, I hope you think this costume of our people is respectful toward them?"

"Very," Bethany said, and laughed. "I love it!" She waved good-bye, then clicked a nonexistent communicator on her wrist. "Bethany, ready to beam back to the future!" she said to

no one, then jumped back out of the book, figuring her "time travel" would account for her just disappearing.

As soon as she hit her bed, she got on her computer and searched the online catalog at the library. The first few books she found, she dismissed. It couldn't be anything too obvious, or too big. Nothing that was still going. Had to be a series that was over, and one that as few people as possible had read.

There. Perfect. She clicked the reserve button, just to make sure it was there tomorrow.

Detective books. Why hadn't she thought of this before? When someone went missing, of *course* you went to a detective.

And thanks to the library, she had just reserved one of the greatest detectives of all time.

01:28:49

Kiel rubbed his aching head as he pushed himself off the alleyway's wall, where he'd been leaning after the last memory hit. That one had come out of nowhere (and wasn't the most useful for the current situation) but at least his memories were returning, if slowly.

Still, sometimes magic really *did* create headaches.

But there was no time to waste feeling sorry for himself. Bethany had a little less than ninety minutes before he'd never see her again, and Kiel was no closer now than he'd been twenty minutes ago.

Why couldn't he have his magic? This would be done in seconds! Or even Charm? She always knew what to do in these situations. Sure, Kiel liked to give her a hard time, but only because she enjoyed it so much. And without Charm, he'd

never have found so much as the First Key to the Source of Magic, let alone any of the others.

But Charm was far away in Quanterium, and he was stuck in the nonfictional world. Here, he needed an expert on the boring and normal. Here, he needed *Owen*.

With a groan, Kiel started back out toward the police station, each extra minute weighing heavily on his mind. What if he ran out of time and was too late to rescue Bethany? Sure, he couldn't remember the past month or so of their time together, but what Kiel could remember made him smile. And not the smile he flashed for other people, the one designed to put them at ease, to make them think Kiel had a plan and knew what he was doing. Not even the smile he gave Charm to make her secretly enjoy herself in spite of everything.

No, this smile was just for *himself*, and that . . . that was something Kiel had never really felt before.

Bethany was just so unlike anyone he'd ever known. All her rules, all her worries made him want to grab her hand and jump off a cliff with her, just to see her excitement break through. The times when she had just let go and gone fictional, she'd seemed so happy, and the memory gave Kiel a warm feeling throughout his chest.

The sight of the police station, though, killed that feeling. He paused a block away, watching the police cars skidding to a stop outside of it and the steady flow of criminals in and police officers out. Busy night, apparently.

Kiel wiped his hands on his pants, not sure why his palms were so sweaty. He'd done this before, been in police stations dozens of times. The Science Police had picked him up constantly when he was just a thief on the streets.

So why was he so nervous? Kiel Gnomenfoot didn't do nervous . . . at least not so anyone could tell. What would his fans all think if they knew that he was terrified half the time? They'd be let down, and that was something Kiel wasn't ever going to let happen.

He wiped his hands again, pasted a smug grin on his face, and stepped confidently toward the police station. He'd find Owen, they'd escape, and together they'd find Bethany in minutes. Owen would know what to do. This was his world, and he knew this Doyle guy.

It'd all be okay. It'd definitely all be okay.

So why wasn't he moving?

Kiel looked down at his traitorous lower limbs. *Hmm.* Apparently his feet were making this more difficult than it

needed to be. He gave them an annoyed look and forced his leg to step forward.

It refused, staying put exactly where he'd had it.

What was happening? Kiel Gnomenfoot, boy magician and savior of all Magisteria, was scared of being caught by the police? Just because he had no magic and no idea what he was doing in this world? Just because for the first time in his life, he honestly wasn't sure he'd be able to get back out once he stepped inside the police station?

Maybe his feet knew more than he did.

Kiel backed away into the shadows, realizing his heart was racing. This was ridiculous! He was Kiel Gnomenfoot! He'd faced down dragons, fought crazy clones of himself, and even gone past the edge of existence. Just because he was completely powerless now, that didn't mean that he couldn't handle himself.

And yet, somehow his palms were sweaty again.

"You made it!" said a voice to his side, and Kiel quickly turned to find a girl about his age with light-brown skin, her long black hair held down with a tight black hat, which matched the rest of her dark clothes. She was also grinning hugely.

Kiel instantly flashed a smile at her in return, letting himself fall back into old habits. It felt good, actually. "I did," he said, unsure what she was talking about.

Before he could ask, the girl threw her arms around him and hugged him quickly. "I thought you'd *never* show up," the girl continued, pushing him away. "This is so exciting, isn't it?"

Ah, a fan. "You must think I look like the dashing hero of the Kiel Gnomenfoot series," he said, using his smug grin.

The girl laughed. "*Nothing* you say makes sense. *Love it.* Never change! Where've you been? I've been waiting forever for you!"

"I get that a lot," Kiel told the girl, then winked.

The girl laughed, then winked back immediately.

Kiel paused, not entirely sure what to do with that. He winked again, and she did too.

"What's happening here?" he said.

"Like *I* know?" the girl said, grinning widely as she shook her head. "I followed that other guy here, like, a half hour ago, but I thought you got lost or something. But you're here now, so we can get moving, my handsome little koala! Time to set this plan into motion, am I right?" She winked again.

This was *not* how these things usually went. "Can we step back a bit?" Kiel asked. "I'm honestly not one hundred percent sure who you are."

The girl nodded. "You're so right. Who are *any* of us? Let's seriously get moving, though." With that, she shoved Kiel forward, out into the road leading to the police station.

Kiel immediately jumped back into the shadows. "Wait a second. *I don't know who you are.*"

The girl gave him an odd look. "You don't?" She looked down at herself. "I mean, I'm in my work clothes, but I don't look that different. Are you just messing with me?" She slowly grinned at him. "You're *totally* messing with me. *I love this.* You guys are so fun!"

Kiel just looked at her helplessly for a moment, then put up his hands in apology. "No, I mean . . . I've had some problems with my memory. It's a whole thing. Magic and all."

"Oh, *totally*," the girl said, and winked. "Magic. Of course."

"Stop that!" Kiel shouted, then put his hands back up as the girl's smile faded into a more dangerous look. "Look, sorry, it's just hard to concentrate when you keep doing that."

The girl gave him a careful look, then shrugged, the smile exploding back over her face. "No need to apologize. Let's just

get going!" She grabbed his arm and pulled him back toward the police station.

This was clearly another missing memory, so all he had to do was trigger it. Kiel pulled the girl to a stop, then when she turned around, stared her right in the face for a good ten seconds. Then he closed his eyes, focusing on her face, willing the memory to come. Anticipating the pain, he gritted his teeth and waited for the memory to smack him across the face.

Instead of the memory, though, he got an actual slap.

"Wake up!" the girl said. "I think I lost you there. Did you faint? You fainted, didn't you. You stared at me for a second, then looked like you had to go to the bathroom. Kind of like a koala, weirdly. Is this normal for you?"

Kiel put a hand up to his cheek, which throbbed where she'd slapped him. "Not even a little bit."

"Then follow the plan, my magical koala." She laughed, then grabbed his arm and pulled him toward the police station again.

"Um, we're going to get caught if we get any closer," Kiel told her.

"Uh, *yeah?*" she said. "That's the idea!" Then she turned toward the station and raised her voice. "Hey, cops! Aren't you

96

looking for this guy? I found him. Kiel Gnomenfoot. Come and get him!"

And with that, every police officer around the station glanced up. Kiel's eyes widened and he turned to run, only to feel a jolt like lightning hit his side, and he dropped to the ground, twitching.

The girl in black stood over him, a small sparking device in her hand shooting little blue bolts. "Wow, that was *fun*," she said. "Hope it didn't hurt much. Did it? A lot? Sorry. But still, *how much do I love my Taser?* Anyway, enjoy!"

And with that, she ran off, laughing as Kiel twitched on the ground, police officers surrounding him on all sides.

CHAPTER 18

01:18:12

Owen sat in a different room in the police station, this one a bit more comfortable than the interrogation room, but with the door no less locked. It didn't escape him that there wasn't even a window. Apparently, the police were taking no chances.

After the last memory attack, Inspector Brown had given him some aspirin and said that his mother was on her way now, which almost made Owen's head ache even more. Beyond having to explain exactly what he'd been doing in the library (um, *not lighting it on fire!*), there was the fact that she'd told the police he was still in bed. What did that mean? Was she trying to cover for him, somehow? He snorted. *His* mom? But what else could it be?

All of this would be so much easier if he could just remember what had happened before he'd woken up in the library!

Owen growled in frustration and smacked his head over and over, hoping to jar out some more memories. All of this was beginning to feel like one of those terrible stories, where half of it took place in the present, and the rest was told in flashbacks. So irritating. You knew the characters would be okay during the flashbacks because you were seeing them in the present too, so the flashbacks were always boring. Why couldn't those writers just tell the story the *normal* way?

Again, a tiny part of Owen's brain began trying to tell him something, but he couldn't quite get ahold of it, like it was a slippery water balloon covered in oil. Whatever it was could wait, though. Right now, he needed to remember.

Maybe the flashback thing could help? Sure, it was more of a fictional thing. You didn't flash back in the real world, you just remembered things. But it's not like anything was happening like it was supposed to tonight. There was no record of Bethany anywhere, a second Owen was home asleep, and his library had just been burned down by a fictional character.

At this point thinking a little fictionally might help. Besides, what else did he have to do here in the police station? Wait to either be thrown in jail by the cops or grounded until he was a million by his mom?

Owen took a deep breath and focused on flashing backward, trying to mentally push himself into the past. He brought up the first memory that'd hit him, the day when Kiel had gone back into his series to recover his spell book. That'd been a quick memory, just Kiel and Bethany as Charm (sigh . . .) jumping out of the book. But the next flashback had been much longer, when Kiel had used the finder spell to find Bethany's dad.

But what had happened next? Bethany had told them she didn't want to go into any more books, and . . . and *what*?

"Flash . . . *back*," he whispered, rubbing his temples. "Flash-back! Flassssssh baaaaaack." Ugh. Nothing. He swung his head in circles, trying to drag the memories to the surface, but that didn't help either. Finally, out of options, he scrunched his eyes closed, took a deep breath, then banged his head on the table.

"AH!" he shouted, grabbing his poor skull, still entirely memoryless. Clearly, forcing a flashback was just not going to happen.

Not without, maybe, something *bigger*, at least. Owen glanced around the room for something to hit himself over the head with, but other than the table (which he'd just tried), there wasn't anything too promising.

Ugh. This was so frustrating! He glanced at his watch, and realized that in another eighty-five minutes or so, Bethany really *would* disappear. Maybe that's what had happened? Had Doyle somehow removed all record of her from the police database? And maybe he'd been the one to put a fake Owen in Owen's real bed!

But why would he have done those things? Why would he have done *any* of these things? Owen sighed, dropping his head into his hands.

At least Kiel was out there, looking for Bethany. Kiel the hero would actually get the job done, unlike Owen, sitting here uselessly in a police station, powerless, planless, hopeless. Kiel had been right. He should have trusted the magician, and not turned himself in to the police. That's what a nonfictional sidekick did, not a fictional awesome person.

Kiel Gnomenfoot would never be caught dead in a police station. Not *Kiel Gnomenfoot, Magic Thief.*

The door flew open, and Kiel Gnomenfoot, magic thief, stumbled inside, looking shaken and weirdly twitchy. A police officer smirked at Owen, then closed the door behind Kiel and locked it.

"Kiel?!" Owen shouted, standing up just in time to have the

boy magician slump into his arms. "What are you doing here? Did you get caught?"

Kiel gave him a dazed look. "I think? I came to rescue you. But then there was this *odd* girl, and things went downhill from there."

For some reason Owen suddenly wanted to hit the boy magician, and he briefly considered dropping Kiel to the floor. "You're supposed to be finding Bethany, not rescuing me! Get out of here and go find her!"

"Find her where?" Kiel said, using Owen's shoulders to steady himself. "I had no idea where to even look, Owen. I need your help. You're from around here. Where do we start?"

"We don't start *anywhere*, not now!" Owen said, shouting again. "We're both locked up in the police station, meaning neither of us is saving Bethany!"

"I thought you said this was the right thing to do," Kiel said, giving Owen a half-annoyed, half-still-dazed look. "Isn't this what you wanted?"

"No. *Yes.* I thought so, but they won't listen to me. They keep saying she doesn't exist." Owen dropped into his seat in frustration. "They think *we* did it. I have no idea what else to say. How could Bethany not be in their records? I don't get it!"

"Forget about the police," Kiel said, sitting down thankfully in the seat across from Owen. "Focus on the *enemy*. If we find Doyle, we find Bethany. Have you figured out his clues?"

"Clues?" Owen said. "You mean how he said he did this by the book? All that means is he did things the official way, according to the rules. What does that even mean? There aren't any rules for kidnapping someone and setting fire to a library. And if there are, then I feel like that's really messed up!"

"He also said we'd understand if we knew where we were," Kiel pointed out.

Owen's eyes widened. "I think I've made it pretty clear! We're in the police station, and we're not getting out!"

"Calm down," Kiel said, forcing a shaky grin. "You're with *Kiel Gnomenfoot*, remember? I've got this. I'll get us out of here in no time." He winced. "Assuming I don't have another stupid memory come back."

Owen's eyes widened. "You got those too? I've had two memories, one of you getting your spell book back—"

"And the other of us using the finder spell," Kiel finished, giving him a confused look. "Hmm. I must have modified the forget spell I used on us somehow so our memories would return." He grinned for real this time. "I'm amazing!"

"There has to be a reason Doyle made us forget everything," Owen said. "There has to be something important that we've forgotten. Like how he got out of his book, or where Bethany is. Or how he knows who we are in the first place."

"Well, I'm not just sitting here until I remember," Kiel said. "And neither are you. We're going to escape, and then you and I are going to find Bethany, memories or no."

Owen just shook his head. "Don't you get it? If I leave now, I'll be a fugitive. They won't stop until they find me, and then I'll go to a juvenile detention center or something. For the rest of my *life*, Kiel. I can't leave. You'll have to go."

Kiel frowned. "Bethany's life is in danger, remember? Nothing else matters."

"But *you're* going to save her. That's what you do!"

Kiel shrugged. "Of course I do. And now you will too. You saved Charm, and you basically defeated Dr. Verity—"

"No, *you* did that. I messed everything up." Owen shook his head. "It's okay, you don't need to pep-talk me. I know I'm sort of the sidekick here. You have magic, and Bethany has her half-fictional powers, and all I have is that I've read a lot of books. Not exactly a superpower, you know?"

Kiel gave him a long look, then shook his head. "You're com-

ing. And you're going to be a hero, just like I am. And then I'm going to wink, and it's going to be amazing." And he winked, and Owen couldn't help but smile.

"Kiel, this is something you don't come back from," he said.

Kiel nodded, ignoring Owen as he stood up and moved closer to the door, pulling out a small wire from his cloak. Kiel inserted the wire into the door, and a moment later, something clicked. Kiel grinned at Owen, then quietly opened the door.

"The hall's clear," Kiel whispered. "As soon as I say go, follow me as quickly as you can, okay?"

"Kiel, I *can't*—"

"One," Kiel said, watching the hallway. "Two—"

The door flew open, and Inspector Brown and two police officers stood in it. "Three," Inspector Brown said. "Grab Mr. Gnomenfoot for me, will you boys? It's his turn for questioning."

Kiel tried to duck under their arms, but there was nowhere to go, and a second later they had Kiel's hands cuffed behind his back.

"Bring him to interrogation," Inspector Brown said, gesturing out into the hall with his thumb. "I'll be there in a second."

The two police officers nodded and carried out a still-struggling Kiel Gnomenfoot. "Don't worry, Owen!" Kiel shouted as he left. "I'll be back to rescue you."

Inspector Brown shook his head. "That kid's going to be very disappointed. If there's one thing I've learned in my time with Doyle Holmes, it's that no one escapes him."

Owen's eyes widened as Inspector Brown left, locking the door behind him. Inspector Brown knew Doyle Holmes? How was that possible? How could the nonfictional police know a fictional character, act like they'd known him for years?

And maybe just as important, was Inspector Brown right? Was Doyle that good, like he was everywhere at once?

Holmes . . . everywhere . . .

And just like that, another crystal-clear memory hit Owen, right across the face. Ugh. This was getting a bit ridicul—

MISSING CHAPTER 4

Yesterday . . .

Owen sat at the checkout counter, staring blankly at his math homework. His pencil slowly doodled on his homework, sketching a smiling half-robotic girl.

Sometimes he just felt so useless. It'd been a month since he'd seen Bethany, and Kiel seemed to be getting more and more antsy, being trapped in the nonfictional world and going to school. But what could Owen do? Bethany wouldn't take his calls, and it's not like he really knew what to say anyway. Sorry you didn't find your dad, and that magic thinks he's trapped in every single book in the library?

This was the problem. Owen was just the sidekick, maybe not even that. At least Robin knew how to fight, and he had his own comic sometimes. Owen's comic would be all about Kiel

and Bethany rescuing him because he bumbled into some new trap every issue. And it'd be canceled after, like, the third one. Maybe the second.

He sighed, sketching some hair on the half-robot girl. If only there was something he could say to Bethany to cheer her up, make her realize that they were still on her side. Even if they never jumped into another book, Bethany was still his friend, and he wanted to be there for her. To help her.

But how?

Someone placed a pile of books on the counter in front of him, and Owen looked up from his doodling to see a boy a few years younger than him looking annoyed. Owen smiled politely. "Do you have your library card?" he asked.

"Why are there so many Sherlock Holmes books now?" the boy said, glaring at Owen. "He's everywhere. I don't get it."

Owen shrugged. "I think he's just popular. Things go in waves sometimes."

"But look at this," the boy said, sliding a book over to Owen. "Since when is he even in the Bad Time Orphan Bunch series?"

Owen raised an eyebrow and took the book. The Bad Time

Orphan Bunch: *Life Becomes Unbearable*. Fun series, but Owen hadn't read it in a while.

"There's no Sherlock Holmes in this," he said, holding the book out to the boy.

"Open it!" the kid said, pushing it back.

Owen sighed and turned to the first page.

Chapter 1

I hope you're sitting down. I hope you've had your fill of fairy tales and nursery rhymes and stories where good conquers evil, or good sits down with evil over tea and talks out evil's problems, because this is not that. This is an altogether different thing than that. Good does not win. Good doesn't even show up on time for the fight.

Good, my beloved readers, decided to stay home and take a nap instead.

So get a blanket. You're going to need it to hide under. Get a teddy bear or your mother or whatever it takes to keep you reading well past when the fear reaches up your spine and into your brain, teasing out

the terror. This is that kind of story. The kind of story I'm shaking just *considering* telling you.

This is the story of fourteen children, each one an orphan, though somehow they formed a family. A bunch, if you will. Like bananas, or a random amount of things. That's what these orphans were. A random amount of things.

Let me introduce them to you. Here we are, their home, the ramshacklest of ramshackle houses, officially called the Sunshine Home for Happy Kids, but known to our orphans as the House of Moldy Porridge.

You don't want to know why. But I'm going to tell you.

Here, I'll open the door for you. Walk on inside, and . . . eh?

"I've got this."

This is odd. There's a boy in a mask, a mask adorned with a question mark. And he seems to be wearing an odd sort of hat and coat. He's not one of the orphans though. Who might this—

"Doyle Holmes," the boy says, not sticking out

his hand. "Great-great-great-great-great-grandson of Sherlock Holmes. I solved the mystery of these orphans, missing parents. They've all been returned home, and the missing diamonds were recovered."

But . . . you weren't even supposed to learn of the diamonds for several books yet. This isn't how this tale is supposed to go!

"Don't worry, I know the part you played in this too," this Doyle boy says. "The police are on their way. Don't bother running, I can track you anywhere."

The police? What? Sirens blare in the air behind me, and I turn to find several cars pulling up at once.

Is this truly the end, before any of it began?

Um. This was *not* how the book was supposed to go. Owen turned the page, and his eyes widened.

The next page was blank.

So were the next two hundred and fifty pages.

"It's not the only one like that," the boy said in disgust. "This masked Sherlock Holmes grandson guy shows up in a ton of books. Not fantasy or science fiction, just the regular kind of books. Jason Scout: *International Spy of Pancakes*,

Robin of Sherwood Lakes Subdivision, and a bunch more." He sighed. "Is this some kind of stupid crossover? 'Cause I never liked his first book anyway."

"What first book?" Owen asked, barely able to breathe.

"*The Baker Street* something or other," the boy said. "Anyway, this is all lame. I don't even want them. But you should complain to the companies that make these."

"The writers?" Owen asked absently, not even looking up.

"Whatever," the boy said. "Tell them crossovers are terrible, and no one wants them. I just want the Orphan Bunch."

And with that, he left, still mumbling to himself.

Owen was out of his chair instantly, practically running to the children's section. He scanned the shelves for a moment, then yanked out the book he was looking for.

The Baker Street School for Irregular Children.

He flipped it over and quickly read the back.

The great-great-great-great-great-grandson of Sherlock Holmes has inherited the family school, named after Sherlock's Irregulars, the group of children who used to help the great detective solve his mysteries. But Doyle Holmes wants to do more

than just help troubled children learn from their mistakes. He's ready to solve the biggest mysteries, capture the most dangerous crooks, and share his adventures with his trusty computer, W.A.T.S.O.N.!

The cover confirmed it. There was Doyle Holmes, a boy in a Sherlock Holmes coat and hat, wearing a question-mark mask. *The criminals don't know his true identity, so they can never see him coming,* the cover said.

Wow. *Yikes.* That did not sound good.

But somehow, this Doyle Holmes character was getting into other books, other stories, and solving mysteries, apparently before those stories even started. How was that possible? It wasn't like he, Bethany, and Kiel had ever visited this book, so at least it wasn't their fault. But still!

Wait a second. What was he thinking? *This was his chance.* Not only to distract Bethany from what'd been happening with her father, but also to show that he wasn't completely useless! Maybe that'd be Owen's thing—being the research guy! Finding books with characters who were escaping their stories, and he'd send Bethany in to stop them? Maybe give her all the plans and cool gadgets, then make jokes when they came back,

maybe every so often a hug, so Bethany knew he cared. Maybe this was his thing all along, to be the one finding important things for her to investigate!

Or maybe this *was* just some stupid marketing attempt to get people reading the Baker Street series, since it looked like only one book in the series ever came out, and that was years ago.

Either way, he'd take it to Bethany, and she'd have to check it out, with him and Kiel, too. And maybe this was the start of them doing some good now, instead of just having cool adventures and enjoying themselves.

That thought made Owen feel just a bit proud of himself as he carried *The Baker Street School for Irregular Children* back to the checkout desk, where he dialed Bethany's number.

Just a bit? No. A *lot* proud.

After all, this was completely Owen. He was going to totally get the credit for this.

"AUGH!" Owen shouted into the empty room in the police station, in spite of his pounding head. "Not again! It can't be all my fault *again*!"

CHAPTER 19

01:11:12

"Mr. Gnomenfoot," a man in a suit said to Kiel. "I'm Inspector Brown. I'm quite interested in who you are, to be honest. According to our files, you don't actually exist."

"You're not the first person to tell me that," Kiel said, still feeling a bit woozy but giving the detective a wink anyway. "That's a whole other story, but trust me, it was a fun time."

The man didn't seem to notice his wink, which was unusual. "I'm told by a reliable source that you're actually some sort of magician." The man leaned back in his chair. "I love magic, myself. It's like a puzzle, figuring out how the tricks are done. Haven't had one magician fool me yet, though."

Kiel raised an eyebrow. "They're not tricks, Inspector Brown. And I already figured out how magic works. Came from science, it was a whole thing." He shrugged. "Still kind of turns

my stomach, but it's probably just time to accept that."

"Not a trick, huh?" Inspector Brown said. "Let's see some. I bet I can tell you how you do it."

Kiel sighed. "I'm currently powerless. No magic." He shook his head sadly. "Otherwise, this conversation would probably be going very differently." He winked again, just to see if maybe it didn't take the first time.

"You seem to have an eye twitch," Inspector Brown said.

"I can see why your parents named you Inspector," Kiel said.

". . . They didn't. It's a title."

Kiel grinned. "I've got seven of those myself. Some are a little more clever than others. I like *Kiel Gnomenfoot and the End of Everything* best, I think. It's got the most appropriate level of importance."

"Enough games, Mr. Gnomenfoot," the inspector said. "We have an eyewitness claiming that you set fire to the local library with your friend, Owen Conners. Owen's already given us everything we need. He claims *you* did it."

Kiel frowned. "That doesn't sound like him. Especially since that's not true."

The inspector smirked. "Really? Because Owen couldn't wait to throw you under the bus. I didn't even need to ask. Volun-

teered that you covered the library in gasoline, lit the match, the whole deal. Are you saying that *he's* actually the one who did it?"

"Oh," Kiel said, smacking his head. "I get it. You're trying to get me to turn on Owen by lying about what he said. That's fantastic, I didn't realize the police still used that old trick."

Inspector Brown narrowed his eyes. "Why don't you tell me exactly what you were doing in the library, Mr. Gnomenfoot?"

"I'd like to, but I don't remember," Kiel said, tapping his forehead. "Magic spell. You should ask your eyewitness about that. I'm fairly sure he was the one who made me cast it."

"You don't remember." The inspector looked annoyed.

"Not a thing," Kiel said, then caught himself. "That's not entirely true, actually. Every so often I get this flash of memory, usually when something comes along to trigger it. You could maybe try saying different words, that might jog something, but I wouldn't count on it."

"This could go a lot easier on you if you cooperated, Mr. Gnomenfoot," Inspector Brown said.

"Honestly, I don't even have time for it to go easily," Kiel whispered, leaning forward. "If I don't rescue my friend

Bethany before this watch counts down, then something bad happens, and I never see her again. You'd think that the police would be interested in something like that. Doesn't that sort of thing fall into your jurisdiction? Or am I getting things wrong in this world?"

"In this world?" the inspector said, shaking his head. "I'm getting tired of this act, Mr. Gnomenfoot. Maybe let the fantasy stuff rest and just answer the questions?"

"Fantasy stuff?" Kiel said, giving the inspector an indignant look. "You police are the ones working with a kid in a question-mark mask! Why not ask him about Bethany, and see what he says?"

"I can keep you here overnight, Mr. Gnomenfoot," the inspector said. "If your friend really is in danger, I'll be happy to help, but I'm going to need you to be honest with me and tell me exactly what happened at the library. If not, we can talk again in the morning."

"Owen and I woke up in the library with no memory of how we got there. Then a guy named Doyle Holmes told us about Bethany, and burnt the place down," Kiel said, starting to get slightly irritated. "I'm guessing Owen already covered this, didn't he?"

The inspector started to say something, but stopped and hit a button on the wall. "Yes?" he said.

"Inspector, you're needed downstairs," said a voice muffled by a speaker on the wall with the mirror. "We found some sort of incendiary device in the evidence room."

The inspector's eyes widened. "I'm on my way." He jumped to his feet and pointed a finger at Kiel. "You're staying here until I get back, and then we're continuing this discussion."

"Don't worry, I'll have broken out by the time you're back," Kiel said, giving the inspector a broad smile.

The inspector finally smiled back. *"Good luck."* He gave a brief nod, then walked out, locking the door behind him.

"You'll see!" Kiel shouted, jumping up and yelling right through the closed door. "I've broken out of prisons a lot more robotic than this one!"

The door burst open, missing Kiel's face by inches, and the girl in all black from before grabbed him by the wrist and yanked him out the door.

"Hey!" he shouted at her, pulling his hand back. "I was making a point!" His eyes widened and he immediately jumped backward. "You!"

The girl covered his entire face with her hand. "Shh!" she

whispered, giving him an excited look. "You're so right, it *is* me! We'll talk later. We don't want the police hearing you! Though that'd create all sorts of interesting challenges." She giggled quietly. "You'd probably have to pay me more gold, though, if you wanted me to save you from *that*."

Kiel slowly pulled the girl's hand off of his face, just staring at her. Pay her gold? Who *was* she? Why was she helping him escape now, after she'd just helped hand him over?

He paused, waiting for a memory to flash into his head as the girl just grinned at him.

"Weird," he said. "I really thought that this would trigger some kind of memory."

"What an odd thing to say," she said with a shrug. "You crack me up! C'mon, Magical Koala. Can I call you MK? Let's go find that other kid, and then we'll get you out of here."

Without waiting for a response, the girl turned and walked carefully down the hall, moving so silently that even Kiel was impressed. Seriously, who was this girl? Had they really hired her in some way?

And where had they found gold?!

CHAPTER 20

So Doyle Holmes had somehow been invading other people's stories, and it'd been Owen's idea to investigate. Which meant that all of this was his fault, just like when he'd messed everything up with Kiel and the Magister. Perfect! Was there anything that Owen didn't ruin?!

Owen lay with his face on the table, his head still aching from the flashback, which, granted, had told him a lot about why he was here now. But what had happened when Owen had gone to Bethany about Doyle? Had she listened, or left him to mess it up even further somehow? If Doyle was getting into other stories, did that mean he had found a way out of the fictional world? That'd explain a lot. But not how he knew who Bethany was, or Owen and Kiel, for that matter.

ARGH. Mysteries were so annoying! And this whole

flashback thing really was starting to get on his nerves. Why did he have to remember in pieces? Why couldn't his whole memory just pop back into place at once?

This was feeling more and more like a badly written story, and if there was one thing Owen hated more than mysteries, it was bad writing. At least with mysteries, you could flip to the end and see who the killer was.

If only he could do that here, just flip to the end, and see where Bethany was, or why Doyle was doing all of this. Stupid real world. Not that the real world was acting very real right now. But that had to be Doyle's doing. It *had* to be.

Hadn't it?

Owen knocked his knuckles against his forehead, trying to bring back more memories when the door opened, and a girl dressed in all black pushed Kiel inside the room, then closed the door silently. Owen blinked in surprise. "Um, hello?"

"Owen!" the girl said, grinning widely. "*Boom*, job fulfilled. Well, started. Isn't this exciting? I'm having *such* a good time. Thank you for thinking of me!"

Owen slowly stood up, having no idea how to react to any of that. "Uh, who is this?" he whispered to Kiel.

"I have *no* idea," Kiel whispered back. "Apparently, we know

her." He shrugged. "Oh, and she's the one who got me caught by the police. I haven't entirely wrapped my head around all of it yet."

The girl giggled at him. "You're being *so crazy* right now, MK, I love it. It was all part of the plan, Owen! I needed you both together, and that was the easiest way." She shrugged. "Kiel's cape was going to lead to all kinds of interesting questions if I tried sneaking him in. Though I love it. *I love it.* I'm getting one. I have to have one."

"Who are you, again?" Owen asked, completely confused.

The girl laughed, then leaped forward and hugged him. "That gets me every time!" She pushed him away hard, and Owen went falling back into the table as she ran a hand down over her face, making herself serious. "Now, back to business. When I give the signal, you both follow me, doing exactly as I do, okay? Let's keep those mouths of yours clamped shut, boys. Let me do the talking. Good?"

Owen opened his mouth to ask a question, and immediately the girl reached over and pushed it closed. "No talking!" she said, and laughed again. As he stared at her in shock, she went to the door, opened it slightly, and nodded outside.

On the other side of the police station, a loud bang went off,

and smoke began to fill the halls. The fire alarm blared, and everyone began running everywhere.

"Quiet faces, you guys!" the girl said, and snuck out of the room. Kiel flashed Owen a huge grin, then took off after her, while Owen sighed and quickly did the same. This was it. He was officially a fugitive and was going to go to jail for the rest of his life. And his mother would show up at the police station only to find him missing. Apart from the him that was home, apparently.

The hallway outside was chaos, with smoke, running people, and irritating sirens. A police officer ran up and grabbed the girl by her hand. "Where are you three going?" he demanded.

"Inspector Brown told us to go to his office until this was over," the girl said, her face a mask of innocence and confusion. "Is that wrong?"

"No, do what he says," the officer said, already starting to run toward the source of the smoke. "Just hurry."

"Yes, sir," the girl said, then stuck out her tongue at him as soon as the officer turned around.

Through the chaos, the girl led them to a door that actually said INSPECTOR BROWN.

"We're *really* going to his office?" Owen asked.

"Quiet faces," she whispered, then tried the handle, which didn't turn. "Hmm."

"I can get this," Kiel said, stepping forward and taking out the small wire he'd used before. "I've got some experience with locked doors."

The girl giggled. "Really, MK?" she said as her hands flew over the doorknob, then turned it. "You'll have to teach me some new tricks!" The door opened and she shoved the two boys inside, then quietly shut it, locking the knob again.

"How did you do that so fast?" Kiel said, his eyes wide with admiration.

"Runs in the family," she told Kiel, shrugging. "Now, get yourself out that window and quit being so crazy." And to Owen, "Let's push this desk against the door. Just for safety."

Kiel ran for the window and yanked it open. "Four floors up," he said, grinning at Owen. "I like your style, Ms. Whoever-You-Are."

The girl sighed as she and Owen pushed the desk against the door. "I still don't get this joke. How could you not remember who I am?"

"It's been an interesting night," Owen told her. She made

125

a kissy face at him, then raced to the window, where Kiel was stepping out onto the ledge.

Owen frowned, hating his memory right then. Why would they have someone to help them? Where had they found her? And who was she, opening a locked door so quickly and setting off smoke bombs in a police station?

He stared at the girl as hard as he could, willing the flashback to start. GIRL. GIRL. GIRL.

And then a memory hit him right in the face.

"Who can tell me the name of the president of the United States during World War II?" Mr. Barberry asked.

No one raised their hand.

"Really? No one knows?" Mr. Barberry said. *"This was homework, people!"*

Owen gasped, but mostly at the boringness of the memory. That one had barely even hurt. What had happened? Had the flashback broken somehow?

"Come *on* already!" the girl said with a huge smile, yanking him forward. "The plan takes exact timing, Owen. Get your silly behind out on that ledge before I kick you off of it!"

Owen stepped out of the window and put a shaking foot out onto the incredibly shallow ledge. Who built ledges like

this, anyway? Either they were big enough to walk on or they weren't! Why split the difference?

"This way," Kiel said from one side.

"Uh-uh," the girl said, pushing Owen out of her way to climb out as well. "That way gets us caught, MK. *This* way!"

Owen looked down at the police cars below and the flashing red fire-alarm lights. They were so tiny, and so far away, it made them look almost adorable.

Less adorable was Inspector Brown, who stepped outside, looking in all directions, before turning around and glancing up. Then he smiled like he'd just seen through a magic trick or something.

And that's when another memory hit, which was just terrible timing at that exact mome—

MISSING CHAPTER 5

Yesterday...

Bethany!" her mom shouted from downstairs. "Owen and Kiel are here."

Bethany looked up at her bedroom door from where she was lying on the floor, her feet up on her bed. What were they doing here? She hadn't talked to them since, well, the finding spell night. And with what she'd done since . . .

The last thing she wanted to do was face either one of them.

"Tell them I'm busy!" she yelled down, then covered her head with a pillow. They probably wanted to check on her or something, and their sweetness made it even worse that she couldn't face them.

Her bedroom door opened, and Bethany tore the pillow off her face to find her mother staring down at her. "You realize I'm

not your butler, right?" her mother said. "Come on in, boys."

Bethany gave her mom an annoyed look, and her mother threw her one right back as Owen and Kiel stepped into her bedroom. "Don't work too hard on that homework project," her mom said as she left, leaving the door open.

"We won't," Owen said, then began to blush. "I mean, we will!"

"Looking lovely as usual, Mrs. Sanderson," Kiel said, waving as her mom left.

"What are you doing here?" Bethany hissed at them as quietly as she could. "I told you guys I didn't want to talk."

"I know," Owen said, taking some books out of his bag. "But something came up that couldn't wait. Something big."

"What, a real homework project?" Bethany asked, looking at the papers in his hand.

Owen shook his head and handed her the papers. She glared at him, then flipped through them in annoyance. They were all newspaper articles that he'd printed out.

Sherlock Holmes Takes Over the Literary Scene.

The Game Is Afoot: Sherlock Crossovers the New Big Thing?

Sherlock—

She tossed the papers back at Owen, and he fumbled them all, dropping them. "I already said no to jumping into Sherlock Holmes," Bethany told them, shaking her head. "And I *told* you guys. We're done!"

"Did you read them?" Owen said. "Look." He picked up the *Crossovers* article. "Sherlock Holmes is showing up *everywhere* right now. Well, at least his great-great-great-something-grandson. Doyle Holmes is appearing in other people's series, Bethany, and the authors say they didn't even know it was happening. Some are even suing their publishers. People think it's one big publicity stunt."

Bethany's heart almost stopped when Owen said the name Doyle Holmes. "Okay," she said, taking the article and swallowing hard as she pretended to skim it. "So it probably *is* just a publicity thing for this Doyle Holmes book."

No, no, no, *no*. What was Doyle *doing*?

"Have you ever heard of fictional characters crossing over into other series?" Owen asked her.

Every mention of a book in the article made her feel worse. The Orphan Bunch books, really?! "How is this my problem?" Bethany said, not looking Owen in the eye. "*We* didn't do it, right?"

"Not yet!" Kiel said, giving her a grin.

Bethany had to swallow hard to keep from throwing up.

Owen pulled a book out of his backpack and handed it to her. *The Baker Street School for Irregular Children.* The same one she'd checked out two weeks ago. "This is the book Doyle Holmes comes from," he told her. "I think we should go in and investigate. You know, be detectives, kind of."

"Detectives that take this kid down," Kiel said, juggling a wand on her bed. "It's way too long since I've had a good fight. I'm starting to get worried I'm not as impressive as I used to be."

"No fights," Bethany told him, ripping the book from Owen's hands. This was the exact same copy she'd used. If Owen had looked in the computer, he could have seen her name listed as checking it out.

"Maybe we can help," Owen said quietly to her. "Take a quick look and see if it *is* just a publicity thing, or if there's a fictional character who's figured out how to cross into other stories. If it's the second one, don't you think we should do something about it?"

"Why?" Bethany said, realizing how whiny her voice sounded, even to her. "We're not the *story police,* Owen. We

don't have to fix every problem." In her head, she begged Owen to just let it go, leave her alone, so that he and Kiel wouldn't find out what she'd done.

"I vote we're not the *anything* police," Kiel said. "Let's be thieves. That's a lot more fun."

"It's up to us because who else can fix it?" Owen said. "I know it's a lot to take in, but I'll handle it all. I'll read up on Doyle today, and have a plan ready for tonight. I'll take care of everything. You just have to jump us in and out."

"I'll handle the fighting," Kiel said, back to juggling. "Hopefully there are monsters. Oooh, or dragons! I *miss* dragons."

"We *can't* do this," Bethany said, almost pleading with them. "This goes against all the rules." The same rules that she'd broken. "It'll be interfering with a story." A story that she'd already *completely* interfered with. "You know I can't do this."

"This isn't about saving the Magister this time, Bethany," Owen said. "I promise. I'm being completely up front. I just want us to take a look and make sure it's not something horrible and world-ending. Think what would happen if a character like that got out into other stories. He's the world's greatest detective—"

"I thought that was the Bat guy you like," Kiel said.

"And there's no end to the stories he could ruin," Owen finished, then nodded at Kiel. "You're right, my mistake. *Batman* is the world's greatest detective. Sherlock Holmes was the world's greatest Victorian detective. Huge difference."

"Thank you," Kiel said, nodding at him.

They weren't going to let this go, and a part of Bethany realized they were right not to. It did look really bad, honestly. The only thing was, she knew something they didn't.

She knew that it was all her fault.

"I'll go alone," she told Owen, trying not to hyperventilate. "There, satisfied? I'll check it out and let you know what I find."

"Never!" Kiel shouted, and jumped up from the bed. "One for all and whatever else that musketeer guy told us. You need our help."

"Don't worry, I'm going to be useful too," Owen said, and his hopefulness almost broke her heart. "I've totally got a plan. I've even got a *backup* plan." He gave her a guilty look. "It's a bit weird, but when you go up against a Sherlock Holmes character, it doesn't hurt to have a little help on your side."

"Just let me just do this," Bethany said, not sure what else to say. "Please?"

"Nope," Kiel said, hugging them both. "We're in this together, until the dragons come, at which point I call the first two. No, first three!"

Owen smiled nervously at her, and Bethany sighed. "All right. Tonight at the library. But you guys have to do *exactly* what I say."

"Deal," Owen said.

"Deal!" Kiel said. "There's no way this can possibly go wrong!"

CHAPTER 21

01:04:23

Bethany sat shivering on the back of the chair, her chains curled up on the seat beneath her as the water slowly rose up toward her neck. Soon she was going to have to move, and there weren't that many more places to go. The shelves nearby rose another few feet higher than the chair did, but even they didn't get close to the ceiling.

Not only that, the water seemed to be flowing in faster now, as if it'd doubled at some point. Perfect.

As the water rocked her back and forth, all she could think about was the day before, when Kiel and Owen had come to her with *The Baker Street School for Irregular Children*. Why hadn't she just called it off? Doyle could do whatever he wanted, as far as she was concerned. And then none of them would be in this mess.

Except she wouldn't have let it go, because it was already too late by then. She'd have gone back into the book anyway, and been caught. Though at least then, it'd have just been her.

Jump, part of herself said. *You're going to by the end anyway. Kiel and Owen are never going to find you. Why put yourself through this?*

Because she deserved it.

You don't *deserve this. You did the only thing you could to find Dad.*

And look what had happened.

MISSING CHAPTER 6

Two weeks ago . . .

"Mr. Holmes will see you now," said a giant bald man wearing a white shirt printed with the words THE BAKER STREET SCHOOL. Despite having arms thicker than her head, his heavy English accent somehow made her feel a bit more comfortable as he held open a thick wooden door. Bethany nodded at him, then stepped inside the headmaster's office.

The entire room was covered in wood and leather. Chairs so deep you could dive into them sat in front of a roaring fireplace, which was topped with a violin hanging above the mantle. A pistol in a glass case labeled THIRD ACT also sat on the mantle, probably some sort of trophy from a previous case. An enormous desk filled the far part of the room, and a tall leather chair was currently turned around, facing a wall of monitors behind it.

Each of the monitors showed either a classroom or what looked like a cellblock, and the images switched so fast that Bethany could barely keep up.

"Yes?" said a voice from behind the chair's tall back. "State your business. I have little enough time as it is."

Bethany frowned. Maybe this hadn't been a good idea. She could have at least found a nicer detective. Still, a Holmes was a Holmes, and there was no one better. Except maybe Batman, but that was something else entirely. "I came to hire you to find a missing person," she said quietly.

"Obviously," said the voice, and the chair swiveled around, revealing a boy wearing a question-mark mask, a Sherlock Holmes hat, and a big brown overcoat. Bethany grimaced in spite of herself. Seriously, a question-mark mask? Who wore that?

Doyle Holmes snapped his fingers, not even looking up from his desk. "Give me whatever information you have."

Bethany stepped closer and laid down a folder full of photos on the table, most from before she was born, a few from after. Doyle ignored the folder, instead glancing up at her.

"I've seen you before," he said quietly. "But not like this. You looked different somehow. And there's something very *off* about you."

"I'm not from around here," Bethany said, taking a step back nervously. This was already breaking all of her rules, *every single one*, about not interacting with fictional characters, let alone the main ones. But this was the end of Doyle's only book, right? It's not like there'd be any more to come. And things seemed to have gone okay with EarthGirl, so maybe it'd all be fine!

But honestly? Even if this messed up Doyle's entire story, she was just beyond caring. If he helped find her dad, it'd all be worth it. *Be more fictional*, Kiel had said. Well, here she was, throwing out all of her responsible rules and careful plans.

And if even after all this, she *still* couldn't find her father . . . no. She wouldn't even think about that. This boy would find him. He was a Holmes.

Doyle stared at her for another moment, then opened the file and flipped through the pictures before pushing them aside and turning back to her. "Missing father. Mother has same odd quality that you do, something off about her, as well. Just more so. Something I've never seen before." He glanced up at Bethany. "And that's not something I say lightly."

"I've heard you're very good at what you do," she said, trying to change the subject. "Do you think you can find him?"

"Of course," Doyle said, sitting back in his chair and

steepling his fingers. "That is, if he's still alive." He paused. "I'm sure I've seen your face before. Not a photograph, though. A drawing. A book." Another pause, then he abruptly sat straight up in his chair, his hands slapping the desk. "*Story Thieves!*"

"I'm sorry?" Bethany said, taking another step backward.

Doyle stood up slowly, his masked face giving no indication of what he was thinking. "Do you know the story of my great-great-great-great-great-grandfather's supposed death?" he asked Bethany quietly. "What am I saying, of *course* you do. Everyone's seen the news articles. *Sherlock Holmes dies in fall over Reichenbach Falls. A Nation Mourns.*"

"Sure, I know it," Bethany said nervously, stepping back again. "Who doesn't?"

"Later it was all revealed to be a hoax, so he could take down Professor Moriarty's criminal network," Doyle said, getting closer. "Moriarty being his greatest enemy. But do you know that he actually *should* have died that day? That he did go over the falls, but somehow lived?"

Bethany took another step backward. *Of course* she knew that. She'd been there, taunting the Magister about it, since the wizard had broken Sherlock Holmes's fall with his own magi-

cally flying body. "I . . . I didn't know that," she said, her voice cracking.

"My family has kept it a secret," Doyle said, stepping closer. "No one was to know. We couldn't let the world find out that the great rationalist Sherlock Holmes believed he was saved by a flying man, of all things."

Bethany swallowed hard. "I should be going."

Doyle crossed his arms, and for some reason she thought he was smiling behind the mask. "Of course. I'll start the investigation. But we haven't spoken about my payment."

Relief flooded Bethany's body, and she almost felt weak. "Of course! Payment. I've got gold, if that works."

"Gold?" Doyle said. "That's unique. Most offer a more standard currency. But that can wait. I'll let you know what the information I find will cost once I know your father's whereabouts. I shall contact you when I'm finished."

Bethany shook her head. "I'm usually not very contactable. Can I just come back in a few weeks or something?"

"Why?" Doyle asked, taking another step toward her. "Going somewhere?"

She tried to shrug nonchalantly. "It's just much easier if I come to you. Thank you. And please, don't tell anyone about

this. It's between us. I can pay extra for that."

Doyle slowly nodded, then gestured toward the door. "Interesting to meet you, Ms. Sanderson," he said.

"Same to you," Bethany said, then stepped outside and closed the door behind her.

And for the first time since the finding spell had failed, Bethany actually felt hope again. Doyle Holmes *had* to be able to find her father. Part of her mind was screaming at her that this was wrong, that she was changing Doyle's story, that even if Doyle found her father, what else would that tell Doyle? Her father might come from any story, after all. Could Doyle even cross into different stories? Was that possible?

But that part of her mind got shouted down by one simple thought: *I am finding my father! I don't care what it takes, I am making this right!*

It wasn't until the enormous guard led her back to the front gate of the Baker Street School that she realized she'd never told Doyle that her last name was Sanderson.

CHAPTER 22

01:03:29

Owen grabbed his head from the pain of the flashback and unconsciously took a step forward . . . into nothingness.

His eyes flew open, and he realized he was falling straight off the ledge, forty feet above the police parking lot below. Suddenly the pain in his head was replaced by a shrieking terror.

Something grabbed him from behind and yanked him backward. "Whoa there, killer," the girl in black said. "Going somewhere? You're not an owl, Owen. Mostly you look more like an adorable panda who's always sad. Sad Panda."

Owen tried to answer, but he couldn't get a word out, or catch his breath even. "I . . . I . . ."

"Don't worry, I've got you, SP," the girl said, putting an arm around him. A noise behind them made her twirl around, almost sweeping Owen off the ledge again. Someone was banging on

the door in Inspector Brown's office. "Whoops, time to go!"

But Owen couldn't move any more than he could speak. His heart wouldn't stop racing, and all he could think about was how far down it was. One step and he'd be falling into nothingness, and then . . . *splat.*

"You've done scarier things than this, Owen," Kiel said. "Think of what you did with Charm. That was *far* more dangerous than this is!"

"That was . . . a book," Owen said between breaths. "This is . . . real. No . . . happy . . . endings if . . . I fall."

The girl in black stepped in front of Owen, barely still on the ledge, and gave him a sympathetic look. "I get it, SP," she said. "You're freezing, but I'm here to help. You just need a little incentive. Get moving, okay, or *I'll throw you off this ledge.*"

Owen's eyes widened and he took an unconscious step to the right, trying to get away from her. "See?" she said. "That got you moving. Look at you go!" And with that, she pushed him onward. "Yay, SP! You're killing the game!"

"You two go on, I'll take care of them," Kiel said from the other side of the window. His hands went down to his belt and he sighed. "It would have been a lot more fun with magic, but

oh well." He started to climb back inside the window, but the girl yanked him back out onto the ledge.

"No one gets left *behind*!" she said in a singsong voice. "Including people trying to be heroes."

"You three, stop this instant and go back inside!" Inspector Brown shouted in a bullhorn from the parking lot. "There's nowhere for you to run. We don't want you to get hurt."

Owen paused at this, but the girl gave him a not-so-small push, and he continued moving along the ledge. He picked up speed and slid carefully farther toward the edge of the building.

Unfortunately, there wasn't much farther to go. The ledge ran out just past a few more windows. "So when you say you know what you're doing . . . ," he whispered to the girl.

"Oh, I've *so* got this," she said, patting him on the shoulder.

"So I'm guessing you just had a memory return too?" Kiel called to him.

"Yup," Owen said. "I convinced Bethany to look into Doyle, Kiel. This is all my fault."

"We both went to her," Kiel said. "Don't blame yourself."

"It was my idea," Owen said. "But I said I had a backup plan. Did you get that memory yet?"

"Nope," Kiel said, sounding a bit frustrated. Not having his

magic must be tough for him, Owen realized. He had seemed a bit different ever since he'd arrived at the police station. Not down so much as just . . . less *Kiel*.

"Turn around and go back inside!" Inspector Brown shouted into the bullhorn. "This isn't helping your case. Come in and we'll talk."

"They'd rather die, cop!" the girl shouted back, her voice harsh and threatening. "You'll *never* take them alive!"

"*What?!*" Owen said.

"I agree with the theory, but let's not go overboard," Kiel said.

"Follow my lead," she whispered to them, grinning. "Trust me, it's more fun that way!"

Owen gave Kiel a look, who shrugged, then smiled his Kiel smile. "Might as well," the smile said. "It could be fun!"

"Who *are* you?" Owen whispered to the girl.

"Just a criminal genius who could probably stand a haircut at this point," she told him. "Why, who are *you*?"

"Stop right there!" a police officer yelled from the ledge, coming out of Inspector Brown's window behind them. They must have broken down his door.

"Oh, they're calling our bluff!" the girl whispered, her eyes

lighting up. "Looks like we're jumping to *extreme measures*."

Then she grabbed Owen by the back of his shirt and pushed him off the ledge.

"Aaah!" he screamed, terror exploding through his body as he fell into nothingness. He paused in midair just like last time, only this time the girl didn't yank him back to the wall. Instead, she left him hanging there, her grip on his shirt the only thing keeping him from splatting.

"Let us go or I drop the kid!" the girl shouted at the assembled police. "I swear I'll do it!"

"No dropping!" Owen shouted, his heart trying to break his chest open.

"If he falls," Kiel said, his voice low and scary, *"you* go next."

"Turn off those spotlights!" the girl shouted, then turned to the police officer in the window. "And you, back inside. Now!"

The police officer glared at her, but slowly retreated back into the window, while below the spotlights clicked off one by one.

"Don't you love when plans just go perfectly?" the girl asked quietly, her voice back to normal. She pulled Owen back onto the ledge, and he pushed against the building as hard as he could, so thankful to feel hard concrete.

"Never do that again!" he hissed at her, his voice cracking.

"No promises," she said with a huge smile. "Let's go. Don't fall behind, MK."

"Would you call me Kiel?" Kiel whispered, but started sliding along the ledge again.

"On the side of the building, there's a drainpipe," the girl whispered to them. "We're going to climb up it to the roof."

The roof? Climbing? A *drainpipe*? "Other than that being a great way to die, won't we just be trapped up there?" Owen asked, trying to be as polite as possible to this crazy person.

"You'd *think* so!" she told him. "I guess we'll see!" She pushed his shoulder again, and Owen sidled on down the ledge until he was just out of sight of the police below.

This side of the building was empty, filled mostly with garbage cans, and surrounded on two sides by bushes. The third side was an open alley down the block, and even from this high, Owen could hear running feet. They wouldn't be out of sight for long.

"Up we go," The girl shoved him into the drainpipe, then playfully kicked him in the bottom.

"Stop that!" he whispered as angrily as he could, then began climbing, trying not to look down. The pipe was small, yes,

but it was firmly latched into place, which made for convenient footholds. This girl had done her research. Either that, or she had gotten lucky. Owen didn't particularly want to know which.

After a harrowing fight against gravity, Owen pulled his trembling body up and over the edge of the roof and tumbled down onto it. He considered kissing the roof, like he'd seen people do when they landed from crazy plane rides, but honestly, it looked pretty disgusting, so he passed.

A moment later the other two joined him, neither one having any trouble with the climb.

"Now what?" Owen asked, trying to cover the fear in his voice.

"Now you see where some of your money is going," the girl said, looking proud of herself as she pointed back down. Owen groaned, then pushed himself to his feet, and with a tight hold on the edge of the roof, looked down.

On the ground below, a girl and two boys about their size jumped out from between the garbage cans and pushed through the bushes, just as police officers reached the alley.

"Stop!" the officers shouted, and Owen heard one talking into his radio. "They're on the street, on foot, heading for Alexander Road." The officers sprinted past the garbage cans

and pushed through the bushes, following the fleeing kids.

Owen stepped back away from the roof and turned slowly toward the girl, staring at her in awe. "You have . . . decoys?"

The girl shrugged. "Minions, really. I've worked with them before. Quality henchpeople. Five stars, would hire again."

"But the police will be able to see that we're not them," Kiel said, then mumbled something about "Not even a disguise spell or anything."

"Not in the *dark*," she said, looking far too excited. "Besides, they won't catch up. My people have done this before. We give them two minutes, then climb down the drainpipe and head in the opposite direction. See? Perfect plan! And it was so easy! Then you just pay me the rest of what you owe me, and we all hug, maybe a few tears, promise to stay in touch, and then we go home!"

". . . Pay you?" Owen said.

The girl's smile slowly faded, and her eyes narrowed. "You don't have the other half of the *gold*?"

"Other half?" Owen said, a second before the memory slammed into him like a freight train to the face, and he fell backward onto the roof. Kiel managed to stay on his feet, but didn't look any happier.

"Are you okay?" the girl said, helping Owen stand up. "What keeps happening to you two?"

"Memories," Kiel said.

"I know who you are," Owen told her quietly. "I *remember* now!"

The girl give him a confused smile. "And who exactly am I, then?"

Owen swallowed hard. "You're my backup plan. You're a *Moriarty*."

Yesterday . . .

O ur backup plan," Owen whispered from their hiding spot in the bushes, nodding at the girl with long black hair being led out of a police station in handcuffs. A detective unlocked her cuffs, then sighed, putting his keys away as he sat down on the steps of the police station.

For a moment the girl just looked at him sadly, then started to walk away, but the detective called for her. "Moira Gonzalez," he said, "get *back* here."

The girl froze. "You already questioned me. What more do you want?"

"That was the official interrogation," the detective said, patting the stairs next to him. "This is for me."

Moira turned around and slowly walked back, then dropped to the stair beside the detective.

"She's a criminal?" Bethany asked.

"Sort of," Owen said. "She's trying not to be, but she's the great-great-great-great-great-granddaughter of Professor Moriarty, Sherlock Holmes's greatest enemy. So she's got crazy natural talent."

"Do you want to talk about this?" the detective asked the girl.

"Not even a little bit," she said, her chin on her palms as she watched traffic go by.

The detective nodded. "I know you want to find your mother. But she's *gone*, M. And everything you did to find her just led you here."

Bethany seemed to stiffen next to Owen, and he realized too late the similarities. Ugh. Still, the damage was done. And maybe Bethany would be more willing to get Moira's help with so much in common?

"Her mother is Moriarty's descendent," Owen whispered. "Her dad, on the other hand . . ."

"Is that all, Detective Gonzalez?" Moira asked, not looking at her father.

"I miss her too, you know," the detective said, putting his arm around his daughter's shoulders. "Every day. But your mom made terrible choices in life, probably including

marrying me. The only good thing that came from it is you, and I'm not going to let even her memory change that. I know you're not like her, M. You're too good a person to keep . . . well . . ."

"Breaking the law?" Moira said. "I'm trying, Dad. I really am. I know it doesn't look like it—"

"*You just robbed four banks—*"

"They got their money back!" Moira said, then grinned at him. "It was way too easy, by the way. They should *thank* me for highlighting their weaknesses—"

"*Moira!*"

"I know, okay?" she said, her smile disappearing. "I just thought maybe mom was watching, to see if I had what it took. I thought she might have noticed if I did something big."

Her father sighed. "Your mother loves you, Moira. And let's hope she's staying away because she's trying to do the right thing, which is not bring you into her world. But I need you to stop this. You're lucky none of the charges stuck. You think I want to investigate my own daughter?"

"They'd never have put you on the case, Dad," Moira said, grinning at him. "You know that's a conflict of interest."

The detective stared at her, and she rolled her eyes. "Okay, I'm sorry." She paused. "But just so we're clear, none of the charges stuck because I'm really good. You know that, right?"

Her father glared at her for a second, then smiled. "Yes, fine, you were amazing."

"Woo!" she shouted, and threw her arms around him. "That's all I want. Take pride in what you've got, Dad!"

He laughed and hugged her back, then pulled away. "You know I *am* proud of you, right? You can do so much with your life, and I just don't want you following your mom down the wrong path. Promise me, M. Promise me you'll be good from now on."

Moira sighed loudly. "I mean, what's 'good' exactly?"

"No law breaking, no criminal activity of any kind, and definitely no bank robbing!"

"Fine, I promise," Moira said, shaking her head sadly. "But you're definitely going to need to raise my allowance then. I needed that extra cash from the banks!"

Her father stared at her hard.

"We'll talk about it," she said, then leaned over and kissed his cheek.

"Remember, you promised," her dad told her, standing up.

155

"I know, I know," she said, standing up too and hugging him. "See you tonight."

"Let's make it at home this time, instead of in jail," the detective said, then tousled her hair and walked back into the police station.

"That's the end of the book right there," Owen whispered, staying hidden in the bushes as Moira came closer.

"This is the girl you want to help us against Doyle?" Bethany hissed as Moira passed by. "She's a criminal!"

"So was I," Kiel said, grinning at her. "Don't you trust *me*?"

"That's different," Bethany told him. "You were stealing to live. She's doing it because it's fun. And because . . . she's trying to find—"

"She's perfect!" Owen lied, trying to avoid the topic of Moira's missing mother. "She's like Doyle's opposite. I'm surprised they're not in the same series. They're both descended from some of the greatest minds who ever lived. Who better to help us?"

"He's right," Moira said from the sidewalk. "You clearly need help if you're trying to be inconspicuous." She turned around and gave them an excited look. "*Please* tell me you're from my mother?"

For a moment, not a proud one, the thought of answering yes passed through Owen's head. It'd get her help, wouldn't it? And maybe Bethany could actually find her mother in the book somewhere.

One look at Bethany's face killed that thought, though. "Uh, no. We were hoping to hire you, actually."

"Owen," Bethany hissed at him, but before she could say anything else, Moira grabbed Owen by his shirt with both hands and kissed his forehead.

"*Thank you!*" she shouted. "Do you have any idea how long it's been since I've done something I shouldn't?! I'm so bored I've been wondering if I'm in a coma!"

"It's not anything criminal," Owen said, blushing hard from her kiss. "We just want you to be ready in case we need your help with anything. We're investigating this guy—"

"You want me to rob him?" Moira said, her eyes widening. "*No*, identify theft?" She gasped, then frowned. "You don't want me to kill him, do you? I've got a line. Though I might be able to recommend someone—"

"Whoa!" Bethany shouted. "Definitely no killing!"

"I can't tell you too much," Owen said. "But we're going to this school, the Baker Street School for Irregular Children, and—"

"I've heard of that," Moira said, shrugging. "You trying to break someone out? That's always fun! I haven't done a break-out in, like, weeks!"

Owen froze. She'd heard of that? How could she have heard of a school in a different book? "Uh, no, no breakouts," he said, trying to stay on track. "Just, like, protection—"

"You want me to make the school pay protection money?" she said, frowning. "I might need a bunch of muscle for this, then. How much can you pay?"

"Owen," Bethany said, yanking him backward, "this is a bad idea!"

"Just backup, not a protection racket," Owen said quickly. "Do you . . . know who runs the Baker Street School?"

Moira shrugged. "I don't know, a principal? Who cares. It's like juvie for big-timers. I've heard some of the older kids talking about it. They're all afraid, so I think the cops use it to scare them." She smirked. "Don't worry, it's not a concern. I *never* get caught."

"You just got caught now," Kiel said, nodding at the police station.

"Ha, good point!" Moira said, and smacked his shoulder. "But I'm free, aren't I? I never get charged. Speaking of charging, this

is going to cost a lot. My fee, travel expenses—though I'll prob-ably just steal a car—and incidentals. Let's call it ten grand."

"What?!" Bethany shouted.

"Would you take gold?" Owen asked, taking a step away from Bethany.

"What?!" Bethany shouted, this time at Owen.

He gave her an embarrassed look, then handed her a page from *Kiel Gnomenfoot, Magic Thief,* specifically the page talking about the dragon's lair filled with treasure, within which Kiel and Charm were going to have to find their first key.

"The dragon won't miss it," Owen pointed out.

Bethany just stared at him, her mouth opening and closing. She was never going to go for this, he realized. This was break-ing *way* too many rules. But this was all he had. He didn't have Kiel's magic or her power, so all Owen could do was try to be clever and come up with plans. And this one actually made sense, sort of. You fought fire with fire.

"Fine," Bethany whispered, and turned around.

"Gold's good," Moira said, trying to see over Bethany's shoulder. "I'll have to look up the exchange rate . . ."

"Do the math later," Bethany said, passing her a handful of gold coins.

Moira's eyes lit up. "This is probably close to half . . ."

Bethany turned away, then dumped another bunch into Moira's hands. "We'll get you the rest after the job, then."

Moira nodded, not looking at her. "I'm just *so happy* right now. So, so happy. So, so, *so*!"

"Didn't you make your father a promise?" Bethany asked her, and Owen sighed. He knew she'd agreed too easily.

"Sure," Moira said, not looking up from the gold. "And I kept it all the way over to you guys. That's a lot for me!"

"Be at the school tonight," Owen said. "And make sure you don't let anyone see you."

This finally made Moira glance up. "You're just adorable, you silly little man," she said. "I just want to eat you alive for saying something so cute. No one sees me when I don't want them to. Trust me, I'm an expert!"

They exchanged phone numbers, so Owen could call her in case of emergency while they were in the school. Then Moira turned and walked away, murmuring to her gold. "You're so pretty, aren't you?" She held it up to her face. "So pretty and shiny and *worth so much*."

"Thank you for going along with this," Owen told Bethany as she took his and Kiel's hands, ready to jump them out.

Bethany looked at him for a moment like she wanted to say something, then sighed. "I don't even know what to say anymore. Everything's weird and crazy now, Owen. Let's just hope this all works out."

He nodded, inwardly screaming at himself over Moira's mother. Why hadn't he looked closer at her story? The last thing he wanted to do was make Bethany's life *worse*.

00:58:42

"You really weren't kidding about forgetting, were you," Moira said, still looking confused. "But I'm not a Moriarty. My mom was, but I'm a Gonzalez. Come from a long line of law enforcement." She glanced at Owen and Kiel. "Yeah, okay, that wasn't going to hold up. I'm a Moriarty. So?"

"Hold on," Owen said, squinting against the pain in his head. Remembering who Moira was helped, but that wasn't the bigger deal. No, it was something in the memory.

Moira had heard of Doyle's school. Which meant that their stories were taking place in the same world.

"Owen, we should get off the roof," Kiel said.

"One second," Owen said, putting a finger up. "Something's *very* wrong."

He sat down in the middle of the roof, covering his eyes with his palms. Wait. Okay. So if Moira and Doyle's stories took place in the same world, did that mean that *every* story did? At least the ones that took place in a real-world setting?

That would explain how Doyle had shown up in other books. It wasn't about switching stories so much as just finding a main character and getting in their way. But why hadn't it happened before? Why hadn't fictional characters ever crossed over into each other's stories?

Except maybe they *had*, but since there was no reason for one main character to recognize another, why would they? If a boy with a lightning scar on his forehead happened to be sitting next to you and you'd never heard of Harry Potter, why would you even notice?

So was there an entire realistic planet, then, in the fictional world? Right down to the same cities and countries? Right down to the streets? To the buildings?

Right down to the libraries? And even to the people?

Oh, oh *no.*

"Kiel," Owen whispered, dropping his hands from his eyes

and looking up at the boy magician with horror. "I think I know where we are."

"Look at you, you're like a map!" Moira said. "I love it. But are we going to leave, or . . ."

Kiel bent down and helped Owen to his feet. Owen pulled him a few feet away and grabbed Kiel by the shirt. "I think we're in the fictional world," he said, his voice shaking.

Kiel frowned, looking around. "You realize we're in your hometown, right? Did that memory hit you too hard?" He felt around Owen's head. "You seem okay, but maybe it's, like, internal damage."

"No, I'm fine," Owen hissed. "But it all makes sense. Listen." He raised his voice. "Moira, did the three of us and our friend Bethany ever all hold hands and, you know, *jump*? And then you ended up here?"

"Unless that's a funny way of saying 'I stole a car and drove here,' then probably not," Moira said. "Can I use that though? I *jumped* a car to get here. I like it!"

Kiel's eyes widened. "How could she have gotten here, then? Maybe she found a way out, like Bethany's father?"

"*This is the fictional world,*" Owen said. "Listen to me.

164

We've jumped into stories that take place in a world exactly like ours, right? Well, they all had to exist somewhere, and apparently it's here. Together, in one place. That's how Moira had heard of the Baker Street School." Again to Moira, he said, "And how did you track us down?"

"I watched the school, like you paid me to do," Moira said with a shrug. "You two and that girl came out all tied up, and they threw you in a truck. I followed it to that library, which then blew up. I saw you two get out, but not the girl." She made a face. "Hope they left her in the truck, actually. That pulled away a little bit after dropping you off."

Kiel almost collapsed, but Owen caught him. "No, she wasn't in the library!" he said. "Remember, Doyle said she would disappear in . . . less than an hour from now. She couldn't have died."

"Not unless he was lying," Kiel said, his eyes squeezed shut. "If she's hurt, Owen, I swear to you that Doyle will—"

"We'll find her," Owen told him. "And that's good news. We know she's not at the school anymore, so she's probably somewhere in town. But that explains everything, Kiel. Why there's a second me still in his bed at my house, why the

police acted like they were in a movie, even why . . ." But he stopped. Why *was* there no record of Bethany? If there was an Owen, why no Bethany?

Unless there was a fictional Owen because there was a non-fictional Owen. The worlds must be connected somehow? And maybe there was only one Bethany, because she was from both?

It didn't matter. What mattered is that Owen now understood. Everything made more sense. They were still in a book! That's how Doyle was here, that's how the police had heard of him, and that's why they believed everything he said when Doyle framed them.

"If we're in the fictional world, then why is Bethany trapped?" Kiel said, and this time Owen looked at him in confusion.

"Seriously, my crazy co-caper-comrades, we're going to get caught up here if we stay much longer," Moira said, not looking quite as excited as she usually did. "And we really need to talk about the rest of my gold."

"One second," Owen told her, then turned back to Kiel. "I don't know . . . it doesn't make sense. He said that we'd never see her again, but if she jumped out, she could just come back into the book and find us."

"Except we're not exactly anywhere close to Doyle's story anymore, are we?" Kiel said.

Owen paused, then looked around, his entire body going ice cold. They weren't, were they? And that meant if Bethany jumped out, she might never find them again. She could search Doyle's story for years, and never think to look in her own hometown. She'd probably never even considered that it might be in the book.

Which meant that it wasn't Bethany who needed rescuing. *They* were the ones who needed to be rescued by *her*, before she jumped back out of the book. Otherwise they'd be stuck in this book, maybe forever. After all, she hadn't been able to find her father. Even if she used Kiel's finder spell and it pointed to *The Baker Street School for Irregular Children*, there was a whole world for her to look through before she found them.

"*We need to find her,*" Owen said. "She's going to be fine—we're the ones who might never go home!"

Kiel nodded, and together they turned back to Moira, who was looking less and less thrilled as the minutes passed. "We need your help," Owen told her.

"I think we already covered that," she said, smiling just

slightly. "That's why I'm asking for my money, remember? I rescued you guys. You asked for protection, and I protected."

"We paid you to protect us all," Kiel pointed out. "We never did find Bethany."

Moira narrowed her eyes and didn't say anything, but she was no longer smiling. Suddenly Owen remembered some of the crimes she'd committed, and the happy, excited girl seemed very far away. "We'll pay you double," Owen said quickly. "Triple! Just help us find Bethany, and you can have as much gold as you can carry."

Instantly the smile returned, bigger than ever. "Oh, these arms are *made* for carrying!" she shouted. "I'm in! Yay! Let's go find her. Where is she?"

Kiel and Owen looked at each other. "No idea," Owen said. "But you said you'd worked with people here before. Do you know of anyone in town who we could go to for information?" Detectives always got clues from criminal informants, didn't they? Sounded right, anyway.

Moira sighed. "There's a local crime family, they might know something. But they're not exactly friends with my family. Specifically, they've tried to kill my mother a bunch of times. So not, like, best-best friends."

"Sounds like they're our only option," Kiel said, sounding a bit more excited himself.

"Whoa, wait a second," Owen said. "They're not our only option. There's a world of possibilities out there!"

"Where is this crime family?" Kiel asked.

Moira shrugged. "Not too far. Sweet, let's go!" She stopped abruptly and gave them both a serious look. "But if I say run, you *run*, got it? Because that might be our only chance to escape." She stared at them for a moment, then broke out laughing. "I'm just kidding, once we go in, there'll be no escape. *Let's do it!*"

CHAPTER 24

00:53:01

With the chains hanging over her shoulder, Bethany carefully climbed the metal shelves, which were over half-submerged. Her chair had gone under a few minutes ago, and though she'd tried standing on the back of it, the water moved too much to stand securely.

And falling meant going under, then having to pull the chains back to the surface with her. Given their weight, that was quickly becoming impossible, as cold and tired as she was.

The shelves were a thin metal and not too stable themselves, but she'd pushed the chair over for some extra support. And it's not like she had any choice now. More importantly, the shelves could hold her chains, and she wouldn't have to hold them and tread water as the water filled the room.

Of course, once the water rose three or four feet higher than

the top of the shelves, she was going to be holding the chains no matter what. The ceiling was easily fifteen feet high, which was seven or eight feet taller than the shelves. And that meant she was going to hold the chains or drown, or . . .

Or jump out, and abandon Kiel and Owen. Just like she had her father. Not to mention that Doyle's cameras would capture it all, and potentially give Doyle . . . what? What could he possibly do with that? It was *her* power! Could the world's greatest detective really learn how to jump between the fictional and nonfictional worlds just by closely watching *her* do it?

But what if he could?

She'd stay until the very last moment. *The very last.*

"How's the water?" said a voice from above her. Bethany gasped in surprise, then climbed as best she could to the top of the shelves, where she found a computer tablet displaying a mask she recognized, even if the voice was a bit hard to hear over the noise of the water.

"They're going to find me!" Bethany shouted at the tablet. "And after they do, we're going to find *you*. And then—"

"You're quite mistaken, Ms. Sanderson," Doyle said. "As we speak, Kiel and Owen are locked away safely. No, you have only one way out."

No. "If I jump, I'll be back, Doyle," she said, trying to make herself sound intimidating despite her teeth chattering from the cold water. "I'll find them, no matter where you hide them!"

"Like you found your father?" Doyle asked.

Bethany's entire body burned with anger, and she desperately wanted to toss the tablet into the water, but she was half afraid the movement would knock over the shelves, dropping her into the water too.

"I won't leave them," she said, trying to calm herself down.

"Then you'll die," Doyle said. "And we'll all lose. Well, you more than me, of course."

She'd never hated anyone so much in her life. Not even the Magister. But this guy was a Holmes, wasn't he? Wasn't there *some* way to reason with him? "If I jump out, and you learn whatever it is you're trying to get from me, will you give me back my friends?"

"Of course not," Doyle said. "Why would I do such a thing? Contrary to your bravado, you'll soon leave, and I'll get exactly what I want without rewarding you for having humiliated my family."

Bethany started to say something, only to yell in surprise as her chains slid off the shelves, yanking her off as well. Their

weight dragged her down below the surface of the water, all the way to the floor.

Her mouth still open as she plunged in, Bethany swallowed water and struggled to kick back up to the surface. The chains held her just below it, though, and she couldn't get her mouth high enough to breathe.

Finally, she dove to the bottom and gathered up all the chains in her arms, then dropped them onto the seat of the chair. Then she climbed up the chair and shot back up to the surface just as everything began to go dark.

She felt air hit her face and coughed up water, then immediately sucked in as much oxygen as she could get, barely an inch above water.

"*That* looked dangerous," she heard Doyle say from the tablet, still on top of the shelves. "I really would jump out, if I were you. But it's your choice. Good luck!"

And with that, the tablet went silent, leaving Bethany gasping for air and wishing she'd left Owen and Kiel behind in the first place, like she'd intended.

Yesterday . . .

Bethany entered the library an hour ahead of the time she was supposed to meet Owen and Kiel, using the key that Owen had given her. The entire place was dark except for emergency lighting, but she knew where Owen kept the books they planned on jumping into, and she quickly found the one she wanted.

The Baker Street School for Irregular Children.

If she wanted to learn what Doyle had found out about her father, it'd have to be now, before Owen and Kiel arrived and the three went in to investigate Doyle. There was no more time to procrastinate, no more time to worry either way. He'd either found her dad or he hadn't. She took a deep breath, carried the book into Owen's mother's office, then slipped into the last page.

The Baker Street School itself was just as intimidating now as it had been the last time. Thunder cracked above and lightning lit the black iron gates as she hit the intercom button, glad that it at least hadn't started raining.

"Ms. Sanderson," said a voice with an English accent. "He's been expecting you."

Bethany shuddered as the gates squeaked open loudly. *Why are you doing this? Just jump out now and come back with Kiel and Owen. Kiel can take this guy down with magic, and then you can find out what Doyle knows safely.*

But then Owen and Kiel would know what she'd done. After everything she'd told them since day one about following the rules, never speaking to main characters, never messing up stories, how could she possibly face them now if they found out?

Bethany pushed through the gates and walked quickly through the courtyard, trying to shut down the loud, annoying part of her brain that kept telling her to jump out and come back with her friends. Sometimes you had to do something wrong to make things right. That's just the way it was. Wasn't it?

It'd all be worth it in the end, when she was hugging her father. It would. It *had* to be.

The same enormous bald guard from the last time waited for her at the entrance, holding one of the gigantic wooden doors open for her. "Right this way," the guard said, and led her through the candlelit entry hall and up the double staircase at the back. She passed by classrooms filled with children, but she barely noticed them as she went. All she could think about was what Doyle might have found.

The guard led her to the doors labeled HEADMASTER'S OFFICE again and knocked gently.

"Let her in," said a voice, and the guard opened the door, waving formally for her to enter. As she did, the guard closed the door softly behind her.

And then she heard the lock turn.

That hadn't happened last time.

This was bad. She shouldn't have come alone. This was way too dangerous. Doyle was obviously up to something, if he was visiting other stories somehow, and she shouldn't be here, not without Kiel and his magic. Even having Owen here would have been more of a comfort than standing alone, shivering in the flickering candlelight.

Just like last time, the tall leather chair at the enormous wooden desk was turned to face away from the door. This time,

however, the monitors showed the empty cellblocks, as all the students were in class. In fact, it looked like only one of the cells even had a light on.

"I expected you sooner," said a voice from the other side of the chair. Just as it had last time, the chair slowly twisted around, revealing Doyle in his mask and Sherlock Holmes hat and coat, his fingers steepled in front of him.

"I've been busy," Bethany said, trying not to sound nervous and failing completely.

"I suppose you'd like to know what I found concerning your father's whereabouts?" Doyle asked.

Bethany started to speak, but her mouth was so dry, she could barely move her tongue. She swallowed hard, then again, and finally was able to form a word. "Yes."

Doyle stood up from the chair, then slowly walked around to the front of the desk and leaned back against it, his arms crossed behind him, not saying a word. A moment passed, then another, and Bethany could feel sweat dripping down her neck, despite the room being chilly and the lack of fire in the fireplace.

"We haven't discussed the matter of payment," Doyle said finally.

Bethany let out a huge breath, wiping her hands on her pants. "Of course," she said. "I can pay you however you'd like. Would gold be okay?" She'd given some to a Moriarty now, after all. Why not a Holmes?

Doyle, though, slowly shook his head. "It will *not* be okay, actually. I require something more rare."

"What?" Bethany asked, getting a bit impatient. Were they really going to haggle over the price? "Diamonds? Platinum? What do you want?"

"I want *books*," Doyle said simply.

Books? Bethany's mind began screaming at her to jump out, to come back with Kiel and Owen. "What books?"

Doyle reached behind him and took a book off his desk. "All of the books in your friend Owen's library."

It took Bethany a second to accept that she'd really heard what she thought she had. "*Whose* library?" she whispered.

"If you want to find your father," Doyle said, stepping closer to her with the book in his hands, "then you will get me a digital copy of every single book in Owen's library. You can ignore the nonfiction. That means nothing to me. I want the *fiction*."

"Who . . . who's Owen?" Bethany said, stepping back away from Doyle. "I don't know anyone by that name."

"Oh, but you *do*," Doyle said, and he held the book in his hand out to her.

Bethany shook her head, taking another step back, only to run into the door. *Jump!* her mind shouted. *Jump now!* But if she did, Doyle would see it all.

He stepped closer, holding the book out to her. "Take it," he said. "This one you can have for free."

Bethany reached out a trembling hand and took the book from him, then brought it close enough to read the title in the flickering candlelight.

"*Story Thieves?*" she said, then glanced down at the drawing of two kids leaping into a book. The girl had red hair, and the boy wore all black and carried wand-knives.

"Oh, didn't you know?" Doyle said, his voice sounding like it was a million miles away as Bethany stared at the cover, not believing what she was seeing. "The fictional world's been enjoying your exploits for a few months now. None realized it was a true story, of course. Not even me. Though I did wonder how exactly this author, James Riley, knew of my great-great-great-great-great-grandfather's claim of being saved by a flying man." He paused. "Turns out, my family's embarrassment was all thanks to you."

179

Bethany couldn't speak, could barely breathe. This book was about her? How was that possible? She wasn't fictional! Half, maybe, but she wasn't living in the fictional world. How could someone see what she was doing? People were reading about her? People knew her secrets?

"I know where your father is, Bethany Sanderson," Doyle continued. "I know what you and your friends are doing. And I know what you *are*. So now you're going to provide me with all the books in your library. That is the payment I require. You'll pay it, or you'll never see your father again. Now, please: Jump out of my book. I'd rather not look at you a moment longer than I have to."

And with that, he turned his back, and Bethany immediately jumped straight out of the book, screaming at the top of her lungs.

00:46:02

"I come here all the time!" Owen said, pointing at the Napoleon Bakery storefront. "You're telling me this is just a front for the mob?"

"Nah, they're not mob, SP," Moira said, crinkling her nose. "Your town isn't really that big, so they're unaffiliated. But they're trying, so you have to give them that! They've made a few big moves, just enough to get on the radar."

"Like trying to kill your mother," Owen said, giving Kiel a glance. The boy magician, though, barely seemed to notice where they were, and just kept looking at the countdown watch. Owen nudged him with his shoulder, and Kiel looked up and winked, but then he got the same faraway look in his eye.

"On the bright side, they would have had to know where

she was in order to off her!" Moira said, pushing the door open. "So let's see what they know, shall we?"

"The sign says 'closed,'" Owen pointed out. It was after midnight, after all.

"That's for the regular people," Moira said, sticking out her tongue at him. "You're with me now, you adorable little monkey. And besides, the door's open. They *want* us to come in!"

The inside of the fictional Napoleon Bakery looked exactly like the nonfictional version that Owen had been to so many times, just darker, considering that most of the lights were off. Small white metal tables filled the front of the bakery, each with two or three chairs around them, while a large display case filled the back, empty now, but usually complete with every possible sweet or baked goodie you could ever want.

Lights shone in from behind the case, and fun smells drifted in from the kitchen. They were probably up baking already for the next day.

Was his version a front for a crime boss too? Did his hometown actually *have* a crime family, or was this just the fictional world? So much of this was confusing!

"I'm going to do the talking, okay?" Moira told Owen and Kiel. "Usually I love hearing what you two crazies come up

with, but in the hopes of at least one of us getting out alive, let me handle things."

"This is such a bad idea," Owen told her, wondering if he'd ever have been willing to go along with this in the real world. Did it feel less dangerous just because it was fictional, and things tended to work out in this world? Or was he just so tired and headachy that following Moira just seemed easier?

She blinked at him and Kiel. "A wink for each of you!" she said, then shoved them forward through the door to the kitchen. "Pretend you're my bodyguards!"

As Owen passed through the door, all action in the kitchen stopped, and ten different bakers, all in white, immediately stopped what they were doing and pulled out guns, each one aimed at them.

Owen swallowed harder than he had in his life, struggling to not just collapse in a heap. "Bodyguard," Kiel whispered, and Owen fought through the terror to try to look tough and bodyguard-like, then just as quickly realized he had no idea how to do that.

"Tell the Piemaker that Moira Gonzalez is here to see him," said a dangerous voice behind Owen, and he turned to find Moira, a deadly calm look on her face, staring the kitchen

down. The excited girl from a minute ago had completely disappeared, and again Owen remembered that in spite of her demeanor, this girl was a criminal.

No one moved in the kitchen for a moment, then Moira snapped her fingers, and Kiel shoved a cart full of pans over. The clatter made Owen almost jump out of his shirt, but he wasn't sure which was more surprising . . . the noise, or that Kiel had embraced his role so quickly.

"The lady said to move!" Kiel shouted, then turned to wink at Owen, his face still filled with anger. At least he was having some fun.

From a room toward the back, an enormously fat man in a chef's hat and a business suit emerged, drying his hands on a towel. He glanced in their direction, then snorted. "Back to work!" he shouted, and immediately the kitchen jumped to it, the bakers putting their guns away and returning to whatever it was they were doing. One baker even started picking up the pans that Kiel had just knocked over.

"Sorry about that," Owen whispered, and Moira smacked him.

"Moira Gonzalez," said the man in the suit. "This is a surprise. And what might you be doing here?"

"I'm here for information, Piemaker," Moira said. "I hear you're the one to talk to in this pathetic little town."

Hey! Owen wanted to yell, but kept his mouth shut to avoid getting smacked again.

"And why exactly would I help you?" the Piemaker said, walking toward them slowly while glancing over the shoulders of his bakers. "Seems to me I ought to bake you and your little guards there into a pie and send it to your mother as a warning, instead."

"She lets you operate because you're not a threat," Moira said, dipping her finger into one of the baker's chocolaty bowls and tasting it. "Not bad. No, you're not going to touch me *or* my friends. And you're going to give me exactly what I want. Or you and this bakery will disappear in twenty-four hours like you never existed."

The Piemaker laughed. "Not a threat? Tell your mother that next time we sink her boat, she'll be chained to it."

Moira paused, then turned to the Piemaker, her eyes burning. "*Enough.* I was going to let you bluster to impress your people here, but that's all over now." She pulled out her phone and began dialing.

The Piemaker's eyes widened, and he leaped forward, only to

stop short as Kiel grabbed a knife from the counter and held it almost casually between them. Behind them, Moira began to murmur into her phone. "Yup, he's not cooperating. I think his bakery's about to go bankrupt."

"No!" the Piemaker shouted. "I'm cooperating! This was all just a big misunderstanding!"

Moira paused, then said, "Hold on," into the phone. She turned to the Piemaker. "Apologize."

The large man looked around at his bakers, who were staring at him. "I can't—"

"Apologize."

The Piemaker swallowed hard, then nodded. "I'm deeply sorry if—"

"On your knees."

The man started to protest, but Moira just put the phone back to her ear, and he immediately sank to his knees. "I'm deeply, *truly* sorry if I offended you. I am happy to help in any way I can."

Moira nodded, then put the phone to her ear. "Okay," she said, then hung up. "My mother says that she's now bored of this game where you try to disappear her. One more attempt and *you* go away. Am I clear?"

The Piemaker nodded vigorously. "*Crystal* clear, Ms. Gonzalez."

"Good," Moira said. "Now, get me a croissant or something. You've got two minutes."

Exactly two minutes later, the three of them all had pastries and coffee, while the Piemaker sat across from them at one of the small metal tables, visibly sweating. "Of course I've heard of Doyle Holmes," he said, after Owen filled him in on their questions. "The families are watching him, just to make sure he doesn't get too far in his family business. But he's mostly stuck to little stuff. He was here a few weeks ago, but that's the last I heard of him."

Doyle was here a few weeks ago? That was news!

"Oh, he's back," Moira said. "And he's got a friend of mine. What was he doing here before? Give me something, Piemaker, or my mother's going to be *very* disappointed."

The man started breathing hard, and despite the fact that the Piemaker was a criminal, Owen still felt bad about all of this. "Nothing, I swear! All he did was go to the local library. That's it!"

The library? Why would he have gone there? Maybe to get it ready to burn down? But that was ridiculous, Owen's mother,

or her fictional version at least, would have noticed something.

"What did he do there?" Owen asked.

"Just talked to some kid, that was it," the Piemaker said. "They left together. Guess he's the son of the librarian or something. We looked into him but didn't find anything. And Doyle left soon after. So I'm sure it was nothing."

Owen's hands began to shake, and he had to grab the table to stop them. Doyle Holmes had spoken to his fictional self a few weeks earlier? What was *happening*?

CHAPTER 26

00:35:12

re you sure meeting yourself is a good idea?" Kiel asked for the fourth time as they hid in the bushes outside of the fictional Owen's house.

"Nope," Owen said. "But if Doyle spoke to this Owen, then he's involved somehow. His mom's library just got burned down, and he and I are being blamed. If Inspector Brown is right, Doyle even got our fingerprints on the gas cans. Doyle must have put us in the library for a reason. Maybe it was just to throw us off and make us think we were in the nonfictional world, but maybe not. Either way, right now this is the only clue we have."

"I just feel like we're losing time and are no closer to finding Bethany," Kiel said, shifting from foot to foot. Owen glanced at him, not sure how well the magician was holding up. His

books had always given Kiel a clear goal, with the Magister telling him what to do, and then Charm helping him get there. Now, though, everything was so nebulous, and nothing was certain. That and not having his magic must be making the magician crazy.

At least Kiel *had* power when he had his wands and spells. The best Owen could do was let a criminal genius get the clues for him, and then question a version of himself.

Like he didn't question himself enough already.

"What do *you* think?" Owen whispered to Moira.

"I love this plan, Sad Panda!" she said, patting him on the shoulder. "I suggest we hang this kid outside his window by his ankles until he talks. If that's uncomfortable for you, I'm happy to do it."

Very helpful, as always.

"Follow me," Owen said, and crept toward the back door. His . . . fictional Owen's mother *should* be down at the police station by now, but who knew when she'd be back. For all he knew, there'd be police cars on their way to the house, too.

Fortunately, there was no need to break in, as Owen had a key. Assuming his nonfictional key worked in the fictional lock.

He pulled his keys out quietly and began to slip the key into the door, before Moira excitedly shoved him out of the way and unlocked it herself, then pushed the door open.

"Sorry, I *love* picking locks," she said, grinning at him. "There's just something so satisfying about it."

Owen stared at her for a moment, desperately missing Charm, then slipped inside a very familiar-looking kitchen.

Everything looked exactly the same as the house he'd left just . . . well, who knew how many hours earlier. The same stove, the same report cards and photos up on the refrigerator, the same nicks in the countertop where he'd learned to slice potatoes years ago. How could it all be so similar, but so different? How connected *were* these worlds?

"I should be upstairs," Owen whispered, then grabbed Moira's arm and yanked her backward before she could take the lead. After the ankle comment, there was no way he was letting her take charge, not with his fictional self. Kiel brought up the rear, seeming more and more uncomfortable with this whole thing.

In the living room something small, furry, and extremely unexpected rubbed up against Owen's leg, and he almost shrieked before leaping backward. He quickly looked down to

find a black cat with a white fur spike in the middle of its face staring back at him, purring.

His fictional self had a cat?! Owen didn't have a cat! When did *this* happen?

"Aw, kitty!" Moira whispered, and the cat immediately trotted away, then stopped a few feet away, blinking at Owen. "Hmm," she said, her eyes narrowing. "*Not* cool."

Kiel absently scratched the cat on its head as they passed, Owen giving the animal one last look. A cat? Really? But he'd always wanted a dog.

On his way up to his own bedroom, Owen avoided the creaky stair just by habit, and Moira followed his lead, but Kiel stepped directly on it, which at least confirmed that not everything changed. The noise didn't seem to wake anyone up, so Owen continued the climb, and after quickly confirming that his mother's room was empty, he walked quietly down the hallway toward his own bedroom.

That was an odd feeling, walking toward your own room but knowing that it wasn't yours.

"Let me talk to him," Owen whispered to the other two. "Out of all of us, I'm probably going to freak him out the least." He paused. "And that's saying something."

Moira silently clapped her hands excitedly. "And *then* we hang him out the window!"

"No hanging anyone out windows!" he whispered to her. "Kiel, you okay?"

Kiel just nodded quietly, so Owen slowly turned the doorknob to his bedroom.

Just like his own room, Fictional Owen's bedroom was a bit of a book graveyard. All the library books too beaten up to last on the shelves inevitably were either given to Owen or sold at fundraising sales, so his bedroom tended to look like the night of the living dead books.

The curtains let in just a bit of light, enough to show someone sleeping in Owen's bed (which sent an unpleasant chill down his spine), but not enough to see the titles of the books on the floor. Owen considered stopping for a moment just to see what kind of books Fictional Owen would have, but sighed, figuring that was probably not going to help things right now.

Instead, Owen crept toward the bed, trying not to make a sound, and took a deep breath.

Then he turned on the light.

There, sleeping in his bed, was Fictional Owen, looking

exactly like the Owen that Owen saw in the mirror every morning. As soon as the light hit them, Fictional Owen's eyes flew open, and he proceeded to lose it.

"AH! What's going on?" he shouted, shoving himself away from the intruders until he hit the wall.

"It's okay!" Owen shouted at his fictional self. "Don't freak out! It's just me! It's you! I'm you, I mean!"

"AH!" Fictional Owen shouted again, his eyes frantically switching from Kiel to Moira to Owen and back. "Who are you? What do you want?" And with that, Owen saw his fictional self reaching for a nearby bat.

The same bat that Owen had used to knock out Dr. Verity, actually.

"This is *amazing*!" Moira said, starting forward with her Taser. "He looks *just* like you! I'm so in love with this I want to marry it. How'd you do this, anyway?"

Owen caught her by her shirt and yanked her backward. "No!" he shouted. "Let me *handle* this."

She gave him a sad look, then sighed and put the Taser away. "You're starting to sound like my dad."

"Good!" he told her, then turned back to his fictional self. "Owen, it really is me, so, *you*. You know how you've always

thought there was more to the world than school and home-work and chores? Well, you're right, and I'm the proof! I come from a different world, and I need your help."

Fictional Owen paused, looking closely at Owen. Then his eyes widened, and he jumped to his feet. "You're *real.* He said you were real, but I didn't believe it. I *couldn't* believe it. You're here, you're really here!" He turned toward the boy magician. "And *you* must be Kiel!"

Uh-oh. "You know Kiel?" Owen asked, his stomach drop-ping into his shoes.

Fictional Owen nodded. "And is that Bethany?" He leaned forward and squinted. "You don't look like the version of you on the cover."

"Nope!" Moira said. "I'm *Moira!*" She stuck out her hand, but Owen noticed the Taser behind her back, so he quickly pulled her away from his other self.

"Bethany?" Owen said to the other Owen, his mind racing. "Where did you hear that name? How do you know Kiel?"

"He told me you would come," Fictional Owen said, shak-ing his head. "I can't believe it. You're actually here! All this time, I thought this was just a weird joke by that James Riley writer. I couldn't believe that he used my name and my mom's

library in his book. But you're real! You actually exist!"

With that, his other self began rooting around on the books on the ground. Finally, he found what he was looking for and handed it to Owen.

"See?" Fictional Owen said. "*Story Thieves.* And you're really here! He was right! Doyle said you'd come, and you did!"

Owen reached out a trembling hand and took the book from his fictional self. *Story Thieves,* by James Riley.

And on the cover was a drawing of Bethany holding Kiel's hand and jumping with him into a book.

"Ah, congratulations!" Kiel said, leaning over his shoulder. "Looks like we're both in a series of books!" He clapped Owen on the back. "Think about all those people who've read all about you, Owen. Just think about it!"

Owen did. And then he threw up right on the floor of his fictional self's room.

CHAPTER 27

00:30:56

Bethany's face was the only thing that could still reach above the water. Her chains were on the highest of the shelves, and her arms were so tired of holding them that she wasn't sure she could keep swimming even if the chains weren't there at this point.

There was nothing else to it. What help would she be to Owen and Kiel if she drowned? None. She'd just have to go find them in whatever book Doyle hid them in. She could do it. It wasn't like what happened with her father, because this time . . .

This time, she'd brought them in on purpose. That made it even *worse*.

Bethany gasped for breath, slowly kicking as she pulled the chains up just a bit more, trying to keep her face above water.

Could she just jump a little ways out? Just enough to keep breathing, then slip back in it? But the chains would still be there, dragging her back in.

But maybe she could leave the chains behind?

She'd never actually tried that. Every time she'd been carrying something or touching someone's hand, she'd *wanted* to pull them in or out with her. What if she tried to leave the chains behind, in spite of them being on her wrists?

She focused hard on just one hand, then took a deep breath and dropped back into the water to stare at it. Instead of thinking about jumping, she concentrated on just that one hand, up to her forearm, rising up out of the pages of *The Baker Street School for Irregular Children*.

Her hand began to transform into letters and words, then disappear as it shifted to the nonfictional world, and she could feel the pages of the book on her fingers. She grabbed the pages and held on.

But the chain was changing into words too, and disappearing along with her hand. NO!

She yanked her hand back inside the book and, with her lungs burning, pushed back up to the surface, barely able to reach it this time. She gasped for air, kicking desperately to keep

her head above water. The water had finally risen high enough that she'd have to hold the chains with her if she wanted to breathe.

It was now or never.

She dropped back into the water, let the chain hit the shelves again, and concentrated harder. Only her hand. Only the words "skin, bone, fingers, fingernails, thumb, veins, blood, wrist," everything that made up her hand, and nothing else. Her hand began transforming again, and disappearing, but this time, before the chain itself could follow, she grabbed the chain and pulled it up and over her wrist, right where her missing hand had been.

The chain briefly turned into the word "chain" as it passed her missing hand, then solidified back into metal and tumbled down to the bottom of the floor.

She wanted to scream in happiness, but she didn't have enough air left. Quickly she brought her missing hand back to the fictional world, then concentrated on slowly pushing her other hand out, her lungs screaming for air.

Her left hand disappeared, and she immediately tried to yank the chain off her wrist, but it disappeared too.

Her vision started to blacken at the edges as she panicked,

bringing both hand and chain back for another try.

All she wanted to do was breathe. If she didn't leave now, she'd pass out and drown. *Jump!* her brain screamed at her. *Jump out! You can't stay, you'll die!*

She shook her head and concentrated on her hand. It disappeared more quickly this time, and Bethany frantically tried slipping the chain off her wrist.

It felt like the chain disappeared, but everything was turning numb, and she couldn't fight the impulse to just breathe in. Instead, she kicked as hard as she could, barely sure which way was even up, her legs burning with exhaustion, her lungs about to explode.

Then she felt cool air on her face, and she opened her mouth to gasp for air. She drank it in, sweet breath filling her lungs, and realized there was nothing pulling on her arms anymore.

The chains were both gone, coiled up at the bottom of the room.

Bethany let herself float for a moment, her face gently swaying in the water as she breathed in over and over, her body rising with each inhale, falling a bit with each exhale.

For a moment she let the water buoy her, just feeling what it

was like to not be chained down. Her wrists still felt like they'd been torn up, but they'd heal.

And then she caught sight of the countdown on her watch: 00:27:18.

In twenty-seven minutes, she'd have to leave Owen and Kiel behind forever.

CHAPTER 28

00:26:11

T his couldn't be real. There was no way. Owen opened the copy of *Story Thieves* and flipped through it. It had to be a joke, some kind of prank.

Owen thought back to all the books he knew, and what he could remember about the ends of chapters. Most seemed to stop on some kind of ironic one-liner, or a cliffhanger. Cliffhangers would be a bit tough in here, with no cliffs to hang off of, but maybe he could trick the book into chaptering by saying something horribly ironic, and then waiting for it to (*surprise!*) happen.

That . . . that had *happened*. He'd thought those things, when he'd been trapped by the Magister between pages. How

could this author have known that? Was someone seeing his thoughts right now? Was he a made-up character too?

Was someone reading about him right at this very moment?!

"Cool, huh?" Fictional Owen said, grinning widely. "You're *so* lucky. I mean, you're not on the cover, and basically Bethany and Kiel do all the cool stuff and are the heroes of the book, and you're just the jerky guy who messes everything up, but other than that, it's pure awesome!"

Owen just stared at his fictional self, his mouth hanging open but nothing coming out. He barely even noticed as Kiel grabbed the book from his hands and gave the cover a quick glance. "A bit stylized, but it does look like me. Glad to see I didn't stop with just the first series." He grinned, almost looking like his old self. "These readers just can't get enough of me, can they?"

"Someone wrote a book about you?" Moira asked, trying to grab the book out of his hands, but Kiel moved it out of her way too quickly.

"Wait your turn," Kiel told her with a smile.

Fictional Owen gave Moira a strange look. "I don't remember a Moira in the book, so you must be new. A lot's probably changed since the first book, I guess. Hey, what's the title of this one?"

"Title?" Owen asked, still barely able to follow the conversation.

"Yeah, I mean, the first one was just *Story Thieves*, but the second one must have a title, right?" Fictional Owen said. "The book you're living out now. What's it called?" He frowned. "Though honestly, I wasn't altogether clear on who the story thieves were. *You* obviously were stealing Kiel's story, but it's almost like the nonfictional authors are the real thieves, since they're the ones saying they made up stories, when really they're just somehow watching fictional people's lives. There's no way someone made us up. That's just ridiculous. The Magister should have realized that." He shrugged. "Guy needed to relax, honestly. Even if he *was* made-up, who cares? That's, like, the first step to breaking out of the story and becoming real anyway."

"You're not . . . we're *not* made-up," Owen said, slowly shaking his head. They weren't, right? Owen wasn't, that was for sure. . . . Was he?

"We've been through this," Kiel said. "Probably in that book right there, actually. How about we hold off on the life-changing revelations until we find Bethany? Then we can all come to terms with whether we're real or just made-up by some-

one named Jonathan Porterhouse, of all things. Who'd you get?" He glanced at the book and made a face. "James Riley. Okay, not much better."

"Oh, that Riley guy isn't real," Fictional Owen said. "That's what Doyle said, at least. He looked for him for days and found nothing. Said it's a fake name to hide the real person. Probably some nobody."

This finally pulled Owen out of his fog. "So you do know Doyle?" he asked his fictional self. "Did he say anything about us? About Bethany?"

"Well, *yeah*," Fictional Owen said. "That's why he came to me. I guess she showed up a few weeks ago hiring him to find her father. Doyle realized he recognized her from the book, which of course he didn't think was real. He just figured someone wrote about her, or she was a big fan and was pretending to be the book's Bethany. But when he started investigating, and it turned out the author didn't exist but that an Owen Conners did, he came to me." He grinned. "It's a whole story, actually."

"Let's hear it!" Moira shouted.

"I'm not sure we have the time to waste," Kiel pointed out.

"This is important," Owen said to the magician. "Owen . . . can I call you Fictional Owen?"

Owen paused, tilting his head as if considering it. "Um, no?"

"*Fowen,*" Moira declared. "There you go."

Fowen gave her an annoyed look, but she just jumped onto the bed and bounced excitedly, waiting for him to start his story.

"Doyle has Bethany somewhere," Owen told Fowen. "We need to find her in the next . . . twenty-three minutes, or we're going to be stuck in your world forever. We could really use your help. Honestly, we have no idea where to find either Doyle *or* Bethany. If you know anything about where he might have put her—"

"That's not much time," Fowen said, glancing at his watch. "And I really don't want to get in trouble if my mom catches me." He paused, trying not to smile, then laughed loudly. "Ha, don't worry. I'm *kidding,* I've waited my whole life for this. Let's go!"

"Go?" Owen said. "We don't need to go anywhere. You just need to tell us everything you know about Doyle."

Fowen frowned. "Don't you think that getting out of here would be smarter? Aren't they after you?"

Before Owen could respond, sirens began blaring from down the street. How did Doyle know everything they were doing?!

"Oooh, this Doyle guy is *good,*" Moira said, glancing out

the blinds. "How does he always know where we are?"

"That's his whole thing," Fowen said, pulling on pants over his pajamas and then throwing on a sweatshirt. "He's the greatest detective that ever lived. He can see what you're going to do before you do it. Knows everything about you, from what you ate for breakfast to which movies make you cry."

"Wait till you see the movie of *Kiel Gnomenfoot, Magic Thief,*" Kiel said. "There will *definitely* be tears. That's what Jonathan Porterhouse told me, at least. He said he was crying the whole time he was signing the contracts."

Fowen gave Kiel a weird look, then leaned in close to Owen. "I get that you like him for some reason, but you should *really* read your book. He's kind of annoying, and totally steals all the credit for everything you did. You should have been on the cover, Owen." He slowly grinned, his eyes widening. "Hey, I bet we're *both* on the cover of this next one!"

"There *isn't* a next one!" Owen shouted, running to the window to peek past the curtains at the cop cars outside. "We're not in a book, *that* book isn't real, and none of this is happening!"

Two squad cars parked in front of Owen's house, while another two sped down the street, then hit the brakes two

houses away to both skid perfectly into place right next to the first two. Of course they did.

"We need to go out the back," Owen whispered.

"Way ahead of you," Fowen said, handing him a rope that led out his bedroom window. "I've been preparing for this day ever since Doyle told me you guys were real!"

The Amazing (But True!) Adventures of Owen Conners, the Unknown Chosen One

CHAPTER 1

Owen wanted to scream at the horror before him. But the sound wouldn't come and the nightmare only continued, forcing Owen to ask himself, deep down, one question:

"Can anyone tell me what year the Declaration of Independence was signed?"

Mr. Barberry stood at the board at the front of Owen's classroom, his arms folded, waiting for a hand to raise.

No, not *that* question. The real question was this: Was there anything in the world that could possibly be more boring than history? Owen frowned as Mr. Barberry gave up on volunteers and just picked someone. "Huck? What year?"

Waiting in a two-week-long line for the chance to wait in another line? That'd be pretty boring. But not *history* boring—

Something hit Owen on the shoulder, and he glanced down to find a folded-up note on the floor next to him.

"1776," Huck said, then covered a huge yawn.

"That one was easy," Mr. Barberry said. "Who can tell me *where* it was signed?"

Owen slowly reached down and picked up the note between two fingers, than carefully brought it up to his lap, making sure Mr. Barberry didn't see him.

"Emma?" the teacher said, turning away, so Owen unfolded the note.

Have lunch with me? I have so many questions! —B

Well. *That* was new.

Class went on for another thirteen or fourteen hours before the bell rang, finally releasing them to lunch. Owen stood up slowly to hide his excitement, then walked to the cafeteria with his most confident strut. There, he quickly grabbed some food and sat down at a table, waiting.

Less than a minute later, a girl with long bronze hair sat down across from him.

"So?" Brianne said, smiling at him for probably the first time ever. "Do you *know* him? Are you two friends?"

For some reason, her smile made Owen's mouth dry up, and

he had to swallow a few times. "Do I—" he croaked, then took a quick drink of water. "Do I know him? Him *who* him? I mean, who him?"

Brianne's smile faded momentarily, only to reappear as she slammed a book down on the table. "The author of *Story Thieves!*"

Hmm. *That's* something he'd never been asked before. In his daydreams, when girls admitted they'd always had a secret crush on him, the conversation went very differently.

Still, he could work with this. "Huh?" Owen said, trying to sound smart.

This time the smile disappeared completely as Brianne gave him a suspicious look. *"Story Thieves,"* she said, pointing at the cover. "You've never heard of it? The book's all about *you!*"

Owen glanced at the cover showing a redheaded girl and a black-haired boy in some kind of costume jumping into a book. "Um, which one am I supposed to be?" he asked, really hoping it was the black-haired boy.

Brianne narrowed her eyes. "I don't get this. I thought you knew the author or something. I wanted to know what's going to happen in the second book."

Owen fought hard against his instincts to keep asking questions or just look confused, so instead he nodded. "Right," he said. "Of course. The second book." He paused. "Is . . . *this* the second book?"

Brianne growled, and opened the book to the first chapter. "How have you not heard about this? It's about a boy named Owen Conners whose mother works at a library, and—"

"Um, *I'm* Owen Conners," Owen said. "And *my* mother—"

"I *know*, I'm the one telling you about this," Brianne said, looking much more irritated now. "There's this half-fictional girl named Bethany, and Owen catches her popping out of a book in the library—"

"A half-what now?"

"That part's all made-up, obviously," Brianne said. "There's never been a girl named Bethany in our class, but Mr. Barberry's in here too! I thought you had to have known about this." She paused. "Shouldn't they have gotten your permission? You know, to use your name like this?"

Owen picked up the book and read the back. Apparently the half-fictional girl took him into some book, and then things got clearly *awesome*. "How . . . how is this real?" he asked, though inside he knew the answer. This was *The Sign*. The Sign that

said Owen Conners was never meant to live such a boring life, that all along he'd just been waiting for Fate to come along and Choose Him. There was no way someone boring and ordinary would ever have a book series about him. This was it!

"I'm a *hero*," Owen whispered, staring at the book in awe.

"Uh, not really," Brianne said. "It's just a book."

"But I'm the hero of the book!"

"More like the sidekick, honestly," she said, making a face. "Bethany's the real hero. Her and Kiel. You just mess things up. Listen, Mari's father is a lawyer, maybe you should talk to her about suing this author? He's probably got tons of money. I hear authors are all rich."

Suing? Because the author had made Owen the not-actually-the-sidekick hero in a book? The *last* thing he'd ever do was sue! "*Story Thieves*," he said, running a hand over the cover. Why wasn't the Owen character on the cover, anyway? Was that Owen too busy being amazing and doing all kinds of cool things? "Can I borrow this?"

Brianne smiled, and he smiled back. "Nope," she said. "But let me know if you track the author down. I want to know who Bethany's father is. I think the whole thing with Nobody is too obvious, and it's kind of annoying that she didn't find him in

the first book. Way to leave things on a cliffhanger, right?"

"Totally," Owen breathed as Brianne grabbed the book and walked away.

He had to get a copy, of course.

He had to get a copy *now*.

The school library didn't have one, and a quick phone call to his mother from the payphone outside the school's office told him that neither did her library. That explained why he hadn't seen it. He asked his mother to order a copy, and she said she'd look it up, but why was it so urgent?

"Because I've been waiting for this my entire life," he told her.

"Owen," she said, sighing. "What did I say about you being the chosen one, destined to save the world?"

He rolled his eyes. "That the real world is exciting enough, and that I can find plenty of fun things here."

"Without . . ."

"Without being the long-lost son of a king or a secret wizard."

"Or . . ."

"Mom, I have to go!"

"Or . . . ?"

"Or an orphan who grows up to fight crime."

214

"That one was always a bit insulting, honestly," his mom said. "I'll look into this book. Get back to class."

Owen put down the phone with a sigh. She could say those things all she wanted (or, well, make *him* say them), but it didn't matter. He knew the truth, and right now the truth was that some author had made Owen Conners the hero of a book called *Story Thieves*, and that meant . . .

Well, that meant *something* amazing. Now all he had to do was find out what!

"Bethany," he whispered out into the school hall. "If you're actually out there, and if you're really real, *come get me*, okay? That's all I ask. Come get me and bring me into your world. Deal?"

No one answered, so Owen quietly whispered in a girl's voice, "Deal. I can't wait to meet you, Owen!"

"You too, Bethany," he whispered back with a smile. *"You too."*

Later that night Owen sat at the checkout counter of the library, trying to research this James Riley author. There was weirdly very little on the Internet about him, and even his author photo was apparently just an actor or something. That was odd . . . why bother? Who even *looked* at author photos?

"I'm going to start closing up," Owen's mother said, tapping him on the shoulder. "Start putting those books away." She

pointed at an enormous pile next to Owen, which he'd been ignoring all night.

He started to object, but he saw her face and sighed, then nodded. She smiled at him, and headed into her office, while Owen carefully picked up the pile of books and walked it toward the children's section.

Carefully balancing the pile, Owen had walked it slowly to the back of the library, trying to make sure he didn't trip over anything. The pile was so large, though, it wasn't easy to see around.

"Owen Conners?" said a deep voice from just inches in front of him, and Owen shrieked, dropping every single book.

"You scared me—" Owen started to say, then lost his train of thought when he saw who he'd almost walked into. There, standing in front of him, was a boy in an overcoat, wearing a hunter's hat and a mask with a question mark on it.

"WHOA!" Owen shouted. "You're—"

"Doyle Holmes," the boy said, extending his hand. "World's greatest detective. And you're clearly Owen."

Owen's mouth dropped. The incredibly famous detective *Doyle Holmes* knew *his* name! "I . . . I am!" he said, much too loudly, and took Doyle's hand.

"Everything all right in there?" Owen's mom yelled from her office.

"Tell her it's fine," Doyle said softly, taking a step backward. "What I have to say is for your ears only."

"It's fine, Mom!" Owen yelled, then whispered to Doyle, "I'm your biggest fan! I knew you were real. The Internet says you're just an urban legend, but I knew you had to be real. Things couldn't be as boring as they look!"

"I encourage those rumors to keep from being overrun by idiots," Doyle said, sounding bored. "But apparently, now I need one's help. I'm investigating someone, and you are sadly my only lead."

"You want my help?" Owen said, his eyes widening in awesomeness. "Of course! Who are you investigating?"

"The man who wrote *this*," Doyle said, and handed Owen a copy of *Story Thieves*.

This. Was. The. Greatest. Day. EVER.

00:21:42

And that's how I met Doyle," Fowen finished, then sighed heavily. "Only, after he found out that I'd never heard of the *Story Thieves* author either, he left, and I never saw him again."

Owen peeked above some bushes at the police cars still outside his house. *Fowen's* house. He kept forgetting. Either way, how was Doyle able to track them this fast? Even the greatest detective in the world shouldn't have been able to know where they'd be headed, right when they got there. How had he found them so quickly? Had someone seen them sneaking around in the backyards?

And seriously, even his fictional self was having flashbacks now? More importantly, why hadn't *Owen* had one in a while?

"Why did you tell us what happened like it was a chapter in a book?" he asked Fowen quietly.

"Because obviously someone's going to want to make a book about *me* someday," Fowen told him. "I've been trying to decide where it should start, and that seemed like a good place, since that's when my life finally got interesting. Your authors can't write about *everyone* here, since it'd be too boring most of the time. But look what Doyle's done. This is totally exciting enough for a book!"

"None of this helps us find Bethany," Kiel said, his joy at finding out he was in a second series of books apparently wearing off. "We can't keep wasting time. We're down to twenty minutes!"

"Doyle must have given you some clue," Fowen said. "He wouldn't have been able to resist. It's just how he thinks. Maybe I can help?"

"Aren't you on the wrong side here?" Moira said. "I mean, don't get me wrong, you seem absolutely delightful as a human being, and I'm sure we're going to be best friends until we're being chased and I end up tripping you so the cops get you instead of me. But you just said you were helping Doyle."

"I didn't realize he was trying to hurt you guys!" Fowen said. "Of course I'm on your side. Your side *is* my side."

Moira laughed. "I still don't at all get this. You guys are twins

or something? No, don't tell me, I like the mystery. Shh, *no*, don't explain!"

"If he can help, then we're all on the same side," Kiel said, throwing an arm around Fowen's shoulders.

Fowen glanced over at Owen and rolled his eyes.

"All Doyle said was that we didn't even know where we were, which was true. We knew we were in the library—" He froze, realizing that Fowen didn't know. "But we were confused about other things. We got that part. The only other thing he said was that he was doing it by the book. Whatever that means." Owen sighed. Why did mysteries have to involve so many things to solve? No wonder Owen hated them.

"Hmm," Fowen said, his eyes lighting up. "I just love mysteries. See? It's all about noticing the things that don't seem important. Like what Doyle said. It sounds almost like a riddle to me."

"I love riddles!" Moira said. "Have you heard of the sphinx that ate people who answered his riddle wrong? That sphinx definitely had it *all* figured out."

"What do you mean, a riddle?" Owen asked Fowen, trying to ignore Moira.

"Think about it," Fowen said. "Doyle said he was doing things by the book, right? What if that didn't mean doing things the

official way? Maybe it was a clue to where Bethany actually is."

Owen started to respond but instantly went quiet as he heard a familiar voice. "Check the surrounding areas," Inspector Brown said from less than ten yards away. "Doyle said they were here not ten minutes ago, so they can't have gotten far."

Moira's smile disappeared, and Kiel jumped to his feet.

"What are you doing?" Owen hissed at him.

"Running isn't getting us anywhere," Kiel said, forcing a grin. "It's time to *fight*."

"Fight the police?" Fowen said. "With what? You said you don't have magic, and isn't that all you can do?"

Kiel's eyes widened, and he paused for a moment. "There's more to me than magic," he said quietly, then began silently moving through the bushes toward Inspector Brown.

What was he doing? They needed to run! There was no time for this. Kiel was acting like he was still in a fantasy series instead of a mystery book. Mysteries involved thinking, not fighting!

"Over there!" a policeman yelled, and Owen pushed out of the bushes to see what was happening, only to fall backward a second later, as a police car almost ran him over.

"Get in!" Kiel yelled from the driver's seat as police officers ran at them from every direction.

"Oh, you did *not* steal a police car!" Moira shouted, and tried to push Kiel out of the front seat. "I'm officially completely in love with you, Magical Koala!"

Kiel pushed her back to the passenger's side as Owen considered what he was about to get into. This was probably the *worst* way possible to avoid getting caught.

But weren't they basically caught already? He sighed, pulled open the back door, and jumped in. A moment later Fowen followed, his eyes gleaming with excitement.

Well, at least *one* of them was having fun.

"Hold on," Kiel said, turning around to flash a real, honest smile at Owen. "I'm not entirely sure how to work this thing."

Okay, maybe two of them, then.

As Kiel looked out the back window to reverse, the car jumped forward, taking out a mailbox first, then a stop sign, and narrowly missing two police officers, who had to leap out of the way.

"Stop!" someone shouted from behind them, and Owen heard the squeal of tires as two other cars raced after them.

"Never!" Moira shouted out the window, then slammed her foot over Kiel's on the gas pedal.

And three of them. Fantastic.

The car's acceleration sent Owen crashing against the back-

seat, then straight into Fowen as Kiel skidded around a corner, jumping the curb before crashing back onto the street.

"He's going to get us caught for sure!" Fowen shouted at Owen as the two banged against each other when Kiel took another corner hard. "If not *killed*."

"Kiel, we have to stop!" Owen said, trying to sit upright. "You've got the sirens on. They're going to follow us everywhere!"

"Good point," Kiel said, taking his eyes off the road as they spun out onto a major street with oncoming traffic. "How do I turn them off? We need to be stealthy."

"Here, I've got it," Moira said, reaching past Kiel to turn off not only the sirens but also the car's headlights as a truck barreled toward them.

Maybe if this really is *a book, then we won't die,* Owen thought to himself. Then he remembered how that had worked out for him in *Kiel Gnomenfoot and the Source of Magic,* and how his heart was now robotic, and decided that maybe it wasn't a good idea to take the chance. Not to mention that this was potentially *his* book, and given his luck, he should probably be expecting bad things.

"Watch out!" Fowen shouted as the truck's headlights blinded them, its horn blaring.

"Wow, someone has no idea how to drive," Kiel said, turning the wheel hard. The car jerked almost ninety degrees to the right, and the truck passed within inches of them.

The two cop cars behind them weren't so lucky. One managed to follow them, but the other went careening off the road and crashed right into a huge pile of trash.

"Good thing that garbage was there," Fowen shouted from next to Owen.

It's how things work in fiction, Owen wanted to say, but he just sighed in relief before falling straight into his fictional self as Kiel took another hard turn.

"Where should we go?" the boy magician said, turning back to Owen.

"Who cares?" Moira shouted, grabbing the wheel from Kiel momentarily, a wild look in her eyes as she aimed them toward an empty newsstand on the side of the road. Newspapers went flying, smacking into the windshield of the police car right behind them, which caused the car to turn widely and skid to a stop against some nearby parked cars.

"How'd you know that would happen?" Owen asked in awe.

Moira looked confused, then glanced behind them. "Oh, perfect! I'd just wanted to hit the newsstand."

"Okay, *we're stopping right now*!" Owen declared. "Kiel, pull over!"

Kiel slammed on the brakes, despite Moira's loud groan, and Owen and Fowen both crashed against the seat in front of them. Through the pain, Owen tried hard to be thankful that at least they weren't dead. "Everyone out!" Owen shouted, then went to push open his door, only there was no handle.

"Police car back doors don't open from the inside," Fowen told him. "It's to keep criminals in."

Criminals. *That* was appropriate. Even if they hadn't set the library on fire, now they'd stolen a police car. Oh, and resisted arrest, broken out of a police station, and about a dozen other things. Could Owen really argue now with Inspector Brown that he was innocent?

Kiel opened Owen's door from the outside, and Owen spilled out onto the sidewalk, then crawled away from the car before standing, Fowen just behind him. "We're doing this all wrong," Owen said as more sirens began sounding in the distance. "We keep running from place to place instead of *thinking*. That's not how you win mysteries!"

"You don't really win mysteries," Fowen said.

"Fine, you solve them, or whatever," Owen said, wondering

if *he* was ever that annoying. "Which means investigating, and finding clues, then putting those together in the only way that makes sense."

"Enough thinking!" Kiel said. "Sometimes it's good to just take action."

"That's not the kind of story we're in, Kiel," Owen said. "We need to use our heads!"

"Think about the clue Doyle gave you!" Fowen said as the sirens got closer.

Owen sighed. "It's not a clue. It doesn't mean anything! By the book? All that means is . . ." And then he stopped. By the book. As in *by* the *book*.

It *had* been a clue all along, and Owen hadn't even noticed. Doyle had practically told them exactly where Bethany was, and it took Fowen to point it out.

"I know where we're going," Owen said. "Come on!" And with that, he took off at a sprint.

Fowen ran after him, a big grin on his face, followed by Kiel and finally Moira, who looked longingly at the police car they left behind. "I'll come back for you, my love!" she said. "Don't forget me, or our all-too-short time together. You'll always be in my heart!"

CHAPTER 30

00:10:34

"Um, we've been here already," Kiel said, staring at the still-smoking library. A second fire engine had arrived at some point, and even after this long, the firemen still had hoses turned on the smoldering building.

Owen almost couldn't look at the library, even knowing it wasn't exactly his version. Did that really make a difference? Sure, it was fictional, but this was still a place that people could visit and find doorways to other worlds. All those books, gone. What would his fictional mother be thinking right now? How much had her entire life been torn apart?

He turned to Fowen, not sure what to say. If his fictional self felt a fraction of the sadness and horror he felt, then Fowen was going to be devastated.

"I should have told you," Owen told him.

But Fowen didn't seem to hear him, and just stared at the library. "Doyle really is evil, and must be stopped," he said quietly. "This is going to take a true hero, nothing less."

Owen paused, then touched Fowen's shoulder. "Are you okay?"

Fowen jumped as if he were surprised that Owen was there. "So what's the plan?" Fowen asked, his eyes burning with excitement. "Where do you think Bethany is?"

"Aw, I hope she didn't burn up," Moira said, looking sadly at the remains of the library. "I'm *so* going to miss my gold. . . ."

Owen just stared at her for a moment, then sighed and glanced around, no idea what he was looking for. There *had* to be a reason that Doyle had left them in the library. And the "by the book" line seemed almost like bragging, now that Owen realized what it meant. Or might mean.

It *better* mean what he hoped it did, because they were down to ten minutes.

But if Bethany *had* been in the library, it was way too late to find her now. She'd for sure have jumped back to the non-fictional world, which meant Owen and Kiel were stuck here in the fictional world, probably for good.

And not only did that make one too many Owens, but he, Kiel, and Moira were all wanted by the police. Not to mention he'd

never see his mother again, or the outside of a jail cell, probably.

"She's here," Owen said, faking confidence, trying to be more like Kiel. Just to prove it, he glanced at the boy magician and gave him an awkward wink.

Kiel gave him an odd look back. "Are you sure?" he said. "I don't feel my spell book anywhere close. If Doyle has them and he's with her, then she's not here, Owen." He glanced around, his hands opening and closing anxiously.

"I'm *not* wrong," Owen said, hoping he was telling the truth. "Doyle put us here to taunt us. We were here all along, and she was right under our noses! We just have to find her. Split up, but don't let anyone see you."

"I've got *all* the faith in you guys!" Moira said, leaning back on the ground and closing her eyes. "Let me know if you find her and need to get rid of the body or something."

Owen glared at her, which she didn't see, then set off with Kiel and Fowen, Kiel moving one way, Owen the other, with Fowen following Owen.

"*I* think you're right," Fowen said, his eyes on Owen. "She's got to be here. That's exactly how villains work, you know?"

"That's the weird thing," Owen said, picking his way slowly through the bushes around the side of the library, trying to

stay out of the lights of the fire engines. "Since when is the great-something-grandson of Sherlock Holmes a villain? Why is he doing all of this? What could he possibly get out of locking me and Kiel away and making Bethany leave us behind? I think he wants something."

Fowen shrugged. "All he ever said to me was that he was looking for Bethany's father, and that your author—"

"He's not *my* author," Owen said, far more angrily then he expected. "I'm *real*."

"That your author isn't real," Fowen finished, then raised an eyebrow. "So wait, you don't think *I'm* real?"

Whoops. "Of course you are," Owen said, glancing at his watch. "That's not what I meant. I just . . ." He groaned. There was no time for this right now. "Look, *you* don't have an author either. You and me, we're just extras, background characters for important people. No one's writing stories about us, you know?"

Fowen shook his head. "You're *wrong*. Look at you right now. *You're* the one saving the supposedly important people. Where's Kiel? Bumbling around, useless without his magic. Bethany's captured and needs saving—"

"Actually, I think she's the one who's going to save *us*," Owen said quietly.

"And you're the hero of *Story Thieves*," Fowen finished. "The book doesn't make you out to be, but you are. Or you *should* have been! You're a bigger hero than either Bethany or Kiel were, for sure. You saved the Magister, Charm, *and* Kiel, even if they didn't all deserve it."

For a moment Owen let himself imagine it was Charm standing next to him instead of his fictional double. "He's not wrong," Imaginary Charm told him. "But why are you wasting time with doubting yourself? Bethany needs you."

"I'm looking for her, but I feel like I'm missing something," he told Charm in his mind.

"Of course you're missing something," Charm said, her robotic eye shining on him. "Why would Doyle put her here, then light it on fire? What happens when something burns down?"

"The fire department comes," Owen said, glancing at the trucks.

"And what do *they* do?"

"Put out the fire?"

"With?"

Owen's eyes flashed to the hoses still spraying water on the various small fires around the building. Most of the library was

now soaked down, with excess water running down the side-walks and into the sewer.

Oh!

Ohhhhhh.

Oh *no*.

"You've got it," Imaginary Charm said, and gave him a half smile.

"I miss you," Owen said as she faded out.

"You do?" Fowen said, giving him an odd look.

Owen started to blush, but grabbed Fowen's hand and pulled him back to where Moira waited. He whistled softly, then waved when Kiel turned back. The boy magician quickly returned too, and Owen gathered them all in a huddle.

"I think I know where Bethany is," he said. "I—"

And then police sirens sounded down the street, and Owen shook his head. "Just follow me, okay?"

With that, Owen took off, following the flow of excess water from the library.

"Where is she?" Kiel asked. "Owen, we're almost out of time, and—"

"Doyle burnt down the library with us in it and started the clock when he heard the fire engines," Owen said, wincing as

the sirens got closer. "If the two are related, then Bethany's danger had something to do with the fire. What if the clock had to do with the fire department putting out the fire?"

"Nothing like a ticking clock to make things more exciting," Moira said, yawning.

"I'm not following," Kiel said, as Fowen began nodding vigorously. "What would that have to do with Bethany?"

The water flowed down the sidewalk and into a sewer grate, and from within, Owen could hear a deep splashing. *There.* "What if it's not the fire that's the danger," he said, "but the water?"

CHAPTER 31

00:04:17

Bethany had never felt so tired in her life. Every muscle in her body ached, and all she wanted to do was slip below the surface of the water for a minute, maybe two, and just . . . relax. Close her eyes and stop kicking, stop treading water. It was just so tempting to let the water hold her up, do all the work. Not for too long . . .

Her lungs began to burn, and her eyes burst open. She *was* underwater!

Her legs were so tired they refused to respond, so she frantically pumped her barely functioning arms until her face broke the surface, less than a foot from the ceiling now, and rising.

This was it. She'd failed them. Kiel and Owen were going to be trapped in the fictional world, but she just couldn't hold out any longer.

The guilt felt like a truck parked on her back between her shoulders, but alongside that was a feeling almost like relief. She'd hung on until the very last moment, hadn't she? She'd almost drowned a few hundred times over the past two hours, and now . . . now she could just let go, and jump back to reality.

. . . Where she'd have explain to Owen's mother why her son had gone missing, and probably was never coming back.

She forced her dead legs to slowly kick, switching up between her numb, dead limbs as the water rose and her face got closer and closer to the ceiling.

Of course they hadn't found her. How could they? Doyle had hidden her away somewhere secret, and neither Owen nor Kiel was a detective. Not that Moira would have been a help either, if she'd even shown up. That girl was the opposite of a detective. She should have made Owen find someone better. Or just left them both behind and come alone.

Bethany sank below the water level again, this time letting herself drop deeper until she was suspended weightlessly, her legs and arms crying out in thanks. She closed her eyes and tried to ignore the fact that soon there'd be nowhere in the room for her to breathe, and she'd have no choice.

She'd look for them. Of *course* she would. Every bit as long and hard as she had for her father. And maybe it'd even be easier. After all, she knew they'd have to be in some sort of realistic world. Doyle had crossed into other stories somehow, but they'd all been set in the real world.

Unless he figured out how to do whatever it was she did when she jumped out in a minute. Then he could take them wherever he wanted, and Kiel and Owen were both going to be just as lost as her father. Lost in a book, or worse, lost in an unwritten book, stuck somewhere she could *never* find them.

Her lungs began burning again, but she didn't bother kicking back up to the surface. There was no point. They weren't going to find her. It was all impossible.

Be more fictional, Kiel had said before she faced the Magister. And she had been. She'd taken the advice, and when his finder spell hadn't worked, she'd broken her own rules, broken *all* the rules when she'd hired Doyle.

And for that, she was paying the price. Doyle had won.

Something inside of her screamed in rage and anger at that thought, and in spite of everything, her legs began kicking again. Part of her tried to quiet the screams, just wanting to stay underwater where everything was silent, but the scream-

ing part was too wild, too angry. It forced her to the surface, forced her to push her mouth up just inches from the ceiling, and breathe in, even as the air tasted far too stale and made her light-headed.

She stayed there, windmilling her arms behind her, practically kissing the ceiling for a minute.

Then another.

And another.

And then, finally, her watch blinked 00:00:00 and the water rose above her face.

Everything felt weird and sleepy as she sank back into the water. She'd stopped noticing the cold a long time ago, but her arms and legs began feeling weirdly warm now, like she was floating in a warm bathtub, completely comfortable.

Some part of her was still screaming about her friends, about Kiel and Owen, but that part needed to shush. It was really too loud. And the water was so warm, and everything was just nice and relaxing.

Jump, something in her head said. *You* need *to jump.*

But that was the last thing she needed to do. Not when she could just float effortlessly, letting the current of the water do all the work.

Sorry, guys, she thought, but had to struggle to remember what she was apologizing for. Had she done something wrong? And to who?

And why was she holding her mouth closed? Her lungs were saying they needed air, so why not open her mouth and just breathe in?

She parted her lips, and the cold water hit her tongue, just enough to jolt her back to awareness. *JUMP!* her mind screamed. *JUMP OUT NOW!*

Bethany began to jump, pushing her aching, nonresponsive muscles to cross from the fictional world to the nonfictional one before she drowned.

Weirdly, though, instead of pushing up and out of the book, she felt like she was being pulled down instead. Down toward the bottom of the room, where she could hear a roaring even under the water.

Jump! her mind screamed again, and she tried, pushing her arms and legs as hard as she could.

But the water pulled her down toward the roaring, and between the fog in her mind and the ache in her lungs and muscles, she just couldn't make herself fight it.

Kiel, Owen! she screamed soundlessly. *I'm so sorry. I deserve this! I deserve what's happening! It's all my fault. I'm so, so sorry.*

And then the water pulled her down to the floor, and her eyes closed, her breath completely gone as everything went black.

CHAPTER 32

0:00:00

"Y ou're putting two worlds in danger just by being here," the stranger behind her said.

"You brought this on yourself," Doyle Holmes said from behind his mask.

"You *promised* you wouldn't go to the fictional world," Bethany's mom said. "You've broken my heart!"

"You left us behind, Bethany," Kiel said.

"Just like you did your father," Owen said.

"Give her mouth to mouth," said a second Owen.

. . . Wait. *Two* Owens?

"I'm not sure how!" said the first Owen, just above her.

"Oh, *you guys*," said a girl's voice. "What would you ever do without me?"

Then silence.

Abruptly, Bethany began choking, coughing up water, and her eyes slowly opened.

Moira, criminal genius and great-great-great-great-great-granddaughter of Professor Moriarty, Sherlock Holmes's greatest enemy, was bent over her, giving her a disgusted look. "I get that you were almost dead and all," she said, wiping water off of her face, "but basically you just puked on me. You're honestly not my favorite person in the world right now."

"Bethany!" Owen shouted, and pushed Moira out of the way. Bethany weakly let Owen hug her, relief and confusion fighting for dominance in her brain. They'd found her? She hadn't left them behind? But *how* had they found her? And were those sirens in the distance?

She looked around over Owen's shoulder, and saw they were at the bottom of a ladder leading up to a manhole, letting in the only light around them. The smell confirmed what the slippery walls and dank floor hinted at: They were in the sewer.

"I'm so sorry," she whispered to Owen, her throat raw from coughing. "I waited for you two as long as I could. It's all my fault."

"It's *my* fault," Owen whispered back. "I never should have told you about Doyle in the first place."

"No, she's right," said a *second* Owen, and Bethany's eyes widened. She hadn't been imagining it . . . there really were two Owens. What exactly had she missed? "She came to Doyle before you even knew about him, Owen," the other Owen continued. "She's the whole reason you're in this mess."

The first Owen let her lie back down, and Bethany turned from one Owen to another, having trouble finding the words. Finally, she pointed at the Owen closer to her. "Who?" she said.

Mercifully, Kiel swooped in for a hug at that point and held her close. "The one farther away is the fictional version of Owen," he whispered in her ear. "We didn't really have a choice. Turns out he's met Doyle." Kiel squeezed her hard then, and for a moment she couldn't breathe again but didn't really care. Instead, she just hugged him back and didn't let go, trying not to worry about anything else.

Then Kiel pulled away, and reality came flooding back. A *fictional* version of Owen? And they'd gotten him involved? He must know everything by now! What had they been thinking? How *could* they—

No. She wasn't going to blame them for breaking the rules, not after she'd done it herself. And it sounded like involving this Owen was her fault too, if Doyle had spoken to him.

"How did you find me?" she whispered, her throat still raw.

"Owen figured it out," Kiel said, and Bethany caught a slight bit of disappointment in his voice. "After Doyle set his mother's library on fire—"

"*WHAT?*"

"The fictional version of her library," Owen said quickly.

"He's a *monster*," said the other Owen, the fictional version. The one who's mother's library had just burned down. "You need to take him down, or who knows what he'll do next!"

"What did Doyle want with you?" the real Owen asked her. She gave him a confused look. "You were there when he took us."

Kiel and regular Owen looked at each other. "We, uh, haven't really remembered everything," Owen said.

"Doyle made me use the forget spell on the two of us," Kiel said, looking embarrassed now. "I modified it when I cast it so we'd gradually get our memories back, but it's taking longer than I'd like. I was never that great at changing spells, honestly."

"So?" Fictional Owen said. "What did Doyle want?"

"Books," Bethany whispered. "He wanted books."

"That's it?" Kiel said, raising an eyebrow. "All of this over a few books?"

"Not a few books," Bethany said. "*Every* book. He wanted me to bring him an electronic copy of every book in the library. *Our* library. All the fiction books it had."

Owen gasped, but Kiel looked confused. "Why would he want those?"

"He'd have known every secret in the fictional world," Owen said quietly. "He'd know what people were thinking, what they planned on doing, and when. What more could a detective want? He could solve every mystery before it even started."

Moira waved a hand at Bethany. "I love this craziness, I really do, but I kinda need to get home soon. Don't want my father finding out I've been gone. Want to pay me now, or . . ."

"I'm still not seeing why the books thing is so bad," Kiel said. "Granted, he's evil, but solving mysteries isn't the worst thing."

"It is if you see everyone as a criminal," Fictional Owen said. "Look what he did to you two, and you're not exactly hardened criminals."

"Wait, hold up," Moira said, raising an eyebrow. "What's this, now, about hardened criminals? Tell me you didn't give Doyle this information."

Bethany looked away, not saying anything.

There was silence for a moment, other than the sound of people shouting above them somewhere.

"So that's it, then," Fictional Owen said finally. "You've unleashed a monster on us. *Great job*, Bethany."

"It's not her fault," Kiel said, stepping between Bethany and the fictional Owen.

"We'll fix this, don't worry," regular Owen said. "She just needs a chance to rest."

"So what, we just sit here while Doyle begins his reign of terror?" Fictional Owen said. "You guys can do that if you want. I'm not going to let this happen, though."

"Hey, just wait for a second," regular Owen said to, well, himself. "We'll figure something out, and—"

"He's right," Bethany said, then went silent as the sirens stopped and red and blue lights flashed down through the manhole. That couldn't be good.

She started to get to her feet, and Kiel moved to help, but she pushed him away gently. "Look at what Doyle's done," she said. "And that was just to punish us. We can't let him have those books. We need to fix this. *I* need to fix this."

"Even if we get the books back, he'll still know all about you, about the real world," Owen whispered to her.

"Nonfictional world," Fictional Owen said.

"Then we use Kiel's forget spell on *him*," Bethany said.

"Small problem with that," Kiel said, pointing at his waist. "Doyle has my wands and spell book."

"Then we get you replacements first," she said, getting irritated. "Not like we haven't visited the Magister once already."

"The wands I can re-create," Kiel said. "But that was my last spell book. The only other one would be my master's, and that's the one Owen ended up using. We can't take that away from him, he'll die."

"Then we get your spell book back from Doyle," Bethany shouted, not sure why everyone had to argue. "I'm sure it's in that school of his!"

"That school is the most heavily guarded place on earth," Fictional Owen told her. "And ignoring the surveillance cameras, the guards, and the electrified fences and doors, *Doyle* is there. He knows what you'll do before you do it. You'd need a miracle to even get close to him."

"We've got her," Bethany said, nodding at Moira.

Moira laughed. "Do you? You already owe me more gold than you can possibly pay. Oh, *don't worry*, that's just an expression, you'll totally find a way to pay it. But after that, I'm done.

This has been a hugely fun time for me, but I can't be caught doing this. My father finds out, I'm done for."

"Really?" Bethany said. "A chance to steal something from the descendant of Sherlock Holmes, right out from under his nose? You don't want in?"

Moira snorted. "You'd think I'd care about that, wouldn't you! But that's my mom's thing, not mine."

"Then it'd be the kind of thing she might notice," Bethany said quietly, feeling terrible for even mentioning it.

Moira went silent, just staring at her. Finally, she sighed. "I'm in." There was no excitement or joy in her voice, just resignation.

"I hear voices!" someone shouted from above. "Inspector Brown, I think they're in the sewers!"

They all looked up, but Fictional Owen was the first to move. "Go," he hissed. "I'll distract the police."

"What?" Owen said. "You can't, they'll think you're me and throw you in jail!"

Fictional Owen paused for a second, then shook his head and smiled. "They'll have to catch me first. Now go! Go beat Doyle, and get him to admit to everything he's done. The police won't be able to hold me if you win. And you *will* win,

Owen. I have faith in you. Be the hero you're meant to be. You can do it. I *know* you can!" And with that, he ran to the ladder and began scampering up it as they saw flashlights approaching through the manhole.

"NO!" Owen shouted, and tried to catch his other self, but Bethany grabbed his hand and stopped him.

"We have to go," she said, pulling him toward Moira and Kiel. "We'll fix this, and get him out. I promise."

Owen just looked at her, and she'd never seen so much doubt in his eyes. But finally he nodded, and Bethany grabbed the hands of the other two and jumped them out of the book.

She was so weak, they barely made it past the cover of the book, slipping out in a pile to land on the floor of the library.

One by one, they all stood up, and Bethany faced them each in turn. Kiel, the magicless magician, who still managed to wink at her, though somehow it seemed more forced than usual. Moira, who looked around with wide eyes, then turned back to the book they'd just left in amazement. They'd need Kiel's forget spell for her, too.

And finally, Owen, who met her gaze for just a moment, then turned away, shaking his head.

UGH. She deserved that. But she'd make it up to him. She'd

make it up to his fictional self too, and the entire fictional world. She'd fix this, she'd fix *all* of it. She had to.

"Hold up," Moira said, pointing at *The Baker Street School for Irregular Children* on the floor with a shaking finger. "Did anyone else just see us pop out of that book?" She began to laugh nervously.

Bethany nodded, too tired to talk.

Her visitor had been right. Jumping into books was just too dangerous. As soon as she fixed things with Doyle, that'd be it.

She'd never step foot in the fictional world again.

Owen wandered through the library's bookshelves, partly to pick out books that Bethany might be able to use as weapons if she needed to, and partly just to reassure himself that the library was still standing. In spite of the craziness of the night, he found himself yawning every few minutes and realized how late it must be. *Wow*, had it been a long night.

And it was only going to get longer for Fowen now.

Why had his other self done it? Bethany could have taken Fowen out too. But instead, he'd done the heroic thing, and now he was probably locked up in jail. Or *worse*, facing his horrified mother.

And in spite of all that, Fowen still believed in him. In both of them. Why? All Owen had done was mess things up. He wasn't the hero that Kiel was. He wasn't even the hero that his fictional self was!

Through the shelves, Owen saw Moira reading *The Baker Street School for Irregular Children*, preparing for the break-in. He and Kiel had managed to calm her down a bit since they'd jumped out. They'd even shown her a copy of her own book. She refused to look at it, though, and only had one question: Did it say anything about where her mother was?

Owen had shaken his head, and since then, she'd just jumped into planning. She'd even come up with a list of tools she'd need, but they'd all been easy to find. In fact, he'd simply had Bethany reach into Moira's book for most of them. Not that he'd told Moira that.

"This is all so crazy, isn't it?" he said to Moira. "That there's a world where people read about you? I just found out the same thing about me today, so I know what it's like."

"It doesn't matter," Moira said, not looking up.

"It doesn't bother you at all?" Owen asked.

"*You're* bothering me." There wasn't a trace of her excited energy now, just annoyance.

"Think about it. Someone can see into your head," Owen said. Abruptly, he glanced around, wondering if he could see any readers. And then the worst thing in the world occurred to him. "Wait! What about the bathroom? They

251

don't read about you going to the bathroom, do they?"

Moira sighed loudly, but Owen barely heard her. "Maybe that's why they never show people going to the bathroom in books?" He had to go now, in fact, but like *that* was going to happen. If necessary, he'd just hold it for the rest of his life. . . .

"Are you not busy?" Moira said, looking up at the ceiling. "Do you need more to do? Because I can give you a job, or I can shut you up permanently. Those are your two options."

Owen paused for a moment. "What's bothering you, Moira?"

The Baker Street School for Irregular Children slammed shut, and Moira's face appeared on the other side of the shelves an instant later. "Permanently it is!" she said, and a hand shot through an empty space to grab for him.

Owen leaped back out of reach. "Just think of this as more rule breaking," he said. "Because you're totally breaking all kinds of laws of physics just being here!"

Moira didn't reply, and instead tried to shove her arm farther through the shelves.

"Isn't that your whole thing? You love being bad?" Owen asked, stepping back again.

"That's not what this is!" Moira shouted. "Don't you get it?"

"No?" Owen asked. Moira's hand disappeared, and he real-

ized she was coming around the shelves at him, so he quickly circled around, keeping the shelves between them.

"Before, when I was helping you and my Magical Koala escape, that was fun! I love that kind of thing because it doesn't matter. If you two got caught again, it's not like I'd be in trouble."

"Hey!" Owen said, moving quicker now as she continued following him around the shelves.

"But this?" she said. "This is *important*. I've been trying to get my mother's attention all my life, and nothing I do works." She stopped abruptly, then switched directions, causing Owen to do the same. "And now we're trying to break into a place that, if I'm reading it right, has some of the best security I've ever heard of. So excuse me if I'm taking this a bit more seriously!"

Owen gave her a confused look. "So it's not because there's a book about you?"

"Who cares!" Moira shouted at him. "What does it matter if people read about me? They should, I'm brilliant! There should be classes taught in how I commit crimes!" She slowed down and sighed. "I'm sorry, Sad Panda. I shouldn't be taking this out on you. I always get a little more stressed out when I'm trying something big. And it doesn't get bigger than this."

253

"But you're a criminal genius," Owen told her. "If anyone can do this, you can."

"Obviously," she said, cracking a smile. "But what if *no one* can? That's the part that worries me, Owen. And failing on this kind of stage not only is embarrassing, but will get back to my dad. More importantly, it'll get back to my *mom*. She might not want anything to do with me after that."

"Your mom loves you," Owen said, coming around to her side of the shelves, still ready to run if necessary. "Your father said so, and he hates her, so why would he lie?"

Moira snorted. "I don't need a pep talk. All I want is a way to bypass a security system designed to counter every break-in tool that exists."

Owen paused for a moment, then walked over to the science-fiction shelf, grabbed a book, and tossed it to her. "Then it's good that we can get you things that *don't* exist."

Moira started to say something, then stopped, staring at the cover. "Huh," she said.

"What?" he asked, suddenly nervous.

She looked up at him, a huge grin on her face. "So Bethany can just reach in and grab stuff for us, right? Anything we might need?"

"As long as it doesn't interrupt the story somehow, she can."

Moira smiled even wider, then started pulling book after book off the shelf. "This might actually be fun after all," she whispered, then switched shelves.

Owen moved with her. "So you have a plan now?"

"Always!" She threw some books on the floor, and Owen winced.

"Try to not beat them up?"

"Eesh, you're right," she said, glancing down at the books. "What if by dropping them, I'm causing earthquakes or something in all those stories?" She kicked one, then bent down and put her ear to the cover.

"I don't think that's how it works," he told her. "It's just that the better you take care of a book, the longer you get to read it."

She laughed. "You're *adorable*, SP. You sound like someone's mom! I love it!"

That was fair. He *did* sound exactly like his mother, he realized. "So what?"

"Sew buttons!" she said, then dropped a pile of books in his arms. "This is going to be *so much fun*!"

Kiel slid down the wall next to where Bethany had collapsed earlier and handed her a copy of *What's to Come in the Future*, a book of made-up futuristic inventions. He'd opened to the page about Recovery Pills, which claimed, *You'll feel like you've had a week of sleep with just one pill!* She reached into the page and grabbed one, trying not to look out the nearby windows at the rising sun.

There wasn't much time before Owen's mother would be showing up to open the library. If they hadn't made it back by then, they'd get caught for sure.

Right now that seemed like it wouldn't be the worst thing.

"This can wait, you know," Kiel said. "We don't have to go back in just yet."

"He's too dangerous," Bethany said, not looking up. "The longer he has the books, the more damage he can do. And we

need your magic back as soon as possible. Besides, I'm feeling fine." She swallowed the Recovery Pill, then started to push herself up the wall to a standing position, but Kiel gently put his hand on her shoulder.

"Just relax," he said. "Rest for a minute. And don't worry, we'll beat him." He gave her a Kiel smile.

"Will we?" Bethany said, still looking at the ground. "He's a Holmes. You think he doesn't know we're coming? He's probably prepared for everything we do before we even do it." She shivered.

"You're afraid," Kiel said, and he wasn't asking.

She nodded slowly. "Our only real way to fix this is to make Doyle forget it all, Kiel. What happens if we can't get your spell book back? Think of what someone like him could do."

Kiel nodded. "I have been. It's . . . unpleasant. But what made you think you had to go to him in the first place?"

She dropped her head into her arms. "I just . . . *there was no other way.* Once your spell failed, what else could I do? It was either this, or just give up completely."

"But why hide it?" Kiel asked. "Why not tell Owen and me?"

Bethany raised her head. "And what would you have said?"

Kiel grinned. "I'm in?"

"No, you wouldn't have," Bethany said. "You'd have said it was a bad idea. And Owen would have been even more against it. And you'd have both been *right*. But I had to try one last time. And the worst thing?" She sighed. "I think he might know where my father is."

Kiel paused. "Then we'll get that from him."

"He won't tell us," Bethany said. "Don't you get it? Say we outwit him, which we won't. How do we force him to tell us anything?"

"There's magic for that."

"Magic that he knows about," Bethany said, then pushed to her feet. "We need to get going."

"We still have time," Kiel said from the floor, staring up at her. "You're not telling me something, Bethany. What are you still hiding?"

Bethany turned away, not looking at him. There was *so* much she wasn't telling him at this point. That some stranger had seen her in Argon VI and claimed it was dangerous for her to be in the fictional world. That the stranger knew her father. That she wasn't sure what she'd do if Doyle offered her the location of her father in exchange for letting him keep his memory.

That after all of this, she'd decided enough was enough,

and she was done jumping into books. Which meant that she'd need to bring Kiel back into his books and say good-bye for good.

"I'm just exhausted," she said, forcing a smile at him and giving him her hand to help him up.

Kiel took the offered hand and slowly stood. "Don't worry. We'll get my magic back, wipe Doyle's memory, and be back before breakfast."

"Oooh, pancakes," Bethany said, her stomach rumbling maniacally. When had she even eaten last? Dinner last night? It felt like weeks ago.

She led Kiel back to the checkout counter, where Owen was waiting with an enormous pile of books. Moira appeared a minute later from Owen's mother's office and tossed *The Baker Street School for Irregular Children* onto the counter. "*That* was poorly written!" she said, grinning.

"What were you doing in there?" Bethany asked her.

"Research," Moira said. "I've got a plan now. An *unbeatable* plan!"

"Before we start, can I make a suggestion?" Owen said, not looking at Bethany. "Whenever people go over plans in books or movies, they always fail. It's the plans that stay secret that

work. So maybe we should just let Moira fill us in as we go."

"You're such an adorable panda, aren't you," Moira said.

"That's just so the readers can get a twist," Bethany said, giving Owen a tired smile. "It's not like we've got that problem here. It's just us. We're not in the fictional world."

"Bethany," Owen said, still not looking at her. "There's a chance that someone's writing about us."

"*Story Thieves*, I know," she said. "I've been trying not to think about that. Maybe fictional authors can see us like our authors can see fictional people?"

"So what if we're in a sequel?" Owen asked. "I'm just saying, we have to be careful, especially giving plans away. If someone's writing this up, then that means anyone could find out about our plan. Just think of it as not jinxing ourselves."

"Like a baby panda holding a teddy bear!" Moira said.

Owen sighed. "Maybe if we *are* in the *Story Thieves* sequel, it'll change chapters right now and skip over the plan. If that happens, at least we'll still have a chance."

Okay, here's the plan," Moira said, grabbing some paper. She quickly sketched out a box with big, intimidating lines in front of it. "This is what I like to call the Baker Street School," she said.

Owen raised one eyebrow. "Seriously?"

"I really do call it that, yes," Moira said, nodding at him.

He sighed. "And that's the fence?"

"You have an eye for detail, my little panda!" Moira said, and quickly started marking spots around the box. "There are cameras every five feet surrounding the courtyard, as well as inside the school. The gate is ten feet tall and electrified. The walls are *eleven* feet tall, just to be different, and topped with barbed wire, which is *also* electrified. But that's the easy stuff."

"Which part of that is easy?" Bethany asked.

Moira laughed. "The challenging part is the computer

system. It sounds like it handles security for the school *and* helps Doyle solve his cases. It's got some weird acronym that doesn't mean anything."

"W.A.T.S.O.N.," Owen pointed out. "Because that was the name of Sherlock Holmes's best friend and assistant, Dr. Watson."

Bethany groaned and smiled at Owen. He forced a smile back, then looked away.

"In spite of W.A.T.S.O.N.'s adorable lineage," Moira continued, "it sounds like the computer is basically our worst nightmare. It monitors all the cameras as well as a whole suite of motion and thermal detectors. So basically if anything moves or even just exists at a higher temperature than seventy-two degrees, then W.A.T.S.O.N. knows it's there."

"How are we going to get past it, then?" Bethany asked.

Moira winked at her, then patted the pile of books. "You can thank my Sad Panda over there for the idea. We've got it covered."

"Thanks, Sad Panda," Bethany told Owen, and smiled at him again. This time he didn't return it.

"What does W.A.T.S.O.N. do if it detects you?" Owen asked, still trying not to look at Bethany.

"All *kinds* of fun things!" Moira told him. "Every door in the

school can be electrified. Even some floors, it sounds like. The book was a little vague. It can also release sleeping gas in any room in the school, alert the guards, call the police, anticipate your next move, wake you up in the morning, and I think do the laundry. That part was vague too."

"You mentioned guards," Kiel said. "How many?"

"You don't remember them yet?" Bethany asked.

Kiel shook his head. "Should I?"

"They're enormous," Bethany said, shuddering. "They're all big and bald and look exactly the same."

"They're ex–British Special Air Service, the SAS," Moira said. "Like our navy seals. Top of their field, the toughest of the worst. And Doyle has about thirty of them, all armed to the teeth."

Owen swallowed hard. This had sounded good when Doyle had been describing it in the book as a way to keep the hardened criminal kids he caught locked away in his rehabilitation school, but from this side it felt a lot less comforting and a lot more impossible.

"Why don't we just jump into a page already inside the school?" Kiel asked, flipping through the book.

"Because those scenes all take place before Bethany went

in the first time," Owen told him. "If we're going to get your magic back and erase Doyle's memory, we need to go in after she hired him."

"Can we talk about this whole wiping his memory thing?" Moira said, giving them a suspicious glance. "Don't think I haven't noticed how it keeps coming up. You don't plan on doing that to *me*, do you?"

Bethany, Kiel, and Owen all stared at the floor.

"*What?!*" Moira shouted. "How *could* you! I thought we were all friends!"

"You're charging us all the gold you can carry," Bethany said, giving her a guilty look.

"Right, I'm charging my *friends*. You're going to wipe my memory?" She shook her head. "No way. I'm out. Keep your gold. Or better yet, don't wipe my memory and give me all the gold."

"You know," Owen said, shrugging a bit, "if you did have your memory wiped, you'd be able to deny doing anything wrong this whole time. If your father asked, you'd be able to tell him you lived up to your promise."

Moira stared at Owen for a second, then burst into a huge grin. "My silly, sad little panda," she said. "I love when you get

underhanded. Okay, you can wipe my memory too, but you better still pay me. Memory or not, I know when I've been cheated, and I'm giving you guys a *great* plan here."

"Which part of this has been your plan?" Bethany said. "All I'm hearing so far is how impossible it's going to be to break in there."

"That's what *I* thought too," Moira yelled excitedly. "But we'll get to that! So it sounds like Doyle keeps all of his important treasures in a safe in his office. The book doesn't say where the safe is, only that it's hidden, and he's the sole keeper of the combination. Supposedly even W.A.T.S.O.N. doesn't know it." She beamed. "So *that* will be a fun challenge. If it takes me any more than two minutes to crack it, I'll give back every gold coin you're going to pay me."

"So what are these books for?" Bethany said, taking the top one off the pile. *"Alpha Predator?"*

"Invisibility suits that also hide our heat," Owen pointed out. "The book's about this race of aliens that hunt down humanity, and the only survivors have to wear these suits to go about their lives. And if the suit gets ripped even a little—"

"I get it," Bethany said, frowning. "I hope there's a less scary place to jump in and grab some of those suits."

"This one has hover shoes, in case the floors get electrified,"

Owen said, handing Bethany a book called *RoboJones*. "Then there's *Boxing Day 2150* with its knockout gloves. They use them in these crazy fighting tournaments. It's actually a terrible book."

"I'm not hearing how that'll help us against W.A.T.S.O.N.," Bethany said, taking the books from Owen.

"That's the best one!" Moira said, and knocked over the rest of the books in her excitement to grab the bottom one. "Take a look!" She shoved the book into Bethany's hands, then stepped back, giving Owen a smug look. "Nailed this one. I'm *so* proud of us."

"*Do Computers Worry About Electric Cooties?*" Bethany said, then slowly looked up at Owen and Moira. "Are you kidding me?"

"It's about a virus that teaches computers how to love," Owen pointed out, blushing. "It ends up creating this whole dystopian world because every computer stops working, and humanity loses all of its technology."

"Electric cooties," Bethany repeated, still holding the book.

"We can just grab a drive with the virus on it, then plug it into W.A.T.S.O.N.," Owen told her. "It should only take a few seconds after that."

"Before W.A.T.S.O.N. falls in love."

"Isn't it sweet?" Moira said.

Bethany tossed the book onto the table. "You guys seem to have done a lot of work here, and I think it all makes sense. Sort of."

Owen glanced from the books to Moira grinning proudly, and back. It *could* work. It was elaborate enough. But the edges of an idea tickled his brain just enough to make him pause. "You know, there might be another way," he said quietly.

Moira and Bethany looked at each other. "Set the place on fire?" Moira asked.

"It's a school!" Bethany said, her eyes widening in horror.

Moira shrugged. "Yeah, but it'd get us in pretty quick. I'm not *suggesting* it, I just thought maybe that's what he had in mind!"

"Not exactly," Owen said, frowning as the idea formed. "It'd be dangerous, but it doesn't involve actually hurting anyone or making computers fall in love."

"It's fire, got to be," Moira said, grinning widely.

Owen looked down at the table. "Nope. No fire. Just me surrendering to Doyle."

CHAPTER 36

Though it was early morning, the Baker Street School for Irregular Children was covered in a dreary, almost sticky fog that clung to streetlamps and the front gate as if it were alive.

Owen slowly approached the front gate, wishing the others hadn't let him go through with this idiotic plan. Why had he even mentioned it? Moira was the criminal genius. Why hadn't he just followed her lead?

I believe in you, Fowen said in his head, and Owen nodded. That was why.

It was time to prove once and for all that the Owens of the world weren't just sidekicks, weren't just someone to be rescued. No, the Owens might be comic relief, but they could also come up with a pretty clever plan, if he did say so himself.

His breath quickening, Owen reached a trembling finger out to push the intercom button.

It beeped, then a voice with an English accent answered. "Yes?"

"My name is Owen Conners," Owen said, leaning forward to talk into the speaker. "I'm here to turn myself in to Mr. Holmes."

The line went silent for a moment, and Owen wondered if the plan was over before it started. Maybe it wasn't too late to go with the computer love virus after all?

But then the front gates clicked and ponderously swung inward as an enormous bald man opened the double doors at the opposite end of the courtyard.

"Mr. Holmes has been expecting you," the guard said, and held the door open for Owen.

Doyle was expecting him? No way. That had to be a bluff. "Thank you," Owen said, and forced himself to step into the courtyard, remembering the cameras that Moira had mentioned. All were probably aimed at him right now, which didn't exactly help his confidence.

He held the envelope in his hand tighter, took a deep breath, and hurried across the empty courtyard to the doors. The guard looked twice as big up close and seemed to know something was up, given his suspicious look.

Or was that just his face? It was hard to tell.

"This way, please," the guard said, and led Owen inside to the

foyer, with its huge staircase that split halfway up, turning on both sides to lead to the second floor. Owen followed the guard up the stairs and past a bunch of classrooms, all empty at this time of morning.

Good. That'd make things easier.

Owen glanced at his watch, the same one Doyle had placed on his wrist: 00:04:23. Four more minutes until the plan kicked into Phase Two, as he called it. Things were going right on schedule.

The guard led Owen to another set of double doors, this time labeled HEADMASTER'S OFFICE. The guard knocked quietly, then turned the knob, opening the door for Owen without entering. Owen nodded at the guard, then stepped into Doyle's darkened office, lit only by flickering electrical candles and a fire in the fireplace, which was close to going out.

As soon as he was inside, the guard closed the door and Owen heard the lock click. Great. There was no turning back now.

At the opposite end of the room behind an enormous desk, a bank of monitors showed various cellblocks, all quiet with no movement. The desk's tall chair was turned toward the monitors, so Owen couldn't even tell if Doyle was there.

"Hello?" he said, then rolled his eyes at his own nervousness.

He cleared his throat and tried again. "Mr. Holmes, I'd like a word with you."

That was better. And would have been even more impressive if his voice hadn't cracked.

The chair slowly rotated around, and Owen almost stopped breathing when he saw the question-mark mask and the Sherlock Holmes hat.

"Mr. Conners," said the same deep, fake-sounding voice he'd heard in the library. "Right on time."

Owen's heart stopped. It was a bluff. There was no way Doyle knew his plan. *No way.*

"I'm here to give you a message from Bethany," Owen told Doyle, and stepped closer to the desk. "We're surrendering, but only under our terms."

Doyle didn't say anything, so Owen quickly laid the envelope he'd been carrying down on the desk and took a few steps back. He knew better than to look at his watch, but the time must be getting close.

"And these are your terms?" Doyle said, picking up the envelope without opening it. "Why send only you? Where are Kiel and Bethany?"

"I'm the messenger," Owen said. "Bethany is ready to pull

me out at any moment, if you don't agree to our terms."

Doyle slammed his hand down on the desk. "You're *not* just the messenger, Owen. What is wrong with you? You need to Owen what you're doing!"

Owen gasped. "You mean own it?"

Doyle paused. "That's what I said." He stood up and carried the envelope over to the fire. While his back was turned, Owen glanced down at his watch: 00:00:59.

Just one more minute.

"I don't think these are surrender terms," Doyle said, looking at Owen over his shoulder. "No, I think this is a trick."

Owen could almost hear his own heartbeat, it was beating so hard. "I don't know what you're talking about. Bethany agrees not to trespass in anyone's story ever again, as long as you tell the police that Kiel and I didn't set the fire. Agree to that, and you'll never have to worry about us again. And you can keep the books. That'll be the end of it."

"No, I don't believe it will be," Doyle said, then absently tossed the envelope into the fire.

"NO!" Owen screamed, and leaped forward, but Doyle swept a leg out, knocking Owen to the ground. Before Owen could move, Doyle had Owen's arms behind his back and a knee to

Owen's neck. "I am the greatest detective who ever lived," Doyle said, his fake voice sounding even more eerie up close. "Did you really think you could trick me like this?"

Owen watched as the envelope slowly caught fire, burning away to reveal a page from a book, before that too went up in flame. "No," he said again, quieter this time, as behind him his watch began to beep.

"So let me see if I have the plan correct," Doyle said. "You come in, ostensibly surrendering, but carrying a page from a book that Bethany and friends are hiding within. At a designated time, right now, it sounds like, Bethany jumps out of that page to take me by surprise, bypassing all of my security in one swoop. Do I have it correct?"

Owen groaned and tried to free himself, but Doyle just yanked Owen's arms up painfully, and Owen stopped moving.

"Shall we see if they're coming?" Doyle said as the book page shriveled up in the fire, blackening into ash.

Finally, the page disappeared entirely into the flames, and Owen dropped his head to the floor, unable to even look anymore.

"Ah," Doyle said, releasing Owen's hands and standing up. "*Now* I will accept your surrender."

"Don't be so melodramatic," Doyle said, using a poker to stir up the ashes from the book page. "It's not like they're trapped in that story. If they jump out now, they'll just end up back with the rest of the book."

"How can you know that?" Owen said quietly.

Doyle turned and looked at him in what Owen assumed was a sarcastic way. "I'm Doyle Holmes. I've cataloged Bethany's powers multiple times, and know exactly how she does it. But that's for later."

Owen's eyes widened. Could he be telling the truth? Had Doyle really figured out how Bethany's powers worked? The Magister had used magic to re-create her abilities, after all. Maybe Doyle's science had done the same thing.

"So was this it?" Doyle asked, pulling Owen to his feet. "Was this your entire plan? Sneak a page of a book into my

office, and then what? Pull me out of the book with you?"

Owen wouldn't look him in the eyes, or, well, question-mark mask. "Thought we'd get Kiel's wands and spell book off of you and then make you forget any of this ever happened."

Doyle snorted beneath the mask. "You never had a chance, Mr. Conners. None of you did. I was two steps ahead of you this entire time. Three or four, for most of it." He moved over to his mantle, lifted a glass case off a pistol labeled THIRD ACT, and pulled on the gun.

It raised just an inch, and something behind the desk began to rumble. Owen turned to find the bank of monitors pulling aside to reveal a safe with fourteen different combination locks. "No peeking," Doyle said, and started working his way through each one.

For a moment Owen considered just jumping Doyle and try-ing to knock him out. All he'd need was a weapon. His thoughts turned back to the pistol on the mantle, wondering if it came off, or was just part of the safe mechanism. The rest of the office was strangely empty of anything weapony, unfortunately. The chairs were far too big to pick up, and the desk was completely out.

"Just another minute, if you don't mind," Doyle said, almost taunting Owen by not bothering to turn around. Owen nodded

to himself and crouched down, ready to simply tackle Doyle right into the wall.

"And before you move, you might want to consider that countdown band on your wrist," Doyle said, still not looking. "Every student at the Baker Street School wears one. Most of the time it's just a watch, but within the school grounds it also works as a deterrent. Try to leave the school or act up in any way, and you'll be twitching on the ground in seconds."

Owen's eyes widened, and he immediately went to take the band off, only to get a shock that sent him to his knees.

"Oh, and I wouldn't try taking it off," Doyle said, finally turning around as he pulled the safe door open. "Sorry, probably should have mentioned." He shrugged, then reached into the safe and pulled out Kiel's wands and spell book. "Beautiful, aren't they? I know they shouldn't exist, and that as a man of science I should reject them outright, but I simply can't put them down." The spell book tried to bite his head, but Doyle smacked it hard against the desk, and the book started whimpering.

"What are you going to do with those?" Owen asked quietly.

"What do you think?" Doyle said. "Come, let me show you something." He gestured for Owen to follow, then led the way out of his office.

Owen paused, then followed slowly, glancing behind him at the still-open safe. Was there anything else in there that—

And then the safe door slammed closed, and all fourteen combination locks whirled around.

Maybe not, then.

"Put the school on lockdown," Doyle was telling the guard outside of his office. "I want a total quarantine. No one in or out. I'm expecting some visitors will be arriving in a matter of minutes, and they may be using technology you've never seen. Just ensure that all doors and windows are electronically sealed."

The guard nodded and jogged off, barking orders into a tiny device on the neck of his T-shirt while Doyle gestured for Owen to follow him. "I'd really like to go over my plan now, if you don't mind? There won't be time once Bethany and Kiel show."

"Maybe they're not the only ones," Owen said. If Doyle didn't know they had a Moriarty on their side—

"What, Moira Gonzalez?" Doyle said. "I've been watching her for years, waiting until she might present a bit of a challenge. Didn't want to just cut her legs out from under her before she could hold her own at the game. She has potential, but nothing like the original."

And that was that. Doyle knew every last bit of advantage they had.

"Was that what you've been hiding?" the detective asked, throwing a look Owen's way. "Your body language has been virtually screaming that you were keeping something from me."

Owen nodded sadly. "I thought she'd be our secret weapon. What better way to fight a Holmes?"

"That's just it, Mr. Conners," Doyle said, sliding his hand down a portion of the wall near the stairway. "You can't."

The wall next to him split apart, revealing an elevator filled with newspaper articles framed in gold. Owen looked at the first few and realized they were about the actual Sherlock Holmes. *Consulting Detective Solves Murder; Doctor to Publish Account.* That was their first case. *Holmes Uncovers Hound Hoax. Holmes Not Charmed By Murderous Snake.* All of the famous cases of Sherlock Holmes, here in actual newspaper articles. Some even had drawings.

"All we had was his reputation," Doyle said quietly, staring into one of the mirrors as the elevator shook, then began to descend. "That's all the family had. We were of the house of *Holmes*. And that meant something until your little book arrived on the scene and gave away our family secret, even if

it was in what everyone thought was a made-up story."

"What secret?" Owen asked quietly.

"That my great-great-great-great-great-grandfather was saved from his death at Reichenbach Falls by a flying man," Doyle said, practically spitting. "Sherlock Holmes then spent the next *three years* looking for that man, tracking down magicians and yogis of various sorts, trying to learn the secret of flight. Do you understand how humiliating that'd be if it got out? That this great man of science and deduction was taken in by magic, of all things?"

Owen just shook his head as the elevator rumbled to a stop, and the doors opened into a dark, dank hallway.

"Bethany will pay for what she put my family through," Doyle said, then stepped out of the elevator. "And she's given me the tools to do just that."

"Where are you taking me?" Owen asked, wondering if Doyle was going to leave him down here to starve. Or worse, make Owen start attending his school.

"Thanks to Bethany, I now have copies of every single fictional story in your library," Doyle said, ignoring Owen's question as he walked farther down the dark hall, forcing Owen to jog to catch up. "And since I have Kiel's magic, I can follow

the Magister's example and re-create Bethany's powers with a simple spell. All I need now is the girl herself, and I'll have access to every fictional world ever."

No. This couldn't happen! Owen stopped dead in the hall as Doyle reached his destination, a lone cell door, too shadowed to see inside.

"You don't have to do this," Owen told him, backing away. "You're supposed to be a good guy. You're supposed to be a Holmes! You just said that your reputation was everything. Well, taking over the fictional world and becoming a tyrant is the last thing a Holmes should do! You're better than that. You're better than this!"

Doyle raised a finger and beckoned Owen to come closer.

"No," Owen said quietly. "I won't let you hide me away down here."

"I need you to see this," Doyle said. "I need you to understand what I've done." He beckoned again with his finger, and Owen swallowed hard.

What choice did he have, though? Doyle could just electrocute him again through the band on his wrist if he didn't do what the detective said. So Owen stepped forward slowly, dreading what he was about to find. The bones of Sherlock

Holmes? A jar for Bethany's essence? A robot W.A.T.S.O.N. with a mustache like the real Watson?

Owen passed Doyle and put his face up to the bars, peering into the darkness.

Two eyes filled with hatred glared right back.

Owen gasped and stepped away as the boy stood up and moved to the front of the cage. A gag covered his mouth, so he couldn't speak, but the boy's eyes were filled with rage as well as something else. A cold, dead, calculating stare. A stare that looked right through Owen, that took in every detail and spit out secrets.

"This can't be," Owen said, barely able to breathe.

"Meet Doyle Holmes, Mr. Conners," said the boy in the mask. "I'm sure he'd like to introduce himself, but he's far too smart for me to take off that gag while I'm not wearing earplugs. I hate when he deduces strange things about me. It's creepy."

Owen turned around and stared at the question-mark mask. "If he's Doyle . . ."

The boy reached up and took off his mask, revealing a very familiar face.

"I'm so disappointed in you," Fowen said, shaking his head. "How did you not figure this out?"

"How are you here?" Owen asked, backing away from his fictional self. "I thought you gave yourself up to the police?"

Fowen snorted, holding up the question-mark mask. "I had the mask on the second I was out of the manhole, Owen. Catch up here. How are you this slow?"

No. *No.* "Did you . . . did you beat Doyle? Is that how you have his mask?"

"Are you kidding?" Fowen shouted. "I've *been* Doyle. At least, the only Doyle you ever met. I was the one who found what I figured were other stories and messed them up, just to bait you guys in. The real Doyle's been down here since a few days after he came by the library."

Owen turned around to look at the ordinary boy in the jail cell, who now was glaring at both of them, his eyes burning,

his nostrils flaring as he breathed hard over his gag. "You were Doyle . . . this whole time?"

"Try to follow along, Owen," Fowen said. "You're making me embarrassed for us both. Don't you get it? This was all me. I set this up. I told Bethany I wanted to be paid in fictional books. I framed you and Kiel for the library burning down, which *I did*." He snorted. "How did you not see through me? You think the real Doyle is actually smart enough to know where you are at all times? I was alerting the police because I was standing next to you! I even told you that your own fingerprints were on the gas cans. How did you not suspect me when you found out that I existed?" He shook his head. "They're right about you. You *are* useless, aren't you. I'm doing you a favor with all of this, I really am. I'm doing *us* a favor."

Owen tried to breathe, but it felt like an anvil was sitting on his chest. He backed into a wall and slid down, not looking at his fictional self. This couldn't be true. He was dreaming. "Why . . . why would you do this?" he said, his heart pounding in his ears.

"Why?" Fowen's eyes widened. "Have you *seen* everything I did? I was amazing, Owen! You stole Kiel's story to live it out, but I *built* you a story. I created this for you, and gave you the

chance to fight a really great villain! Sure, it happened to be you in disguise, but you didn't know that. I gave you that! I gave you one of the greatest adventures of all time, and you sit there asking me why? If you'd done this for me, I'd be thanking you!"

"You burned down your library!" Owen said, finally able to look at Fowen. "You almost drowned Bethany. You stole Kiel's magic. All just to give me an adventure?"

"Oh, not at all," Fowen said. "I just thought you'd be a little more grateful. No, I did all of this because I wanted to be the hero, and to do that, I needed a big, awesome adventure to hero in. And when Doyle showed up, I realized I'd found one."

Fowen slowly walked toward the bars, where Doyle stood, giving him a look of death. "Only, Doyle gave up," Fowen said softly. "Doyle, boy genius and famous detective, up and quit. He recognized Bethany from *Story Thieves* and was all offended by the whole family-secret thing getting out. But once he realized that James Riley, the author, didn't exist, and he couldn't find any trace of who'd actually written the book . . . well, he just decided that this was all a waste of time. He just wasn't smart enough to see the whole story."

Abruptly, Doyle launched his arms through the bars of the

cell, but Fowen leaped backward, grinning. "Nice try, smart guy," he said, then gave Owen an almost embarrassed look. "He tries that every time I bring him his food. See, Doyle was all lonely up in this school and wanted a friend. A Watson to his Holmes, someone who'd tell him how great he was and how smart his deductions were. So I played that for him, I became his Watson. And he told me *everything*, all of this school's secrets. Even how to access the camera system." He shrugged. "Wasn't hard to find out where he kept his safe after that, and even zoom in for the combinations. It was all in the security recordings."

"You've kept him imprisoned down here because he didn't do what you wanted?" Owen said, pushing himself back up to his feet.

"You make it sound so petty," Fowen said. "I put him down here because Doyle gave up on the *greatest thing to ever happen to me*. Someone made up a whole story about *me*, Owen, and I needed to find out why, and who, and most importantly, what if it were actually real? I needed to meet Bethany, Owen. And if she really *was* real . . . then that left me only one option."

"Drown her?" Owen asked.

"You're so melodramatic," Fowen told him. "She was never

in any danger. I was watching her the whole time. I had to be, after all. I had Kiel's magic working on her."

Owen's eyes widened. "You were—"

"Magistering her? Yup. I was stealing her power, little by little. Took me a few minutes to locate the spell the Magister used in *Story Thieves*, but I found it and stole some of her power just like he did. I haven't tried it just yet, but I can't wait to!" Fowen looked straight up and sighed. "Can you imagine where I'm going to go? Fantasy lands, space, the past, the future, shrink down to the size of nothing . . . so many options."

"But why torture her?" Owen said. "Why almost drown her?"

Fowen shrugged. "I had to make her think I really wanted her to jump out, so she wouldn't. Reverse psychology, Owen. I suppose I could have just told her that, but death traps are so much more villainous, and she's going to need to believe Doyle's truly bad for all this to work."

"The Magister used up her power," Owen told him. "So will you. And then you'll be stuck in whatever book you jumped into."

"Nah," Fowen said. "Because she'll be close by whenever I need a charge." He turned to Owen and slowly grinned.

No. "You're not—"

"That's right!" Fowen shouted. "I'm taking over, Owen. I'm stealing your story. I'm going to be you, and you're staying here. Haven't you always wanted to live in a fictional world?" He frowned. "I do feel a little bad about the whole framing you for the library-burning-down thing, but I can't just have you running after me, or telling anyone what I did. So 'Doyle' will speak to the police. You're going to stay here, at the school, to pay for your crimes." He shook his head sadly. "Don't worry, though. You'll meet all kinds of interesting kids. It definitely won't be boring! And plus, I'll leave you a copy of all the fictional books. I can make one easily enough. I just needed them so I could pass for you, since you've read everything anyway."

This was all too much. How could it be real? How could he be doing this to himself?! "Why? Why would you do this to me?"

Fowen sighed. "Don't you see, Owen?" he said, giving him a pitying look. "You're wasting what could be the greatest life any person could ever live! You could keep jumping into stories with Bethany and Kiel forever, and having the biggest adventures possible. You could be a hero, you could learn magic, you could fly spaceships! But instead, you got all mopey because Charm was in danger and stories were hard, and suddenly you're not into it anymore?"

"I had just had my heart taken out," Owen pointed out quietly, wincing through the pain.

"I wouldn't have let that stop *me*," Fowen told him. "Look at what I was willing to do, Owen! I made Doyle a villain, I framed you and Kiel, I almost drowned Bethany, all so I could be the one to save everyone. Well, not save Doyle, but you get the point. I made up this story, and now I'm going to be its *hero*."

"But it's not just a story!" Owen shouted. "That's what I didn't get before. This is people's *lives*. You can't just go in and mess with them because it sounds fun. You need to take them seriously!"

Fowen leaned in and looked Owen straight in the eye. "*I burned down my mother's library*, Owen," he said. "You don't think I'm taking this seriously?" He stood back up, shaking his head. "It's honestly embarrassing, reading about you as the bumbling sidekick, the comic relief. I'll take care of things. I'll make a name for us both, a heroic one. And you can benefit too! Just tell people the book was written about you, and everyone will love you."

"I don't care about that. You're trying to steal my *life*!"

Fowen made a face. "I can, though. But don't worry. There aren't any hard feelings on my end. Really, I think this is all for the best."

Owen stared at him for a moment, then leaped straight at Fowen. Before he made it two feet, though, the band on his wrist sent a powerful jolt through his entire body. For a moment he completely forgot what was happening and just wondered why he couldn't stop jerking around on the floor. Somewhere close by he heard a muffled groan of pain, and something hit the floor, but he couldn't concentrate on that while he was twitching out of control.

He felt hands under his shoulders, and someone dragged him a short distance. Finally, Owen looked up to see Fowen close the cell door in front of him, with Doyle's unconscious body now outside. "Relax here for a bit," Fowen told him. "I have to go get the guards to help me carry this guy upstairs. You'll enjoy this . . . I'm going to have it set up in his office so when Bethany and Kiel finally get in, they'll see me, Owen, having just defeated Doyle all by myself. *I'll* be the hero that you never could be, and we'll go back to your home dimension and have the coolest, most awesome adventures ever. Maybe I'll even come back and tell you about them."

"*You're a monster,*" Owen whispered, struggling to sit up.

"No, I'm *you,*" Fowen said, and grinned.

"You're not me," Owen said. "You're the *evil* version of me."

"I'm the *better* version of you," Fowen said. "Speaking of, I brought my cat, Spike, with me here. I couldn't bear to leave him home without me. Would you mind taking care of him? It's the least you can do."

"It's the *least* I can do?!"

Fowen gave him an annoyed look. "He's a *cat*. Don't take out your issues on him." He turned and started to drag Doyle to the door, then stopped. "Oh, one last thing. See if you can figure out *this* mystery, at least. Who actually wrote *Story Thieves*? Who's the real James Riley?" He grinned. "I'm pretty sure I know, but you'll have plenty of time here to figure it out. Let me know what you come up with!"

And with that, he took Doyle's unconscious body and closed the door behind him, locking it. Owen tried to call out Fowen's name, but an enormous pain hit him in the face like a hammer.

What, a flashback? Now?! NO, this was the *worst*—

MISSING CHAPTER 9

Yesterday . . .

*J*ust because Doyle let us in, doesn't mean we should trust him," Owen whispered to Bethany and Kiel as an enormous guard with an English accent led them down the full hallways of the Baker Street School for Irregular Children. Everywhere he looked, kids walked quickly to class, their eyes shifting nervously at the slightest sound.

"I don't like how scared they are," Kiel said. He stopped near one and stuck out his hand. "Hello," he said, grinning widely.

The boy, an enormous fourteen-year-old with more muscles in his arms than Owen had in his entire body, gave Kiel a terrified look, then sidestepped the magician and hurried away, not looking back.

Kiel frowned, his eyes going up to the moving cameras above them.

"Please don't speak to the children," the guard in front of them said. "It interferes with their rehabilitation efforts."

The guard turned around, and Kiel stuck out his tongue at him, which caused a nearby student to snort. The student immediately clamped her hands over her mouth, but it was too late. Something beeped, and a teacher stepped out of the nearest classroom, beckoning the student in. The girl dropped her head and followed, and the teacher, flashing a suspicious look at Kiel, Bethany, and Owen, quietly closed the door behind her.

"How exactly are they rehabilitated?" Bethany asked the guard.

"Very carefully," the guard said, then smiled. "Shouldn't keep Mr. Holmes waiting."

During the rest of the walk, Owen made sure not to even look at the students, for fear of getting them in trouble. Sure, these were all criminals of one kind or another, but still, he wasn't comfortable with any of it. None of this had been in the book.

And it didn't explain how Doyle was crossing over into other stories, either.

"Remember the plan," Owen whispered to the other two as they approached the double doors at the end of the hall, doors that said HEADMASTER'S OFFICE. "We grab him and jump out. No messing around. We'll deal with whatever he's done from the real world."

"Nonfictional world," Kiel murmured.

"Shh, both of you," Bethany said, shifting from foot to foot. "And forget the plan. Don't do anything until I say so, okay? I'll handle this."

Huh? Owen glanced over at her, but Bethany's eyes were focused on the door. This was odd. She had barely said a word when they were discussing how to handle Doyle—had just nodded along. And now she wanted to take care of things?

And why were her hands shaking?

The guard knocked lightly on the door, then opened it and waved for them to go in. All three stepped into the head-master's office, and the guard closed the door gently behind them.

And then the lock clicked. *That* wasn't a great sign.

"Come in," said a voice from the far end of the room, and Owen turned his attention to the enormous wooden desk and a high-backed chair that was turned away from the door.

"Mr. Holmes?" Bethany said, stepping forward. "We'd like to speak to you about some of your latest . . . cases."

"I know why you're here, Bethany Sanderson."

Owen gasped at her name, but Bethany looked more . . . *guilty* than anything.

"Mr. Holmes," she whispered, "*please* tell me you found my father."

Owen's eyes widened. What had she done?

"*What* did you say?" Kiel asked, giving her a shocked look.

She didn't answer, her eyes fixed on the chair. "Tell me what you found, Mr. Holmes," she said, her voice wavering, her hands shaking even worse. "Everything else can wait."

Was *that* what this was all about? Doyle had crossed stories. Why would he do that if not looking for someone lost throughout the fictional world? Bethany had hired him to look for her father and caused this whole mess to begin with. Maybe her showing up here in the first place had done it. Doyle Holmes could probably tell she was half-fictional just by looking at her!

"I do have information for you," Doyle said, and he swiveled around in the chair, a boy wearing a question-mark mask, a Sherlock Holmes hat and coat. The books made it sound

almost like a superhero costume, but in person it felt like something out of a horror movie. "But first, let's discuss the matter of my payment."

Payment? Not only had she broken *all* of her own rules, she'd promised to pay the guy?

"I brought what you asked for," Bethany said, reaching into her bag and pulling out a tiny black device. She laid it on the desk, while Doyle stared at her with his fingers steepled before reaching out and taking it.

"Before we continue, I'll need to confirm this is what you say it is," Doyle said, plugging the device into his desk.

Behind Doyle a bank of monitors had been showing classrooms full of kids. Now, though, the monitors began displaying book covers, *real* books, switching so fast that Owen could barely keep up. There were so many . . . what had Bethany given him?!

"It's a copy of every e-book that the library had," she said, sounding miserable, and Owen gasped loudly. She'd given a fictional character real books? But why? What use could he have for them? This was insane!

"Bethany, jump him out now!" Owen shouted, then moved to grab Doyle.

"I wouldn't," the detective said, raising a hand to stop him. "Not if Bethany wants to know what happened to her father."

The room went silent, and Owen slowly turned toward Bethany, who had grabbed his arm and was pulling him away from Doyle.

"Please," she said. "I need to know. I shouldn't have done this, *I know* I shouldn't have, but I *had* to. Don't you get it?"

Owen just stared at her. "No. I don't."

She looked away as Doyle stood up. "Payment accepted," he said. "However, I regret to inform you that I won't be handing over my findings."

"What?" Bethany said, pushing past Owen. "But I paid you! I did exactly what you asked!"

Doyle hit a button on his desk, and the door opened behind them. Guards flooded into the room, one grabbing Kiel and another grabbing Owen. Bethany, though, they left free.

"That you did," Doyle said. "But you're a *thief*, Bethany Sanderson. You steal from books, you trespass in stories that aren't your own, and you just paid me in stolen property. I can't encourage that, now, can I?"

296

"Let them go!" Bethany shouted, moving toward Doyle. Was she going to jump him out and leave the two of them behind? Owen tried to free himself, but he couldn't even budge in the guard's strong grip.

"Ah-ah," Doyle said to Bethany, and the guards holding Owen and Kiel began squeezing. Owen shouted in pain, while Kiel gritted his teeth. "Touch me, and your friends suffer. Now, let's discuss your punishment for your crimes."

"Punish me, but let them go," Bethany said, practically begging the detective. "They didn't do anything wrong!"

"Of course they did," Doyle snapped. "Owen stole Kiel's story. And Kiel was a thief for half of his life. *All of you* will be punished."

What? How did Doyle know all about them?

"Jump out, Bethany!" Kiel shouted. "Don't worry about us!"

"Worry about us a *little*!" Owen said. If she left them behind, Doyle might hide them somewhere. They might be stuck in the book forever!

Bethany turned to look at them and shook her head sadly. "I did this. This is my fault. I'm not going to just leave you two to pay for it."

"Remove her," Doyle told the guards, and they stepped

forward to grab Bethany by her shoulders. Kiel struggled again, but the guard just held him tight enough to make the magician groan in pain.

"I'm not leaving without you two," Bethany said as she passed between them, her eyes watering. "I *promise*."

And then she was gone, the doors slamming behind her.

"And now, Kiel," Doyle said, "you're going to do a little magic."

Magic? What was Doyle talking about?

"Gladly," Kiel said. "Let me go and I'll be happy to turn you into a toad and squish you."

Doyle sighed. "How charming. No, you're going to use your magic on yourself and Owen. You're going to wipe your memories, all the way back to when you first moved to the nonfictional world, Kiel. All of those memories were made by breaking the rules, and I don't intend to let you keep stolen property."

Owen gasped. He couldn't be serious. Their memories? "And why exactly would I do such a thing?" Kiel asked.

Doyle nodded at the guard holding Owen, and the guard squeezed until Owen almost burst. "And worse will happen to Bethany," Doyle said.

Pain filled Owen's head and he screamed, so he barely

heard Kiel yell for Doyle to stop. "I'll do it!" Kiel shouted. "Let him go!"

The guard stopped squeezing, and Owen would have collapsed to the ground if the enormous man hadn't still been holding him. "Perfect," Doyle said, then paused. "I shouldn't do this. I shouldn't gloat. It's not becoming. But I can't help it. You have to know. And besides, you won't remember any of this."

He gestured, and the guards holding Kiel and Owen both let go, then left the room. Owen, barely holding his feet, looked at Kiel. Should they attack?

Kiel barely shook his head. He was right. Doyle still had Bethany, and who knew what he'd do to her.

"You won't appreciate this right now," the detective said, his hands on his mask. "But trust me, I'm enjoying it enough for all of us."

And with that, he pulled his mask off, and Owen found himself looking in a mirror.

What? Was that . . . him? Was this some kind of evil weird future time travel thing? "Please tell me you're not my future self," Owen said, practically begging.

"Oh, I'm you," his other self said. "Just your fictional self. Impressed?"

Impressed? Owen could barely breathe! What was happening?

"How is this possible?" Kiel said, sounding as shocked as Owen felt.

"Life's a mystery, I suppose," Owen/Doyle said, putting his mask back on. "Now it's time for you two to forget." He held up a small button on a thin box. "If you say any spell other than the forget spell, or aim your wands at anyone besides yourself and Owen, then I push this button. You don't want me to push this button. *Bethany* doesn't want me to push this button."

Kiel gritted his teeth. "I'll find her. Her *and* you. And I'll make you pay for this."

Owen/Doyle shook his head. "No, actually, I don't believe you will. You're not the hero anymore, Kiel. Not this time. This story is *mine*, from start to finish. But you won't have to worry about that, not anymore."

Kiel gave Owen/Doyle a look of pure hatred, then turned to Owen, his wand in his hand. "We'll find her, Owen," he said quietly. "And we'll figure this all out. Trust me." And then he winked.

The wink was the last thing Owen remembered before the spell hit. The magic filled Owen's brain, and for some reason

he lost control of his body, dropping to the floor. A familiar face leaned over him.

"Your story is *mine* now," his other self said.

"No!" Owen screamed, but his clone's hands reached for him, and then everything turned into a weird dreamlike fog.

CHAPTER 132

Never wear a mask. That was the lesson of all of this.

"Put him right there, in the chair at the desk," Owen said, trying to suck in air through the stupid question-mark mask. The guards carried Doyle's limp body over to the chair and carefully arranged him in it so he didn't slide off.

"Perfect," Owen said, the mask changing his voice into the deeper, scarier version that he loved. Okay, so that part was awesome. "Now turn off the extra security. I'm going to have some visitors, and I want you to let them right in."

"Mr. Holmes, are you sure?" one of the guards said.

Did he just question a direct order? Owen slowly turned around, doing his best Doyle impression, and stared in the guard's general direction, not sure which had actually spoken. All four guards stared at the floor, silent. "Have I ever been unsure?" Owen said.

"Apologies, Mr. Holmes," one of the guards said, and all four bowed, then left quickly, closing the office door behind them.

Owen quickly pulled the stupid mask off and sucked in air. He hadn't been able to do that downstairs, while explaining everything to his nonfictional self, which had been annoying. But who else would appreciate his grand, complicated, amazing plan if not himself?

Well, he'd appreciate it after he'd calmed down a bit. When he realized how truly for the best it was.

Nowen (as Owen liked to call the nonfictional Owen in his head) couldn't do anything right! Before seeing him fail all over town, Owen had been convinced Nowen would be able to find Bethany instantly. *By the book.* They were in a *library*! What more of a clue did his other self need? Eventually he practically had to slap Nowen in the face with the clue.

Honestly. Other selves could just be such a letdown.

A noise from the desk chair made Owen turn. Doyle was stirring, moaning in pain.

Let's see how *he* liked his mask back.

Owen untied Doyle's gag as the detective tried to lift his head up, looking around in a daze. "Don't worry," Owen told

him, sliding the mask down over his face. "In a minute, this is all going to be just a bad memory."

He could have done this before, of course. There'd been plenty of time since he'd taken Kiel's spell book and wands. But Owen wanted every detail just right for when Bethany and Kiel burst in to find that he, Owen, had just beaten Doyle. And that meant that Doyle had to still be woozy from getting his memory erased.

Taking the wands and shrunken spell book from his Sherlock Holmes coat pocket, he laid them on the desk, then draped the coat over Doyle. Getting the detective's arms into the coat was more annoying than Owen would have thought, but there wasn't a whole lot of choice in the matter.

By the time Owen popped the deerstalker hat above the mask, Doyle was starting to stand.

"You," he said, his whole body shaking as he made it to his feet.

"Yup!" Owen shouted, his grin about as wide as his face. "Sorry about these last few weeks. Really. You didn't do much wrong, other than let me down completely. But like I said, you won't have to remember any of it, so it won't be *so* bad."

"You moronic *pustule* of an excuse for a human being," Doyle said, leaning heavily on his desk. "I will see you locked

in the same cell you put me in for the rest of your days. I will *personally*—"

Then he paused abruptly and collapsed face-first onto the desk.

Owen put down the wand, having cast the memory spell. His eyes wide, he shook his head. "I can't believe I'm giving you guys up," he told the wand and spell book. "Seriously. I want to keep you forever."

Preparing himself, he tossed the wand into the air, caught it, and whirled around, expecting Bethany and Kiel to burst their way in, now that the school was open again.

Nothing happened.

He frowned. How bad exactly was their timing? Hadn't they been waiting at the gates? It couldn't have taken them *that* long to figure out they weren't in Doyle's office, like they thought they'd be when they jumped out of whatever book Owen had carried a page from. Why did they have to mess everything up?

A noise from outside made him stand up straight, and just as he thought the doors would open, Owen tossed Kiel's wand into the air again, then caught it.

No one came in.

What was the problem here? Why weren't they bursting in

already? Were even *they* tired of rescuing Nowen, so taking their sweet time?

Suddenly Owen felt a chill go down his spine. What if they *hadn't* been able to jump out of the unburned pages of that book? What if by setting that page on fire, Owen had actually *trapped* Bethany and Kiel in the book forever?

No, no, no, *no*. That couldn't have happened. He'd been so sure, and it'd been such a cool thing to do in front of Nowen! Sure, it wasn't the safest move, but honestly Nowen had surprised him a bit with the whole Trojan Horse plan. He'd assumed that all three would show up together, and he'd just use Kiel's magic to knock Bethany and Kiel out first, then when they woke up, he'd be the only Owen around, with a newly beaten Doyle. But no, Nowen had improvised and messed everything up.

"Nooooo," Owen whined, tapping his foot in annoyance. "Why does life have to be so hard?"

The doors burst open, and Bethany and Kiel stepped inside, followed by that annoying girl, Moira. Despite getting caught whining, Owen had to admit that their entrance was pretty cool. It was practically in slow motion, it was so awesome. If there'd just been an explosion behind them—

"Owen?" Bethany said, giving him a strange look as Moira closed the door, locking it. "*You* beat Doyle?"

Now *this*, Owen had planned for! He awesomely raised one eyebrow, tossed Kiel's wand up, then caught it. "*Someone* needed to do it. And it might as well have been me."

"Gasp!" Moira said, grinning widely. "Look at how cool my Sad Panda's gotten!"

Bethany flashed her a look, and Moira looked embarrassed, then shut her mouth. Bethany then turned back to Owen. "What did you do to him?"

"I just used Kiel's magic against him," Owen said, shrugging. "No big deal. He took our memories, I took his. It's called quid pro go."

"Not really!" Moira shouted, and got another look from Bethany. What was happening here?

"So he's forgotten everything?" Bethany asked as Kiel slowly stepped closer to Owen. "He doesn't remember me, or what I can do?"

"Not a thing," Owen said. Kiel reached out a hand, and Owen sadly handed over his wands and the spell book, which tried to bite both of them. Kiel shushed it, then began leafing through the book. Bethany watched him until he nodded, then sighed.

"Now," she said.

"Now?" Owen said, raising his other eyebrow.

"Now," said a familiar voice from right in front of him.

And then something punched Owen right in the face, so hard in the face that he spun around to land on the desk, staring right at the question-mark mask. He quickly looked over his shoulder. "Who did that?" he shouted.

"Just me," said the same voice, and from out of thin air, a zipper appeared, then pulled down, revealing a very, *very* angry Nowen.

"I can't believe you didn't figure it out, *Fowen*," his non-fictional self said. "Guess who's here to take his *life* back?"

CHAPTER 39

Thirty minutes earlier . . .

*T*hese kinds of stories always need a double twist," Owen said. "The plan has to look like it's failing, while actually going exactly how you intended it to go."

Owen walked up to the gate of the Baker Street School, holding an envelope with a book page in it.

At his side Bethany, Kiel, and Moira stood waiting in silence, all wearing heat-masking invisibility suits from *Alpha Predator*.

Owen reached out and pushed the intercom button.

"*Doyle thinks he knows everything,*" Owen said. "*So let's let him think that. Let's give him a trick to see right through. Something just a step below obvious, so he can think we really thought we were getting away with something. He thinks we're that stupid anyway, so let's just confirm it.*"

Doyle threw the envelope into the fire, and Owen, acting like he was truly horrified, leaped after it. Doyle tripped him, and through the suit's special goggles Bethany saw Kiel start forward, but she grabbed his arm and held him back. It wasn't time yet. Doyle hadn't opened his safe, and they still needed Kiel's wands and spell book. She watched as Doyle cruelly pulled Owen's arms behind his back.

Just one more thing he was going to pay for.

"All we have to do is let him beat us," Owen said. *"Here's the idea. I take a page from some random book and hide it in an envelope. I'll tell Doyle that the envelope has, I don't know, terms of surrender or something, from Bethany. But it's going to look like I'm smuggling you in, like a Trojan horse. And that at the right moment, you're going to jump out."*

"So let me see if I have the plan correct," Doyle said. "You come in, ostensibly surrendering, but carrying a page from a book that Bethany and friends are hiding within. At a designated time, right now, it sounds like, Bethany jumps out of that page to take me by surprise, bypassing all of my security in one swoop. Do I have it correct?"

"But instead, you're wearing the invisibility suits the whole time," Owen continued. *"But it's not about just getting you guys*

310

inside. It's about making Doyle think he's won, so he starts doing stupid things, like revealing his entire plan, and hopefully opening his safe."

"Don't be so melodramatic," Doyle said, using a poker to stir up the ashes from the book page. "It's not like they're trapped in that story. If they jump out now, they'll just end up back with the rest of the book."

Bethany narrowed her eyes. Was he right? Would they have been able to just jump back out of the other pages? Possibly, she guessed, but there was no way Doyle knew that for sure. Basically he'd just risked trapping them forever in that book, and that was something *else* he'd pay for.

Doyle bragged some more, and Bethany wanted to punch him. Open the safe, already! Show them how smart you were, and how little you had to worry about!

"Thought we'd get Kiel's wands and spell book off of you and then make you forget any of this ever happened," Owen told him, and Bethany grinned. That was genius of him, bringing that up. But would Doyle take the bait?

Doyle snorted beneath the mask. "You never had a chance, Mr. Conners. None of you did. I was two steps ahead of you this entire time. Three or four, for most of it."

And then he did exactly what they all hoped he'd do. He revealed the safe, and began opening it.

"This is the part I'm most worried about," Owen said. *"He's going to really have to think he's beaten us here, or there's no way he's just going to open his safe. It's like his most guarded secret. I'm going to have to be as convincing as possible that he just utterly destroyed us here."*

"And before you move, you might want to consider that countdown band on your wrist," Doyle said, his eyes on the combination locks. "Every student at the Baker Street School wears one. Most of the time it's just a watch, but within the school grounds it also works as a deterrent. Try to leave the school or act up in any way, and you'll be twitching on the ground in seconds."

Uh-oh. *That* wasn't part of the plan. She and Kiel looked down at the bands still on their wrists. But what if they just pulled them off?

Before Bethany could move, Owen touched his band, then began twitching and jerking, collapsing to the floor. She gasped, but the sound was covered by Owen's painful flailing, and this time Kiel held *her* back.

Doyle. Would. *Pay.*

As Owen writhed in pain, Doyle pulled Kiel's wands and spell book out of the safe. "Beautiful, aren't they?" he said. "I know they shouldn't exist, and that as a man of science I should reject them outright, but I simply can't put them down." The spell book tried to bite his head, but Doyle smacked it hard against the desk, and the book started whimpering.

"If he does reveal the spell book and wands, then we have him," Owen said. *"You guys just jump him invisibly, Kiel gets his magic back, and we wipe Doyle's memory for good. Done and done!"*

This was all getting to be too much. Bethany moved around behind Doyle, ready to grab him as Kiel silently got into place at her side, waiting for her signal. She nodded at him, then held up three fingers. Three . . . two . . .

"Come, let me show you something," Doyle said, and walked out of the office.

Owen got up and glanced at the safe, where Moira was standing, just as it closed, all fourteen locks whirring. Kiel and Bethany quickly followed Fowen and Owen, while Moira jogged to catch up. "Got you a present from the safe," she whispered to Bethany. "You're *welcome!*"

Great. What had she stolen now?

Doyle led them all into an elevator, where Kiel seemed ready

to jump the detective, but Bethany shook her head. It was way too close a space. If they attacked now, they'd probably end up hitting each other and Owen as much as Doyle. Instead, the three of them flattened against the side walls in order to avoid touching Doyle or even Owen by accident, not wanting to startle him.

For a moment Owen looked right through Bethany at some articles on the wall behind her, which was eerie. But then Doyle started going on about how Bethany had ruined his family's reputation, and Owen played for time, trying to get details out of Doyle as much as possible.

In spite of the danger, Bethany couldn't help feeling proud of Owen. This was his plan, and he was doing everything right.

"If things go wrong, then we can improvise," Owen said. "But don't worry about me. Doyle's going to think of me as bait, so he won't do anything too bad to me. Just stay with us, and I'll try to get whatever I can out of him, no matter what."

Owen kept Doyle talking, though the detective seemed to think that revealing his plan painfully slowly was the only way to go. Finally, they came to a cell at the end of a long hallway, too shadowy to see into. Moira gleefully bounded forward and stared through the bars as Doyle beckoned Owen forward.

"I need you to see this," Doyle said. "I need you to under-stand what I've done."

Moira turned around, and even through her goggles Bethany could see her eyes were huge. What had she seen? She looked from Doyle to the cell and back, then quickly pulled Bethany and Kiel away.

"Something's wrong," she whispered. "There's a boy in that cell, and something's very wrong."

"This can't be," Owen said as he looked into the cell himself as Doyle backed away.

"Meet Doyle Holmes, Mr. Conners," said the boy in the mask. "I'm sure he'd like to introduce himself, but he's far too smart for me to take off that gag while I'm not wearing ear-plugs. I hate when he deduces strange things about me. It's creepy."

What? Doyle was in the cell? Then who was . . .

Doyle took off his mask, and Bethany wanted to scream.

Owen? The fictional Owen?!

Fowen proceeded to electrocute both the real Doyle and Owen, insulting Owen the entire time. Bethany's hands curled into fists, and she desperately wanted to attack, but this time Moira barred both Bethany's and Kiel's way. "This isn't what we

thought," she whispered. "We need to know what he's doing."

"Magistering her?" Fowen said. "Yup. I was stealing her power, little by little. Took me a few minutes to locate the spell the Magister used in *Story Thieves*, but I found it and stole some of her power just like he did. I haven't tried it just yet, but I can't wait to!" Fowen looked straight up and sighed. "Can you imagine where I'm going to go? Fantasy lands, space, the past, the future, shrink down to the size of nothing . . . so many options."

Bethany surged forward, but again Moira held her back. "Not yet," she hissed at Bethany.

"That's right!" Fowen shouted. "I'm taking over, Owen. I'm stealing your story. I'm going to be you, and you're staying here. Haven't you always wanted to live in a fictional world?"

And there it was. The reason for all of this. Fictional Owen just wanted to have an adventure, so he'd written his own story for them to act out, for them to play the parts of victims, so he could be the hero.

Fowen dragged Doyle's unconscious body down the hall-way, saying something about how the author of *Story Thieves* was some nobody. Kiel looked at Bethany, ready to attack, but Bethany held up a hand to wait.

So Fowen wanted to play the hero, huh? Well, they were going to let him.

"Moira, open that cell," Bethany said. "Kiel, give Owen the extra suit. We're going to go let Fowen have his win and be the hero. And then we're going to *tear his story apart.*"

T his can't be happening!" Fowen shouted. "You're messing up the whole story!"

"Apparently, that's what I do," Owen said, standing over his other self, trying to stay calm. After everything Fowen had done, all Owen felt like doing was hitting. Hitting and hitting and *more* hitting. "Now you're going to give up, and Kiel's going to wipe *your* memory."

Fowen glared at him, then snorted. "Not likely." He reached into a pocket and pulled out a small button, then pushed it over and over.

Immediately Owen, Kiel, Bethany, and Moira all collapsed to the ground, writhing in pain as electricity shot through the bands on their wrists.

Fowen wiped the back of his arm over his mouth, then stood up to his full height. "You really are the worst Owen, you know,"

he said to Owen, then kicked him. "This wasn't personal before. You could have just let me have your life. I rearranged *my* entire life for you, making it exciting and awesome. I built an entire mystery out of boringness, out of my regular everyday world. And you reject it?" He kicked him again. "No! You don't get to mess up *this* story, Nowen."

Owen tried to move, to think, to do anything, but the shock jolting his system wouldn't stop, and he kept jerking around on the floor as Fowen stepped over him.

"I'll be taking these back, then," Fowen said, grabbing Kiel's spell book and wands from the floor. "You all think you won. But I'm the one telling this story. And I say that if it doesn't end how I want it to, then we *start all over.*"

He opened the spell book to the forget spell page and held up a wand. "Don't worry," Fowen told them. "You won't remember any of this happening. We'll start from scratch, and this time, I'll know how Nowen's going to try to mess this up. We'll just keep going until it ends the right way. *My* way."

"No," Kiel groaned, but through the pain, Owen saw the spell fill Fowen with an unearthly light as he aimed a wand at Bethany.

And then, out of nowhere, the electricity stopped. And

though Owen's muscles still jerked out of his control, suddenly he could think again.

"What?" Fowen said, and jammed a hand into his pocket, then pulled it out empty. "Where did the button go?!"

"Someone didn't pay attention to the clues," said a voice behind him. Fowen whirled around to find Moira tossing the button into the air and catching it. "First, you should have remembered that I never had one of those wristbands. That was clue number *one*." She grinned, then threw the button as hard as she could into the wall, where it split into pieces.

All of their wristbands immediately unlocked and fell to the floor. Fowen gasped, turning his wand on Moira.

"Clue number two is that I'm smart enough to know when to act," Moira said, pulling out her Taser and zapping it a few times, sending electricity shooting out the top. "And clue number three? I'm a criminal genius. I could have picked your pocket before I knew how to walk."

Fowen began chanting, and Moira leaped for him, her Taser sparking.

But she was just a bit too far away.

The forget spell slammed into Moira face-first, and Owen could see the awareness of where she was disappearing from

her eyes as she fell to the floor unconscious, just inches away from Fowen.

"You never belonged here anyway," Fowen spat at her, frantically trying to find the forget spell again in the spell book, since each spell could only be cast once before you had to relearn it.

Owen heard Kiel muttering words, but he couldn't make them out. Abruptly, though, the spell book began to grow in Fowen's hands. He dropped the book in surprise, but the spell book stayed exactly where it was in midair, getting bigger and bigger until it was almost the size of Fowen. It roared at the fictional boy, and Fowen screamed, running behind the desk to hide.

The enormous spell book turned toward Kiel and roared again, then picked up Kiel's wands in its pages and disappeared completely.

"What was *that*?" Fowen shouted. "What did you do?!"

"Set . . . it . . . free," Kiel said, slowly pushing himself off the floor. "Won't . . . let you . . . *have it*!"

Fowen gasped, his eyes wide in surprise. "Set it free? It's a book! You can't set a book free! Get it back here!"

"The magic's . . . gone, Fowen," Kiel said, just about at his feet. "Your story ends . . . now."

"You're going to get that book *back* for me," Fowen said, grabbing Moira's Taser and advancing on Kiel. "I don't care what it takes. I'm going to have that magic, and I'm going to redo this story until I'm the one living Owen's life. Me! I deserve this. I've waited my entire life to be the hero, and I made it happen. All it took was becoming the villain for a bit, but that's a small price to pay. Give me the life I deserve!"

Owen slowly pushed himself to his feet, his muscles beginning to actually listen to him again. Across the room Bethany was doing the same as Fowen advanced on Kiel.

"It's not coming back," Kiel told him, circling around Fowen just out of reach of the Taser. "And that was the only one I had. You're now just as magicless as the day you were born."

"Stop acting like you've won!" Fowen shouted, sparks shooting out of the Taser. "You don't get to win. This was *my* plan. I deserve Nowen's life, not him! He's wasting it. He's not good enough at it. I'd be the best Owen ever!"

Bethany kicked him in the back of the knees, and Fowen dropped to the floor, the Taser flying from his hands.

"That's what you don't get," Bethany said, standing over him. "Owen *is* Owen. No one gets to tell him how to live his life. Not you, not me, and not some author nobody. Owen gets

to choose how his life story goes, and no one, let alone his idiot fictional self, gets to take that away from him."

"I think he's doing okay," Kiel said. "He won here, didn't he?"

"Because he had help!" Fowen shouted, quickly crawling away back toward the desk. "He couldn't have done any of this without his friends."

Owen took a slightly shaky step forward. "You're totally right," he said, trying to ignore the ache in his muscles. "I'm only here because of my friends. Just think what you might have done if you'd tried to be friends with them too, instead of manipulating them."

Bethany turned to Kiel. "We need to make him forget. Can you still do that?"

Kiel looked at her sadly. "No, I meant what I told Fowen. The spell book is gone." He paused, looking away. "I . . . I won't be doing magic anymore."

Owen tried to think of something to say to Kiel to help, but he realized now was probably not the time. "Then what do we do with Fowen?" he asked. "We can't just leave him here like this. He knows everything. And he's still got some of your power, Bethany."

"Oh, you're not going to do anything with me," Fowen said,

then ran between them, knocking Bethany and Kiel off their still-shaky feet. He barreled into Owen, pushing him hard into the wall, then stopped behind the desk and grabbed a book. "I *do* still have your power, Bethany," he said, practically spitting. "And there's always another way to take what should be mine."

And with that, he opened the book on the table to a specific page, then jumped in headfirst.

"No!" Owen shouted, and moved over to the desk as quickly as he could on his aching legs. He grabbed the book before the page could be lost, then gasped.

"This is bad," he said quietly. "Very, *very* bad."

"What book is it?" Bethany asked.

Owen held it up, not saying a word, and showed her the cover of a redheaded girl and a boy in a black cape jumping into a book. "It's *our* book," he said quietly. "It's *Story Thieves*."

Bethany stared at him for a moment, then nodded. "Hold it open," she said.

"What?" Owen said, just as she ran straight at him. He opened the book wide in front of him, and Bethany dove right in.

The Amazing (But True!) Adventures of Owen Conners, the Unknown Chosen One

CHAPTER 134

As her fingers touched the page, they melted and re-formed, becoming various words like "knuckles" and "fingernail" and "thumb," all describing whatever part they'd been. Those words then spread over the page like brownie batter, absorbing right into the book. Finally, she just shoved her arm in up to her shoulder.

"I'm wriggling my fingers at you right now in Wonderland," she told him.

Owen laughed oddly, then made a weird face and fell backward to the floor, unconscious.

Bethany sighed, shaking her head. "Alien invasions and rocking-horse-flies are fine, but *this* you faint at?"

Owen watched Bethany nervously look around, wishing he could electrocute her some more. But instead, she just gave his

nonfictional, unconscious self an apologetic look, then ran off into the library.

"Owen?" his mom said from the front. "Are you almost done?"

Owen stepped out from behind some shelves, staring at Nowen on the ground. "Oh, not going to answer your mom?" he whispered. "Guess I'll help you out, just this once." Then louder, "Give me, like, two minutes, Mom!"

"Don't think I forgot about your homework!" his mom shouted back. "I'll be done soon, so get to it!"

Owen nodded, then looked around for an appropriate book. His eyes settled on one, and he grinned. "Don't like mysteries, huh?" he said, opening the book. "Guess you won't enjoy your time in this one, then."

And with that, he took the book and ran it over Nowen's unconscious body, using Bethany's power to send Nowen into the pages. Then, with his other self gone, he cleaned up the children's section a bit, and went back to the front of the library.

He had homework to do, after all.

Later that night, lying in a bedroom that looked creepily familiar, Owen ran through the next day. He couldn't remember everything his other self had said in the next chapter, but

that was okay. He'd get close enough. And as soon as *he* met Bethany, he'd be the only Owen she ever knew about.

Story officially stolen.

He turned over in bed, a contented look on his face. Sure, he might end up jeopardizing all of existence with some sort of time travel paradox, but that was the risk you took. And if reality *did* fall apart, then wasn't it really Bethany and Nowen's fault? He'd tried to take over Nowen's life in the present, but *noooooo*. They had to insist he take the riskier approach.

The only truly horrible part was that he could never tell them how badly he'd beaten them. He closed his eyes, drifting off to sleep, imagining how it'd go.

"You did what?" Bethany would say.

"I'm actually the Owen from the fictional world," he'd tell her, bragging. "I completely stole nonfictional Owen's story out from under him. You had no idea!"

"Ha-ha," she'd laugh. "You're so smart!"

"I sure am," he'd say.

The daydream was so nice that it was all the more jarring when his eyes flew open. What was *that*?

Had something just . . . skittered across the floor?

Owen slowly sat up in bed, trying to see something in the

dark bedroom. The curtains shut out even the moonlight, though, and all he could make out were dark shapes. There was his desk, and his bookshelves overflowing with broken books missing their covers, and—

Wait, *something just moved*!

"Hello?" he said quietly, flailing a hand for his light, not taking his eyes off the spot where he'd seen . . . whatever. "Is someone there?"

Nothing answered, but on his other side, he heard the skittering again.

"Hello?" he said again, his voice barely above a squeak.

"Little boy," said a high-pitched voice. "You've been baaaaaaaaad."

Owen's eyes widened, and he frantically pawed at the lamp, trying to turn it on, only to knock it to the ground. He almost screamed in frustration and fright, but instead dove after it, desperate to turn it on, his body hanging over the side of his bed.

His fingers closed around the lamp's knob, and he switched it on, light flooding the room.

Upside down, Owen looked beneath his bed to the other side. There he saw two red shoes about the size of doll's feet. And

then slowly, ever so slowly, something on the other side of the bed bent down.

It was a doll. A clown doll.

A clown doll with teeth that smiled at him.

"Little boYYYYyyyy," it said, "I've COOOOME for you . . ."

Owen started to scream for all he was worth, only to have an enormous book come out of nowhere and slam into his head. He instantly crashed to the ground, falling the rest of the way off the bed, and watched in horror as the clown doll came skittering at him.

"Bad boys get EEEATEN!" the clown said, and Owen covered his eyes in terror.

But nothing happened.

Finally, he opened his eyes one by one and found something even worse than a clown doll standing over him.

Bethany dropped an enormous book of horror stories right onto his stomach, knocking the air out of him. As Owen struggled to breathe, she bent down and smiled. "Welcome to every night for the rest of your life," she whispered to him. "I know where you live, Fowen. And I know what you've done. I don't care how much it changes my story, my past, none of it. I will make sure you *pay* each and every night for the rest of

329

your life. You'll never get a wink of sleep. Every time you close your eyes, I'll be there. And there's a whole horror section in the library, with new books coming in all the time."

"No," he moaned, covering his eyes again. "No, *please.*"

"Where's my Owen?" Bethany asked him.

He opened his eyes again. "*I'm* your Owen. . . ."

Bethany grabbed the horror book and began leafing through its pages. "Oooh, ghosts. I'll probably have a harder time getting those out before they drive you insane, since they're so hard to touch and all. Want to try?"

"He's in there!" Fowen shouted, pointing at a book on his shelf. "I swear, he's in there. Just grab him from page four, he won't have been in too long if you take him from there."

Bethany glanced at the book, then glared at Fowen. Without pausing, she reached her head and hand into the book, then pulled her head back out and walked the book over to Owen's bed. There she pulled her arm out and gently ran the book down the length of the bed, spilling a still fainted Nowen out onto his bed.

"He wakes up there in the next chapter," Fowen told her, still squeaking a bit. "I didn't even change the book. Please . . . no more!"

"Sorry, Fowen," Bethany said. "You know too much, and now there are no forget spells to take care of that. You're going into the horror book!"

"No, please!"

"It's either that, or this one," she said, holding up the book he'd stuck Nowen in. "You put your other self in there, it's only fair."

Owen glanced between the two books for a second, then sighed, tapping the second one.

"Good choice," Bethany said. "Now, I know you can jump out on your own until my powers you stole wear off, so I just want to warn you: I see that cover lift even an inch, and you're clown food. We understand each other?"

Owen nodded sadly and held out his hand.

"And just so you know," she said, shoving him into the book, "you're the worst Owen *ever*."

S o what now?" Bethany asked as she, Kiel, and Owen stood in Doyle's office.

Owen shook his head. What *did* they do now? So much had just happened that he could barely take it all in. Fowen was trapped in a book, which Bethany held close to her, ready to grab him if he tried escaping. It'd only be a day or so before his power ran out, though, and then he'd just be stuck there.

"We should tell Fowen's mother where he is," Kiel said.

Owen shook his head, walking over to the still-unconscious Doyle. "I think I have a better idea." He pulled the mask off and saw the voice changer inside. "Let me make a quick phone call."

Two minutes later Inspector Brown had been informed by "Doyle" that Owen Conners would now be attending the Baker Street School for Irregular Children to be rehabilitated over setting fire to his mother's library. Inspector Brown prom-

ised to inform Fowen's mother, and thanked "Doyle" for taking care of all of this. Owen then buzzed a guard and asked to have Fowen's cat, Spike, brought up from wherever he'd hidden him.

He might be Fowen's, but his other self had been right about one thing: It wasn't the cat's fault that his owner was evil. And Owen wasn't going to just leave the cat here.

While Owen retrieved the cat in his carrier from the guard, Kiel and Bethany stood over Moira.

"What about her?" Kiel asked. "She won't remember anything she's done here."

"No, she won't," Bethany said. "But we still owe her. I'll take care of it. We'll bring her back with us." She bent down to grab the hand of the unconscious criminal genius, then paused. "What's this?"

A curled-up piece of paper stuck out of Moira's back pocket. Bethany pulled it out and unrolled it, then went deathly white.

"It's from Doyle's file," she said, her voice barely above a whisper. "The one on my dad."

Kiel and Owen both kneeled down next to her, watching in silence as she read it. Finally, she began shaking, and dropped the paper. She immediately threw her arms around Kiel and shoved her face into his shoulder, her back heaving.

333

Owen picked up the paper and quickly read it. Doyle had actually been fairly thorough, investigating pretty much the entire fictional real world. And at the bottom in bold was his conclusion.

Client's father is presumed dead. There is no record nor trace of him anywhere. Case closed.

A few minutes went by in silence, with Bethany crying into Kiel's shoulder, and Kiel hugging her close. Finally, she pulled away, sniffing loudly and wiping her face on her sleeve. "Let's get out of here," she said. "I never want to see this place again."

"Agreed," Kiel said, not looking much happier than Bethany.

"I can't believe you did that," Owen told him, taking Bethany's hand. "You gave up all your magic to save us. I don't even know what to say."

Kiel nodded. "I suppose I could always find a new master and go through the trial of wills and courage to bind a new book to my service." He shrugged. "Right now, I just want to sleep."

"Me too," Bethany said quietly, then took Kiel's hand. Together, Kiel and Owen grabbed both of Moira's hands,

with Owen's other hand on the cat carrier, Fowen's terrified cat watching them all with fright. And then Bethany jumped them all out of the book.

"Moira, you're still asleep?" someone yelled. Moira's eyes flew open, and she immediately sat up in bed. Wait, she was asleep? Hadn't she just been somewhere else? Somewhere more incredibly fun?

Her father stood over her, shaking his head. "Promising to be good includes being on time to school, kiddo."

"I'm up," she said, stifling a yawn as her eyelids slid closed again. So tired. So very, very tired. What had she been doing all night?

"By the way, this came for you," her father said, and she felt something light hit her in the lap. She made a face and opened her eyes to find a letter from some school. "Looks like I'm not the only one keeping an eye on you."

Moira glanced at the letter, suddenly feeling more awake. The Baker Street School for Irregular Children? That was the place all the teenage criminals were so afraid of being sent off to. She wrinkled her nose. How bad could a boarding school really be, though?

"I'll pass," she said, handing the letter back to her father as she slid out of bed. She kissed his cheek, then went to her closet to find some clothes for school.

Her father grunted. "Just keep your promise and neither of us will have to worry about this," he said, pointing at the envelope. "You *have* been good, right?"

"*Dad,*" Moira said, her hand on the closet doorknob. "It's me! Of *course* I've been good. Angel-like, even! Future civilizations will mark this moment as the goodest anyone's ever been. In fact, I've been *better* than good. I've been *best!*"

Her dad gave her a suspicious look for a moment, then smiled despite himself. "Get dressed, I'll make breakfast." With that, he left her room, closing the door behind him.

The Baker Street School. Moira rolled her eyes. Like she'd ever get caught doing something bad enough to get sent *there*.

She opened her closet door . . . and found herself staring at ten overflowing bags of gold coins.

Huh.

Moira reached quietly out and closed the closet door, her hands shaking both from excitement and panic. Not getting caught was suddenly going to be a *lot* more interesting.

CHAPTER 42

Owen didn't see Kiel or Bethany for a week after returning home, apart from school. After everything that had happened, none of them even brought it up. They all needed a chance to breathe and to decide exactly how to feel about everything that had happened.

Finally, Bethany tossed a note at Owen in Mr. Barberry's class, and Owen saw one hit Kiel, too.

Library tonight?
—B

Owen crumpled up the note and gave the slightest nod back to Bethany. Even knowing it wouldn't happen for hours, his palms began to sweat. He had so much to say, but it all just made him so nervous. Would he really be able to go through with it?

For the rest of the school day, Owen avoided looking at either Kiel or Bethany, not wanting them to see how anxious he was. That wasn't really fair to them, not after everything they'd been through.

Working at the library that night before it closed, Owen wandered around the shelves, looking at all the different books they'd visited. The Narnia books, Sherlock Holmes, and so many more. Finally, he took down *Kiel Gnomenfoot and the Source of Magic* and flipped through, going straight to the end as he usually did.

Reading about Charm just made everything better.

Finally, time came for the library to close, and he walked back to his house with his mother, carrying a pile of books that were too broken to keep lending out, so were destined for the book graveyard in Owen's bedroom.

"Don't read those all tonight," his mother warned him. "I saw that you didn't do any homework at the library, so that gets done first."

"I know," Owen said, thinking for the first time that home-work might actually be a good distraction.

Needless to say, it wasn't, and was just as horrible as every other time he'd done homework. *Some* things, at least, didn't change.

Eventually his mother turned off her light long after Owen had pretended to go to sleep himself, his new cat, Spike, lying on his chest. Either Spike thought Owen was Fowen, or the cat had decided Owen was close enough, as he followed Owen around everywhere.

A fictional cat now lived in his house. That went well with his robotic heart.

Owen gave his mother another hour to fall asleep, just lying in his bed and petting Spike, wondering how Bethany and Kiel were going to take things tonight.

Several times during that hour, he considered not going. It could wait, after all. But getting it over with seemed like the smarter thing to do, and didn't he owe them the truth, at least?

In his mind, Fowen mocked him. "You're so useless, you're scared to tell your friends what you're thinking," he said, giving Owen a disgusted look.

"Don't listen to him," said a different voice in Owen's head, and Charm's robot hand exploded out of her arm, punching Fowen right in the face. "You'll always be the best Kiel ever, Owen." Then she sighed. "But I'm not real. I'm just you telling yourself these things, so maybe don't listen to me."

Owen shook the daydream out of his head, sighed, and got up.

It was time. Probably past time. He'd be late if he didn't hurry.

He *didn't* hurry. In fact, he was even later than he'd thought he'd be.

Kiel and Bethany were both waiting inside, having used the keys Owen had given them months ago. Neither one was speaking when he walked in, and for a second he wondered if they were nervous about tonight too.

Then Kiel winked, and Owen immediately felt better. Whatever funk had come over Kiel during their time in *The Baker Street School for Irregular Children* seemed to have disappeared, so that was good news.

"Sorry I'm late," Owen mumbled, taking his seat at their usual table. "What's the plan tonight? Back into looking for your father, or just having fun?"

Bethany didn't look at him. "Neither. I have something to tell you both."

"Me too," Owen said quietly.

"I do, as well," Kiel said. "But you two can go first."

Bethany glanced up at both of them, and shook her head. "No no, you go."

Kiel waved her on. "I insist."

They continued doing this for another few seconds until

Owen slapped the table. "I'll go first," he said, not looking at either of them. "I just wanted to tell you both that . . . I'm done. I'm done with all of this. I'm not jumping into books anymore. We're messing with a whole other world, and I just can't take it anymore."

Kiel and Bethany both went absolutely silent, and Owen could actually hear his heart beating in his ears. Granted, it was going a mile a minute, but still. Finally, he looked up at both of them.

Weirdly, neither looked surprised.

"I'm finished as well," Kiel said. "It's time I went back home." He sighed. "I don't know who I am anymore. Without my magic, what am I? Fowen was right about that, at least. I need to find what life has in store for me now, and I think the place to start is back where I belong." He looked up at Bethany. "I came here tonight to ask you to take me back into my books."

Bethany just stared at him sadly for a moment, then nodded. "I was going to tell you that I had to take you back tonight too, Kiel. Because I'm done *too*, too."

Both Kiel and Owen stared at her in surprise. "But your father!" Owen said.

"Doyle's file was wrong," Kiel told her. "You can't just give up!"

"You know he's out there, Bethany," Owen said. "Doyle couldn't explore *all* the worlds . . ."

"I can't keep letting this make me crazy," she said, staring at the table. "I've been looking for him for, like, half my life, and I'm no closer now than when I started. It's just too big a world, and I've got no leads. But beyond that, *look what I did.* I almost set loose a horrible, evil boy on the entire fictional world." Realizing what she said, she blushed deeply, then gave Owen an embarrassed look. "Sorry. You know what I mean."

"No, he's the worst," Owen said.

"I don't hate *anyone*, and I hated him," Kiel admitted.

"I'm so with you on that!" Bethany said, almost smiling.

"Okay, we get the point," Owen said, trying not to sound as irritated as he felt. "Can we get back to your dad? You're really going to just let it go?"

"I think it's past time," Bethany told him. "It's like Kiel said. I'm not sure I even know who I am without that. I can't just keep living the same story. I have to find my own now."

She went silent, and for a moment no one spoke.

"I was actually thinking about writing, maybe," Owen said.

"About Charm?" Kiel asked, raising an eyebrow.

"*No?*" Owen said, probably a bit too fast to be believable. "I

have some other ideas. Maybe they already exist on some fictional world somewhere, and maybe they don't. But I thought it'd be fun to just see what happened, see where a story in my head goes for a change. Hopefully, I won't mess up too many fictional characters' lives *that* way. Or at least in any way they're not meant to be."

Bethany smiled. "You're definitely going to have to let me read it."

That idea sent a chill down Owen's spine. "Uh, we'll see."

Bethany turned to Kiel, and for a moment it looked like she wanted to say something. Finally, she just shook her head. "When do you want to go back?"

Kiel's face dropped, and he looked more miserable than Owen had ever seen him. "Right now, if that's okay. I'm not sure waiting will help."

Bethany nodded slowly and stood up. "I'll go get the book."

As she walked away, Owen reached out and hugged Kiel, who hugged him right back even harder.

"I'm going to miss you," Owen told him. "You're always going to be my favorite hero."

"You're a true friend, and I couldn't ask for a better one," Kiel said. "You've lived my life, Owen Conners, and that connects

us. Like brothers, only closer. I hope you read of my adventures someday and imagine yourself by my side, as that's what I'll be doing."

Owen sat back, his eyes wide. "That's . . . a good way to say good-bye."

Kiel just winked.

When Bethany returned, Kiel stood up, and together they walked farther back into the library. Owen let them go, giving them a chance to say good-bye by themselves. At one point he thought he heard the book hit the floor, but it was several minutes before Bethany returned, her eyes wet. She didn't bother sitting, instead nodding toward the front door.

"Let's just go," she said. "I don't really want to be here anymore."

Owen nodded and led them outside. As he locked the library door, he glanced up at Bethany, who was crying without any sort of embarrassment now. "You okay?"

She nodded, then shook her head. Owen stood up and hugged her tightly until she let go, then stepped back. "We don't have to jump into books to be friends, you know."

She smiled, sniffing through her tears. "Of course we don't. Our friendship just won't mess up anybody's stories from now

on. Maybe we can just see some movies and do normal things for once."

"Video games too," Owen said.

Bethany laughed at that. "Just no jumping into them."

Owen's eyes widened. "Can you . . . do that?"

Bethany's laugh died, and she gave him a death look. "Owen Conners, do *not* even think about it!"

Bethany sat in her bedroom, collecting all the books she'd accumulated over the years. Some she'd be keeping, like *Goodnight Moon* and *The Little Prince*, just for emergencies. Most, though, she was going to give to Owen for the library.

She didn't need the temptation.

Still, there was *one* last thing she had to do. She still owed someone a thank-you.

The green sun of Argon VI warmed Bethany up as she slowly floated to the ground behind EarthGirl. "Hey," she said quietly, knowing Gwen could hear her from miles away.

EarthGirl turned around faster than the speed of sound and shouted in joy. "Bethany!" She immediately hugged Bethany hard enough to crack a mountain in half. "You're back! Did you find your father?"

"No," Bethany said quickly. "But I did realize I had something that might help *you*."

"Help *me*?" EarthGirl said, giving her a curious look. "But how?"

Bethany took Gwen's hand in hers, smiled, then jumped them both out of the book.

The two of them landed on Bethany's bed, and Bethany turned to the shocked Gwen with a finger over her mouth. Gwen looked like she wanted to scream in surprise, but she just nodded silently.

Bethany went to the door and listened to hear if her mom was still up. She could hear the TV still on downstairs, so Bethany grabbed Gwen's hand and walked her quietly down the stairs, then out into the kitchen.

"You're still up, Beth?" her mom said from the living room at the front of the house.

"Yeah, just going to get a snack and look at the stars for a bit," Bethany said loudly.

"Okay, but only for a minute. You've got school," her mom said.

Bethany started to leave but realized Gwen was staring in the direction of the living room in amazement. Right. Bethany

quietly led her to the door, where they could both see Bethany's mother sitting on their old couch, watching some late-night news show. Gwen's eyes began to water, and Bethany quickly pulled her back into the kitchen, then out the back door into her fenced-in yard and the cool night air.

"This is . . . this is Earth?" Gwen said, one tear slowly sliding down her cheek. "But how?"

"I'm a time traveler, remember?" she said. "I sometimes visit here. That's my . . . my adopted mom. I just thought you'd want to see what your home planet looked like."

Gwen swallowed hard, tears flowing quicker now. "Would . . . would *my* parents—"

"*No,*" Bethany said, probably a little too quickly. "No," she repeated, more gently this time. "This is still a hundred years before your time."

"But . . . but we can save them, then!" Gwen said, gesturing to the houses all around them. "We can save *everyone!*"

Bethany sighed. *Of course* EarthGirl would want to save her planet. Who wouldn't? "It's already happened in your future. If we changed it, then you wouldn't exist to help me save it, you know? It'd be a paradox, and that'd explode the entire universe."

Gwen shook her head. "I don't accept that. There's *always*

a way, Bethany. We just have to find it! You traveled through time, and we both have superpowers—"

"Not here," Bethany pointed out. "Try flying."

Gwen gave her an odd look, then leaped into the air, only to immediately drop back down to the ground. "No green sun?" she said.

"It's yellow, actually," Bethany told her. "I need to take you back now, but I just wanted you to see what Earth was like. It's not much, but I hope it helps."

Gwen reluctantly nodded, then faster than Bethany could react, Gwen threw her arms around her and hugged her tightly. "I can't *begin* to thank you for this," she said. "Not even a little bit."

Bethany nodded, getting choked up herself, then led Gwen back into the house.

"Get some sleep now," Bethany's mom said, and Gwen froze in place.

Bethany looked at her, then gestured for her to go ahead.

"Okay, I will," Gwen said, just loud enough for Bethany's mom to hear.

"Okay, good night then, sweetie," Bethany's mom said, and Gwen almost giggled, even as tears fell down her face.

Bethany quietly walked them both back upstairs, then took Gwen's hand. "Close your eyes," she told EarthGirl, and when she had, Bethany touched the open page of the book and jumped them back to Argon VI.

As the heat of the green sun beat down on them again, Gwen opened her eyes, and floated into the air, twirling slowly in circles. Finally, she hugged herself tightly, then turned to Bethany. "I can never repay you," EarthGirl told her. "Never ever, Bethany. But let me at least show you *my* home here."

"I . . . I need to get back to my own time," Bethany lied. "Got to get to bed. You heard my mom." She smiled.

Gwen nodded. "If you ever want help looking for your father . . . or with anything at all, you don't even need to ask. I'm there. *Always.* We're partners now, like detectives. And partners support each other."

"I think I'm good, actually," Bethany said, looking up at the bright-green sun in the sky. "I don't know why, but all of a sudden . . . I think things will be okay."

UNCHAPTERED

Nobody wrote "The End" in Story Thieves: *The Stolen Chapters*, and placed it on his shelf. While that was taken care of, things were progressing much faster than he'd like, and he needed to be prepared.

And that meant taking another quick trip.

He turned the page, pulling fictional reality apart, then stepped through to what he knew was just another story, but looked like an entirely new world, this one foggy, with cobblestone streets and gas lamps smelling of kerosene. The *clip-clop* of horses alerted him to someone coming, so he quickly created clothes and a face, making himself resemble an average citizen of Victorian England, then stepped out of the street.

It didn't take long for him to find who he was looking for.

A man in a deerstalker hat and brown coat was speaking to a group of children, mostly young ones, but a few a bit older.

Right in the middle was a boy covered in dirt, whispering something into the man's ear. The man dropped some coins in the boy's hand, and the boy quickly burst out of the group as the other children gathered around the man, hoping for more of the same.

Nobody stepped into the way of the boy with the coins and grabbed him by the back of his shirt, pulling him to a stop.

"You would be one of Sherlock Holmes's irregulars, would you not?" he asked quietly.

The boy stopped in the middle of the sidewalk and gave him a suspicious look. "No one here knows that name."

"Neither of us are from around here, are we, Owen Conners," Nobody said, and for just an instant flashed his normal, featureless face at Owen before returning to his Victorian disguise.

"*Nobody,*" the fictional Owen Conners said, his eyes lighting up. "I was wondering when you'd show up!"

"You knew I'd come?" Nobody asked, a hint of a smile playing over his reforming face.

"*Of course,*" Owen said. "I saw you walking away with the Magister's textbook at the end of *Story Thieves*, so of course you'd come for me, too. I mean, it didn't say for sure that it was the Magister's textbook, but it had to be. And that meant I was next!"

"And why would you think I'd do that?" Nobody asked.

Owen just smiled. "We're not in the book right now, are we?"

Nobody looked up, directly at you, the reader, then turned back to Owen and shook his head. "No one can see you."

"Then I think you're not Bethany's father, because you're secretly her enemy," Owen said, whispering in spite of Nobody's assurances. "I think you're putting together a group of her worst enemies to take her down. Like the Avengers or the Justice League or something, only evil."

"And you would want to fight against her, then?" Nobody asked, raising an eyebrow.

"As long as I get to take down my nonfictional self, too," Owen said, his eyes narrowing. "I owe Nowen big time. Him and that idiot, Kiel."

"So you've learned nothing," Nobody said, and reached out to the boy. Owen just watched in confusion as Nobody's hand touched his arm, at which point he screamed. The scream cut off instantly as Owen's mouth closed on itself, while his flailing arms and legs began to retract into his body.

Moments later Nobody held just a small ball in his hand, which he put into his pocket. "Of the two Owens, I thought I'd be doing this to your nonfictional self a lot sooner than to you,"

he said, almost sadly. "You disappointed me, fictional Owen."

With that, he stepped into an alley, then pulled the pages of Victorian England apart, and stepped back into his own library. He deposited the fictional Owen Conners into a jar on a shelf, next to a copy of a math textbook, before sighing.

"Things are happening much too fast, Bethany," he said, staring at the copy of Story Thieves: *The Stolen Chapters*. "You're causing more trouble than I can keep hidden." He sighed, then opened a new, empty book titled Story Thieves: *Secret Origins*, and put his pen onto the first page.

"I suppose there's nothing for it. It's time that you meet your father."

ACKNOWLEDGMENTS

Liesa Abrams Mignogna stared at the pages, wondering what James Riley could be thinking. Was he actually saying that he was a character in the Story Thieves books? Was he crazy? Was this some sort of ego thing, putting himself in a book?

Did he really believe it?

And the acknowledgments page was even stranger than the rest of the book. "He's writing about *me*?" she said, straightening her Batman cape across her shoulders. "Is this . . . a joke?"

Apparently, Acknowledgments-Liesa was thinking the same thing, as "'Is this . . . a joke?' asked Liesa" was right there at the top.

Sometimes being an editor was a lot harder than anyone knew. Especially with *this* author.

"Did you see this?" Liesa said to Emma Sector, her coeditor on the books. "*This* is what I've been dealing with since *Half Upon a Time*."

Emma shook her head. "He's got you going over a list of everyone he's thanking. Look."

Liesa glanced down and saw that Acknowledgments-Liesa was running over a list of who James had thanked: Michael Bourret, his agent; Mara Anastas and Mary Marotta, his publishers; Carolyn Swerdloff, Teresa Ronquillo, Matt Pantoliano, and Lucille Rettino in marketing; Faye Bi, his publicist; Katherine Devendorf in managing editorial; Adam Smith, the copy editor; Sara Berko in production; Laura Lyn DiSiena, who designed the book; Chris Eliopoulos, his interior illustrator, and Vivienne To, his cover artist; Michelle Leo and the education/library team; Christina Pecorale and the rest of the sales team; and Stephanie Voros and the subrights group. All the people who worked really hard, basically to give James the chance to narcissistically insert himself into his own book.

Those poor, poor people, Acknowledgments-Liesa thought.

Real Liesa shook her head, wondering again why she put up with this. Why did *everything* have to be so meta with James? "Can't he do it the easy way, just once?" she murmured. And how was he going to thank his friends and family, his loved ones, if this was all written from her perspective? She shook her head.

Her e-mail beeped, as it did every 1.2 seconds, and she

thankfully turned away from the acknowledgments to look over at her computer.

Except, of course, it was him. It was *always* him.

> Subject: Whoops!
> LIESA!!!!!
> I totally forgot to add in all my friends and family and loved ones! Obviously, I need Corinne in there, like, right at the top of everything. And my parents, who probably still wonder what they did wrong. My family. Everyone who's supported me. The Laird family, Katie, Heather, Mark, and Kim. My readers, ESPECIALLY my readers, who are the greatest, most kindest, wonderfulest people ever.
> Also can we put a thank-you in to J. K. Rowling as if she and I are friends? Something like "and most importantly, thanks to J. K. Rowling (or Jo, as I call her) for all those long talks we had over coffee, where we just laughed together over nothing." That's legal, right?
> James

Liesa banged her head against her desk twice, took a deep breath, then hit reply.

> Subject: Re: Whoops!
> Hey,
> No, that would be sort of odd, since you don't know

her. Speaking of odd, why don't you just maybe write your acknowledgments in a more normal way? Then you don't have to confuse everyone even more, especially right when they're finishing the book.

Speaking of confusing, are you actually trying to say you're Nobody in this book?

The reply came just seconds later.

Subject: Re: Whoops!

;)

"And NOPE!" Liesa shouted, shutting her computer down. "It's OVER! It's just OVER!" She grabbed the acknowledgments, planning on ripping them up, then glanced down at the pages and saw that Acknowledgments-Liesa was doing exactly that too.

"ARRRGH!" she shouted, both in real life and on the page, then collapsed into a heap on her desk, shuddering every few seconds. *Why? Why do I do this?!*

"Writers," Emma said quietly from the doorway as she clicked off the light, then closed Liesa's door. "They really *are* just pure evil."

THE STOLEN CHAPTERS

"We need someone who can do everything," she'd said. "Painting and carpentry and blocked drains and radiators. Can you do everything?"

"Yup," Jonah said. "That window sash's loose, s'gonna rattle in the wind."

20th November 1966

Dear Mum and Dad,

I'm sorry to have been so long in writing, but we've been really busy getting the hotel ready for opening before Christmas. We've pretty much finished now—today we put up a Christmas tree in the reception and that was our last job. Everything looks really beautiful, and our first guests are arriving next week. Last night Annabelle and Peter took me out for dinner to celebrate. We went to a posh restaurant called the Gay Hussar—it serves Hungarian food, which was delicious. We had Champagne to celebrate and they gave me a really beautiful watch.

How are you both? Have the twins gone to sea yet? Is Tom coming home for Christmas? What stage is he at in his degree? I forget. Are Peter and Corey behaving themselves? How is Adam? I'd really love a picture of him. Would you ask Tom to take one while he's home and send it to me?

Has anything interesting happened in Struan lately? I'd love to hear all the news when you have time to write.

Love, Megan

PS I am enclosing a brochure of the hotel so you can see what it looks like.

8th December 1966

Dear Megan,
—Megan could hear her father's voice in his
handwriting, but strangely it was the voice she imagined
him using at the bank rather than at home: measured
and rather formal, as opposed to irritated and
impatient—

Thank you for your letter. It is good to know that your
hotel is up and running. Your employers sound like nice
people. Regarding your celebratory dinner out, the Gay
Hussar is a curious name. The Hussars were light
horsemen in the Hungarian army, dating back to the 15th
century. They were an elite regiment and no doubt had
more to be happy about than the average foot soldier
(hence "gay").
Thank you for sending the brochure of the hotel. It
looks a stylish place. I was interested to see that it is near
the V&A Museum, which is world-famous for its art and
design. Its founding principle was that works of art should
be available to all—quite an advanced idea in its time (the
early 1850s). If it is as close to your hotel as it appears to
be in your brochure, you could easily walk there in your
lunch hour.
We are all well. Your mother is writing to you also and
will no doubt pass on such news as there is.
All the best.

Tuesday

Dear Megan,
—Her mother she saw, rather than heard: her smooth, pale face and large, always anxious eyes, her soft fair hair, so fine that it drifted about her, defying all efforts to pin it down—

It was very nice to hear from you. Your hotel looks expensive. Could you afford to stay there yourself?

Yes, the twins have gone. Their ship is the HMCS St. Laurent and they are on NATO patrol. I don't know where and I don't know if they're enjoying it because they haven't written a single letter. I expected the house to seem very quiet when they left but Peter and Corey make so much noise it hasn't changed much.

There isn't much news. You remember I told you Tom's friend, Robert Thomas, accidentally killed a child on a bike in the summer? It turned out that he was drunk at the time. After the inquest he had some sort of breakdown and didn't go back to university. It was a terrible thing.

Tom is coming on Friday but going back to Toronto straight after Christmas. He has exams quite soon. He's doing a second degree on top of the first one. He always was crazy about planes.

Adam is growing very fast. You will hardly know him when you get home. You still haven't said when that will be. Soon, I hope!

Love, Mum

Did they simply not see her request for a photo of Adam? Or did they see it but couldn't be bothered even to comment, far less to act? She had written to Tom twice herself but of course he hadn't replied. Though maybe he was preoccupied with worry about Robert. That at least would be understandable. She couldn't imagine how you went about comforting someone who had killed a child.

Her parents, though, had no excuse. Why do you keep trying? she asked herself angrily. You're just setting yourself up for more disappointment.

But it was astonishing how much she still missed Adam. It felt wrong, fundamentally wrong, not to know what he looked like.

She was about to throw the envelope away when she saw that her mother had written something on the back. *"A letter has come for you from Cora Manning. I will put it in this envelope. But why has she written to you? Aren't you living with her?"*

You're getting worse, Megan said to her mother inside her head. She checked the envelope: there was nothing in it. Par for the course.

She'd almost forgotten Cora; it was as if she belonged to another place and time. She wondered whether they would ever meet again. It was strange to think someone could have such a huge effect on your life and at the same time vanish from it completely.

On the way to John Lewis on Oxford Street to look at bed linen (they needed a considerable amount and were hoping to do a deal) Megan's eye was caught by a display of tiny cars in the window of a newsagent. She stopped and peered in. The cars were very cute and there were lots of them, including—best of all—a bright red London bus and a shiny black London taxi. Megan turned and went in.

"I'll have those two," she said to the newsagent, not bothering to ask the price. She didn't care about the price, she who was always so careful about money. Each car had its own neat little box with its picture and the word "Matchbox" on it. They were smaller than the Dinky Toys the other boys had had, which in any case had been lost or smashed to bits years ago. She'd never seen the point of giving toys to very small children—they were just as happy playing with a spoon—but this was different; this was for her as much as for Adam.

She imagined her mother unwrapping the cars for him one at a time and exclaiming over them. "These are from Megan, Adam! From your sister, Megan, way over in England! Aren't they cute?" She imagined Adam's grin as he seized them. He would try to eat them—he was nearly two and a half now—but they were too big to swallow and looked sturdy enough to survive, and he would enjoy them more and more as he got older. She would send the bus and taxi now, by airmail, expensive though it would be. All the Christmas presents had gone by surface mail weeks ago but this would be a little something extra. From now on she would send him another every couple of months until he had the whole set. It would be her way of keeping in touch with him.

The night before the Montrose opened for business they had a hotel-warming party and invited people from the press and the AA and the RAC and anyone else they thought might be interesting or useful. There were nibbles from Harrods and Champagne in tall glasses. Megan's job was to circulate and keep people's glasses topped up.

She wore a slim black trouser suit of impeccable cut, a surprise gift from Annabelle and Peter. (She'd been planning to wear a perfectly acceptable black skirt and white blouse.)

"But you gave me the watch!" she'd protested when Annabelle lifted the suit from its layers of tissue paper.

"That was a thank you," Annabelle said. "This is your uniform for when you're front of house, and you shouldn't have to pay for your uniform. And these go with it." She lifted a pair of shiny black stilettos out of a shopping bag, then laughed at Megan's expression. "You don't have to wear them ever again, they're just in honor of the occasion. Try them on, and if they kill you I'll take them back."

When she came downstairs in all her finery just before the first guests arrived Peter did a double-take and said, "Good God, Meg, you're a stunner!"

"She is, isn't she?" Annabelle said. She studied Megan as if she were a newly decorated room still in need of a little something. "I like your hair tied back like that, it's very chic, but I wonder if you should loosen it a bit. Like this." She carefully eased the knot in the fat black ribbon tying Megan's hair back. They were standing in front of the huge mirror in the lounge (another junkshop find). "There. What do you think?"

Megan considered the effect. It softened her face, gentled her firm chin. "It's nice," she admitted, "but it will be all over the place in a few hours."

"The party will be over in a few hours," Annabelle said. Her own hair fell in ravishing curls from a pile on top of her head. She wore a very short, very red dress with shoes to match and would have stopped the traffic in the streets. "How are the shoes?"

"Bearable for a bit, I guess," Megan said, she who had always sworn she would suffer the pain of silly shoes for no one.

So during the evening, when Megan—circulating with the Champagne bottle and smiling politely and explaining that no, she wasn't American she was Canadian, and yes, she was enjoying her stay in England—caught sight of herself in the mirror in the lounge she should have been pleased, but in fact her appearance startled her and made her uneasy. It wasn't her, that elegant girl. Not that she wanted to look like a country hick but she did want to look like herself. Anyone looking at her would think she was one of them, but the minute she opened her mouth they would know that she wasn't and would think she'd been pretending. For the first time since meeting Annabelle and Peter, she felt unsure of herself.

But then, halfway through the evening, she was rescued quite unintentionally by a photographer from the *Evening Standard* who asked her to pose by the fireplace in the lounge and then tried to chat her up. He wore a black leather jacket and had hair like the Beatles, and Megan suspected he spent a lot of time in front of a mirror, like the twins. (They'd spent hours and hours in the bathroom, heads together, slicking back their hair and admiring themselves while various desperate brothers pounded on the bathroom door. Megan had tried confiscating the key so that they could be barged in upon but there was a general riot so she'd had to put it back. Finally, much against her better judgment, because in her view the only thing more pathetic than a vain female was a vain male, she'd put a mirror in their room.)

"What are you doing afterwards?" the photographer asked, taking a shot, moving six inches to the right, crouching down and taking another. "When everyone's gone."

"Going to bed," Megan said.

"Alone?" he said, with blinding predictability, leering at her over his camera.

And all at once Megan felt just fine. The photographer looked exceedingly sophisticated and maybe he was, but at heart he was an idiot, and with the exception of Annabelle and Peter, that probably applied to everyone in the room. Megan knew where she was with idiots; she'd been dealing with them all her life.

=

In later years, when she looked back on her time at the Montrose, Megan had trouble remembering the order of things. The events of the first few months were easy to place—the hotel-warming party, for instance, was immediately followed by her first Christmas in England (spent with Annabelle and Peter and wonderful apart from a phone call home, during which her mother wept and her father almost audibly counted the cost of each second). That was followed by a quiet patch—so quiet that they wondered if the hotel was going to go bust before it had a chance to show the world how good it was—during which Megan made use of her free time to lose her virginity to the Scot named Douglas.

Then came her second English spring, which was remarkable because it was such a contrast to the first. It was still wet, of course, but when the sun did come out London was transformed. Buildings that mere days ago had looked old and grimy suddenly became majestic. Trees burst into flower, covering themselves in great billows of pink blossoms and lolling about in the breeze. After a few weeks the petals loosened their grip and began blowing around like snow and that was more beautiful still; they flowed across the pavements in gentle drifts, then picked themselves up and whirled off again. Small parks ("squares," they were called, though many of them weren't square) sprouted up everywhere, with trees and flower beds and carefully tended grass. They must have been there all along, but somehow she had failed to notice them before. During lunch hours the parks erupted with office workers eating sandwiches and reading books. As soon as it was warm enough—in fact, before it was warm enough—they stripped themselves of every permitted layer of clothing and sprawled on the grass, present-ing their bodies and faces to the sun as if they'd turned into plants themselves.

Megan couldn't recall seeing any of this the previous spring. She must have been blinded by homesickness.

In April business picked up. There were several favorable reviews of the Montrose in the right publications and they were now often full to capacity, which meant that the room Megan had been using was needed for guests, so she moved in to a tiny room on the top floor that they ultimately intended to use as a linen cupboard. Annabelle in particular was distressed about this—"Megan, it's disgraceful! What if someone were to find out that we keep our housekeeper in a linen cupboard! It would be a scandal!" ("Great publicity, though," Peter said. "Maybe I'll leak it to the press.")

But Megan had been adamant. In due course she would have a place of her own but it was early days in her career as housekeeper and she was still doing things for the first time— the first Easter, with its flood of tourists all arriving at the same time and the lobby overflowing with luggage, the first complaint by a guest (noise from the room next door—a tricky one), the first overflowing toilet (Jonah muttering about "wimmin's things" under his breath). She wanted to be on hand to deal with such problems herself.

In any case, as linen cupboards went it was a sizeable one, Buckingham Palace compared to the box room in Lansdown Terrace. It even had a light and a rail to hang her clothes on and shelves where she could put a kettle and a hotplate.

How long had she slept in there? It felt like just a couple of months but it must have been more like a year. She was there when letters from her parents arrived telling her of the suicide of Robert Thomas—she knew that because she remembered holding the thin airmail sheets up to the ceiling light and reading her mother's letter through several times, trying to take it in. She couldn't make it seem real. She'd known Robert quite well, but reading the letter, his death seemed so distant—that part of her life seemed so distant—it was as if he'd existed only in her memory: an idea, not a person. She couldn't feel the horror she should, and that worried her, because it emphasized how far away from home she was, in every sense.

There'd been something else troubling in the letter as well, quite apart from its content. Her mother had always been very good at spelling but she'd written, *"he jumped of the clif down at the gorge."* She'd also failed to sign the letter or even send her love, which was unlike her too. Maybe it was because she was upset by Robert's death—the accompanying letter from Megan's father had suggested that. He'd said, *"The entire community has been very shocked, as you can imagine. Your mother has been in rather a state over it."* So perhaps that was the explanation—her mother was merely more distracted than usual.

From then on, though, her mother's spelling was unreliable even when there wasn't any obvious excuse. But over time the unreliability became normal and Megan stopped noticing.

She was still in the linen cupboard in the autumn when she went out with a policeman who came to investigate the theft of their color television from the lounge. That relationship lasted a couple of weeks. Then there was the businessman who took Megan to a party and introduced her as "my little colonial" as if she were a pet chimpanzee and then tried to make love to her in a taxi on the way back to the hotel. That one lasted about five hours. After that there was a very nice but rather dim dentist who took her home to meet his mother on the first date. After that, astonishingly, it was the hotel's first birthday (free Champagne in the lounge for the guests and a nostalgic dinner at the Gay Hussar for Megan, Annabelle and Peter), followed immediately by Christmas and New Year's. And then, incredibly, it was 1968 and Megan had been in England for two years.

Sometimes it felt like a couple of months. Mostly it seemed like a lifetime.

=====

In March 1968 Megan decided it was time she had a place of her own. She'd resigned herself to a bedsit; a bedroom-cum-living room with either its own kitchen or its own bathroom but not both. Annabelle and Peter paid her well but even so there was no way she could afford a flat of her own anywhere near the hotel; it was either a bedsit or sharing a flat with a group of others, as in Lansdown Terrace, and she wasn't going to do that again.

She wasn't in a rush and she was very picky, so it took a while—three months, in fact. In the end she saw it in the window of the newsagent's where she bought Adam's Matchbox cars, printed neatly on a postcard, stuck up alongside notices about lost cats and cleaning ladies: a bedsit with its own kitchen and a bathroom shared with just one other person. And the address was a ten-minute walk from the hotel.

The room was on the top floor of an old house, up under the eaves, so it was full of odd corners and sloping ceilings and there were a good many places where you couldn't stand upright, but that merely added to its charm in Megan's view. It was painted a drab green but she would change that—the landlady seemed to have no objection. The kitchen, stretched along one wall and closed off from the rest of the room by means of a sliding door, contained all the essentials, including the smallest refrigerator Megan had ever seen. Its interior measured one cubic foot. Megan mentally measured it for milk, butter, orange juice, meat and cheese, and decided it would be fine. Perfect, in fact; no wasted space. She was delighted with it; she was delighted with everything. Even the shared bathroom was fine: it was clean, which was all she asked.

"I'll take it," she said to the landlady, a tired-looking woman with a small girl clinging to her knee.

"But Mummy, you *said*," the child said. She had a well-practiced whine that made the hairs on the back of Megan's neck stand on end.

"All right, darling, in a minute," her mother said. To Megan she said, "Oh good, I'm so glad."

"But Mummy!"

"Who do I share the bathroom with?" Megan asked.

"Mummy, you *said*!" the little girl was hauling on her mother's skirt.

Give me five minutes alone with that child, Megan thought.

To the mother she said politely, "Do you live here too?" because much as she loved the room, if she had to listen to that whine it would be a deal-breaker.

"Yes, on the ground floor. The first floor is a flat and then the second and third each have two bedsits."

Excellent, Megan thought. Two full floors of insulation should do it. "And who do I share the bathroom with?"

"Mummy, you said!"

Megan's mouth went tight. Maybe not, she thought. Maybe I couldn't even stand hearing it occasionally on the stairs.

Across the hall a door opened and a man came out. He gave the child a look of intense disapproval, then looked at Megan and smiled.

"Hello," he said. "Are you taking the room next door?"

Megan looked at him. Looked again. "Yes," she said decidedly. "Yes. I am."

CHAPTER ELEVEN

Edward

Struan, March 1969

Sometimes I am tempted to move in to the bank. Take up residence there rather than coming home to a fresh set of problems every night. An added bonus would be that the bank doesn't smell; there's a very unpleasant smell in this house. Initially it was just upstairs but now you can smell it in the living room too. Emily isn't keeping up with the laundry—the towels in the bathroom haven't been changed for a long time—but I don't think that's enough to account for it.

And then there are the everlasting problems with the boys. Yesterday evening when I got in there was a letter waiting from Ralph Robertson, the principal of the high school, asking Emily and me to come in and talk to him about Peter and Corey. I took it up to Emily to ask if she knew what it was about, but of course she didn't, so I went down the hall and knocked on Peter and Corey's door. They opened it a crack, looking furtive.

"I have here," I said, pushing the door farther open, "a letter from your principal asking your mother and me to come in and talk to him about the two of you. What's it about, do you suppose?"

They glanced quickly at each other and then at the floor, looking guilty of virtually any crime you'd care to suggest.

"Well?" I said when the silence showed no sign of coming to an end. I don't know what it is about the two of them that makes my blood pressure rise so fast and so high. They are indescribably annoying. They give the impression that as far as they're concerned you don't exist, you're just a hazard to be avoided, like a hole in the road.

"Dunno," Peter said, studying his feet. Corey did likewise.

"Everything's been going all right at school, then?" I said. "Neither of you is in any kind of trouble?"

Peter gave a minimal shrug. Corey did likewise.

I managed to simply turn and leave, which was an achievement. My father would have knocked them both across the room.

Just for the record, I did not want any of this. A home and a family, a job in a bank. It was the very last thing I wanted. I am not blaming Emily. I did blame her for a long time but I see now that she lost as much as I did. She proposed to me rather than the other way around, but she is not to blame for the fact that I said yes.

That phrase they use in a court of law—"The balance of his mind was disturbed"—sums it up very well. I married Emily while the balance of my mind was disturbed.

Back downstairs I noticed Tom, sitting in that damn chair. He has it partially turned toward the wall so as to block off the rest of the room. Either he doesn't want to see us or he doesn't want us to see him. Or both. I know the feeling. I considered suggesting that he come into my study so that we could try yet again to have a talk, but I was feeling too annoyed about the boys.

There was a time when I found it possible to talk to Tom. Him alone, of all the children. I remember having quite a long conversation when he was in his early teens about the building of the Canadian Pacific Railway. The cost in lives, whether the end justified the means, that sort of thing. It was the first time we'd had a proper discussion and I remember being impressed by the seriousness with which he considered all sides of the matter.

We had other discussions over the years. Not many, but one or two. In his final undergraduate year we had a talk about whether or not he should go on and do his master's in aeronautical engineering. He was at the Institute for Aerospace Studies at the University of Toronto and wanted to do his MSc there. It was going to cost a fair bit of money and he asked rather tentatively if I would fund him. There was never the slightest risk of my saying no but I asked him a good many questions purely for the pleasure of hearing him talk about this great interest of his.

I wish I'd talked to him more. Not just then but earlier. The fact is, I didn't know how to go about it and still don't. You can't just decide to have a conversation with someone, or at least I can't. It's easy at work because there's always a point to the discussion, a reason for it. I have no trouble with that. Or with talking to Betty. Books provide the starting point there.

He did extremely well in his MSc—Tom, that is. Just over eighteen months ago, when he finished the course, which coincided more or less with the suicide of his friend, both Boeing and de Havilland contacted him via the university inviting him for interviews. Boeing is based in Seattle. Imagine being paid to go and work in Seattle.

He didn't even reply to their letters. It made me almost sick with frustration. Still does.

====

I've taken to visiting the library in my lunch hour. I'm not in love with Betty, nothing so foolish. I like her and admire her and I enjoy our conversations very much and generally feel better for them, although today, in fact, I did not.

We've never talked about our families before but today she asked how Tom was. The difficulty was that I couldn't think what to reply. Finally I said that he seemed to be having a hard time getting over the death of his friend and that I suspected he felt responsible in some way. I said he didn't seem to want to talk about it and that I didn't know what to do for the best. I told her I was considering kicking him out, purely for his own good.

Betty nodded, then asked what Emily thought about it. Another straightforward question but again I was stuck for an answer. I couldn't very well say, "I haven't asked her" without explaining why I hadn't asked her, which would involve discussing Emily herself and her inability to focus on anything more than six inches from the end of her nose. Finally I said she was rather preoccupied with the new baby and Betty smiled in that particular way all women do at the mere mention of babies and asked how he was and what we were going to call him and so on and so forth, and we sailed safely into the calm waters of new babyhood.

Betty hasn't had an easy life herself. She has just one child, who was born with some form of brain problem. I don't know the details. Dr. Christopherson sent the boy down to the Hospital for Sick Children in Toronto but nothing could be done. He's in his teens now and as far as I know isn't a particular problem aside from the fact that he'll never be able to fend for himself. So Betty is serving a life sentence, you might say. Though possibly she doesn't see it that way. Her husband clearly did—he took off a long time ago.

As she'd brought up the subject of children, when we'd finished with babyhood I asked how her son was making out (by some miracle I managed to remember that his name is Owen). She said he never varied much. There was a short pause while I tried to think what to say to that. Finally I said something about it not being easy.

"Oh, well," Betty said, with a smile. "Whoever said it would be? Never mind. Ever onward."

Ever onward. I imagine that sums up her attitude to life. I find it admirable and rather shaming.

When I got home I went up to Emily's room. She was talking to the baby while changing his diaper—I heard her as I opened the door, though she stopped when I came in. The baby was waving his arms and legs about like they do, his eyes fixed avidly on Emily's face. He was naked and looked alarmingly small and vulnerable but at the same time entirely content. Emily glanced up when I came in and said hello as if she wasn't entirely sure who I was.

"How are you both?" I said with an attempt at a smile, inclining my head at the baby.

"We're fine," she said cautiously. "We're both very well. How are you?"

"I'm fine too," I said. "I'd like to talk to you. Do you have a minute?"

"Talk?" she said, looking alarmed. I tried not to let it irritate me.

"About Tom."

"Oh."

For some reason that seemed to relieve her. She pulled a tiny woolen undershirt over the baby's—I must stop calling him that; his name is Dominic—over Dominic's head and deftly eased him into a many-buttoned sack-type thing that contained his feet. I was reminded of Betty and her sleeping bag.

"You'll have noticed Tom's still here," I said, though there was no guarantee of that. "It's been more than eighteen months since his friend died but he seems unable to get over it. At least I assume that's at the root of the problem. I was wondering what we should do about it. He can't just sit in the living room for the rest of his life."

"Can't he?" Emily asked vaguely, doing up buttons.

"No, he cannot," I said, unable to keep the annoyance out of my voice. She'd switched off—it was perfectly evident—and I can't believe it isn't deliberate; she simply prefers not to think about anything difficult or unpleasant. "He's wasting his life and it's time he pulled himself together. I've been trying to think what we could do or say to help him and I wondered if you had any thoughts on the subject."

"Me?"

"You are his mother, Emily. What do you think we ought to do?"

She looked at me and just for a moment it was as if a fog had lifted and she'd actually heard me and taken in what I'd said. Then it was gone. She turned back to the baby and gathered him up, cupping his small bald head in her hand. "I don't know what to do about anything," she said to him. "Except you. I always know what to do about you."

———

This morning I phoned Ralph Robertson at the high school. I explained that Emily was fully occupied with a new baby and I was very busy and asked if we could have our chat about Peter and Corey over the phone instead of my going to see him. He said he'd rather I came in, which is irritating. We've fixed a date for next week.

On the plus side, a letter has arrived from Megan. She wrote and posted it more than three months ago, so it predates several we've had since then. God knows where it's been in the interim. Anyway, it seems that a mere three years after arriving in England Megan has finally paid a visit to the National Gallery. If I were a drinking man I'd have a drink in celebration. She describes it as "really amazing." High praise. She enclosed a postcard of *The Execution of Lady Jane Grey* by Paul Delaroche, of whom I'd never heard. A strange choice of picture on Megan's part, I would have thought, but Delaroche is clearly very good, I will have to look him up. Lady Jane Grey I have heard of. I believe she was a pawn in the games of powerful men around the time of Henry VIII and ended up having her head cut off. I'll look her up too.

I took the letter up to Emily and found her drifting around the room in her nightgown with the baby over her shoulder—it made me wonder if she's been dressed at all today. When I said there was a letter from Megan she gave me an angelic smile and continued drifting. I put the letter on the bed for her to read when she comes back to earth. I didn't give her the card. I thought the subject might disturb her.

She was looking quite beautiful. That is the one thing about Emily that has not declined over the years; if anything, I'd say she is more beautiful now than she was when I first met her. Not that beauty matters, but for some reason when you're young you think it does. Though possibly when you're young you just don't think.

Emily's father became the principal at our high school during my final year—the family moved up from Hamilton in order for him to take the job. From my point of view the timing was good because by then things had become very bad between me and my father, and Emily was a welcome diversion, you might say.

In addition to being the best-looking girl I'd ever seen, I thought she was the cleverest, though it turned out I was wrong about that. Coming from an educated family she spoke well, and I mistook that for intelligence. I'm not saying Emily is stupid, just that she isn't as smart as she sounds.

Even so she was the only one of my classmates I was ever able to talk to. I don't recall now what we talked about but travel and art certainly came into it. She let on she shared my dreams of seeing the world and I was innocent enough to believe her.

That isn't fair. It suggests she was like a spider, spinning a trap, and I don't suppose she consciously did that. No doubt she imagined herself in love with me and was trying to be interested in my interests. I imagined myself in love with her too. It has always struck me as a mistake on Mother Nature's part that we make the most important decisions of our lives when we're too young to have any idea of the consequences.

═══

I've returned to Mother's diaries—the final section. I've been putting it off, but having started this venture I feel I owe it to her to finish it. Then I will know her story, as much as it can be known.

I would have been in my teens when she wrote the last of the entries that survived the fire, and by then we had been on the farm for some years. Our lives were incomparably easier there than they had been in the early days, so it is ironic that this was when the deterioration in her writing began.

The farm was a gift from my mother's parents. I didn't realize that until today and it explains a lot, but it puzzled me considerably when I read it. For eight years she had refused to see or accept help of any kind from her family and then all of a sudden she capitulated and accepted a farm. That was quite a climb-down. There was nothing in the diaries to account for it and it wasn't until I was working out how old we children were when we moved to the farm that it suddenly made sense.

I was seven and Alan and Harry were eight. School age. Out of loyalty to my father my mother had been prepared to sacrifice almost anything, but she couldn't bring herself to sacrifice our schooling. She'd been teaching us herself for several years but she would have been aware of her own limitations. The only solution was for us to stop traipsing around the North and settle down near a town with a school, and her parents offered her the only means of making that happen.

She must have agonized over that decision. She would have known how my father would take it, the message it would send to him. But she'd also have known there was no other choice. He'd been prospecting for the better part of a decade by then, promising the earth and delivering nothing, and had walked out of or been fired from every job he'd ever had.

"*Stanley says he will not work for fools,*" she has scribbled on a scrap of newsprint not much bigger than my thumb, *"and that they are all fools."*

Quite.

The farm was certainly a generous gift but probably not as extravagant as it sounds. It was 1929 when we moved there. The price of silver was falling and the mines were closing. Towns that had grown up around them were dwindling away until in some places nothing was left of them but the giant corrugated iron head frames that towered over the landscape. Some of the head frames are still there. They are magnificent in their way. Like giant rusted dinosaurs.

With the miners gone, the surrounding farms had no one to sell their produce to. Eventually many of the farmers just upped and left—walked out of their farmhouses with nothing but what they could carry on their backs and headed south, looking for work. Their loss was our gain; my mother's father would have picked up the farm for a fraction of what it was worth. It was thirty miles from his own farm. I'm sure he and my grandmother would have preferred it to be closer, but my mother would have drawn the line at that.

To anyone accustomed to a halfway normal existence the farm would have looked alarmingly primitive but from my mother's point of view it must have been luxury. It was just three miles from the lumber town of Jonesville, which is a ghost town now, but back then it boasted a church, a post office and a general store as well as the all-important school. After the isolation of the mining camps it must have seemed like a metropolis.

The farmhouse itself was only a log cabin but it was large and well-built, with three good bedrooms and a big living room/ kitchen with a fireplace at one end and a range at the other. We children thought it was a palace and after so long in the bush I imagine my mother did too. I remember her standing in the center of the living room on the day we arrived, very slowly turning full circle to take it all in—the rounded, well-chinked logs, the solid floor and neat, tightly fitted windows—her expression a curious mixture of disapproval and delight: disapproval because an easier life for herself had not been her goal; delight because she was a woman, after all, and a home meant a great deal to her. She was probably trying not to love it. Trying but failing. I remember when she'd completed her circle she walked over to the range and bent down and kissed one of the stove lids, then straightened up and turned to face us, laughing, her mouth and nose all black from the stove, her face luminous with relief and joy.

It is hard to overstate the difference it must have made to her life. Up until then we had moved so often there had never been time to get a vegetable garden established or enough land cleared to raise a single cow. It was a hand-to-mouth existence in those early mining camps, and that is desperate enough if you have only yourself to feed. The farm, by contrast, although small—just fifty acres—came complete with four cows, half a dozen chickens and a large kitchen garden. It was far enough from town that there was game around and from the first snowfall each year we would put out a couple of handfuls of hay every day to attract the deer and whenever we needed meat we'd shoot one. There were ducks and geese in season, there were eggs from the chickens and milk, cheese and butter from the cows. In the summer there were wild blueberries and strawberries, which Mother bottled and sold in the town along with any surplus from the garden.

I'm making it sound idyllic. It was subsistence farming and

grindingly hard work, but now at least there was always something to put on the table at suppertime. You had to grow it or catch it or shoot it and you had to know where to look for it and you had to know how to preserve it, but having come from a pioneering background my mother knew all of those things.

My father did not.

Stanley says farming is work for a peasant, not for a man with anything about him. I asked was it not satisfying to watch things grow, to provide food for your family through the work of your own hands. It was foolish of me to say such a thing. Stanley became furious, thinking that I was saying he could not provide for us, which is not what I meant at all. He upset the table and everything crashed to the floor.

She was right, it was a foolish thing to say.

I wonder if he knew, deep down, that he was not very smart and had no talents and no skills and nothing special to offer the world. I've always assumed the opposite—that he had a ludicrously high opinion of himself—but maybe that wasn't so. Maybe in the darkest hours of the night a cold chill of self-knowledge stole in and he saw that by his own definition he was a nobody. A failure. Maybe that was at the heart of his anger.

In which case when my mother, breaking her promise to him, accepted the farm from her parents, he would have seen it as proof that she saw him for what he really was.

Is that enough to explain the change in my mother's writing and the bruises we hid under our clothes? I think it could be. Back then a man who couldn't support his family was not a man. The farm would have reminded him of that every day.

Why didn't he leave us? God knows I for one fervently wished that he would. But he wasn't one to let anything go, my father. My mother was his and so the farm was his, no matter that he despised it. It gave him free bed and board, and if my mother managed to sell some of the produce from the kitchen garden, well, the money was his too. It kept him in drink.

I have found something—it caught my eye because of the name on it. My mother wrote it on the back of a brown paper bag, the sort that flour and sugar used to come in.

> *Yesterday I spoke to Mr. Sabatini and he said that he was certain Edward had a great future if only he could stay on at school. I dare not mention it to Stanley—he is taking against Edward more and more—but I wish there were someone with whom I could share my happiness. I thanked Mr. Sabatini from the bottom of my heart.*

Mr. Sabatini was my geography teacher. A remarkable man; Italian, as his name suggests. He had a flair for languages and had been everywhere, not as a tourist but living and working in each country for a year or more, generally as a teacher. I don't know how he ended up so far north. Perhaps he was running from something, or perhaps someone told him that the essence of this country is not to be found in its cities but in its wilderness. Either way, I was fortunate that he did.

For the two years he taught us, our geography classes included history, art, philosophy, politics, religion—just about everything, an education in the fullest sense of the word. He started off by introducing us to the countries of the Mediterranean and by way of illustration brought in a selection of his own photographs for us to see. I was stunned by them. The photographs themselves were extraordinary, but more than that, I'd never imagined such astonishing places existed. When we were dismissed at the end of the day I went back to his classroom and asked if I could look at the photographs again while he was tidying up. The next day he brought in several of his own books on art and architecture and said I could borrow them.

I hid them under my bed. I wasn't afraid my younger sisters would get hold of them, I was afraid my father would.

I'm sure Mr. Sabatini guessed that things were not good at home. I remember him telling me that he'd been flung into jail once in some foreign port and to keep himself from despair he would call up in his mind the wonderful places he had still not seen, and plan the order in which he would visit them when he got out. It can't have been mere chance that he told me that.

It would be an exaggeration to say that he changed my life but he certainly made the one I had more bearable. He gave me something to dream about, something to strive for. I'll never achieve it now but just having the dream was valuable. It has broadened what has otherwise been a very narrow life.

Here's an ironic thing: after all my dreams of traveling the world I am the only one of my siblings still in the North. Alan and Harry live on adjoining farms in Manitoba. They married sisters and have at least a dozen children between them. Margaret married a Toronto man and seems quite happy down there. They have four children. My other sisters are dotted across the country. Margaret's the only good letter-writer in the family. She keeps the rest of us up to date.

One way or another this has been quite a night. I was sitting here at my desk, thinking about Mr. Sabatini, when the door of my study opened and there stood Emily in the doorway.

She was looking . . . I'm not sure how to describe it. She was looking unlike herself. For a start she wasn't holding the baby, and Emily looks incomplete without a baby, but more than that she looked wide awake and much more focused than usual, rather as she did for a moment a few days ago when I went up to speak to her about Tom.

Before I could speak she said, "Edward, what did I do wrong?"

Her voice was unsteady but she asked the question with such directness that I was taken aback.

"What do you mean?" I asked.

She said, "I must have done something wrong but I don't know what it was. I've never known. You never said."

I said, "Emily, what are you talking about? I don't know what you're referring to."

"You and me," she said. "You used to love me and then you didn't, and I don't know what I did wrong."

She wasn't crying but her lips were trembling. I felt the most crushing sense of shame. I stood up quickly and went around the desk and stood for a moment, uncertain, and then put my arms around her. I don't tend to do that sort of thing but I couldn't think what else to do.

She gave a little start but she didn't pull back, just stood with her head bowed, her forehead not quite touching my shoulder.

I said, "You didn't do anything wrong, Emily. I'm sorry. It wasn't your fault. None of it was your fault. It was mine."

We stood for a minute like that. I didn't know what else to say, so I said again that I was sorry.

"It's all right," she whispered. "It doesn't matter."

That made me feel even worse—her saying it didn't matter. As if her life didn't matter. Or as if she assumed I would think that.

I said, "Yes, it does. It does matter. I'm sorry," knowing that repeating those trite words couldn't make anything right.

After a moment she stepped back and looked up at me and said, "I want to go back to bed."

"All right," I said. "I'll come up with you."

I followed her upstairs. The baby—Dominic—was asleep in a tangle of bedding, his mouth making those involuntary sucking motions Mother Nature has programmed into them.

Emily looked up at me anxiously.

"What is it?" I said.

"I only want to go to sleep. By myself."

"That's fine," I said, somewhat stiffly. "That's what I thought you meant." I have never insisted on "relations." I've left it to her to make the advances.

I went back downstairs, still with this terrible weight of shame. I didn't know what to do with myself. I didn't want to read; I didn't want to think. I went into the entrance hall and pulled on my outdoor clothing and went out into the dark. I walked fast into town.

Walking from one end of Struan to the other takes less than ten minutes. If you kept walking south and east eventually you would hit civilization; if you kept walking north and west you would hit Crow Lake, where the road comes to an end. In either case you'd freeze to death long before you got there. When I reached the gas station at the far northern end of town I turned around and walked home.

I knew there was no point in going to bed, so I went into the kitchen and got myself a bowl of cornflakes, more for something to do than because I was hungry. I took it into my study thinking that I'd look through one of the books on Rome while I ate, but I found I didn't want to think about Rome. I ate the cornflakes staring at my desk. When I'd finished I decided to go through the few remaining scraps of Mother's diaries. I felt so terrible already that I thought nothing I found there could make me feel worse.

In the end, only one of the entries was complete enough to make any sense, and Mother's writing was so shaky that in some places I couldn't make it out at all, but it reported an incident I remember only too clearly. I can date it exactly because Mother wrote it in the margins of a page torn from the *Temiskaming Speaker* and the date is still legible—18th September 1934. I would have been twelve.

> . . . *the children were screaming and all three of the boys tried to shield me but that made him angrier still, and he turned on them savagely, knocking them away, first one and then another, and all the while I was pleading with him to stop but that only made him worse, and it wasn't until he had worn himself out that he finally stopped and left the house. All of us were crying, myself as well. I have never cried in front of them before and it terrified them. It was more than an hour before I had calmed them all down and got them into bed. I believe my arm is broken, and my eye is very bad, but worse than that, worse by far, is that the children witnessed it.*
>
> *After about an hour Edward came out from his bedroom. His face was red and swollen, partly from*

Stanley's blows and partly from tears. He stood in front of
me and said, "Mother, if he does that again I will kill him."
I was so horrified I almost cried out. I said he must
never, ever, allow himself even to think such a thing again.
I tried to make him promise, but he wouldn't promise . . .

The next bit is indecipherable but at the bottom of the page
there are several more lines.

Edward has been my joy, my consolation. To see his
intelligence develop, to watch his face as he reads and see
him so transported, has given me hope that he will escape
all this and that some good will have come of my life. But
now I am fearful for him. Very fearful. I believed he had
the strength of character to rise above hatred and bitterness
against his father, but now I am not sure. But I must have
faith in him. Those were words spoken in anger and he is
still very young. I must have faith. He is a kind and loving
person; he will put this behind him. I know he will.

I sat until after midnight, reading and rereading those lines.
I don't know how to deal with them. I don't even know what to
feel.

CHAPTER TWELVE

Tom

Struan, March 1969

Eleven inches of snow in one dump. Marcel took it personally; in a fit of fury he drove the snowplow just that little bit too fast and the heavy snow shooting off the end of the plow created a vortex, a mini tornado, and demolished six road signs in the blink of an eye.

"Rip' 'em right off der posts," Marcel raged. "Now I gotta go an' put 'em up agin, gonna take me a week. I piss on it! I piss on dis goddam' snow!" and he unzipped his pants and did so.

On Crow Lake Road there was an exposed stretch where the wind played tricks, scooping snow into fantastical shapes on one side, scouring it down to bare ice on the other. Tom was heading home at the end of his shift when a truck in a hurry overtook the plow, hit a patch of ice, went into a spin and shot off into the bush. Tom stopped the plow so fast it was a miracle he didn't leave the road himself. He leapt out and ran down the track left by the truck, cursing as he went. The truck's driver was cursing too—Tom could hear him as he came up, so at least that meant he was okay. He was trying to get out, but the truck had embedded itself in deep snow and he couldn't get the door open. Tom shoveled the snow away with his hands. It was heavy work and he was panting by the time he was done.

"Thanks," the driver said as he climbed out, but he sounded madder than hell. "Thanks very much, but God damn it!"

"You okay?" Tom asked, still breathless.

"Yeah, but I'm gonna be late! I have to meet this guy . . ." The man stopped, recognizing Tom at the same moment Tom recognized him—the man who'd rescued him from the coleslaw at Harper's restaurant. "Hi," the man said, calming down a little. "Didn't realize you drove the plow. Thanks for stopping."

"That's okay," Tom said. To anyone else he would have said, "What do you think you're doing going that fast on a road like this?" but he owed the guy. "Want a tow out?"

The man looked at his watch and shook his head. "Thanks, but it'd take too long. Could I hitch a lift? I'll get it towed out later."

"Sure."

"Just gotta get some stuff from the truck."

The sign on the truck said, "Luke's Rustic Furniture." The man—Luke, presumably—disappeared inside the cab and reappeared with a large cardboard box. "Samples," he said. "And they're not broken, so that's something. This is great of you. I appreciate it."

The hurry, it turned out, was because he had an appointment with the boss of the hotel/hunting lodge that was being built out along the lakeshore. He was hoping to get the contract to make the furniture for the lodge.

"The boss-guy phoned from Toronto first thing this morning," the man said when they were under way. He was cradling
the box of samples on his lap. "Said he was going to take advantage of the weather and fly up for the day. He's got some people
to talk to, said would I like to meet him for lunch and discuss
things. I heard the plane fly over about an hour ago, so he's
here."

He looked across at Tom. "I'm Luke Morrison, by the way.
And thanks again."

"Tom Cartwright," Tom said. "No problem."

That was it for a couple of miles. Luke sat in silence, seemingly mesmerized by the plume of snow streaming off the blade
of the plow. It was hypnotic, Tom knew: he'd had to train himself not to look at it.

Eventually Luke stirred himself. "Cartwright, did you say?"

"That's right."

"Your dad manager of the bank?"

"Yeah."

"He helped me a lot when I was starting up my furniture
business," Luke said. "Ten, fifteen years ago. I was just a kid,
really, knew nothin' about nothin'. I went to him for a loan. He
showed me how to draw up a business plan, work out what I
needed to borrow—all that sort of stuff. He took a lot of time
over it. Really helpful."

"No kidding," Tom said, trying not to sound as sour as he felt.

Luke nodded. "Nice guy."

Dr. Jekyll and Mr. Hyde, Tom thought bitterly. Maybe he
should make an appointment to see his father at the bank. That
way, he might get ten minutes of his time.

More miles went by. A couple of inches of new snow covered
the road, easy for the plow to deal with. What it couldn't deal

with was the treacherous layer of compressed snow underneath, hard as ice and just as lethal. Chains were the only answer to that and most cars had them, but even so people ended up in the ditch on a regular basis.

"Speaking of families," Luke said. "The . . . ah . . . waitress at Harper's the other day? Sorry about her, she's a pain in the ass. Best thing is to ignore her."

"You're related?" It seemed polite to pretend he hadn't worked that out.

"She's my sister."

Tom tried to think of an appropriate response. "Sorry to hear that," might be a little impolite. "She seems to have a thing about vegetables," he said at last.

"Been going on about them for years."

"That must be kind of . . ." he searched for a word . . . "wearing."

"You cannot imagine," Luke said.

Tom laughed. He hadn't laughed for a long time and it felt good, felt as if it loosened things that had been clenched up inside him.

"What do your parents think?" he asked.

"They're dead, so they don't have to deal with it."

"Oh. Sorry."

Luke lifted a hand dismissively. "Years ago."

Ahead of them a moose stepped out of the bush, ambled into the middle of the road and stopped. Tom touched the brakes carefully, then stepped on them harder, and the snowplow slewed sideways, straightened up again and came to a stop. The moose paid no attention. He was gazing into the woods on the far side of the road, lost in thought.

"Sometimes they don't seem any too swift," Luke said.

"That's for sure." Tom honked the horn. The moose swung his head around, gave them a baleful look and sauntered on.

After that they sat and watched the snow-laden trees go by until they got to Struan, where Tom realized he'd not only managed to carry on a whole conversation without breaking into a sweat but had passed the turnoff to the ravine without even noticing.

Luke Morrison was meeting the boss-guy at Harper's, so Tom dropped him off there and went and parked the snowplow. When he got to Harper's himself, Luke and a bald guy in a suit were ensconced in one of the bigger booths. Along with their lunches there was furniture—dollhouse size—all over the table. The bald guy was forking fries into his mouth with one hand and picking up pieces of furniture with the other, turning them this way and that. ". . . As many as you need," Luke was saying as Tom walked by. "The numbers wouldn't be a problem."

Tom stole a quick look at the models as he went past. They looked good. There were three or four different designs, some of them fancy, some of them plain, all of them sturdy and graceful-looking. He'd have liked a closer look at them himself.

He'd picked up a copy of *The Globe and Mail* on his way to Harper's but before he could spread it out the Amazon sped by carrying two plates of hamburgers and fries. She delivered them to a table near the front, then headed back toward the kitchen, pausing, as if purely in the pursuit of duty, at Luke's table.

"How's your dinner, sir?" she asked the bald man solicitously, inclining her head to show her genuine interest and concern. "Are you enjoying the hot turkey sandwich? How about the coleslaw—isn't it just the best?"

From where he sat Tom could see the man's face and Luke's

back. Luke was running his fingers through his hair—a gesture of stress, Tom guessed. You could bet this wouldn't have been his choice of meeting place. But the bald guy smiled widely. "It's real good," he said. "All of it, coleslaw included. What's your name, miss, if you don't mind my asking?"

"Bo," the Amazon said. "Good, that's what I like to hear, a rave review. And you, sir," she turned graciously to Luke, tipping her head to the other side. "Are you enjoying your meal?"

Tom looked away—it seemed cruel to watch. Luke must have forbidden her to let on they so much as knew each other and she was having so much fun with the situation she hardly knew what to do with herself.

"Well, there we go!" Tom heard her say. "Two rave reviews. The chef will be so pleased. Now how about dessert? There's blueberry pie, apple pie, lemon meringue pie, black cherry pie, pecan pie and Mrs. Harper's world-famous brownies, all with cream or ice cream. My own personal recommendation would be the blueberry pie because our blueberries up here are the best in the country, but they're all delicious."

"Well, I for one am going to have exactly what you recommend," the bald man said. "And some more of your excellent coffee."

Luke's hair was starting to resemble a well-plowed field. He muttered something and the Amazon said, "Excellent choice, sir! Coming right up!" and bounced off to the kitchen. The bald man followed her with his eyes.

"Now she is something else," he said admiringly. "Didn't know you grew them like that up here!" He was all but licking his lips.

You dirty bastard, Tom thought, with disgust. You've got to be pushing fifty!

———

On the way home he took a detour down to the lake to have a look at the plane. It was sitting on its skis out on the ice, a Beaver, as Tom had guessed it would be, a single-engine, propeller-driven little workhorse designed by de Havilland Canada and purpose-built for the rigors of the Canadian bush. Back when he was four or five he'd been playing on the beach one day when an unimaginably wonderful machine had swooped down out of the sky, skidded along the top of the water, settled down on its floats and taxied right up to the shore. The door opened and a man leapt out and splashed barefoot to the beach, pausing just long enough to tousle Tom's hair as he went by. Tom had been so astonished he couldn't speak.

He'd been hooked then and there. The miracle of flight—the glamour of it, the romance, the nonchalant ease with which man defied the law of gravity—everything about it enthralled him. Two decades later, still enthralled and studying aerodynamics in Toronto, he'd come to realize that the truly astonishing thing was that it *wasn't* a miracle: man had worked out that it could be done and therefore he had done it; it was as simple as that. Now man had taken on space itself; he had broken free of Earth's gravity and orbited the moon. Soon he would land on it. No miracles required, just a little imagination and a lot of math.

Tom's own particular passion wasn't outer space, it was supersonic flight, and it seemed to him that if there were a miracle involved it was that he happened to be born when he was, because in the whole history of flight there had never been a better time to be an aeronautical engineer. Over in Europe, Concorde was under development; out in Seattle, Boeing was working on the supersonic transport program; down at the Institute for

Aerospace Studies in Toronto, having completed his final exams, Tom was called into his professor's office and told that his name had been put forward to both Boeing and de Havilland and he would probably be receiving letters inviting him for interviews shortly. If that wasn't a miracle for a boy from the bush, what was?

Three weeks later, back at home for the summer, he had rounded the corner of a sheer rock face and seen the crumpled heap of his friend's body at the foot of it, and twenty years of passion had vanished in a heartbeat.

Now Tom walked around the little plane trying to work out what he was feeling. Nothing much. But he didn't think he'd have been able to come and look at it a couple of months ago, so maybe that was progress.

He walked along the shore, keeping close to the edge, where the wind had left enough snow to provide some traction. The sun had gone and a few large soft flakes were drifting down—the plane would have to leave soon or not at all. Once he rounded the point that sheltered Low Down Bay from the wind, the snow was thigh deep and within yards he was breathless and sweating. As soon as Lower Beach Road came into view he stopped. No need to go farther.

The bay looked entirely different in winter, barren and hostile, the point where land and water met erased by ice and snow, the curve of the rocks obscured by drifts. The trees were so burdened with snow they looked like figures hunched against the wind.

The cottages were deserted—they had no insulation, so were only for summer use. The one the little girl and her parents had been staying in was at the far end of the road, with the beach on its doorstep and its back to the woods. It was the one they always stayed in. They came for a month every summer to enjoy the beach and the lake and the wide curving beauty of the bay. They loved the peace and quiet, the child's mother had said that day in court, her mouth so distorted with grief and rage that the words had to be squeezed out one by one. The peace and the quiet and, in particular, the lack of traffic.

Robert was convicted of manslaughter, which surprised no one. What surprised them all was the sentence passed down by the Crown attorney: three months of service in the community. Robert had looked stunned by it. He'd expected a prison sentence.

Tom had been standing beside Robert when the child's mother came up after the trial—Robert's parents were on the other side—so he heard what she said. She was shaking so hard with anger that the words came out in fractured syllables, but they were still comprehensible. She said that justice had not been done and that Robert knew it. She said she hoped that the image of her child's dead body would be at the forefront of Robert's mind every minute of every day from now until the day he died. She said that Robert had destroyed her child's past for her as well as her present and her future; she could no longer see her daughter in her mind's eye as a baby or a toddler or a little girl learning to ride a bike—her memory no longer held those pictures. The only picture it held, the only thing left to her, was the image of her child's dead body, head lolling back, mouth gaping open, as they had lifted her into the doctor's car. And therefore her prayer now, her constant prayer, was that it would be all Robert would ever see either, now and forever.

Tom had known he should stop her; he'd known he should step between her and Robert and say, "Ma'am, excuse me, but you don't want to say those things, you really mustn't say those things, please come away now." He should have put an arm around her and steered her away, forcibly if necessary, given her into the safekeeping of someone, anyone, so that she could not let loose into the world words that should never, ever, have been spoken. He knew he should do that but he was unable to move. He felt rather than saw Robert stagger back, though the woman hadn't struck him with anything but words. Later he saw that Robert's mother had collapsed and that people were gathered around her. He also saw Robert's father, Reverend Thomas, standing as if carved from stone, one hand partially raised as though to stop the appalling words before they reached his son, his mouth half open as if he'd tried to say something but at this, the most critical moment of his life, had lost the power of speech.

By a stroke of luck Shelley the Slut wasn't there when he got home. Adam was in the living room playing with his cars. Tom sat down in his chair, leaned his head back and closed his eyes. Apart from the sound of Adam's cars there was silence, a rare and beautiful thing in this house. He thought he might even fall asleep, and then thought he was asleep, and then he woke up because the sound of cars had stopped and he smelled an odorous presence. He opened his eyes a slit. Adam was standing by his knee looking at him with serious eyes.

"Hello," Tom said, not bothering to lift his head.

"Are you sad?" Adam asked.

"I guess a bit," Tom said.

"Why?"

Tom sighed and straightened up. "A friend of mine died. It was a while ago, but it's still sad."

The by now familiar crease appeared between Adam's eye-brows. "What *is* died?" he said.

Tom opened his mouth to say, "Like that mouse we found" but stopped himself. The concept was difficult enough without the kid thinking that everybody ended their days upside down in a jar of honey.

"It's like . . . you just aren't there anymore. It's kind of hard to explain."

"Where do you go?"

"Nobody knows. Nowhere bad, though."

Adam thought about it long and hard. Finally he held out a car he'd been clutching. "This is my new car," he said.

"That's called a change of subject," Tom said, taking the car. "This is new, is it? It's very shiny. Do you know what kind it is?"

A shake of the head.

"It's a Mercedes sports car. They can go really fast."

A vigorous nod. "Is that color called silver?"

"It is. Where did you get it?"

"It was on the table."

"What do you mean, on the table? In a box or something?"

Adam shot off and returned with a little Matchbox box and handed it over.

"I see," Tom said, examining the box. It had been consider-ably squashed. "That's very neat. Where did it come from?"

"It came with the letters."

"Someone sent it to you? That's nice of them. Do you know who it was?"

A shake of the head.

"Do you have the paper it was wrapped in?"

Adam shot off again and returned with a jumble of brown paper.

"Right," Tom said, smoothing out the paper on his knee and fitting pieces together. "Somewhere here there should be a return address . . . look at the stamps, they're different—well hey! Whaddya know—it's from Meg. Do you remember Meg? I guess you wouldn't; she left a long time ago. She's your big sister. She lives in England."

Adam hauled up his T-shirt, releasing a fresh puff of stink, then hauled it down again. "Why doesn't she live here with us?"

"That's a good question," Tom said. "I wish she did, then you wouldn't smell like you do and we wouldn't be in this mess. Have all your cars come like this?"

"Yes."

"So Meg sent you all those cars. Wow! That's really nice of her, isn't it? I think she must like you. She's never sent me anything."

Adam looked thoughtful. For a moment he seemed to debate something with himself, then abruptly he disappeared behind the chair, rattled cars briefly and reappeared with a red and yellow dump truck that had seen better days.

"You can have this," he said.

"You mean to keep?"

"Yes."

"Thank you," Tom said. "That's very generous of you. I'm touched."

CHAPTER THIRTEEN

Megan

London, July 1968

His name was Andrew Bannerman and, apart from having an attractive smile, there was nothing remarkable about him. He had brown hair in need of a cut and a pleasant enough face and dirty jeans and a sweater that was unraveling at the collar. His bedsit room, across the landing from her own, was a shambles—at least the bit she caught a glimpse of through the open doorway was. Clothes and books and papers everywhere.

A standard male, in other words. He was on his way out when she met him on the landing and said he'd be away for a couple of weeks but would knock and introduce himself properly when he got back, so she only had that one brief look at him and he was nothing special. That was what she decided.

He seems nice enough, she told herself as she painted the window frame. It'll be good to have someone nice across the landing. Did I just paint that bit or not?

———

Annabelle and Peter came over to view the room the evening after Megan signed the lease, bearing a bottle of wine and a set of wineglasses with delicate twisted stems.

"To your new home!" Peter said, raising a glass. "This is a real find, Meg. And that's quite a view." He went over to the big sash window. (Megan had washed it, inside and out, at no little risk to life and limb, as soon as she took possession of the room.)

"You've got your own private nature sanctuary," Peter said. Birds were flitting about, squirrels were flowing up and down the trees. It was like a miniature forest, and from the road you'd never have guessed it was there. Just before Annabelle and Peter arrived there'd been a short but vigorous downpour and now the evening sun was glancing off the rooftops as if the whole thing had been stage-managed for the specific purpose of impressing Megan's visitors.

Annabelle turned back from the window and contemplated the room with a decorator's eye. They had offered to help Megan do up the flat before she moved in. "Have you decided on the color?"

"Pale yellow-gold." (Two years ago she would have painted everything white and never given it another thought.)

"Perfect," Annabelle said. "I think you need another arm-chair for when someone comes around. Would you like the Windsor chair in the office? We never use it."

Megan imagined Andrew Bannerman sitting in it, glass of wine in hand.

She took a week off to paint and decorate the room. Janet, her assistant housekeeper at the hotel, was quite capable of filling in for her now, and in any case Megan was still sleeping at the hotel, so she could keep an eye on things. Annabelle and Peter came around on a couple of evenings to help out and it was just like old times, though in fact it was the days on her own that Megan enjoyed most. She'd never had a holiday before, at least not since she was too young to remember. In between coats of emulsion she sat at the table by the window, looking down into people's back gardens and thinking about the strangeness of the past two and a half years: the desperate homesickness of the early days, how close she had come to giving up and going home, how much she would have missed if she'd done so. Here she was in a place of her own, paid for with her own money, earned by doing a job she loved. And who knew what tomorrow would bring?

When the decorating was finished she went shopping. Around the corner there was a hardware store that sold all kinds of things for the kitchen. She bought a set of crockery (plain white, four of everything), cutlery, saucepans, a bread board, a chopping board, kitchen utensils and a fat brown tea pot. Then she went to John Lewis ("Never knowingly undersold") and bought an electric kettle, a toaster, a coffee percolator and a casserole dish nice enough to put on the table should she happen to invite someone for dinner. She had to take a taxi to get everything home.

On Sunday, the final day of her week off, Megan moved in. It didn't take long; apart from her recent purchases she still had very few possessions. She'd invited Annabelle and Peter for dinner that evening to celebrate, so after sorting out where everything went she started cooking. She made a chicken pie for the main course, just to check that she hadn't lost the knack of making pastry, and fresh poached plums for dessert. Then, because she'd been wanting to make them for two and a half years and now she finally could, she made Chelsea buns to serve with the plums. They weren't considered a dessert, but so what? She served them warm with custard and they were a triumph.

Megan was so happy that day she almost burst with it, so it was strange that she had a disturbing dream that night. In the dream she went back to see her family and they weren't there anymore. Nothing was there: not the people, not the house, not even Struan itself. It and they no longer existed. The dream didn't provide any explanation. Megan awoke to a feeling of loss and grief she hadn't felt since her days at Lansdown Terrace. Why would you have a dream like that at a time like this?

On Monday morning she got a letter from her father—just her father, which was unusual; normally her parents wrote at the same time so as to economize on stamps. Megan opened it with a vague sense of apprehension (the dream was still lingering in the back of her mind) but by the time she finished reading the letter it was no longer apprehension she felt but outrage.

6th August 1968

Dear Megan,
Thank you for your letter dated 15th July. I am glad you have found an apartment close to your place of work. That will be a considerable advantage, saving time as well as travel fares. Provided the roof is sound, being on the top floor will be an advantage too, as there will be no noise from above.

Things here are much as usual. Your brother Tom is driving a lumber truck for the summer and appears to have

*no plans to return to his chosen career. We've had no word
from the twins for a good while, so we don't know where
they are, but there is nothing new in that. Your mother is
expecting another baby after Christmas.*

*That's about all the news, apart from the fact that we
have had a spell of dry weather so the mosquitoes are not
as bad as they were earlier, which is a considerable relief.*

Everyone is well. I hope you are too.

The way he slipped it in: "*Your mother is expecting another
baby after Christmas.*" As if it was of no particular consequence.
As if he hadn't been told, straight out, by Dr. Christopherson—
Megan had heard it with her own ears—that there were to be no
more babies. Her mother wouldn't be able to cope, the place
would be utter chaos. But more important than that, much
more important, was Adam: who would look after him while his
mother fell in love with the new arrival? Megan was so furious
she wanted to phone her father and shout, "You're a disgrace!"
down the phone line.

Fortunately, things were busy at the hotel. Mondays were
Annabelle's day off, so in addition to her other duties, Megan
was front of house. An elderly lady guest had been taken by
surprise by a spider in the bath and had to be soothed and
brought tea and the spider disposed of. Someone had stolen a
bottle of Harveys Bristol Cream, a bottle of Courvoisier and the
contents of the honesty box from the bar. (A guest? A member
of staff? Someone off the street? There was no way of knowing.)
Megan grimly made a note of it and sent Janet out to buy more.
Doing the rounds with Jonah (he of the single tooth), she happened to catch sight of his hand, which he had stabbed with a
screwdriver the previous week. Megan didn't like the look of it.

"That's infected," she told him. "Go to the doctor. Go this minute." Jonah said he didn't have a doctor, he'd never had a doctor,
he didn't believe in doctors. Megan phoned the nearest surgery,
made an appointment for him and threatened to escort him if
he didn't go at once. An American couple arrived with no luggage: they'd flown overnight from New York to Heathrow while
their luggage had flown from New York to Singapore. Megan
was very sympathetic—she didn't have to pretend. She gave
them complimentary toothpaste and toothbrushes and promised to make the airline's life hell until the luggage was returned.

Whenever her father's letter entered her mind she reminded
herself that her mother had coped without her for two and a half
years now and Mrs. Jarvis came in twice a week and would
doubtless come more often if necessary. And Adam was nearly
four and, unless he had changed his personality since she'd left
(and he wouldn't have—in Megan's experience they were who
they were from the moment they drew breath), was a steady
little soul. He'll be fine, she told herself, just fine.

She did a reasonable job of convincing herself, but back at
her bedsit that evening she reread her father's letter and saw
something she had failed to take in earlier—that Tom was still
at home—and that made her mad all over again. Neither of her
parents had mentioned him for a while and she'd assumed he'd
managed to pull himself together and get on with his life. She
should have known better. Tom had always been a brooder. As a
child, when any little thing had gone wrong—someone stepping
on his Lancaster bomber, his prize penknife vanishing—he'd
withdrawn into himself and brooded for days.

She decided to write to him. Somebody had to do something
or he'd sit there for the rest of his life. She got a pen and an
airmail form from the kitchen drawer she'd dedicated to such

things and sat down at the table by the window. *"Dear Tom,"* she wrote, and paused. What she wanted to say was, *"Dear Tom, I know Robert's death was terrible, but I hear from Dad that you are still at home sitting on your backside brooding about it and I was wondering exactly what you thought you were achieving by that and when you were going to get on with your life,"* but she suspected that would be a mistake. She was still puzzling over it when there was a tap at the door. She answered it absent-mindedly, pen in hand.

"Hi," Andrew Bannerman said. "I've come to say welcome to the top floor. Oh . . . ," he broke off, noticing the pen. "Sorry. You're in the middle of something. I'll come back another time. But welcome anyway." He gave her his very nice smile and started to turn away.

"No," Megan said hastily. "It doesn't matter. I was just writing a letter. I can do it later. Please come in."

"Just for a sec," he said. "I can't stay—I was just going to say hello. Wow!" He looked around the room. "What a difference! It looks amazing. It's a great color."

"It was easy because it was empty," Megan said, ridiculously pleased. "I did it before I moved in."

He looked at her uncertainly. "I'm useless at accents but I think I detect one. Where are you from?" (How could you fail to like someone who phrased it like that?)

"Canada."

"Canada," he said, looking thoughtful. He seemed to be mulling Canada over.

"It's above the United States," Megan said dryly. (She was used to this now but nonetheless a little disappointed—she'd expected better of him.) She pointed upwards. "North."

He looked down at his feet and grinned. "I did know that

much, believe it or not. I was just wondering if I knew anything else. I know it's big and there's a lot of snow. Let's see: there's the Northwest Passage and the Franklin Expedition—they all died. Polar bears. Mounties, of course, always getting their man. Lumberjacks—there are lots of lumberjacks, right?"

"Some," Megan said. He was joking but she didn't mind. He was older than she'd thought, maybe close to thirty, and much better-looking. How could she have thought his face merely pleasant?

"I think that's about it," he said. "Sorry."

"That's okay," Megan said. "That's more than I knew about England when I came. Would you like some coffee?"

He had the nicest eyes she'd ever seen. Honest eyes. They were blue (unusual with such dark brown hair) and direct, and you didn't get the feeling that behind them he was wondering how soon he could get you into bed.

"I'd love to," he said. "But I can't just now. I have a deadline. But definitely another time. Or you come over to my place, except I'll have to clean it first."

He only stayed a minute after that, just long enough to say that he sometimes had the radio on when he was writing up his "stuff" (he was a journalist) and if it disturbed her she should knock and he'd turn it down. So he couldn't have been there longer than five minutes in total, but still, by the time he left, Megan felt as though she were running a temperature. She went over to the window, opened it fully and stood looking out over the quiet gardens. Don't you get carried away, her rational self said. He's nice—I'll grant you that. He's very nice. You like him and he likes you—because he did—she had felt that immediately—but that's all there is to it, so don't pretend there's more.

But another self, a self that despite the absurdity of pop song lyrics did indeed seem to be located somewhere down near the heart, safely beyond the reach of common sense or reason, said, This is it. He's the one.

When she finally turned from the window and saw the air-mail form lying on the table, for a moment she couldn't remember who she'd been writing to. Then she picked it up, refolded it and put it back in the kitchen drawer. Not tonight, she said to Tom in her head. Sorry. I can't think about you tonight.

══

Three weeks after he first knocked on her door Megan decided to invite Andrew Bannerman to dinner. She'd thought about it long and hard beforehand. The man was supposed to do the asking—it was silly but that was how it was, which was why she'd spent three weeks waiting for him to invite her over for coffee. The fact that he hadn't was disappointing, but she reasoned that it didn't necessarily mean he wasn't interested. It was possible, of course, that he already had a girlfriend, though if so he never brought her back to his room in the evenings. It was also possible that he hadn't had the time—certainly she heard his typewriter rattling away at all hours of the day and night. But the most likely reason, from what Megan knew of the male sex, was that he was chronically disorganized and simply hadn't got around to it yet.

It seemed to Megan that inviting him for dinner would do no harm. If she made it a casual, spur-of-the-moment, "I just happened to make too much of this stew" sort of invitation, it would look like a neighborly gesture rather than anything more. Where was the harm in that?

She considered the menu carefully. It needed to be something tempting, something really good, but it also needed to be the sort of thing she'd cook for herself or he'd smell a rat. Men loved pies, but no one made pies for themselves. They loved steak, but you couldn't "accidentally" buy twice as much steak as you could eat. She went to a bookstore on her lunch hour and browsed through cookbooks, looking for inspiration, and found it in the form of something called coq au vin. It sounded delicious. It also sounded posh, but she could call it a chicken casserole and he'd never know.

She left work early and bought the ingredients on the way home: a chicken, streaky bacon, butter, olive oil (she'd never heard of it), garlic (ditto), button onions (ditto), button mushrooms (ditto), herbs (mostly ditto), a quarter bottle of brandy (you only needed two tablespoons but you couldn't buy two tablespoons) and a bottle of Burgundy (you only needed half a bottle but they'd drink the rest). It cost a fortune but she didn't care. She carted it all home, the plastic bags cutting into her fingers. It was an oppressively hot day but she didn't care about that either. It took her the better part of an hour to bone the chicken and peel the onions and make the stock and cream the butter and flour for the roux, and she loved every minute of it. It wasn't until she'd put the dish in the oven and was standing back, hands on hips, smiling at the wreckage of her tiny kitchen, that she suddenly caught sight of herself in her mind's eye and realized she was behaving *exactly* like the sort of female she most despised, the sort she'd seen in ads on the television in the bar at the hotel, the sort who longed for nothing more than to spend her life chopping onions in order to please a man.

Worse still, she was deceiving herself. If he'd been interested in her, he would have shown it by now. And he wasn't stupid; if she knocked on his door with some story about having made too much stew, he would know precisely what she was doing and why.

Megan, already hot from slaving over the stove, went hotter still with shame. I will *not,* she said, silently but furiously, not just with her rational self but with every molecule, every atom of her being, I will *not* make myself ridiculous for any man. I will eat it myself. It will keep a couple of days in the fridge. And I'll drink the wine too.

She had a cool bath to lower her temperature and put on jeans and a none-too-clean shirt and her Scholl sandals and was on her way back to her room when Andrew's door opened and he came out, stopped dead in his tracks and said, "My God, Megan, what are you cooking? It smells fantastic out here!"

He was originally from Leicester, where his parents still lived, but when he was young the family had spent a couple of years in Edinburgh and in the summers they'd gone to the Isle of Skye for their holidays and stayed in a small town called, of all things, Struan. He was twenty-nine and had an older brother and a younger sister. He'd always wanted to be a journalist. (The problem was, he said, so did everyone else, so it was a crowded field, which was why he was permanently broke.)

He had a habit of looking down at his feet when he was joking or expressing an opinion, as if he thought he shouldn't force it on you, but then when he looked up he met your eyes so directly that it made you feel he was looking straight into your soul.

He seemed fascinated by Megan's description of life in Struan. His interest made her feel interesting, though afterwards she worried that she'd talked about herself too much. She told him about never having been to a city before she came to

London, and he shook his head in amazement. She told him about her arrival at 31 Lansdown Terrace and losing her suitcase. She laughed as she told the story, remembering how naive she'd been, but he didn't laugh. He said, "That isn't funny, it's terrible. What an introduction to England!" so she hastily told him about Mrs. Jamison at Dickins & Jones and Annabelle and Peter and how she loved working at the Montrose.

When they'd finished their dinner (she'd explained the coq au vin away as part of her plan to teach herself some fancy European cooking), he insisted on helping with the washing up— the first time she'd ever known a man to do that. As he was leaving he said, "That was a really great meal, Meg—thank you. Next time you have to come to me if you're brave enough. I'm not up to your standards but I do a mean spaghetti bolognese."

———

Three weeks. Four. They ran into each other frequently on the landing and he always seemed pleased to see her and never seemed in the least embarrassed or apologetic about the passage of time since the spaghetti invitation. Maybe he hadn't meant it. Or maybe he was the sort of person who took relationships seriously and didn't rush into them. Which, of course, was good.

Once she came up the stairs just as he was on his way back to his room from the bathroom, wrapped only in a very small towel. His hair was wet and he looked so astonishingly beautiful that Megan felt the blood rush to her face. Fortunately, he misinterpreted it. "Sorry, Meg," he said. "Timed it wrong." He didn't try to make anything of it, as she suspected most men would have done.

His door didn't latch properly unless he leaned against it, so generally it was open a few inches and if Megan left her door open too, she could see his right elbow as he sat at his desk. Now and again he'd tap at her door and say, "Coffee?" and her heart would give an enormous lurch and warmth would flood through her like a tide.

On and off he was away for a few days. The top floor felt wrong then. The silence echoed, and sometimes Megan heard the whining brat downstairs.

=====

"We've been thinking," Peter said.

They were in the office, behind the reception desk. It was three in the afternoon, a quiet time of day.

"We think we're going to sell the Montrose."

Megan stared. The front door opened and the young couple from Paris came in. Megan got up automatically, went out to the desk, smiled, gave them their room key and returned to the office.

"That was not a good way to break it to her, Peter," Annabelle said. "Megan, you've gone pale. You're not going to be out of a job. We want to buy another old hotel and do the same as we did with this, and of course we want you to be part of it. We wouldn't dream of doing it without you."

"We'll get a good price for the Montrose," Peter said. "It's the right time to sell. And we'll buy something a bit bigger, twenty to thirty rooms."

"It'll be a challenge," Annabelle said, smiling at her. "And we know you like a challenge."

Sell the Montrose? They wanted to sell the Montrose? She couldn't believe it. The Montrose was theirs—they had made it, the three of them. They had poured their hearts into it. They *were* the Montrose. How could they sell it?

Annabelle and Peter were watching her.

"It's not going to happen straight away," Peter said. "Probably not until next year, unless we stumble on the perfect place before then. Come on, Meg, you look as if someone had died. Think what fun it was last time."

Megan collected herself. "Yes," she said. "Yes, of course. Of course."

At home that evening she sat at her small table watching the swaying of the trees against the darkening sky. Cold rain splattered against the window. It was October and the nights were closing in. When Peter had made his announcement it was as if the world had tilted—everything that had seemed fixed was suddenly shown to be precarious.

With hindsight, Megan thought, there had been signs recently that Peter was restless; he'd taken to standing on the porch of the hotel, hands in his pockets, looking out at the road as if he was waiting for something to happen. It had crossed her mind that he didn't have enough to do, but she'd thought no further about it. Now she saw that Peter having too little to do was the source of the problem. The Montrose was running smoothly, they were frequently fully booked and their accounts were in good order. All of those things were a source of satisfaction to the three of them, but for Peter they also meant that the hotel was no longer a challenge. He was the one who liked a challenge. And what Peter wanted, Annabelle would persuade herself she wanted too.

At least, Megan thought, they're looking for another property in London. They could have decided to start up a hotel in France, or Italy, or Spain. They could still decide that. They both spoke several languages and loved going abroad. But if that happened, she would not want to go with them. She had no gift for languages and in any case it would be one step too far. She wasn't an adventurous person. She knew that now.

So what would she do? If Peter and Annabelle left London or tired of the hotel business, or if there was some other unforeseen eventuality, what would she do? She'd have to start over and she didn't want to start over—it was too hard. She saw that it wasn't England or even London she'd been living in for the past almost-three years, it was the Montrose Hotel. Outside its walls she was still a stranger here. It was her own fault: she should have pushed herself, met more people, tried new things. But it had been easier not to.

There was a tap at the door. Megan went over and opened it. Andrew Bannerman, wearing an apron and holding a glass of red wine in each hand, said, "Spaghetti?"

She'd never known anyone who listened as intently as he did. She told him about Peter's announcement, making light of her reaction to it, but he saw through that. "New things are scary, but nothing stays the same, Meg. You have to go with it, grab opportunities when they come along."

"I know," she said. "I know."

He smiled. "Sorry. Unasked-for advice. Have some more spaghetti."

She liked the fact that he gave unasked-for advice. It was a sign that he was interested. But she didn't want to talk about herself again, she wanted to know more about him. She asked about journalism and he described his early days in London, trying to sell his work. It had been a struggle, he said, and she guessed it had got him down sometimes; he wasn't as laid-back as he looked. He was the only member of his family who wasn't a doctor—two grandfathers, father, mother, brother and sister.

"They don't think journalism is a real job," he said ruefully. "They're all infuriatingly patronizing, even my little sister. *Especially* my little sister."

Megan nodded. "My older brother used to patronize me. He did it all the time. I got so fed up I banned it, in the end."

"Banned it?" Andrew said with a grin. "How do you ban being patronizing?"

"Well, there were certain phrases he used that made me mad because they didn't sound rude but you knew they were. You know, things like 'If you think about it,' which means you're not thinking about it, and 'With respect,' which basically means without respect. 'I think you'll find' is another one. I fined him twenty-five cents every time he said something like that."

Andrew let out a whoop of laughter. "Brilliant!" he said. "Did he pay up?"

"I was in charge of the pocket money, so I just deducted it. Some weeks he didn't get any at all."

Which Andrew thought was funnier still.

Megan wasn't sure what he found so amusing. Though now, looking back, she suddenly wondered if Tom had found it funny too, funny enough, in fact, to be worth sacrificing his pocket money for—that possibility hadn't occurred to her at the time. But regardless of the reason, she was glad she could make Andrew laugh. There was no reserve in his laughter and she was becoming aware of a shadow of reserve in him the rest of the time. Not exactly guardedness. "Carefulness" would be a better word. Maybe he'd been hurt in a previous relationship. But then, the English were famous for their reserve, weren't they? So maybe it was just that.

She asked what he was working on at the moment and he said he was doing a piece on a painting at the National Gallery.

"Have you been to the National Gallery?" he asked.

"No," Megan said. "I haven't been anywhere." She'd been dreading that question—it was bound to come up sooner or later.

But if he was horrified he didn't show it. "Buckingham Palace? Hampton Court?"

"No," she said. "Nothing like that. I don't know anything about history or art or anything, so I'm afraid I wouldn't get a lot out of it. To be honest."

"You don't need to know anything. I don't know much myself. It doesn't matter. Look, I'm going to see the painting again on Thursday—I need another look at it. Do you want to come? Can you get time off? Say, Thursday afternoon?"

"Yes," Megan said. "Yes, I can get time off. Yes, I'd like to come."

Who'd have believed she would ever accept an invitation to the National Gallery with such a leap of the heart?

Though when it came to it, the gallery was just as she'd thought it would be, only bigger. Room after enormous room filled with paintings of absurdly dressed men and women looking down their noses at you or unreal landscapes or ships being tossed about in storms or pictures of angels and saints with golden halos. They left Megan cold.

Andrew pretended not to be watching her. Every now and then he'd tell her who someone was or the story behind a painting.

"You recognize this guy?"

A skinny-looking guy wearing armor and sitting on a horse with a head too small for the rest of it.

"No, but I can read. It's Charles I—it's on the plaque." Much as she loved him, she wasn't going to let him patronize her.

"Ah, so it is." She could hear his grin.

They entered yet another room, filled with yet more paintings. Andrew steered her over to a large picture with several figures in it, all of them in dark clothing, the room behind them dark, everything dark apart from the central figure of a pale girl in a pearl white dress with a blindfold over her eyes.

"This is the one I'm doing a piece on," Andrew said. *The Execution of Lady Jane Grey.* The National Gallery's just acquired it."

"Who was she?"

"She was queen of England back in 1553. She reigned for nine days and then she was sent to the Tower. And after a bit they chopped her head off."

The blindfold covered almost half of the girl's face, but nonetheless you could see that she was very young, and you could also see that she was absolutely terrified. Her lips, which looked very soft, like a child's, were slightly parted and she was reaching out her arms as you would if you couldn't see what was in front of you. What was in front of her was a chopping block. Beside it was a man dressed in dark red tights, leaning casually on an axe. An old man in a fur-lined coat was guiding the girl down toward the block, helping her to kneel. In one corner, two women were swooning against the wall.

"How old was she?"

"Sixteen."

"Sixteen!"

If you reached out and touched her hand it would be like ice.

"Who are the other women—the ones against the wall?"

"Her ladies in waiting, I imagine. Overcome with horror and grief."

Megan studied them, her lips tight. Get up, she thought. Go over to her, kneel down beside her and talk to her. Stay there until she's dead. Then you can be overcome with horror and grief.

"It wouldn't have happened quite like he's painted it," Andrew said. "For a start they wouldn't have executed her indoors; they'd have taken her outside and done it on Tower Green. And her dress is wrong for the time."

Who cares where it happened or what she was wearing, Megan thought. She was astonished by the intensity of emotion the painting conveyed. Who'd have thought you could paint terror and dread?

"It's powerful, isn't it?" Andrew said. "I've always been interested in her because she lived very close to where I grew up. Her home was in Bradgate Park, up near Leicester. The day her head was cut off, her household lopped off the tops of all the oak trees. Decapitated them as a gesture of respect for her. A few of them are still there."

Megan tore her eyes from the girl's face. "The actual trees? Didn't you say it was 15-something?"

"That's right." He studied her, smiling at her interest. "Would you like to see them? I'm going up there next week—I want to mention them in the piece I'm writing, and I need a photo. I'm borrowing a car, so if you want to, you could come and see them for yourself."

They arranged to go on Tuesday, Megan's day off. She spent the intervening days storming around the Montrose with an energy born of joy. She reorganized the linen cupboard, harried Jonah to check and bleed the radiators in preparation for winter, took down and cleaned the chandeliers on the landings, rehung the curtains in room 8. In the evenings she spring-cleaned her flat as well. It didn't need it but she had energy to burn. She wanted it perfect to come home to, in honor of the fact that, although ostensibly everything would be the same as when they set off, in reality everything was going to be different.

====

It was a three-hour drive to Bradgate Park, and they were going up and back in a day, so they set off early. The sky was overcast and the landscape en route flat and uninteresting but when they finally arrived, the park made up for it. It was bigger than Megan had expected and wilder and far more beautiful. Hills covered with bracken, their surfaces broken here and there by granite outcrops, areas of woodland, a wide clear stream. The leaves were turning. They didn't have the drama of Fall at home—the colors were softer and more muted—but with every gust of wind the leaves went swirling through the air in clouds of russet and gold.

They came across several of the ancient oaks straight away: huge trunks abruptly sliced off about ten feet from the ground, topped by a mass of smaller branches sticking up like fingers on a hand. One of the trees was dead, its mutilated body stark against the sky. Megan thought of the girl with the childish lips and icy hands; thought of her seeing that tree when both she and it were young. She might have sought out its shade on a hot day, sat under it peacefully. Not knowing its Fate. Not knowing her own.

It had never struck her before that the people you read about in history books had actually lived. Theoretically you knew they had, but in practice they'd been no more than words on a page. The tree was proof. It made Megan wonder who had killed the girl and why, but she didn't ask Andrew because if she had he would have told her, and that would have turned it into a history lesson and destroyed her feeling of connection with the girl. She would ask him another day.

They wandered, Andrew stopping now and then to take photographs. One tree in particular seemed to please him. They passed it early on and after exploring elsewhere they returned to it and he spent a long time photographing it from different angles. At some stage in its history it had been struck by lightning— one side had been partially burned away, leaving a great black cave at its heart. Incredibly, several branches were still reaching up, topped with small crowns of crisp brown leaves. As Megan watched, a gust of wind made the leaves shiver; several of them lost their grip and whirled away.

"A true survivor," Andrew said. "Still soldiering on."

A few yards away there was a log. Megan sat down and wrapped her arms around herself. The wind was cold. While they'd been walking the sky had clouded over, and her feeling of closeness with the place and its history had drained away. She was just herself now; herself, sitting on a log, trying not to think about the fact that time was passing and the day was more than half gone. In a few minutes Andrew was going to say he had enough photos. They'd go back to the car and drive somewhere for lunch, and then they'd head home and the trip would be over.

Which would have been fine if the trip had been truly and solely about Lady Jane Grey, but it was not. Megan had imagined herself and Andrew walking through this park hand in hand; she'd seen him leaning back against one of the ancient trees, wrapping his arms around her. Kissing her. Holding her to him. Ridiculous women's magazine images, but it turned out there was a core of truth in them because—she knew this now—when you were in love with someone you wanted to be as close to them as it was possible to get, you wanted to weld yourself to them, become part of them, make them part of you. You needed to touch them, you needed them to touch you. And he hadn't touched her. He'd never touched her and had shown no sign of wanting to. Never kissed her. She'd been certain that today, finally, would mark a turning point in their relationship, but once again, nothing had changed.

Andrew had climbed up as far as he could get into the ancient trunk and was taking a photo down into its hollowed-out innards. "I have fond memories of this particular tree," he said. "My brother and I used to pretend it was a castle—we had to defend it against all comers. Our parents, in other words. Our parents and our little sister. She was a ravening wolf. She didn't want to be a ravening wolf, she wanted to be inside the castle with us, but we needed a ravening wolf and she was it. Very mean."

A response was required. Megan said, "So this is really close to where you lived, then?"

"About ten miles. We came here a lot at weekends."

She tried to imagine him young, scrambling over the rocks with his brother, but she could only see him now.

"I'm nearly done," he said from inside the trunk. "Are you cold?"

"No, I'm fine." She wasn't fine. She was wretched.

"Good. I'll . . . Bugger, that's the end of the roll. I guess it'll have to do." He climbed out of the tree and came and sat down beside her. "There's a pub in the village," he said, opening the back of his camera. "We'll get some lunch there and warm up before heading back." He took out the roll of film and put it in his pocket. Then he looked at her and smiled. "So what did you think of the trees? I hope it hasn't been a waste of a day off."

"No," Megan said. "They're amazing."

She wanted him so badly she didn't dare look at him; he would see it in her eyes.

A minute passed. Andrew said, "You okay, Meg?"

"Yes, of course. I'm fine," she said, not looking at him. "Do you want to stop and see your parents on the way back?"

"No, not this time."

She could feel him watching her and tried to pull herself together. "Are you sure? Because I'm not in a hurry, if you want to." She had assumed he would—she'd wondered if they would like her.

"It wouldn't be smart," he said.

Which was such an odd thing to say that she looked at him. He was watching her. There was something in his eyes she couldn't read.

He said, "Meg, there's something I think you should know." He hesitated, and looked away for a minute, then looked back and smiled. She couldn't read the smile either. "You've probably guessed, but I need to be sure, because I like you a lot—really a lot—and I don't want you to get the wrong idea. I'm getting the feeling—maybe I'm wrong, in which case everything's fine—but I'm getting the feeling that maybe you'd like there to be more to our friendship than just . . . friendship."

She looked down at her feet. She was cold right through to her bones. If he was telling her he already had a girlfriend hidden away somewhere, she wished he would say so.

Andrew said, "Basically, what it boils down to is I'm not good boyfriend material."

What did he mean by that? She was getting angry with him. Was he saying he was married?

"Are you married?" she said, looking at him fiercely.

He smiled, but his smile was tired, as if he'd had this conversation before and would rather not be having it again. "No. No, I'm not married. And I don't have a girlfriend. I've never had a girlfriend. I'm homosexual."

Megan felt a jolt go through her, felt color flood her face. She turned sharply away. On the hillside to the right of them there was another of the ancient oaks, dead but still standing, black against the sky.

He said, "You didn't realize. Sorry. I should have told you sooner."

She couldn't look at him. She kept her eyes on the ancient oak.

He said gently, "Megan, say something. You've heard of homosexuality, right? Even in Northern Ontario they've heard of homosexuality?"

She had heard of homosexuality but only as a term, as a concept. She'd never met anyone—or at least never knowingly met anyone—who was homosexual. Mostly it just seemed to be a term of abuse used against boys by other boys. "*Homo.*"

In the trees behind them some rooks were squabbling. Apart from that there was no sound.

Andrew said quietly, "You are making this hard for me, Meg."

She had to say something. She cleared her throat. "I've never understood it," she said.

"Okay, good. You're talking." Relief in his voice. "What don't you understand?"

"I don't understand why it would happen. Why would such a thing . . . ?"

"Yes, well, the problem with these 'why?' questions is there's no one to ask. It just happens. Always has, always will, unless they find some way of wiping us all out, which no doubt they're working on."

It just didn't make sense. Surely, Megan thought, surely if he were homosexual then her love for him—this incessant, desperate longing—would not have come about; her body would have known that his body didn't want hers and that would have been the end of it. Instead of which she had loved and wanted him more every time she saw him. Surely that meant it couldn't be true.

"But, Andrew, how can you be sure? I mean—"

He stood up quickly, cutting her off, and walked away and stood with his back to her, hands in his pockets, looking out over the park.

She saw that his back was taut with strain, that there was strain in every line of his body. She saw that telling her had not been easy for him. That nothing about it was easy for him. That he would not have said it unless it was true.

She wanted to go home. Not home to London, home to Struan. She wanted to go home to her own bed in her own room and stay there because life was too much for her. Too complicated, too painful.

Finally he came and sat down beside her again.

"Sorry," he said. "Difficult subject." He reached out and rubbed her back. "Let's go and have lunch."

It was the first time he'd ever touched her.

How are you supposed to stop loving someone you love?

CHAPTER FOURTEEN

Edward

Struan, March 1969

I need some time off. I don't mean from work. I'm entitled to two weeks' annual vacation, which I never take because being at work is so much less stressful than being at home. I mean time off from the escalating chaos in this family. There are things I need to think about and they're important, because it seems to me that if I could get a sense of perspective on the past I'd be able to deal better with the present, but there's no time; the present goes from one crisis to the next so fast that there's scarcely time to draw breath, far less think.

This afternoon I had the interview with Ralph Robertson, the principal at the high school. It was very inconvenient to have to go—there were a great many papers waiting on my desk at the bank—but I went. Robertson is a gray man. He wears gray and he looks gray. He greeted me rather anxiously, I thought, and spent an unnecessarily long time on the pleasantries, but eventually I managed to steer the conversation around to the purpose of our meeting.

"You wanted to see me about Peter and Corey," I said when we were both sitting down.

"Yes," he said, frowning at his pen. "Yes, I thought perhaps we should have a word . . ."

I nodded encouragingly. I was recalling that he has a wife and three teenage daughters, all of whom disappear off to Sudbury with his checkbook from time to time and manage to spend more in an afternoon than he earns in a month. I wondered if they'd done it again and seeing me reminded him of his bank account and that was why he was looking anxious.

"Nice boys," he was saying. "Though at a difficult age, of course."

"I take it they've been misbehaving," I said, trying to speed things along.

"Not seriously," he said. "Well, by and large not seriously. By and large just the usual things, fighting in the schoolyard, smoking in the toilets, failing to do homework, that sort—"

"Smoking?" I said. It's the most ridiculous habit known to man; quite apart from its effect on your health, you might as well roll up a dollar bill and set fire to it.

"They all do it," he said, taking off his glasses and rubbing his eyes. "It's because it's forbidden. And now there's all this new stuff, marijuana, LSD, who knows what else. LSD hasn't reached us up here yet—or at least I don't think it has. Makes them go out of their minds, apparently, but with some of ours it can be hard to tell. In my view we should make it compulsory, all of it, then they'd stop." He put his glasses back on. "But with Peter and Corey the greatest concern at the moment is the absenteeism and the—"

"Absenteeism?"

"Yes, lately they've been regularly missing a day or two a week, sometimes more. They weren't in at all last week and only on Tuesday the week before. Our secretary, Mrs. Turner, phoned your wife several times to see if they had colds, but there was no reply. So I thought it would be a good idea to speak to you."

It didn't surprise me that Emily hadn't answered the phone—she probably can't even hear it, up in her room with the door closed—but the boys playing truant was something else. It wasn't only the fact of them missing lessons that concerned me, it was also the thought of what they might be up to instead.

"Also," Ralph Robertson said. He was hunched over his desk with his shoulders up around his ears and his hands clasped in front of him, and I suddenly noticed that he was twiddling his thumbs. Literally twiddling them—they were spinning around each other like little turbines. I've never seen anyone actually do that before. I thought it was a figure of speech. If I were Robertson, that is a habit I would break. His pupils must love it.

"Also—and this I can't verify, it is merely hearsay, but I thought I should tell you just in case—one afternoon last week they, or two boys looking very like them, were seen down at the sawmill apparently trying to set fire to one of the old shacks. Well, partially succeeding—it was the smoke that drew attention to them. Though I believe it soon went out. The wood, of course, was very wet."

I was frozen to my chair.

"As I say, the boys weren't identified for certain, but I thought I should pass it on to you. Because your two weren't in school at the time."

All sorts of images were scrolling through my head. Archie Giles's hay barn. The charred sticks behind the bank. Joel Pickett and his sons. Sergeant Moynihan filling the doorway to my office.

"I see," I said.

I stood up. Ralph Robertson stood up as well.

I said, "Thank you for telling me. Are they here now? At school?"

"Er, no. I don't think they've been in today."

I didn't go home to see if they were there. I didn't dare. I was so angry I didn't trust myself anywhere near them. I drove directly to the police station. Fortunately Gerry Moynihan was there. He offered me a chair and I sat down but I was so agitated it was all I could do to stay seated.

"It was my sons," I said to Gerry without preamble. "Peter and Corey. They burned down Archie Giles's hay barn. You don't need to look any further. It goes without saying that I will—"

Gerry raised his hand and I stopped. He said, very calmly, "Sorry, Mr. Cartwright, can we start again? What's happened? Take your time, sir. We've got plenty of time."

I took a breath. My lungs didn't seem to be expanding properly. It was as if they were in a cage that had become too small, too tight. It took a huge effort to speak normally—in fact, it took a huge effort not to shout—but I managed to relate the details of my interview with Ralph Robertson. Gerry listened quietly, looking attentive but unperturbed.

"So it was them," I said when I'd given him the facts. "It goes without saying that I will repay Archie every cent he lost, the barn, animal feed, any expenses, anything. The question is—"

Gerry raised his hand again. "Hold on, Mr. Cartwright," he said. "Hold on. I appreciate you comin' to tell me this—not everybody would—but I'm pretty sure your kids didn't burn down that barn."

I was concentrating so hard on trying to keep a lid on my fury that I didn't hear him properly at first, but after a minute the words sank in, and even though I was sure he was wrong I'd never heard sweeter words in my life.

"I've thought all along the jobs were different," Gerry said. "Whoever did Giles's barn meant business. They used gasoline, gave it a real soaking. Whereas with the fire behind the bank, your boys, if it was your boys—"

"It was," I said. "Thank you, but I know it was."

"Well, no, you don't, sir," Gerry said mildly. "There's no evidence it was them, nobody saw them, and from what you tell me there wasn't a positive identification down at the sawmill either, so you don't know, you're just suspicious."

"All right," I said. "I'm suspicious. I'm very, very suspicious."

"Okay. So what I was sayin' is, whoever set that little fire at your bank was an amateur. Didn't know the first thing about it. Struck me the minute I saw it. I reckoned it was kids and they were copy-catting. They'd heard about the Giles's fire and thought it'd be kinda fun to try it. Same applies down at the sawmill. I'll go take a look at it but from what you say they didn't even manage to get the fire properly started."

He paused, watching me. After a minute he went on.

"So the question is, what're we gonna do about it. Seein' that there's no proof it was them and no damage has been done."

"What would you normally do in such circumstances?" I said tightly. "I don't want them treated any differently from anyone else. No differently at all."

Gerry cleared his throat. "Well, I'll tell you, the theory is all kids are the same so all kids get treated the same, but the fact is they aren't and what I do depends on what I think of their parents. In cases such as yourself, a good family, I would normally just report my suspicions to the parents, let them handle it. If I thought the parents wouldn't care too much or had no control over their children, I'd haul the kids in to the station here, ask 'em a few questions, maybe show 'em what a prison cell looks like. Give 'em a little bit of a scare, you might say.

"This case is a bit unusual in that you've come to tell me rather than the other way 'round, which I appreciate. And because of that and because I know you, I'm not inclined to do anythin' more." He paused, studying my face, and then added, "Unless you want me to, of course."

I sat for a minute. It wasn't only a matter of how much control I had over the boys, it was also a matter of how much control I had over myself. I was still so angry I didn't want to be within ten miles of them. Added to that, I strongly suspected they would pay no attention to anything I said.

"If it's all right with you, I'd like you to talk to them," I said at last.

"Do you want me to bring 'em here? Into the jail?"

"Maybe at home—at our house. If you would do that."

He nodded. "Sure," he said. "Fine by me. I'll come knockin' on your door tonight."

"What if they're not in?" I realized I had no idea how the boys spent their evenings.

"I'll find 'em."

He would too. The relief of handing the whole business over to someone who knew what he was doing was indescribable.

"Thank you," I said. "Thank you very much."

I started to get up but Gerry said, "One more thing I should say, Mr. Cartwright. Arson's a serious crime and you were right to come in and tell me about it, but your boys, if it was them, aren't the first to do somethin' like this. They're young and they're male and that means they're stupid, it doesn't mean they're criminals. I'm just telling you that in case you're feeling a little . . . upset."

He came at eight, in uniform, looking as if he meant business. The boys were in. I hadn't seen them—I took care not to see them—but the usual thumps and yells were reverberating through the house. I called them downstairs and when they saw Gerry their faces went almost green. Frankly, I felt a bit sick myself. I showed the three of them into my study—Tom and Adam were in the living room—and retreated to the kitchen. I couldn't sit down. I paced back and forth, back and forth. I kept thinking about what Gerry had said: if it was a good family, he told the parents and let them handle it. He classed ours as a good family and no doubt anyone from outside would say the same. But what people actually mean by that phrase, when you take it apart and look at it, is a family that lives in a nice house with a father who earns a decent wage. I was thinking as I paced that if you knew what went on inside our family, by no sensible criteria could you call it "good." Right now, in my study, a policeman—who as it happens isn't married and has no children of his own—was talking to my sons because I, their father, was afraid that I might do them actual bodily harm if I tried to do it myself, and also because I was afraid that they would pay no attention to me regardless of what I said. Meanwhile, upstairs, my wife had just produced another son, on whom she would dote for a year and whose upbringing thereafter she would totally neglect. A son who might well turn out to be a disgrace to us and a menace to society. I thought about this community we live in and how hard I have tried over the years to be a useful and respected member of it. I thought about my good name. It is hard to say whether rage or shame was uppermost in my mind.

After a while I heard the boys come out of the study. I waited until I heard them go upstairs and then went in to see Gerry.

"Well, we had a little talk," he said easily, leaning back in my chair. "It was like I thought: they did the fires at the bank and the sawmill, but not the barn. I doubt they'll do anythin' of that sort again. They're not bad kids, Mr. Cartwright."

"Thank you," I said. I wanted to ask him what I should do now. How I should go about managing them from here on, because I had absolutely no idea. I wanted to explain to Gerry that I had never wanted to be a father and lacked the qualities necessary to do the job. I wanted to ask if he'd do it for me, if he'd just take them off my hands.

I offered him coffee but he declined. I showed him to the door and thanked him again and he gave that salute of his and set off into the snow.

I went back in. As I passed his chair Tom looked up from his newspaper.

"Trouble?" he said.

It was the first time in a year and a half that I'd heard Tom initiate a conversation but I was in no state to be encouraged by it.

"Arson," I said, bitterly.

He raised his eyebrows. "Anything major?"

"Not yet. But only because they're incompetent."

"They were probably just messing around," he said. "You know them." He watched me for a minute and then added,

"Anyway, he read them the riot act. They looked pretty scared when they came out."

He went back to his paper. I went into my study and closed the door.

I sat at my desk, remembering the first time I heard the police knock on the door. I'd have been about ten. There were two of them and sagging between them was my father, mumbling drivel and stinking of vomit. It happened many times after that but I remember that first occasion vividly. The shame of it. I'd wanted to deny all knowledge of him, all connection. I'd wanted them to lock him up and throw away the key.

Now, sitting in my study, I thought, Here we are again. From the police knocking on the door, back to the police knocking on the door, in two generations. Never mind that I'd asked Gerry to come; in essence it was the same.

After a while I heard Tom and Adam go up to bed. I stayed where I was, in a kind of daze of confusion and incomprehension, trying to figure out how my life had become what it was. I thought about the five sons I had sleeping upstairs. Two more on the far side of the world. One in the cemetery beside the church. One daughter, three thousand miles away.

I wondered how I had come to father all those beings, having wanted none. I wondered, for the hundredth time, how I had come to marry Emily, given that I didn't love her. I decided there were many reasons, none of them good. I married her because she was in love with me and I was amazed and flattered by that. I married her because I mistakenly thought we wanted the same things out of life. Because she was beautiful. Because I was grateful to her parents for accepting me as a suitable partner for their daughter despite my father being a drunkard and a fool. Because I was about to go off to war and would be killed and wanted to have sex before I died. I married her because she asked me to and it would have been impolite to say no. I married her because the stench of the fire was still in my nostrils and the balance of my mind was disturbed.

=====

We seem to be programmed to seek answers. Something happens and we need to know why. We chase around inside our heads, trying on this theory and that theory, searching for one that fits. But often there are no answers, or too many. You could say, for instance, that what happened during the fire was a consequence of my doing well at school. You could say it was a consequence of my brothers Alan and Harry going off to war. They may seem like tenuous links but they're real and they're important. Without them, what happened wouldn't have happened.

That bit in her diary where my mother wrote that she didn't dare tell my father how well I was doing at school because he was "taking against" me more and more: that was true. The others came in for their share of abuse but I was the one he hated and it was at least in part because I was a whole lot smarter than he was and he knew it and knew that I knew it. Worse still, I was smart in the way he despised and envied most: I was book-learning smart.

My mother was book-learning smart too but she took care not to let it show. I'd have had an easier time of it if I'd done the same and I knew that; I just couldn't put it into practice. My hatred of my father for the way he treated us—my mother in particular—was so great that when he came into the room I would start to shake. It was loathing, not fear, but I knew it looked like fear and for my own self-respect I had to find a way of standing up to him. Physically I stood no chance—he was a big man and his fists were hard as stone—so I fought him with my intelligence. I fought him with irony.

In the evenings I'd do my homework at the kitchen table and he'd come in after a hard day drinking or chipping away at rocks—the last man in Canada to realize there was no longer a market for silver—and find me with my head in a book and instantly he'd be furious. It was like flicking a switch. He'd say, his voice low and dangerous, "What you sittin' there for, doin' nothin' like you own the place?" and I'd quickly get to my feet and stand almost, but not quite, to attention, hands at my sides, willing my body to be still, and say something like, "I'm sorry, Father, I need to work out these equations for school. But I can do them later if there's something you want me to do." Very earnestly, very respectfully, with not the faintest hint of sarcasm in my voice—or only the faintest hint. He'd look at me with eyes like slits. Not sure.

I loved that look. The suspicion, the uncertainty in his eyes. I paid a high price, but it was worth it. I never did it when my mother was in the room, though. Which I suppose is another way of saying I knew it was wrong.

The twins saw what I was doing and they thought I was crazy. I remember one night in our bedroom when I was studying my bruises, Harry said, "Just stay out of his way, for Christ's sake, Ed! Do your bloody homework in here where he can't see you."

I said I had a right to do my homework wherever I liked. Harry shook his head in disgust and said, "Thought you were supposed to be smart."

With hindsight the twins were remarkably good to me. We had nothing in common but it didn't seem to matter. Both of them left school at sixteen to help with the farm, whereas I stayed on. It meant I didn't do my share of the farm work but they didn't hold it against me. School was my refuge and I guess they knew that. I had my eye on university and had decided that when I had my degree I would do what Mr. Sabatini had done: teach my way around the world. When Emily arrived on the scene I confessed my dream to her and thereafter she dreamed it too, or let on she did. The two of us were going to travel the world together.

The dreams of the young. They're particularly tragic, it seems to me, because they are based on the assumption that you control your own destiny. On the third of September 1939 a lot of dreams came to an end, including ours. I was seventeen, too young to sign up, but the twins were eighteen. I remember the evening they told me they were going. "It's your turn now, kid," Alan said, meaning my turn to quit school and look after the farm.

I felt as if I'd been kicked in the stomach, and it must have shown, because he punched me lightly on the shoulder and said it wouldn't be for long; the war would be over by Christmas and if it wasn't, then as soon as I turned eighteen I could join them.

I knew that wasn't so. There was no way all three of us could go, leaving our mother with only the girls to help with the heavy farm work and, more than that, leaving her at the mercy of our father. It felt like the end of everything, the end of the world.

I hadn't realized the extent to which the twins had acted as a buffer, shielding me from my father. Once they left, things became very bad between us. I was big enough by then that he hesitated to attack me when he was sober but he was sober less and less of the time, and when he was drunk he was savage. I couldn't stay out of his way because I didn't dare leave my mother alone when he was around.

My schooling was over, and with it my contact with the outside world. Emily and I saw each other only at church on Sunday and for an hour or two in the evenings if I was sure my father was off on one of his prolonged binges. Those few hours aside, I was a prisoner on the farm.

I prayed every night for the war to end so that Alan and Harry would come home and rescue me. I don't know why it took me so long to work out that they never would. It finally dawned on me one night when I was sitting in the doctor's office in town. My father had arrived home raging drunk and when I tried to bar the door he smashed his way in and came at me with a broken bottle. I raised my arm to shield my face and the glass sliced through my arm from wrist to elbow. With my other hand I grabbed a kitchen chair and hit him so hard I knocked him cold. I believe I would have gone on to kill him then, had my mother and Margaret not stopped me.

Margaret drove me to the doctor's and it was while he was stitching me up that it suddenly came to me that, even if they survived the war, Alan and Harry would not be coming home. Why would they? The farm wasn't worth much, certainly not enough to compensate for life with our father. They'd made their escape and I couldn't blame them; they'd have been crazy to come back. That was when I realized that while my father was alive I was never going to be able to leave. So that was when I started lying awake at night planning how to kill him.

The phrase "every cloud has a silver lining"—I'd like to know who thought that up. One morning late in the summer of 1942, almost three years after Alan and Harry went off to war, I stepped out onto the porch and saw a strange cloud on the horizon. At first I thought it was a storm cloud and I was glad to see it—there had been no rain for six weeks and the fields were parched. During the morning the cloud continued to build and when I came out after lunch the underbelly had taken on a lurid light. I called out my mother and Margaret to have a look and the three of us watched it uneasily. We live in a tinderbox up here. We're surrounded on all sides by thousands upon thousands of square miles of grade-A firewood.

At length Mother said, "I think it's a fire."

It was a long way west of us and I remember thinking we'd be okay unless the wind changed. By three o'clock you could see flames beneath the cloud of smoke. I propped a ladder against the house and climbed up onto the roof to get a better look and saw a vast curtain of fire at least twenty miles wide. I still thought it would miss us but I decided to take the cattle down to the lake, half a mile away through the woods, just in case.

By four o'clock great billows of smoke were beginning to block out the sun. Fires create a ferocious updraft, sucking up air as the heat rises, and from the roof I could see flaming tree-tops being tossed miles ahead of the fire itself. It was still a long way off but the danger lay in a stray gust blowing smaller branches or twigs in our direction, so I decided to soak the roof of the house as a precaution. My mother and Margaret took turns at the pump and those of my sisters who were big enough formed a chain and passed the buckets up to me.

We were in the midst of this when my father showed up. We hadn't seen him for several days, which generally meant he'd been off on a bender, but either he hadn't had all that much to drink or the sight of the fire sobered him because he seemed to grasp what was needed. I left him on the roof slinging water on the shingles and went down to take my turn at the pump.

The next time I went up the ladder, the sky to the north and west of us was dark with smoke and beneath it the flames seemed to fill the whole horizon.

"It's getting too close," I said. "Time we left."

My father said, "We ain't leavin' this house to burn, so you can put that idea out of your head. Get back to the pump."

As he spoke I felt a breath of hot air on my face. Just a breath, very slight. Then a moment later, another one.

I didn't bother replying to my father. I turned and went down the ladder fast. My mother and the girls had left the pump and were clustered together at the foot of the ladder, looking up at us. Amy, the smallest, was clutching Margaret's legs and crying with fear.

I said quietly to my mother, "I think the wind's changing. You need to take the girls to the lake before it gets too dark to see the path."

She was nearly wringing her hands with distress. She said, "Edward, we cannot leave the house to burn. We cannot."

From the top of the ladder my father roared, "Bring up the buckets! What're you waitin' for?"

My mother started to run back to the pump but I grabbed her arm. "Mother! You have to take the girls! It might still miss us, but we can't take the chance."

My mother turned to Margaret and said, "Margaret, you take them. Edward and I will stay and help your father."

"I will not!" Margaret said, furious and terrified. "We will all go together!"

My mother didn't reply. She was looking past me, over my shoulder. She said, "Edward . . ." her voice scarcely above a whisper.

I turned and saw that the wind had swung around and was blowing the fire straight toward us. Above it, darkness was rolling out across the sky.

The worst thing, the most terrifying thing, the thing that has stayed with me over all these years, was not the sight of the fire's approach, though it seemed to be coming at the speed of an express train, but the *sound*. It was like nothing I had ever heard. It bore no relation whatsoever to the spit and crackle of branches when you throw wood on a campfire; it was a deep, cavernous *howl,* like some gigantic creature gone insane. Trees were exploding at its approach—they weren't "catching fire," they weren't "bursting into flames," they were literally exploding—huge fireballs belching 150 feet into the air, clouds of smoke and sparks roaring upwards. The *sound* of it. I'll never forget it. If hell has a sound, that is it.

For a moment I couldn't even draw breath. Then I turned. Margaret was holding Amy. I picked up Jane and tried to press her into my mother's arms.

"Take her!" I said. "Go! Now!"

But my mother wouldn't take her. She backed away from me. "You have to go with them, Edward. I'm not leaving your father."

"I'll bring him!" I shouted. "We can run faster than you!"

"He won't come with you, you know that! He won't listen to you!"

"I'll make him!" I shouted, or started to shout, because at that moment there was the most desperate, terrifying shriek and we turned and saw that my sister Becky's hair was alight. It was flaming out around her and she was spinning in terror, shrieking above the roar of the flames. I ran, tearing off my jacket, and flung it over her head and Mother joined me and we put out the flames. The other girls were screaming hysterically. I lifted Becky and gave her to my mother and put my mouth to my mother's ear and said, "Take them now, Mother, or they will die. We will catch up with you."

She was shaking violently but she nodded, and kissed me, and she and Margaret gathered the girls together and they ran.

When I turned back to the house my father was standing on the roof, silhouetted against a sky that seemed itself to be exploding with flame. The urgency of the situation had driven everything else, even the state of war between us, from my mind, and until that moment I hadn't given him a thought. Now, as I watched, he raised his fists to the flames and roared his defiance and I suddenly realized that after all those sleepless nights planning his death, all I had to do was turn around and walk away. Just leave him, because left to himself you could guarantee that he would leave it too late. Just walk away, and all our problems would be solved.

I would like to be able to say that I couldn't do it, that in the name of humanity I could not leave without at least trying to make him come down. Or that in the horror of that moment I had some sort of revelation and saw in my father, this man who had battled the Fates and lost time and time again, a nobility that I hadn't recognized before. But it's the truth I'm trying to write here and the truth is, I could have walked away without a qualm. The sole reason I didn't was because I couldn't have faced my mother if I had.

I ran to the foot of the ladder and shouted up to him, but he couldn't hear me above the roar of the fire. Cursing, my guts cramping with terror and frustration, I climbed the ladder and scrambled across the roof to him. He was standing with his back to me, facing the approaching flames. I grabbed his arm and he turned and looked at me. I yelled, "Come on! If you don't come now it'll be too late!"

I don't think he even knew me. He was covered in soot and ash and his hair was wild and his eyes, bloodshot and streaming from the smoke, were completely mad. He batted me off as if I were an insect, a mere distraction, and turned back to the fire, and I realized that God himself could not have made him leave. I turned to go, but a flaming branch landed on the roof beside us and instantly the roof shingles caught alight. Before I'd managed to stamp them out another firebrand landed, and then a third. I yelled a warning but my father didn't even turn to look. That was it for me. My courage broke and I scrambled back to the ladder and climbed down, coughing and choking from the smoke, and ran.

When I reached the path I looked back and saw him, almost obscured by smoke and flame but still facing that towering wall of fire, arms raised, fists clenched. And that is my last memory of my father: shaking his fists at the sky. *Shaking his fists,* for the love of God! Shaking his fists at a holocaust.

By the time I reached the lake it was so dark and the air so full of smoke that you couldn't see two feet in front of your face, so it wasn't until the fire burnt itself out early the following morning that I found the others. They were sitting on a small crescent of beach, soaking wet from having spent most of the night in the lake, huddled together like refugees from some bloody but nameless war.

My mother stood up when she saw me and came to meet me. There was no question in her face—there could only be one reason why I was alone. I told her that I had tried. I am glad I was able to say that.

I have comforted myself over the years with the thought that the fact that I tried means that, strong though my father's influence on me was, my mother's was stronger still. I don't know if that is true.

We made our way back along the shore until we reached the edge of the fire's destruction and then worked inland back to Jonesville. I was afraid there would be nothing left of the town, but though the stench of burning was thick in the air and a layer of ash covered everything, it had largely escaped the fire. Emily's parents took us in. After a few days with them, we went by truck and train to my mother's family, thirty miles away. When everyone had settled in I told my mother I had decided to enlist. She didn't try to stop me. I imagine she knew that I had to get away.

Emily did try to stop me. I returned to Jonesville to tell her and she wept and pleaded with me not to go. Finally, when she saw that I was adamant, she asked me to marry her, saying she'd be able to bear it better if we were married. I said yes. I could see no reason not to, given that I was sure I'd be killed.

The following day we were married. I was still so dazed from the fire that I have no recollection of the wedding. We had one night together before I was shipped off to training camp and six more nights before I was sent overseas. During one of those nights we created Tom.

CHAPTER FIFTEEN

Tom

Struan, March 1969

Overnight the wind swung around to the south and when he left the house in the morning he could feel the difference in the air and hear it in the snow under his feet—a wet crunch rather than a dry squeak. He knew better than to think spring had arrived—another blizzard was on its way—but it gave you hope.

When he passed Reverend Thomas's house the porch light was on again. Tom slowed down and anxiously scanned the house and front yard but there was no sign of the old man, barefoot or otherwise. He was so busy looking for him he almost failed to notice that the car had been partially cleared of snow. The top, and the sides down as far as the bottom of the windows, were exposed; it no longer looked like a hump but instead like an island or the back of a whale. The driveway hadn't been cleared, so Reverend Thomas couldn't have gone anywhere even if he'd been able to open the doors, but maybe that would come next.

Tom searched around in his mind for conclusions to be drawn and decided it was a good sign. If you lived in the center of town like Reverend Thomas did, you didn't really need the car on a day-to-day basis, so it suggested he wanted to go somewhere, and that in itself could be considered a positive thing. Maybe he was thinking of driving down to wherever it was his wife had gone. Maybe eventually they'd be okay. Not happy, of course, but okay.

Luke Morrison was in Harper's reading the paper, the box of models beside him on the bench seat. He glanced up when Tom came in and nodded a greeting. Tom paused at his table.

"How'd the interview go?"

"Okay," Luke said. "Nothing definite but I think he liked the stuff."

"That's great."

"He's bringing his wife up today. Wants her to see the models, help decide which ones they want to go for."

"They're here," Tom said. "I saw the plane coming in just now."

"Thanks. Better get things out, I guess." He opened the box and started unpacking various pieces of furniture.

Tom slid into his half-booth, across from Luke and one row down, and spread out his paper. Nobody dead on the front page. Prime Minister Trudeau was shaking hands with a sleazy-looking guy with dark glasses. They were smiling at each other like sharks.

A glass of water landed on the table.

"Same old thing?" the Amazon asked.

"Yes. Thanks."

"Boring, boring." She sped away.

The door opened and the boss-guy came in accompanied by a woman wearing dark glasses and more dead animals than Tom had ever seen all together in one place before. Fur from head to toe. The hat on its own had to be a whole silver fox, the coat . . . Tom did a quick count and reckoned it had to be at least fifty mink, maybe double that. Her feet and legs up to mid-calf were each inside a baby seal. Conversation in Harper's ceased altogether for a count of ten, then resumed in an awed murmur.

The woman seemed at ease with that. She stood in the doorway, smiling faintly behind her dark glasses, and waited to be shown to her seat.

The boss-guy spotted Luke, waved to him, then guided his wife down the aisle. Luke got up and stepped out of the booth. His back was to Tom, which was a pity, Tom thought, because he would have liked to see his face, but on the other hand he got to see the woman and that was an experience you didn't get every day.

"This here is Luke Morrison, furniture-maker extraordinaire," the boss-guy said with a wide smile. "Luke, I'd like you to meet my dear wife, Cherie. She's the brains of the business. As well as being the beauty, of course."

"Nice to meet you, ma'am," Luke said.

The woman took off her dark glasses and smiled at him. Her face was a work of art.

"Isn't this a cute place you have here," she said. She allowed her husband to help her out of her coat and slid into the booth opposite Luke. Without the coat she was a bundle of twigs.

"And this is the furniture," she said. "And isn't it cute too."

The men sat down and watched her. The whole of Harper's watched her. She picked up a miniature circular table, turned it around, turned it over, put it down, picked up a chair.

A hot beef sandwich and fries appeared in front of Tom. Perched on top of the sandwich was a solitary pea. Tom's retinas registered the pea but the optic nerves were busy with the woman and failed to pass the message on to his brain. Despite five years in Toronto he'd never seen anyone who looked quite as unreal as the boss-guy's wife. Every eyelash looked as if it had been meticulously crafted and glued in place that very morning.

Bo was setting down iced water in front of the newcomers. Seeing her beside the woman, Tom suddenly realized that Bo was a knockout. He wondered how he'd failed to notice it before; maybe he'd never really looked at her, in case she started talking to him. In addition to being tall and blond, she was clear-eyed and long-legged and looked fit as hell. If the boss-guy's wife worked at it for a million years she'd never come close to looking as good as Bo did without lifting a finger, which when you thought about it was kind of unfair.

"Very nice to see you again, sir," Bo was saying. "How are you today, ma'am? Isn't it a lovely day?"

"Lovely," said the woman.

"Are you ready to order yet?"

"Um, no," said Luke quickly. "Give us a minute."

"Absolutely, sir," Bo said. "No problem. The menu's on the table mat in front of you when you're ready, ma'am."

"I know what I'm having," the woman said, making a little rocking chair rock with the tip of her finger. "This is delightful," she said, smiling at Luke. "May I have this?"

"Sure," Luke said. "Sure, of course."

"I'll have an omelet," the woman said. She balanced the rocking chair on the palm of her hand and raised it to eye level. Everyone watched.

"That's a good choice, ma'am," Bo said, taking out her note-book.

"Please tell the chef to use two eggs, fill it with fresh spinach and grate a little Parmesan on top."

"Fresh spinach?" Bo said, her pencil pausing.

The woman looked at her for the first time. "You don't have fresh spinach?"

"Not at the moment," Bo said, looking out of the window at several million square miles of snow.

"I wasn't assuming you grew it in your garden," the woman said, her mouth going thin. "I was assuming you would have it flown in."

"I'm afraid not, ma'am," Bo said. "I'm pretty sure we have tinned spinach, though. Would that do?"

"It's not that kind of town, Cherie," the boss-guy said jovially. "This is the *North*."

"Have you *frozen* spinach?"

"I'm afraid we don't have that either. How about peas? We have frozen peas."

"A *pea* omelet?" the woman asked glacially.

"Or how about potatoes?" Bo said, warming to the subject. "They're fresh. Potatoes are great in an omelet. And onions—how about a potato and onion omelet with cheddar cheese? That would be delicious! We could add some peas as well for color if you like. It would be healthy too."

"Are you saying you have no fresh vegetables apart from po-tatoes and onions?"

"Oh no, we have carrots, cabbage, squash, turnips . . . a tur-nip omelet would be different. How about that?" There was a dangerous light in Bo's eyes.

Luke was squirming in his seat. Tom knew it would have been a kindness to look away, but it was too good to miss.

The boss-guy said, "Why don't you have one of their hot beef sandwiches, Cher? They're damned good and it wouldn't hurt you for once. I eat them all the time and look at me."

"I have looked at you," his wife said, not looking at him. "I'd like to speak to the chef."

"Sure," Bo said. "I'll just get her." She sailed away.

"Do you think people who have enough money to be flown all the way up here by seaplane will be happy to stay in a place where there are no fresh vegetables?" the woman asked her husband. Her tone was enough to freeze your balls off, Tom thought. Which might explain why the guy looked as if he didn't have any. It was funny, when you thought about it, how many rich guys looked like eunuchs.

"We can get them flown in if they really want them," the man was saying. "But this isn't Toronto, Cher. That's the whole point! People will be coming up here for a new and absolutely authentic experience." He stretched his arms out to encompass the magnificence of the Canadian North. "That's what we're offering them—that's why it's so special. They'll experience the North as it really is, up to and including the food of the region."

"I think you should be very worried about this," his wife said, scanning the menu.

"Not everybody likes raw spinach, dear. Some people prefer normal—"

"I think you should be losing sleep."

Luke was scrabbling frantically around in his box of models. He brought out something wrapped in newspaper and began unwrapping it with great care.

"I, um, brought this in to show you," he said. "Just in case you were interested. It isn't something I could do in quantity; each piece takes a long time to make. But I thought . . . you know . . . you might be interested in having one or two."

He set a small chair down on the table in front of the woman. The seat was a smooth silver-gray disc of driftwood resting on slender legs. The back was formed from a delicate branch, or maybe several branches, each twig arching up or curving around to lend itself to the whole.

Wife and husband looked at it.

"I want twelve," the woman said.

"Twelve?" her husband said. "I mean it's gorgeous, I agree, but do you think it's right for what we—"

"Not for the hotel," the woman said impatiently. "People up here wouldn't appreciate how unique they are. I want them for us. For the dining room."

She turned to Luke. "Can you do me twelve? And I want a table to match. I'll leave the design to you."

"I couldn't do it in the time frame we're talking about, ma'am. I'm sorry, but they're handmade and each one depends on me finding just the right-shaped branches. Takes a really long time, so they'd be kind of expensive. Actually, very expensive."

Mrs. Harper appeared, Bo at her elbow. "I'm the chef," Mrs. Harper said. "Bo here says you wanted to see me."

"Just bring me a plain omelet," the woman said. "I'm sure it will be fine." To Luke she said, "You can discuss the price with my husband. It doesn't matter how long it takes, send me each one as you finish it. As for furniture for the hotel, I think this style here would be most suitable for the lounge . . ."

Tom found he was sitting with both elbows on the table, his

knife and fork sticking straight up in the air. Bo, passing by, said, "That's what I like to see. An empty plate. How are you feeling?"

"What?" Tom said.

"How do you feel? Sometimes when your body's not used to a certain food it can upset your stomach a little bit to begin with. That's why it's a good idea to build up gradually."

"What?" Tom said.

"Never mind," she said kindly. "If you feel a little strange this evening just lie down for ten minutes. You'll be fine."

"I'm going to need more guys," Luke said. "Want a job?"

"Making furniture? I've never done anything like that." Tom was examining the models—he'd taken a seat in Luke's booth. "This is really nice stuff. I'm not surprised they want it."

"These are all machine-made," Luke said. "Not hard to learn."

Tom would have liked to have a close look at the branching handmade chair, but the woman had taken it with her.

"You have work lined up for after the snow goes?" Luke said.

"Not sure. Last summer I drove a lumber truck. Is your workshop out at Crow Lake?"

"Yeah. It's in the garage. I'm going to need to extend it, get more machines. I've got to go see your dad, talk to him about money."

Tom put down a chair and picked up the circular table with its central leg and three elegant feet.

"I did aeronautical engineering," he said. He hadn't realized he was going to say it until it was out. "I was working on supersonic flight."

Luke raised his eyebrows. "Wow! Sounds really interesting."

"Yeah. It was. But things got a bit . . . messy, a year or two back. Personal things."

Luke nodded.

Bo appeared with more coffee. "Make him treat you to a brownie," she said. "He's going to be rich."

"Want a brownie?" Luke said.

"I'm okay, thanks."

Bo smiled at him and vanished.

Luke started wrapping up the models and putting them back in the box. "Well, like I said, I need to talk to your dad again, arrange some financial stuff before I know how much I can offer money-wise, but I definitely need more guys, so the job's there if you want it."

"Thanks. I'll bear it in mind. And congratulations, by the way. Glad you got the contract."

While he'd been in Harper's the wind had changed again and tiny stinging flakes were driving into his face as he walked home. He wondered what it would be like to work with a bunch of other guys. Six months ago—even six weeks ago—he couldn't have considered it, but he liked Luke. He was a straightforward sort of guy and working with him might be okay. As for the others, if there were machines going, they probably didn't talk much anyway. He could just keep himself to himself. It would be a completely different life from the one he'd imagined for himself, but that in itself might be good.

The downside would be that, to start with at least, he'd have to live at home and he'd been thinking it was time he got out. Things seemed to be falling apart there and it was definitely no longer a refuge. He needed to give the whole thing some serious thought.

As he was walking up the drive he noticed the sled he'd borrowed from Marshall's Grocery leaning against the side of the house. He'd meant to return it weeks ago. He looked at his watch, then studied the sky. If he took it back right now he'd have time to get home before the weather got serious.

He flipped the sled over and towed it around to the front of the house. As he passed the living room window something made him look up. Adam was standing right up against the glass, hands clenched under his chin.

"Shit!" Tom said to his feet. "Shit, shit, *shit!*" He dropped the tow rope and went in. Sherry was bashing about in the kitchen. Adam was watching him, his whole body taut with longing.

"I'm taking the sled back to the grocery store," Tom said sharply. "You can ride there but you'll have to walk home. Can you walk that far?"

Adam didn't waste time replying. He shot into the entrance hall and started pulling things from the rubble. "Is this your coat?" Tom asked, taking a coat off the hooks.

"Yes." Adam's face was shining like a candle; it made Tom want to smash the wall with his fist.

"Boots," he said. "Scarf, hat, mitts. That hat isn't warm enough—put this one on top of it. Okay, we're off."

The wind had dropped, which was something. He walked fast, listening to the swish of the sled's runners on the hard-packed snow. Each time he looked back Adam grinned up at him like a jack-o'-lantern. You'd have thought he'd never been on a sled before. The thought made him wonder if Adam *had* ever been on a sled before. It's not your bloody fault, he said to himself. It's not up to you, it's nothing to do with you, it's not as if he's starving or living in a doghouse, just fuck off and leave me alone.

Marshall's was on the same side of the road as Harper's and three stores farther along. The worst thing that could possibly have happened, the thing so bad that even he with his genius for imagining disaster hadn't thought of it, was that as they passed Harper's Bo would be serving someone in one of the window booths and would happen to look out and see them.

She was out the door in a split second.

"And who is this?" she demanded, hands on hips, looking down at Adam with astonishment. "Who is this and why haven't I met him before? Hello, gorgeous, what's your name?"

"Adam," said Adam.

"Adam is a wonderful name," said Bo, "and you have the biggest eyes I've ever seen in my *life*. Is this your daddy?"

She gestured at Tom without looking at him.

"No," said Adam.

"We have to go," Tom said. "Sorry, but we're in a hurry."

"So, if he's not your daddy, who is he?"

"Tom," Adam said. "My brother."

"Okay, good. I know all about brothers. Is he nice to you?"

"Yes," Adam said. He'd tipped his head back as far as it would go in order to take in all of her, which made his mouth hang open and his parka hood come down over his eyes.

"That's good," Bo said, "because otherwise I was going to have to kill him. Would you like to come in and have some ice cream?"

"We can't," Tom said, very fast. "We have to get this sled back and get home before the storm sets in."

"What storm?" Bo said, still looking at Adam. "How would it be if you came in while your brother takes the sled back, which will take him quite a long time because he'll have to apologize *profusely* to Mr. Marshall for keeping it so long. Does that sound like a good idea to you?"

Adam looked anxiously at Tom. Tom couldn't look at him.

"We don't have time," he said. "I'm sorry. I'll bring him back another day but we don't have time now."

"You do if I get Luke to drive you home," Bo said. She looked him in the eye. "Small boys need ice cream," she said. "This is a fact."

His fear was that when Adam took his coat off Bo would recoil with shock at the stench. In the event, maybe due to all the other odors in the place, it didn't seem too bad, but Tom was still in a sweat of anxiety the whole time. He declined Luke's offer of a lift home because the cab of the truck was so small Luke would be bound to notice the smell and anyway, there was a whole lot of stuff jostling around in his mind and he needed to think and walking was good for thinking. Things couldn't go on as they were, that was the gist of it. It just couldn't go on.

He walked faster than he should have, but Adam trotted beside him, uncomplaining. His uncomplainingness was one of the things that bothered Tom most. If he'd whined and sulked and been a pain in the ass like other kids, it would have been easier to ignore him; it was the fact that he was so good and had such low expectations of everyone around him that got you in the guts.

When they got in, when he was helping Adam take off his boots, Adam said, "I liked it."

Tom looked at him. His eyes were still shining.

"What did you like?" Tom said.

"The lady and the ice cream and the room with all the people. Mostly the lady and the ice cream."

Tom forced a smile, but it was hard. He hauled off his own coat and boots and went into the living room and then paused. Sherry was still in the kitchen. He'd thought she'd have gone but maybe it was good that she hadn't. He crossed the room and went upstairs.

Pushed out of his mind these past weeks, because to acknowledge it would mean dealing with it, was the knowledge that only one thing could be causing his four-year-old brother to smell like he did. When he opened the door of Adam's room the stench almost made him retch. In the week or two since he'd last been in, it had become far worse. He crossed over to the bed. It had been made, but badly, the bedspread hauled up over crumpled blankets and sheets. He pulled it away and stepped back, covering his nose and mouth with one hand, his eyes stinging from the ammonia. Sheets, blankets, everything sodden. He grabbed the bedding, tore it off, flung it on the floor, took the mattress by one corner and heaved it up. It was saturated—it sagged under the weight. How did the kid climb into that bed every night? How did he even stay in the room?

He went out into the hall, closing the door behind him, and stood for a few minutes, head down, taking deep breaths. Adam was standing at the top of the stairs, looking at him.

"Go into Mum's room," Tom said. "And stay there."

He felt amazingly calm; a flat calm, quiet and still. He waited until Adam had disappeared and then went downstairs. Sherry turned around as he came into the kitchen and her face lit up.

"Well hiya, Tom," she said. "It's a long time since I seen you. How you bin?"

"Come upstairs," he said. "There's something I want you to see."

"Well now, that's a nice invitation," she said, tipping her head down and looking up at him under her eyelashes.

"Upstairs," he said.

She rolled her hips up the stairs ahead of him. When they reached the top she headed for his bedroom but he put a hand on her back and steered her along to Adam's room. "In here," he said.

"We ain't goin' in there," she said, stopping abruptly. "I don't like that room."

"Why is that, Sherry?" Tom asked. "This is a nice room. Why don't you like it?" He gripped her arm with one hand and opened the door with the other.

"I ain't goin' in there!" Sherry said, louder, pushing against him, but he shoved her in and stepped in behind her and closed the door.

"Okay," he said. "You wanted a bed. Here's a bed."

"You leave me alone, Tom Cartwright!" Her voice was shrill. "You don't—"

"Don't you want to lie down, Sherry? You were so keen a minute ago."

She tried to get to the door but he blocked her.

"Lie down, Sherry."

"You let me outta here, Tom Cartwright, or I'm gonna say you raped me!"

"Now why do I think you'd have trouble getting anyone to believe that, Sherry? A girl with a nice clean reputation like yours. I just want to know why you won't lie down on this bed but are happy for a four-year-old kid to sleep in it every night for weeks on end."

"It ain't my job to clean up after some filthy, stinkin' kid who wets his bed!"

"Yes, it is. It is exactly your job. You are paid to clean this house. Would you call this a clean room? At the very least, at the very *least,* you should have told my mother he was wetting the bed."

"Your mum ain't right in the head! I could'a told her ten times and she'd never do nothin'. And if you din't know about it yourself, that's 'cause you din't want to know, 'cause anyone could smell that stink a mile off."

"Get out," he said, sick with disgust, because there was no answer to her accusations. She was right in every respect. "Just get out."

"I ain't goin' without my money!"

"Oh, but you are." He opened the door and propelled her out. "You are going now. You haven't earned a goddamned cent since you came into this house. I could sue you for taking money under false pretenses. In fact, maybe I will. Down the stairs. Down." He grabbed her arm, forced her down the stairs.

"You let go of me!" Sherry screamed. "You let go of me, you bastard!"

"And out we go," he said, propelling her across the living room and into the entrance hall, opening the two doors and heaving her out into the snow, which was coming down fast now, spearing through the dark.

"One coat!" he yelled, throwing it out after her. "One pair of boots!"

He closed the doors, leaned against them, then pushed himself off and back up the stairs. Adam and his mother, holding the baby, were at the top, looking down.

"Go back to bed, Mum," Tom said. "Adam, go with her. I told you to stay in her room."

He went into the bedroom, gathered up the sodden sheets and blankets, took them down the stairs and into the kitchen, opened the back door and threw them out. He went back upstairs.

Adam was there again. He was crying. "I'm sorry," he said. "I'm sorry."

In the past year and a half Tom had never seen him cry. Not once. He pointed a shaking finger at him. "Stop crying," he said. "And stop saying you're sorry. It isn't your fault. It. Is. Not. Your. Fault. Do you get that? Do you understand? So stop crying."

He went back to the bedroom, heaved the mattress off the bed and out the door and down the stairs and through the kitchen and out the back door to join the blankets. He washed his hands at the kitchen sink and went back upstairs to his mother's room. Adam wasn't there but his mother was in bed, holding the baby to her. She looked at him with wide eyes.

"Mum, Adam's started wetting his bed," Tom said. "He needs to have a diaper at night."

"Oh," his mother whispered. "All right."

She wasn't taking it in. Tom went back downstairs. Adam was standing in the living room. Tears were still rolling down his face but maybe he couldn't stop them.

"I need the paper your new car was wrapped in," Tom said. "Do you know where it went?"

Adam ducked into the space beside Tom's chair and came back with the paper. Tom smoothed it out on the table, then took it over to the telephone. He phoned International Inquiries and asked for the number of the Montrose Hotel. He glanced at his watch, then dialed the number. There was a pause, then a couple of clicks, and a phone rang twice.

"The Montrose Hotel," Megan's voice said crisply. "May I help you?"

"Hi, Meg," Tom said. "It's Tom."

CHAPTER SIXTEEN

Megan

London, December 1968

Most of the time things were very good. In the evenings, if Megan wasn't on duty at the hotel and Andrew wasn't out researching, they would sometimes eat together. She would cook or he would cook and they would share a bottle of Mateus Rosé or Chianti and talk about their days and then Andrew would go back to his desk and carry on with his work. Often they left their doors open and then really it was like having one large flat instead of two small ones. It was like being married, Megan decided, thinking of her father shut in his study. But hers and Andrew's was a much better marriage than her parents', more like Annabelle and Peter's. Though, of course, without the sex.

If you didn't want children, which she didn't, sex was no big deal, was it? You can't have everything. Most of the time she was able to convince herself of that.

A couple of times, when her day off coincided with Andrew having some free time, he took her to see something famous, something he thought she really shouldn't miss, such as the Tower of London (amazing) or Buckingham Palace (disappointing) or Hampton Court (wonderful curling chimneys). Megan sent postcards home to please her father.

So most of the time things were very good. It was when her body refused to listen to her head that it became difficult. She had worked very hard at making Andrew think that what he'd told her in Bradgate Park was of no particular importance to her—that she considered him just a friend—with the consequence that the guardedness she'd noticed previously had left him. Not that he walked around naked or was given to displays of affection, but sometimes he'd put an arm around her in a brotherly fashion, rather as Tom used to do. (Though Tom only did it when he was teasing or trying to get something out of her.)

That was what she found difficult. Being so close to him. Touching, but not properly touching. Sometimes that hurt so much she wanted to cry.

Occasionally he was out very late. She couldn't sleep until she heard him come in and then she couldn't sleep for wondering where he had been and with whom.

Once he seemed low and when she asked, cautiously, if he was all right he said he'd met someone he liked but it hadn't worked out. Then he'd smiled at her and shrugged and said, "Never mind. It'll happen."

That was very, very hard. To know that he wanted someone, but not her.

Most of the time, though, she was able to not think about it and things were good.

One night Andrew said, "When am I going to see this hotel of yours?" so she took him there on one of her evenings off. Annabelle and Peter were supposed to be out for dinner with friends but as it happened the friends had canceled and they were still at the hotel. Megan had carefully never spoken about Andrew, so they were a little surprised when she showed up with a strange man, but they were friendly and gracious, as she'd known they would be.

"This is Andrew Bannerman," Megan said casually. "He lives across the hall from me." (She'd worked out how she'd introduce him just in case something like this happened.)

"We'll give you a guided tour," Peter said expansively. "This is the bar, which is the perfect place to start. You'll need to fortify yourself for the tour; it's very strenuous. What'll you have?"

It turned out that Peter hadn't yet unbooked the table they'd booked, so after the tour the four of them went out for dinner. Megan sat in a haze of happiness, watching these three people she loved so much. Peter and Andrew got onto the subject of old cars: if it didn't have a solid chassis it didn't rate as old, they agreed.

"How about the Jowett Jupiter?" Peter said. "Now that was a great, great car."

"It was," Andrew agreed, "but it was ugly."

"Ugly!"

"All right, not ugly. But put it alongside the Morgan Plus 4, for instance. Poetry in motion."

"If you two don't stop," Annabelle said, "Megan and I will go elsewhere. Won't we?"

"Yes," Megan said. But she would have gladly stayed there forever, watching them, basking in the wonderfulness of them getting on so instantly and so well. They could talk about whatever they liked.

"Megan, he's one of the nicest men I ever met," Annabelle

said afterwards, "but promise me you won't fall in love with him. You do know he's homosexual, don't you?"

Fortunately Megan was hanging up her coat, so Annabelle couldn't see her face.

You're too late, she wanted to say. Just as Andrew himself had been too late that day in Bradgate Park, when he'd said he didn't want her to get "the wrong idea." Love was not an idea; you couldn't choose to get it or not get it any more than you could choose to catch or not catch flu.

====

She'd hoped they could spend Christmas together but Andrew said he'd be going home. His parents had a big house and always hosted a family Christmas. His brother and his brother's wife and three kids and his sister and her husband and a one-year-old and another on the way—they all stayed over and it was four days of bedlam.

"Do you enjoy it?" Megan asked.

"Mostly. It's great seeing them all. Though the past few years it's been a little . . . awkward at times. You know parents. They keep wondering when I'm going to bring home a girl."

"Don't they know?" Megan asked cautiously. It was the first time they'd mentioned the subject since Bradgate Park.

"My brother and sister do. Not my parents."

"Aren't you going to tell them?"

He smiled at her, the same strained smile he'd had that day. "No. I love them and it would hurt them. They wouldn't understand. Their generation grew up thinking it was something you chose to be." He changed the subject. "How about you? Do you miss your family at Christmas—your parents and all those brothers of yours?"

Megan thought about it. Christmases had always gone by in a haze. From the moment she got out of bed on Christmas morning, she'd been either in the kitchen or whirling around tidying up. With hindsight she could see that it had been her own fault. She remembered coming into the living room—it was her last Christmas at home and Tom had arrived back from university the night before—to find it once again strewn with paper and discarded presents and dirty plates and half-empty cups of coffee, standing with her hands on her hips and saying, "I don't know why I bother." Tom, who was sitting on the sofa fiddling with a 3-D puzzle the twins had given him, looked up and said, "I don't know why you bother either, Meg. Nobody else cares if it's a mess. Sit down, why don't you?" He'd patted the empty seat beside him. "Tell me what you've been doing lately. How's life treating you?"

She'd snapped at him, saying he'd be the first to complain if the turkey didn't get cooked, and he'd said cheerfully, "No, I wouldn't. I'd have another piece of Christmas cake."

But of course she'd gone back to the turkey.

If she could do it again, she thought, she'd sit down and talk to him. She'd always admired Tom, although he'd driven her at least as mad as the others, but she'd never really got to know him and she regretted that.

The only thing she'd actively enjoyed that Christmas was Adam, whose first real Christmas it had been. He'd loved the noise and the fuss and had chewed his way through quantities of wrapping paper and grinned like a maniac the whole day long. She'd carried him about with her, quite unnecessarily—he was perfectly happy on the floor—because she'd known by then that she'd be leaving home soon and wanted to store up the feel of him. She had no idea what it was about Adam that tugged at her so hard; at that age the others had left her cold.

"I do miss them," she admitted now to Andrew. "Some of them more than others."

"Have you thought of going home for Christmas?"

"I've thought of it, but I can't go now because my mother's expecting another baby and if I went home I know I'd get sucked into it all again."

As usual she spent Christmas Day with Annabelle and Peter. They had Christmas lunch out (a different restaurant every year) and opened their presents over coffee, and it was easy and uncomplicated. After lunch the three of them returned to the hotel to pass around mince pies and Champagne to the guests, and that was fine too. At four P.M. Megan phoned home—the one bit of Christmas she dreaded. She could have gone back to her flat to make the call—there was a pay phone in the hall on the ground floor of the house—but it felt too public for such a conversation and it was simpler to use the phone in the office. On her father's instructions she reversed the charges but then spent the call counting the seconds because she knew he'd be counting them too.

Her mother answered the phone. She sounded serene rather than flustered, which meant the baby was going to arrive any day—Megan knew the signs. She was so calm she didn't even ask when Megan was coming home. Everyone was well, she said. Yes, yes, she had everything ready for the birth.

Megan asked how Adam was; her mother said he was fine, just fine.

"Has he opened my present to him yet?" She'd been hoping to

hear the sound of Matchbox-size collisions in the background but there was only the distant sound of Peter and Corey fighting.

"I don't think so," her mother said vaguely.

"What do you mean you don't think so, Mum? Have the rest of you opened my presents?"

"I'm not sure who's opened what . . ." Her mother's voice trailed off.

This was what she was like before a baby and wasn't in itself a cause for concern, but that didn't make it any less frustrating.

Next Megan spoke to her father, who wasn't sure her mother had got around to the presents yet. Megan wanted to yell, What do you mean you're not sure? Either you've opened your presents or you haven't opened your presents. You live there, you're not unconscious, you must know! She controlled herself and thanked him for the check he'd sent—the only Christmas present she'd received from her family, but at least it was a generous one.

Next she asked to speak to Adam, who turned out to be asleep although it was eleven in the morning their time. So Megan asked to speak to Tom, who was out on the snowplow—there'd been another blizzard, and Christmas or not, the main roads had to be kept open. Then she spoke to Peter, who said Merry Christmas and vanished before she could reply, and finally the phone was passed to Corey, who was eating toffee and couldn't disengage his teeth. Nobody mentioned her presents, which was absolutely par for the course.

When she'd put down the phone Megan went up to the linen cupboard, shut the door behind her and cried, another thing she did every year now. Then she washed her face and redid her hair and went down to make coffee and be pleasant to the guests.

———

For 364 days of the year, her family seemed so far away and long ago they might have been characters in a book she'd once read, and yet the minute she heard their voices they became so painfully, infuriatingly, achingly close she might as well not have left home at all.

———

Early in the New Year Annabelle and Peter found a hotel they liked the look of and, rather to her surprise, Megan liked it too. It was very different from the Montrose—art nouveau rather than Victorian, according to Peter. It had tall stained glass windows and sculpted cornices and a curling wrought iron staircase spiraling up the four flights of stairs. It also had collapsed ceilings in half the rooms and wallpaper hanging off the walls in great damp sheets.

"That's the only reason we can afford it," Peter said. "There was a leak—more like a flood, in fact—in the water tank in the loft. It's too big a job to do ourselves, we'd need help, so the first step is a structural survey and then we'll get some quotes from builders. Then we'll decide if it makes sense to take it on."

Megan found herself hoping that it would make sense. For her the Montrose would always be special, but the idea of a new challenge was growing on her too. Conveniently, the new hotel was only a mile away from her bedsit; she wouldn't even have to move to be near it.

She talked about it with Andrew—in fact, they all did—they went out as a foursome from time to time. He demanded another grand tour, so they took him to see it.

"Whoa," he said, looking at the sagging ceiling in the main reception room. "Looks as if an elephant sat on it. You're sure about this, are you?"

"Well no," Peter said. "Not sure. We're waiting for the results of the survey."

"Will you sell the Montrose to finance it?"

"We thought we'd have to but now we're wondering if maybe we could keep it—get another mortgage on the strength of it."

They adjourned to the pub on the corner and spent the evening talking about bankruptcy. Peter seemed to find the subject funny, which made Megan anxious. Sometimes it seemed to her that Peter treated the whole business of money as a joke.

Andrew didn't. At heart Andrew was quite a serious person. It was another thing she loved about him.

Later Annabelle said, "Megan, I know it's none of my business but I'm worried about you. Because it looks to me as if you're in love with Andrew."

Megan felt herself flushing but she said calmly, "He's just a good friend. A very good friend."

"Good," Annabelle said, still sounding doubtful. "Because it wouldn't work, you know."

It was the first time Megan had ever been cross with her. Who was she to say what would or would not work, as if there were rules?

——

On a Wednesday morning toward the end of January a letter arrived from Megan's father telling her that she had another brother. His name was Dominic John. He and his mother were both doing well.

Megan phoned and spoke to her mother, who said everything was fine, just fine.

"Brother number eight," Megan said, tight-lipped, to Andrew

that evening. "Though Henry died when he was a baby, so there are only seven."

Weeks ago she'd bought a tiny Babygro—yellow to allow for either sex—and wrapped it and stuck it in an envelope. Now she was wrapping two Matchbox cars for Adam, to enclose in the package—or at least she would be if Andrew would stop playing with them.

"Are they Catholic?" Andrew asked, opening and closing a car door.

"No. They have no excuse whatsoever. Our doctor told them after Adam was born that there were to be no more babies—I heard him, I was there. But here we are. It's irresponsible and it's disgraceful."

Andrew grinned.

"It's not funny," Megan said.

Andrew blew his nose and hid the grin in his handkerchief. "Sorry. It's just that you do disapproval so well. Why does it make you angry?"

"Because they're not capable of looking after the ones they have and I know what's going to happen. The house is going to fall apart and my mother is going to write and ask me to come home and sort it out, and I'm not going."

"Well, why be angry about it? Just tell her no."

"You don't understand," Megan said.

"The graveyards are full of indispensable people, Meg. You've been away three years and they've managed without you all that time. Things change in three years—people change."

"Not my parents," Megan said.

"I bet they have. In fact, I literally bet they have. I'll bet you five pounds your mother doesn't write that letter."

"Done," Megan said.

In a sense he won the bet. The weeks ticked by and no letter arrived, and Megan was getting ready to pay up when the phone in the office rang one evening toward the end of March and Tom's voice said, "Hi, Meg. It's Tom."

"Tom," Megan said, instantly gripped by an icy dread. Tom had never phoned her, never so much as written to her. Nothing but a catastrophe would drive him to this.

"How are you?" Tom said. "How're things?"

"Is it Mum?" Megan said, seeing her mother dead, herself not there with her at the end.

"What?" Tom said. "Oh. No, Mum's fine. At least, not exactly fine, but she's not sick."

"What's the matter with her?"

"I don't really know. Maybe nothing . . ."

Megan's hands were shaking. "Tom, what is this phone call about?"

"Well, I guess it's mainly about Adam."

Her heart seemed to stop beating altogether. "Is he sick?"

"No, but things haven't been great here lately, Meg. Mum's kind of . . . lost it. Nothing's getting done."

"She's always like that after a baby. Tell me about Adam. List every single thing that is wrong with Adam, starting now."

"Okay. Well, for a start, sometimes there isn't any food in the house and I think a couple of times he's actually gone hungry. And also, he's started wetting his bed and nobody's done anything about it, so he's been sleeping in a wet bed for weeks and he really stinks. And Mum's completely wrapped up in the new baby and Dad's at work and even when he's home he's not at home—you know how he is. And I'm at work, so Adam's on his own a lot and he's . . . unhappy, I think. He seems kind of . . . lost. So basically that's the state of things. I thought you'd want to know."

Megan was so angry her jaws were locked. The phone line hummed back and forth across the Atlantic.

"Meg? You there?"

She drew a breath. "You thought I'd want to know that Adam's been hungry because there isn't any food in the house and he's been sleeping in a wet bed for weeks?"

"Megan—"

"There are three adults in that house, Tom! *Three adults!* And you've phoned to tell me that none of them can be bothered to see to the *basic needs* of one four-year-old boy!"

"Stop yelling at me, Meg. I've been doing my best, but I'm going to be leaving in a few weeks' time. I just called to tell you that things really aren't good here. Mum's genuinely kind of nuts, and Dad doesn't want to know. We even had the cops here the other night—well, Sergeant Moynihan—because it turns out Peter and Corey have been setting fire to things. The cleaning lady hasn't been in months and Mum got someone else to come who was completely crap and I've just thrown her out. Like, literally thrown her out. I've also had to throw out the mattress on Adam's bed because it was saturated with piss—all the sheets and blankets, everything's soaked. So I'm sorry if I've disturbed you, but I thought you'd want to know. In fact, I thought you'd be extremely upset if nobody told you. That's why I phoned."

The phone line hummed.

"Megan?"

"Where's Dad in all this?" Her hands were still shaking.

"In his study. Where else?"

"It's his responsibility."

"Maybe you could phone and tell him that. I've tried."

"You want me to come home—three thousand miles—and sort it out. That's why you phoned, isn't it?"

"No, it isn't, I—"

"Yes, it is."

"Look, obviously it would be great if you came home, Meg, even if you just came for a week or two, but I don't expect you to do it. Why should you? You did it for years, and now you've got your own life to live. Adam will survive. I'll get in lots of biscuits and stuff before I leave—stuff he can open by himself. But I've been wondering about this bed-wetting business. Can kids put on their own diapers? 'Cause that's going to be a tricky one."

"I'm going to kill him," Megan said. "It would be worth going home just to kill him."

Annabelle said, "Megan, we can manage here, you know. Janet's very capable. Why don't you go for a week or two?"

"There are three adults in that house. There isn't a single thing I could do that they couldn't do just as easily. I am not going."

"He's trying to blackmail me," she said to Andrew. "He's trying to make me so worried about Adam that I'll have to go home."

"I get the feeling he's succeeding," Andrew said.

"No, he isn't. He is not."

"That's okay, then," Andrew said. "Anyway, I thought you said he said he didn't expect you to come."

"That's because he's smart. Tom is very smart."

"You could go just for a week or two. For your own peace of mind."

"It wouldn't give me peace of mind because I'd see how *use-less* they all are and I'd never be able to leave."

"Buy a return ticket. Tell them from the outset that you aren't staying. Go for two weeks, sort things out and then come back . . . Megan, are you crying?"

He got up and came around the table and put his arms around her, the first time he had ever done such a thing, and she was too upset to savor it.

"I'm just so mad," she said between sobs. "The idea of Adam sleeping for *weeks* in a soaking wet bed. And being actually *hungry*. I'm just so *furious* with them all."

"I'll meet you at the airport when you get back," Andrew said. "You can come home and have a nap and then in the evening we'll go out for dinner and you can rage about them to your heart's content."

"I'm not going," Megan said. "I am *not* going."

CHAPTER SEVENTEEN

Edward

Struan, March 1969

I've just had a visit from Reverend Thomas. I was on my way upstairs to bed—the rest of the household had retired long ago—when there was a knock at the door. Needless to say I was reminded of his non-visit a couple of weeks ago and sure enough when I opened the door there he was in his big black coat, looking so ill I thought he might collapse on the doorstep.

Before I had time to open my mouth he said, "I'm sorry to trouble you, Edward. I know you don't relish my company but I'm afraid I must talk with you."

I invited him in, of course. I took his hat and coat and hung them up and led him through to my study. When we were seated I asked what I could do for him. He didn't reply for a moment; just sat, looking vaguely at my desk. It crossed my mind that he might have had a turn of some kind, a small stroke perhaps, and I wondered if I should call John Christopherson. But then he pulled himself together.

"I won't keep you long," he said, finally raising his eyes to mine. "There are only two things I need to say. The first is an apology. Some years ago you and I had a disagreement about Joel Pickett. I expect you remember."

I nodded. There was no danger of my forgetting.

"Subsequently I used my position—my pulpit, you might say"—there was a trace of that smile I dislike so much—"to . . . vent my anger against you. What I implied about you was untrue and did you damage. It was wrong of me and I am sorry. I hope you will accept my apology."

That was something I had never expected to hear. Given the man's overwhelming pride and arrogance, it must have cost him a great deal to say those words.

"Thank you," I said. "I do accept it."

He nodded, and then looked away again and sat for a bit studying the titles of the books in the bookcase behind me. I imagine his home is full of books too. In another life Reverend Thomas and I might have found we had something in common.

"The second thing is harder to say," he said finally. "Harder to tell. I need to make a confession and I have decided that you are the right person to confess to."

That startled me, I have to say—I would have thought I'd be the very last person he would want to confess anything to—but he certainly had my attention.

He drew his gaze back from the books. "You remember my son, Robert's, trial."

"Yes."

"You remember he was given a very light sentence. The sentence, as I'm sure you know, is decided by the Crown attorney. In Robert's case, a term in jail was expected, but instead he got off with three months' service to the community."

I nodded. The sentence had been particularly surprising because the current Crown attorney is known to be very tough on the drink and drive issue, particularly where young men are concerned.

"He is a friend of mine," Reverend Thomas said. "The Crown attorney, Gilbert Mitchell. We have been friends since university. Several weeks before the trial I went down to North Bay to see him. I told him Robert had suffered enormously for his crime already, which was true. I said that he was a sensitive boy, which was also true, and that he would be utterly crushed by a period in jail, that he would be destroyed by it. Which was not true. Robert was desperate to atone, he would have positively welcomed a prison sentence. I knew that. The truth is . . ."

His voice was shaking and he stopped. He swallowed, the sound of it painfully loud in the silence of the room. I couldn't look at him. I focused on a splatter of ink on the blotter on my desk. I was so alarmed by the thought that he might break down in front of me that I found I was holding my breath. I could hear his breathing shuddering with the effort of control, and I willed him to achieve it. Gradually, he did.

"The truth is," he said finally, his voice steadier but harsh with the effort of forcing out the words, "I could not stand the idea of a child of mine going to jail. The idea of everybody knowing that my son was in jail.

"So justice was not done and the child's mother could not bear it and said things to Robert that he could not live with. And he killed himself. But the truth is, I killed him. For the sake of my pride."

He stopped again. I think he expected me to say something, but I was so shocked, so appalled, I couldn't speak. After a moment he carried on.

"It has destroyed my wife and I know it has harmed your son as well, Edward. I don't know if he has been blaming himself in any way, but I want to be sure he knows that he could not have prevented Robert's suicide. No one could have. I would be grateful if you would tell him that and apologize to him on my behalf. I would do it myself but I think he might find that . . . painful, and I don't want to add to his burden. Whereas you would know how to put it."

I have to say I felt the most profound admiration for him at that moment. I couldn't imagine how he had managed to say what he had just said, how he had brought himself to come here. That previous night when he had come to the door, it must have been to say this. He had knocked and waited, but I had delayed so long in answering that his courage had failed him. I thought of the weight he must have been carrying for the past year and a half; it must have been like being crushed by rocks. It struck me as astonishing, in such circumstances, that he'd still been able to think of what Tom was going through and had come to try to put it right.

Finally I managed to look at him. "Thank you," I said. "Thank you very much. I will tell Tom."

He nodded but didn't reply. After a minute, knowing that nothing I could say would make any difference but having to try, nonetheless, I said, "I've always understood that the Christian god is a forgiving god, Reverend. Surely if we're supposed to forgive others, we're also supposed to forgive ourselves."

He looked away.

"God has been silent on the subject," he said after a minute. "He has been silent on all subjects since the day Robert died."

I imagined him, alone in his house, waking each day to the knowledge of what he had done, listening for some message—

any message—from his god, hearing nothing but the howling of his own mind. Here is a strange thing: I found myself *loathing* his god for abandoning him at such a time. Hardly a rational thought for a non-believer.

We sat for some time, not speaking. Finally, with an effort, he got to his feet. I would have encouraged him to stay—I felt no resentment toward him anymore; what had happened between us years ago seemed utterly trivial now—but it was clear he had said what he had come to say and wanted to go.

As he was leaving, he held out his hand and I took it. He said, "Thank you for listening, Edward. I wanted you to know."

When he'd gone I returned to my study. After a moment the floorboards creaked above me and then I heard someone coming downstairs and knew it would be Tom.

"Come in," I said when he appeared in the doorway. "Sit down."

"Was that Reverend Thomas?" he said.

"Yes, it was."

He sat down. "What did he want?"

I told him what Reverend Thomas had said. How he had fixed the trial, how he felt he was to blame for Robert's suicide.

Tom put his head in his hands. "Oh God," he said when I'd finished. "Oh God."

I said, "He asked me to apologize to you on his behalf, Tom, for what you've been through. He was afraid you might have been thinking you could have prevented Robert's suicide. He asked me to tell you that no one could have."

He didn't reply. I got up and went out to the entrance hall and brought back a coat and draped it over him—he was wearing only pajamas. I risked putting a hand on his shoulder, just briefly. Then I sat down again. Outside the wind had picked up and snowflakes were splattering against the window, melting and trickling down.

When he seemed to have collected himself I said, "You and I have to talk, Tom. But not tonight. You should go back to bed."

He nodded and after a moment he straightened up and left without looking at me so that I wouldn't see that he'd been crying. I sat on for a while and then went upstairs myself. I was afraid I might dream about Reverend Thomas, but when it came to it I didn't dream at all.

——

I am glad Betty is a librarian. It means I have a reason to see her frequently, and there is something about her that gladdens the heart. She has ditched her sleeping bag. When I went to the library at lunchtime she was wearing only her coat (with three layers underneath, so she informed me), hat, scarf, boots and gloves with the fingers missing.

"Reborn, like a butterfly!" she announced, wafting her arms. "Emerging from my chrysalis. Summer's coming."

I was enjoying the idea of Betty as a butterfly—she is on the hefty side—but I urged caution. Another blizzard is forecast for this evening.

"Nonsense," Betty said. "What do they know?"

I told her that I had not had time to do justice to the books on Rome, which are due back at the library in Toronto next week, and she said she would try to get an extension for me. I hadn't known that was possible. Apparently, if someone else is waiting for them I'll be out of luck, but otherwise I can hold on to them for a while longer.

She asked how things were at home and I said better, which

isn't strictly true. I considered telling her about Peter and Co-rey's little forays into arson but decided against it. She would suggest that I talk to them. I've got as far as imagining knocking on their bedroom door but I can't imagine what comes next.

I also thought of telling her about Reverend Thomas's visit but decided that would be breaking a confidence.

When I got back to the bank I saw in my desk diary that Luke Morrison had made an appointment to see me. I can guess what it's about: Sam Waller of the building firm Waller and Sons has been up here recruiting for the new hunting lodge/hotel, and my guess is that Luke Morrison has won the contract to make the furniture for them. I hope very much that is so. It's good to see talent and hard work rewarded.

Luke Morrison and I have a connection he is probably not aware of. His father was the senior accountant at the bank when I joined it after the war and was therefore my first boss. He was an exceedingly nice man. It was he who encouraged me to study accountancy by correspondence course and saw to it that I had time off to get the qualifications. He and his wife were killed in a collision with a logging truck about fifteen years ago. A terrible thing. Several of us from the bank went to the funeral out in Crow Lake. I remember thinking the children—there were four of them—behaved with great dignity.

But as a result of that accident, the job of senior accountant at the bank became vacant and I was given it. And then a few years later, when Craig Stewart retired, I became manager. You could say I benefitted directly from that family's tragedy, and I confess I've never been entirely comfortable with that.

So a few years later when his eldest son—Luke—came into the bank wanting to borrow money to set up a furniture-making business, I dealt with his request myself and gave him as much help and support as I could. He has done very well and when Sam Waller dropped in last week and asked what I knew about Luke, I was able to give him a very good reference. If he does get this new contract, it will set him up nicely.

In contrast to last night this has been a remarkably pleasant day. Reverend Gordon came into the bank this afternoon. I believe I said before that he has been hauled out of retirement by the church until a replacement for Reverend Thomas can be found. It seems to me unreasonable, given his age—he must be in his seventies; he was at least fifty when we were in Italy during the war—but he claims to be enjoying it.

He came in to discuss his finances. His pension is very small but so are his outgoings, and I was able to reassure him there was no cause for concern. When the business side of things was out of the way we sat on for a few minutes (his was my last appointment of the day) and talked about this and that, mostly about the new hotel and what it will mean for the town. There will be more tourists—always a mixed blessing—but it will bring money into the area and create a good number of jobs and we agreed that on balance it would be a good thing.

We didn't talk about the war. We never do. We shared what you could call an intense experience in the course of it but it wasn't the sort of thing you talk about afterwards. He sat with me during what was unquestionably the worst night of my life. About a dozen of us, myself and another badly wounded man, had taken shelter from a bombardment in a deserted villa on the outskirts of Motta in southern Italy. In the end, after a day and a night of bloody battle, our forces did take the town, but that was no thanks to me; I was out of it by then.

I have several very clear memories from that day, one of which I have tried unsuccessfully to wipe from my mind ever since. I was on a stretcher—this was shortly after I was wounded—being carried to the villa. Pain had set in, and a desperate thirst, and no one had any water. I lifted my head, looking for someone to appeal to for a drink, and what I saw instead was a flame-thrower in action, simultaneously coating its target—and inevitably the men who were manning that target—in fuel and setting fire to it. And therefore to them.

Both sides had flame-throwers, I know that. But all I knew then was that this one was being used by us. By our side—the side that God was on. I remember hearing screaming and realizing it was coming from me.

Then I remember nothing until I came around in the villa and found myself lying on a heap of blankets beside the other injured man, with a padre sitting on his rucksack on the floor between us. The padre was Reverend Gordon. I didn't know him at that stage and had no idea he was also from the North. He was the minister of the church in Struan, and Emily and I didn't move here until 1948, when I got the job at the bank, so our paths had never crossed. He was just a man in a padre's uniform, sitting on a rucksack.

We were in a large, imposing room with grand furniture and several magnificent paintings hanging on the walls. From outside I could hear the bombardment still going on. Inside, my fellow soldiers, who had discovered a wine cellar in the basement and were in exceedingly high spirits, were breaking up the furniture and throwing it on the fire. As I watched, two of them climbed onto a table, wrenched a painting off the wall and started hacking it up for the fire as well.

I guess I went a little mad. I remember shouting at them,

struggling to get up and fighting savagely with Reverend Gordon, who was trying to restrain me, until eventually I was too exhausted to continue and fell back on the blankets.

Sometime after that the injured man next to me started calling for his mother and I heard Reverend Gordon say that his mother was here, right here beside him, and then he prayed with him and in the course of the praying the man died. I remember thinking that his death didn't matter, that no man's death mattered because the entire human race deserved to be wiped from the face of the earth.

My final memory from that day is of an exchange I had with Reverend Gordon in the middle of the night when the men had drunk themselves into a stupor and there was silence apart from the never-ending hammer of the guns. I was in terrible pain and certain that I was about to die. If I'd had any religious faith before that day, the flame-thrower had put an end to it, and I just wanted to depart this world as swiftly as possible. Reverend Gordon was still beside me—he never moved from my side all that night—and I remember saying to him, "Just don't talk to me about God," (though he hadn't been) and him saying, "All right."

"And don't pray for me. I don't want to be prayed for."

"All right," he said. "Have some water. It's very good—there's a well in the garden."

And then later still, feeling the warmth of his hand on my arm, I opened my eyes and saw that although he was still sitting upright, his eyes were closed, which made me suspicious, so I said, "You promised not to pray for me."

He smiled and opened his eyes and said, "I'm doing my best not to, Edward. But I'm praying a kind of general prayer and you'll have to forgive me if sometimes you slip in. Not often, though. I'm trying to keep it to a minimum."

———

As I say, not the sort of thing you talk about sitting in a bank thirty years later. But not the sort of thing you forget either. I hope he knows I am grateful. I have no doubt he would say there is nothing to be grateful for.

The events of that day—in particular the flame-thrower— coming as they did hard on the heels of the forest fire and my father's death, pretty much finished me off, mentally speaking. I had what they now call a mental breakdown and for several years I was not in good shape.

Physically I recovered almost in spite of myself. I spent six months in a hospital in England and it was while I was there that I received a letter from my sister Margaret telling me that my mother had died. Her lungs had been affected by smoke inhalation during the fire and she died of pneumonia. I remember the gaping chasm that opened within me when I read that letter. It—the chasm—is there still, though I am not aware of it so often.

A matter of days later I received a letter from Emily—it had been written before Margaret's but it had spent some time in Italy and was two months old by the time I got it—in which she told me I was going to be a father.

I read and reread that letter, trying to make it say something other than what it said. While I was still in Italy I'd realized that if I had ever been in love with Emily I no longer was. I'd worked out that as soon as I got home I would tell her that the war had changed me, which was certainly true, and that I no longer wished to be married and wanted a divorce. Her pregnancy made that impossible. Abandoning her with a child was not something I could bring myself to do even in the state I was in.

With hindsight, of course, it might have been better for Emily if I had.

Very little account was taken of your emotional or mental health back then. When I was considered physically well enough to be moved I was transferred to a hospital ship and sent to Toronto, and after a spell in hospital there I was sent home. By the time I got there Tom had arrived. I remember Emily, delightedly, ecstatically, holding out to me this small bundle that was our son, and the way her expression changed when I made no move to take him, merely looked at him and said, "This is him, then." Hardly knowing what I was looking at.

Her parents had rented a very small house for us so that we could be on our own and I could "get back on my feet"—very kind of them, of course. We were there for two years. It felt to me like being in a steel box barely big enough to stand in, containing scarcely enough air to breathe. I circled around and around inside that box. Around and around. It's a wonder I didn't wear a groove in the floor.

It's also a wonder Emily didn't get out the rifle and shoot me, now that I think of it. It must have been very hard for her.

At one stage I thought the endless babies were Emily's way of punishing me for not loving her, but I don't think that anymore. Emily isn't vindictive. More likely she's never quite got over Henry's death. Or maybe it's simply that I don't make her happy and babies do. The problem is, they refuse to stay babies. She tries to hold on to them but one after another they slip away.

===

It is now Friday night. Another weekend in the bosom of my family. This evening when I got home there was blood on the rug in the living room. My first thought was that Emily had had some sort of post-childbirth problem. I took the stairs two at a time—there were splotches of blood on them as well—and went into her room, to find her peacefully feeding the baby. After asking if she was all right I went back out onto the landing and then, of course, noticed that the splotches led to Peter and Corey's room, from which came the usual sounds of battle.

I knocked on the door. There was instant silence. I opened the door and found them frozen, Peter with Corey in a head-lock; Corey with blood dripping from his nose.

"Let go of your brother," I said to Peter, and he did so. Corey continued to drip. The two of them looked terrified. Probably they were afraid I'd summon Gerry Moynihan again.

"There is blood all over this house," I said. "You have fifteen minutes to clean it up."

I went down to my study and shut the door.

I still have no idea what to do about them. You'd think we'd know how to bring up our own young. Other animals seem to. Generally the job seems to fall to the females, but Emily, many times a mother, doesn't have the first idea, whereas Megan was seemingly born knowing everything there is to know.

I've tried to remember how my mother achieved discipline—I don't remember her ever shouting at us, nor do I remember us ever misbehaving. I wish I could ask her how she did it. I would like her advice on a good many things.

I've felt her presence very much the past few days. It's as if the past has sidled up alongside the present for a while. She doesn't seem to be either approving or disapproving, merely there. A bonus is that I haven't had a visitation from my father for several weeks now. I don't know if he's gone for good—

gave me the book. It was quite literally my most treasured possession. It was destroyed in the fire and when I tried to buy a copy after the war it was out of print.

But there on my desk was the same photograph, every bit as heart-stopping as it had been the first time I saw it.

It depicts in dazzling white marble the moment when Daphne is transformed into a laurel tree. Apollo is pursuing her, mad with love and lust, and Daphne is fleeing from him, her hair flying, her back arched in a desperate attempt to evade his grasp. But Apollo's too fast, he has grabbed her, hard—you can see the indentations his fingers are making on her hip. In panic, Daphne cries out to her father, Peneus, for help, and to save her Peneus turns her into a laurel tree. You can see it happening right before your eyes: leaves are sprouting from her fingers and a root is flowing down from her heel into the ground. It is all over for her. She has escaped Apollo's advances but she will never walk the earth again.

Spellbinding.

One day, I will get to Rome.

maybe he's off on a binge like old times and will come stag₂
back. But in the meantime I'm sleeping better.

I went upstairs an hour ago, thinking I'd have an early night,
saw that the light was still on in Emily's room, so I went in.
was asleep with the baby curled beside her. I stepped forwar₍
switch off the light and suddenly realized that the baby
Dominic—wasn't asleep. His eyes, which are dark and astonis
ingly clear, were open and were looking intently into my ow
He seemed very interested. His fists knotted and unknotte
themselves several times and he blew a small bubble but hi
gaze never wavered. I wondered what he was thinking, or in
deed if he was thinking—it's difficult to imagine how you go
about thinking without words.

There was a chair in the corner of the room. I brought it
closer to the bed and sat down, but in the moment I had been
out of his line of vision he'd fallen asleep. I sat for a while watching him sleep beside his mother. I wondered who he was—who
he would turn out to be.

I wondered if there were any possibility that I could be a
good father to him, this late in the day.

That last thought was so unsettling that I gave up on the idea
of an early night and went back downstairs, thinking I'd leaf
through one of the books on Rome to distract myself. I pulled
the largest of them over to my side of the desk, opened it at
random and found myself transfixed by a magnificent full-page
photograph of a sculpture by Bernini of Apollo pursuing Daphne.

The remarkable thing is, that very photograph was on the
cover of one of the books Mr. Sabatini let me take home all
those years ago, and of all the works of art he introduced me to,
it was the one that moved me most. When he left the school he

CHAPTER EIGHTEEN

Tom

Struan, March 1969

He stood looking at the phone when he'd hung up, wondering if he'd said the right things. He thought he knew his sister pretty well, but she'd been away three years and people change; he himself was proof of that.

There was a sound on the stairs—Adam, coming down again. Tom had sent him up to their mother's room while he was speaking to Meg. Now Adam crept in and stood by the table, watching him fearfully. At least he was no longer crying.

"I think I got her," Tom said slowly, more to himself than to Adam. "But I'm not sure. But I think so." She'd been madder than hell within a second and a half, which he took as a good sign; it meant she was still the same old Meg in that respect at least, still reacted with her guts instead of her brain.

Adam was still looking fearful.

"The aim of the game is to make her come home," Tom said. "Basically that has to happen. There's no other solution."

He noticed Adam's clenched hands sliding up toward his chin.

"This is Meg we're talking about. Your sister, Meg. Nobody you need to be scared of. The rest of us need to be scared of her all right, but not you. She's the one who sends you the cars."

The fists came down and, for maybe the first time ever, a look of cautious hope appeared. "When is she coming?"

Now he'd set the kid up for something that might not happen. Megan's final words, in fact, had been "I am not coming!" which on the face of it wasn't all that hopeful.

"I don't know for certain she is, I just hope so. Meantime we're going to have to sort you out. You can sleep in the twins' room. But you'll need a diaper at night. Don't start crying!" (Tears were welling.) "Just don't start! It is not your fault and it's not a problem—that's what diapers are for. Let's go and ask Mum about it."

Now that Meg was coming (he still thought she was—you didn't want to pay any attention to what Megan said; it bore no relation at all to what she eventually did), even the prospect of having to think about diapers didn't bother him unduly.

Their mother looked baffled but pointed to a neat pile of muslin squares. They were snowy white—evidently they still got washed, unlike everything else in the house.

Tom looked at them dubiously. "I don't think they're big enough."

"The toweling ones are in the cupboard," his mother said. "But he won't be needing them for a long time yet."

"I don't think we're talking about the same backside," Tom said, his head in the cupboard. Sure enough, there was a great stack of toweling diapers. He lifted out a foot-high pile.

"What else do we need?" he asked, but his mother had gone back to communing with the baby.

"Safety pins," Adam said. "And plastic pants."

"Do you know where she keeps them?"

Adam nodded, burrowed around and came up with the goods. It was a good thing he was smart, Tom thought, or getting through the day in this house would be completely impossible. They took everything through to the twins' room and heaped it on one of the beds.

"What does she do with the dirty ones?" Tom asked, trying not to think about dirty ones.

"There's a bucket."

"Good. When you take it off in the morning, put it in the bucket. Do you know how to put it on yourself?"

"You have to fold it first."

Tom shook out a diaper. There was no shape to it; it was nothing but a big square of toweling. "So how do you fold it?"

"There's a special way," Adam said.

"Do you know it?"

Adam shook his head.

"Right," Tom said slowly. Looking at the square reminded him of the paper-plane-making contests they'd had every year at university. Each of them would be given a single sheet of paper—just that and nothing else. No glue or tape was allowed; it all had to be done by folding. There was a prize for the longest sustained flight and another one for hitting a target. He'd won the sustained flight two years running but he was crap on accuracy.

"Wonder if we can make an airplane out of it," he said. "If we fold it like this" (taking two corners of the diaper and suiting action to words) "and then like that" (folding a previous fold in on itself) "we've got an acute-angle triangle. This is a good shape we've got here. These are the wings, see? Think of the lift you'll get when the air flows over the front edge there. This is going to be the world's first and finest aerodynamic diaper."

Adam was grinning at him, bouncing up and down on his toes for all the world like a four-year-old kid, and Tom was suddenly swamped by a tidal wave of dread and doubt. You have to come home, Meg, he thought. Because what the fuck is going to happen to him if you don't?

=====

In the morning the air had a softness to it that had been absent for months and the snow was mushy underfoot. It smelled like spring, which was impossible—the ground was still buried under a couple of feet of snow—but still, some sense you couldn't put a name to knew it was happening; shoots were stirring down there in the dark.

When he drove past Reverend Thomas's house he saw that, apart from an inch or so that had fallen overnight, the car was now clear of snow and the driveway had been partially cleared as well. There'd been no repeat of bare feet on the porch. Maybe things were finally getting better for the Reverend too.

Out by the New Liskeard turn there was a car in a ditch. The driver was trying to shovel it out, so Tom stopped and they attached a tow rope and got it back on the road. It made him late getting back to town and when he went to buy a newspaper they were sold out, but generally someone left one lying around in Harper's and anyway so much was going on in there nowadays that the paper wasn't the necessity it used to be. The town was buzzing. The boss-guy was due to start recruiting any day and everyone wanted to get a look at him first and—more fascinating still—get a look at his wife. She'd visited twice now and people just couldn't get enough of her: the furs, the sunglasses, the makeup, the voice—the whole package was riveting.

Tom himself was not immune. The last time she was in Harper's he'd got hooked on the way she ate—each morsel taken delicately off the fork, masticated primly (eyes cast down) and finally squeezed down her gullet—as if eating were an uncouth business you'd rather not be seen doing in public. After each bite she'd wipe her mouth, twice, inwards from each corner, for fear a gross crumb might be left on her lips. Tom had watched, mesmerized. She made him want to stick a finger up his nose.

But there'd been no sign of the sea plane today and Harper's was relatively quiet, which meant that Bo wasn't rushed off her feet. She pounced on him the minute he stepped in the door.

"So where is he?" she demanded.

"Who?" Tom said. He tried to edge past her but she blocked the way.

"Why haven't you brought him with you? Give me one good reason."

"I've just finished my shift," Tom said. "And I'm hungry. That's two good reasons."

He took a step toward her and she had to take a step back or he'd have been right on top of her, so he kept that up until they reached Luke's table. Tom slid in opposite him for moral support.

"How long would it take you to go home and pick him up?" Bo said, hands on hips. "Ten minutes? If you're too lazy to walk you could've picked him up in the snowplow on your way here. Think how much a four-year-old boy would love riding in a snowplow. Just think about it."

"Any suggestions?" Tom said to Luke.

"About kids and snowplows or about her?"

"About her."

"Nothing works," Luke said. "Just stick a couple of pieces of Juicy Fruit in your ears and get on with your life."

Beside Luke's plate there was a page torn from a newspaper. It was creased all over as if it had been crumpled and then spread out again. Luke passed it across to Tom.

"Brought this in for you," he said. "It was wrapped around some tools I had sent up from Sudbury, caught my eye when I unwrapped it. It's a couple of weeks old—there was that blizzard, newspapers didn't make it as far as here. Thought you might not have seen it."

The headline read "The Big Bird Flies." Beneath it was a photograph of what had to be the most beautiful aircraft that had ever existed or ever would exist, sailing up into the sky. "Concorde makes faultless maiden flight," the sub-headline read.

"Holy Moses," Tom said. "Holy Moses."

He'd seen interpretive drawings and artists' impressions and photos of the prototypes and plans of the profile of those incredible wings, but the finished plane was so much more beautiful than anything he'd imagined it made him go hot and cold all over just looking at it.

"Says it only went three hundred miles per hour, though," Luke said. "Wasn't it meant to go faster than the speed of sound?"

Bo walked off, disgusted. Neither of them saw her go.

"Yeah, it does," Tom said. "The top speed's something like thirteen hundred miles per hour, but they wouldn't take it to the limit on its first flight. You need to warm things up a little."

He couldn't take his eyes off it—that incredible fusion of beauty and function. Even in the grainy photograph you could almost see the air streaming over those wings. He could see exactly how it would work.

His dinner landed with a thump on top of the newspaper. Tom looked up to warn Bo that if she splashed gravy on the photo he would tear her head off but she was already halfway down the aisle.

"She's giving you the silent treatment," Luke said.

"Hallelujah," Tom said. "Long may it last." Though the fact was, when he'd been face-to-face with her a few minutes ago, it had been disconcertingly difficult to resist getting a little bit closer. Ever since noticing how good-looking she was he hadn't been able to stop noticing it. Grow up, he told himself. You're as bad as the boss-guy. She must be ten years younger than you. Eight, anyway. If you want to look at something sexy, look at Concorde.

"Could I have this?" he asked Luke. "To keep, I mean."

"Sure. That's what I brought it in for." He was looking thoughtfully at Tom.

"What?" Tom said, suddenly nervous.

"I was just wondering if you really want to spend your life making furniture."

"Oh," Tom said, relieved. He lifted his plate, folded the paper carefully and set it to one side. "I don't know," he said honestly. "I've been thinking about it, but I still don't know."

There'd been moments lately when going back to it did seem possible. And just now, looking at Concorde, he'd felt stirrings of a kind of hunger he'd thought had left him forever. Imagine working on something like that. It had to be the most amazing job on the planet. But would he be up to it? It would be a challenge and he wasn't sure he was ready for a challenge. A couple of months back he'd had a letter from Simon, who'd been with him down in the ravine that day. Simon was working for Boeing now, out in Seattle, and after a cautiously worded inquiry about how things were going, he'd said that Boeing had a new project under development and in a few months' time would be taking on more aeronautical engineers.

"Don't know if you're interested," he'd written, *"but there's some great stuff going on out here."*

At the time, Tom had been unable even to contemplate it. Now, though . . .

"I need to think about it a little more," he said to Luke. "I'm still not sure."

"That's okay," Luke said. "I talked with your dad this morning and I'm going to be extending the workshop and buying more equipment, so I won't need more guys for a few weeks yet."

Bo sailed by carrying three dinners, a jug of coffee and a foil-wrapped package tucked under her chin. It seemed to Tom she stirred the air in a certain way when she passed, as if she generated a strong magnetic field. He had to resist the urge to turn and follow her with his eyes.

On her return trip she stopped at their table. Tom concentrated on his hot beef sandwich. She's too young for you, he reminded himself, forking in a mouthful.

"This is a brownie," Bo said grimly, depositing the foil-wrapped package in front of him. "It is not for you, it is for Adam. I imagine you'll eat it yourself on the way home but that's a risk I have to take."

Tom swallowed his mouthful. "I thought the silent treatment lasted for days," he said to Luke. "I was counting on it."

Luke shook his head. "'Fraid not. Half an hour's her limit. After that her mouth snaps open like it's on a spring."

===

That night, just as he was sinking into sleep, there was a knock at the front door. It wasn't loud, but nonetheless it jolted him awake, almost as if he'd been waiting for it. He heard his father answer the door, heard voices faintly. He knew it was Reverend Thomas. He stayed where he was, lying on his back, staring at the darkness, until finally he heard the front door open and close again. Then he got up and went downstairs.

Afterwards, when his father had told him what Reverend Thomas had said, he went back up to his room. He didn't go to bed straight away; instead, he went over to the window and stood for a while looking out at the night. The wind had picked up and it was snowing again, the snow creating a shifting, swirling halo around the light at the end of the drive. For a moment he saw Rob and himself staggering down the road in the wake of the snowplow, laughing like idiots, Rob clutching the hubcap he'd found in the snow.

He thought about Robert's death—allowed himself to think about it, for the first time didn't try to suppress it.

A car went by, a cloud of snow whirling up behind it. The wind caught it and sent it spiraling upwards and then it paused and drifted down.

He thought about Reverend Thomas, coming out on such a night, driven by the unendurable need to unburden himself to another mortal soul. And also to absolve him, Tom, of blame.

Grateful though he was, Tom wasn't sure the Reverend was right that no one could have prevented Rob's suicide, but he could see now that it was possible; that someone might be in so much pain they couldn't even hear what anyone else said, far less be comforted by it.

You're never going to know, he said to himself, watching the snow. You're going to have to live with that. There's nothing you can do but face it, and accept it. That's all. Just let it be.

════

Late the following evening there was another knock on the door and when Tom opened it Sergeant Moynihan was standing on the doorstep.

"I need to speak to you and your dad," the sergeant said. You could see by his face that it was bad news. Tom took him through to his father's study and the three of them sat down.

The sergeant spoke heavily, directing his words at the floor. He told them that earlier in the afternoon he'd been driving along Whitewater Road. As he passed the turnoff to the ravine he saw a glint of metal through the trees and decided to investigate. The glint of metal turned out to be Reverend Thomas's car, stuck in a snowdrift. Reverend Thomas was inside.

"Wasn't carbon monoxide poisoning," the sergeant said, "'cause the engine was switched off. The doc says it could have been a heart attack. He can't say for sure until the post-mortem. He says it could have been just the cold. Got down to minus eighteen last night."

When he stopped speaking there was no sound in the room. Tom watched snowflakes hitting the windows, spearing out of the dark. The snow had been heavier still last night. He thought of it drifting silently down around the car, the old man watching it, perhaps even marveling at its beauty, as the cold crept in.

The sergeant had been studying his boots but now he looked up.

"Haven't found a note," he said. "So could have been an accident. But he hasn't been lookin' too good lately. My guess is he just couldn't make sense of things anymore. Couldn't find a reason to go on."

CHAPTER NINETEEN

Megan

Struan, March 1969

When she arrived, Tom was standing in the middle of the kitchen eating cornflakes. His shoulders were hunched in order to shorten the distance the spoon had to travel and he looked thin and disheveled, just as he always had. The unexpected rush of gladness at seeing him was so great that for a moment Megan didn't notice that he was eating out of the upturned lid of a saucepan. Then she noticed and, looking beyond him to the kitchen counter, saw why he was eating out of the lid of a saucepan and she almost turned around right then and there and went back to England.

"Why are you eating out of a saucepan lid?" she asked.

Tom turned and saw her and his face lit up.

"Well hey!" he said. "It's Meg! Hi! You came! How are you? How was the trip?"

"Long. Why are you eating out of a saucepan lid?" She wanted to hear him say it. She was floating in a haze of fatigue—

the Toronto airport had been closed by snow and the plane diverted to Montreal, adding many hours to an already painfully long trip—and she was not in a tolerant or forgiving frame of mind.

Tom said, "There aren't any clean bowls. It's really good to see you, Meg. No kidding, it really is."

"You look terrible," Megan said, because that was the next thing she noticed. There were bruise-like shadows around his eyes and he looked about forty.

"Yeah, well. You don't look too great yourself but I imagine we'll both survive." He tipped his head back and shouted, "Adam! Come see who's here!"

Adam appeared in the doorway. Megan forgot about the saucepan lid and being tired. He had their mother's eyes and soft fair hair, and no photograph could possibly have done him justice. She forbade herself to scoop him up in her arms—he didn't know her and it might frighten him—but she knelt down to be on his level.

"Hello, Adam," she said.

"Hello," he said. He studied her gravely. "Are you Meg?"

"Yes," Megan said. "I'm Meg."

He held out a car. It was the silver Mercedes. "This is my favorite," he said.

Next she went up to see her mother.

"Hello, Mum," she said from the doorway. "How are you?"

"We're fine, dear," her mother said, rubbing the baby's back. "We're both just fine. How are you?"

"I'm fine too," Megan said, though a chill went through her. She crossed to the bed and took a look at her youngest brother (he looked exactly like the rest had at that stage), kissed her mother and sat down on the bed beside her. She wanted to hug her but her mother looked too fragile.

"I've been away a long time," she said. "Did you miss me?"

Her mother looked down at the baby.

"Mum?" Megan said.

Her mother looked up. There was bewilderment in her eyes. She searched Megan's face as if for clues.

Megan wrapped her arms tightly around herself. She looked away, fear like a taste in her mouth. Then she smiled at her mother, leaned forward and kissed her forehead. "It's okay," she said gently. "Don't worry. Everything's fine."

She went downstairs, phoned Dr. Christopherson and made an appointment for a house-call the following morning. When she'd hung up the phone she sat down stiffly on a kitchen chair and tried to talk some sense into herself. Don't start imagining things, she said silently. It could be something quite simple. Something to do with her hormones, maybe. Probably in the morning Doctor Christopherson would give her mother a pill, and she'd be fine.

From the living room came the sound of a mini pileup. For some reason Megan found it comforting. She drew a deep breath, stood up and surveyed the kitchen. Now then, she thought. From an untouched pile in a kitchen drawer she dug out two clean tea towels, summoned Tom and Adam, gave them a towel each and together they washed every dish in the house. Then she made out a shopping list and gave it to Tom.

"This is just to tide us over till tomorrow," she said, steering him toward the front door. "I'll do a proper shopping then."

Then she went down to the basement to put in a load of laundry and then she came up and gave Adam a bath.

"Do you have any clean clothes?" she asked him, toweling his thin little body. Not dangerously thin, though, she thought. He's okay. He hasn't actually starved.

"I don't think so," Adam said.

"We'll put on dirty ones for now, then."

Downstairs the outer door slammed and then the inner door.

"Who do you think that is?" she asked Adam, listening to the ruckus.

"Peter and Corey," Adam said.

"I think so too. Let's go downstairs and surprise them."

Peter and Corey had fought their way through the living room to the kitchen and were locked in mortal combat on the floor.

"Hello, boys," Megan said, standing in the doorway. "Remember me?"

"We need to talk," she said to her father, "but not tonight."

That was the second thing she said to him. The first (apart from hello) was that she was flying back to England in two weeks minus a day. "I'm tired and I'm going to bed now. But Dr. Christopherson is coming to have a look at Mum at eight thirty tomorrow morning and you're going to need to be here. Can you manage eight thirty or should I change the appointment?"

"I believe I can manage that," her father said. He had trouble meeting her eyes and Megan hoped it was because he was ashamed, because if he wasn't he should be.

"Megan," he said as she turned to go. "It's very nice to see you. And very good of you to come."

So he was ashamed, which was something. "It's nice to see you too," she said, because strangely, in spite of everything, it was.

———

"I'm sleeping in here with you," she said to Adam, unpacking her exceedingly small suitcase. "Is that all right?" They were in the twins' room.

"Yes," Adam said. He was looking anxious, though. She guessed it was the diaper question.

"It's your bedtime too," she said, "so we can both get ready. Do you know how to fold your diaper? I put them on the chest of drawers." She said it as if it was a perfectly normal thing for four-year-olds who had been dry for some time to suddenly need to wear diapers again, and it seemed to do the trick; the anxiety cleared.

"Yes," he said.

"Show me, then."

He took a diaper from the pile, spread it out on the bed, took two of the corners and folded them in, then folded one of the folds in on itself, then the other.

"Um . . . ," Megan said doubtfully.

"It's aerodynamic like this," Adam explained. "These are the wings and the air blows over the top of them like that and lifts it into the sky."

"I see," Megan said, forgiving Tom all sins past, present and still to come. "Fair enough. But how do you put it on?"

"You have to pull it apart a bit at the front and fold it down and then bring the back around and pin it, but I can't do the pinning."

"Okay. I'll do that."

In the night she heard the wind and the creaking of the house and she was back where she started. Andrew, Peter, Annabelle, the Montrose, her much-loved bedsit, her lost suitcase, the trip to England—all ghostly figments of a dream. She went back to sleep and Andrew was there but she couldn't touch him and every time she tried he disappeared.

When she woke she washed and dressed and supervised Adam doing the same and hammered on Peter and Corey's door and went down and got breakfast on the table and took tea and toast up to her mother and hammered on the boys' door again and went down to make their lunches for school.

As the boys were leaving, Dr. Christopherson arrived. He stayed for an hour. He was very kind and very gentle with her mother, and then very kind but very honest with Megan and her father. When he had gone Megan and her father sat on in the kitchen for some time, not speaking.

Early-onset dementia, he had called it. Megan had never heard of it.

"Have you heard of it?" she said to her father at last.

He stirred himself and rubbed his hands over his face. "I think it's what used to be called premature senility," he said. "Though I'm not sure." He looked very strained.

Whatever it was called, Megan couldn't reconcile it with the person who was her mother. But maybe it was something else, something less serious. Dr. Christopherson had said they'd know more once they'd seen a specialist in Toronto.

Megan pulled herself together. "We need to talk about the practical side of things. Can we do it now or do you want to wait until tonight?"

"Now will do."

"Dr. Christopherson seemed to think that she could stay at this stage for quite a while," Megan said. "If the specialist agrees, then that's really good, especially for Dominic's sake.

But you're going to have to get someone reliable to do the house-work and the cooking and keep an eye on Mum. What happened to Mrs. Jarvis?"

"Mrs. Jarvis?"

"She used to come in to help Mum."

"Ah. I believe she was ill."

"Oh. Well, would you like me to make some inquiries?"

"That would be good of you, Megan."

"All right, I'll ask around. Now, regarding Peter and Corey . . ."

Her father visibly flinched.

"You are all they're going to have," Megan said.

Her father picked up his pen, removed the top, put the top back on, set the pen down. Megan waited. Finally he met her eyes.

"You're all they're going to have," Megan said again, because he had to understand that, and accept it, or nothing was going to work. "They need a firm hand, they need routine and they need supervision, and you can't expect someone who comes in to cook and clean to do that. Which leaves you."

She waited for it to sink in. Then she added, gently but very firmly, "And, Dad, you won't be able to do it from your study."

She felt like the executioner with red tights in the painting of Lady Jane Grey.

"And then there's Adam," she said that night after Adam was in bed. She and Tom were in the living room. Their father was in his study while he still could be.

"Yes."

"Are you all right, by the way?" she asked.

"Yes. Things have been a little rocky. But yes."

"You said on the phone you were leaving soon. Where are you going?"

He hesitated. "There's a guy, Luke Morrison, out in Crow Lake who makes furniture—he's got the contract for this swanky new hotel they're building out along the lakeshore, so he's taking people on. He asked if I'd like a job. I might do that for a bit."

"Why?" Megan said. It was just plain ridiculous. He'd been mad about planes for his entire life; he'd just made a flying *diaper,* for goodness sake.

"Why not? He's a nice guy."

"What's that got to do with anything? You're a . . . whatever it's called, an aerodynamic engineer."

"Aeronautical," Tom said. He shrugged and looked evasive. "I might see if Boeing or de Havilland have any vacancies. I'll see how it goes."

Megan decided that meant he was going back to planes, he just wasn't going to say it out loud yet. He had always hated committing himself. He'd keep saying "I'll see how it goes" until he had his suitcase packed and one foot out the door.

"How about you?" Tom said. "You're sold on England, are you?"

"I love my job."

"You run a hotel, right?"

"Yes."

"You'd be good at it."

He scraped at a spot on his jeans with a fingernail. Shifted in his chair. Cleared his throat. "Look, I'm not saying what I'm about to say with any ulterior motive. I'm just telling you because it happens to be true. Okay?"

"Just say it," Megan said.

"Right. The guy who owns this new hotel is up here at the moment recruiting staff. There's a list of the jobs in the *Temis-kaming Speaker* today and one of them is for a hotel manager. I'm just telling you, okay? It was in the paper and I saw it and I'm telling you, that's all."

Megan forgot that she had forgiven him all his sins. "I looked after this family for *fifteen years!*" she said. "And I'm *not* coming back!"

"Okay. I know. I don't blame you. Though it's a live-in job, so you wouldn't exactly be back, you'd be a couple of miles away. But I don't blame you."

There was silence apart from the sound of the wind.

Tom said, "The boss-guy of the hotel is a bit of an idiot but he seems pretty nice, pretty flexible. He might not mind if you had Adam with you." He lifted his hands. "Okay, okay. I was just thinking out loud."

"Well, *stop!*"

"Okay. I've stopped."

He arched his back stiffly. "I'm going to bed. I have to be up at five fifteen."

The wind was making whooping noises in the chimney, which meant it was from the west. Strange, Megan thought, the things you remember and the things you forget.

Tom stood up, hesitated, sat down again.

"Have you met someone over there, Meg?"

She saw Andrew. He'd be at his desk now. Fretting over a word, a comma. In a while he'd get up and stretch and wander across the hall to her room, but she wouldn't be there.

"I think that's a yes," Tom said after a minute. "That changes things all right. If you've found the right person, well . . . that's the rest of your life you're talking about. Obviously you have to go back."

He went up to bed shortly after that. Megan tidied the few things that needed tidying and listened to the wind and the creaking of the house. The sounds of her childhood. Sounds she had known long before she knew there was a world out there beyond the frozen North.

When she went upstairs to get ready for bed she left the bedroom door ajar a few inches rather than switching on the light, but Adam woke up anyway. He sat up in bed, looking at her, eyes wide.

"It's all right," Megan said quietly. "It's just me."

"I didn't know if you were real," he said.

Megan smiled at him. "I'm real. Are you real?"

"Yes."

"Good," Megan said. "I'm very glad about that." Once again she resisted the urge to pick him up and hold him to her because if she did that she'd start to cry and she didn't want him to see her cry. She closed the door and climbed into the bed beside his and reached out across the space between them and took his hand. "Let's go to sleep, shall we?"

"Okay," he said.

She waited until she was sure he was asleep before she retrieved her hand and let the tears roll, welling up out of the great sea of grief and loss within her. She wept for her mother, who was slipping away from them all, and for Adam and Dominic—and even for Peter and Corey, nuisance though they were—all of whom were going to finish their growing up without a mother. She wept for England, for her beautiful bedsit, which someone else would move into now and paint a horrible color, and the Montrose, and Annabelle and Peter. But above all, she cried to ease the terrible ache for Andrew, whom she would phone to-morrow and who would tell her she was doing the right thing and mean it, because it was the right thing, and who at the end of the call would ask her, quietly, if she was all right, if she would be all right. She wept for his laugh and the sound of the typewriter, which had always been the first thing to greet her when she got home at the end of the day, and she wept at her own foolishness in pretending they were right for each other and could make a life together.

When she'd finished crying she lay in the darkness, listening to the quiet rise and fall of Adam's breathing, until, finally, she fell asleep.

In the morning she got everyone up and dressed and break-fasted and packed Peter and Corey off to school and told Adam she was going out but would be back shortly. And then she went out into the billowing snow to find the boss-guy and get herself a job.

ACKNOWLEDGMENTS

The town of Struan is an invention, but in my mind it is located at the northern edge of the vast and beautiful area of lakes, rocks and forests known as the Canadian Shield, in Northern Ontario. I imagine it west and a little north of the real towns of New Liskeard, Haileybury and Cobalt, the last of which was the site of a spectacular silver rush back in 1903.

When researching the section of the novel that deals with that silver rush, I consulted a number of books, among them *Two Thousand Miles of Gold,* by J.B. MacDougall (McClelland & Stewart, 1946); *Six War Years, 1939–45: Memories of Canadians at Home and Abroad,* by Barry Broadfoot (PaperJacks, 1974); *Ten Lost Years, 1929–39: Memories of Canadians Who Survived the Depression,* also by Barry Broadfoot (PaperJacks, 1975); *Cobalt, Ontario,* by Michael Barnes (Looking Back Press, 2004); and in particular *We Lived a Life and Then Some: The Life, Death, and Life of a Mining Town,* by Charlie Angus and Brit

Griffin (Between the Lines, 1996). I am indebted to Paul McLaren, owner of the wonderful Chat Noir Books in New Liskeard, Ontario, not only for telling me of the existence of this excellent and invaluable book, but for giving me his own copy.

In a section of *Road Ends* set in England, there is reference to a painting by Paul Delaroche entitled *The Execution of Lady Jane Grey,* which hangs in the National Gallery in London. A character in the book (Megan) is very moved by the painting when she visits the gallery in 1969. Art historians will be aware that, in fact, the painting did not go on display there until 1975. My excuse is that I myself was very moved when I first saw the painting, and I so badly wanted Megan to have the same experience that I played a little fast and loose with the dates. My apologies. But after all, this is fiction.

I would like to thank the following: in Canada, Patricia Anderson of the town of Cobalt for a fascinating tour of a silver mine; Tamara Fishley and Breanna Bigelow at the Cobalt Mining Museum for their help, advice and hours of photocopying from the *Daily Nugget,* back copies of which, along with the *Temiskaming Speaker,* provided a vivid picture of life in Northern Ontario over the years; Eddie Sagle and Chris Callaghan, former snowplow drivers on Manitoulin Island, Ontario, for the lowdown on plowing northern roads; Malcolm Loucks, formerly of Montreal, for suggesting the Sicard snowplow; and Denise Organ of Manitoulin Island for sharing her memories of life in the early mining communities.

In the UK, my thanks to Steve and Elleen Warren, owners of the fabulous Penally Abbey Country House Hotel, near Tenby in Pembrokeshire, for their memories of running a small hotel in London "back then"; Amanda Grant, for her insightful reading and sound suggestions; and Carolyn and Nigel Davies for en-

couragement and support through good times and bad—and
Nigel in particular for all things relating to aerodynamics. The
flying diaper would never have come into being without him.

Heartfelt thanks to my peerless agent, Felicity Rubinstein of
Lutyens & Rubinstein, and to my wonderful editors and publishers: Louise Dennys and Marion Garner in Canada, Clara
Farmer and Poppy Hampson in the UK and Susan Kamil in
New York. Special thanks to Alison Samuel for her great patience, encouragement and tact, and for the remarkable skill
with which she kept all the editorial balls in the air.

Last, but definitely not least, I would like to thank my family
on both sides of the Atlantic, without whom I would never have
managed to write one book, far less three: my brothers, George
and Bill, for their meticulous reading and advice on everything
from the use of flame-throwers in the Second World War to the
northern limit of poplar trees in Ontario; my sons, Nick and
Nathaniel, for their perceptive reading and their unwavering
support; and above all, my husband, Richard, and my sister, El-
eanor, who, as with both *Crow Lake* and *The Other Side of the
Bridge,* were involved every step of the way. For both of them,
once again, thanks are not enough.

Mary Lawson, 2013

MARY LAWSON was born and brought up in a small farming community in Ontario. She is the author of two previous novels, *Crow Lake* and *The Other Side of the Bridge,* both international bestsellers. She lives in England but returns to North America frequently.